EXOSKELETON III

OMNISCIENT

THE EXOSKELETON SERIES

SHANE STADLER

Copyright © 2019 by Shane Stadler

All rights reserved.

No part of this book may be reproduced in any form or by any electronic or mechanical means, including information storage and retrieval systems, without written permission from the author, except for the use of brief quotations in a book review.

Other than for review or evaluation purposes, dissemination of this book, or portions of this book, is forbidden.

CHAPTER 1

Nothing is forever.

William Thompson wondered if he had spoken the words aloud as he sat up and wiped his damp brow with the back of his hand.

He squinted into the sunlight that beamed through the floor-to-ceiling windows on the southeast side of his flat. He'd fallen asleep on the couch for the third straight night. He grabbed his phone from the coffee table next to the couch: it was 6:04 a.m. on Sunday, July 19th, and no messages.

He set the phone back on the table, next to a whiskey glass. The aromas emanating from the brown residue that glazed the bottom of the tumbler amplified the lingering taste of scotch in the back of his throat. He swallowed hard, but it did little good at eliminating the stale aftertaste.

He kneaded the back of his neck with the heel of his hand as he tried to recall what his mind had revealed during the night. His dreams had often been enlightening, but those illuminations sometimes cast dark shadows. Even as a child, his dreams had transformed his perceptions of reality.

The recent ones were better classified as nightmares, but not of the usual type. The latest was that of a blue planet fading to a pale-gray orb, like Earth's dead moon. It was a complete death that incited a melancholy so deep that it made his ribs tighten to the point of cracking. The physical symptoms of these nightly terrors usually subsided after a few hours. The effects on his mind, however, remained, and accumulated.

There were other nightmares that he knew derived from actual events: he was haunted by the screaming faces of those he'd killed. There were many.

A milder dream of a few nights prior was of his late friend, Horace. The last words the 99-year-old man had spoken to him before he'd died were at the front of Will's mind. "Go to the Nazi base," Horace had said. "You will find answers there – about yourself and, more importantly, about the things to come."

He'd been convinced the instant Horace had spoken the words. But Will had to persuade the others. The base was located in Antarctica, and could only be accessed by submarine. The US Navy would have to take him there.

He drank a glass of water, brushed his teeth, and got dressed. He then exited his apartment and crossed the hall, to the gym. It was one of many amenities offered to guests at the Space Systems building. Afterwards, he'd resume his daily chores of searching his mind for foreign memories – those he'd acquired during his encounter with the being in the probe – and practicing his separation abilities. Those were two things no one else in the world would be doing on this sunny July morning in Washington, DC.

NOTHING IS FOREVER, Jacob Hale thought as he sighed and stared at the tops of his brown leather shoes. It was a phrase his late uncle had uttered often. His words had always been intended for comfort, as if to say that time cured all things. Now, however, they seemed to carry a different meaning.

The anticipation of disappointment induced a clammy sweat on the back of Jacob's neck. It was the feeling of awkward embarrassment that comes from people pitying you, but saying nothing.

Shadows of branches thickened on the white, semi-transparent curtains on the French doors at the front of the room as the late afternoon sun descended behind the trees in the courtyard behind the building. The scents of cologne and perfume mixed with that of sweat reminded him of his own anxiety. He struggled to keep his hopes at bay.

He knew that, no matter what the outcome, he had no right to complain. He'd been twelve years old when his family had been murdered and Uncle Theodore had taken him into his home. Theo was actually the uncle of Jacob's mother, so he was Jacob's *great* uncle. But Jacob had always addressed him as "Uncle Theo."

In the fifteen years that followed, Uncle Theo had sent him to prestigious prep schools, and then to college and graduate school in engineering. And Theo had always made him feel welcome in the family. Jacob just hoped that, after all of that time with his uncle, there'd be something for him in the will – some small crumb from the massive estate. After all, he'd saved Theo's life.

Jacob leaned back in his chair and propped his right foot on his left knee. His three cousins – who were more like siblings to him – sat to his left. More than a dozen others, most of whom Jacob recognized but didn't know, sat in the rows of folding chairs facing the attorney's massive desk.

Of his cousins, Jacob had the strongest connection with Tabitha. Now 33 years old, she was just two years older than him. Kenneth and Janet were older, both in their 40s. Jacob and Tabitha had similar interests: she'd always been more intellectually inquisitive than the older cousins, and had recently finished her Ph.D. in anthropology. With her being married, and a child on the way, he wondered whether she'd ever put her education into practice. He was inclined to believe that her child-rearing would be only a temporary delay.

Like his uncle, Jacob and Tabitha both loved to read and solve puzzles. Every day, from the time he'd arrived on the estate until the day he'd left for college, they'd solve at least one conundrum or brainteaser. It could be a word puzzle, a cipher, or a math problem – whatever they found that seemed interesting. Other times they'd tackle spatial problems, like constructing a model airplane without the instructions. All of these challenges had led him to the field of engineering and uniquely prepared him for his current job.

The lawyer behind the desk commenced the reading. Almost everything had been divided amongst Theo's wife, Aunt Rebecca, and his three children. Their combined take included over twenty properties, 500 million dollars spread through various accounts, millions in stocks, and another 50 million in other assets, including a magnificent sailboat that went to Kenneth, the oldest of the three. Finally, there were trust funds for their children, and future grandchildren. Jacob was not mentioned.

He knew the estate was large, but the actual size was overwhelming: over a billion dollars. And just when he thought everything had been given away, there was more.

The final round of bequeathing focused on charities, schools, and universities. With the many millions of dollars flowing around him like leaves in a dust devil, he hoped he might catch just one. A million dollars would make an enormous impact on his life: he'd finally propose to Paulina, his girlfriend of four years, and buy a house.

"And finally," the lawyer said, reading Theo's words, "for saving my life on the waters of the Long Island Sound on that cold, overcast afternoon, I have something special for Jacob F. Hale."

Jacob's heart sputtered in his chest like a cracked garden hose.

The lawyer looked over her glasses into the crowd.

Jacob raised his hand, and she resumed.

"Your love of reading, mysteries, and puzzles should be well satisfied by the acquisition of my favorite book. Even though it is quite rare, it doesn't have significant monetary value. It was, however, worth more than anything to me, save my family, including you, Jacob. May you find the happiness and adventure in it that I have found." The attorney looked up and waved Jacob forward.

Jacob stood, weaved his way around feet and legs into the aisle, and walked to the lawyer's desk. She handed him a brown, letter-sized envelope – too small for a book.

As he walked back to his seat, something small but heavy slid back and forth inside the envelope. It felt like a key. A light, metallic clinking noise indicated that there were at least two inside.

He took his seat and put the envelope in the inner pocket of his jacket. He'd open it later.

Although Uncle Theo was well-loved, and deeply missed by his children and many others, there were no tears during the reading of the will. The man had been nearly 100 years old. Even though his death had come without warning, it hadn't shocked anyone, including his children. Theo had married late, and he'd had his last child while in his sixties. Jacob wondered if his cousins also found it difficult to imagine him as a young man.

"This concludes the reading of the final will and testament of Mr. Theodore Horace Leatherby," the lawyer said and stood up behind her desk. The attendees bustled about and murmured as they filed out of the room.

The reading was followed by an early dinner at a fine local restaurant. Jacob managed to keep his demeanor light. He guessed only Tabitha sensed that something was bothering him, and he was sure she knew why. She didn't bring it up.

Jacob's flight from Boston to Washington, DC's Reagan International Airport left at midnight. Sleep eluded him.

AFTER 12 YEARS, the name *Jiang Tao* still looked foreign to Chang Wei. He examined his updated false documents scattered on the table. They all carried his alias, which he should have been used to after more than a decade. He was supposed to have returned to China by now, but that plan had changed when his predecessor had been eliminated.

By orders from above, "Jiang Tao" would have to step down from his leadership position in the intelligence network to replace the late

Hicham Cho. He'd been informed that Cho's mission was of great importance, but Tao didn't understand it. It was probably a political move to get Tao removed as the director of North American Chinese intelligence operations so that some bureaucrat could get his nephew into a cushy post. After all, that's how the late Cho had gotten his position. But Tao forced himself to bury his theories about unfair treatment. Cho had been killed, which meant his new post came with some risk.

Tao walked out of the office and onto the work floor. The stench of old motor oil and gasoline seemed to permeate everything in the transformed vehicle repair shop. Although it was an unpleasant place, the site had many useful features, including sublevels that had once been used to access the underbellies of cars.

Except for the two guards at the roll-up exterior door, the place was empty. The new safe house wouldn't be functional for another week, after security equipment was installed, including soundproof rooms and an underground vault.

He stepped through the open roll-up door into the morning sunlight and took a deep breath of dewy air. His grounds crew had mowed the previous evening, and the scents of freshly cut grass filled his senses. It was a fragrance he could only describe as a cross between the aromas of hay chaff and green tea. It was going to be a hot and muggy day, not unusual for mid-summer in Washington, DC.

Tao's briefing on Cho's work had been a surreal experience. The Americans supposedly had a man who had developed the ability to separate his soul from his body, and could do strange things while in that state. Tao, however, was skeptical of the farfetched stories he'd heard. Of what use was such a capability, even if the man's soul could pass through walls and kill people? China had nuclear weapons and submarines. What else did they need?

But Tao would follow through on the assignment with strong determination. He was awaiting the delivery of information that would get him up to speed on the American Red Wraith project – the project through which this supposed "ghost-man" had been developed. Until then, he had work to do.

The first item on his predecessor's list of unfinished tasks was a simple collection assignment, which meant low-risk burglary or robbery, although such operations sometimes got more complicated. These kinds of jobs were best assigned to local contractors.

Tao was fortunate that much of Cho's network was still intact. He'd assign a dependable asset – a former American operative – to carry out the operation. Tao made a call to a man named Lenny.

JACOB FLIPPED down the visor to shield his eyes from the morning sunlight that glinted from the cars around him. The highway was jammed and moving slowly with testy commuters on their way to work.

He turned on BBC News radio for what was supposed to be a 25-minute drive from his apartment in Alexandria, VA to Washington, DC. His employer, Interstellar Dynamics, was located in the Washington Loop, in an area occupied by numerous other government agencies and contractors.

He mostly enjoyed the science segments on the BBC, but he also thought their world news coverage was better than those of the other networks. Today they reported on a skirmish between the American and Chinese navies in the seas near Antarctica, and described a devastating fire that had broken out on a Chinese carrier that had claimed many lives. The event had occurred weeks earlier, but the story had just broken.

China blamed the United States which, of course, claimed no involvement. The situation had been diffused, but the already fragile relationship between the two countries had become confrontational. There was even talk of a new Cold War. The feuding countries could agree on one thing, however: the Russians were responsible for a malfunctioning spacecraft that was broadcasting a signal that interfered with AM radio all over the world. The problem was that the malfunctioning device was expected to broadcast for years. The only solution was to send up another vessel to destroy it, but that was prohibitively costly, and would take time.

Jacob was curious, so he tuned his car radio to the AM band they were discussing. A few minutes later, he thought he found the interference. It just sounded like intense static.

He chuckled. The Russians would deny it until their satellite fell out of orbit sometime in the next decade. Meanwhile, no one could use that part of the AM spectrum.

Jacob turned onto Interstellar Drive and got in a line behind a dozen other cars that led into a concrete-walled roundabout designed to prevent vehicles from crashing through the gate. He got his identification card ready and was on the other side five minutes later. He was already running late, and was relieved that he hadn't been selected for a random car search.

He pulled into his assigned parking spot in front of the seven-story concrete building a few minutes past 8:00 a.m., pulled his knapsack from the back seat, and walked to the front entrance. He slid his security card through a reader, opened the large glass door, and entered a foyer with an iris scanner mounted on the wall next to another door. After getting the green light from the device, he walked through a metal detector, where uniformed security personnel met him.

"Good morning, Dr. Hale," a large man said with a smile, his right hand on his holstered weapon.

"Good for a Monday, Bill," Jacob replied.

The big man chuckled. "Please open the backpack," he said.

"Phone, please," another man said.

Jacob complied, as usual. He'd never liked the idea of them holding his phone all day, but he understood the security protocol. What he didn't like was that they downloaded the data from his phone – including location information. And he wasn't supposed to have an extra personal phone. They claimed that they couldn't vouch for the security of another device, but he knew the real reason was to keep tabs on him. He'd kept another phone anyway – an untraceable "burner" phone, for emergency purposes. The company didn't own him.

After passing through security, he entered an elevator, punched a code on a number pad, and pressed the button for the fourth floor. A minute later he stepped out, greeted the woman at the reception desk, and walked to his office where he punched in yet another access code to unlock the door. He stepped inside and set his backpack on a small table next to the lone window. At six feet tall and eight inches wide, the window didn't provide enough light to work by comfortably. He switched on the overhead lights.

Jacob had found the ideal job. He loved to solve puzzles, and that's what Interstellar Dynamics paid him to do. He was tasked with reverse engineering things "acquired" from foreign governments and companies. Although he wasn't privy to the means by which these objects had been collected, he had his suspicions as to how operations were carried out. The things that reached his desk included everything from weapons and communication systems to medical devices. Once, he even had to reverse-engineer an electric razor.

In order to reverse engineer any device, such as an electric razor, many things needed to be unraveled. First, its mechanical operation – all moving parts – needed to be well understood. This involved gears, levers, actuators, and the like. Next, the functions of all electronic circuits had to be determined and carefully mapped. Then came the control systems – programmed computer chips used to make automatic decisions based on user input or external sensing. The control systems included computer codes that could be extracted from the permanent memory of the programmable chips. In most cases, these codes needed to be fully understood before a device could be cloned. Finally, they needed to determine the materials of which the device components were composed. For instance, a razor blade was made of hardened steel, and an artificial hip was composed of biocompatible materials such as titanium. Each new device had a cornucopia of puzzles to solve, and Jacob loved it all.

When reverse engineering a benign piece, such as a surgical

device, one could often disassemble it and work on each system in piecewise fashion. Dealing with military devices, however, was another story. Tampering traps, which could initiate self-destruct events, were often built into the systems. In some cases, the device would burn its electronics, rendering it useless. In other cases, there were lethal traps. These ranged from high-voltage shocks to explosives, and even poison.

Jacob recalled a case where an Interstellar Dynamics employee had been assigned to reverse engineer a Russian missile guidance system. It had been so riddled with booby-traps that they'd ultimately concluded that the intelligence operative who had acquired the device had been compromised; they'd collected a dummy device designed to send its collector a message. That engineer had been good, or *lucky*, enough to identify the problem before falling victim to it.

Jacob sat at his desk and rubbed his eyes as he logged into his computer. He never slept well after a late flight. His uncle's will kept running through his mind. Paulina had gotten it into his head that Theo was going to give him something significant. She insisted it would be money – in the millions – and he'd started believing her. *Wait until she hears what I actually got*, he thought. A book. He hadn't even opened the envelope. He wondered if he ever would.

He tried to shake the feeling, but it was clear that his disappointment had grown overnight. Uncle Theo couldn't even float him *one* million dollars out of the half-billion he'd given to his own children?

He wondered more now about how his uncle had gotten his money in the first place. He'd had the impression that it was old money – that Theo had inherited it just as his three children had just done. But Theo had never mentioned it. The other possibility was that he had earned it through business or investments – but, again, completely unknown.

Jacob didn't even know what his uncle had done for a living. He'd asked on a number of occasions, but never got a definitive answer. All he knew was that Theo had been gone most of the time, working in Washington, DC, or traveling the globe. He'd supposedly died right after one of his mysterious trips. On his deathbed, he'd been reminiscing about his last adventure on a submarine. Jacob's aunt said Theo must've thought he was back in World War II.

A knock on the door interrupted Jacob's thoughts.

"Come in," Jacob said.

A tall, wiry man with a shaved head, black goatee, and gold-rimmed glasses entered and leaned against the doorframe. The stench of noxious cologne soon filled the office. It was Terrence Fleming, his supervisor. He wasn't a person Jacob wanted to see first thing on a Monday morning, or at any other time.

"Just checking how you're progressing on the magnetic car bomb," Terrence said.

Jacob was supposed to inform Terrence of everything he did, and submit regular progress reports. Jacob wasn't always completely forthcoming, however, and for good reason. On more than one occasion, Terrence had reassigned him to another project right after Jacob had untangled all of the complicated puzzle work. Terrence would then finish the job – or get his staff to do it – and then take full credit. To Jacob, it felt like he'd just hooked a big fish, and then someone else grabbed the rod, reeled it in, and claimed it for their own.

"It's going slowly," Jacob lied. "I'm a little worried about tamper mechanisms."

"In the car bomb?" Terrence asked, seemingly skeptical. "They're handmade."

"They're Israeli-made," Jacob argued. The Israelis were known for sophisticated work on almost everything they did.

Terrence nodded but still didn't seem to buy it. "I want to discuss the details this afternoon," he said, and then left.

A knock one door down indicated that Terrence was now shaking down Hassaan, the next engineer on the block.

All of the junior engineers were aware of Terrence's methods, but it wasn't clear whether upper management had yet caught wind of his behavior. He wondered if it even mattered. Their group had been extremely successful since Jacob and a few others had been hired. He only worried that the stolen credit would give Terrence too much power – input on who got raises or promoted. Or *fired*. It reminded him, once again, about being shortchanged by his uncle.

Jacob walked down the hall to the restroom, relieved himself, and washed his hands. He took off his glasses and splashed his face with water in front of a mirror. He looked horrible. His fine, blonde hair was sticking up all over – he needed a haircut, and a shave. His eyes were those of a man who had gotten a poor night's sleep, and he was as pale as wax paper. How Paulina could be attracted to that face and skinny body he didn't understand.

He dried his face with a paper towel and put on his glasses. He walked down the hall, skipped his office, and then passed Hassaan's, where Terrence was still conducting his shakedown. He continued down the corridor until he reached a metal door on his left, punched in a code, and entered.

A young woman with black hair looked up from a microscope, smiled, and went back to her work. A large, bearded man in a lab coat and safety glasses waved to him from the opposite side of the lab. It was Sheldon, the electronics specialist.

Jacob walked over. "How's it going?"

"I figured out the actuator switch," Sheldon explained. "The countdown time is pre-programmed, and it has some nice safety features."

The Israelis' magnetic car bomb had made news years ago when it had been used to assassinate an Iranian nuclear scientist: an Israeli operative on a motorcycle stuck it on the man's car door and drove away. A few seconds later it detonated, and the target had been eliminated. Although Interstellar Dynamics wanted to understand the workings of the entire device, they were most interested in its explosion-focusing properties. A highly directed explosion did two things. First, by virtue of the need for less explosive material, the device could be made smaller, making it easier to deploy. Second, it greatly reduced collateral damage. The Israelis had perfected it.

"How is it armed?" Jacob asked.

"It's just like programming an alarm clock," Sheldon explained as he reached into an explosion-proof hood and extracted a device about the size of a hockey puck.

Jacob widened his eyes and looked at the device, and then to Sheldon.

"The explosive charge has been removed," Sheldon explained, apparently realizing Jacob's concern.

Jacob nodded for him to continue.

On the top of the puck were a digital display and three buttons. The display read "00:00."

Sheldon pushed a button and the digits started blinking, and then another button and the time display counted upwards. He stopped at twenty seconds.

"If you want to clear it and start over, you press the first and third buttons simultaneously," he explained and demonstrated. He then set it to ten seconds. "Now, once the countdown time is set, the device is activated by pressing the third button." He pressed it.

Jacob watched the timer. "It's not counting down."

Sheldon nodded. He then walked to the side of the metal explosion hood and brought the puck up to the outer wall. The device snapped to it with a metallic clang.

"Look at the timer now," Sheldon said, pointing.

It was counting down. It made perfect sense: you wouldn't want to have the thing counting down while it was in your hands.

"To disarm," Sheldon continued, "press the first and third buttons again." He demonstrated the operation and the puck fell off the metal hood.

"So the magnet is shielded when it's not armed?" Jacob asked.

Sheldon nodded. "That's a mechanical component – the only moving part."

"Nice feature," Jacob said. "That's a strong magnet. You wouldn't want it to stick to anything prematurely."

Sheldon reset the timer for fifteen seconds and again stuck the device to the metal casing of the hood. This time he positioned it so a part of the puck where the outer casing had been removed was visible.

"You can see what happens internally when it detonates," Sheldon explained.

After a few more seconds, Jacob jumped in response to a loud snapping sound and a brilliant flash.

"Bang," Sheldon said, smiling. "Easy as pie."

"The discharge is more than strong enough to detonate the plastic explosive this thing carries," Jacob said, "but we need to have numbers on that – voltage and power delivery. And we still need to understand the explosive focusing."

"Will do," Sheldon said. He deactivated the magnet and the device fell into his hands.

Jacob walked over to Elise, who looked up from her microscope and pushed her chair back from the table. "It's a custom chip," she explained as she tightened the band around her long ponytail. "The circuit will fry it if we try to remove it, even with the battery removed."

"A storage capacitor?" Jacob asked, knowing the answer. In some devices, like old television sets, even if the power source is removed, the internal electronics remain energized for some period of time.

"Yes," Elise said. "We'll need to bleed the stored charge before removing it."

"Good," he said. "And you've already mapped out the printed circuits?"

She nodded and said, "And downloaded the computer code from the chip. Sent it to you already."

"Thanks," he said, grinning. Finally, he thought, *a puzzle*. Deciphering computer code was one of his specialties. He enjoyed the logic. And it was even more fun if it was encrypted. For a simple device like the magnetic car bomb, it would take him only a few hours, but it could take weeks for more complicated systems. During those times Pauli would sometimes complain of neglect; his brain was always somewhere else.

He went back to his office to work on the code. He needed a few hours of escape.

The plastic seat creaked as Lenny Butrolsky leaned back and gazed through the enormous wall of windows facing the tarmac. Atlanta airport's international terminal was breathtaking, and he tried to enjoy what was probably his last cup of coffee in the United States. It was never easy to relax.

It had been a grueling and dangerous few weeks, but it was the last push. Now he could retire.

He hadn't chosen Costa Rica for the weather alone. Costa Ricans were the happiest people on the planet, and he hoped to emulate them. He had enough money to buy a modest house and live the remainder of his life in peace. The plan was to live in San Jose, the capital, but it wasn't essential. His only requirement was year-round warm weather, which ruled out the mountains.

As it got closer to his departure time, passengers trickled into the terminal and filled up the seats around him. He was suspicious of every one of them, save the children. After more than thirty years in his business, it would be difficult to reprogram his brain.

An elderly Asian man took the seat next to him on the right.

Lenny moved his carry-on bag and set it between his feet to give the man more space. He then leaned forward, rested his elbows on his knees, and rubbed his eyes with the heels of his hands. He just wanted to be in the air and on his way to Guatemala. Once in Guatemala City, he could manage an alternative route to San Jose if flying became problematic. Airports were dangerous places for those on the run.

He flinched at a tap on his right shoulder.

"Do you have the time?" the old man next to him asked in a thick Chinese accent.

Lenny looked at his watch. "Three-thirty," he replied. He turned his gaze back to the windows just as the afternoon sun glinted from the wings of a silvery jet lifting from the runway at a steep angle.

The elderly man thanked him, and then asked, "Tell me, sir, why are you leaving?"

Lenny stiffened his back, sat up, and turned to the man. "What do you mean?" he asked.

The man repeated the question.

Lenny didn't know what to say.

"You don't answer your phone. You still have work to do," the man said, and then passed him a business card.

Lenny grabbed it. The front of the card read Syncorp, Inc., followed by some Chinese script he couldn't read. He flipped it over: an address was written beneath *Tomorrow 2:00 p.m.*

Lenny's stomach turned sour. He again looked at his watch – his flight was due to board in twenty minutes. The plane had arrived and was waiting.

"I strongly recommend that you show," the man said as he stood, and then walked away, out of sight.

Lenny belched up a burning concoction of coffee and stomach acid that seared his throat. He took a sip of coffee but it didn't help. He stared at the card. He should have known better; getting out of his line of work wasn't easy. He should've waited until the last minute to destroy the contact phone. With his luck, they'd probably called the minute he'd smashed it.

One of Lenny's most serious concerns was that he no longer knew the identity of his employer. As the card suggested, however, whomever he worked for was still connected with Syncorp. But that didn't clarify anything: Syncorp had changed hands.

It worried him that they'd been able to track him down so quickly. He'd only made the flight reservations that morning, and under an alias. He'd been working under numerous identities, but he was currently using a new one. If they were that efficient, they'd find him in Costa Rica as well. They'd find him anywhere. Perhaps it was best to finish his business with them and break away clean. But he knew that might not be possible.

Lenny slung his bag over his shoulder, threw his coffee cup in the trash, and left the terminal.

Jacob entered the I-495 traffic jam at 5:00 p.m., just in time for the top-of-the-hour news report on BBC. They led with the Russian AM radio debacle and speculated about the technical aspects of the malfunction. The Russians emphatically denied the story, but the US and UK, and then Israel, Australia, and China, pressed on with their accusations. France was still undecided.

He turned off the radio and opened the windows. The car's air conditioner wasn't keeping up when the traffic came to a standstill.

The heat and exhaust fumes shifted his level of frustration up a notch. In addition to the traffic, and everything else he'd experienced in the past 24 hours, he'd struggled the entire afternoon on a simple computer code that should have taken him an hour. Terrence Fleming had interrupted him just as he'd started making progress. The half-hour interlude had blown his concentration.

Jacob loved his work, but was becoming increasingly dissatisfied with the results. In the beginning, a perfectly reverse-engineered device had given him a sense of accomplishment. At the end of the day, however, it seemed to have little impact. Even deconstructing weapons systems had little effect, other than the discovery of some tiny detail that might find its way into future American devices. But even if one did, he'd never see it in action, or even know whether it had been used. To top it off, his boss was taking the credit.

His thoughts projected a half-hour into the future, when he'd arrive home and see Paulina for the first time since leaving for Boston. The conversation about the will should be short – he got nothing. But Pauli wasn't the type to let things go, even if there was nothing that could be done about it.

He shook his head and sighed. He had to get over it. His uncle had done a lot for him, and he had to stop acting like a spoiled brat. Theo had provided him with an excellent education, and the means to take care of himself.

He turned the radio back on and listened to a debate about the skirmish in the Southern Seas. He learned that the Russian Navy had also been involved. It was peculiar that three adversarial countries would have a simultaneous military presence in such a strange place.

Not to mention it was winter in the southern hemisphere. Something seemed fishy.

After a 50-minute drive in slow, hot traffic, he exited the Capitol Beltway toward Alexandria, Virginia. He navigated a maze of surface streets, pulled his Toyota Corolla into its assigned parking spot at his apartment, and got out and grabbed his backpack from the back seat.

As he made his way to the entrance, he spotted Paulina's BMW in one of the visitor spaces. She'd be waiting for him in his third-floor apartment, probably hungry like he was. They'd have to go out, or order in.

He walked into the main lobby, retrieved his mail, and continued to the elevator. On the way up, he paged through the stack. It always annoyed him that so many of his bills still came through the normal mail even though he always paid them electronically. Even more irritating was the volume of junk mail that came along with it.

He walked down a carpeted hallway to his apartment and pulled out his keys. The door opened before he could unlock it. Pauli stood in the doorway in white shorts and a green t-shirt. Her blonde hair was tied up in a messy twist. She looked as if she'd been napping.

"It's been a long three days," she said as she hugged him and planted a kiss on his lips, and then his cheek. She stepped backward, into the apartment. "How'd it go?"

Jacob looked down at his feet for a second before answering. "Not well," he said, walked in, and closed the door behind him.

"Tell me."

"No money, no property. Just a rare book of some sort that he said wasn't worth much money."

Her lips pursed, and she shook her head. "I don't understand," she said. "I thought you were like one of his own kids."

Jacob had thought so, too.

"You saved his life for Christ's sake," she added, clearly agitated. "His kids ever do anything for him?"

Jacob was trying to let it go and didn't want to argue. "Let's get something to eat," he suggested.

"How are we ever going to buy a house?" she asked. "That could have lifted us off of the ground."

"Come on, Pauli, we can do it ourselves," he said. "My uncle paid for my education – I can earn a living." *Not to mention you're a well-paid lawyer*, he didn't add. No reason to get into a full-blown argument over money that had never belonged to either of them. "Now, food. I'm starving."

Pauli changed her clothes, and twenty minutes later they were in Paglio's Bistro, a local Italian restaurant just around the corner from his apartment building. The aroma of pizza baking in the wood oven made his stomach grumble until theirs finally came.

Against his better judgment, he described the magnitude of the estate as they ate.

Her face turned gaunt, and she hardly touched the pizza. "How can you live with this?" she finally asked.

He'd been thinking about it constantly, but he'd already accepted the reality of it. "First, even though I lived with them, I never experienced having a lot of money – no big allowance or anything," he explained. "Second, it wasn't mine to take – Uncle Theo could do whatever he wanted with his money."

"It could have changed our lives," Pauli blurted.

"We're doing pretty well," he argued. "I know I am, and you make twice what I do."

"What we have isn't real money," she scoffed. "Even renting modest apartments, in this area we can hardly save anything. It's going to take us forever to get a house."

"You realize a million dollars wouldn't change our lives very much," he said. "It could get us a nice house in this area, but then we couldn't afford the taxes."

"But *fifty* million would have changed our lives drastically," she said.

"You really didn't think I'd inherit fifty – "

"Why not?" she said. "What did his kids get? A hundred?"

Much more, he figured, with the properties.

"And he gave you *a book*?" she said, squinting her eyes. "What could it possibly be worth?"

He shrugged.

She pulled out her phone and tapped on it while he finished his slice and grabbed another. A few minutes later she said, "Unless it's Leonardo da Vinci's notebook, or *The Magna Carta*, it's not going to be worth much."

He didn't know anything about rare books. He preferred informative ones. "Theo said it was a book he enjoyed – so I doubt it's very valuable."

The waiter brought a box for the leftovers and handed Jacob the check – it was his turn to pay. A few minutes later they were out into the night, and walking back to his apartment. As they approached the front entrance, she said, "I think I'll go home tonight."

It was odd. It was going on ten o'clock, and she'd usually spend the night unless something big was going on the next day.

He shrugged. "Okay."

She kissed him on the cheek, and then trotted to her Beamer and drove away.

He went up to his apartment, changed into shorts and a t-shirt, and sat in silence on the couch facing a large, fully packed set of bookshelves. He'd known Pauli was going to be disappointed, but her reaction was more than he'd expected. He'd figured she'd feel bad for him, and that he'd have to tell her he was okay. Instead, it seemed she was upset for herself. What was she thinking? They weren't married. They weren't even living together.

Jacob took a shower and went to bed. He had a long week ahead of him.

It was going on midnight as Will sipped the 14-year, single-malt scotch – *The Balvenie* brand that Daniel and Sylvia had given him as a welcome gift. That had been over three weeks ago, when he'd moved into the Space Systems building. The fifth was almost gone.

He leaned back on the leather couch and looked out at the sky. The black abyss between the stars had always summoned a hope that freed him from the existence in which he was trapped.

Where in the hell is Denise? he wondered. She should have been in DC by now. He knew she and her mentor, Jonathan McDougal, had a lot to arrange before they could leave their posts in Chicago. But three weeks should have been enough time. Jonathan's exit would take more effort since he'd been running the DNA Foundation. The institution employed hundreds of lawyers and law students to research old cases where verdicts could be refuted or confirmed through DNA evidence. Jonathan would have to find someone to manage it in his absence, possibly permanently. Denise, on the other hand, would only have to tie up some loose ends – a few pending cases – and sublet her apartment. But she'd probably stay to help Jonathan, which meant it might be a while.

What was worse, Will thought, was that he and Denise weren't allowed to communicate in any way. They couldn't risk revealing his location.

The logic-driven part of his mind rejected the idea of developing a romantic relationship with Denise. More pressing, existential issues should be the priority. It seemed that all parts of his brain agreed on this point, but things were developing between them nonetheless. It was more than just wanting to be with her. Instead, it was as if they were connected through the situation that was arising.

He took a sip of scotch, set the glass on the coffee table in front of him, and picked up his notebook. He'd written over 100 pages of notes over the past three weeks that read like the ramblings of a madman. They were ideas, thoughts, or dreams that he couldn't connect to places, people, or experiences that were in his memory before he'd encountered the being inside the probe – the so-called Judge. Some seemed like random thoughts. Others were like scenes from science-fiction movies.

Emotions also rode upon those memories. He likened it to a device that had the option to record video or sound or both. Some memories carried images with minimal emotions, like the trip to a local art museum he'd gone on in grade school. In that case, he recalled paintings and statues, but minimal emotional information. In contrast, he remembered going to the funeral of one of his cousins who'd been killed in a motorcycle accident. Will had been only eight years old at the time, but the images and emotions were recorded in his memory with high resolution. Many of the untraceable memories – those he suspected weren't his own – were of the latter type, some with an emotional component that exceeded even that of his first memory of death.

The memory that affected him the most was one that caused the most prevalent nightmare: a blue planet turning pale. It conveyed the emotions of billions of deaths. He concentrated on a mental image of the planet while it was still blue: there were continents and seas and clouds and, on the dark half, the lights of cities. He didn't recognize the continents, and the collection of lights on the dark side was unusually dense. It wasn't Earth. But the threat was clear. What had caused the destruction was unknown.

There were other dreams that didn't seem threatening at all, and carried feelings of happiness and excitement. In one, he was on a beautiful island with a woman – he seemed to know her – and they were trying to solve a mystery, the details of which he couldn't recall. In another, he'd awakened on a paved trail in the middle of a desert of white sand. With the sun beating down on him, his only option was to follow the path. Both dreams carried positive, adventurous feelings.

Will flinched at a loud knock on the door, and then went over and peered through the peephole. It was James Thackett, the CIA director. It was late, but he'd informed Thackett that he was usually up past 2:00 a.m. Thackett was no night owl, but he'd visited after midnight on multiple occasions in the past three weeks. Will opened the door and Thackett stepped inside.

"I just came to check how things were going," Thackett said. "Any revelations?"

Will shook his head. "Sorry."

Thackett walked over to a set of two facing chairs with a small round table between them. He sat in one and gestured for Will to sit in the other.

"Setting up a trip to the base is not trivial," Thackett explained. "Naval Command wants only the *North Dakota* and its original crew to do it – because of their experience with the navigation and knowledge of the base and, of course, for secrecy purposes. As you know, the *North Dakota* is undergoing repairs, and the original crew has 200 days on land."

Will was well aware of the damages suffered by the submarine – he'd been onboard when they'd occurred. He also knew how the "gold" crew was to be swapped out with the "blue" crew, the latter of which had no experience with the probe, tunnel, or the base.

"We need to get there as soon as possible," Will said. "I don't think it would be in our best interest to wait 200 days."

"Can you give me any new information to strengthen the case for those who can make this happen?"

Will shook his head. "You heard what Horace told me," he replied. "Other than a feeling of urgency, all I have are his words."

Thackett sighed and nodded slowly. "I have a few strings I can pull to at least give the *North Dakota* priority in repairs. I don't know what will happen regarding the crew – there are stringent rules in place, many of which address the mental health of the men."

"I don't think they'd be deployed for too long – a few weeks," Will said. "And, imagining myself in the place of one of the crew, it would be another adventure."

"Maybe you'd be less enthusiastic if you'd been away from your family for six months."

"Probably," Will admitted. Maybe if they understood the urgency of the situation they'd realize that what they were doing was for everyone, including their families. He thought it was likely that many of them did sense that urgency. Will only wished he could explain what was causing his own anxiety – to them, and to himself.

"I'll see what I can do," Thackett said. "Let me know if you come up with anything new."

He nodded and followed Thackett to the door. "I will," he said as Thackett exited.

Will closed the door and grabbed the scotch bottle on his way to the couch. He added two fingers worth to his glass, downed half of it, and looked out at the sky. The nearly full moon seemed larger than usual, and its pale-white face made his nerves quiver as if an electric current were flowing through his body.

They had to get back to the base. Something was there.

THE NIGHT FLEW BY, and the next morning Jacob was running late for the second straight day. He didn't have time to make his usual stop for coffee, which was a good thing since he was presently caught in traffic and his bladder was near full capacity. With the congestion, it would be another 30 minutes before he got to Interstellar Dynamics.

He couldn't get the conversation with Pauli out of his mind. He was more disturbed by her reaction than by his disappointing inheritance. He hoped she'd calm down by the time he got home after work.

He turned on BBC News. The host interviewed a man who was convinced that the AM radio interference came from an alien spacecraft. He argued that the signal contained an encrypted message. The host turned to a British scientist who agreed that the signal was not merely noise: it came from a Russian communications device that was broadcasting an encrypted radio signal to correspond with its Earth-based control center. The encryption was standard practice, he explained. A Russian scientist followed, and denied any responsibility for the disturbance.

Jacob chuckled. They'd have a hard time getting the Russians to acknowledge that the satellite even belonged to them, much less that it was malfunctioning.

BBC followed with a science segment on the observation of gravitational waves that resulted in a Nobel Prize in Physics a few years ago.

The two colossal structures located in the US that had detected the first gravitational waves, and many others since that initial discovery, were undergoing repairs and upgrades due to recent erroneous detections. Experts debated whether the 200 million dollar price tag was worth it. Jacob was on the fence: he'd always been pro-science, but many other good things could be done with funding of that magnitude.

Jacob's bladder felt like it was going to explode as he turned onto Interstellar Drive, and the line of cars was longer than usual. After a full ten minutes, it was finally his turn to go through the concrete roundabout. He flashed his ID badge and a guard waved him over to a parking spot where two uniformed men were waiting.

Great, he thought. He hadn't been selected for a random search in six months, and they picked a day when he was running late, and about to wet himself.

It took them ten minutes to search his person and vehicle, and then he was racing to the main building where he'd have to go through another wave of security.

He turned into the parking lot and couldn't believe his eyes. Someone had parked in his assigned spot.

He looked at the clock: 8:36 a.m. He was late and the parking lot was packed. He found a spot about 75 yards from the entrance. As he got out of his car, the strain on his gut made it difficult for him to fully straighten. He opened the back door, pulled out his backpack, and swung the door closed, the jolt of which nearly made him let go of his bladder.

The walk to the building was slow and excruciating. He made it to security, where Bill, the largest of the guards, greeted him. Jacob felt a cold bead of sweat run down the side of his face as the man tried to make small talk.

Bill let him through, and Jacob made his way to the elevator and pressed the up button. It seemed to stop at every floor on its way down. When it finally arrived, he had to wait for a half-dozen people to exit before he could enter. As he walked in, three other employees joined him and pressed buttons for the second and third floors and entered their codes. Jacob pressed the button for the fourth floor and entered his pin.

He exited on the third stop, walked toward his office, and spotted his supervisor knocking on his door. Jacob would have to pass by him on the way to the bathroom, but he was at the stage where it no longer mattered.

As he approached, Terrence spotted him and walked in his direction.

"We need to talk," Terrence said.

Jacob pressed past him as he said, "Give me a minute. I'm about to explode."

He went into the bathroom, set his backpack on a sink, and found the urinal. It was the greatest relief he'd felt in weeks. He wondered if he'd done any permanent damage to his kidneys or bladder. Afterwards, he washed his hands and walked back to his office, where Terrence was waiting.

"You're late," Terrence said, leaning against the doorframe.

"Sorry," Jacob said, feeling his face flush. It wasn't like him.

"Again."

"It's been a rough couple of days."

Jacob punched in the code for his office and they walked in.

"How can I help you, Terrence?" Jacob asked.

"Your last two projects have been taking longer than anticipated," Terrence said.

Jacob noticed something in Terrence's voice, and in the way he looked at the floor when he spoke. What the hell was going on?

He got his answer when the two security guards stepped into the doorway, one of whom was Bill from the building's entrance.

"You have to be kidding me," Jacob said, and shook his head. "You're firing me?"

Terrence shrugged. "It was a team decision."

"Team?" Jacob said. "Who, exactly?"

"Me and the branch head," he replied.

Jacob had never interacted with the branch head, so he knew that the only input regarding his performance had come from Terrence.

His face became hot. "Who are you going to steal credit from now, Terrence?" Jacob said, his voice increasing in volume. "You have no skills – you can't do this work."

Terrence looked to Bill. "Get him out of here," he ordered.

Bill moved forward, looked at Jacob, and shrugged.

Jacob raised his hands. "I'm going," he said. "But I'm writing a letter to the branch head to let him know exactly what you've been doing here. And not only what you've been doing to me, but to the rest of the engineering staff."

"The branch head thinks I'm doing a fine job with the group, and has just made me the lone manager – Jackson was fired as well," Terrence said smugly, referring to his now former co-manager.

"Does he know you're a snake?" Jacob asked.

Jacob, who had never gotten into a fistfight in his life, purposely knocked his shoulder into Terrence's as he passed.

"Have a nice life, asshole," Terrence said.

Jacob stopped instantly. While he contemplated turning around and throwing a punch, a heavy hand grabbed his right upper arm.

Bill guided him out the door, and Jacob didn't resist. A few steps away from the office Bill let go of his arm, followed him to the elevator, and got in with him.

"That guy's an ass to all of us," Bill said as the door closed. "I had half a mind to let you slug him."

"You saw that."

Bill nodded, and the corners of his mouth turned up slightly. "Tough luck, fella," he said. "You're a young, smart guy. I bet you'll have a job by the end of the week – a *better* one."

On the ground floor, another security guard collected his badge and ID card but didn't return his phone – it belonged to the company.

Bill escorted him to the door. Seconds later, Jacob was in the parking lot.

When he was about halfway to his car, he felt strange. Something was wrong. It took him a few seconds to figure it out.

He was smiling.

WILL SAT on the leather couch that faced the southeastern windows of his flat. It was just after 9:00 a.m. The sun had risen above the lip of the overhang so that there was no direct sunlight, and he had a good view of the dense forest below. It was mostly spruce trees, like those at the summer cottage he used to visit as a kid. He could almost smell them from memory.

His mind was like a slowly melting icicle, dripping imprinted thoughts and memories from his subconscious into accessible images and feelings. So far, the alien thoughts were mostly just the ingredients of nightmares. But he knew they were also threads of unique and critical knowledge, the importance of which he was desperate to understand.

He sat down for an hour every morning and evening to extract memories from his encounter with the being in the probe. It was something that was difficult to explain to anyone who hadn't experienced separating their soul from their body, and then occupying another. There were no points of reference to help describe the muddy-warm feeling of slipping into the possession of an empty body.

While inside the probe, he and the Judge had occupied pristine bodies in order to communicate. When they'd exited the bodies afterwards, the Judge slipped into the body Will had vacated and stole his imprinted memories. Will had responded by pulling the same trick on the Judge – he occupied the body the Judge had exited – and stole the Judge's memories. The Judge used Will's memories to condemn the human race. The memories Will had stolen from the Judge now haunted him and trickled new information into his mind.

Will had tapped into some of that information weeks ago when he'd deciphered the inscriptions on the White Stone artifact, although that had come too late to be of use. But he was sure there was more useful knowledge locked in his mind, which was why he documented everything that came to him – daydreams, nighttime dreams, nightmares, and any random thoughts that he deemed odd.

He'd considered hallucinogenic drugs or cannabis to accelerate the process, but he'd concluded that it would be too difficult to sort out whether a peculiar memory was from the imprint, or from drug effects.

It was an odd thing trying to record one's thoughts when a distinction had to be made between the authentic and the implanted. The implanted ones would most often present at night, when he was calm. Other times, when his attention was focused on some task, like running on the treadmill or swimming, they'd drop out of his subconscious – if that's where they were stored – and into full view.

Images of the Nazi base kept popping into his mind. He'd never been there, but he'd seen photos of the place. The pictures Daniel and Sylvia had brought back from their trip to the base rarely had people in the frame. When they had, they'd only been in the background, or purposely placed in the photo for scale. But they were also all in modern US Navy uniforms. The people in his memories were either in Nazi uniforms, or naked – the prisoners. He doubted that the images came from photos or documentaries he'd seen. They were too vivid, and entwined with emotions.

Will's phone chirped: it was time for his daily meeting with Thackett and the others. Hopefully they had some information about the trip to Antarctica.

It was midmorning. Rush hour was over and the traffic was light.

As Jacob drove, his mind was blank, and he wasn't as upset as he thought he should have been. Perhaps it was because both events, the reading of the will and his termination, had been out of his control. It was his impression that, in general, people felt more badly about things if they had some part to play in them – if they were at fault somehow. None of it was his fault and, therefore, losing his job started to look more like an opportunity.

He drove past his apartment building and continued two more blocks to a small, hole-in-the-wall coffeehouse called Pine Perk, which was located across Pine Street from Pine Park, a vast public recreation complex. He frequented the running path through Pine Park in the evenings, and Pine Perk for coffee before work and on weekends. Now he found himself in the coffeehouse in the late morning on a weekday. He knew he couldn't endure sitting alone for hours in his apartment waiting for Pauli to get off work.

The barista looked at him with an odd expression as he ordered a dark roast coffee.

"Strange time to see you here on a weekday," she said.

"Vacation," Jacob said. Her name was Lisa and he saw her almost every weekday morning on his way to work. "Taking a few days to relax."

She smiled and handed him a mug.

He took a seat at a small table next to a window with a good view of the park. Kids played soccer, and young mothers pushed strollers with babies. It was a peaceful scene. It was just what he needed.

He opened his knapsack and pulled out a notebook to jot down his thoughts. His first task was to figure out how long he could survive in his current lifestyle without a job. That was easy: he had about seventy thousand dollars he'd been saving for a down payment on a house. If he streamlined his lifestyle, his current expenses added up to about three thousand dollars a month. That gave him about two years. It was more than enough time to find a job and enjoy life for a while. If Pauli moved in and got rid of her apartment, that buffer time would double. She'd been hinting at the idea for a year. Maybe now was the time.

He pulled his laptop out of his backpack and spent the rest of the morning searching job ads and reading a novel. At about 2:00 p.m. he went back to the apartment and cleaned everything – kitchen, bathroom, and laundry. He went for a run in Pine Park, showered, and left again to pick up groceries. Before he knew it, it was 5:00 p.m.

A half-hour later, Pauli called and wanted him to meet her at a restaurant in DC at 7:00 p.m., close to her law firm. She was having a late night at work – something that was more the norm than the exception.

He ironed a shirt and pants, dug up his coat and tie, and hit the road by 6:30 p.m. He couldn't believe that he was finally going to ask her to move in. It was a bittersweet transition for him, and possibly for her, considering his employment situation, but he felt it all would end well. Despite her reaction the night before, he hoped this might put the inheritance situation to rest and they could move on.

The restaurant had mandatory valet parking. The young man to whom he handed his keys looked disappointed as a Porsche pulled in behind his Toyota Corolla. *Tough luck, fella*, Jacob thought.

It was a French restaurant, something Jacob had never learned to appreciate. Even the aroma of the food seemed stuffy to him, but he was hungry, and was thinking about fillet mignon. He'd ask Pauli the question over dessert.

He followed the ceramic-metallic clacking sounds of silverware and plates past the host desk. He spotted Pauli by herself at a table in the center of the main dining room. He realized that he was lucky she was alone: often she'd be with colleagues when they'd meet near her firm.

She wore a blue skirt suit with a white shirt and a red scarf. Her blue jacket was folded over the back of the chair to her right. Her blonde hair was tucked into a tight bun except for a few recalcitrant strands that fell alongside her ears. He saw fatigue in her otherwise bright green eyes.

He walked over and leaned in for a kiss. She turned her face so that he only got to her cheek. He knew she'd been upset by the bad news about the will, but he didn't think it would carry on this long. He sat in the chair across from her and loosened his tie.

"How was your day?" he asked.

"A lot happened," she replied. "Yours?"

"Could've been better," he said, not wanting to deliver the bad news before the good.

She ordered a salad but not wine. Both were unusual. He ordered a steak and had a coke. He could have used a glass of wine.

As he finished his fillet – she barely touched her salad – he got the impression that she had something to say. "Something on your mind?" he asked.

She shifted in her seat and didn't make eye contact. "My firm is transferring me," she said.

"Oh," he said. His stomach tightened. The mechanical tone of her voice carried more meaning than her words. "Where?"

"London," she replied.

Her firm was one of the largest in the world. They had offices in New York and Los Angeles as well. He could find a job in either of those cities, especially LA, but London would be tough. His expertise was suited best for government work, not private industry, and he wasn't a UK citizen.

"Okay," he said, and spent a few confusing seconds with his thoughts. "How long will you be there?"

She shrugged. "It's not just for one case, Jake," she said and stared at him, seemingly assessing whether he understood the implications.

He understood. "So you don't want to try to make this work."

She just stared back at him.

"How did this come about?" he asked.

"One of the senior partners of my firm came into my office today and gave me an offer that I couldn't refuse."

"A raise?"

She nodded. "A huge one. And a flat in London."

"They gave you a flat in London?" he asked, astonished.

She shook her head. "Leased. It's mine as long as I'm with the firm," she explained. "They promised I'll be promoted to partner in six months, and then I'll take over the trademarks branch."

Jacob knew where this was heading, but had to ask. "Again, do you want to try the long-distance – "

She put up her hand and shook her head. "I think it will be too hard. Maybe it's best we make a clean break."

It took him another full minute of convoluted thought to solidify the situation in his mind. Finally, he asked, "This is what you want?" He knew by her expression that she'd already made up her mind.

Her look turned solemn as she nodded, a gesture that Jacob knew indicated that she'd thought about it, and she'd stick with her decision even though it was unpleasant.

Receiving no inheritance hit him hard. Losing his job hurt, but he'd been in good spirits. But his girlfriend of four years leaving him without warning was devastating. He was fed up with all of it. He had no more negative emotions to spill out. The last few days had drained him, and it was clear that he had to clear his plate and start from scratch.

"Okay," he said, waving to the waiter for the check. "You can go – I'll take care of this. I wish you the best."

Paulina's eyes went blank, stunned or confused, he couldn't tell.

"That's it?" she asked.

He stared back at her. "Good luck, Pauli."

A tear streamed down her face as she gathered her purse and folded her jacket over her arm. She walked away at a hurried clip. The waiter came with the check before Pauli exited the restaurant. Jacob delayed paying for a few minutes to avoid an awkward moment; she'd be waiting for the valet to drive up with her Beamer. He'd hit the restroom afterwards just to make sure she was gone.

She was right that a clean break was best. A long-distance relationship with no plan was bad for everyone. The more devastating realization was that she'd chosen her job over him. That wasn't completely fair – the offer sounded like her ideal job. She'd often mentioned how being based in the London office would be a dream for her. And to be promoted to partner in six months – after only two years with the firm – seemed unusual. She'd just recently been elevated to associate. Something didn't sit right with him.

He went to the restroom and relieved himself before the half-hour drive back to his apartment. He was never again going to make the mistake he'd made with his bladder on the morning drive to his last day at Interstellar Dynamics.

Five minutes later, he threw his jacket on the passenger seat of his Corolla, tipped the valet, and was on the road toward his apartment.

He'd lost everything in less than forty-eight hours. It should have been overwhelming, but he tried to keep things in perspective. He had his health and wasn't in any sort of trouble. He was just single and unemployed, and he had enough money to live on for two years, if it came to that.

After ten minutes in traffic, his lack of emotion slowly turned to anger, and then nearly to rage. He was tempted to ram the car in front of him or simply crash his car into a brick wall. He managed to hold himself together by promising himself that there was a bottle of Merlot waiting for him at home.

He got back to the apartment complex without incident and checked his mailbox. He sorted through junk mail as he rode the elevator to the third floor. After entering his apartment, he dumped the mail in the garbage and then threw his coat at a chair. It missed and landed on the floor. Rather than picking it up, he went into the kitchen and grabbed the bottle of wine from the rack on top of the refrigerator. He opened it, poured a heavy glass, and downed it as if he were gulping water after a five-mile run. He refilled, peeled off his shoes, and sat on the couch.

He took swig, and then shook his head and closed his eyes. *What a day*, he thought. *What a couple of days*. He looked around his apartment and sighed. He was starting to see the consequences of inheriting nothing from the Leatherby estate. Although it may have had its part in losing Paulina, it was much more than that.

Not being included in the inheritance was a declaration of exclusion from the family. He was now different than his cousin-siblings. They'd forever be separated by socioeconomic class, and there'd always be an awkwardness between them. Tabitha had already behaved oddly with him at the dinner just after the reading of the will. Was this what Uncle Theo intended? He was a smart man – did he do it on purpose?

He took another gulp of wine and examined his bookshelves, which were packed to full capacity. Many of the books were engineering and computer texts, but the majority were puzzle books. There were at least two hundred of them, and he should've tossed them long ago – he'd solved them all. But he just couldn't get himself to part with books of any kind. They'd been his entire life ever since his family had been murdered.

He finished the glass and stood. Already a little dizzy, he made his way to the counter, poured a third glass, took a gulp, and topped it off.

Maybe he'd never work again. He could get a cheaper place and ride his money until it was gone. After that, who knew? Work a menial job? Jump off a bridge?

As he walked back to the couch he stepped on his jacket, which slid on the slick hardwood floor. He almost fell, and wine splashed onto his white shirt. He cursed as he set the dripping glass on the counter.

He took off his shirt, rushed it to the utility room next to the bathroom, threw it in the washing machine, and started running hot water. He had no idea of the correct thing to do in this situation, but that was what he'd decided. He went to the bedroom, changed into a t-shirt and shorts, and collected some bathroom towels he'd neglected to wash during his cleaning binge in the afternoon. He threw the towels into the washer, added detergent and bleach to their proper dispensers, and then closed the lid and started the wash cycle.

He then went back to the living room and picked up the jacket that had caused the incident. As he walked into the bedroom to hang it up, something fell to the floor. He leaned over and looked to see what it was. In a few seconds, he remembered: it was the envelope he'd gotten at the reading of the will – he'd been wearing that same jacket. He picked up the envelope, threw the jacket on his bed, and went back out to the living room and sat on the couch.

He held the brown, letter-sized envelope up to the light but couldn't see through it. He pressed on it with his fingers. He was sure the two hard objects were keys, although one seemed to be round, like a smooth bolt. He shook it, causing a light, metallic clanging sound.

To him, the envelope represented two things. First, it marked his separation from the Leatherby family. Second, it drew the pity of Paulina, a factor that must have played a part in her decision to go to London. If he'd inherited just one million of the billion dollars doled out that day, he and Pauli might have been browsing for houses rather than going separate ways.

He shook his head. Was that the type of person he wanted to be with the rest of his life – slogging around trying to make sure someone else was satisfied? He respected her decision, but it revealed her priorities.

He opened the envelope and spilled its contents onto the coffee table in front of the couch. Just as he thought, two keys slipped out. One was silver and cylindrical, like that for a bike lock, but longer. The other was a normal key made of tarnished brass. He picked them up and examined them closely. The silver key had some markings etched along the cylindrical shaft – a line of numbers and letters – and the brass one had a small '4' stamped into its circular face. There had to be more.

He picked up the envelope and forced it open, hoping for a note with more information.

Nothing.

It seemed that his uncle had given him a puzzle.

CHAPTER 2

Jacob awakened to a buzzing alarm clock.
He started the morning routine to get to Interstellar Dynamics by 8:00 a.m. He didn't realize his folly until he was halfway through his shower. He didn't have to be anywhere, and didn't have to see anyone. It was a depressing freedom.

He donned khaki shorts and a t-shirt, put his laptop and the envelope that contained the keys into his backpack, and headed to Pine Perk.

Ten minutes later he was sitting at an outdoor table with a dark roast coffee and a clear view of the park. Before eight o'clock the area was populated mostly with runners, but a few people had brought their dogs. He wondered if it was like that every day. If so, it was a tranquility that he hadn't appreciated – something enjoyed by the subculture that got to stay home on weekdays.

He powered up the laptop and connected to Pine Perk's wireless internet service. His task for the day was to gather info and identify the keys.

The brass key was of an ordinary design, like that for a conventional padlock, and only had the number '4' stamped into its head to identify it. It would be impossible to place. The silver one had more detailed identification markings, and resembled a key for a tubular lock, like those often used for bicycle locks. This key, however, differed from a typical tubular lock. It had grooves around the barrel and along the length, and was rounded at the end.

He started by assuming it was the key to a safe deposit box. After just a few minutes of research, it was clear that he'd need more than just a key to get into a safe deposit box: he might need a code, or they'd check his signature. Some banks even required biometric data, like a fingerprint or iris scan.

For the next two hours he read everything he could find about cylindrical keys that resembled the one in his possession. The string of twelve characters engraved along the length of the cylinder contained numbers, a decimal point, and mixed upper and lowercase letters. He searched for the character string, segments of the string, and key labeling protocols, but found nothing useful. He then researched European safe deposit box keys, and found some that resembled the cylindrical design but, in the end, he'd gotten no closer to solving the problem.

He decided to take another approach. He wrote down the markings on the key in his notebook: n7Nat.1SwSWn. He stared at it for a while, assuming it was a word scramble of some kind. It would normally be simple puzzle work for him to rearrange scrambled letters to form a word or phrase, but this string of characters contained numbers and a decimal point, as well as upper and lowercase letters. He thought it could be a physical address – perhaps that of a bank. Assuming both numbers were used in the street number, it could only be 17 or 71. It took him a little over a half hour to figure out the street name because the "NW" appended to the end had thrown him off. Afterwards, he thought it should have been clear since they were uppercase letters.

It was by no means a definitive answer – he could be wrong about it being an address – but he narrowed it down to one of two places: 17 or 71 *Swann St. NW*. He pulled up a map of the area on his computer. The bank was in Washington, DC.

Although they'd only spoken over the phone, Lenny Butrolsky suspected that his new contact in the Syncorp network was at the top of the food chain. He'd sounded older than Lenny's usual handlers and, on top of a moderate Chinese accent, spoke English as if he'd learned it in the UK. But the man had seemed to lack the practical knowledge of someone in his position. It was in the way he'd downplayed the difficulty of the mission, as if it were going to be a simple smash-and-grab job, or a midnight break-in. It made Lenny squirm in his middle seat in the last row of the Boeing 777 as it lifted off from DC's Reagan International Airport. It was going to be much more complicated than that.

Lenny had developed all the skills associated with his profession, but his true talent was assassination. That's what made him nervous about the current job: he had to first extract information from the targets before eliminating them. And it was clear that his interviewees would all have to die. He couldn't have those he encountered warn the others downstream, or identify him later. It was a shame, but a trail of bodies was better than a trail of informants.

The other problem was that interrogations took time. With a simple hit, he could be in and out in minutes. In this case, the job would linger on, and would make noise.

He landed at Boston's Logan International Airport in the late afternoon and checked into an expensive downtown hotel. It was not his usual method of operation – he preferred seedy places where he could pay in cash – but the situation called for it. It was a part of his cover story, and his client was paying extra for this one.

His target was a lawyer, and he'd already set up an interview with her. He was posing as a wealthy man setting up a trust fund for his family. She was a partner in one of the largest law firms in Boston, and he had to find a way to isolate her in a secure and private place. There was going to be a ruckus.

The meeting was at 5:00 p.m. It was time enough to take a shower and get dressed. He was amazed at the size of the bathroom in his suite, which included a hot tub, and wished he'd have more time to enjoy it.

Getting dressed and undressed was always a chore with his shoulder. Although the bullet wound was mostly healed, he had a limited range of motion in his right arm, and it was painful to move in certain directions. He undressed, stepped closer to the marble countertop, and examined the scar in one of the many mirrors. It looked like a quarter-sized hole plugged with flesh-colored bubblegum.

He stepped back and caught the reflection of his naked body from many directions at once. His image disgusted him – especially the view from the side. He looked like a pale ape that had been through a meat grinder. Over the decades, he'd been shot four times, and nearly carved up like a Thanksgiving turkey once by an Iranian in Morocco. The latter, he realized, had happened twenty-five years ago.

He'd always been heavy – thick, not fat. His wide shoulders presented a good target for a bullet, like the one that got him six months ago. He'd always thought his arms were too long, and his hands too large – he really did have ape-like features. But the most striking thing he realized was his age. It was something not as noticeable when observing one's own face straight on. The side view captured it, and he thought it was probably because people didn't see themselves in profile very often. He looked old and haggard. He still had his hair, but it was cut short and was mostly gray. He was 52 but looked much older. He'd been through a lot more than most people had in their tame lives.

He finished his shower and implemented a disguise that subtly changed his facial features and hair. He was good at disguises, but this one took him a full hour to construct. Afterwards, he dressed in a suit and tie, and packed his alias credentials and paperwork in a leather courier bag. He couldn't bring a gun for this one.

The firm was across the street from his hotel.

As he rode the elevator to the lobby, he admired his disguise in the mirror-finish of the door. The goatee made him look younger.

He walked out of the hotel, turned right, and proceeded to the first traffic light. He turned left, crossed the street, and entered the large building on the corner: the law firm of Watts, Turk, and Genobli. He was immediately met by security, and asked for his identification and appointment information.

He gave them the details of his upcoming meeting and his ID, and then passed through a metal detector. They returned his ID and directed him to a large waiting room with leather furnishings and artwork on the walls. A five-gallon stainless steel coffee dispenser with a flame warmer beneath it stood on a table in the far corner. Next to it was a pyramid of porcelain coffee cups.

He walked over, filled a cup, and sat in a chair next to a window facing the street.

It was a comfortable day – clear and warm – but he would rather have been on a beach in Costa Rica. This job would be unusually lucrative, but he'd already accumulated enough wealth to retire, although at a modest level. This one would put him well over the top, but his motivation for money had waned. Now he was doing it for security – for a clean break from his current employers, whoever they were. And this was a good one on which to quit: it was complicated, dangerous, and not well-planned. In fact, "well-planned" was the opposite of what it was – it was pure improvisation. He'd been given five days to accomplish his objective, and this job was just the first of many dangerous steps.

Seven others sat in the lobby, presumably waiting for meetings of their own. A young female receptionist opened a door and called out a name. A middle-aged man with a shaved head and an expensive suit stood and followed her through the door.

A few minutes later, the same receptionist called out Lenny's alias, Leonard Schultz. He followed the woman through the door where he was handed over to an armed security guard. Lenny shuddered at the idea of being unarmed, but he'd been in tighter situations.

The guard led him into an elevator, held a proximity access card to a sensor on the control panel, and pressed the button for the thirty-fifth floor. The elevator door closed with an unusual rapidity and silent efficiency. The building was modern, and it seemed that no expense had been spared. He figured they probably hadn't skimped on security either, and that he should beware of silent alarms and cameras.

Lenny's knees flexed as the elevator accelerated upward, and his ears popped as they reached their destination. The doors opened to a carpeted hallway that resembled those in his five-star hotel. The guard led him to office 3517 and knocked on the large wooden door.

A woman's voice on the other side invited them to enter, and the guard pushed it open and held it.

Lenny walked in and the door closed behind him. The security guard was gone.

A woman, early to mid-30s, with blonde hair and dark-rimmed glasses stood behind a large desk. She walked over and greeted him with an extended arm.

"Nice to meet you in person, Ms. Dixon," he said and smiled. They'd chatted on the phone for two hours that morning to set up the expensive, impromptu service of her firm. They cleared her schedule for the negotiated 2,000 dollar-per-hour fee. The expense was absorbed by his client, and strengthened the ruse.

"Likewise, Mr. Schultz," she said. "But, please, you can call me Jody."

"Thanks again for making room in your schedule," he said. "Call me Lenny."

"You're my last meeting for the day," she said. "Did you bring all of the documents?"

Lenny nodded and took a seat in a chair in front of the desk as Jody moved around to the other side. He handed her a thick manila folder.

She paged through the papers. "Looks like everything's here," she said as she pulled out one of the documents and looked at it. "I can see why you're doing this now – at your young age," she said. "You could put twenty million in a trust and, no matter what happens to the rest of your assets, your family will be set for life."

Lenny nodded. "That's the idea."

Jody pressed a button on her desk phone and a young man

entered. "Please make copies of these," she said and handed him the manila folder.

"Now, let's get to the details of the trust," she said. "What would you like to do?"

Lenny had a long list of requests that he'd prepared with the intent of making the meeting last as long as possible. He wanted it to extend to another appointment. He'd also omitted one of the required documents – she hadn't noticed – as an excuse to meet again, if necessary. He figured she wouldn't be disappointed with more billable hours.

Now that he understood their security procedures, he could devise a plan.

AFTER SPENDING MOST of the afternoon running errands, Jacob went back to his apartment and forced down a nutrition bar. Excitement had suppressed his appetite.

The keys and the address had been on his mind the whole afternoon, but he held off to avoid the DC rush hour traffic. At 7:00 p.m. he took a ride.

He punched in "17 Swann St. NW" into his GPS navigation device and drove. After a half hour in the waning but still slow traffic, he found himself in the trendy Adams Morgan area of northwest Washington, DC. He passed by the French restaurant where his love life had taken a downward turn the previous night, and continued through streets mixed with unique businesses and residential buildings. He turned onto Swann Street and concluded immediately that there would be no bank.

He had two street numbers to check: 17 and 71. He came to 17 first. It was on his right, and he slowed as he approached. It was an old stone building, maybe eight to ten stories tall. There were no entrances or windows facing the street. Based on its design, and those of the buildings in the surrounding neighborhood, it was a residential structure.

He drove a few blocks farther, to street number 71. It was a flower shop.

Damn, he thought. *What else could the markings on the key mean?*

He took a left at the next intersection, and then two lefts and a right, and was again on Swann, heading back toward the first building. He passed 17 on his left, continued on for another block, and did a U-turn. He parked the car on the street and turned off the engine.

He removed the car key from the ignition and examined the two new keys he'd put on his key ring. Neither seemed like they'd be the key to a residence.

He got out of the car and walked down the sidewalk toward the building. Its walls were constructed of square-faced stones that were about the size of car batteries. Smaller, hand-sized stones made up sills and arches of façade windows that were bricked in. In the waning light, the large stones glittered like rough, silver-black granite, and the smaller ones had an amber hue.

He turned onto the walkway that led between 17 and the adjacent building to the right. Both buildings were at least eight stories tall, and were separated by about 30 feet. The little sunlight that made it through the tall oaks on the west side of the street didn't make it into the narrow gap between the buildings. He walked into the shadows.

Halfway down the alley between the buildings was a set of stone steps on his left that led to a porch on 17. The red brick building on the right had no doors or windows facing 17.

At the top of the porch was an enormous wooden door. It was inset about two feet into the stone wall, and looked like it was constructed from railroad ties, or from wood retrieved from a sunken ship. It was about ten feet tall and four feet wide, and arched at the top. There were no visible hinges, and only a black metal plate where the handle was supposed to be.

He walked up the steps and examined the black plate. His heart thumped: there was a circular receptacle, about a quarter inch in diameter, and nothing else.

He looked to his left, toward the street. It was clear. About a hundred feet to his right was a brick wall that extended through the backyards of both buildings – a dead end. He selected the cylindrical key from the ring, and inserted it into the hole. It slid in smoothly.

The key vibrated lightly in his fingers. An instant later, the left side of the door moved – it swung outward a few inches. He removed the key and slid his fingers along the exposed edge of the door. He found a smooth groove that seemed to be designed to provide a grip, and pulled. The door pivoted with little resistance, but he could tell it was massive.

As he pulled and stepped toward the widening opening, he got a view of the door's edge, which was about eight inches thick. The outer wood was just a façade for a massive slab of steel. Inset into the door's left jamb were six circular holes, each two inches in diameter, that were equally spaced from the bottom to the top of the doorframe. The positions of the holes matched those of six steel rods in the open edge of the door that would extend into the jamb when the door was locked. It resembled the door to a vault.

He peered inside. It was dark, and he couldn't see anything. He hesitated, but then trusted that his Uncle Theo would never put him in danger. He entered.

The door automatically inched closed behind him, and a humming and final metallic click indicated that it had locked. A dim light energized about six feet above his head, revealing a square foyer, about twelve feet on a side. Directly across the room, opposite the door he'd just entered, was a shiny steel door. On his left was a three-by-three array of what seemed to be the doors to mailboxes, like those used in apartment buildings, but larger. They were a foot square, and the faces were made of polished brass with numbers engraved into their centers. Each had a slot for a key on the right, near the edge.

With trembling hands, Jacob selected the brass key stamped with a '4' on his key ring, inserted it into the keyhole of the mailbox door with the same number, and twisted. The key vibrated and the door shifted outward about a centimeter on the side nearest the keyhole.

He removed the key and pulled the door. It was much thicker than he'd anticipated – like the door to a small safe. He peered inside and spotted a book and an envelope. He extracted both and then felt around deeper inside with his hand for anything he might have missed. There was nothing, so he closed the door. The locking mechanism immediately engaged with a hum and click.

The leather-bound book was about nine by eleven inches, and over two inches thick. The envelope was similar to the one that had contained the keys, except his name was written on it. It was his uncle's handwriting.

Next, he examined the steel door that led deeper into the building, and wondered if it was of the same design as the outer one. It was smaller but it, too, had a circular keyhole.

He searched the walls and ceiling. He figured a place that committed to security would have cameras. He didn't find any, but he knew they might be miniature and hidden.

He pressed on the sealed envelope with his fingers. There was another cylindrical key inside, and he was sure it was for the inner door. But he wasn't going to go through that door. Not tonight. Instead, he was going to go home and see what was in the book and envelope.

He turned to the outer door. In the low light, he felt around on its metallic surface for a button or a keyhole. His heart picked up pace. There were no features of any kind – it was perfectly smooth. He pushed on it but it didn't budge. He felt along the wall near the door and, to his relief, located a circular button. It was an inch in diameter and illuminated in such a dim green light that it was almost unnoticeable.

He pressed it. The door hummed and then swung open a few inches so that the space between the jamb and the edge of the door revealed the fading light outside. He pushed it open and stepped out, onto the porch. He turned and watched as the door slowly swung closed on its own. The lock engaged with a light hum and click.

He looked toward the street to see if anyone was watching. He didn't know why he was so nervous – he wasn't doing anything wrong.

He went back to his car. His hands shook as he slid the key into the ignition.

Jacob had to concentrate in order to obey the speed limits and safely navigate traffic on the way home. His mind was going a hundred miles per hour.

THINGS WERE RUNNING LATE, just as Lenny had planned. It was 7:50 p.m., and Jody had three billable hours to write in the books. The assistant had gone home at 6:00 p.m., and no one else had interrupted, although she'd received numerous phone calls and texts.

"It looks like you're missing one document," Jody said as she moved her glasses from her eyes to the top of her head and looked at him. "The statement from Travertine Bank, in Iowa. You have quite a bit to transfer from that account."

"Damn," Lenny said. "I'll have to get them to send me the paperwork, but it's after hours. Can we meet again tomorrow?" He considered attempting a run on the operation now. He thought he understood the security layout. It would hinge on her answer.

"I'm all booked up until next week," she replied and pulled something up on her computer. "How does next Tuesday at 9:00 a.m. work for you?"

It didn't work at all. He pulled out his phone, pulled up a calendar, and pretended to mull over the dates. "I'll have to push some things around, but that should work," he said as he stood. "Can you point me to a restroom?"

As she led him out of her office and down the hall, he said, "In the meantime, maybe you can call security to escort me out."

She shook her head. "I can do it. I'm on my way out, too."

That's what Lenny wanted to hear.

He walked down the hall and into an immaculate restroom that had granite countertops and a marble floor. He relieved himself and then went into a stall and closed the door. He pulled two plastic cable ties out of his sock, and fed the front end of one into the back end of the other. He pulled until it clicked a few times, indicating that it had engaged, and then fitted the two loose ends together, making a loop. He slid the loop into his sleeve and walked back into the hall. Jody was waiting in front of her office door.

"Ready?" she asked as he approached.

"My bag," he said. He'd left it in her office on purpose just in case she'd try to lead him out of the building directly from the restroom. He was lucky she hadn't seen it.

"Oh, right," she said and held her proximity card up to the square sensor on the door. When it beeped, she opened the door and held it for him to go inside.

Lenny's skin warmed, and the hair on his neck bristled. He walked in, grabbed his leather courier bag, and walked back. As he started to step through the door toward the hall, he grabbed Jody by the arm, dropped the bag, and yanked her into the room and shut the door. Before she could scream, he got behind her, put his forearm around her throat, and cupped his hand over her mouth. She screamed into his hand.

He squeezed her throat until the scream cut off, and then released the pressure. "I'm going to uncover your mouth," he said in a gruff voice, very different from the tone he'd been using for the past three hours. "If you scream, I'm going to break your neck. Understand?"

The woman nodded, and a tear ran down her cheek and onto Lenny's hand.

He dragged her to a small arrangement of upholstered furniture in the far corner of the room and sat her down. He took her purse from under her arm and dug out her phone.

"My client wants me to get specific information from you, and then kill you," Lenny said. "I'll settle for the information." He pulled the cable-tie noose from his sleeve and showed it to her. "If you scream, or make any other attempt to alarm anyone, I will put this around your neck and tighten it until your head pops off. Understand?"

Jody shook uncontrollably and tears streamed down her face. "What do you want?" she asked a little too loudly.

Lenny held a finger to his lips. "Quieter," he said, as he slipped the noose back into his sleeve and sat next to her, close.

"You handled the estate of Theodore Leatherby," he said, and looked to her for confirmation.

She nodded at least six times and said, "Yes. Yes, I did."

"Relax, you're doing fine," he said. "I'm looking for a specific item, a book, and some keys."

Her eyes got big, and she nodded repeatedly.

"Who has them?"

"His son," she said immediately. "I don't remember the name – the youngest one."

"Where does he live?"

"I don't know," she said, and her face distorted as she started to bawl.

"You need to be quiet," he said sternly and grabbed her upper arm and squeezed.

She started to yelp but caught herself.

"Very good," he said. "I knew you'd be able to keep yourself under control. Do you have records of his location – maybe an address on some paperwork?"

She nodded, and pointed toward her desk.

"On the computer?"

She shook her head. "In a file."

He stood and pulled the slight woman up with him. He dragged her toward a bank of filing cabinets. "Get it," he ordered.

He stood directly behind her as she opened a wide drawer and flipped through file tabs. After about twenty seconds she pulled out a thick folder and set it on her desk. She frantically filtered through its contents and pulled out a paper-clipped multipage form and handed it to him. On it were the names and current addresses of all of the Leatherby next-of-kin, as well as their dates of birth and phone numbers.

He folded up the form and put it in the inner pocket of his jacket.

He had what he needed, and it was time for cleanup. Unfortunately for Jody, he couldn't have her communicating with his next subject, or anyone else for that matter.

He grabbed her face with his hand and pressed the back of her head against his chest, and then slipped the zip-tie noose out of his sleeve and forced it around her neck. As soon as he let go of her mouth, he yanked the zip ties and they ratcheted as they closed in around her throat. He then forced her to the floor, put his right foot on the side of her head, and pulled upward on the end of the noose. It ratcheted tighter ... tick, tick, ... tick ... SNAP! The plastic end of one of the ties broke.

Jody gasped for air, and then tried to scream in a hoarse, ruined voice, "Daddy! Daddy!"

Lenny was confused by her pleas for a few seconds, and then realized she was making noise.

Shit! He'd have to improvise. He stood on her chest with all of his weight, and then stomped on her head as hard as he could. It took at least six stomps before he hit it just right. Her skull caved in like a rotten melon.

He stepped aside as blood pooled around her on the tile floor. He pushed her twitching body under the desk, and then forced the chair in behind it.

It was not his preferred method. It would have been better to strangle her with his hands, but he had a distaste for the technique. It was too up close and personal. It wasn't that he had a weak stomach or anything – quite the opposite. To him, dead was dead was dead, and it didn't matter how one got there. Some methods, however, gave one the opportunity to have a change of plan in the middle of the process. Indecision equaled danger. However, the problem with the mess he'd just made was that it was unprofessional. It made noise, it took time, many things could go wrong, and DNA evidence was on everything.

He looked down at the droplets of blood that speckled his right shoe and pant leg. He wiped them with tissues from a box on the desk. It was a good thing everything he wore was dark.

He decided to take the whole file, put it in his bag, and then grabbed Jody's purse and rummaged through it for her access card. He sped up the process by dumping its contents on the desk and spreading it out. As he did so, he came across Jody's open wallet, exposing her driver's license. She looked somewhat younger in the picture – late 20s rather than mid 30s – but it was the date of birth that struck him. Her birthday was July 30th. He stared at it for a few seconds, but then shook it off and got back on task. He found the access card and put it in his pocket.

He took one more look at the bloody scene behind the desk. They wouldn't find her until morning – maybe even *late* morning.

If he got out of the building without incident, he'd go back to his hotel, discard the disguise and anything else that might connect him to the law firm, and enjoy a good meal.

His next target was not far away.

DESPITE THE EXCITEMENT, Jacob's empty stomach became a priority. His mind was on the leftover pizza in his refrigerator.

His mealtimes were already getting later, and he had a feeling that not having to get up early in the morning was going to shift his normal sleeping and eating patterns. If he weren't careful, he'd revert to his graduate school routine where he stayed up past 3:00 a.m. every night.

He was in the elevator on his way up to his apartment when his phone rang. It was Paulina. He didn't answer. It was a funny thing about being liberated so completely in such a short time; it was like a new life had been magically revealed. There was nothing to constrain him – no obligations, no guilt, no anxiety. It was the only time in his life that he'd ever had such a feeling.

As he approached his apartment door his phone chimed, alerting him to a voice message. Paulina probably wanted her belongings. He'd spent that afternoon gathering them – clothes, toiletries, jewelry, dishes – and packing them in a large cardboard box. He'd send her an email in the morning to let her know that she could pick them up whenever she wished, and to leave him her key.

He went inside, set down his things, and slapped three thick slices of Paglio's pizza on a pizza pan and slid it into the oven. While he waited for the pizza to warm, he sat on the couch and examined the book and envelope on the coffee table.

The leather cover of the book looked old, and had a worn, gold embossed title that read *The Israel Thread*. Beneath the title were two dates: *22 January 1966* and *12 May 1945*. The same information was repeated on the binding. He fanned through it with his thumb. The pages were thin, and their edges looked as if they'd been coated with gold at one time.

The envelope was brown, sealed, and had only 'Jacob' handwritten on its front. He was sure the lump at its center was another key.

The oven timer beeped, and he removed the pizza pan and set it on the stove. He slapped a slice on a plate and grabbed a can of Pepsi from the fridge. He slid the can into a foam sleeve, popped it open, and took a long swig. The ice-cold soda burned the back of his throat on the way down, and the carbonation seemed to bubble through his sinuses, making his eyes water. He gasped and shuddered, and then set it down on the counter.

He paced back and forth between the coffee table and bookshelves with the pizza in hand, periodically taking a bite and glancing at the book and envelope.

What had Uncle Theo given him? What was in the book? And what the hell was that place from which he'd retrieved it? The key in the unopened envelope made it clear that there was more to the puzzle than just the book. There was another door.

He finished the slice and went back for another. He grabbed the soda, guzzled half the can, and belched. He got a knife out of a drawer, went back to the couch, and carefully opened the envelope. He pulled out its contents: a key and a folded piece of paper.

The key was cylindrical, similar to the one for the building's outer door, but gold plated rather than silver. He set it aside and unfolded the paper. It was a typed note.

Dear Jacob,

I knew such a rudimentary puzzle would be no match for your intellect and curiosity. The fact that you are reading this means that you have accessed Swann Street. What I do not know, however, is whether you have gone through the inner door. My guess would be that you have not – you're too careful. This is precisely the reason you have been given this opportunity.

You have an important choice to make. If you ever trusted me, trust me now. You should go through that inner door.

The book in your hands will change your life. But beware: just as the events of that nearly fateful day on the Long Island Sound could have ended either way for me, so could this for you. Do not speak of the book or of Swann Street to anyone.

I have enjoyed my time with you, Jacob. And I hope you will see that what I am offering you is priceless.

Thank you one final time for saving my life.

Your loving uncle,

H

Jacob shivered.

The note was dated a few days before Theo passed away. The signature was confusing: a large cursive 'H' signed by hand, and in green ink. It was Uncle Theo's middle initial, but Jacob had never seen his signature signed in that manner.

He'd always trusted his uncle, and now he flushed with shame that he'd complained about his inheritance.

He picked up the key and compared it to the one on his keychain. The shape and size were identical, but the grooves were different, as was the color. The gold key had no markings. He put it on his keychain with the others.

He picked up the book and started to open it when a loud knock on the door nearly made him jump through the ceiling.

He padded over and looked through the peephole. It was Paulina.

"Shit," he muttered under his breath. She probably wanted her things.

He went back to the table and slid the book onto the shelf amongst the engineering texts and puzzle books. He folded the letter and put it in its envelope, and then into his backpack on his way to the door. He took a deep breath and opened the door.

"Don't you answer your phone?" Paulina asked, seemingly without tempering her irritation.

He shrugged. "I've been busy." He found it strange how seeing her brought out no outward emotional response from him. He knew he still had feelings for her, but they were effectively suppressed. He supposed that losing his job and, through alienation, his family, just put losing her on the growing list of disruptive events. And the excitement of recovering his uncle's book from the mysterious building was an added distraction.

"Can we talk?" she asked.

He really didn't want to – his mind was elsewhere – but he obliged. She hadn't done anything so horrible as to warrant him being indifferent toward her. She had her own life to manage.

"Sure," he said and offered her a beverage. It was already past 10:00 p.m., and he resigned himself to the fact that he wasn't going to get back to the book until the next day. Maybe it was best to approach it with a fresh mind first thing in the morning.

Lenny Butrolsky had stayed up late the previous night. His nerves were always electrified after a hit, which made sense since that was usually when a dangerous escape plan was put into action. Although that had not been the case this time, he was now paying for it with the lack of sleep. And the little sleep he did manage was disrupted by disturbing dreams of the woman yelling for her daddy.

He hadn't experienced lingering effects from a hit since his very first. That had been over 30 years ago. It was an old man working in his garden. Lenny had slit his throat so deeply that his head hung from a flap of skin on the back of his neck. He'd had nightmares about it until he'd carried out his second hit a week later.

It was a shame he'd had to eliminate Jody Dixon, but sometimes people found themselves in unforeseen situations. He was sure she'd never anticipated that a career in estate law would put her in danger.

But there was something else that bothered him. Jody was going to have a birthday in a week – on July 30th. Lenny's daughter was born on the same date, and was about the same age. Misha was only four years old when he'd left her and her mother behind. Memories of them resurfaced from time to time. Guilt would creep up on him until he quashed it with the fact that it was best he hadn't dragged them into his life. They would have been in constant danger.

He hadn't bothered checking out of the hotel since he no longer identified with the alias – the person who had killed the lawyer no longer existed. At 7:00 a.m. he drove off in a car he'd rented in another name and, after 40 minutes of navigating horrible traffic, found himself in the Boston suburb of Weston, west of the city. After reading about the inheritance of the Leatherby children, it was no surprise that Kenneth Leatherby lived in a mansion in a neighborhood filled with similar homes.

What was strange was that Jody Dixon said the items had been given to the youngest son. But it seemed that there was only one son, Kenneth, and two daughters, Janet and Tabitha. Perhaps she meant the youngest daughter. Lenny shrugged. If Kenneth didn't have the items, he'd extract the information he needed from him anyway.

The three Leatherby successors were worth more than 150 million dollars apiece, and he had half a mind to ransom their lives. But he knew that would never work. There was no place in this world to hide, no matter how much money you had.

He drove past the gated driveway of Kenneth Leatherby's estate and checked for security equipment. The entrance was unmanned but packed with modern cameras and high-tech options, including motion detectors and a biometric access device. He recognized the name of a reputable security company on the number pad mounted on a brick pillar next to the gate.

An eight-foot brick fence topped with wrought iron spikes surrounded the entire property. There was no point in trying to defeat the security system and physical obstacles when there was another way. But he had to move quickly before anyone got wind of the foul play that had transpired the night before. He glanced at his phone: it was just after 8:00 a.m., and he wondered if Jody Dixon's body had been discovered yet.

He found one of the many Java Land Cafés in the area, ordered a medium roast to go, and took a seat outside, far away from other patrons. He studied the documents he'd acquired from Jody Dixon and came up with a plan to meet with Kenneth Leatherby.

He tapped a number into his phone and called. A man answered.

"Is this Kenneth Leatherby?" Lenny asked, trying to sound professional and upbeat.

"Yes," the man replied.

"My name is Leonardo Delatorre, from Cadmore Estate Insurance," Lenny said. "You're the son of the late Theodore H. Leatherby?"

"Yes," the man replied. "How can I help you?"

"My condolences for your loss," Lenny said. "I'd like to meet with you to discuss your father's life insurance policy."

"I wasn't aware of any life insurance policies."

"I'm sure you weren't," Lenny said. "This particular policy is something he would not have shared."

After a long silence, the man replied, "I don't understand."

"I'd like to meet, preferably in a place where our conversation will be private," Lenny said. "I would invite you to my hotel room – I'm here in Boston from our New York headquarters. But maybe your home would be more secure."

"Am I a beneficiary?"

Lenny knew he had him. "I'd rather not discuss anything over the phone, and I'd suggest you not share this with anyone, especially your siblings, or even your spouse for now."

"When?"

"How's 11:00 a.m., today?"

"That works," Kenneth replied. "You need the address?"

"According to our records, it's 246 Barclay Estates. Is that correct?"

It was. Lenny hung up, and the meeting was set. He put the phone on the table and picked up his coffee. The sun beat down on his head and he readjusted his sunglasses. He'd use a gun this time.

JACOB COULD HARDLY WAIT to get to Pine Perk. Paulina had kept him up until 3:00 a.m. explaining her side of the story – seemingly trying to justify it in her own mind. However, he sensed that she was holding back – concealing something. But he didn't press her to try to figure out what it was, and even tried to relieve her of any guilt by telling her that he'd have trouble finding work in London, and that the long-distance relationship would be impossible to maintain. He kept it to himself that he was newly unemployed, if anything, to shorten the conversation. After many tears, she took her box of belongings and left. Afterwards, he fell asleep with a sick stomach.

He was still exhausted when he woke up at 7:30 a.m., but his excitement about the day ahead enlivened his brain. His body followed soon thereafter and, a half hour later, he was sitting in Pine Perk with the book on the table in front of him.

Before opening it, he reread his uncle's note just to make sure he hadn't missed anything the night before. He hadn't, but the message seemed even stronger.

He grabbed the book and examined the cover. In gold print was the title: *The Israel Thread*. Beneath it were two dates: *22 January 1966* directly below the title and, closer to the bottom, *12 May 1945*. He didn't understand – which one was the date of publication?

He opened the book and flinched at the green-inked note

addressed to him on the inner cover. It was in his uncle's handwriting.

Dearest Jacob,
   This book is a top-secret document called an integrated monograph. It is something of which you will be seeing more in the future. The task I have passed on to you is to link the information this monograph contains to current events. Ideally, your undertaking the challenge of this grand puzzle would be without the pressure of time, or the risk of conjecture. Unfortunately, time is short, and the events to which this document point, in the past, present, and, most importantly, the future, are of utmost importance. The outcome has existential implications.
   I have bestowed on you this responsibility – to finish the work that time has not allowed me to complete. –H

The hair on the back of Jacob's neck bristled. It was as if he could hear his uncle's voice saying the words as he read them.

Was he really in possession of a top-secret document? Was he *allowed* to possess such a thing? Jacob had a high-level clearance through his former employer, although he was sure it had already been revoked. But even if he still had clearance, top-secret information was compartmentalized in such a way that a person was only allowed to see a highly constrained area of the overall information landscape. A person with top-secret clearance was not allowed to see all top-secret information. And Jacob was sure he wasn't cleared to see anything outside of what he was given at Interstellar Dynamics.

He fanned through the book. The margins were riddled with handwritten notes.

He flipped to the second page, the first chapter of *The Israel Thread*, and read.

LENNY HAD DONE the required preparatory work in the hours leading up to his meeting with Kenneth Leatherby. First, he'd parked his rental car in the parking lot of a large supermarket, and then taken a cab to another car rental place. He'd booked a car under yet another alias, driven it back to the supermarket, and parked it in the lot, far from the first car. He'd then taken the first car to a large truck stop near the highway and changed into business-casual attire. The inner part of his jacket had an extra-long pocket fitted with a holster to accommodate his gun with silencer attached.

He thought this job wouldn't be as tricky as the one the previous night, and the kill should be easier. This time his disguise amounted to nothing but a fake mustache, sunglasses, and a baseball cap. He figured that would be enough for the security cameras at the gate and outside the house. Once he was inside, he'd have to take off the hat and sunglasses and hope that there were no active cameras.

He passed Kenneth Leatherby's house, scanned it for anything unusual, and continued ten miles further west to Theodore Leatherby's estate. Trees lined the gated drive, and a manned guardhouse prevented him from casing the place. He could see nothing of the interior. He made a note to check out the satellite view of the area when it was all over. He was curious to know the extent of the property.

He reversed course to the east, and it was 10:58 a.m. when he arrived at the gate of the Leatherby son's residence. He pushed a button on the intercom mounted on a concrete pillar in the center of the driveway. A few seconds later a voice he recognized as Kenneth Leatherby's projected from the speaker.

"Hello?" Kenneth asked.

"It's Leonardo from Cadmore Estate Insurance," Lenny replied.

The gate split in the middle and rolled open. He squeezed the rental car through as soon as the gap was large enough.

The main house was about a hundred yards from the street and another building – probably a guesthouse – was to the right and behind the mansion. He admired a large fountain in the center of the circular drive as he rolled up to the front entrance.

The house was enormous: three stories, with multiple nooks and crannies under a multifaceted roof. The front was mostly windows through which a chandelier sparkled in the light coming from the windows in the rear of the building. The light from the back windows shimmered, indicating that there was a pool, or a pond, in the backyard.

He got out of the car, grabbed his briefcase from the back seat, and headed for the front entrance. Before he could press the doorbell, someone approached from the inside and opened the door. For an instant, he worried that it might be a maid or butler. He didn't want complications, and he didn't like to kill people who weren't targets. It was unprofessional.

The man who appeared before him looked like he should be on a sailboat, with off-white pants rolled to the calf and a white, untucked, button-down shirt rolled to the elbows.

"I'm Kenneth," the man said and stuck out his hand.

Lenny shook it. "You can call me Lenny."

Kenneth led him through a foyer into an expansive, marble-floored room with curved staircases on each side that led to a common balcony. The stairs were made from the same marble as the floor and each staircase had a red carpet runner in the center. He spotted another wide staircase, similar in design, behind the balcony that led to the third floor. It was like something from a movie.

He followed Kenneth through the large room, past the left staircase, and into a study on the west side of the house. Bookshelves and paintings covered the walls, and inset lights beamed from the wooden, coffered ceiling onto the floor and a cluster of furniture to the left. The room impressed him less than it should have, probably because it appeared to be only for show, and served little purpose. The man was a self-proclaimed entrepreneur, but had built nothing himself. As far as he could tell, old man Leatherby had taken care of everything, including assembling the executive boards that controlled the trust funds and businesses. And the businesses were nothing special, mostly intellectual properties – largely patents that brought in royalties that had to be managed by someone who knew what they were doing. Kenneth Leatherby had an MBA from Harvard, but had done nothing with it. Which was probably the reason why the man was at home in the middle of the afternoon on a weekday, dressed in the equivalent of pajamas.

Kenneth offered him a seat in front of a large wooden desk near a window opposite the door, and then took a seat behind it.

"How can I help you ... uh, Lenny?" Kenneth asked.

Lenny sat in the chair and shifted until he was comfortable. "I think it will be me helping you in this case, Mr. Leatherby," he said. "Are we alone?"

"Everyone's out," Kenneth said. "The groundskeepers just left, and the cleaning service comes tomorrow."

"I'm more concerned about your family," Lenny said. "It was part of your father's nondisclosure option – he didn't want your wife or siblings knowing anything about this."

"Please," Kenneth said, leaning forward in his seat. "We're alone."

"Okay," Lenny said and nodded. "You see, your uncle took out a large life insurance policy the week after you were born, and in your name alone."

Kenneth looked at him suspiciously. "Sounds a little odd," he said. "Why would a man nearly a hundred years old hold on to that – how could anyone insure him?"

"Of course," Lenny chuckled and shook his head. It was a question he had anticipated and researched about an hour before the meeting. "The policy rolled into an annuity almost 30 years ago. The principle has matured and can now be liquidated."

Kenneth shrugged and shook his head. "I've never heard of anything like that," he said. "How much are we talking?"

"Just over 43 million dollars," Lenny replied.

Kenneth raised an eyebrow.

Lenny knew the amount was believable since, as he'd learned from the documents extracted from Jody Dixon, each of the siblings got over 100 million, including the properties. This would put Kenneth well above the others.

"So, what's the process?"

Lenny leaned back and crossed his legs. "We need to make an exchange," Lenny explained. "Your father held something of great value to my firm that he used to ensure that we would cleanly process these funds and transfer them to you upon his death."

"What do you mean by 'cleanly process?'" Kenneth asked with an expression of alarm and disgust.

"The funds were derived from unusual sources," he said. "There was nothing illegal – just difficult to explain."

"Try."

"They came from precious metals and gems – mainly from heirlooms and inheritances that came from his ancestry," Lenny explained. "Our job was to liquidate, invest, and liquidate again when the time was right. Every option was taken to minimize loss through taxes and penalties, and to avoid investigation. We obliged, but your father needed collateral. He was in possession of something that we need back. Now that he has passed, we can settle accounts, so to speak."

"My father was on the cautious side," Kenneth said. "What is it that you want?"

"A book, and the keys to a safe deposit box," Lenny replied.

Kenneth's face went blank and then turned to the ceiling as if he were in deep thought. A few seconds later, his eyes met Lenny's. "I don't know about any book, or keys. And my father never mentioned them."

"Are you sure?" Lenny asked. "They weren't bequeathed to you in the will?"

Kenneth's face went blank again for a few seconds, and then flushed. "That bastard," he hissed.

"What?"

"He found a way to give money to my freeloader cousin."

"What are you talking about?"

"My cousin inherited a book," Kenneth explained. "And he was given an envelope – probably had keys in it – at the reading of the will."

Lenny now thought that Jody Dixon must have panicked and

given him the wrong information. "Can you get me your cousin's name and contact info?" Lenny asked.

"No," Kenneth said. "I'm going to find a way to fight this. That money belongs to the immediate family, not to some orphan who happened to live with us."

Lenny was done with the charade. He pulled the gun out of his jacket and pointed it at Kenneth's face.

Kenneth's eyes seemed to cross, and his expression turned to blank confusion.

"Give me the name of your cousin and his location," Lenny ordered.

Kenneth just stared at him, seemingly trying to process what was happening. After a few seconds, he opened a drawer in the desk.

Lenny stiffened his arm. "Careful."

Kenneth slowed his motion and removed an address book from the drawer. He paged through it, handed it to Lenny, and pointed to an entry. It read, Jacob F. Hale, 1223 Pine Street, Apt. 311, Alexandria, VA 22304.

Lenny tore out the page and put it in his pocket, and then shot Kenneth between the upper lip and nose. The man's eyes stared back blankly as blood poured out over his lip and chin and onto his white shirt. His body slumped to Lenny's left and began to tilt over, along with the chair.

Lenny hopped around the desk and lowered the man gently to the floor. He stood back and fired two more slugs into the man's forehead. The stench of urine and feces filled the air as he shoved the body under the desk and pushed in the chair. He smirked. The desk maneuver was becoming a theme.

He put on his sunglasses and hat, and then walked out of the study, through the giant room with the staircases, through the foyer, and out the front door. He got in his car, navigated the circular drive, and headed toward the gate.

He was a hundred feet away when the gate started to open. He had a bad feeling.

A few seconds later, a white BMW SUV came through, and he

moved to the right. The driver was an attractive blonde woman in dark, oversized sunglasses, and she waved as they passed each other. He waved back to her and also to one of the two young girls in the back seat. He guessed they were both between five and eight years old, and had their mother's blond hair. He didn't envy them.

The gate started to close but reversed direction when he got close. He drove through and took a right.

It was a tense fifteen-minute drive to the supermarket. He seemed to hit every red light along the way. He pulled into the crowded parking lot, grabbed his things from the back seat, and made his way to the other rental car, a hundred yards away. He was careful to obey the speed limits and traffic lights as he drove off. When he was a couple of miles away, he threw the gun out the window as he went around a curve in a densely wooded area, and then the keys to the other rental car a few miles further up the road. He was safe.

He was heading to T. F. Green International Airport in Providence, Rhode Island. His next stop was Alexandria, Virginia.

CHAPTER 3

Jacob had been at it all afternoon at Pine Perk and still couldn't identify exactly what he was reading. It had elements of history, investigation, and intelligence report. Uncle Theo had written dated notes in the margins of almost every page. The annotations were all dated later than 1966, the more recent of the two dates embossed on the spine and cover.

The book started with a summary of interrogations of Nazi war criminals by Israeli intelligence. The text was riddled with reference numbers, each pointing to a resource at the end of each chapter. Included with each reference was a clearance level, most of which were top-secret, although some were open sources.

The interrogation summary, which did not include details that were to come later, expanded into a synopsis of Israel's worldwide hunt for Nazi war criminals. It started with those captured in Europe immediately after the war. The minor offenders, relatively speaking, were given great incentive to provide connections to bigger fish. In some cases, it meant a reduced sentence. In others, it had saved their lives.

The Israelis were pursuing people such as Adolf Eichmann, the man who'd orchestrated the holocaust, and his assistant, Alois Brunner. Also at the top of the list was the infamous Dr. Josef Mengele, the monster who had carried out horrific medical experiments in the concentration camps. The interrogations of the lower-level Nazis had produced information regarding the escape paths of Nazi officers. But other things also emerged, some of which were nothing short of bizarre.

Some crucial information extracted from mid-rank officers included details of ODESSA, the organization of former Nazi SS members assembled to facilitate the escape of high-level Nazis out of Germany. The ratlines, as they'd been called, ferried them to places all around the world, but many led to South America. As noted in the text, ODESSA had been well known at the time of writing, and wasn't the topic of the current monograph.

A more unusual line of information, and one emphasized in Theo's comments in the margins, came from the ramblings of a low-level Nazi officer. The SS *Unterscharführer*, which was equivalent to the rank of sergeant, organized the transport of Auschwitz prisoners to an insane asylum called Kraken, located within a two-hour drive of the infamous concentration camp. When the interrogating officer had made it clear to the sergeant that the dozen or so people he'd transported every Sunday night had been tortured and killed, he seemed to offer up every shred of information he could pull from his mind. Being an accomplice to over a thousand murders would have meant certain execution.

On some occasions, the man explained, Josef Mengele rode with him in the truck's cab during the trips from Auschwitz to Kraken. He'd described how Mengele would say things that seemed like complete lunacy, from the spiritual effects of extreme torture to the creation of a new race. Regarding the latter, the man explained, Mengele hadn't been referring to the Aryan race in the usual context. The doctor was instead referring to a leap in evolution, an elevation to a new species rather than a race.

On another occasion, Mengele described a secret discovery that was going to allow Germany to win the war and change the world.

He'd made it sound as if they would connect with God himself, and humanity would be extinguished and replaced by the *Final Reich*.

The summary of the interrogations ended with Uncle Theo's handwritten message, "The devil is in the details – more to come."

Before Jacob knew it, it was after 6:00 p.m. He'd been at Pine Perk all day, except for an hour interlude for lunch.

His fourth cup of coffee for the day was still three-quarters full, but cold, and his stomach grumbled. The reading was fascinating, and he didn't want to stop, but his mind was drawn to the last two slices of leftover pizza in his refrigerator.

He packed the book in his backpack and walked out of the café and into the mild summer evening. The smell of the wood oven from Paglio's Bistro a block north made his stomach churn even more. He concentrated instead on the aroma of the purple lilacs that lined the edge of Pine Park, carried by the warm breeze that soughed through the trees. It brought forth a melancholy sensation that reminded him of his childhood – days by the lake with his parents. It reminded him how much he missed them.

He took in a deep breath and exhaled strongly, clearing his olfactory pallet and mind.

His burner phone vibrated in the front pocket of his shorts. It reminded him that he needed to get a permanent replacement since Interstellar Dynamics had confiscated the one he'd been using for nearly three years.

He pulled out the phone and discovered he had a voice message from a restricted number. He must have missed the call.

As he dialed the number to retrieve the message, his first thought was that it was Paulina, although he didn't know why she'd call from a restricted number. It was odd to him how relationships were such a struggle between control and insecurity. Pauli was obviously a grade above him in the market – she'd find a new man before he'd find a girlfriend. But he figured she might be having some kind of seller's remorse since his attitude had taken on a complexion of indifference. That wasn't completely accurate; he still cared for her.

The message played and, initially, he didn't recognize the female voice. He finally realized that it was his cousin, Tabitha, and she seemed stressed. Her message was short: "Call me when you get this. It's urgent."

Jacob shivered. He'd never heard Tabitha speak that way – panicked. He picked up the pace and decided he'd call when he got to his apartment.

After a five-minute walk he was in the lobby of his building. As routine dictated, he stopped at his mailbox, pulled out a stack of junk mail, and then rode the elevator to his floor. As he got out and turned the corner toward his door, four people, two of them in police uniforms, froze and looked at him.

Jacob stopped and stared back at them.

A fit, middle-aged man, average height with a brush haircut, spoke as he walked toward Jacob. "Are you Jacob Hale?"

Jacob nodded. A million things went through his brain simultaneously, but the most prominent thought was of his activities the night before, using the key. He brushed it away – he'd done nothing wrong. "How can I help you?"

"I'm Detective Kranz, Alexandria police," the man said as he flipped open his wallet and displayed a badge. "Where are you coming from?"

The two officers stepped toward him. One was a large man, well over six feet tall, and the other a young woman with a dark ponytail that hung out from the back of her hat and settled on the front of her left shoulder. It seemed they thought he might run.

"A coffee place around the block," he replied. "Why?"

"Can you prove that?" Kranz asked.

"What the hell is going on?"

"I asked you a question."

"And I asked you one," Jacob replied, not liking the man's tone. "Go ask the barista at Pine Perk. I was there all day."

Kranz handed one of the officers a photo that Jacob recognized as the one on his ID card from Interstellar Dynamics.

"Where's the place you're talking about?" the other man in plain clothes asked in a thick Boston accent. He was heavy-set and bald, and wore a brown jacket with tan elbow patches that looked like it came from the 1970s. By the looks of him, it had been the decade when he'd been in his prime.

Jacob told him the location of Pine Perk, and the name of the barista. The male uniformed cop then pressed past him and went to the elevator.

"Can we have a look in your apartment?" Detective Kranz asked.

"After you tell me what this is about."

"Kenneth Leatherby was murdered earlier today," Kranz said.

After a few seconds of silence, Jacob could only muster one word. "How?"

"Shot," Kranz replied. "In his home."

Jacob's resistance to the cops subsided. "Go ahead, check out my apartment," he said and tried to walk past them, but the bald man stepped in his path and held up his hand.

Jacob stopped and looked at him.

Kranz held out his hand. "You'll have to stay out here for now," he said. "Keys, please."

The last thing he wanted to do was hand over his keychain with its newest members attached, but he obliged.

Kranz handed them to the woman, and she opened the door. The uniformed cop and the bald man stepped inside, leaving Jacob with Kranz.

"Where were you last night?" Kranz asked.

It was a question he didn't want to answer in complete truth. "I was with my girlfriend, here in my apartment."

"You mean your former girlfriend?"

Jacob nodded. "Yes, thank you, my *former* girlfriend," he said without hiding the sarcasm. Obviously, the detective had already done some homework. "What does last night have to do with what happened today?"

"Do you know someone by the name of Jody Dixon?"

"Sounds familiar," Jacob replied, but he didn't know from where. "I can't place it."

"How about the estate lawyer you met on Sunday afternoon?"

Jacob nodded. "Yeah, that's her. Why?"

"She was murdered last night, in Boston," Kranz said and studied Jacob's face, apparently trying to assess his reaction.

Jacob stared back at the detective. His mind whirred, trying to figure out how the two murders could be connected.

A few minutes later, the other detective and cop came out of his apartment.

"It's clean," the cop said, and then took off her hat and itched her forehead, near the hairline. "Does he have a car?"

Kranz looked to Jacob.

"Of course," Jacob said. "You knew my girlfriend just dumped me, I'd think you'd know if I had a car. The keys are inside." He nodded toward his apartment door and then looked to Kranz. "May I?"

Kranz nodded, and Jacob went into the apartment and took his car keys from a hook on the wall near the refrigerator. He'd separated his car keys from the others the night before – too many keys for one ring.

He turned to the cop, who was following closely, and showed her the keys. "I'll take my apartment keys back, please," he said, and jingled them.

She shrugged and handed him his key ring, and he reciprocated with those for the car. "It's the maroon Corolla in parking slot #11," he said, and then slipped the other set of keys into his front pocket.

As Jacob followed her out of his apartment, the male officer emerged from the elevator and walked up to Kranz. "His story checks out."

"Of course it does," Jacob said. He was getting annoyed with what they'd been implying and by their withholding of information. "Now, could you please tell me why you're questioning me about something I obviously had nothing to do with?"

Kranz sighed and shrugged, and then motioned to the door of the apartment. "Let's talk."

Jacob led them in as the female officer went down to his car. The two detectives took the couch, and the male uniformed officer stood close to the door. Jacob sat in an upholstered chair across from the detectives.

"You've had a few rough days, Mr. Hale," Kranz started. "Lost your job, broke up with your girlfriend, and you were left out of your uncle's will."

"None of that makes me happy," Jacob replied. "But why would I kill my cousin? And, for God's sake, why would I kill the messenger – the lawyer?"

Kranz shook his head. "You were all we had, and it was your late cousin's wife who suggested that you might be angry about the outcome of the will. She said she saw someone driving out of their estate just before she discovered her husband's body, but she didn't get a good look at the guy. She said it could have been you."

"I cannot even express how offensive and irresponsible that is," Jacob said, trying to control his anger. "She has wasted your time, and sidetracked your investigation with a false lead."

Jacob had always sensed that Kira disliked him. She came from old money and was even richer than Kenneth, even after his recent windfall. Jacob, on the other hand, was a low-class orphan. From the first time they'd met, she'd treated him like dirt, and he'd often wondered what Kenneth had told her about him. And jealousy was not the right emotion for what he felt about being cut short on the will. He was offended and embarrassed. Those feelings had turned to anger at times, but not enough to kill anyone.

"Don't worry," Kranz said. "She's a prime suspect. The spouse is always on the top of the list."

"Are you sure the murders are connected?" Jacob asked.

"No."

"Other leads?"

"Yes, regarding the murder of Jody Dixon," Kranz explained. "We can't find the last client she saw the night she was killed. He operated under an alias. We have some video."

"That sounds more promising than what you're pursuing now," Jacob said.

"We follow all leads," Kranz said. "Including the tip from Kira

Leatherby. It was clear that you might be angered by everything that has happened to you in such a short time."

"I certainly was – still am," Jacob said. "And I'm disappointed. But not enough to do something like that."

"And what about the other things – your job and girlfriend?" Kranz asked.

"I'll get another job when I need one," Jacob said. "Same goes for the girlfriend."

He thought he saw the corners of Kranz's mouth curl upward for an instant.

"I suggest you focus your efforts on finding Dixon's last client," Jacob said.

The female officer returned, threw the car keys to Jacob, and looked to Kranz. "It's clean," she said.

Kranz stood. "Sorry it played out like this," he said and handed him a business card with a phone number. "Give me a call if you think of anything that might help."

Jacob led them out and closed the door. He looked out the window, down to the front parking lot. The uniformed officers got into a squad car, and the detectives into an unmarked car. When they drove out of sight, he pulled the keys out of his pocket, looked at them, and sighed. The two murders were undoubtedly linked, and he had a feeling that it all had something to do with the keys in his hand, and the leather-bound book in his bag.

He was in danger.

LENNY HAD ENJOYED the amenities of the five-star hotel in Boston, but reverted to his old ways and checked into a half-star dump in Washington, DC just after 9:30 p.m. Luxurious hotels had their appeal, but fleabag joints like this one took cash, and didn't require official identification. Now, the only connection to his newest alias was the rental car parked in the poorly-lit lot on the opposite side of the building. If things went haywire, and they found the car, they'd have no idea which room he was in, or whether he was even at the hotel.

The downside of the place was that everything smelled like cigarette smoke.

He linked his laptop to his satellite phone and accessed the Internet. He was going to scope out the areas where Jacob Hale lived and worked, and then devise a plan to isolate him.

After just a few minutes it became clear that he wouldn't be able to approach Hale at his workplace. He worked for a defense contractor called Interstellar Dynamics, and the facility was built like a fortress. He'd have to get him at his home.

Hale's apartment building was located in a quiet residential neighborhood in Alexandria, Virginia. It was the center of three buildings of identical design, and near a large park with woods and a running track. In the rear of the building was a large parking lot that abutted a dense residential neighborhood.

His phone vibrated. It was his handler.

Lenny disconnected the Internet link and answered.

"Progress?" a male voice asked. The man was perfectly understandable, but had a strong Chinese accent.

Lenny didn't recognize the voice – it wasn't the same man who'd called to assign his current job. But he wasn't concerned. He'd changed handlers often during the past six months, and was no longer certain of the identity – or the national allegiance – of his employer. And it didn't matter, he wanted out of the business as soon as possible.

Lenny described the events of the past two days, and the man sounded pleased. It seemed that dead bodies equated to progress for these people. It was a typical scorched-earth method of operation: get information, kill the source, and repeat until you got what you needed. He hoped Jacob Hale would be the final event: Lenny would get the items he sought, hand them over to his client, and then leave the scene on good terms. Soon he'd be sipping coconut water on a beach in Costa Rica.

He ended the conversation by explaining his current stage of planning and identifying his next target. *Target* probably wasn't the correct word; he wasn't sure if he'd have to kill Hale since he was the final link in the chain but, more often than not, that was the way it turned out.

He re-established the Internet link and searched for Hale on the web. He found links connecting Hale to three prestigious universities, as well as an abundance of other information, including numerous pictures. Lenny found it disturbing that he was able to find so much information so quickly – it could put a person in danger.

Jacob Hale had been a cross-country runner in high school, and won multiple engineering awards in college. His Ph.D. was in computer and electrical engineering, and his dissertation was on some advanced topic in signal processing and encryption.

Now that Lenny knew what Hale looked like, he'd see if he could spot him before he went to work in the morning. Other than getting a look at the man, and his car, Lenny thought he'd break into his apartment and search for the book and keys, and avoid confrontation altogether. The problem was that he didn't know for what exactly he was searching. How could he be sure he got the right things? What if Hale didn't have the items in his apartment? It was clear that it would be better to question him directly, and make Hale *lead* him to the items. But the other way was worth a shot.

Lenny realized he was starving. He'd eat and then get to bed early since he'd have to be in Alexandria by 6:00 a.m. the next morning to catch Hale before he left for work.

He grabbed his keys and wallet and put them in the inner pocket of his light jacket. He put his gun in the holster under his left arm and walked out of the room and into the mild night.

AFTER TWENTY MINUTES in a zombie-like state on the couch thinking about what had transpired during the past four days, Jacob stood and walked to the refrigerator. He was hungry but didn't feel like eating.

He grabbed a piece of cold pizza anyway. He tried to call Tabitha twice, but it went directly to voicemail.

He gnawed the pizza down to the crust and then took the book out of his bag and flipped through it. He wondered if he should go page by page, or skip directly to the end and figure out what it was all about.

His phone buzzed. It was Tabitha. Before he could finish the word "Hello," she went into an uninterruptable flurry of angry scolding. She was annoyed that he hadn't called her back. She calmed down after he explained what had happened with the police that evening, and that he'd tried to call.

"That's awful," she said. "Kira is going to hear about this."

"Let it go," he said. "She just lost her husband."

"Their marriage had been declining since the honeymoon," she explained. "She should have been the primary suspect from the beginning."

Jacob told her what the detective had said about following all leads, and that Kira was at the top of the list.

"Are *you* okay?" Jacob asked.

A three-hour conversation followed, during which Jacob's legs twitched continually. It was like the anxiety he'd felt in college when he had an important exam the next day and he couldn't find time to get to his books.

The call ended after 1:00 a.m., and he could hardly keep his eyes open. He leaned back on the couch and tucked a pillow under his head. He stared at the ceiling and thought about everything that had happened.

It all began with the reading of Uncle Theo's will. He didn't think *everything* was connected – surely losing his job wasn't – but that Sunday afternoon marked the first link in his chain of misfortune. And there were many links: no inheritance, loss of job, loss of girlfriend, and, finally, his cousin is murdered and he's considered a suspect. Not bad for four days.

He couldn't get his mind off the murders. He wasn't close to his two oldest cousins – they'd been out on their own when Jacob had lived on the estate – but Kenneth was still family.

It reminded Jacob of what had happened to his parents. He felt a painful sadness for Jody Dixon's family – they'd never be the same. He wondered if she had kids. Kenneth's daughters were the ones who'd found him.

He closed his eyes and, after what seemed like just minutes, sunlight woke him from a dream. He sat up in a sense of panic. The clock on the microwave in the kitchen read 6:30 a.m., his usual wake time for the morning routine before work. Evidently, his internal clock was still calibrated for the employed Jacob.

He twitched when his phone buzzed on the coffee table directly in front of him. He picked it up and realized immediately that he had to hurry. It was a programmed reminder that he had a dentist appointment at 7:45 a.m. He recalled making arrangements for arriving late to work, which was no longer an issue. He thought he'd better make it to the appointment since he didn't know how long his dental insurance would extend beyond his termination. He then realized that he'd also have to make new arrangements for medical insurance.

He took a shower, brushed his teeth, grabbed his bag, and was out the door by 7:05 a.m.

LENNY SIPPED orange juice from a glass bottle and listened to the radio as he watched the front door of Jacob Hale's apartment building. It was already a few minutes past 7:00 a.m., and he figured Hale was running late, especially if he had to get to DC by 8:00 a.m., which was going to be trouble in traffic. Then again, he thought, if the guy was a high-level engineer, he probably had some flexibility in his hours.

Lenny had been parked on the street since 5:50 a.m., but it never bothered him to sit and watch for long periods of time. He was patient, like a cat watching a gopher hole, and he'd often devised good plans while laying in wait.

The parking lot had thinned considerably since he'd arrived and, just when he was beginning to think that he'd missed his mark, Hale exited the building. The man was maybe five-foot-ten, with a slight build and sandy-blonde hair. He wore sunglasses.

Hale seemed to be dressed too casually for a professional engineer, but these days the work environment was much different than decades earlier. Now they had open office spaces with foosball tables and video games for the employees. Lenny thought it might have been fun to have had a regular job for a while.

Hale got into an old-model maroon Toyota, drove out of the parking lot, and turned left, toward the highway. Lenny would wait another twenty minutes before he made any moves just to make sure Hale hadn't forgotten something and had to double back.

After listening to the bottom-of-the-hour newscast, he got out of the car and discarded the empty orange juice bottle in a trashcan on the side of the street. He then walked through waist-high bushes that separated the sidewalk from the apartment's front parking lot and weaved between two motorcycles parked near the entrance of the building. He was certain there'd be no doorman, but didn't know if there was a front desk or some other form of front-end security that might prevent him from getting through the lobby. He had a plan for that situation, but it was chancy.

To his relief, the lobby was empty, and he walked directly into an open elevator and pushed the button for the third floor. A half-minute later he was standing in front of a mirrored wall in a small foyer, with the option to go left or right. He chose left, and surmised quickly that he'd guessed correctly. He found apartment number 311 and knocked. He peered down the hall to see if anyone was looking, and then went to work on the lock.

It was a 1980s' vintage lock that he'd have no trouble defeating. However, if the door's deadbolt jammed even slightly, he might have trouble applying enough torque to turn it. Everything went smoothly and he was inside in less than a minute.

It was a single-bedroom apartment that looked much like a college dorm, complete with a crumpled pizza box sticking out of the trashcan. He went directly to the bedroom to make sure no one else was there. The place was dark and small, and it was clear that Hale hadn't spent much money on furniture. A baby cried in the apartment next door, and the mother's muffled voice came through the thin walls. He found it strange that someone connected to the wealthy Leatherby family would live in such a modest place.

He methodically searched through drawers, closets, and cabinets. The thing that took the most time, however, was searching through the massive collection of books on the shelves in the front room. Even though he knew the book's approximate size, and that it had a leather cover, he didn't know its title or subject matter. He also knew that one of the keys was cylindrical, which was somewhat rare, but there were two or three in total, and he didn't know what the others looked like.

After checking the usual overt locations, he searched all of the obvious hiding places. A novice would usually choose a ceiling tile or the underside of a drawer. The only false ceiling was in the bathroom, so that's where he started.

JACOB WAS PLEASED to be out of the dentist's office by quarter to nine with polished teeth and a clean bill of health. On the way back, he drove past his apartment, directly to Pine Perk. He was lucky to find a parking spot: after 9:00 a.m. the park was already crammed with kids and parents, many of whom drove from miles away.

The first thing he had to do was pay his bills. It was a monthly chore that took him half an hour since he did it all online. He bought a coffee, found a table near a window, and then pulled out his laptop and pressed the power button. Rather than the screen illuminating as usual, a red light flashed on the keyboard. The battery was dead.

He swore under his breath. He knew the charger was back in his apartment, plugged into the outlet next to the couch.

He packed up the computer and brought the coffee mug up to the counter. Kirsten, a barista who knew him better than most of the others because their schedules seemed to line up, smiled and waited for the explanation.

"Forgot something," Jacob said. "Hold on to this?"

She shook her head and smiled. "I think we can give you a fresh one when you get back."

Jacob was about to get into his car but, instead, put his wallet in his pocket and locked his backpack in the trunk. He'd walk back to his apartment and try to enjoy the pleasant morning air. It often proved to be a good time to think, and walking had a soothing effect on his mind, like a short nap. However, for some unknown reason, he felt like running. Something was pushing him, and his nerves wouldn't let him relax. All he could think about was the book, and the mysterious building on Swann Street. But he hadn't been able to get back to either, and his brain was about to explode.

Five minutes later he was in the elevator on the way up to his apartment. While he was there, he figured he'd grab a few nutrition bars so that he could work through lunch.

As he stood in front of his door and fanned through the keys on his keychain, a sound, like that of a plastic cup falling on the floor, came from behind the door. He remained still, and listened. A drawer opened and rattled as if it were pulled out completely and dumped over.

It was Paulina. He wondered what he'd forgotten to pack for her, and why he'd neglected to ask her for her key.

He didn't want to have a confrontation with her, and it seemed she didn't either since she'd come when he was supposed to be at work, but he needed to get his computer charger.

He opened the door, walked in, and closed it behind him. His books were strewn all about the front room, and the couch cushions were on the floor. He walked a few steps into the kitchen and detected motion to his left, in the direction of the bathroom. He turned, and froze.

A man who was as wide as the doorway stood in the bathroom.

He was perfectly still and holding an empty drawer in giant purple hands. He was wearing latex gloves.

A million thoughts flashed through Jacob's brain. They converged on fictitious images of his murdered cousin. His vision turned red.

The man dropped the drawer and pounced forward, hitting the doorframe with his shoulder and simultaneously yelping a cussword.

Jacob ran for the exit. The sound of hurried movement behind him put him into a frantic mode of flight. He pulled the door open and flew into the hall. As he yanked the door closed behind him a mass of humanity slammed into it so hard that he thought the entire wall might come down.

He ran to the elevator, but quickly realized it was a mistake: it was too slow, and the hallway on the other side of the elevator led to a dead end. Now he'd have to pass by his apartment to get to the stairs, and it was already too late. Pounding footsteps approached.

Jacob crouched near the wall in the foyer, below the mirror opposite the elevator. As the man ran by and made a wide left turn in front of the elevator, Jacob jumped out behind him and ran in the opposite direction. He passed his open apartment door and continued at maximum speed down the long hallway, toward stairs at the far end that led to an emergency exit. He glanced back as the man, his shoulders nearly as wide as the hallway, sprinted in pursuit. The animal was large, but much quicker than he looked. It was like being chased by a grizzly bear. Jacob ran faster.

He had a horrific thought that there might be a second person waiting for him in the stairwell. But he didn't have a choice – it was the only way out.

If he could only make it out of the building, he knew the thick man couldn't keep up with him on foot. Then his brain sent him another disturbing thought: *you can't outrun a bullet.*

The emergency exit led to the rear parking lot. There wouldn't be many cars there on a weekday, so there wouldn't be much cover.

He kicked open the metal door to the stairwell and jumped down the first set of stairs in one leap, slamming into the wall at the landing and almost twisting his ankle. He took three stairs at a time on the next half-flight and nearly tripped, barely catching himself on the handrail.

As he got to the next landing, an explosive clank from above indicated that his pursuer wasn't far behind. The sound of two feet landing heavily two landings up told him that the man was chasing him at full tilt.

After two more flights, Jacob kicked open the exit door and was out and into the daylight. The building's emergency alarm sounded behind him, but he knew that wouldn't attract much attention: kids that lived in the building were doing it all the time.

He passed a green dumpster that abutted the building to the left, and sprinted into the rear parking lot. He headed for a stone wall about 40 yards away that separated the lot from the adjacent neighborhood. When he was about halfway there, the metal exit door slammed open against the red brick of the apartment building. He glanced back to see the gorilla-like man sprinting, his jacket flapping in the wind. He didn't know if his mind had just conjured up the image, but he thought he saw a gun in the man's purple hand.

Jacob zigzagged, but maintained a full sprint. The wall was about six feet tall, and he worried that he might get caught, or shot, while climbing. About 30 feet in front of him, a black BMW sedan was parked in a spot so that its front bumper was about four feet from the wall. He cut at a 45-degree angle to the right and, when he had a clear path to the hood of the car, turned sharply to the left. He jumped onto the hood and then, in one stride, to the top of the wall. His inertia took him over the top and down, into a thick bush. As he ripped through it, thorns tore through the skin on his waist and legs. He wasn't going to stop.

A few seconds later, a crashing sound came from behind the fence. His pursuer must have failed an attempt at the same maneuver.

Jacob sprinted past a swimming pool, and came to a gate at the far side of the yard, between a house and a wood fence along the lot line of the adjacent property. He opened it and looked back. He spotted the man's gargantuan purple mitts as the beast gripped the edge of the wall and peered over. Jacob got a good look at his face, and then took off running.

He ran past the house and down the driveway. When he got to the street, he took a left, ran a block, took a right, and then another left a few blocks down. On the next corner was a chain drugstore. It was a good place to hide for a while, and to get bandages for the cuts on his body. He noticed his right forearm was bleeding, and a dozen small thorns stuck under the skin on his thighs like giant splinters. He'd need antiseptic.

His heart pounded and he breathed heavily as he tried to calm himself before entering the store. He couldn't go back to the apartment. He had to get to his car. Then he remembered something.

He retrieved his wallet from his front pocket and pulled out a business card: Paul Kranz, Sr. Detective, Alexandria Police Department. He punched in the number.

IT WAS the biggest mistake Lenny had made in a long time. *What was that asshole doing home in the middle of the day?* And it couldn't have been more unfortunate that he'd gotten into a footrace with a cross-country runner.

Still out of breath, he peeled off his latex gloves and threw them into a dumpster. He hurried back to his car and put on a baseball hat and sunglasses. He knew his chances were slim, but he might still find Hale on the street. That reminded him to check Hale's parking spot: it was empty. This gave him three options.

First, he might catch Hale while he was still on foot. Second, he could find his car and wait. Third, if Hale called the police, Lenny might follow them to him. That would only work if they used sirens. There was also a fourth option: Hale would eventually have to go back to his apartment, and Lenny could find him there again after everything cooled down. But that would take too much time. His employer wanted results in the next few days.

He turned off Pine Street into an unnamed alley about a quarter mile from Hale's building. It led in the direction Hale had last been heading. He rolled down the windows and listened for police sirens.

Even if he recovered and got a hold of Hale, he'd already made a horrible blunder. Now Lenny wondered if he'd have to kill him. Probably so.

JACOB HAD NEVER BEEN MORE relieved to see law enforcement. Kranz stepped out of an unmarked car, and two uniformed officers got out of a squad car that parked behind it. One of the two officers was the woman from the night before. He didn't recognize the second, an average-sized man in his 30s with a thin nose, narrow-set eyes, blond hair, and a red mustache reminiscent of small-town cops in movies from the 1970s.

Jacob walked out of the store and met Kranz in the parking lot, near the unmarked car.

"Your card came in handy," Jacob said. "Thanks for coming."

Kranz smiled. "Had a scare?" he asked and then nodded toward the bandages on Jacob's arms and legs. "What's that?"

"Jumped into a rose bush," Jacob replied.

Kranz shook his head. "Tell me what happened."

Jacob explained everything in as much detail as he could remember.

"Your description of the man is consistent with the first murder suspect," Kranz said.

"What do you mean?"

"Large man – crushed Jody Dixon's head like a walnut," Kranz replied.

Jacob felt like throwing up.

"You have somewhere to stay other than your apartment?" Kranz asked.

Jacob nodded.

"Where?" Kranz asked, obviously skeptical.

Jacob just realized that Kranz already knew a lot about him from his investigation. "My ex will let me stay at her place," Jacob replied, not looking forward to that awkward conversation. "It won't be enjoyable."

Kranz shook his head and chuckled. "You're having a hell of a week," he said and slapped him on the shoulder. "Mind giving me your apartment keys? We'll check the place out – maybe find fingerprints – and then lock it up."

"Don't know about fingerprints – he was wearing gloves," Jacob said as he peeled off a key from his key ring and handed it to Kranz.

"Can I give you a lift somewhere?" Kranz asked.

Jacob accepted the offer and Kranz took him to Pine Perk, where his car was parked.

As Jacob opened the door to exit the car, Kranz explained that they would write a report, and that he'd let Jacob know what they'd found in the next day or two. In the meantime, for his own safety, Jacob was not to go near his apartment.

Jacob agreed, thanked him again, and closed the door. Kranz did a U-turn and disappeared into the labyrinth of surface streets.

It was just past 11:00 a.m., and Jacob knew that Paulina wouldn't get home until six o'clock at the earliest. He wouldn't call her until then since he'd have to take time to think up a cover story. In the meantime, he'd do some reading.

He retrieved his knapsack from the car, went into the coffeehouse, and approached the counter. The same barista, Kirsten, who had served him a few hours before, cut her rehearsed greeting short and asked, "What happened?" She was looking at his bandaged arms.

"Chased by a dog through a rose bush," he lied. He backed away from the counter so she could see the bandages on his legs as well.

"That's awful," she said. "Did he get you?"

"Nope," he said, and smiled. "I'm too quick."

She laughed, and then poured him a mug of coffee and set it in front of him. He pulled out his wallet and she held up her hand. "Don't worry about it," she said.

He thanked her and went to the same table he was at in the morning, with a good view of the street and his car. He knew it was unlikely that the man would find him there, but a little paranoia was healthy.

As he opened the book he realized again that he hadn't paid his bills, and still couldn't because his charger was in the apartment. They'd have to wait.

He continued reading the book from where he'd left off. History wasn't his first choice of entertainment, but it was different when there was a puzzle to solve. The writing style was a bit dry, like his uncle, but he trusted every sentence. Anything that might be considered conjecture was footnoted as such, as were statements that weren't verified by multiple sources. He likened the writing style to that of articles published in scientific journals, something he'd read daily as a part of his former job.

So far, the origin of the information in *The Israel Thread* was connected to the interrogations of Nazi war criminals by Israeli intelligence. Although the end-of-war escape plan devised by the Nazi SS, codenamed ODESSA, was described in the monograph, more attention was dedicated to the so-called *Final Reich*, and a long line of events related to it.

In 1938, just before the beginning of World War II, Germany sent an exploration vessel, the *Schwabenland*, to Antarctica. Its official mission was to study the Southern Seas for the whaling industry, which made some sense considering that whale byproducts were used in the production of nitroglycerine for explosives. However, the more suspicious analysts, and this had been corroborated later, had suspected that Germany was looking for places to build submarine bases. This idea was substantiated when a British ship shadowing the *Schwabenland* had observed it rendezvous with a German U-boat in the middle of the Weddell Sea, off the western coast of Antarctica. Handwritten in green ink in the margin was a note indicating that there had been a more insidious reason for the voyage of the *Schwabenland*.

What could be more insidious than a clandestine submarine base? Jacob wondered.

He set the book down and let his mind wander. Why would his

uncle be so protective of a book that presented historic events that meant nothing in the present day? He shook his head. That was wrong: the past and present were always connected. His uncle wouldn't have sent him on a wild goose chase. The building on Swann Street was a testament to that.

The voyage of the *Schwabenland* led to speculation that the Germans were building a secret base in the area. In response, the British launched their own mission, Operation Tabarin, to counter the German efforts, whatever they were. There had been rumors that, late in the war and afterwards, battles had been fought in the Southern Seas, and on the Antarctic mainland, but there was no direct evidence of that.

At half past four, Jacob took a sip of cold coffee and looked up just in time to notice something that instantly accelerated his heart rate. A red subcompact car slowed as it drove by his Corolla. He could see only the back of the driver's head, but he could tell it was unusually large, even beneath the baseball cap.

He watched as the man's head swiveled, undoubtedly looking for a parking spot. It was the one time Jacob was grateful for the lack of parking in the area.

Keeping his eye on the red car, he stowed his things in his backpack, brought his mug up to the counter, and thanked Kirsten. He walked to the door and watched another car pull up behind the red one. The driver of the other car tapped the horn. A third car was pulling out of a spot on the street but, to Jacob's relief, it was too far back; the red car would have to go around the block to get to it.

When the red car made it to the intersection a block ahead, Jacob casually exited the café and walked toward his car. The red vehicle took a left and Jacob immediately ran, unlocked his car with the remote key, opened the door, and threw his knapsack in the passenger seat. A few seconds later, he was on Pine Street, heading in the direction of his apartment.

In the rearview mirror, he saw another car trying to parallel park in the spot he'd just vacated, and the red car turn the corner onto Pine Street far behind.

The red car sped toward him down Pine, but the person trying to park in the spot Jacob previously occupied was having trouble. The red car was stuck.

Jacob turned right and sped toward the highway. He knew how to drive in Alexandria traffic, and thought he'd be hard to catch once he got into the thick of it. But first, he had to get through a thicket of slow stoplights.

Lenny couldn't believe his eyes. Hale's maroon Corolla pulled out of the parking spot in the minute it took him to go around the block. *The man must have a sixth sense.*

Lenny had searched all afternoon. He'd been lucky to find the car, even though he knew it must have been walking distance from Hale's apartment. Hale had made a stupid mistake by staying in the area, but now Lenny thought he might lose him again, stuck behind some moron who couldn't parallel park. Another car blocked him in from behind.

He cursed as Hale turned right at the intersection. He laid on the horn and tried to squeeze past the white SUV in front of him. There was probably an inch of clearance, but Lenny was off the mark. He scraped the entire length of the woman's passenger door and took off her side mirror. He floored the accelerator and turned right at the first intersection.

The street widened to four lanes and was packed with vehicles that barely inched along. It was rush hour. He spotted the Corolla one light ahead.

Lenny was a few cars behind the front of the line at the light, but had some room to maneuver the small car to the front of the right-turn lane, at the noisy protest of the other drivers. A small gap opened in the cross-traffic, and he crossed the intersection through the red light, and entered the next line just two cars behind Hale. It was close enough to maintain a tail, although it would be difficult in the dense traffic if Hale knew what he was doing.

If Lenny had been going for a kill it would have been a much easier operation: he'd just need a clean shot. The problem was that he needed to capture him, which would be difficult if it came down to another footrace. Next time he'd shoot him in the leg. After he got what he needed, he'd plug him twice in the brain.

JACOB CURSED at the red light eight cars ahead, and it looked like he might not make it through the next green light cycle. The thug ran the red light behind him and was now just two cars away.

Jacob was trapped. The man could just get out of his car and shoot him through the window. There'd be a lot of witnesses, but he'd still be dead.

He kept an eye on the red car through his mirrors. If its door opened he'd have to get out and run.

He fumbled around in the pocket of his knapsack and dug out his phone. He searched for the last number he'd called and dialed.

"Detective Kranz," the voice said.

"This is Jacob Hale," Jacob said. "I need your help."

"What's going on?"

"The man from this morning is on my tail – he's in the car behind me."

"Are you sure?" Kranz asked, calmly. "After traumatic events, people often think – "

"– I'm sure. He scoped out my car when it was parked on the street," Jacob said, and then explained the other details.

"Where you headed?"

"I'm at the light on Second and Spruce, going south," Jacob replied.

"I'm a ways away," Kranz said. "Keep heading south. I'm going to get some squads involved, but no lights or sirens. What's the make and model of the car that's following you?"

Jacob gave him the info along with a description of the driver –

Caucasian, baseball cap, sunglasses, and a huge head – and then hung up.

The light turned green and traffic inched through the intersection. The red car slid into a gap that had formed in one lane to the right, which was moving faster. Jacob found a gap to his left and took it, putting him in the left-turn lane, which would take him into a residential neighborhood. As the intersection approached, the red car pulled even with him, but was still separated by a lane of cars.

Jacob made eye contact with the man and, for a reason he didn't know, stuck up his middle finger at him.

The left turn lane moved forward, and the red car tried to edge into the adjacent lane of traffic. As Jacob started the turn, the red car was in the middle of the intersection and already ahead of him, heading for the side street. With an instinctual, last-second maneuver, Jacob pulled an illegal U-turn, and was now heading north on Second Street. The red car was stuck in the intersection in an awkward position, its path blocked by the long line of left-turning traffic.

Northbound Second Street was not as congested, and Jacob floored it. A quarter mile up the road, he took a right onto Pine, and then a quick left on King Street. After a few blocks, he turned right on Oak and then took another right at the light, onto Third Street.

Certain that he'd lost his pursuer, Jacob brought the Corolla back down to legal speed and continued along Third toward the highway. To his horror, the red car reappeared in his rearview mirror. He pushed the accelerator to the floor, and could tell that the red car was doing the same.

He ran a red light, barely avoiding an accident and, not that he cared, red-light cameras snapped his picture. The red car had to slow to navigate the cross-traffic as it ran the same lights, but was still on the move. The man was relentless.

Jacob turned onto US Route 1 and sped toward the Capital Beltway. As he entered the onramp to Interstate Highway 495, his phone rang. It was Kranz.

"Where the hell are you?" Kranz asked.

"Had to improvise," Jacob replied. "I'm getting on 495."

"What the hell? I thought I told you – "

"He was making a move! He's on my ass – gotta go."

Jacob hung up the phone and concentrated on losing his pursuer. His thoughts turned to Paulina. There was no way he was going to stay at her place – he wasn't going to drag her into this. So now he didn't have many options. Hotels required credit cards, and could be tracked. He also wouldn't make the seven-hour drive up to Boston to stay with his cousin. He only had one option.

The 495 Loop was jammed with rush hour traffic, but that was to his advantage. He'd made the drive every day for almost three years, and knew a few tricks. With his pursuer about ten cars behind him, he weaved through traffic and got in front of a semi-trailer. This made him uneasy since he couldn't see anything behind him.

Traffic picked up speed and, a few minutes later, he approached an exit on the right. At the last second, he pulled hard to the right, cut through a small gap in the right lane, and barely slid into the exit. The red car didn't make it.

Jacob doubled back on a surface street, and then reentered the highway and proceeded in the opposite direction. No matter which direction he chose, the I-495 Loop would eventually take him to his destination.

After 45 minutes in slow traffic, he exited the beltway into the same area he'd been two nights before. Five minutes later, he parked his car two streets west of Swann Street, in a residential neighborhood about a quarter mile from the building. He called Detective Kranz and explained that he'd lost his pursuer and was staying with a friend – not Paulina. For ten minutes Kranz interrogated him for the descriptions of the man and his car, and then ordered Jacob to come into the station to fill out a complete report within the next 48 hours. Jacob agreed, but doubted that was going to happen.

He grabbed his knapsack, got out of the car, and walked.

The aromas of grilled meat from local restaurants reminded him that it was nearing dinnertime, and that he'd had nothing to eat all day. His stomach grumbled, but he wasn't going to stop for anything;

he had to get out of the daylight. He relaxed as he walked, and the disturbing events of the day settled into the background of his mind. He was anxious to see what was beyond the inner door at 17 Swann Street, and whether it was a place he could hide out until things cooled down.

The sun was low in the western sky but still peeked through the trees. The air was still, and the temperature was in the mid-70s. He was more relaxed than he'd been in days, but wondered if the feeling was just a side effect of diminishing adrenaline.

He turned right at a cross street, and then another right onto Swann. A few minutes later, he passed the flower shop on his left at number 71.

The thick canopy of oak and spruce trees darkened the street, but his eyes adjusted as he went along. Still a couple of blocks away, the top of the building at 17 was visible above the trees. He still found it odd that it was turned ninety degrees relative to the others. The front entrances of all of the other structures faced the street. That of number 17 faced an alley.

He took a left onto the walkway that led between numbers 17 and 15, walked into the alley, and up the steps to the massive door. He inserted the silver cylindrical key and it vibrated in his fingers. The door pivoted on its unexposed hinges and inched outward on the left side. His fingertips found the grooves on the exposed edge and he pulled. The door swung open, and he stepped through the opening and into the dark foyer.

The door closed gently behind him.

CHAPTER 4

Not unlike his habit when returning to his apartment after work, Jacob went to the mailbox and sorted through his key ring for the brass key stamped with a "4." With a shaking hand, he inserted the key and turned. The door vibrated, and then cracked open a centimeter. He opened it and looked inside. Nothing.

He closed the box and turned to the inner door. He selected the gold cylindrical key and inserted it into the circular keyhole next to the door.

His heart picked up pace as the key vibrated in his hand and the door hummed.

The door slid to the right, revealing a closet-sized compartment. He extracted the key, stepped inside, and turned to face the door as it closed. It was an elevator.

A panel on the wall to the left of the door had over twenty buttons, numbered one through nineteen. The remaining buttons were labeled with letters. Next to each button was a keyhole. The numbered buttons had key slots that took a regular key, but those labeled with letters took the cylindrical type.

He had three keys for the building, two of which were cylindrical. He selected the regular key that opened the mailbox and inserted it into the slot next to the button labeled with the number four. He turned it, and the button lit up in green. He tried to press it and realized it was only an indicator light.

The elevator moved. His knees barely flexed when it started, but he could tell it was ascending. After about 20 seconds, it stopped, and seemed to *rotate* horizontally by about ninety degrees to his right. He took a step backward for balance as the elevator moved *forward*. It stopped after about 15 seconds, turned right again, and then inched forward until it came to a complete stop. A green light illuminated above the door, and it slid open.

He pulled out the key and peeked out, but did not exit the elevator. It was dark, but there was a weak source of light from above. The air was slightly musty, and carried light scents of old leather and pipe tobacco. It was dead silent.

He inched out of the elevator and his eyes, brain, and heart jolted as light suddenly flooded the area. A few seconds later, after his brain had processed the information, he stood in awe of the display before him.

Directly across the room from the elevator was a massive wall of books, making him think that he might be in a library.

The size of the room surprised him – it must have been the entire top floor of the building. He estimated it was 60 or 70 feet wide, over 100 feet long, and looked to have multiple floors. At the top of the arched ceiling, which was easily 40 feet high, were two large hemispherical skylights that glowed with the dark purple hue of the twilight sky. Giant wooden beams spanned the width of the room about two-thirds up, and dozens of others crisscrossed at strange angles near the top in a way that was both functional and beautiful.

Jacob twitched as the elevator door clanked closed behind him.

He took a few steps toward the center of the room where floodlights mounted to one of the thick beams illuminated a long wooden table. The table resembled those found in libraries, and had a line of lamps down its center, all of them lit.

"Hello?" he said, not quietly but not shouting.

No answer.

A burgundy rug with a diamond design pattern spanned the full length of the marble-tiled floor.

The long wall, opposite the elevator, was inset from floor to ceiling with wooden bookshelves. They were filled mostly with books – thousands of them – but they also stored wooden boxes and other objects. A ladder built into the wall on the near end led to two levels of narrow catwalks that spanned the length of the wall, for a total of three tiers of shelves. There were no guardrails. He spotted an identical ladder at the far end.

On the floor level to his right, opposite the bookshelves and beneath an overhang, was a massive wooden desk with a computer monitor and keyboard. To the left of the desk was a printer and a wooden file cabinet and, to its right, a garbage can and a small table stacked with printer paper. Further down, to the left of the file cabinet, was a leather chair and a coffee table. On the table was a pipe turned upside down in an ashtray. An energized light fixture was suspended above the chair.

Jacob went to the center of the room, near the far end of the long table, and surveyed what was above the overhang. It was another level of rooms.

Directly above the desk and open to the large central area was a loft with a bunk-style bed. It was darker deeper inside, but he thought he saw some wooden furniture and a door. On the same level, further to the left, was a kitchen with a counter and stools, and a flat-screen television mounted high on the leftmost wall. He couldn't see deeper inside from below.

The overall layout reminded him of a library building that Uncle Theo had donated to a small college near Boston. In that case, the exposed rooms had been study areas.

At the end of the flat, on the far right, was a wooden staircase that ascended to a landing on the second level, and a second flight that continued up another level to a platform beneath the far skylight. There was furniture on the high platform.

"Hello?" Jacob said again.

No answer. He repeated the call a few times with the same result.

He went to the desk and looked for clues that might reveal the purpose of the place, and the reason his uncle wanted him to go there. On top of the computer keyboard was a brown envelope with his name written on it.

Jacob's heart beat in his temples.

He picked it up. It wasn't sealed. He pulled out a folded piece of paper and read.

Dear Jacob,

Since you are reading this, you have summoned enough courage to go through the second door. You will not be disappointed. You now have a chance to enrich your life in ways you could never have imagined. But first, you will have to accomplish something of great significance and, second, commit to something greater than yourself.

I have spent many decades in this beautiful place, and I urge you to explore it thoroughly. It contains secrets, many of which were first revealed in this very room.

I have just returned from what was undoubtedly my final mission. I am very ill, and I regret that I have to leave this work unfinished. The book I gave you is just the beginning.

Keep the book, this place, and everything you learn here concealed as if your very life depended on it – because it does. In fact, everything you do from this point forward will have existential consequences.

I didn't give you money, Jacob. Instead, I gave you an opportunity. I am sure that, if you haven't already, you will one day question that decision. If you trust me, you will see that I have given you the best gift of all.

Your loving uncle,

Theodore H. Leatherby

P.S. You should consider resigning from your job, moving out of your apartment, and focusing your efforts here. You will be provided with everything you need. And do not lose the keys. There are no replacements.

JACOB'S HANDS trembled as he placed the letter in its envelope. What did Theo mean by *existential consequences*? It was the second time he'd used the phrase. And what could be so important that he should quit his job? That, of course, was no longer an issue, and Theo's words only made him feel better about his sudden termination.

It was the perfect time for this to happen, Jacob thought. He'd lost his job and girlfriend in one week, although he still felt miserable about the latter.

He'd accept his uncle's challenge.

DANIEL PARSONS HAD OFTEN DREAMT of having Horace's job, but it had been a dream based on incomplete information. There were things about the job of which he'd not been aware, and now it was too late to reconsider. But it wasn't as if he'd had a choice. Horace was dead, and the CIA Director, James Thackett, had to appoint someone immediately. Daniel was the obvious choice.

What the hell was "17 Swann Street 4?" It was mentioned in an urgent email from Director Thackett, and they'd set up a meeting to discuss the matter in Daniel's office at 8:00 p.m., which was in ten minutes.

Daniel put the report he'd been reading on the coffee table and stood from the couch on which he'd just spent the better of two hours. He walked to the window where an electric teapot maintained a reserve of hot water, and poured some into a cup with a thrice-used teabag. He sniffed the faint aroma of Earl Grey as he stared blankly into the darkening southeastern sky. His window on the seventh floor of the Space Systems building provided a panoramic view of the pine forest below, above which stars were just starting to peek through the purple-black canvas. It was at times like this that he wished his office windows faced west; he imagined the sunset was magnificent.

His focus readjusted to his reflection in the window. His hair matched the darkness outside, making his pale face stand out in contrast. He looked like hell. His small glasses didn't conceal the bags under his bloodshot eyes, and the graying scruff on his face looked like dirt. He looked much older than his forty-nine years. And, more concerning, he looked gaunt. At five-foot-ten, his body weight shouldn't dip below 140 pounds. He was just two pounds over that last week, and he was sure he was lighter now.

A beep sounded from the far side of the larger room that contained his office, the office of his colleague, Sylvia Barnes, and a large, central work area with various collections of furniture and a kitchenette.

He walked out of his office and into the common area.

Director Thackett entered and closed the door behind him, and then walked toward Daniel. In his fifties, with his dark suit and slick, black-gray hair, Thackett looked like a typical politician. The man's appearance was something that had tainted Daniel's first impression of him, but that had changed quickly. Through direct interaction in dangerous circumstances, it was clear to him that Thackett was a good man, and he trusted him. He was the right man for the job.

Daniel greeted him at a cluster of furniture where they often sat to discuss their work. Two leather chairs and a couch were arranged in a square on a large area rug. At the center of the square was a coffee table. Thackett sat in a chair, and Daniel on the couch directly across the table from him.

"What's Swann Street 4?" Daniel asked.

"It was Horace's workspace."

"He didn't work in the Space Systems building?"

Thackett shook his head. "He had an office here, but rarely used it."

"Why not?" Daniel couldn't imagine someone not enjoying working in the building. His own work area was magnificent, and the building was as secure as any CIA building in existence.

"Horace was old school," Thackett explained. "He was from a time when they'd worked in ultra-secure safe houses in the DC area, and preferred to be seen by no one in the intelligence community."

And it had worked, Daniel thought. He'd been working at the Space Systems building for over twenty years and hadn't seen Horace's face until he'd been introduced to him two months ago.

"What's going on?" Daniel asked.

"Someone accessed the building," Thackett replied, "and got into his safe box."

"Safe box?"

"Like a mailbox, but built like a safe. Even more secure than safe deposit boxes at banks," Thackett explained. "It's the way Horace received classified documents."

Daniel didn't like the idea at all. The protocols for transporting secure documents were clearly defined, and stringent. "So someone got away with classified information?"

Thackett nodded as he pulled a vibrating phone out of an inner pocket in his jacket and read the message. He seemed to read it more than once.

"Looks like it might be more serious than I thought," Thackett said, shaking his head.

"What is it?"

"Someone's in Horace's workspace right now."

"Is there classified information there?"

"Most certainly," Thackett answered. "But only Horace knew exactly what."

"Once he'd passed, I thought all of his things would have been cleaned up."

"They would have, but we can't get into that place," Thackett responded. "There was a special set of keys –"

"Just break in," Daniel cut him off.

Thackett nodded and smiled. "It's nearly impossible," he said. "Especially without drawing attention to the facility."

"Does it matter? Won't we close it down now anyway?"

Thackett shook his head. "We don't want to lose it – we could never build another place like it and keep it secret."

"How did someone get unauthorized access?" Daniel asked.

"I have a theory," Thackett said and smiled.

"What?"

"Horace *gave* the keys to someone."

"To whom?"

"That's what we need to find out," Thackett said.

"You're watching the place?"

"We have people on the way," Thackett replied as he stood. "I'll keep you updated."

Daniel walked him to the door.

"Getting used to your new responsibilities?" Thackett turned and asked as he opened the door.

"There's more to it than I'd anticipated."

Thackett smiled and nodded, and then walked out, leaving Daniel to his thoughts.

Why would Horace risk compromising classified information? Daniel wondered. He had great respect for the man he'd replaced. Horace must have had a good reason.

JACOB WALKED on the tile floor, alongside the narrow rug, to the far end of the room, and then climbed a ladder on the left to the second level of bookshelves. He pulled out a book at random from an eye-level shelf and opened it. It was a monograph similar in style to the one his uncle had given him. It was about the Nazis' version of the Manhattan Project. No author name was given – only two dates appeared on the spine and cover. He put it back and pulled out another a few feet down. It was labeled top-secret.

Jacob had dealt with classified materials all of his professional life. Interstellar Dynamics followed strict protocols, and so had he. He felt strange opening it, but his uncle's note had emboldened him. This one was about a secret CIA surveillance project called Tandem

Pass. He read the abstract and learned that it was a colossal domestic spying mission carried out by the CIA in the 1970s. He knew the CIA wasn't supposed to operate inside US borders.

He put it back, walked a few steps to the left, and pulled another. It also had the top-secret designation. It described an underground nuclear facility constructed by the former USSR in Cuba. He flipped to a page somewhere in the middle and found a detailed diagram of the facility and a few maps. It seemed that the Russians weren't only bringing missiles to Cuba, but building a base and a reactor to fabricate fissionable material on site. They were going to make Cuba a self-sufficient nuclear power. If true, the US had been closer to going to war with the USSR than he'd thought – and it had been pretty damned close as it was.

He put the book back and walked further down the catwalk to a set of shelves with boxes and other objects on them. One object, out in the open on a middle shelf, was an intricate mechanical device about the size of a sewing machine. It had a small circular window, about three inches in diameter, and was riddled with gears and caliper-positioning mechanisms. Next to it was a monograph titled "Theft of the Norden Bombsight." A tag on the device read, "This improved version of the Norden bombsight was discovered in a hidden Nazi facility concealed in the German countryside near Dresden." He read the abstract of the monograph and learned that, before the Allies could even put their new bombsight to use, the Germans were already producing an improved version of it. He sighed and was grateful that the Allies had somehow won the war.

He turned his back to the shelves and looked across the room to the loft on the opposite side. Now, from an elevated perspective, he examined the bedroom and kitchen. Deeper in the kitchen was a furnished lounging area that he couldn't see from the floor. It was strange to see the rooms open to the outside: it was as if he were looking into an open dollhouse.

He scaled down the ladder, crossed the floor to the steep staircase that led to the second level, and climbed the stairs to a landing. To the right was the kitchen, and another flight of stairs that led to the dome was on the left. He went right.

He walked into a combined kitchen and lounging area. An array of inset lights spanned the ten-foot ceiling and illuminated the entire room. To his right was a black granite countertop with two stools that overlooked the first floor, and provided a direct view of the stacks on the opposite side of the facility. On the far end of the counter were a stainless steel sink and a dishwasher. Across the room from the entrance was a refrigerator, and a stove with a microwave mounted above the range. All of the appliances looked to be recent, high-end models. The floor tiles formed a beige mosaic of a compass rose design that spanned the entire footprint of the room. It reminded him of the seal on the floor of the CIA headquarters at Langley.

The inset lighting and luxurious amenities made him feel like he was in an expensive apartment. He checked the refrigerator: it was empty, but clean and cold. He opened drawers and cabinets and found utensils and dishes. He turned a lever on the sink: water flowed and quickly turned hot.

Deeper into the room, to the left of the entrance, was a cluster of furniture including a leather couch, two matching chairs, and a coffee table. A giant flat-screen television – at least 55 inches – was mounted on the wall immediately to the right of the entrance when facing it from the inside.

He went to the opposite side of the kitchen, and then through a door next to the refrigerator that led to a bathroom with a shower. He continued through the bathroom and through another door into a carpeted bedroom with two stacked, bunk-style beds inset into the wall on the left. There was no wall on the right side, which was open to the main library, and had a railing that made it seem like a balcony. An armoire and chest of drawers were on the far wall, opposite the entrance.

As he walked toward the armoire, he flinched at his image in a large mirror on the wall to his left, next to the bunks, and noticed a door next to it. He opened it and found an empty walk-in closet that housed shelves and drawers, and also a stacked, combination clothes washer and dryer.

As he walked back into the kitchen, he noticed a square, steel door, about two feet on a side, on the wall to the left of the sink. He turned the handle on the door and pulled. It opened, revealing an empty cavity that reminded him of the dumbwaiters sometimes found in old restaurants and hotels. He had no idea of its purpose. The door latched with a metallic clank as he closed it.

He walked out of the kitchen to the landing.

He got a better view of the third level on the opposite side, which was another tier of bookshelves. Like the second tier, it had a narrow catwalk that seemed treacherous without a guardrail. He then looked up the staircase that led to one of the domes.

He climbed the stairs to a circular platform. The floor was covered in thick white carpet, and there was a circular leather couch with a round coffee table in the center. He walked through a gap in the circle, took a seat, and looked up into the night sky.

The dome was much larger than it had seemed from the bottom floor, maybe ten or twelve feet in diameter. The platform was positioned high enough to view a wide angle of sky, but nothing else – not even the high treetops of the oaks in the neighborhood. It was a breathtaking view reminiscent of his skiing trips to the mountains in Utah. It made him think of Paulina.

He stood, walked to the guardrail at the edge of the platform, and gazed upon the scene below. It was a magnificent place. He still wasn't sure of its purpose. The fundamental question that had lingered in his mind from the instant he'd read the first of Theo's letters came back to him: *What was he supposed to do?*

THE STUPID BASTARD *thought he lost me on the highway*, Lenny thought.

When someone turned into a residential neighborhood after they thought they were safe, it meant they were probably close to their destination. He'd seen Jacob Hale's Corolla exit to a surface street, double back, and then reenter the highway in the opposite direction. But Hale hadn't seen Lenny take the next exit and double back on the same surface street. Lenny had been fortunate to spot the Corolla again on the highway. He'd then reentered the beltway about a quarter mile behind Hale.

After another 40 minutes in dense highway traffic, Hale had taken an exit to a surface street and then turned right at a light, into a residential neighborhood. At that point, he'd known Hale was near his final destination.

Lenny had exited the highway and turned at the same light as Hale had minutes earlier. When he didn't find the car within a mile down that street, he'd systematically weaved through the adjacent side streets, moving the search radius progressively outward. He'd located Hale's car 30 minutes later.

He parked a block in front of the Corolla, on the opposite side of the street, and waited.

JACOB WENT DOWN to the first floor and sat at the desk with the computer. He pressed a key on the keyboard and the large monitor illuminated. In the center of the display was a file named *Read Me*.

He clicked on it and a text document opened. On the top was written, "How to Use this Facility." He read it.

If everything still worked as described in the instructions, he'd never have to leave the place. He could request classified documents and books, as well as food and other supplies. The physical documents were delivered to the secure mailbox in the building's foyer. Food and supplies were delivered via the dumbwaiter in the kitchen. One thing he hadn't noticed in the kitchen was the garbage drop built into the wall between the counter and the entrance. Finally, he could request the services of a high-security custodial crew to clean the place, but he had to be present since he had the only keys. It looked like Uncle Theo had the place cleaned out before he'd died.

He wondered how long he could carry on like that. Had the

facility been set up by his uncle, or by a government organization? It could have gone either way: even though Uncle Theo had mentioned that his job involved the government, with his wealth he could have set up permanent funding to keep such a place running in perpetuity.

The environment was designed so that a person could think with no distractions. It seemed that his uncle was a professional puzzle solver – if referring to his projects as puzzles wasn't a gross understatement. Now Jacob had a puzzle of his own and, he now recognized, Theo had given him the means to solve it. Apparently, the first part of the puzzle was to identify the puzzle. Up to this point, he knew nothing more than what he'd learned from *The Israel Thread* monograph.

His stomach grumbled, and he decided to get some food. As he contemplated how long the deliveries took, he realized that it wasn't a given that the delivery service was still active. Although, since the "Read Me" file had been created less than a month prior, he was optimistic that everything was still operational. After all, the lights and water were still on.

He followed instructions on the document that led him to an email account. He made a list of items and submitted it. He figured they'd be delivered the next day at the earliest. He couldn't wait that long for food.

Even though he was still in shock or denial about being chased twice in one day by a thug who would undoubtedly appear in his nightmares, he was sure the risk was minimal now. He decided to head out to get something to eat.

THE STREETLIGHTS REACHED into the swaying lower branches of the trees, making the lighting inconsistent. Lenny strained his eyes for over an hour trying to identify people walking toward the Corolla.

Some who approached were joggers, and others were couples walking in the mild evening. On two occasions he'd gotten out of his car and made a move toward someone – lone males who, from far away, could have been Hale. On a third occasion, he went to relieve himself in the bushes between two buildings.

His legs were restless and his mindset edgy. Hale had gotten away twice. He couldn't allow that to happen again.

At 9:00 p.m., he listened to a radio talk show about people who had been abducted by aliens as he sipped on a bottle of water and watched Hale's car. He was getting hungry, but he put it out of his mind. He might be there all night.

As he tuned in a new radio station to avoid a string of commercials, he caught motion under the lights on the opposite side of the street, a couple of blocks behind the Corolla. It was a thin figure, probably male, and he was walking toward the car.

Lenny slid the keys out of the ignition and pulled the door handle. He opened the door with care and put his left foot on the pavement, and then cracked it open a little wider and eased his massive body off the seat and out the door. He winced as the chassis creaked, and he slowed his motion to try to minimize the noise. He then pulled himself completely out of the car and pressed the door closed until it clicked. He straightened up slowly and crossed to the same side of the street as the man, but didn't go all the way to the sidewalk. Instead, he stopped behind a tree that was between the sidewalk and the street. Each yard had a tree in about the same position, forming a long line that he used to conceal himself as he stalked. If he timed it right, he'd beat the man to the car.

When he was about 15 feet from the front of the Corolla, jingling keys warned him that the man was about the same distance behind it. The man stepped out of the tree line and into the street to get to the driver's side of the car. It was Hale.

Just as the car's lights flashed, indicating that it had been unlocked with a remote, Lenny jumped into the street and pointed his gun at Hale's chest.

Hale stopped ten feet behind the car and stared at him with wide eyes. He then dove into the grass to the rear and left of the car.

On any other occasion, the man would've had a bullet in his chest, but Lenny needed him alive.

Lenny charged south, to the rear of the car, just in time to see Hale sprinting north on the sidewalk. He knew he'd never catch him on foot, so it was time to slow him. He stepped onto the sidewalk and took aim at Hale's legs. Before he could get off the shot, the wiry man cut left, into the line of trees. Lenny responded by stepping into the street and caught a glimpse of Hale just as he cut back to the right, trees again interfering with the shot. The bastard was wilier than he'd anticipated.

Lenny ran down the middle of the street, hoping to get a clear shot when Hale weaved to his side. When Hale again emerged from the tree cover, now about 30 yards away, Lenny fired a shot at knee-level.

Hale didn't go down, but disappeared again into the tree line.

Lenny jumped to the sidewalk side and took another shot at him, now 50 yards away – missed by a mile.

He cursed to himself as he watched Hale sprint down the sidewalk, no longer weaving, then dart right at a cross street.

Lenny ran back to his car, did a U-turn, and sped down the street after the man.

Unless Hale was hiding in a yard, he could only have taken the adjacent residential street. Lenny took a right on Lilac, and then another right three blocks down, on Egret Street. Hale was 50 yards in front of him.

JACOB PANICKED when the car screeched around the corner. His shadow grew darker as the headlights closed in behind him. Adrenaline coursed through his veins and he was nearly hyperventilating. He'd never been shot at before. He had to get off the road.

The car was right on his ass, and there were no trees to protect him this time. He recognized the top of the 17 Swann building above the house to his right. As he angled across the lawn toward a driveway to the left of the house, a muffled shot came from the passenger side of the car. He zigzagged, and then cut a hard right, down the driveway.

The car screeched to a halt behind him and he glanced back at the silhouette of a wide-framed man lumbering past the mailbox, and up the driveway. Jacob raced past a garage toward a red brick wall that was about eight feet tall. He hoped he had enough energy to get over it; he'd only have one chance at it. He flew by two garbage cans and a basketball pole, and adjusted his gait to make the jump. He took two long strides and leapt with all of his might for the top of the wall.

He easily got his hands over the top, but the wall cap was wider than he'd anticipated and he didn't get his fingers over the opposite edge. The bark and acorns that had accumulated on its surface cut into his forearms and caused him to slide backward. He lurched upward as hard as he could and hooked the fingertips of his right hand over the opposite edge. As he swung his right leg to the top of the wall, a clanging sound made him flinch and almost fall. The man had taken a shot and hit the basketball pole. He glanced back as his pursuer squared up and shot again, his gun making a spitting sound that nearly coincided with the sound of bricks fracturing near his left leg.

With a final frantic effort, he swung his left leg upward and rolled his body over the wall. He landed heavily on his right shoulder and hit the side of his head on a concrete footing. Now in the alley between the 17 Swann building and the adjacent one, he sprung up and sprinted to the door. He pulled the keys out of his pocket, selected the silver one, and then dropped them onto the stoop. Cursing as he picked them up, he looked toward the wall: no one was coming over the top, but the metallic banging of garbage cans echoed behind it. The man was probably using them to climb over the wall.

Jacob again found the key. His hand shook so violently that he could hardly insert it into the keyhole. The door pivoted, and he pulled on the exposed edge to swing it open. He glanced one more time at the wall at the end of the alley, but the man was not in sight.

He went into the foyer, and pulled on the door in an attempt to speed up its automated closing process. His efforts seemed to have minimal effect, but the door closed, and he was safe.

He bent over, panting, and was on the brink of vomiting. His whole body radiated heat, but his sweat was cold. He straightened himself, selected the key for the elevator, and inserted it. The elevator door opened, he stepped in, inserted the brass key into slot number four, and the elevator took him to what he now realized was his new home.

As the elevator came to a halt, a burning sensation warmed his left thigh. He looked down: his cargo shorts were torn and soaked with blood.

When the elevator door opened, he turned right and rushed across the first floor to the stairs. He ran up to the second floor, through the kitchen, to the bathroom. He took off the shorts and was relieved to see that he'd only been nicked. There was a groove across the outer part of his left thigh, maybe an eighth of an inch deep, a quarter inch wide, and an inch long. He washed it out in the shower with soap. He found no bandages in the cabinets or drawers, so he pressed a washcloth against it and held it there. The bleeding immediately slowed, but it was the kind of injury that would bleed for a while.

He looked around for something to wear – but the drawers and closet in the bedroom were empty. He finally found a white bathrobe in the bathroom closet.

All he knew was that he wasn't going to be leaving the building for a while, and he needed bandages and antiseptic. He'd also need new bandages for the thorn wounds on his thighs and forearms from the rose bushes he'd encountered during the chase that morning.

He went down to the first-floor computer and placed his second order.

DANIEL PARSONS ARRIVED at the Space Systems building on Saturday morning at 6:38 a.m., went through the extensive security checks, and was in room 713 by 7:15 a.m.

He was still adjusting to his new responsibilities. Organizing the efforts of the entire group, just over twenty people, took serious work. But it came with an enormous advantage: other than the CIA director, he was the only one who saw the full picture. The others had specific, focused efforts, and didn't have knowledge of anyone else's work. They didn't even know who the others were.

Sylvia, his colleague and officemate, hadn't yet arrived. She was still an individual researcher, like the others, but she was a special case. Against protocol, she and Daniel had been thrown together to work on an important project before Horace had passed away. They'd done so well together that they'd kept their working arrangement despite Daniel being promoted to the lead position. By virtue of her close proximity to him and CIA Director Thackett, Sylvia had an unusually wide view of the information landscape, although she wasn't privy to certain details.

Before his forced collaboration with Sylvia, and their mandatory office cohabitation, Daniel had relished isolation. The absence of interpersonal relationships, and the general quiet, made his work environment conducive to deep thought. His mind had worked in a state that he could only describe as meditation. At first, he'd worried about their new arrangement – that his concentration would be affected – but it had worked out well.

Their office space took up half of the seventh floor of the Space Systems building. He hardly knew Sylvia was there most of the time, even though the layout was completely open. And he didn't mind the occasional company during breaks for tea. His wife had left him over a month ago. It was something that lingered in his subconscious, giving him a melancholy feeling when his thoughts were allowed to wander. He felt guilty about it – it was his fault. A person could only be neglected for so long before they'd finally had enough. He'd deserted her for his job. But he'd come to realize that this had been inevitable.

He logged into his email: 23 messages. Most were from the group's general researchers who had written a few sentences describing the progress they'd made the previous day. It was strange for him to be on this side of the reporting. When he'd been on the other side, it was as if he'd been writing to an organization, or a machine. He had no idea that he'd been giving his updates to *one person* – that person being Horace at the time. He'd also had a feeling of complete anonymity – no one knew who he was, and he knew no one else's identity. Now he knew all of them. He preferred the old way.

He worked through the emails. There was nothing of great importance until he opened a message forwarded by Director Thackett. Whoever was in 17 Swann 4 had requested food, clothes, and, most disconcertingly, bandages and antiseptic. It looked like they were planning on staying for a while. It was probably a good thing: if they were there to steal information they would've gotten in and out as quickly as possible.

The situation at 17 Swann wasn't Daniel's responsibility – it was Thackett's. The director was only keeping him apprised of the situation. Daniel just hoped that Horace hadn't been keeping information about the members of the group at 17 Swann.

The next message was also from Thackett. Two operatives had been stationed at 17 Swann at midnight, but hadn't seen anything. They'd reported the license plates of all of the cars parked in the immediate area. The results were currently being processed and they'd have the information soon.

Daniel read the remaining emails and then went to his tea kettle, poured hot water into a cup, dipped in a fresh bag of English Breakfast tea, and moved it up and down by the string. He gazed out the window over the treetops and let the sun warm his face.

There was a lot to do. First, they needed to determine from where, exactly, the radio signals were originating. Next, they needed to decipher the encoded message. Finally, they'd have to figure out what it all meant.

His motivation was driven by anxiety, but dampened by a feeling of futility: whatever they were doing might not make a difference.

JACOB WOKE up and stared at the low wooden ceiling. He knew where he was, but was in disbelief. He was on the lower of two wooden bunk beds inset into the bedroom wall in 17 Swann Street number 4.

The polished wood construction of the beds and walls, and the room's coffered ceiling, had the look and feel of the lavish lower deck of a fancy sailboat. It reminded him of the *Omni*, the sailboat that had belonged to Uncle Theo, and then to Theo's now-deceased son, Kenneth. He wondered who would now take possession of the beautiful craft.

Opposite the wall with the beds was a railing that separated the bedroom from the large open space of the main room. It was a little awkward, but something he could get used to after living alone in the place for a while. Besides, someone would have to be on the second tier of the stacks to see into the bedroom.

He put his feet on the carpeted floor and leaned forward as he massaged his temples with the heels of his hands. It was as if the events of the previous night, and the past few days, had all been some crazy dream. The bullet graze on his thigh, the deep gouges from the rose bushes on his legs and arms, and the bump on his head from the concrete footing below the brick wall, were evidence that it had all really happened. He would be uncomfortable for a few days.

He got out of bed and put on the bathrobe. He looked at his phone: he had a message from Paulina. It was 8:07 a.m. His stomach grumbled – he hadn't eaten in over 24 hours – and his attention turned to the dumbwaiter in the next room.

He walked into the kitchen and opened the door to the dumbwaiter. To his delight, it was packed to capacity with clothes, food, and medical supplies. Whoever was in charge of the operation was on the ball.

He took out the clothes – shorts, underwear, shirts, and socks – and moved them into the bedroom, and then the medical supplies into a cabinet in the bathroom. He stowed the food in the kitchen and then went back to the bathroom and took a shower. He dressed his wounds. The thorn gouges had scabbed over, but the bullet graze continued to ooze. He still found it hard to accept that *someone had tried to kill him.*

He got dressed, went to the kitchen, and fried some eggs and bacon. After eating, he made coffee and went to the desk on the first floor. The computer seemed to have only two functions: to request supplies and to order classified documents.

Now that he had effectively moved into the place, it was time to concentrate all of his efforts on the task his uncle had given him. Two things had become clear in the past two days. First, his Uncle Theo was a mysterious man, involved with the government – at least he hoped it was the government. Second, the task his uncle had given him, although he didn't yet completely understand it, was not a puzzle for his entertainment. It was something with "existential consequences." It was serious business.

He went to the large library table at the center of the first floor and sat in one of four heavy wooden chairs. He pulled *The Israel Thread*, his notebook, and Theo's letter from his knapsack and placed them on the table. He reread Theo's letters – the one left for him on the computer desk, and the one that came with the monograph. In his mind the words took his uncle's voice, making the messages even more powerful. They conveyed a sense of urgency.

He opened the book and continued reading from where he'd stopped the day before. The gist of it up to that point was that the Germans had been nosing around Antarctica before and during World War II. The Brits reacted by conducting an operation of their own, Operation Tabarin, where they'd set up tiny lookout bases and may have conducted small-scale military operations on the continent.

It also noted that, well after the war, the United States had executed a large-scale operation called Operation Highjump. Theo had written a note in the margin questioning the Americans' claim that it was a training mission to prepare for a possible Arctic conflict with the Russians. *Why not train in Alaska?* Theo had written, and then, *Were the true motives for the current exercises near Antarctica related to those of 1946?* All of Theo's notes were dated – this one, just a month ago.

The recent naval conflict around Antarctica was all over the news. The so-called exercises had ended a few weeks ago – after a scuffle with a Chinese carrier group. The Chinese carrier was badly damaged – set on fire – and they blamed the US.

He read for the next few hours, learning detailed history that he assumed couldn't be found in anything published on the outside. Just before he decided to take a break, he read a short annotation written in the margin: *Everything leads to Red Falcon.* It was dated just a few weeks before Theo's death. Jacob had no idea what *Red Falcon* was. He looked up to the thousands of books on the shelves to his left. Perhaps he'd find it in the massive stacks.

Or maybe he'd make his first request for classified documents.

"He requested Red Falcon files?" Daniel asked, stunned. It was information that no civilian should even know existed.

Thackett nodded from across the coffee table. "Just an hour ago."

"You think Horace had this information at 17 Swann?"

"Clearly, there was something there that made reference to it," Thackett responded. "But there shouldn't be much there about our current project. Our breakthroughs happened only recently and, as you know, Horace didn't have much time to do anything after that."

It wasn't just the "current project," Daniel thought. It was the most important thing in which he'd ever been involved, and probably ever would be. It was a vast and complicated situation that had global consequences, and Red Falcon was the origin of all of it.

"We're not going to deliver the documents, right?" Daniel asked.

Thackett shrugged.

"You're not really considering – "

"Daniel," Thackett held up his hands, grinning. "I have more to tell you."

Daniel leaned back in his chair, and Thackett did the same, making the leather couch squeak beneath his rump.

"Two things happened today," Thackett said. "First, we got a list of names of the owners of all of the cars parked near 17 Swann. Detailed investigations have not yet been completed, but are in process. There are over 400 of them."

"And the second thing?"

"I got an email from Horace," Thackett said, his face remaining blank.

"What?" Daniel gasped. "I thought he was – "

Thackett held up his hands and shook his head. "He is, he is," he said, almost apologetically. "It was a delayed email that Horace set up before he died. It explains what's happening at 17 Swann Street."

"Who is it?"

"His nephew," Thackett replied. "That's not exactly right. Horace was his great uncle – it's his niece's son – but he refers to him as his nephew. His name is Jacob F. Hale."

"Is 'Hale' Horace's last name?"

"No," Thackett replied. "Horace's full name is Theodore Horace Leatherby."

Daniel nodded. Horace had used his middle name. "Why did Horace let this man –"

"You knew Horace," Thackett said, "and I knew him even better. He did it for a reason. You know, his nephew saved his life a decade ago."

Daniel nodded and sighed. "We should be grateful for that, but that's no reason to give him access to such sensitive information."

"I don't think this was Horace's idea of a reward for his nephew," Thackett said. "I think he thought that Jacob could help."

"How?" Daniel asked, skeptical.

Thackett sat forward. "Let me explain."

ON THE DESK computer was a program with a search function that cataloged the vast collection of books, but Jacob found nothing about Red Falcon in the stacks. He decided to continue reading *The Israel Thread* until the requested information arrived. He was still skeptical, however, that they'd send him anything that was classified.

He moved from the large table on the first floor to the third-floor dome. He leaned back on the circular couch and put his feet up on the coffee table at its center.

The next section of the monograph was a formal, fact-ridden history of events of which he'd never before heard. It was a history of Antarctica starting in 1773, when Captain James Cook first crossed the Antarctic Circle. The passage about Cook was referenced to another monograph labeled with two dates. The first date on the Cook monograph was different from the first date on *The Israel Thread*. By the way the references were written, he concluded that the first dates on monographs were likely their dates of publication. However, he noticed that the second dates on the two monographs were the same: 12 May 1945. He had no explanation for this, unless the second date identified the author somehow.

"The first observation" was written in the margin in green ink, next to the reference to the Captain Cook monograph.

Observation of what? Jacob wondered. Curious, he took the stairs down to the first floor and punched the dates on the monograph reference into the catalog program. The monograph was in the stacks, on the third level.

As he climbed the ladder to the third tier, he was grateful that the bullet from the night before had only grazed his thigh. He wondered how Theo had managed the climbing, being in his late nineties. Although, he thought, Theo had been in pretty good shape: he'd sailed and hiked until the very end.

He found the monograph and took it up to the dome. The title was *Myths and Facts of the Second Antarctic Voyage of Commander James Cook*.

Jacob had never heard of the storied Captain Cook being called "Commander," but it was clear that he hadn't yet been promoted. He thumbed through it and found, near the middle, two facing pages, each a map of Antarctica. The one on the left was made in the 1700s, the one on the right in the 1960s. They were qualitatively similar, but the 60s' version had more details and labels. The older one had elaborate artwork that illustrated important events of Cook's voyage.

One of the sketches in the old map was circled in green ink, and a page number was written next to it. It seemed Uncle Theo had also made notes in this monograph.

He turned to the indicated page and read. Cook's ship, the *HMS Resolution*, had suffered damage to its rudder and had to stop for repairs somewhere in what was now called the Weddell Sea, about 150 kilometers off the west coast of Antarctica. They'd been fortunate for unusually calm waters, and were able to repair it in just two days. But something strange had occurred during that time.

The repair operation involved members of the crew submerging themselves into the icy water. Each could only handle the cold for a minute, and then they'd be hoisted back to the deck as another man was lowered in to continue the work. It was a repair that would have taken less than an hour in port.

The men who had been submerged reported a strange pulsing sound in the water. At first, Cook thought someone was causing the noise from inside the ship, but could not identify who was doing it. With fear spreading throughout the crew, he'd ordered everyone on deck before lowering the next man into the water. The noise persisted.

Everyone thought the sound was mechanical, but couldn't be certain – so Cook himself went into the water. In his log, he described it as a metallic strum, like someone striking all of the keys of a harpsichord simultaneously, and then damping it. The short bursts of sound didn't seem loud, but pained the ears. They came at a rate of about two per second.

Cook didn't explore it any further. His men were spooked and, so it seemed, was he. Once the rudder was repaired, they'd left.

Jacob was astonished. It was a great mystery. How could there be a mechanical noise of any kind in an area in which humans had never trod?

A green note in the margin made Jacob's heart leap: *It all started here.*

Daniel listened as Thackett described the email he'd received from the late Horace.

"The email wasn't programmed to send on a specific date," Thackett explained. "Rather, it was set to send five days after his email account received an email from the attorney responsible for his will. She was to send it within twenty-four hours of handing the keys to 17 Swann to his nephew. That must have happened last Sunday, since I got Horace's delayed email last night."

That was Friday night, Daniel realized, which meant that today was Saturday. He hardly noticed that it was the weekend.

"According to Horace, it was likely that, by that time, his nephew would have already retrieved a monograph from Swann 4," Thackett explained. "It was in the safe box."

"Which monograph?" Daniel asked. The most sensitive information was contained in the monographs that Horace, and those working under him, had authored for their elite CIA organization. The highest level of clearance was required for handling such information, and he was sure Horace's nephew didn't have it.

"I'm not sure," Thackett answered, "but it has already led him to Red Falcon."

"Horace trusts this guy," Daniel said. "You said there was more to it than being family, or that his nephew had saved his life."

Thackett nodded. "Jacob is extremely talented – he has degrees in mechanical, electrical, and computer engineering."

"Having degrees is not convincing," Daniel said, still skeptical. "There's a lot of vetting to find people suitable to handle this kind of information. Mistakes could be devastating."

"He said his nephew is more than just talented – he's a genius, a puzzle solver."

Daniel agreed that puzzle-solving was a required skill for his own work, but it wasn't only about solving tricky math problems or physical puzzles. It involved following threads of clues through history and connecting them to others, both in the past and the present.

"What, precisely, is Hale's expertise?" Daniel asked.

"He worked at a place called Interstellar Dynamics," Thackett replied. "He did classified work, reverse engineering foreign technologies – from weapons systems to industrial devices."

It made Daniel feel a little better that Hale at least had some level of clearance. "What do you mean 'worked,' past tense?"

"He was terminated this past Tuesday," Thackett said.

Daniel didn't like the sound of that. "Why?"

"Unknown – but not for leaking information. We would've heard about it already."

"What's his technical specialty?"

"His Ph.D. research was on some special kind of advanced signal processing, including encryption."

Daniel's mind whirred. "And his work at Interstellar Dynamics?"

"Reverse engineering encrypted control programs and communications codes used in military devices," Thackett said, "including satellite communications."

Daniel started to see the relevance of Jacob Hale. "Are you going to approve his document request?"

"I was leaning that way," Thackett replied. "But I wanted to run it by you first."

Daniel didn't think giving Hale the Red Falcon documents would be a risk to their current work. Besides, there was time pressure, and the more brains working on it, the better. Daniel took a sip of tea and looked to Thackett. "Send it to him."

JACOB MULLED over the implications of the noise in the Southern Seas. Cook was supposedly the first human to have crossed the Antarctic Circle. Therefore, the mechanical disturbance they'd heard must have come from somewhere on the ship – despite the measures taken to ensure that this wasn't the case. It was either that, or the noise had been from a natural phenomenon – perhaps a geological disturbance of some kind. He had no idea of the likelihood of the latter, but the prospect that it was of human making, and not originating from the ship, seemed improbable.

The noise being a natural phenomenon would be interesting to scientists – probably geologists – but it didn't seem to fit with the attention it had been given.

Assuming it was human-made raised other questions. What would be the purpose of such a thing, and how did it get there? How could it operate in cold saltwater? In the early 1700s, there were no power sources that could operate in that environment, unless it was a spring-loaded device, like a clock. But again, why?

He finished reading the Cook monograph just after 2:00 p.m. Realizing he'd skipped lunch, he climbed down from the dome loft to the kitchen and made a sandwich. His attention turned to the TV mounted near the entrance.

He found the remote on the coffee table in the lounge area. He sat on a stool at the counter, swiveled to face the screen, and pressed the power button on the remote.

BBC News came on, and the volume was up too high. It reminded him that Uncle Theo had been hard of hearing. He reduced the volume and changed the station. CNN News came up first, then Fox News, Al Jazeera, and a half-dozen others from foreign countries. It finally cycled back to BBC. He hadn't known Theo to be a news junkie, but now it seemed to fit.

BBC gave updates on two stories that piqued his attention. The first regarded the AM interference from the Russian spacecraft. The offending radio waves were in the middle of the AM Band – between 1140 and 1150 on the dial – and were causing problems around the world. It was more of a nuisance than a threat, but the Russians still denied it came from their disabled craft.

The second was about the skirmish between the US and China in the Southern Sea near Antarctica. It seemed that the United Kingdom and Russia had also been involved at some lower level, and there were new rumors that two Chinese subs had been sunk.

He wondered if it was just a coincidence that, in one day, he'd been exposed to both the earliest and latest events to occur in the Antarctic Circle.

BBC then segued into a science segment about the gravitational-wave detection facilities in the US, and interviewed one of the project's lead scientists. The conversation rehashed the debate he'd heard on BBC Radio a few days ago in his car regarding upgrades and repairs to the facilities that carried a price tag of over 200 million dollars. The scientist from LIGO – the Laser Interferometer Gravitational-Wave Observatory – explained that problems had cropped up weeks ago when they'd started detecting anomalous gravitational wave signals and could not identify the source of the problem. The detectors were hypersensitive to mechanical vibrations, temperature variations, and sound, but they suspected that it was an electronics malfunction.

Just as they were about to go into the details of the glitches, Jacob's phone rang.

He'd been getting calls from unknown numbers all day, but this time it was Paulina. He didn't want to answer. It wasn't because he was angry with her – that had waned – but because he didn't want to get distracted. He'd ignored an earlier call from her, so decided to answer. Otherwise, he'd be preoccupied, anticipating yet another call, or wondering what she wanted.

He stood, turned down the TV volume with the remote, and answered.

"Jake?" she asked.

Her voice sounded strange to him, stressed.

"Jake?" she asked again, her voice crackling as if she had been crying.

"Hi Pauli, something wrong?"

"We need to talk."

The last thing Jacob wanted to do was discuss the breakup – or reconciliation. It wasn't that he didn't want to work things out, but there were more pressing things on his mind. It then occurred to him that it was two o'clock in the afternoon. He needed to get back to work.

"Can we talk later, after I get – "

"I know something about your uncle," she said.

Jacob flinched. After a few seconds of awkward silence, he spoke. "What do you mean?"

"Jake, please, you might be in danger."

Her words resonated in his skull. If she knew he was in danger, *she* could be in danger. His mind whirred and, before he made the conscious decision to speak, he said, "You remember where we went for lunch on your birthday last year?"

After a few seconds of silence, Pauli responded, "Yes."

She seemed to catch on immediately that he didn't want to reveal the location over the phone.

"Let's meet there in an hour."

Jacob hung up, turned back to the counter, and stared out at the stacks. Sunlight from the domes barely hit the lower shelves, creating a warm wood-leather hue that calmed his mind for just an instant. He didn't want to go outside – not in the dark, and certainly not in the daylight.

What he needed was a gun. He figured his uncle had to have one around. He'd start the search in the bedroom.

IT WAS BECOMING INCREASINGLY difficult for Daniel to think. He was constantly getting emails from the others in the group, and his job was to provide guidance. He had his own project within the larger one on which they all focused, and it was going slowly.

He shook his head and sighed as Thackett came through the

main entrance. The distractions were endless, and he wondered if Sylvia had also been agitated by the activity. He had to find a way to accommodate the new conditions and responsibilities, and become productive again.

Thackett walked at a fast clip and waved to Daniel to join him as he approached the cluster of furniture at the center of the room.

"Something wrong?" Daniel asked as he came out of his office.

"We've intercepted a phone call between Jacob Hale and his girlfriend, Paulina Erikkson," Thackett explained. "He's leaving 17 Swann to meet with her right now."

"Is that a problem?"

"Could be," Thackett replied. "We've been doing some investigating and discovered that, just yesterday, Hale was chased out of his apartment in Alexandria by a man wielding a gun. His cousin – Horace's son – was murdered early last week, as was the lawyer responsible for Horace's estate."

"My God," Daniel gasped. "So now they're after Hale?"

"Maybe him, or something he has."

Daniel clenched his fists and released them. That "something" could be anything – possibly information that exposed the Space Systems building and its personnel. "What are you going to do?"

"We have operatives following Hale: four men, two cars," Thackett explained. "Hale is on his way to Alexandria right now. A third team is currently staking out his apartment."

Motion in his peripheral vision made Daniel flinch and look to his right. It was Sylvia. She was cleaning her glasses with her shirt as she approached. Her red-streaked dark hair was a mess, and her eyes were puffy as if she'd just awakened from a long nap. But Daniel knew better. She'd been absorbed in her work.

"What's going on?" she asked.

It was unclear to Daniel how much he could share with his younger officemate, so he looked to Thackett who gave her the rundown.

"Are you going to take him in?" she asked.

"We were thinking about it," Thackett said. "First, we want to see if he draws any other attention."

"What do you mean?" Daniel asked.

"The people pursuing Hale are professionals," Thackett explained, "and might still be on his track. Maybe we can nab one of them."

"Sounds risky," Daniel said. "What if they get sensitive information and get away?"

"What information?" Sylvia asked.

"A monograph from Horace," Daniel replied.

"Is there anything in any of the monographs that even matters anymore?" Sylvia argued. "The most important things are already known to everyone."

Daniel considered it for a moment and shrugged. Maybe she was right. What could anyone do with the information? "But what if he got into 17 Swann?"

Thackett shrugged. "We're watching the place now. Anyone but Hale will be intercepted before they get inside."

"What's in that place that's so important?" Sylvia asked.

"We don't know," Thackett answered.

"Shouldn't we by now?" Daniel asked. "Why haven't we broken into the place and, if not taken everything away and shut it down, at least evaluated the risk?"

Thackett rubbed his hands together and sighed. "As I explained before, we can't," he said. "The security is more sophisticated than you'd expect by the appearance of the building from the outside. If the security system detects a successful break-in, it may self-destruct."

"How was this allowed to happen?" Sylvia asked. "Security was supposed to be the highest priority for our group."

"Horace was the first of your kind," Thackett replied. "He was given a lot of freedom and resources."

"Keys are required for access," Daniel said. "Mechanical locks can't be impossible to defeat."

"They're special locks – not simply mechanical," Thackett said. "The keys are nearly impossible to duplicate, and the doors are like those to a vault. I'm not sure about the other security features but, knowing Horace, they're formidable."

"What could be the most damaging thing found there?" Sylvia asked.

"To start, something that reveals Space Systems," Thackett replied.

Daniel shuddered. The Space Systems building was home to the most important human intelligence resources of the United States. Most people thought that the Langley CIA Headquarters was the hub of the American espionage community. It was its business and political center, but any covert operative would not be seen anywhere near the place. It was well known that foreign intelligence services photographed everyone coming and going from Langley. With advances in facial recognition software, countries have constructed databases of people who have accessed foreign intelligence hubs all over the world. Whenever they are suspicious of someone, they run their photos through facial recognition software. How could someone claiming to have no affiliation with the American government explain a visit to CIA headquarters?

"It would be a disaster," Sylvia said. "How many people work at this place, a thousand? They'd all be compromised, and those that operate overseas would be in grave danger. It would set our human intelligence capabilities back thirty years."

Daniel nodded. He couldn't add anything to strengthen her argument. He looked to Thackett. "Is there a chance that information about Red Wraith is in there?" If details of the American Red Wraith project went public it would be a political disaster.

Thackett shrugged. "It's likely," he said. "But the most recent information is not – I don't know how Horace could have collected anything after we got back from Antarctica. He was in the hospital for most of the time from then until he passed."

"Horace had been keeping notes in a book during that entire operation," Sylvia said. "It was a monograph that he authored. I bet that's the book he's given his nephew. Anything could be in that book – including names."

Thackett's face turned pale. "The most sensitive identity has already been compromised."

Daniel twitched. In his mind, that identity – that person – was the most important of them all. He wasn't a member of their group. He wasn't even in the intelligence community – not officially anyway. But he was living in the Space Systems building.

"Do we intercept Hale before he gets to his destination?" Sylvia asked. "Or do we collect him and his pursuers all in one place?"

"We don't know where he's going," Daniel said. "But it seems the plan is to let him get there."

Thackett nodded. "That's right."

"How long before it goes down?" Sylvia asked.

"If anything happens at all," Thackett replied, "it will happen within the hour."

Daniel shook his head. There was no way he was going to concentrate on anything useful for the rest of the afternoon.

Jacob exited the highway and navigated surface streets past his apartment toward Paglio's Bistro, two blocks behind Pine Perk. They'd gone there the night he'd returned from Boston, after the reading of the will. It was Pauli's favorite place in Alexandria.

It was just past 6:00 p.m. and the lot was starting to fill up. He spotted Pauli's car in the front, near the entrance. He parked in the rear lot with his car facing toward the exit.

He turned off the car and put the keys in the front pocket of his shorts. He patted his hand on his chest and felt the lump beneath his half-zipped fleece jacket. He'd found the gun in a small compartment inset into the wall at the head of the lower bunk. It was a Glock 40, the same model his uncle had taught him to shoot when he was a kid. The magazine was full of hollow points. A round was in the chamber. Uncle Theo had been ready to defend himself.

He'd found a light Velcro holster in the chest of drawers. The Glock was now packed tightly under his left armpit. He'd found his zip-down fleece in the car, and wore a pair of loose khaki shorts with short socks and tennis shoes. The clothes allowed him to move easily.

He took a deep breath and calmed himself. Even though it made him nervous, he had no choice but to bring the keys to 17 Swann along with him. He didn't trust them in his car, or anywhere else but on his person. He'd guard them with his life.

He got out of the car, locked it with the remote, and headed for the entrance.

He entered the restaurant and went into a bar that separated two large dining rooms. He spotted Pauli in a high-backed booth on the far side of the room to the left of the bar. She stood as he approached.

Her hair was a mess and her clothes were wrinkled. Her skin seemed pale and her face was shiny, as if she'd been sweating. He thought maybe she was ill.

"You okay?" he asked.

She nodded toward the booth. They sat across from each other.

She grabbed his right hand across the table and examined the Band-Aids on his forearm. There were two on his right and three on his left. "What happened?"

"Got chased by a dog and ran through a rosebush," he said, sticking with the same story he'd told the barista at Pine Perk. "There are more on my legs. What's going on?"

She let go of his hand and started to speak, but stopped and reached her trembling hand for a glass of water.

Jacob's nerves seemed to channel electric current through his body. His stomach churned in response. He sat still and silent, and waited a full minute before Pauli spoke.

"The day after you came back from Boston, a man visited me at my office and invited me to lunch."

"A headhunter?" Jacob asked, referring to the act of professional poaching that often occurred between competing firms.

She shook her head. "Sort of, but not quite. He was a client who needed someone at the London office, and was wondering if I'd consider it."

Jacob nodded. It seemed consistent with the end result – her going to London.

She continued, "That afternoon is when my boss approached me with the offer – the one I couldn't refuse."

Jacob could tell something was deeply bothering her, but his patience and attention were waning. "You said you knew something about my uncle."

"I'm getting to that," she said. "My boss brought me into his office last night. He said he was offered one million dollars to transfer me to London."

"They must've really wanted you," he said. "That's like what – four years of your salary?"

She grabbed his hand and squeezed. "Jake, the money was offered to my boss personally – not to the firm."

That was strange, Jacob thought. "The client must have really liked your work."

She shook her head. "I'm not even the best trademark lawyer in the DC office, much less in the entire firm," she explained. "It's inexplicable unless, rather than wanting me in London, someone wanted me out of DC."

"And you think my uncle was involved?" he said.

"The client gave me his card," she continued. "I was up all night researching him, and his company. I got help from some of my friends."

Jacob knew the friends to whom she referred. One was in the bank fraud office of the FBI, and the other an upper-level investigator in the Internal Revenue Service. "And?"

"We traced him back to the law firm of Watts, Turk, and Genobli, in Boston," she explained.

Jacob twitched. He remembered that name for good reason: they'd handled his uncle's estate. He even had a copy of a signed form printed on their letterhead.

"I tried to contact the attorney that handled the account of the client – the one that wanted to use our trademark services," she said as her voice quivered. She tried to speak but stopped and took a sip of water.

He knew what she was going to say.

"That attorney is dead, Jake," she said. "She was murdered in her office."

Jake stared at her. He wanted to tell her about his late cousin, but held back.

"That same attorney handled your uncle's estate," she added. "That same firm handles the company that employs the London client – the one that gave me the offer. It's called Green Iris Industries. It's a shell company – it has no physical assets, and does no particular business."

At that moment, something in Jacob's peripheral vision caught his attention. He looked over his left shoulder and caught a glimpse of a man the size of a Volkswagen Bug near the entrance. The restaurant had gotten busier since he'd arrived, and the high back of the booth concealed him entirely. It seemed the man hadn't spotted him. Pauli, however, was visible from the bar, and he was sure the man would make his way over to see who was sitting across from her.

Jacob monitored the man's movements via his reflection in the glass doors of a fireplace at the far end of the room, opposite the bar. The man disappeared into the other dining room.

"We have to go," he said as he grabbed Pauli's wrist.

She froze, and stared at him with wide eyes.

"Now, Pauli!" he whispered with a coarse voice. The urgency in his own voice frightened him.

She seemed to detect his desperation and cooperated.

He released his grasp on her arm and grabbed her hand, and led the way into the bar. He located an emergency exit in an open area behind the bar where the restrooms were located, and headed in that direction.

"Where are we going?" she asked.

"Out the back door."

Just as they passed the back of the bar, the man reappeared at the front and looked in their direction. Jacob made eye contact with the monster for a split second and his legs responded before his brain made the order to move. He jerked Pauli's arm violently, causing her to stumble as he dragged her toward the exit.

Jacob simultaneously hit the release bar with his hip and the door with his shoulder. An instant later they leapt from a cement stoop and were in the rear parking lot. The emergency alarm sounded inside the restaurant, adding to the panic that was already surging through his brain. He weaved through parked cars toward his Corolla.

As he fumbled for his keys, the sound of the emergency alarm increased and then decreased, indicating that the door had opened and closed. Jacob turned as the man jumped off the stoop and lumbered into the lot. He had a gun, silencer attached.

"Jacob," the man yelled as he slowed to a walk. "Just give me the book and keys, and I'll be on my way. No one needs to get hurt."

"Bullshit," Jacob yelled back, still moving with Pauli in tow. He tried to keep two cars between them. "Did you say the same thing to my cousin?"

The large man turned suddenly to his right and fired a shot in that direction, and then ducked as two shots came from somewhere Jacob couldn't locate. The man ran to his left, past an overflowing dumpster, and disappeared through a gate into a residential neighborhood. Two men sprinted into view, guns in hand, and then followed the same path.

"Let's go," Jacob said as he squeezed Pauli's hand and started for his car.

They were almost to the Corolla when a tall man emerged from behind a van and walked toward them. He was clean-cut, with brown hair, khaki pants, and a blue, short-sleeved polo shirt.

Jacob froze.

"Mr. Hale?" the man said, now less than 20 feet away.

Jacob let go of Pauli's hand and pulled the gun from its holster under his arm. He pointed it at the man's face.

"Stop, and put your hands where I can see them!" Jacob yelled. He turned to Paulina. She was frozen. "Pauli, get in your car," he said, keeping the gun trained on the man who stood as still as the large oak tree behind him. Jacob was set to pull the trigger; there would be no hesitation if the man made a move.

Jacob walked closer to the man and, as he did, realized that he was large – well over six feet tall and at least 220 pounds. The man remained as still as stone, and his blue eyes were as calm as the water at the bottom of a well. His composure had the opposite effect on Jacob.

Paulina backed her car out of the parking spot. Jacob walked backward with the gun still aimed to kill. A few seconds later, he got to the car and climbed inside. It was moving before he closed the door.

Next thing he knew, they were driving east on Pine Street, heading for the highway.

Daniel put his cup of lukewarm tea on the table and met Director Thackett and Sylvia in the common area. He wasn't expecting Thackett so soon – they'd spoken just 40 minutes earlier.

"Our people got there in time," Thackett started.

"What happened?" Sylvia asked. She sat on the edge of the leather couch.

Thackett sat beside her and nodded to Daniel to take the chair across from him. "The man after Hale was most likely responsible for the two murders in Boston. He escaped."

"And Hale?" Daniel blurted.

Thackett smiled and shook his head. "He's a wily guy. He had a gun. He and his girlfriend got away. One of our operatives had a chance to talk him down, but Hale was having no part of it."

"Won't the man make another attempt to get to him? Does he know about Swann Street?" Daniel asked.

Thackett shrugged. "It's doubtful that he knows about Swann Street. If he knew, he would've hung around there for a while and waited for Hale to come back, and then forced his way in with a gun.

Our guess is that he found Hale's car and put a tracker on it, and that's how he found them at the restaurant. Swann Street is secure for now."

"You think Hale will go back to Swann after this scare?" Sylvia asked.

Thackett nodded. "Yes."

"I still don't understand why you don't just bring him in," Daniel said.

Thackett leaned forward, wringing his hands. "For what, exactly?"

"I'm not suggesting he's a criminal," Daniel said, "but isn't 17 Swann government property?"

Thackett shrugged. "Yes and no," he said. "But I think we should trust Horace's judgment on this and let his nephew continue. He seems quite resourceful, and has already gone to great lengths to preserve the information."

"Especially considering that he's had no training," Sylvia added.

"What are you expecting from this?" Daniel asked.

"From the looks of his document requests," Thackett explained, "Hale is quickly following up on our work, and will soon be up to speed. Either he will discover something we haven't, or he will be another brain with the proper background to help us move forward."

Daniel nodded. They could use all the help they could get. Time was running out. Time was running out for everyone.

JACOB HUNG UP THE PHONE. "Go left here," he said to Pauli and pointed to an intersection a block ahead of them.

"Where are we going?" she asked.

"The police station on Coriander Street."

She kept her eyes ahead, both hands gripping the wheel so tightly that the tendons in her wrists trembled. Her face was pale except for dark streaks where tears carried mascara down her cheeks. He knew she was horrified by what had just happened. So was he.

"What the hell did that man want from you?" she finally blurted. "What book was he asking you for?"

"The book my uncle gave me."

She was quiet for a few seconds, seemingly processing his words. "He was willing to kill for it?"

"He was going to kill us both," Jacob said.

She turned her head and looked at him. More tears welled in her eyes and she just stared.

"The road," he said and grabbed the wheel with his left hand until she turned her head forward.

"Kill us?"

"He murdered my cousin and the attorney who managed my uncle's will."

"What?" she asked, eyes bulging. "Your cousin is dead? Which one?"

"Kenneth," he replied.

"For the book? But you said it wasn't worth anything."

"The book itself doesn't have real monetary value, but the information it contains is important," Jacob said. "I had no idea."

"He said something about keys, too," she said.

"Keys to a safe deposit box that contained the book and some other information," he said, omitting the sensitive details that would only lead to more questions he didn't want to answer.

She pulled into the Alexandria police department parking lot and turned off the engine. She looked over to Jacob and touched his hand. Her face was still moist with tears. "I love you."

He wasn't prepared for her words, but it didn't matter. His feelings for her were perfectly clear to him. "I love you, too."

They went into the building and found Detective Kranz in a small office on the second floor. The odors of burnt coffee and stale potato chips filled the air, and Jacob realized he was parched.

For the next hour, Kranz took their statements and asked questions. The detective still had no idea who Jacob's pursuer was – or who had chased him away. When asked what the man wanted, Jacob replied that it was a rare book willed to him by his uncle. He overplayed its value, and it seemed that Paulina caught on that he wanted to keep the details of the book secret.

"Where is it now?" Kranz asked.

"In a safe deposit box," Jacob replied.

After a few more general questions, Kranz said, "I think that's it. If you think of anything important, call me." He handed Paulina a business card. "Meanwhile, you should both find somewhere else to stay."

They left the station, got into the car, and headed back toward Alexandria.

"Why are we going back?" Paulina asked.

"To get my car," he replied. "There must be a GPS tracker on it. Otherwise, I don't know how those guys would have found us. I just want to move it to my apartment."

"Where will you stay?" she asked.

"With a friend from work for a few days," he lied. "After that, we'll see. Maybe they'll arrest the guy by then. Where are you going?"

"My sister's place."

Jacob cringed. Her older sister had three kids between the ages of six months and four years, and lived in a townhouse in DC. "Sleeping might be a problem."

"I don't mind," she said. "She's going to freak out when she finds out what happened."

They picked up Jacob's car at Paglio's Bistro and Pauli followed him to his apartment. He parked the car and got back into her Beamer.

It was after 8:00 p.m. and the sun was setting deep into the trees. The cool evening air carried the scents of flowers and grilled food from restaurants as they passed them.

"All of this has been about a book? – the murders, my job offer, the man chasing you?" she asked.

"Not sure about the purpose of the job offer," he said.

"Can you tell me what's in it?"

"The book? Afraid not," he replied. "Uncle Theo's wishes were that no one would ever see it. Some personal things in there."

"Like a diary?"

Jacob nodded. "Maybe it contains some dirt on Theo's family."

This seemed to satisfy her curiosity without offending her.

After 30 minutes in dense highway traffic, and another ten on surface streets, he directed her to stop in front of a large apartment building two streets east and about a quarter mile north of 17 Swann.

Jacob watched from the lobby of the building as she drove away. He pretended to talk on the phone for a few minutes under the eyes of a security guard, and then walked out into the dusk. Fifteen minutes later, he was on the stoop of 17 Swann. He inserted the key, entered the foyer, and then opened box number four. There was something inside.

He pulled out a black mobile phone and a handwritten note. It read, "Use this from now on. Destroy your other phone, and abandon your car."

He took out his burner phone, powered it down, and pulled out the battery and sim card. He powered up the new phone.

A message was waiting.

CHAPTER 5

Back inside the protective confines of 17 Swann, Jacob preheated the oven to make a frozen pizza. It was 9:17 p.m. and he was starving. He turned on the television, more to calm his nerves than to watch the news.

He browsed the contents of his new phone, and jotted down the phone number. It had no applications or high-tech features other than a good camera. The writing on the case said it was waterproof and shock-resistant. It was a satellite phone.

An icon indicated that he had voicemail. He pressed a button on the touchscreen to access it, and a mechanical voice instructed him to say his mother's maiden surname. It was odd. Her name was Leatherby, like his uncle's. It worked. *Whoever was operating behind the curtain knew who he was.*

He was then taken through a procedure to change the password, after which the message played. An electronically modified voice said, "Greetings, Mr. Hale. Discard your current phone if you haven't already, and do not let this device get into anyone else's hands. The tracking option is active. This is for your safety, not surveillance. We are aware of your presence in 17 Swann number 4. We do not intend to disturb you. However, if you discover anything of significance –

meaning something related to current events – we request that you report it to us immediately. You can do this using the same email you have been using to order supplies and documents. We wish you the best of luck." The message ended and Jacob hung up.

It was the strangest voicemail he'd ever received. They'd used his name – they *did* know his identity. Who were they? And what were they expecting him to do?

The TV volume was too low so he turned it up. He flipped to an Israeli newscast in English about the possibility of war with Iran over uranium enrichment. He then turned to CNN News where a Swedish scientist was accusing the Russians of intentionally causing the AM interference. A Russian official argued that they had no motive for such a thing. He then flipped to BBC News where they played footage of a US aircraft carrier off the coast of Argentina, and rehashed the recent scuffle with the Russian and Chinese navies in the waters near Antarctica.

BBC followed with a replay of an interview with a gravitational-wave scientist who tried to justify new costs for repairs and upgrades. The man was reluctant to answer specific questions about the malfunction, and wouldn't give details regarding the types of glitches they were observing. He did divulge, however, that they'd been having identical problems at both facilities. Jacob found it odd since the two mammoth detectors, one in Livingston, Louisiana and the other in Hanford, Washington, were separated by over two thousand miles.

He put the pizza in the oven and set the timer for 18 minutes. He grabbed a can of Pepsi from the refrigerator, popped it open, and took a long swig. The ice-cold soda burned his throat, a sensation that was both painful and comforting.

As the pizza baked, he changed the bandage on the graze wound on his leg, and put an antibiotic gel on the thorn injuries. He still found it hard to believe a bullet had nicked him. It reminded him of how the man who had pursued him did so with a frightening relentlessness. And the man was still out there, searching for him like a starving polar bear stalking a seal.

Who was that man, and what did he want with the book and keys? And who had chased the thug away during the scene at the restaurant? He realized now that he'd probably pointed his gun at a man who had been there to help him.

The oven timer beeped, and he extracted the pizza and set the pan on the stovetop. As it cooled, he ran down to the desk and returned with a notebook and a pen. He cut the pizza, put two slices on a plate, and sat at the counter in direct view of the television. He flipped through the channels, but settled again on BBC News – they covered world news better than any other network.

The instant he took the first bite of pizza he realized he was famished. It was thin-crust style with all of the toppings, and the sauce was sweet and perfectly seasoned. The two slices were gone in just a couple of minutes, and he went to the stove and slapped two more on his plate.

As he ate, he wrote down the topics of the most highly covered stories. Almost everything was related to the three he'd seen at the beginning: the Iranians, the AM interference, and the Antarctic conflict. The science segments focused mainly on medical advances, various space program topics, and the gravitational-wave research funding controversy. For the next half hour, he wrote down details of the main three geopolitical stories, and also those of a few other minor events.

He was stuffed after eating half of the pizza, and his eyelids felt like sandbags. He considered taking a nap but decided against it. He cleaned up the kitchen, grabbed *The Israel Thread* and another Pepsi, and went up to the dome.

He picked up where he'd left off that afternoon, when his reading session had been interrupted by the strange phone call from Pauli. It was surreal for him to be continuing his studies just a few hours later. Both he and Pauli were lucky the way things had turned out. He was safe, and he was confident that she was as well.

His previous reading session had ended with the cryptic words of his uncle, implying that the discovery by the storied Captain –

Commander – Cook of a noise in the waters in the Antarctic Circle was the beginning of something significant.

He opened *The Israel Thread*, the title of which had so far seemed irrelevant. Since the initial summary of Mossad interrogations of Nazis, he'd encountered few references to Israel. Most of what he'd read so far had occurred before 1948, before Israel had even been born. Nonetheless, the skeleton of a story was forming. He looked over his notes to reestablish context.

The first point on the timeline was Commander Cook discovering the repetitive noise in the seas around Antarctica. Two centuries later, just before the Second World War, the Germans sent out the *Schwabenland* to explore Antarctica and the surrounding waters. A British recon vessel witnessed the *Schwabenland* making a rendezvous with a German U-Boat off the west coast of Antarctica. The Brits then countered with Operation Tabarin, setting up bases and outposts on and near Antarctica. The odd thing about that, as noted by his uncle, was that it had occurred during wartime, when the Allies could ill-afford such an effort unless it had some deeper significance. After the war, the Americans carried out a full-scale invasion of the Antarctic continent, called Operation Highjump. The official explanation was that Highjump was just a training exercise.

Jacob now speculated, as his uncle had, that the reasons for the recent events in the Southern Seas were the same as those of the past: the noise in the deep – the very same disturbance discovered by Commander Cook over two centuries ago.

Jacob shuddered. It was fascinating. He put the book on the table in front of him and picked up the soda can and took a gulp. He leaned back and looked at the stars through the dome. What sort of thing could make a noise for that length of time? If it were human-made, rather than a natural phenomenon, how could it have been accomplished in the 1700s?

He drew two conclusions. First, with modern technology, they would have already determined whether or not it was natural. Therefore, it was *not* natural. It would make no sense to have a military conflict over a scientific curiosity. Second, assuming that James Cook was the first human to venture into the Antarctic Circle, whatever had made the sounds *was not put there by humans.*

DANIEL WAS STARTING to admire Jacob Hale.

He leaned back next to Sylvia on the leather couch and took a bite of one of the glazed donuts Thackett brought as a consolation for keeping them late. It was only 11:30 p.m. – which might have been late for Thackett, but not for him. He and Sylvia were just getting their second winds, and would work well into the morning hours. He took a deep breath and exhaled; it wasn't as if someone were waiting for him at home.

"Any more leads on the suspect?" Daniel asked.

Thackett shook his head. "Persistent son of a bitch," he said from the chair across the coffee table. "A professional."

Daniel had researched hundreds of missions that dated back more than five decades, and found it was rare for anyone to escape a trap of the sort set by the CIA team. The CIA wasn't supposed to operate inside US borders but, then again, politicians weren't supposed to cheat on their tax returns. The rules were bent until someone was caught breaking them. Even then, such transgressions were usually swept under the rug. Besides, a failed mission of this sort would not be a political disaster since no one was killed. That the six-man team had failed to bring in either of the individuals – Hale, or the thug operative – was disappointing.

"Hale is already back at 17 Swann," Thackett said.

Daniel didn't know whether Hale's move was brilliant or foolish. He knew Hale would be perfectly safe there, but there was no way for Hale to know that for certain. Perhaps he trusted his uncle, and Daniel supposed that was justified. "So we'll just let him operate as he has been, with access to classified documents?" Daniel asked.

Thackett shrugged and nodded. "I've learned a bit more about him in the past few hours."

"Yes, he carries a gun and can outsmart CIA operatives," Sylvia said.

"There wasn't much outsmarting going on there," Thackett rebutted. "What I meant was that we've done some deeper background work on him."

They already knew that Hale was an engineer with expertise in signal analysis and encryption. He might be useful for their current project, but the CIA already had some of the best people in the world working on that part of the task – engineers, physicists, and mathematicians.

"As we know, he worked at Interstellar Dynamics," Thackett explained, "a defense contractor that specializes in reverse engineering highly technical devices acquired by us – the CIA – and by defense intelligence."

It was a unique skill, Daniel thought. It took rare talent to deconstruct a complex device and understand it well enough to clone it. The Chinese did it all the time – they had no choice but to steal technologies that were otherwise beyond their developmental capabilities.

"But there was one project that he completed that was of particular interest," Thackett continued. "It was a signal encryption mechanism on a Chinese spy satellite that went down in the South China Sea. A Navy SEAL team recovered it before the Chinese could get to it. They were suspicious, but couldn't prove we'd recovered it. Hale didn't even know what he was working on but, in the end, put Chinese military communications in great jeopardy. It will take them years to recover – that is, if they've even discovered the problem. Hale is a hero of sorts – to CIA and defense intelligence – but doesn't know it."

"How did we not know it?" Sylvia asked.

"Hale's name isn't listed in the final report on that project," Thackett explained. "That's for his own protection."

"So why on earth would his company fire him?" Daniel asked.

"They fired him?" Sylvia asked with wide eyes, and looking to

Thackett for an explanation. Daniel had already known, but Sylvia hadn't been in on all of their previous conversations.

Thackett nodded. "Initially, it was a red flag," he admitted. "But I've read his confidential employee evaluations, and he was considered the best engineer in the entire company – and they'd actually just done a ranking because of impending layoffs."

"What did he do wrong?" Sylvia asked.

"That's what I wondered," Thackett answered. "I was concerned they'd deemed him a security risk for some reason. But that wasn't the case."

"So, why then?" Daniel asked as he sat forward and slid to the edge of the couch.

"Horace had him fired," Thackett said.

"What?" Daniel gasped. "How?"

Thackett smiled. "Horace had it arranged so that, after the reading of his will, someone would bribe Jacob's supervisor – and those above him – with large sums of money to carry out his termination."

"But why?" Sylvia asked.

"It's my theory that Horace wanted to make sure that his nephew had no choice but to join our efforts. I think he had great faith in him," Thackett said. "And now I'm convinced that we're doing the right thing by letting him continue."

Daniel was still wary, even though Hale's past success with the Chinese communications device seemed to prove him a perfect fit. "But we should keep a close eye on him – for our sake, and his."

Thackett nodded. "He's already ditched his car, and we've swapped his phone with one of ours."

"And he took it? He complied?" Sylvia asked.

Thackett nodded. "Like I said, it seems Jacob trusted his uncle."

And hopefully he trusts us, as well, Daniel thought.

JACOB READ past midnight in the dome with the help of three cans of Pepsi. He'd soon be out of the caffeine-laced elixir that was once his trusted study companion. His usual prescription of stimulants had been a continuous stream of coffee in the mornings, tea in the afternoons, and a heavy dose of Pepsi in the evenings. An energy drink of some sort could sometimes substitute for the latter. He'd known it wasn't sustainable behavior, but it had been a routine that produced results, from the beginning of college through the end of grad school. He could now see himself reverting back to his old habits.

He'd completed the first section of *The Israel Thread* monograph, which amounted to historical introductions to three time periods. The first two were Commander Cook's era and the World War II era. He was now in the third period, the modern era, and new conflicts in Antarctica.

What he had from *The Israel Thread* were the bare facts – what happened and when, and some speculative comments from Theo written in the margins. What he didn't have were the answers to his most pressing questions. First, what was making the noise in the Southern Seas? Second, what were the Germans doing there? And third, how was it all connected to the recent conflict in the Antarctic Circle?

The next section went into more detail on the invasion of Antarctica in the southern summer of 1946. Uncle Theo had scribbled "BS" next to the line that said it was a training exercise. Jacob assumed the annotation was shorthand for "bullshit." He smiled. He'd heard his uncle use the term many times, and could almost hear him saying it now.

As he read on, it seemed that the monograph was finally going to go in the direction indicated by its title. The state of Israel was born in 1948. Starting even before the formal creation of their country, the Israelis had captured, interrogated, tried, and punished Nazi war criminals. The *thread* to which the title referred was woven through time, starting with these interrogations. The monograph began with a synopsis of one of the first important interrogations, but there had been many others. Unfortunately, the corresponding transcripts were heavily redacted at the time *The Israel Thread* monograph was completed. However, green-ink annotations dated just a month ago indicated that Theo had recovered the unredacted transcripts – and that they "were of utmost importance." In parentheses was written *Red Falcon*.

Jacob had already requested info on Red Falcon and hoped it would be in the safe box in the morning. Now he'd also request the unredacted Israeli interrogations.

He read on. The Israelis had interrogated hundreds of Nazis, from prison camp guards to officers at the highest levels within the Nazi regime. The most notable was Adolf Eichmann, the man responsible for the murder of millions of Jews. After the war, Eichmann had assumed a false identity as an SS officer and spent time in a prisoner-of-war camp before escaping during a work detail. He'd escaped Germany, but had been captured in Argentina in 1960 by the Israeli Mossad, interrogated, tried, and hanged in 1962. From the transcripts, it was clear that the Israelis wanted information about other war criminals, and most of the conversations had to do with the Nazi escape plan, ODESSA.

In most cases, the interrogations of high-level officers had large fractions of information redacted in the transcripts. This seemed logical since they would have been privy to more sensitive information. But his uncle had noted something peculiar. There were a few low-level personnel whose interrogation transcripts were more than eighty percent blacked out.

At 2:00 a.m. Jacob closed the book for the night. His mind still hummed with the new information, and the events of the day, and he'd have to find a way to wind down. He thought about giving Paulina a call but figured she'd be asleep. Instead, he'd eat a slice of cold pizza and watch the news for a few minutes. But first, he'd go to the computer and request the interrogation transcripts.

Jacob stared at the green numbers on the clock on the inset shelf at the head of the bed. After a few seconds he realized where he was. The Swann Street facility was already feeling like home.

It was 6:42 a.m. He usually needed more than five hours of sleep, but he was anxious to get the information he'd requested.

He took a shower, got dressed, and was in the kitchen eating oatmeal within 15 minutes. He turned on BBC News, which only recapped old stories.

He finished breakfast, stepped onto the outer walkway just outside the kitchen, and looked down upon the floor below. Light filtered in through the two glass domes and illuminated the tile floor and table. Together with the massive bookshelves, the place looked like an old library. It was a breathtaking view that he admired for a few seconds.

He padded down the stairs in sneakers and took the elevator to the foyer. He opened the safe box and his heart picked up pace – there was something inside. He pulled out an envelope that was more than five inches thick and bound with two loops of steel wire. Another small envelope was tucked under one of the wires.

He closed the mailbox and rode the elevator back up to the flat. He set the package on the first-floor table, extracted the small envelope, and opened it. It was a handwritten message addressed to him. It said: "These documents are never to leave the facility." Jacob understood well the protocols when dealing with top-secret information.

Next, he tried to slip the steel wires off the larger envelope, which was more like a cardboard box, but they were too tight. He went to the desk and searched through the drawers. He figured his uncle had regularly dealt with the same types of packages. He found a wire cutter in a lower right-hand drawer. The wires snapped loudly on the table as he snipped them, and the package expanded and relaxed under the reduced tension.

He returned the tool to the drawer, coiled the wires, and put them in a trash can next to the desk. He then went back to the table, opened the large envelope, and removed the contents. He fanned out the documents on the table like a deck of cards, making sure to maintain their order in case they had been sorted in some way. He didn't see anything that resembled interrogation transcripts.

Although he'd thought the Red Falcon information might come in the form of a book – a monograph – he wasn't surprised to see multiple documents. The first thing he noticed was the letterhead of the cover pages. Some had an emblem at the top that consisted of a swastika being carried by an eagle. Others had a similar but clearly different emblem; it was a more complex-looking swastika carried by some other bird of prey, which he assumed was a falcon. The modified swastika looked like a hashtag symbol with swastika-like tails. All of the files with Nazi letterhead were written in German. The other documents were from US, UK, and Israeli sources.

He picked up one of the Nazi documents and flipped through it. He was relieved to see that every page had a corresponding English translation on the following page. He picked up the most recent document – a CIA report – and read.

It started with some general information, but then delved into graphic details. His stomach got more and more queasy as he read. About 25 pages into the 100-page document, he put it down, walked over to the trash can, and leaned over it. His gut churned as he stared at the bottom of the can, but that was all. His reaction surprised him; he wasn't usually the squeamish type.

When he was beyond the risk of vomiting, he took a deep breath and went up to the kitchen and started the coffee maker. *What the hell had the Nazis done?* They were a disgusting stain on humanity. He'd been aware of the medical experiments they'd carried out, most of which involved torture of various types, but nothing like what he'd just read.

It was evident that the CIA document was the most recent synopsis of the Red Falcon project. A footnote indicated that it was part of a monograph to be completed in the next year.

The Red Falcon project had been multifaceted, and occurred in stages, beginning before the onset of World War II. Only the upper echelon of the Nazi regime knew its real objectives, and most of the technical aspects were developed and carried out by Dr. Josef

Mengele – the infamous medical research scientist who had murdered thousands of Jews while conducting horrific medical tests in the concentration camps.

Mengele's well-documented medical experiments included subjecting prisoners to extreme temperatures, hyperbaric chambers, amputations, drugs and chemicals, radiation, and explosions. But other things described in the CIA document made Jacob's intestines twist.

As alluded to at the beginning of *The Israel Thread*, Mengele and his accomplices had systematically tortured people at an insane asylum, called Kraken, not far from Auschwitz. Ten or more Auschwitz prisoners would be selected each week, taken to Kraken, and tortured to death.

The document before him now went into more details. The most common torture technique was to amputate limbs by sawing off an inch at a time. Every effort was made to keep the victims alive for as long as possible, but they usually didn't last more than a week.

The coffeemaker beeped.

Jacob ran upstairs, filled a mug, and returned to the first-floor table. In the hour that followed, he learned that the heinous activities of Red Falcon had involved much more than the operations at Kraken. The torture, as horrible as it was, was not as disturbing as the overall objective of the project.

As a victim was being tortured, he or she was secured to a chair, or confined to the inside of a medieval, cage-like device, so that movement was impossible. As the torture proceeded, the subjects were ordered to carry out some action that would be impossible while confined – like tipping over an object on the other side of the room, or pushing a button that was far out of reach.

It was therefore clear to Jacob that one objective of Red Falcon was to develop telekinetic-like abilities. But that wasn't all. The experiments had been designed to test a hypothesis developed by a German psychiatrist named Nestler. It was termed *Nestler's Conjecture*, and the idea was that, if a person were subjected to extreme pain with no way to escape it – great lengths were taken to keep them alive –

then the person's soul would separate from their body. Since it would still be connected to a healthy, albeit *suffering*, body, the soul would remain localized, or connected to its body, and capable of interacting with the physical world.

Josef Mengele's experiments on twins took this idea a step further. In this case, it was suggested that the souls of twins were entangled. Here, the term *entangled* didn't mean like that which happens to two fishing lines that cross and twist. Rather, it referred to the term from quantum physics used to describe the behavior of a pair of electrons that interacted in such a way that they were aware of each other's condition even when they were far apart.

Mengele had carried out horrible experiments to test the idea. In one procedure, a set of twins was separated – put into different rooms far apart from one another. Then, unbeknownst to the other, one twin would be tortured and killed while the other was carefully observed for a reaction. Mengele was looking for some "action at a distance" response.

The results of the twin experiments were inconclusive. However, the Nazis observed a few strange events in their other torture experiments. These amounted to a small number of cases where some unexplained event occurred in the torture room – like something falling from a shelf or, in a few cases, a Nazi scientist losing his or her balance and falling to the floor. Most were minor occurrences. However, there was one major event that was the impetus for scaling up the project.

Five or six Russian soldiers had been taken to an unspecified facility and chained to chairs in separate rooms of a vacated barracks. They'd been subjected to daily amputation treatments, and at least two had survived for nearly three weeks. Late one evening, near the end of the third week, the guards heard more than the usual singular screams emanating from one of the rooms. They rushed in to find the tortured Russian still alive and confined to the chair. However, five other men, including the doctors, had been massacred. And it wasn't pretty: the bodies had been mangled to such an extent that it was deemed humanly impossible for a man to do such a thing with his bare hands. Specific details included a crushed skull and a leg ripped off a body at mid-thigh, breaking the femur in the process.

Jacob put the report on the table, stood with his coffee mug, and paced slowly along the rug that spanned the length of the room. His neck and shoulders warmed as he passed through an oval patch of sunlight from one of the domes. On the return trip, he stopped in the sun and mulled over what he'd just learned.

The Nazis were truly mad. They'd had no inhibitions and no constraints in accomplishing what they'd set out to do. But what, exactly, had that been? And what the hell did any of it have to do with his uncle's book, or current events? He felt he'd gotten the gist of the Red Falcon project and decided to go back to reading *The Israel Thread* monograph. He could always go back to the Red Falcon documents if needed.

He grabbed the book, and then refilled his coffee mug in the kitchen on his way up to the dome. He sat on the circular couch, put his feet on the coffee table, and continued reading from where he'd left off.

The new topic was the Nazi *Schutzstaffel,* also known as the SS. He'd already known that it was a sinister and brutal organization, but hadn't been aware of its connections to the occult and mysticism. After some reading, he understood how SS members could have fallen for the bizarre premises of the Red Falcon project. Their beliefs included everything from demonic possession to extraterrestrials and, of course, they believed in a New World Order dominated by a Germanic Aryan race. What was not as commonly known, however, was that they'd also believed that Aryans had ruled the Earth *in the past.* Although Hitler had been obsessed with the idea, even more so was Heinrich Himmler, Reichsführer of the SS.

Himmler founded the Ahnenerbe Institute in 1935 to research the archaeological and cultural history of the Aryan race. The underlying objective had been to prove that a Germanic Aryan race had ruled the world in the past, justifying their actions to rule it in the future. Teams had been sent around the world to collect evidence to support their claims, but they'd sought much more than cultural materials.

They'd gone to the edges of the Earth searching for and acquiring artifacts. Documents indicated they'd been to South America, Egypt, Jordan, Nepal, North America, Europe, and even Antarctica, and they'd bribed, cheated, stolen, and killed to get what they wanted.

A note was written in the margin in green ink: *The collections from Egypt are of great importance. See the White Stone.* The comment was dated just a month earlier.

What was the White Stone? he wondered.

His stomach grumbled and he looked at his watch: 1:00 p.m. He'd been reading for hours and missed lunch. Before grabbing food, he went down to the computer and searched the information stored in the stacks. There was a lot of material on the Ahnenerbe Institute, but he found nothing regarding Egyptian collections. He then made a document request through email for information on the Ahnenerbe Institute and its Egyptian collections – specifically the White Stone. He hoped there'd be a monograph on the latter.

He sent the email, and then went up to the kitchen and pulled the last two pieces of pizza from the refrigerator. They were starting to dry out and harden, but he took a bite without hesitation. It seemed to him that he'd never outgrow his old college tastes, or lack thereof.

He grabbed a can of soda from the fridge, sat at the counter, and flipped on the television. CNN News was reporting on a failed experimental corrections program in America in which inmates had allegedly been mistreated. He recalled hearing about it a while back, but such stories resurfaced constantly. He flipped the channel to BBC where they discussed the mounting tension between the United States and China.

He flinched at a vibrating sensation in his pocket. It was his phone. He picked it up and looked at the screen; it was a Virginia area code but he didn't recognize the number.

"Hello?" he said.

"Jake?"

"Pauli? How'd you get this number?" he asked, confused.

After a short pause, she asked, "What do you mean? I dialed your number."

He then realized that incoming calls to his previous phone must have been forwarded. "I got a new phone," he explained. "And a new number." He found it on his phone and read it to her. "You doing okay?"

"Yes, I'm at my sister's place. Can we have dinner tonight?" she asked. She spoke in a tone that was different somehow – it was softer.

He contemplated the logistics of leaving the facility and meeting her. He had no car, and he couldn't have her pick him up at 17 Swann. Not having a job was something that he still hadn't reconciled in his mind. But he didn't have a home, either. It flooded him with an anxiety that he hadn't experienced since his family had been killed.

"Jake?"

"I'll have to get back to you," he finally replied. "I have a few things to take care of."

"You okay?" she asked.

"I'm fine," he said. "I'll let you know about dinner later this afternoon."

They ended the call and he sat in silence for a few seconds. Was he just using his uncle's puzzle to distract him from the rest of his life? He'd been fired from his job. He had no home – or at least he couldn't go back to the one he had. And he couldn't get a new place without proof of income. Uncle Theo was dead, and his cousin murdered. Pauli was moving to London. His world was drastically different than it had been just a week earlier. His life had instantly become unstable – more than it had ever been in his adult life. *What if they kicked him out of this place?* he wondered.

He held his anxiety at bay by reminding himself that he had enough money to live on for a couple of years, if he had to stretch it that long. It made him wonder if his final paycheck from Interstellar Dynamics had been deposited.

He went down to the computer and logged in to one of his online banking accounts. It took his brain a few seconds to process what his eyes were reporting: *zero balance*. His hands trembled as he logged out and navigated to his other online bank. He'd always been careful not to put all of his money in one place. He logged in, and his stomach twisted in his gut. The account had also been zeroed, and marked as closed.

He turned the chair, leaned back, and gazed through one of the skylights at white clouds as they bubbled slowly across the light blue sky. *What the hell was happening?*

DANIEL REREAD the email and then called Sylvia from her office to the common area. With her frazzled hair and sleepy eyes, she looked like she needed a midafternoon nap. Daniel felt the same.

"What's up?" she asked as she walked past him to the refrigerator in the small kitchenette across from his office.

"Jacob Hale just requested the unredacted Israeli interrogations," he explained.

"He moves fast," she said as she twisted open a bottle of iced tea.

"He must have help," Daniel said, not hiding his skepticism. "He's asking too many of the right questions."

"Who could be helping him?"

"Horace," he replied. "He must have given him hints."

Sylvia rubbed her temples and closed her eyes. "Horace was keeping notes just as we were," she said. "He must've given them to him."

"Yes," he replied and then added, "some really strange things have happened to Hale in the past week."

"I'd say," she huffed. "He was attacked multiple times, and lost his job."

"There's more," Daniel said. "I've been reading the file from his background investigation. Did you know that Horace was wealthy? We're talking *billionaire*."

She raised an eyebrow but said nothing.

"As a boy, Jacob saved Horace from drowning," he continued. "But Horace didn't give him a penny in the will."

"Did they have a falling out?"

"No evidence of that."

"But Horace had him fired," she argued. "There must've been something going on between them."

"It may be that Horace wanted to force Jacob to work on this project," Daniel continued.

Sylvia shook her head. "Why didn't Horace just explain it to him before he died, and try to convince him?"

"There would have been too much to explain in too short of a time," Daniel argued. "Besides, once he told Jacob what was happening, there'd be no taking back the information. He might have put his nephew in danger."

"Seems he did that anyway."

"There's more," Daniel said. "Hale's bank accounts have been zeroed out and closed."

"What the hell?" Sylvia gasped.

"I can't confirm whether Horace had anything to do with that," he said, "but it fits in with everything else."

"Hale is being forced down a chute," she said with an expression of disbelief.

Daniel nodded. "No job or inheritance and, now, no financial means of any kind. He has no choice other than to live at 17 Swann."

"And carry out the task his uncle assigned," she added. "It's as if Horace is still assigning projects from the grave."

He smirked and nodded. "And it's working."

"And what about our work?" Sylvia said. "Making progress?"

He shook his head. It had been slow ever since they'd returned from Antarctica. Slow wasn't the right word; they'd all been overwhelmed with trying to figure out what had happened there and, more importantly, what was coming next. It made it impossible to concentrate.

The ruse that the AM radio interference was from a malfunctioning Russian satellite was genius. The Russian denial would be business as usual, even though it really wasn't them this time. The real source was concealed from the public, but it was only a matter of time before the cat was out of the bag. He'd found it interesting that the conspiracy theorists were getting this one right and didn't even know it. And it seemed that the other governments were playing along: they'd known immediately that the signal wasn't coming from the Russians. They were keeping it quiet so as not to frighten the public. The arguing back and forth was just for show. They were all trying to figure out what was happening.

"There's still a mountain of things from the base to go through," she said. "But I doubt there's anything new that could help. Most of the books and files had to do with the White Stone inscription. The rest was old psychology and biomedical information."

Daniel agreed. She was referring to the crates of books, documents, and artifacts they'd collected from the Nazi base in Antarctica. And there was a hundred times more still there due to the limited space on the submarine. But, as she'd said, they'd probably not be of much help regarding the AM interference. They already knew that the real source of the AM disturbance had nothing to do with Earth-based satellites. However, they hadn't yet decoded the signal, and had no idea of its purpose.

"Hale is an expert in signal analysis and encryption," Sylvia said, as if she were reading his mind. "But could he really add to the efforts of the multitude of experts already working on it?"

Daniel shrugged. "I don't know. But that's not what he's doing now anyway. He's researching things we already know."

"You think it's a waste of time?"

"We could get him there more quickly," he said. "But maybe that's not the best way."

"What do you mean?"

"As Thackett suggested, let's see if he draws the same conclusions," Daniel said. "Maybe he'll find something different. That's also why we need to go back to the base."

Sylvia nodded and sighed. "We won't get back to Antarctica for a while. What are we supposed to do in the meantime?"

He didn't have an answer, but his anxiety was ratcheting as they remained idle, and the signal emerging from the darkness of space continued its broadcast for those on Earth, and elsewhere, to hear.

JACOB CALLED Paulina back and they made a dinner date for 7:30 p.m.

At 7:15 p.m. he started the walk toward the apartment building where she'd dropped him off the day before, about a quarter mile northeast of Swann Street. Even though he'd taken some time to contemplate her London offer and the payoff to her boss, he couldn't come up with a reason for it. Pauli had traced it back to entities associated with his uncle, but it wasn't definitive that Theo was responsible for it. There didn't seem to be a motive.

By 7:25 p.m. he was sitting on a concrete bench outside the building, waiting for Paulina and thinking about what he'd learned that day. The information was becoming addictive – an obsession, like some of the puzzles he'd fought through as a kid.

He popped up his head in response to a car horn. It was Paulina's white BMW.

He jogged down the walk and got in the car. It was nearing dusk, but she still wore her usual oversized sunglasses.

"You okay after all this?" he asked.

"I don't think my brain believes it really happened." She kept her eyes on the road as she spoke, but he could tell that she was still shaken.

Ten minutes later they pulled into the parking lot of their regular Thai restaurant and got a table. They ordered drinks – green tea for both – and looked over the menus.

Tears welled in the corner of Pauli's eyes until one streamed down her cheek. She caught it with her napkin before it got to her chin.

"What's wrong?" he asked.

She shook her head and then tried to speak but stopped. Just as she was about to try again, the server came with hot tea and asked for their orders. They ordered entrées and, when the server left, she cleared her throat and took a sip of tea.

"I don't think you can break up with me again," he said, trying to lighten the mood.

She smiled, but still avoided eye contact.

"What is it?" he asked, anxious.

"What's going on with you?" she asked finally, tears welling again. "What are you involved in?"

Jacob was taken aback by the question. He just looked back at her and remained silent.

"Is it just the book?" she asked. "Or is it more than that? Why would someone want to get me out of your life?"

Jacob shook his head. "Pauli, you heard the guy – he wanted the book."

"It still doesn't explain why someone would want me out of the picture," she argued. "What could be the purpose of that?"

He didn't know, but it seemed to fall in line with everything else – losing his job, no inheritance, and bank accounts zeroed. It now made him think that his being fired had been accomplished in the same manner as Pauli's promotion. It all pointed to one person: *Uncle Theo*.

The food came and they spent the next 40 minutes eating and speculating about the recent events.

When their plates were empty she wiped her mouth with a napkin and looked at him. "I want us to stay together," she said.

"Might be tough with you in London."

"I do have to go," she said. "My boss is spooked. He thought he better follow through since he'd already taken the money. He has no idea who he's dealing with."

"Neither do we," Jacob added.

"I'm not going to stay at the London office very long," she said. "My firm already relocated the person I'm replacing, so I'll have to go for a short time to cover – probably around six months. But I won't stay after that."

"Why?"

"I didn't earn it," she replied. "I'll never be comfortable knowing I got there only because someone got paid off."

It didn't surprise him. It was one of the reasons he loved her.

"If six months is too long, and you still want to break up, I'll understand," she said and smirked.

Jake just shook his head. "I think my position has been clear all along," he said. Although he was pleased with the way things seemed to be working out, he welcomed the space for the short term. That she'd be out of the picture was best for her own safety. "When will you leave?"

"My flight to London departs at 5:30 a.m. tomorrow. I have to choose furniture for my apartment and office," she replied. "I'll come back to DC at the end of the week to move out of my apartment and pack the clothes I want to ship."

The server placed the check on the table, and Jacob grabbed it.

"No, Jake," she protested. "My turn."

"Actually, I got the last two. And this one is your goodbye dinner," he retorted and gave the server his credit card. "You have the next three – including the first one when I come to visit you in London." He was pretty sure he wouldn't be making it to London in the next few months.

"You must have some vacation time built up again," she said.

Jacob nodded. He was on permanent vacation. "We'll plan something soon."

"I have one more question for you," she said. "Where did you get the gun?"

Jacob's mind went blank for a second, not expecting the question nor having a prepared answer. Just as he was about to stammer out an improvised explanation, the server returned.

"Sir," the man said, looking less friendly than he had while working their table, "this card was rejected. Do you have another?"

Jacob looked over to Paulina, whose eyes widened. He pulled out another card from his wallet and exchanged it with the server who disappeared into the restaurant's foyer.

"What the hell?" Paulina said. "This is getting creepy."

The man returned a minute later with another person who looked to be a manager. "This card was also rejected, sir," the manager said. "Would you like to use cash?"

Jacob was dumbfounded. First his bank accounts, now his credit cards. What the hell was going on? He looked to Paulina and shook his head.

She extracted a card from her handbag and handed it to the man. As he and the server left to carry out the transaction, she said, "I'm really worried about you. What are you going to do? How can I help?"

"Don't worry," he replied. "Just a glitch of some kind." As far as general living, there was only one thing he could do for the time being: Swann Street.

A few minutes later the server came back with her card and a receipt, and they left the restaurant. On the way back to Jacob's alleged apartment, Pauli made a withdrawal at a drive-through ATM and gave him $300. Five minutes later they were parked in front of the building with the car running.

"I'm going to be worried if you don't contact me every day. Understand?" she said.

Jacob nodded, kissed her, and got out of the car. He got a sick feeling in his stomach as she drove away and disappeared around the corner. His emotions were mixed. She had to go – for her own safety and to give him space to work. But he knew there was a chance that he'd never see her again.

He took the long way back to Swann Street. The light breeze that swirled the upper canopies of the tall spruce and oak trees dipped through the lower branches and soughed through his hair. He took a deep breath and detected the aroma of grilled meat.

His mind mediated between feelings of contentment and disquiet. It was strange how anxiety for the future could be balanced by the equanimity of being free from everything the world imposed. Everything that required his attention – job, fiancée, family – was no longer his concern. Maybe Uncle Theo's plan – if he were indeed responsible for everything that was happening – was a blessing.

IT WAS NEARLY dark as Jacob fumbled for the key and opened the massive door of 17 Swann. He checked the safe box and his adrenaline picked up as he extracted a thick envelope: the transcripts of the Israeli - Nazi interrogations, he presumed. Whoever handled document delivery was quick.

He rode the elevator up to the facility, put the envelope on the table on the lower level, and then went to the kitchen and got a Pepsi from the refrigerator. It was going to be a three-can night and, fortunately, that was how many cans were left. He went back downstairs and opened the envelope.

The interrogations were presented in sets of four documents. Each file had one version with portions blacked out, another with nothing redacted, and then English and Hebrew translations from the original German.

The first transcript was the interrogation of Lieutenant Hans Demler, a Nazi prison guard and courier at Auschwitz who had hand-selected prisoners for delivery to the asylum, Kraken, a two-hour drive from the city. Jacob figured it was the first interrogation referenced in *The Israel Thread*.

At first, the man had been reluctant to speak. But when the Israeli interrogator informed him that the people he'd selected had been tortured and killed, and that he was an accomplice in over a thousand murders, Demler cracked and started spilling information.

After describing all of the mundane details of how he'd selected prisoners and transported them, Demler started revealing shocking information. First, Kraken was run by Dr. Josef Mengele. Demler hadn't known the details of the medical experiments – for which Jacob was grateful since he'd already read that in the Red Falcon documents – but he described his conversations with Mengele during the long drives from Auschwitz to Kraken. Although it was clear that someone would have to be severely disturbed to carry out what he'd done in the concentration camps, it was confirmed from Demler's account that Mengele was completely mad.

Mengele had told Demler that his experiments were going to bring humanity into a new existence. A new world was going to be born with an advanced Aryan race capable of things beyond imagination, allowing them to access facets of reality beyond the reach of current humanity. Further, this had been the underlying purpose of the war, and Germany would win because of their new discoveries.

Jacob thought it sounded like the usual superstitious indoctrination to which the Nazi SS had been subjected. With their belief in the occult and mysticism, they were brainwashed into collecting religious artifacts from all corners of the planet in the hope that they'd reveal some great power to help them conquer the world. What he was reading was just more of the usual craziness.

The interrogator prodded Demler for more details, and the man explained that Mengele had described a secret place where they'd discovered something of great importance. The Nazis had invested much effort in both exploring it, and keeping it concealed. When asked where this place was, Demler said it was in one of the coldest and most isolated places on Earth – accessible only by submarine.

Jacob shivered. His thoughts turned to Commander Cook, Germany's *Schwabenland*, and the current events around Antarctica.

That was all the information they'd gotten from Demler, which was no doubt all he had to give. His life had been on the line and, based on a handwritten note at the end of the transcript, it had been spared. The next subject, however, hadn't been as fortunate.

Nazi SS Obersturmbannführer, Otto Adolf Eichmann, was captured by the Israeli Mossad in Argentina in 1960. A scribbled notation indicated that the man's title meant "lieutenant colonel," and another informed that tape recordings were available.

Jacob already knew a lot about Eichmann from documentary films. An oil salesman in his early life, Eichmann had worked his way up the ranks of the SS and, in the end, was responsible for sending millions to their deaths with the stroke of a pen. Having been the major orchestrator of the holocaust, handling the logistics of transporting the Jews to concentration camps, he'd become known as the "desk murderer."

In the interview, Eichmann explained that the purpose of the concentration camps had been to exterminate Jews, but the objectives were different from what had been assumed by the rest of the world. The Nazis wanted to exterminate the other peoples of the Earth not to clear the planet for the Aryan race in its present form, but for the *transformed* race that was coming. There would soon be a refined Aryan race that transcended the current form of human existence.

Eichmann had referred to the Red Falcon project several times during the interrogation – the first instance of which had been initiated by him. The interrogator had led him in that direction, but had never mentioned the name of the project. In the end, Eichmann hadn't known the details of Red Falcon. However, he made one reference that Jacob could tell confused the interrogator. He said there was a *New Order rising from cold waters*. It was this *Last Reich* that would be the transformed version of humanity, and Eichmann suggested that it would rise before he'd be executed.

Eichmann had also claimed that Hitler wasn't dead, nor were many of the others at the top of the Nazi hierarchy. They had escaped from Germany through the Nazi SS operation ODESSA, and would rise again from the south.

Eichmann was executed in 1962.

It was well past midnight when Jacob stopped reading the transcripts. So far he'd only collected two solid pieces of information. First, Josef Mengele's research was directly connected to Red Falcon. Second, everything was connected to Antarctica. Beyond that, all he had were some crazy stories about Hitler being alive after the war, and that the *Last Reich* would rise out of the south. It was all in line with the beliefs of the SS.

After his last can of Pepsi, around 1:30 a.m., he trekked to the computer and ordered more supplies, and then to the bathroom to get ready for bed. Although he was too tired to hold his eyes open while he brushed his teeth, his mind seemed to twitch in his skull. He'd learned a lot, but it didn't seem to get him any closer to the final destination – whatever that was.

He went to the lower bunk and turned off the lights. As he closed his eyes, images of the interrogation transcripts flashed through his mind. His brain was comparing the redacted and unredacted versions. It occurred to him that a comparison of the two could expose an emphasis that might be revealing in some way. He'd reread them in the morning.

Lenny was starting to think that it might have been better if the Americans who had pursued him at the restaurant had caught him.

The two Chinese operatives sitting across from him in the booth were overdressed for the diner. There were no other customers in the greasy restaurant at that late hour, except for a taxi driver in the back, near the restrooms. A woman dressed in a stained apron and too old to be awake at 2:00 a.m. poured coffee into a white porcelain cup and handed it to Lenny. The other men declined.

"It would have helped if you'd told me exactly what I was looking for," Lenny said.

"A book, and keys," the man on the right responded. He did all the talking.

"I was alone in Hale's apartment for over an hour," Lenny said. "There were hundreds of books. I had no idea what to look for. A title, sketches of the keys, something."

"You should have been able to extract that information from the boy," the man said.

Lenny didn't see Hale as a "boy." But the man was right – he would have gotten the info if he'd caught him. "It's going to take some time to get another opportunity – "

"No more opportunities," the man cut him off. "You are being reassigned."

The words put Lenny on edge. That phrase often meant something more ominous than getting a new task. He just stared back at them, waiting for them to continue.

"A hit," the man said.

"Who?"

"You have met him before."

"Tell me."

"You helped us to collect him recently," the man said, apparently not wanting to say the name.

Lenny remembered. He'd helped kidnap the American and deliver him to Cho, the CEO of Syncorp at the time. He'd heard Cho had recently been killed. "You mean the man got away?"

Both men lowered their eyes for an instant. The man who did the talking expelled a burst of foul breath and hissed, "That does not concern you."

It is virtually impossible to escape from an intelligence or military organization unless a rescue operation is executed. Even then, the person being rescued is often killed. "And you want me to capture him again?" Lenny said, rubbing it in. "Or just the hit?"

"Just eliminate him."

Lenny stared at the man, waiting for further explanation, but there was none.

Lenny took a sip of coffee. "I don't believe this was part of our deal," he said. "I'm supposed to collect the book and keys. That's all. Any killing that transpires was to be necessary for that mission alone."

"This one is separate," the operative said. "One million dollars."

Lenny tried not to react, but his eyes started to water. It was five times his usual payment for a hit. He set down his coffee. "What's the catch?"

Both men stared at him blankly.

He rephrased the question. "Are there any special circumstances that you are not telling me?"

The man on the right shook his head. "He's extremely important to the United States. He's a difficult target. He must pay for his crimes against the People's Republic of China."

Lenny remembered the man well, and wondered what his crimes against the PRC had been. The man in question had once been a subject of the Red Wraith program – a supposed success, whatever that meant. Lenny hadn't been the one to deliver him to Cho, exactly, but he'd been a part of the operation. The man had been taken to a Chinese naval vessel. *How in the hell had he gotten away?* "Why don't you take care of this yourselves?"

The man shook his head. "This is now your first priority. Stand by for instructions."

Lenny nodded.

The men left.

Lenny took a swig of coffee and stared out the window and watched as the operatives got into a car and drove away.

He was relieved that he could stop pursuing the book and keys – and Hale – for the time being anyway. That whole endeavor he'd chalk up as a miserable failure. Going after Hale would be too risky now, anyway. Others were watching out for him – like the CIA, which had disrupted the operation at the restaurant. The whole area would be too hot for him to show his face. Actually, his body gave him away even more. Good to lay low and pursue something else.

The lady came back and refilled his mug. The coffee seemed to be freshly brewed, and the aroma pleased him and roused his brain.

He was used to being alone, but it was times like these that he dreaded. When left in silence, he could hear his thoughts – the deeper ones with muffled voices. They reminded him constantly that he was getting old, and that time was running short. They also reminded him of what he was – what he'd been – all of his life. How many had he killed? A hundred? He knew the exact number, but kept that information buried at a deeper level, never to be spoken.

He finished his coffee, paid the bill, and walked out into the gentle summer night.

JACOB SHOWERED, ate cold cereal, and was at the table on the first level by 6:30 a.m. with a mug of hot coffee in hand. By 8:00 a.m., he'd reread the interrogation transcripts and another 25 pages of Theo's monograph. He took detailed notes on both.

As he progressed through the monograph, now about a third of the way through, Theo's green-inked notes became more frequent.

He fanned through the book as he looked at it edgewise. The density of green ink increased as it went toward the end. He was tempted to skip ahead but didn't want to miss anything. Up to this point there had been many details that he'd had to explore further using additional sources to give him proper context.

The latest reference he'd encountered had to do with the Red Wraith project, the supposed American extension of the Nazi's Red Falcon. That Red Wraith was related to the horrid German project made him light-headed. *Did the US torture people?* He suspected they had, especially during wartime, but didn't think it had been carried out on the same scale, or for the same purpose.

He went to the computer and sent a request for Red Wraith information. He was after one file in particular that Theo had described as a recent CIA activity report on the project.

He went upstairs to use the bathroom and refill his coffee. He turned on the television and flipped through the news channels to see if there were any new developments. Nothing interesting was happening, so he returned to the downstairs table and continued reading.

The Israelis had boiled down all of the information they'd gathered through the interrogations of Nazi war criminals and other sources to a succinct theory they'd called, simply, *the thread,* and hence the title of Theo's monograph. *The thread* was a hidden history, from before World War II to the date of publication of the monograph in 1966. From his uncle's annotations, it was clear that the thread carried through to the present day.

The origin of the thread was defined as the voyage of Germany's *Schwabenland* to Antarctica in 1938. However, Theo had argued that the discovery of an artifact had started it earlier. He'd written, 'White Stone discovered, Giza, 1932, started everything.' He'd also noted that Germany had initiated the war just months after the return of the *Schwabenland. Coincidence?* he'd written.

Jacob took a break to check the safe box and found that the information on the White Stone he'd requested hadn't yet been delivered. He'd give it another 24 hours and then submit the request again.

He ate lunch, and continued his work through the afternoon. At 7:00 p.m., a crack of thunder roused him from a slumber. He'd fallen asleep on the circular couch while reading under the skylight. The rain that pattered on the dome was soothing until it came down harder and reverberated like a drum. Storm clouds darkened the sky.

His phone rang, and he took the stairs down to the second level so that he could hear over the rain. It was Paulina.

"I miss you," she said.

She'd taken a direct flight from Washington Dulles to London Heathrow and was now in the Corinthia Hotel for a few days until her flat in the posh Kensington W8 district was furnished. At the end of the week, she'd fly back to DC, close out her apartment, and head back to London for good.

"It's more expensive here than in DC," she said. "But I like it so far. I suppose it's easy to like a place when you don't have to pay for anything."

Jacob agreed. He didn't add that he was also staying somewhere nice, free of charge.

They ended the call and he headed to the fridge to get a Pepsi. As he popped the top he was grateful for the morning's delivery of supplies. He made a mental note to order more eggs and bacon, and a few more frozen pizzas. The idea of food reminded him of money.

He decided to try to get at least one of his credit cards reactivated. Although he'd only use it in an emergency, he felt helpless without an active card. He pulled out his laptop and set it on the counter. When he tried to power it up, a red light flashed. The battery was dead. He muttered a curse as he realized that the charger was still back in his apartment.

He went downstairs to the desktop, sent a request for a new charger and other supplies, and then attempted to log into his credit card account. His login information was invalid. He shouldn't have been surprised, but it ratcheted up his anxiety another notch. He'd try again from his laptop when he got the new charger.

He climbed the stairs back to the dome. The storm had subsided, and the skies above had turned to a deep purple. He leaned back, took a long swig of soda, and contemplated what he'd recently learned.

The American Red Wraith project was the continuation of the Nazis' Red Falcon research. The prime objective of the latter was to torture someone until their soul left their body and could perform telekinetic acts.

It was absurd. He understood to some degree why the brainwashed Nazi SS would fall for such idiocy. That the United States would continue such a thing, however, implied that there was something to it. But he refused to believe it was for the same reason, or that they'd pursued the conjecture of a madman the likes of Nestler, or Josef Mengele. He'd find out more once he received the Red Wraith documents, which he assumed would arrive the next morning.

But what if the US had believed that the Nazi research had credibility? What did that imply – we have souls? We can exist outside our bodies? He brushed it out of his mind, and flipped open *The Israel Thread*.

He read through a terse description of the White Stone artifact acquired by the Germans in 1932. Theo had marked up the margins just weeks earlier with a more detailed description. The object was about two feet in diameter and four inches thick, and was inscribed with five concentric rings of symbols that resembled hieroglyphics. He'd written: "Deciphered by W.T." in the margin.

Who is W. T.? Jacob wondered.

Theo had also mentioned that the artifact was composed of an unidentified material, off-white in color and harder than diamond. He then wrote, "Same material as the beacon?"

What the hell was "the beacon?" Jacob wondered.

At 1:15 a.m. he went to the first floor and sent email requests for information on the beacon, and a repeated request for information on the White Stone. He then wrote, "Who is W.T.?" on the outside chance that he'd get a response.

CHAPTER 6

Jonathan McDougal deplaned and headed for the baggage claim. Checking bags was always a risk, but this time he'd packed for an extended stay. Even though he wasn't pleased that his flight had departed Chicago after 10:00 p.m., he was grateful for the direct flight to Reagan International. His long legs were not conducive to comfort on extended flights.

He'd never liked Washington, DC. His trips to the national capital had always been for official business, and were always of an antagonistic nature. This time the journey was again for something other than leisure, but it was important.

Jonathan loved his life as a law professor, but something greater still burned in his heart. Being over sixty years old gave him the feeling that time was running out, but that condition was the same for young and old alike, whether they knew it or not.

His tenured professorship at the university would be held for him for a while – not that it mattered – but his position as the head of the DNA Foundation was already reassigned. He'd exonerated many innocent people through the Foundation – based on DNA evidence, as the title suggested – and was responsible for the moratorium on the death penalty in Illinois. In the big picture, however, it seemed to be of little consequence. A clock was ticking, and no one knew what was going to happen when it struck the dark hour.

He was going to DC to help with an investigation, as was his assistant who'd arrive the next day, but they both knew the real reason why they were needed there. Of course, he and Denise Walker were both excellent problem solvers, and could think on their feet. But they'd also function as handlers. They'd earned the trust of one person in particular, and the CIA wanted him to be as comfortable as possible. And he was to be comforted. The person in question was responsible for the current situation – a situation that had existential implications.

As Jonathan yanked the larger of his two suitcases from the luggage carousel, a man approached him. He'd never seen the bespectacled Daniel Parsons in jeans; they revealed how thin he was. He didn't look healthy.

"Hello, Jonathan," Daniel said and stretched out his hand. "Good flight?"

Jonathan shook his hand. "Uneventful," he replied. "Sorry to drag you out so late."

Daniel shrugged. "Not that late for us these days."

It was worrying: Jonathan hadn't been able to stay up much past eleven since returning from the Antarctic Circle a few weeks ago. It was either the fatigue of that adventure, or that his sleep routine had become so chaotic from the long and irregular hours that he hadn't yet recovered.

Daniel grabbed one of Jonathan's bags, pulled out the handle, and rolled it behind him as he led the way to the parking garage. Ten minutes later they were piling into Daniel's small Toyota and were on the highway.

"How's William doing?" Jonathan asked.

"In better spirits, I think."

"You make any progress?"

"None."

Jonathan was not surprised. When they'd returned to the States, everyone was still confused. "I'm sorry to hear about Horace."

"I'm sure the trip south didn't help his condition," Daniel said, "but I think it was old age that finally got him. Even so, Horace is still having influence."

Jonathan turned to Daniel, whose attention was now on entering the freeway. "How so?"

Daniel explained about Horace's nephew and his precarious situation.

"Isn't that a security risk?" Jonathan asked.

"Yes and no. One could argue that Jacob Hale is about as well vetted as anyone could be. He'd been under his uncle's nose all of his life."

"Does he understand the security protocols?"

Daniel nodded. "He worked for a defense contractor called Interstellar Dynamics and had a high-level clearance – before he was fired, that is."

"Fired?"

"It seems that Horace had something to do with it."

"Why? To force him to work for the CIA?"

"Maybe," Daniel said and shrugged. "The thing is, Jacob Hale has no idea who he's working for right now. But it seems that he's on to the idea that Horace set up everything – his losing his job, assets, even his girlfriend."

"Girlfriend? I don't understand."

"Horace paid his girlfriend's employer to relocate her. Maybe to keep her out of danger, or to eliminate distractions."

"The kid must be in a bad place right now."

"You'd think so, but he seems to be working fine."

They hit heavy traffic and, a half hour later, exited the highway and turned onto a narrow drive. A minute later they stopped at a fortified and guarded gate at the entrance of a parking garage. Daniel got them through, drove down a few levels, and parked.

They got out, and Daniel opened the trunk and pulled out Jonathan's luggage. "We're going to drop these off at a security station and then go to the main lobby to be screened," Daniel explained.

"I'm staying here? In this building?"

Daniel nodded. "It's one of the most secure surface buildings on the planet."

That might have been true, but Jonathan wondered how comfortable it would be. He would've preferred a hotel.

They dropped off the bags, and Jonathan was informed that they'd be delivered to his room after they were examined.

Jonathan then endured a rigorous security screening that he found to be borderline violating. The background check had been conducted weeks ago, but now they collected all sorts of biometric data, including iris scans and dental X-rays. Daniel finally delivered him to his room on the nineteenth floor just after 2:30 a.m.

Upon entering the flat, Jonathan recognized immediately that he'd been wrong about the place: it was magnificent. His room looked like an upscale two-bedroom apartment with every amenity. The study was beautiful, and the kitchen was stocked. Denise's room was one door down the hall.

He spotted his luggage leaning against the side of the couch in the center of the room.

"Get some sleep," Daniel said. "We meet at eight o'clock in the morning. Come to room 713. Don't forget your ID badge – they're pretty serious about that."

Daniel left.

Jonathan walked over to a bank of windows that made up the entire wall opposite the couch. He was on the nineteenth floor, giving him a view of streetlights and sparse traffic below. He looked up to the sky and was able to spot a few stars through the high, motionless clouds. He wondered what the coming days would bring.

JACOB WOKE up at 5:18 a.m., got dressed, and then went to the dumbwaiter and unloaded the supplies he'd ordered the day before. He put away the food items, and then unpacked the new computer charger. He plugged the charger into a floor outlet and then into his laptop, on the counter.

He finished breakfast and then took the elevator to the safe box in the foyer. He retrieved a wire-bound cardboard package and a brown, letter-sized envelope, and took the elevator back upstairs.

He set the package on the table, but took the envelope to the desk where he found a letter opener and sliced the flap with care. He opened it and found a note, and a black credit card in a leather sheath. The card had his name on it. The note read, "We are aware of your financial situation. This is not a standard credit card. You can use it as a normal credit card, or to get cash from ATMs (pin 8392). Use it sparingly."

He shook his head and smiled. That small gesture somehow made him feel like he wasn't alone.

He cut the wires on the package and put them in the trash. He went back to the table, removed the documents, and sorted through them until he found the one he was looking for: a recent CIA activity report on the Red Wraith project.

For the next two hours, he read the hundred-page document and, at the end, was devastated. The Americans had done exactly what he'd feared: Red Wraith had picked up where Red Falcon left off. The difference was that the scale of Red Wraith was even larger – much larger. The US government had funded the project at a level that exceeded that of the Manhattan Project, and had kept it concealed from the public since its inception. It was made to look as if so-called *dark money* had funded multiple projects, and was spread through numerous defense contractors. But it really funded a singular project with one objective: separate a human soul from its body using the same, although refined, brutality of the Nazis' Red Falcon program – rife with torture and an overwhelming disregard for life. Jacob was ashamed.

Apart from the horrific actions of Red Wraith, it was the absurdity of the concept itself that made him uneasy. If the idea – separating a person's soul and body – had come from an individual, or even a group of scientists, he would've immediately written them all off as lunatics. But the fact that the governments of major countries had embarked on such a vast venture, and at such great cost and risk, made him wonder if it were really possible.

If it were, the implications were profound: we exist beyond our bodies – beyond the physical world. It implied life after death, if death could even be defined anymore. It was a wondrous idea, and a horrifying one, but Jacob would never believe it without seeing it for himself. And he rejected the idea that anyone else truly believed it either.

Belief was not a controllable function. It was no more possible to force oneself to believe something than it was to will oneself to grow a foot taller overnight. His assertion was that belief was often confused with hope, or assumption. One could assume something was true based on faith, but could not truly believe it unless it was directly witnessed. There was even doubt in direct observation because the senses couldn't be fully trusted – nor could memory. It was proven time and again with eyewitnesses to crimes.

The amount of proof would have to be overwhelming for him to believe something as mind-boggling as a soul leaving a body, conducting something resembling telekinetic activity, and then returning. And what he'd read so far did not fulfill that requirement. But the fact still remained that the US government had bought into it, and he didn't know why.

He finished the CIA report just past noon and took a break. He went to the bathroom and then grabbed a can of Pepsi from the fridge. He powered up his laptop to access his credit card account, but soon realized he had no internet connection. He checked for wireless signals, but there was only one, and it was extremely weak and password-protected. He figured the computer on the desk on the first floor must have a direct connection.

He decided to look into the wireless connectivity later, and climbed up to the dome with Theo's monograph.

The topic changed to Operation Highjump, the American invasion of Antarctica in 1946. The cover story was that it was a military exercise to prepare for possible future arctic conflicts with Russia. According to the monograph, and Theo's handwritten notes, however, its true objective was to find a secret Nazi base somewhere on the continent. A green, ink scribble indicated that there was a good reason why they hadn't found it – it was only accessible by submarine. The note was dated just four weeks earlier, a week before Theo's death.

Evidently, Uncle Theo's ramblings on his deathbed about a trip in a submarine hadn't been delusional. Had they discovered a base?

His mind whirred and made some connections. The Germans had been nosing around Antarctica before and during the war, instigating a response by the Brits in the form of Operation Tabarin. The Americans followed with an invasion of Antarctica immediately after the war. And, just weeks earlier, Uncle Theo claimed to have carried out a mission on a submarine. And, just like the CIA report, *The Israel Thread* connected the Nazi Red Falcon research to the American Red Wraith project.

Everything pointed to Antarctica.

LENNY YAWNED and took a swig of water as he watched the terminal exit inside Reagan International Airport. He'd received the call at 5:00 a.m., which gave him an hour to get to the airport from his fleabag hotel on the other side of the city, but was cutting it close with Tuesday morning traffic in DC.

The network had kept close tabs on Denise Walker and her boss, Jonathan McDougal, both of whom had been deeply involved in Red Wraith and, most importantly, with William Thompson. They'd missed McDougal's departure from Chicago the night before, but learned of Ms. Walker's just in time. It was the first time the Syncorp network had given him timely, actionable information. However, it was becoming clear that Syncorp was nothing but a hub for Chinese intelligence. He'd always assumed they'd been involved, but now he suspected the Chinese government was in complete control.

Lenny knew that if they tracked Denise Walker long enough

she'd eventually lead them to William Thompson. The implication was that Walker and Thompson were involved on a personal level.

He spotted Walker at the baggage claim where she met up with a thin woman with red and black hair. He stepped outside and waved to the kid he'd hired to watch his rental car, indicating that it would be a few more minutes, and then observed the women through glass doors as they collected Walker's luggage. Ten minutes later, the women got into a silver Honda Civic parked illegally on the street.

Lenny hustled to his car, handed the teenager a 20-dollar bill, and got behind the wheel. From there it was an easy follow, and the slow traffic worked in his favor. A half-hour later, the women arrived at their destination. Lenny parked out of sight as he studied his options.

The building into which the Honda Civic had disappeared resembled the others in the area, many of which were either technology companies or government contractor offices. But he had to be careful: any one of them could be a CIA facility. It was something of which he had become acutely aware while working for his former boss, the late Heinrich Bergman, who had used such buildings to keep the Red Wraith project secure. They all had generic names like Kinetic Industries, Marine Technologies, and Engineering Solutions. The one the Honda Civic had just entered was called Space Systems. It was the only one that had underground parking, and was therefore more secure than the others.

Lenny drove around the block and examined the perimeter of the building and the property. The only way inside was through the gated entrance to the parking garage. He'd have to find a way to stake out the area and nab William Thompson or Denise Walker when they exited.

Having probed around the Space Systems building, it was likely that his rental car had been picked up by its exterior electronic surveillance. After scoping out the entire area, he returned the car, picked up a sport utility vehicle at another rental company under a different alias, and drove to a coffeehouse. He pulled out his laptop and sent the vehicle license plate number of the silver Honda Civic to his Syncorp contacts. Ten minutes later he got a response stating that it was a restricted plate. It was a definitive indication that the owner was a sensitive government employee. The facility was undoubtedly a CIA or NSA hub.

He found a satellite map online and scouted the area for a good place to set up a stakeout. It wasn't going to be easy. There were no residential neighborhoods with a good view. Southeast of the Space Systems building was a large forest, but he was sure that it was filled with electronic surveillance gadgets since it was so close to the building. For the time being, he'd have to park in the lot of a nearby building, but he'd need binoculars, or a camera with zoom, both of which would quickly become tiring, and would rouse suspicion if noticed.

Lenny was tired, but satisfied. It was likely that William Thompson was in the Space Systems building.

Jonathan awakened to the light from the overcast sky that came through the floor-to-ceiling windows in his bedroom. He'd neglected to close the curtains before going to sleep, but decided he'd leave them open again for the next morning. It was a pleasant way to wake up.

He showered, got dressed, and had a bowl of cereal in the kitchen. The Space Systems building was a comfortable place, and they'd spared no amenity, but it still felt like a hotel. It was something he couldn't fully enjoy without his wife. Julie was back in Chicago, and he was missing out on a visit from his daughter and grandchildren.

He took the elevator down to the seventh floor, approached a man behind the reception desk, and told him his name.

The man examined his badge, and then pointed to Jonathan's right and said, "713."

Jonathan walked past the desk and down a carpeted hallway until he reached two doors at the very end. Room 713 was on the right. A number pad next to the handle had a small inset light illuminated red. He knocked.

Ten seconds later the door opened and a man he recognized as

James Thackett, the CIA Director, ushered him in and closed the door.

"Glad you're here, Jonathan," Thackett said and extended his hand.

Jonathan shook it. "Happy to help."

The room was enormous. The far wall, opposite the entrance, was composed entirely of windows, from the tiled floor to the high ceiling. To the left, nearest the entrance, was a wooden conference table and chairs. In opposite corners of the flat, abutting the wall of windows, were two open offices. At the far end of the room, to the right of the entrance, was a collection of leather furniture and a coffee table atop an area rug. A little further to the right, on the far wall, was a kitchenette with a stove, sink, and refrigerator. The room seemed to cover half of the seventh floor.

Daniel walked out of the office nearest the kitchenette. "Jonathan," he said and smiled. "How did you sleep?"

"Well," Jonathan replied. "It's a beautiful place."

"It's the most secure open facility we have," Thackett replied.

"Open?" Jonathan said.

"It means not fortified, or buried," Daniel explained.

"Those places are too inconvenient, and draw attention," Thackett added, and then motioned to the leather furniture. "Coffee?"

Jonathan sat on a couch, facing away from the windows, and Daniel and Thackett took chairs on the opposite side of the coffee table, Daniel to his left and Thackett to his right. At the center of the table was a stack of white porcelain coffee mugs, along with a silver carafe, spoons, and sugar and cream.

Thackett turned over three mugs, filled them, and slid one over to Jonathan.

Jonathan stirred in some cream and waited as the others got situated. "Where's Sylvia?" he asked.

"She went to pick up Denise from the airport," Daniel replied. "They should be here any minute."

Jonathan knew Denise was anxious to get to work, but she was even more eager to see someone in particular. "Where's Will?" he asked.

"In the building," Thackett replied.

"Is he coming here?"

"Eventually."

"Today?"

"He doesn't know that you and Ms. Walker are arriving today," Thackett explained.

"Why?"

"We didn't want any distractions," Thackett said.

"What's he doing?" Jonathan asked.

"We'll let him explain when you see him," Thackett responded.

"Is he okay?"

Thackett nodded. "He's fine. It's not a secret that we're keeping from you – it's just that he might be able to explain it better."

Jonathan smiled. He was intrigued. Will was capable of many things that were difficult to explain.

Daniel took a few minutes to describe the work they'd been doing since returning from their adventure in the Southern Seas. This mostly amounted to examining and organizing the things they'd brought back from the base. The majority of the cargo was books and files, but there were also a few strange objects of unknown function that they needed to study. Although they hadn't yet been turned over to CIA engineers, they soon would be.

A beeping noise came from Jonathan's right, in the direction of the entrance.

Denise and Sylvia entered and Thackett walked over and greeted them.

"Good flight?" Jonathan asked as they approached the seating area.

"It was early," Denise replied. "Is that coffee?"

Denise sat to the right of Jonathan, on the couch, and Sylvia to her right. When they were settled, Thackett spoke.

"Will agreed to work with us only if you did as well," Thackett explained to Jonathan and Denise. "Your knowledge of Red Wraith and your investigative talents are much-welcomed help."

"Something happening?" Denise asked.

Thackett nodded to Daniel to take the question.

"Two things," Daniel replied. "First, we've learned that Horace had a place in DC where he worked for decades. We're not sure exactly what's there, but it likely contains an abundance of sensitive information. Having classified information off-site, except under extraordinary circumstances, is something we no longer allow."

"Is the place secure?" Jonathan asked.

"Absolutely," Thackett replied.

"Then what's the problem?" Denise asked.

"When Horace passed away, he arranged for his nephew to gain access to the facility," Daniel explained. "He also gave him some crucial information. His nephew already knows about Red Wraith, and is inquiring about all sorts of related things."

"Why not just bring him in?" Jonathan asked. "And then collect everything from the facility?"

"It would be a tricky operation to get into the building," Thackett said. "It's like a vault, and designed with numerous countermeasures to infiltration. Attempting a break-in might destroy the entire building and all of its contents."

"Why would Horace do this?" Jonathan asked.

"There may have been a good reason," Daniel replied. "His nephew, Jacob Hale, is a talented engineer specializing in signal analysis and encryption."

Jonathan nodded. "The incoming signal."

"Precisely," Daniel replied.

"And what's the second thing that's happening?" Denise asked.

Sylvia took over. "Will has made a request," she said. "A big one." She hesitated and glanced at Thackett who nodded for her to continue. She looked to Jonathan and Denise. "He wants to go to the base."

THE MEETING BROKE after Jonathan and Denise were brought up to speed.

Daniel went to his office and chewed some chalky antacid tablets, and followed them with a slug of tepid tea that was on his desk from the night before. With his eating and coffee consumption habits, he wondered how his stomach didn't dissolve away. He went back to the main room, refilled his coffee cup, and sat on the couch across from Thackett who wanted to talk in private.

"Our visitor at 17 Swann is asking more questions," Thackett began. "He's requested info about the beacon and the White Stone."

"He's certainly digging for the right things," Daniel said. He was relieved that the information wasn't particularly sensitive. If it were released to the general public, no one could do anything with it. Most people wouldn't even believe it.

"There's more," Thackett said, as his expression turned more serious. "He's asked about 'W.T.'"

Daniel knew exactly what that meant. It was a security breach worthy of vomiting, and his stomach responded by sending up a chalky belch. "That's not good," he said. He wanted to say more, but it would have involved cursing.

"I didn't want to alarm Jonathan and Denise," Thackett explained.

It was unnerving that Jacob Hale had any knowledge of William Thompson, even if only his initials. "What are you going to do?" Daniel asked.

"We're certainly not giving him anything on Thompson. And nothing yet on the beacon," Thackett replied. "We've just sent him what we have on the White Stone – he's asked multiple times. He should be getting that information soon."

"With the translation of the script?" Daniel asked.

"Yes," Thackett responded.

"Why not?" Sylvia asked as she came out of her office and took a seat on the couch next to Daniel. "We could publish the text in the *New York Times* and it wouldn't matter – too cryptic. It's obvious that Horace wanted him to work on the signal. Why don't we push him in that direction instead?"

"If that's his part in this," Thackett said, "why would Horace give him all of that other information? Why does he need to know about Red Wraith, the White Stone, and William Thompson? Why not just set him up with the signal data and let him get to work?"

Daniel shrugged. "Maybe he felt the urgency of the situation couldn't be fully appreciated without knowing the entire story."

"Or maybe he believed that Jacob Hale could contribute in other ways as well," Sylvia added.

After a few seconds of silence, Daniel said, "Maybe we should let him keep going as he has been so he can catch up with all of the background. I think he'll make a move to study the signal on his own."

Thackett agreed.

As Thackett headed for the door, Sylvia asked, "Where are Denise and Jonathan?"

"They're getting trained on document handling and clearance protocols," Thackett replied. "They'll have their permanent badges by the end of the day."

If it were someone other than Jonathan or Denise, Daniel would have viewed the move as reckless. He hadn't been allowed to set a foot in the Space Systems building – or even know it existed – until he'd undergone two months of training on surveillance and avoidance, and on the handling of sensitive materials. But it no longer mattered. There was too much on the line and time was running out. The only information that mattered was the location of William Thompson, and the new information that he produced.

After the skirmish between the Chinese and US navies weeks before, Daniel was certain China was doing everything it could to find Thompson. The DC area was already swarming with Chinese and Russian operatives. And China might be out for revenge after their last encounter with Thompson.

It made him feel less concerned about the Jacob Hale situation. Hale had information from Horace, and that which he'd requested through the email protocol. That information wasn't irrelevant, but it no longer had much of an impact on anything. When the survival of the human race was on the line, intra-human conflicts were of little importance. And, until now, that's what all secret information was about: geopolitical posturing.

The information William Thompson was producing, however, had deeper implications – even if it wasn't yet clear what they were. Perhaps that would be more apparent when they got to Antarctica.

JACOB MADE a turkey and rye sandwich for lunch and sat down at the counter. He went over what he'd learned that morning as he ate.

He was disappointed in the latest document delivery. First, he got nothing regarding his questions about "W. T." or the beacon. Next, while the translations of the White Stone inscriptions were interesting, they were too vague to be of any use: they read like biblical verses and could mean anything. The one exception was a passage describing the location of something in the Antarctic seabed, which was curious since that's where Cook had heard the sound in the water. He needed more information.

He finished his sandwich, grabbed Theo's monograph, and went to the dome.

After two hours – and now about two-thirds of his way through the book – he thought he'd pieced together the skeleton of the story. There were actually two stories: *The Israel Thread* laid out in print, and the one in green ink, handwritten by his uncle a half-century later. The former suggested that the Nazis were hiding a dark secret that started before the war. The latter indicated that that secret had carried through to the present day. The former was Red Falcon, the latter, Red Wraith. And it was all connected, from the distant past to the present. Everything centered on Antarctica.

He had to give his eyes a rest.

He walked down to the kitchen, grabbed a package of chocolate chip cookies out of a cabinet, and turned on BBC News to watch as he ate. The first story was an update on the skirmish between the Chinese and American navies in the Southern Seas. The Chinese had towed away one of their aircraft carriers weeks ago, but were now trying to locate two sunken submarines. Neither could be retrieved due to the depth. They'd left only a few functioning ships in the area. The Americans, however, left an entire carrier task force in place in the Weddell Sea. Originally there had been two US carrier groups in the area, but one left weeks ago. Jacob wondered if his uncle had been with the one that left.

The news anchor went through a list of stories that seemed to be of no relevance until she came to the Russian satellite story. A British scientist from the University of Leeds claimed that the offending signal couldn't be coming from a satellite. It was some kind of encoded message from another source – and he claimed there were multiple origins. He explained that it was a straightforward task to determine that it wasn't coming from a satellite, and didn't understand why the government was making up a story to refute what was elementary science. He then suggested that it was connected to a wide-band signal anomaly that had occurred weeks earlier, originating at the South Pole.

Jacob twitched. Anything in the news that referred to Antarctica made the hair on his neck bristle. The radio disturbance from the South Pole had been mentioned before, but that signal had subsided and the AM disturbance from the satellite had not. The latter therefore got the most attention.

In the science segment that followed, a physicist from Caltech bickered with a panel of experts about NASA funding, and the funding of LIGO – for the gravitational-wave detection facilities. One man argued that it was a zero-sum game, and that all other science would be underfunded if all of the money went to those programs. A woman on the panel accused the Caltech physicist, who was one of the LIGO directors, of being stingy with releasing data collected at the facility. She argued that it was a public facility, and that the public should have access to all data, not just those published in scientific journals. Jacob agreed.

He put the cookies back in the cupboard, turned off the TV, grabbed a soda, and went back to the dome.

The sky above had turned gray, and a light rain pitter-pattered on the skylight. He turned the knob of a dimmer switch to brighten the inset lighting that encircled the dome, and then leaned back on the couch with the monograph.

Two hours of reading seemed to pass in an instant. He was finally getting some answers. The monograph described the unverified Nazi discovery of an object protruding from the ocean floor near the Antarctic continent. The Nazis had referred to it as "the beacon" – it made a repetitive noise, consistent with Cook's account, seemingly designed to attract something to it. Uncle Theo later called it a *probe*. The word "probe" had a more ominous feel – as if it were actively searching for something.

Jacob read the green handwritten notes in the margin. Dated just weeks earlier, Theo had written that an American sub had located the probe.

"My God! They found it?" Jacob gasped for no one else to hear. He sat up straight and leaned forward, the book in his hands. He had to force his eyes to focus as he read further.

They had disturbed the probe, and it had responded. From a great depth, it had risen to the surface and continued until it reached a height of more than a mile above the water. It then broadcast a powerful electromagnetic signal for over eight hours. Afterward, it retracted beneath the waves and disappeared into the seabed – more than 4,000 meters below the surface.

"What the fuck?" Jacob blurted.

His outburst startled him, but it was an uncontrollable reaction. His mind whirred with implications that seemed absurd, but recurred in his mind the instant he tried to dismiss them. He never would have believed it if he'd only read it, but he'd heard about the electromagnetic broadcast from the Antarctic region multiple times on the news. It was verification that something had happened, and it matched the time period when Uncle Theo had written it.

Jacob's view of the world changed in an instant. It wasn't that his uncle had led a secret life embroiled in espionage and clandestine operations. It wasn't that a professional killer was pursuing him to collect Theo's monograph. It wasn't even that his life had been turned upside down with the loss of his job, apartment, girlfriend, and financial independence.

Jacob realized that the probe, if it really existed, could not have been made by humans. And, if true, then perhaps everything else was true as well – maybe separation of soul and body was also possible. Maybe the two were connected.

He now felt the full weight of the "existential implications" his uncle had expressed to him. And he was beginning to understand Theo's tactics for getting him involved. If Theo had tried to explain it to him directly, rather than letting him discover it himself, Jacob would've concluded that the centenarian's sharp mind was finally starting to succumb to time. Theo would have failed to recruit him when Jacob was precisely the right person to put on the task.

Perhaps it was time for him to put his talents to work.

"He wants what?" Daniel asked as he prepared his 3:00 p.m. tea. Thackett was already sitting in one of the chairs so Daniel sat across from him, on the couch.

"Signal detection and analysis equipment, and a laptop computer with interfacing capabilities," Thackett said and handed him a printout of the list of items.

Daniel looked it over. The list included prices and vendors. "That's about $100,000-worth of instrumentation." He'd assumed that Hale would eventually catch on and start working on the signal, but he thought he'd analyze recorded data rather than detect it himself. He also figured they'd bring him into Space Systems at this stage, and that he'd assimilate into the CIA system and protocol.

Sylvia came out of her office and sat next to Daniel, on the couch. "Looks like we won't have to nudge him toward the signal after all," she said. "What are you going to do?"

"We'll talk to some of our experts about getting him the equipment and whatever else he needs," Thackett said. "That he's already figured out that the radio signal is important gives me confidence in him."

Daniel agreed.

"And what are we going to do about Will?" Sylvia asked.

Daniel knew the underlying question was whether they were going to go back to Antarctica – back to the Nazi base. As he saw it, there were two lines of research that could be explored simultaneously: the base, and the signal. He was less confident that they'd find anything useful at the base, but Will felt differently.

They'd only been at the base for a few days the first time – just enough to figure out what was going on there. But Will had never been there.

It wasn't a pretty sight; a large part of the facility had been designed to carry out the hideous research of the infamous Josef Mengele. It was well known that the Nazi doctor had carried out horrific medical experiments on concentration camp prisoners. What wasn't known until recently, however, was what else he'd carried out during the war, and for over a decade after it had ended. The Antarctic base was the ideal location for Mengele to carry out his every twisted whim. Other than providing complete isolation, it contained an elaborate torture facility, the design of which followed the Nazi method of operation: efficient and merciless. What was still a mystery, however, was how Mengele had acquired new subjects for their experiments after the war, and how they'd been transported to the base.

The base had been the centerpiece of the Red Falcon project. What Daniel and his team found there provided them with the information they'd needed to access the interior of the probe or, more precisely, for Will to access it. Whether entering and activating it was a mistake, only the future would reveal, but they were now in an irreversible situation. But he doubted now that there'd be anything at the base that would help them figure out what would happen next, now that the probe had presumably served its purpose.

There was a library at the base that was filled with books mostly related to deciphering the inscriptions on the White Stone. Those inscriptions had given instructions on how to access the probe, and some obscure forewarnings of future events. There was also a vault at the base that still contained artifacts, and a vast collection of files, most of which were descriptions of torture victims and experimental reports. Again, these were only relevant to accessing the probe, and not to understanding what would come next.

"The *North Dakota* is still undergoing repairs," Thackett explained. "It will take a few more weeks."

Daniel knew that the EM blast from the probe had caused substantial damage to the electronics in the sub. It had limped back to the Naval Submarine Base New London, in Groton, Connecticut, where a technical team from General Dynamics, the contractor that had constructed it, was currently conducting repairs. The plan was to also make some upgrades, including additional external cameras and enhanced sonar systems. The *Little North Dakota*, the remote-controlled deep-sea sub that was lost in the Weddell Sea, was also to be replaced by the advanced *Nodak Mini*, which had a position compensation system that automatically adjusted for currents, and had a homing device for recovery in case something went wrong.

"Afterwards, the *North Dakota* will deploy with the original crew, and will rendezvous with the *Stennis* off the coast of Argentina," Thackett said. "That's where you will board."

Daniel felt dizzy. The idea of being in a submarine had mortified him before his first trip, and he hadn't been looking forward to another adventure so soon. But he did trust the *North Dakota* and its crew.

Sylvia pulled off her glasses and rubbed her eyes. Some of her hair fell from behind her ear to her cheek and she brushed it back with her hand. "Is there an objective?"

Thackett shrugged. "Will says he needs to see the place firsthand. It's because of Horace."

Daniel recalled the meeting between Will and Horace the night Horace had died. He'd told Will that he'd find answers at the base – answers to some cryptic questions that pertained to Will explicitly, and to the situation in general.

"Save the signal – which may contain useful information once it's decoded – we're stewing in redundant information," Thackett argued. "At least there's a chance of finding something new at the base."

It was a good point. Besides, at this point, Will was dictating their plans. He was an untapped source of information. Taking him to the base might be just what was needed to crack open the tap.

"Does Will know?" Daniel asked.

Thackett shook his head. "He's not going to like the delays. I suppose we should fill him in. I'll bring him down here," he said as he pulled out his phone and dialed.

Daniel heard the call go to voicemail. Thackett grimaced, left a message, and hung up. "I'm not used to people not taking my calls."

"Don't take it personally," Daniel said, grinning. "I don't think he likes any of us."

"He just doesn't trust us yet," Sylvia said.

"I guess I don't blame him," Thackett added.

"He'll come around," Daniel said. "We're all on the same side now."

Thackett nodded and put his phone in his pocket. "I'll take a walk up to his room."

Thackett left, and Daniel went back to his office and sent an email to CIA specialists working on the signal to inquire about the electronics Jacob Hale had requested.

He had a hard time imagining what signal analysis and decryption would tell them. Suppose the signal were intended for someone else – instructing them to exterminate Earth of the infestation that was humanity. What good would it do us to know about it? We couldn't stop anything. We have become stagnant in our development – both technologically and socially – and have even gone backwards with many things. Although we have made significant advances in communications and computers, and some progress in medical technologies, anyone around to witness the moon landings in the sixties and seventies had to be disappointed with where we were now. By this time, we were supposed to be inhabiting Mars and exploring the vast unknown beyond our solar system, beyond humanity. Instead, we were trying to keep our economies afloat and feed everyone. And we were still killing each other.

Perhaps the entity in the probe – the Judge – had done the right thing by condemning us.

DENISE KNOCKED on the door and waited. Her heart seemed to rattle in her chest, making her breathing shaky and shallow.

The lock clicked. The door opened and he stood there, facing her. His eyes widened in what seemed to be surprise and confusion.

She stared at him, unable to speak.

Will leapt toward her, lifted her off the ground, and hugged her. He nearly squeezed the breath out of her before letting her go.

"I had no warning you were coming," he said.

She followed him into the apartment and he closed the door behind her.

The instant he turned around she grasped his neck with both hands and kissed him. She didn't know what had come over her. She pressed her cheek against his. "I don't like being away from you anymore," she said.

He hugged her again, more gently this time but still lifting her off the floor. He put her down and grabbed her hand. "I'm glad you're here."

She looked around the room. "Nice place," she said.

It was an understatement. The room took up half the footprint of the building – the same area as the room Daniel and Sylvia were sharing as a workspace. The difference was that Will's was designed for comfort. There were clusters of furniture in various arrangements on area rugs over tiled floors. Bookcases built into the walls reached the high, coffered ceiling in what looked to be a study, and the modern kitchen looked like something she'd seen in a magazine on the flight to DC. She only imagined what the bedroom looked like. "Looks like they're giving you the VIP treatment."

"Overkill," Will said and shrugged. "Under different circumstances, I might enjoy it."

"We'll only be here a few weeks, right?"

"What do you mean?"

"Aren't we going to the base?"

"How do you know that?" he asked.

She explained how she'd arrived that morning, and that she and Jonathan had been updated.

Will nodded. "I'm not sure I've convinced them yet."

"Doesn't seem they have much choice."

Will stared back at her, seemingly confused.

"Looks like you're running the show," she added.

He shook his head. "I haven't made any demands."

She followed him to a wall of windows that overlooked a pine forest far below. She stood beside him as he stared out.

"Horace is the one that suggested we go back to the base," Will said. "I think it's important."

"Your safety is important, too."

He huffed. "Is there really much danger in going there? The waters are secured, the tunnel is well mapped, and the base itself is deserted."

"And what about your efforts here?"

"What? Trying to remember things?" he asked. "I can do that anywhere."

She tried to imagine what it might be like having memories implanted in her mind that weren't hers, and somehow knowing things that she'd never learned. "What could be at the base that will help us?" she asked.

Will shook his head. "I'm not sure," he said. "But much of the base still needs to be explored. I wish Horace had given me more information."

"Where did he get the info?"

His eyes seemed to glass over as if an unpleasant memory had surfaced in his mind. "He got it from someone that only I knew," he replied. "All I know is that we need to go there."

"You've convinced me," she said and shrugged. "I'm ready to go now."

"You're going?" Will said in a tone that wasn't as much a question as it was a resigned statement.

"Of course," she replied, smiling.

He looked at her and shook his head as he repeated her words. "Of course."

"I've been aboard the sub before," she said. "Besides, you just said there was no place safer."

"Quit assuming I mean what I say." He smiled and kissed her.

A doorbell chimed.

At first Will looked confused, but then shrugged. "I guess there's a doorbell."

He walked to the entrance and let Thackett inside.

Denise met the two men in the foyer.

Thackett glanced at her, and then to Will. "I hope I wasn't interrupting anything."

"Not at all," Will said.

"If you'd answer your phone …" Thackett said.

Will patted his right, front pants pocket, and then the other. "Must be in the bedroom, my apologies."

Thackett's expression softened.

"I'm glad you came up," Will said. "Are we heading south?"

Thackett glanced at Denise and then back to Will and nodded. "The *North Dakota* is still undergoing repairs. However, the Gold Crew has already been informed that their 200-day hiatus will be interrupted. We got no complaints."

"I hope you're not interpreting my request to go to the base as a demand of any kind," Will said. "I don't want to put anyone in danger, I just thought that it might be the best use – "

Thackett put up his hand and shook his head. "No," he said. "You've made a convincing argument. There's no logical reason not to go. Other than your safety, that is."

"Am I really safer here?" Will asked. "Seems I'd be easier to find here than in a sub."

Thackett shrugged. "Pros and cons of each, I suppose," he said. "In the meantime, you might consider going through the things we've already retrieved from the base. Might get your mind working."

Will agreed, and then saw Thackett out.

"Where do they keep the stuff from the base?" Denise asked.

"I'll show you later," he replied and motioned back inside. "We have some catching up to do."

Lenny popped the top on a canned espresso drink and grimaced as he took a sip of the bitter concoction. He then downed half the can and set it in a cup holder in the armrest of the SUV.

He'd been on watch since late morning, and the clock now read 9:35 p.m. He didn't know how much longer he'd be able to wait this evening. Stakeouts were always hell, but they were even worse when done alone. And he'd been sitting too long: if he had to get out and run he'd only be able to hobble. His short races with the distance runner who jumped walls told him that it was a young man's game. He was getting too old for this.

Using his laptop computer, Lenny adjusted the settings on the camera that was mounted to the driver's side mirror. It was trained on the gate to the Space Systems building, and was good enough to resolve license plates and faces from two hundred yards in poor lighting. It had a night vision option, but that made the video too fuzzy. Around 7:00 p.m. a blitzkrieg of cars had left the building, but it then calmed down to a trickle and remained that way for hours.

Whenever he had a few minutes of calm, buried thoughts would surface in his mind. They were always there, looking for cracks. His attempts at distraction were like slapping wet mud on holes in a seawall in rough weather.

There was much regret. But there was a more disturbing worry that came with the realization that he might one day have to answer for his life. How had he become what he was? He remembered a specific sunny day on a rocky beach one summer when he was ten years old. His mother had told him that he could be whatever he wanted to be – even if he had to leave the country to do it. He should have left then.

On top of everything else, he'd been having nightmares about Jody Dixon, the Boston lawyer whose head he'd crushed beneath his feet. In his dream, he'd relive the scene. But this time, when he'd come across her driver's license while rifling through her purse, it would be his daughter's face he'd see. And then he'd look down, under the desk where he'd shoved the body, and Misha would be staring back at him, only her face was distorted, and her eyes dead. It stuck with him through the day.

He'd always convinced himself that he'd been born to do what he was doing because he was good at it. He was unique. But that, he realized now, was false. Killing did not take much skill. It took *will*. He got a lot of money to kill people because he was willing to do it. And that said something about him – something that would be used to condemn him in the end. His soul, if he had one, was as dark as night.

The best that could happen to him when his life was over would be to pass into nonexistence, to bypass what he really deserved. He believed that those who were executed for heinous crimes circumvented what they deserved. They avoided the humiliating and painful process of aging, both physically and mentally. They avoided seeing their loved ones pass away, one by one. They avoided the regret that would eventually wick up through the porous surface of conscience. Lenny was experiencing all of it, and had been for a while.

He perked up and closed the valve to the dark part of his mind when a silver Honda Civic passed through the exit gate of the Space Systems building. According to his source, who had taken some time to identify the owner of the restricted plates, it was Sylvia Barnes. She lived in Alexandria, on the opposite side of Pine Park from Jacob Hale's apartment. They might even have crossed paths at some point – probably on the running track. She was alone this time, meaning that Denise Walker was still in the building, and had been since she'd arrived. Jonathan McDougal had arrived in DC the previous night, and was likely there as well. If those two were there, so was William Thompson.

Just as he was deciding whether or not to follow Sylvia Barnes, his phone chimed. It was his Syncorp handler.

The call was short. Other operatives of the Syncorp network were in the area, and had spotted Sylvia Barnes. They would continue the stakeout on the Space Systems building and update him on changes.

In the meantime, Lenny was being given another task.

Tao got a text indicating that the American asset, Lenny, had been removed from his stakeout of the Space Systems building.

He set his phone on the chair next to him and gazed over the light foot-traffic on the streets below his seventh-floor balcony. It was a few minutes to midnight on a Tuesday, and people were still on the streets, partaking in the nightlife of the upscale DC suburb. He wondered how those people maintained employment.

He took a sip of the fine rice baijiu given to him from the head of Chinese intelligence when he was chosen to take over for Cho. Tao usually preferred fine vodka, but he found that baijiu better calmed his nerves, and allowed him to think.

Now that he knew that the Space Systems facility was likely more important than Chinese intelligence had first assessed, it was best to get the American out of the area. He couldn't risk the man getting spotted, or making a mistake. It would ruin any advantage Tao now had.

What was interesting was that Chinese intelligence already had people inside the Space Systems building. Tao chuckled. They had people in every facility: Langley, NSA, the White House. Everywhere. In the case of Space Systems, however, it seemed that the Chinese moles didn't realize what was happening there. The compartmentalized security must have been pretty good. But that would all be moot with a few well-placed moles who were willing to take a few risks.

Tao took another sip of his drink and sat back. He had to be careful not to overreach. Just because Denise Walker was there didn't mean for certain that William Thompson was as well. And it didn't mean that Space Systems was anything more than a fancy holding facility. But it did give him the impetus to press his inside people to arrange for access, and to start collecting information about who was there.

Perhaps Tao would get lucky, and he could take out Thompson, and all of the important people around him. Maybe they'd all be in one place.

For the full year up to Cho's death, the man had been searching for another secret facility, the one to which Jacob Hale supposedly had access. But Tao would now put that on the back burner. He was confident that his people would eventually find the place. Of more urgent priority was the book that Hale possessed. It held one critically important piece of information that China desperately needed.

For the time being, he'd put Lenny on some less sensitive tasks. He'd be sent to collect some things that Tao's predecessor had marked as crucial. More importantly, it would get the American out of DC for a while.

Once Tao's assets inside Space Systems located Thompson, and arranged for access, the American would be called back to carry out the deed. No sense in risking a direct connection to China. Although, Tao knew, the Americans would know who was responsible.

CHAPTER 7

Jacob woke up and went straight to the dumbwaiter. It was empty.
He showered, dressed, and went to the first level to check his email on the desktop computer. There was a message.

Dr. Hale:
If you are intending to use the requested equipment to analyze the AM band radio signal, we suggest that you use the data we have collected rather than use the requested equipment to collect redundant data. Our detection equipment is much more sophisticated, and therefore the data will be of much higher quality. We have given you the raw files – nothing missing – so that you can use software to analyze them. The data include those of the outgoing signal from the beacon as well as the incoming signal (which we continue to record). The latter has been repetitive. We will notify you if any unique data are collected. We have installed signal analysis software on your computer called Wave Tempest. We know from your Ph.D. work that you are familiar with it. If there is anything else that you require, let us know.

--The Staff

JACOB SMILED. They researched his work – whoever "they" were. And he trusted that they'd give him the untouched data. He'd be able to tell anyway.

The Wave Tempest program had been his software of choice since he'd used it continuously through graduate school, and also at Interstellar Dynamics. He searched for the software on the desktop computer but couldn't find it. It was the same for the data files.

He responded to the email sent from the staff, telling them that their solution was acceptable, but that he couldn't find the software or the data.

Jacob walked up to the kitchen and made scrambled eggs, bacon, and coffee as he listened to BBC News. The scuffle between the Americans and Chinese in the Southern Seas had subsided for the moment. There was more about the AM signal, and more experts argued back and forth about its origin, who was at fault, and who was going to fix it. It made him worry how he could be successful in figuring out what was happening when every communications specialist in the world had access to the incoming signal: someone should have figured it out by now.

The subject then turned to the problems at the gravitational-wave detection facilities, and the anchor interviewed the director of the facility located in Hanford, Washington.

"The glitches we are experiencing – at both the Washington and Louisiana sites – render the facilities useless for real measurements," the woman from Hanford explained.

"What is the nature of the problem, and when did it start?" the anchor asked. It was the same man who had hosted the panel debate with the Caltech physicist about funding the facility upgrades the night before.

"Every few minutes there will be a false detection that will last over a second," the woman replied. "We cannot pinpoint the origin, although we suspect at this point that it's electrical noise of some kind."

"And when did it start?"

"Middle of June – over a month ago."

"Other scientists have mentioned that both facilities observe identical glitches," he said. "How do you know that they're not real signals?"

"They're definitely not real," she replied. "For one, the form of the glitches is not consistent with anything we'd expect from a celestial event – colliding black holes or neutron stars, for example. Second, the signal is far too strong. It's not real."

"What about the other gravitational wave detection facilities around the world?" he asked. "Have they reported anything weird?"

The woman shook her head. "The only ones capable of detecting them are currently down because they are being upgraded – as ours should be."

The anchor raised an eyebrow. "Well that's a topic of contention, isn't it? ..."

Jacob turned off the TV.

He filled his coffee mug and brought it with him to the dome. He hoped to press through the rest of *The Israel Thread*. He had to page through his notes to refresh his memory on all of the names of people, operations, and ships, but he was starting to see that those details didn't really matter. It was as if the green ink in the margins of the book boiled it down to its core, and the original print provided a high-resolution historical background.

Jacob isolated the basic facts. The Americans discovered evidence of the Nazi project at the end of World War II, and launched their own, called Red Wraith, to continue it. Unbeknownst to the Allies, the Nazis continued Red Falcon at a secret Antarctic base for more than a decade after the war. The American project continued for the rest of the century and beyond. Both had the same objective: force a human to separate their soul from their body. According to Uncle Theo, the Americans had a single success – a person with the initials "W.T." The same person had translated the White Stone inscription.

He did not understand the geopolitical interest in the Southern Seas. So what if there was a deserted Nazi base in the ice somewhere? Other than its historical significance, and satisfying a morbid curiosity, what of importance could be there?

It occurred to him that it wasn't about the base at all. Instead, it was about the probe, which was in the same general area. The base had been constructed there because of its proximity to the probe. But how was the probe connected to Red Falcon and Red Wraith?

The timing suggested that the incoming AM signal was a response to the broadcast blasted from the probe before it disappeared into the seabed. *For whom was the outgoing signal intended?* he wondered.

He needed to see both the data recorded from the initial blast from the probe and those incoming from space. From the BBC News reports he already knew that the incoming signal had information encoded in it. The governments of all technologically capable nations must have identified the signal's origin – or origins – at least roughly. It gave him an idea.

He went down to the computer and checked his email. He opened an unread message from The Staff. They'd responded to his latest email and explained that the software and files had been uploaded to his laptop.

Jacob was baffled about how they'd been able to do that.

He went to the kitchen and powered up his computer. The first thing he noticed was that he now had a wireless Internet connection. The signal was strong and password protected – the password had already been entered. On the computer's desktop were the icon for Wave Tempest 8.0 – the latest version of the software suite – and a folder labeled "Data" that contained two file folders. How they had accessed his password-protected computer he did not know, but wasn't surprised.

He then responded to their email: *Please tell me the real origin of the extraterrestrial signal sources.* Whether or not they gave him an answer, it might stir the pot for his new friends.

Jacob started up the Wave Tempest program and loaded the data from the blast broadcast from the probe. It was time to start the next phase of his work.

After a bowl of cold cereal for breakfast, Will met Jonathan and Denise at her room, and the three of them took an elevator into the bowels of the Space Systems building.

The elevator door opened, and the scents of musty concrete filled Will's nostrils. At first it reminded him of the basement of his former high school, but then memories of something much more sinister prevailed. An image of narrow, concrete corridors with caged red lights on the walls came to his mind. It was a memory that he wished wasn't his own – that of his first night in the Red Box facility.

"We're looking for room H-18," Denise said, and they started to the right after exiting the elevator.

After passing two doors in that direction, they realized they'd gone the wrong way and turned around. A half-minute later they stood at the door they were seeking.

Denise held a proximity security card up to the door handle and it responded with a beep. She opened the door and the lights inside energized and illuminated a collection of crates and boxes. The room was about the size of a three-car garage, and the cargo transported from Antarctica by the *North Dakota* filled half of it from the back. On the right was a tall rectangular table with two stools.

"I hadn't realized they'd brought so much back," Jonathan said.

"Mostly books and files," Denise said, "but some other things."

Will looked at her and raised an eyebrow. "Is it here?"

Denise's face flushed. "I don't know."

"Is what here?" Jonathan asked.

"Hitler's urn," Denise replied to Jonathan, but looked at Will as she spoke. "Is it going to be a problem?"

Will shook his head. "Nope. He's gone, remember?" He sometimes wondered if they'd ever really believed him about that – that he'd seen Hitler's soul – but it didn't matter.

"This is going to take a while," Jonathan said, nodding in the direction of the stacks.

Will agreed. He just hoped something might jar his memory as they pilfered through it. "Shall we get started?"

Jacob opened a file and mulled over the data from the beacon's initial blast. It contained endless columns of numbers.

Theo had written that the spherical object had risen to a mile above the surface, where it stopped and blasted a signal for several hours. The electromagnetic transmission had been so intense that it had blown out the electronics on a surfaced submarine in the vicinity.

Jacob figured that, at that elevation, source intensity, and frequency range, the signal had overcome any absorptive or reflective effects of the atmosphere. He got a chill when he realized that the signal was still traveling. Of course it was – everything broadcast since the invention of radio communication was traveling at the speed of light toward some distant entity that might detect it. The difference was that the probe's signal was stronger than anything ever broadcast from Earth, and seemed to carry a message that had a specific purpose and, possibly, a definite recipient.

He started the Wave Tempest program and began importing a data file. For an instant, his memory flashed back to graduate school. It had been a simpler time in his life. Signal analysis and encryption was an exciting field at that time with its applications in communications and computers. It had been his talents in this field that had inspired his former employer to hire him, but Jacob had expanded his skills into other areas while at Interstellar Dynamics.

After a few seconds, Wave Tempest displayed a graph of the data from an instant during the initial blast. The signal was like nothing he'd seen before. It was composed of short, broadband blasts that contained the full communications spectrum, from radio waves to sub-millimeter wavelengths. It was unusual because it spanned the full measurable wavelength range of the detection system and, based on the shape of the spectrum, exceeded it on the short wavelength end. That meant that information might be missing from those other, shorter wavelength signals. He'd ask later about the missing data, but would first analyze what he had.

The next thing he noticed, and expected, was that there was a modulation in the signal – some wavelength bands were amplitude modulated, and others were frequency modulated, just like the AM and FM bands of terrestrial radio broadcasts. Modulation was how electromagnetic waves were varied to carry information. Digital information was carried as sequences of "ones" and "zeros," which could be represented by sending a higher intensity pulse as a "one" and a lower intensity pulse as a "zero." This could be done with visible light by varying the brightness, and then carrying the modulated light through fiber-optic cables, as is done with Internet communications. The signal profile displayed on the screen before him was nothing more than that but, instead of a narrow frequency band, which would look like a spike on the screen, it was a wide, bell-curve distribution of different types of signals. Separating the data into decipherable bands was going to be a challenge.

Jacob narrowed in on a vertical slice of the bell curve, loaded new data that corresponded to that specific frequency band, and then processed the data using an operation called a Fourier transform to see how the signal behaved with time. He immediately determined that it was an amplitude-modulated transmission – like AM radio – and extracted the signal data from it. It was a long string of ones and zeros that had no meaning.

Next, he looked at a slice of the data that would appear at the upper end of the FM dial on a civilian radio, and analyzed it. Upon closer look, it was composed of frequency-modulated spikes, just like terrestrial FM radio. Jacob did a few operations on the FM data using the software and extracted another digital signal, and then compared the extracted digital message to that which he had extracted from the first slice, in the AM band. They were different.

He then used Wave Tempest to search for signals that employed a method called phase modulation, or PM, to transmit data, but found nothing.

He continued analyzing slices from other parts of the bell curve spectrum and found them all to be different. It was like tuning in a radio to different stations and getting different music; each band transmitted a different message. Jacob wondered what other experts had already extracted from this data, and whether they'd succeeded in finding a key that turned all of the ones and zeros into an actual message. He would put that question in an email to the staff.

The probe would blast in broadband for a period of just over four minutes followed by a ten-minute broadcast at discrete frequencies. That process repeated for several hours. He pulled up the signals transmitted between the broadband blasts and, instead of a broad bell-type curve, his screen was filled with spikes. They were discrete wavelengths – narrow bands – as one might imagine when tuning in a radio when only a few stations were available. He analyzed one spike and determined that, as he'd suspected, it carried a digital signal. He repeated the process for the other spikes and found they also carried information, except the extracted digital data were all different – each spike was unique. There were also some technically odd things about the signals that he'd have to figure out – but that would be the easy part. There were other things to worry about.

What were they going to do with the sequences of ones and zeros once they were extracted from the signal? Just like emails and other data transmissions over the Internet, this data was probably encrypted, and the only hope of deciphering it was to have the encryption key. Jacob was an expert in encryption and he knew that there were nearly unbreakable encryption techniques. From what he'd seen regarding the advanced technology required to produce the signal, it was likely that the encryption would be just as advanced.

He stood from the table and climbed the stairs to the bathroom. The time had passed just like it used to in grad school. He'd been working on the signal data for more than four hours. He relieved himself, and then walked to the kitchen and grabbed a soda from the fridge. He flipped on the television and watched BBC News. They cycled through the same stories and came to the AM radio disturbance. It was a replay of an earlier interview so he changed the channel to CNN.

CNN had a panel of so-called experts discussing the origin of the AM signal. One member of the panel was a physicist from Stanford University who accused a NASA scientist of misleading the public on the source of the disturbance. A verbal melee ensued as two of the four panelists labeled the others as conspiracy theorists, and the other pair accused the opposing two of being part of the conspiracy. Jacob learned only one thing from the discussion: the signal was becoming a controversy of magnitude that would soon have to be addressed by politicians.

He turned on the oven and pulled a frozen pizza out of the freezer and unwrapped it. He put it onto a pizza sheet, slid it into the oven, and set the timer. He sipped soda as he paced through the kitchen and thought to himself.

There wasn't much else he could do with the signals other than convert everything to the digital data that they carried. He was sure every other communications expert had already done the same. With even moderate knowledge of data compression anyone could get to the base data, which, even though it was transmitted at many frequencies, was not an overwhelming amount of information by today's standards. If the data were text, it would probably take up a few thousands of pages. If there were images, it could be much shorter. Still, the big problem was that it was probably encrypted, which meant they might never access the underlying information. If the outgoing signal were intended for somewhere other than Earth, the encryption might be unbreakable. There was the possibility, however, that the incoming signal had been designed for us to decipher.

The oven timer chimed and Jacob pulled out the pizza and cut it. He put a few slices on a plate and went up to the dome with *The Israel Thread*. He hoped he'd eventually find a point to it all – a final destination.

Will's stomach grumbled as he lifted a large wooden crate and set it on the table. They'd been at it for almost four hours.

The crates were packed with various objects that ranged from keys and electrical components to artifacts such as engravings and small statues. One was identified as Adolf Hitler's urn, filled with ashes that had traveled to Antarctica via Rome, and then to the United States by submarine and surface ship. Many of the objects had been collected from the vault room in the Nazi base, but others were found in some of its countless rooms and side chambers.

The cardboard boxes contained musty books and files from the library, as well as some engineering drawings of the base, collected from an office near its electrical control room.

Will removed the screws from the topside of the crate with an electric drill, and leaned the lid against the wall. The items inside were wrapped in brown paper, and packed in the crate so that they were stable. The packing method varied from crate to crate. More fragile things were sealed in plastic bags and form-fitted in layers of hardening spray-in foam.

Denise reached in and removed some of the loose paper between the objects. "This is crate number six?" she asked as she wrote in a notebook.

"Yes," Will replied as he snapped a picture of the open crate with his phone. "Only about 25 more to go." It was going to take days to catalog everything.

Sylvia had joined them an hour after they'd started, and she and Jonathan worked on the contents of the cardboard boxes, sorting through files and books.

Will reached in and extracted a rectangular object from the crate. It was about the size of a quart of milk and weighed about two pounds. He removed the packing paper to reveal a wooden box. Two pieces of clear tape ensured that the fitted lid would not separate from the box during the move. He scratched at the edge of the tape with his fingernail until a corner peeled up, and worked off the entire piece without tearing it. He repeated the process for the tape on the opposite side and removed the tight-fitting lid.

The box contained a large vacuum tube inset in a felt mold. Will was always amazed by the intricacy of this old technology – an elaborate structure of plates, grids, coils, and wires intermingled with white ceramic insulators, all encased in a glass bulb. Just as with a light bulb, the interior had to be evacuated of all air to ensure that hot filaments would not burn and electrons could pass through the volume without colliding with gas molecules.

"What is it?" Denise asked, admiring it like a piece of art.

"It's a pentode vacuum tube," he replied.

She stared back at him blankly.

"It's old technology," he added and chuckled. "Nothing alien about it."

"Quit laughing. I'm a lawyer, not a scientist," she said.

He put the lid back on the box, replaced the tape, and attached an adhesive tag. He wrote C6-1, for "Crate 6, Item 1."

"What is it again?" Denise asked as she wrote the label identification and description in a notebook.

"Pentode vacuum tube," he repeated. "Vintage, analog technology."

She nodded and then typed it into a spreadsheet on her laptop.

Will reached in and extracted the next item and unwrapped it. This one was a flat, hinged box that was heavier than it looked. He peeled off two pieces of clear tape that safeguarded the lid for the move, released a latch, and opened it to reveal a square slab of gray metal pressed into a felt mold. He pried it out of the depression with his gloved fingertips and set it in the palm of his hand.

The object was about two-by-two inches square, and a little over a quarter-inch thick. All of its corners and edges were smooth, except one corner was chamfered so that the object could be oriented. It was probably supposed to fit into some device, and the chamfered corner was to make sure it was positioned the same way each time.

"What is that?" Denise asked.

Will turned it over multiple times, held it up to the light, and examined all of its edges. Other than the chamfered corner, there were no markings of any kind. "I have no idea," he finally said. "I think it's made of tungsten, or a tungsten alloy, but I'm not sure."

Tungsten was an extremely hard, gray metal, and it had a density close to that of gold, so it was extremely heavy. Other than lead, few common materials were that dense. Something suddenly came to his mind. "We should get this checked for radioactivity," he said.

Denise's eyes widened as she glanced between the object and Will.

"Everything was checked for radioactivity and explosives before it was loaded on the *North Dakota*," Sylvia said from the back of the room. "Who knows what the Germans had in that place – and we know they had their own nuclear bomb program."

Plutonium and uranium both had densities close to that of tungsten. Although the appearance of gold was distinctive, and he knew that tungsten was a dull gray color, he did not know what plutonium and uranium looked like – especially after a long period of time when their surfaces would have oxidized. But Sylvia put his concerns to rest.

He put it back in its holder, and then closed the lid of the container and latched it. He then replaced the tape, stuck a label on the top, and wrote "C6-2" on it.

"What do I call this thing?" Denise asked.

"Just write, two-by-two-inch square tungsten slab with flat on corner," Will answered.

"That's just a description."

"That's all we have," he replied. "You can add, 'In small wooden box.'"

Denise shrugged and wrote it down in the book, and then typed it on her laptop.

Sylvia walked out from the back of the room. "Time for lunch," she said and pointed to her phone. "Just got a text from Daniel – food's ready for a working lunch. He and Director Thackett are in 713."

Will was famished. Although the Space Systems building had a food service, it did not have a cafeteria. Every effort was made to make sure the employees did not interact with each other, or even see each other unless absolutely necessary.

He peeled off his latex gloves and set them on the table. The others did the same, and they all headed for the elevator.

JACOB SPENT most of the day analyzing the outgoing electromagnetic blast from the probe. Although he hadn't had any luck decoding it, he was able to extract digital data. He knew, however, that it was useless without knowing how to decode it.

A peculiar detail had emerged, which seemed to be a weak ghost of the outgoing signal. It was identical to, but much weaker than, the original broadcast, and was delayed by about 18 minutes. He was able to separate the ghost from the original, but was unable to explain why it had occurred. He'd pose that question to the staff in his next correspondence.

He ate a TV dinner of Salisbury steak, mashed potatoes, and gravy while watching the evening news. After downing the peach cobbler dessert, he brewed a pot of coffee and turned his attention to the incoming radio waves – the supposed response signal – impinging upon Earth from multiple directions. Word had gotten out that there were multiple sources – there had to be since the signal was simultaneously detected on opposite sides of the planet – but that was explained away as the Russians' fault again: the rogue satellite controlled a network of others, causing them all to emit the offending broadcast. The Russians denied it.

Based on data collected from different parts of the world, there were seven sources, one of which was stronger than the others by a factor of 10 – and presumably came from the closest source. After a full day of work, he'd noticed four things. One, the incoming signals were longer in duration than the outgoing broadcast from the probe, but were much less complex. Two, they all carried encoded digital information. Three, the six weaker incoming signals carried identical messages to the strongest one, but were out of sync with each other by as much as two hours. Finally, the six weaker signals were all shifted by different amounts to slightly higher or lower frequencies relative to the strongest one.

What he really wanted to know was the locations of the sources of the signals – or at least the directions from which they came, and whether or not those directions were changing. It should have been an easy task to accomplish by the military, or by NASA, but they hadn't gone public with anything. The news reports changed continuously to accommodate the evolution of factual details about the signals. Jacob knew that it was all bullshit, and even the BBC reporter who presented one such evolving story questioned the government's explanation.

Suspicion and anxiety formed in Jacob's mind. Someone knew something and was keeping it from the public, and from him.

He went to the computer and wrote an email to his keepers. *Why are the news networks reporting false information? What is the origin of the strongest incoming signal? What are the origins/directions of the other incoming signals? Why is there a ghost signal in the outgoing broadcast from the beacon with an 18-minute delay?*

He finished with a request for supplies and sent the email.

He swiveled the chair around, leaned back, and gazed at the three stories of bookshelves that covered the opposite wall. It was a library filled with rare books that contained more secrets than he'd ever have time to discover. He inhaled deeply and held it in for a few seconds before he blew it out. The air in the facility was clean except for the subtle mustiness of old books and a hint of cherry pipe tobacco that reminded him of Uncle Theo.

He looked up to the nearest dome, the one above the first-floor table, which was now dimming to a deep purple as the sun descended below the trees to the west of Swann Street. He wanted to go outside and take a walk, but hesitated. His pursuer might still be lurking about.

He climbed the stairs and retrieved the pistol from the bedroom. He donned a light jacket and a baseball cap, and took the elevator to the foyer. He pressed the exit button and the door released. He pushed it open just far enough to peek out into the alley. Sparse patches of fading sunlight warmed the featureless red brick wall of the adjacent building. He was sure that the lack of doors and windows was intended somehow, and he wondered if the same entity that owned his building also controlled the other.

He glanced to the left, toward the dead end that terminated in a brick wall, and then to the right, toward the street. The swaying shadows of trees tricked his eyes for a moment until a car passed and gave him a reference for distance. If the man were waiting for him, he'd better be ready for another chase, and a fight. Jacob wasn't bad with a pistol after all of the target practice he'd had growing up with his uncle and cousins. And, if the man came for him again, he wouldn't hesitate to shoot first. Something changed in a person once they'd experienced someone trying to kill them. It was strange: something that should have made him more fearful had instead emboldened him.

He stepped out and onto the stoop, made sure he had his keys – he couldn't even imagine the disaster it would be if he accidentally locked them inside – and gently pushed the door until the automatic closing mechanism took over. He walked to the street and turned right, toward the flower shop.

The streetlights glowed in the dusk. A light breeze rustled the branches of a line of spruce trees, carrying a scent that reminded him of better times. One of those memories was camping with Paulina. He wondered how she was doing – what she was doing at that very moment – and wanted to be with her.

The fresh air and change of environment allowed his mind to view things from a different perspective. Looking back on what had happened during the past week, he should be suffering post-traumatic stress symptoms. The attempts on his life alone should have been enough, but the loss of his job and savings on top of everything else should have shocked him into a static existence, unable to function. Perhaps the attempt on his life hadn't yet sunk in – like a narrowly avoided car accident. It was the sort of thing that was pushed to the back of one's mind. Losing his job was easier than he'd imagined – he'd been almost grateful for it in the beginning. His relationship with Pauli was in a fragile but improving state. Her being away was a good thing for now. All he knew was that he needed to be on his own for a while to think things through.

He continued past the flower shop on his right and followed Swann Street up another two blocks. He smelled coffee for a full block before arriving at a café called the *Count Cristo Coffee House*. He climbed a short set of concrete stairs, and stopped at a large wooden door. The sign posted on it read: "Open until midnight 7 days a week." It was approaching 9:00 p.m. He went inside.

The place was larger than he'd expected, and bustling with people. He ordered coffee, grabbed a section of an abandoned *New York Times*, and found a seat at a small table near a window that faced Swann Street. He took a sip of his dark roast coffee and paged through the paper, but his attention wasn't on the news. Rather, his mind mulled over the information he'd been feeding it for the past week.

First, the whole world was scrambling to figure out what in the hell the probe had transmitted, and also what was now coming back – from where, and from *whom*. The possible implications were astonishing: there were only a few possibilities, one of which was that the signals were of extraterrestrial – nonhuman – origin. But he was skeptical of the idea. The time between the probe sending the signal and the response from deep space – about a week – indicated that it came from a distance of a small fraction of a light-year, a half of a light-week, away, since the electromagnetic signals traveled at the speed of light. The next closest star was more than four light-years away. So either we didn't understand the physics of space-time, or there were spacecraft positioned relatively close – maybe even inside our solar system. Perhaps they were just probes – hard to tell – but what if they were massive ships, and we were on the verge of an invasion?

Jacob smiled to himself.

"Something funny?" a female voice asked from his left.

Startled, Jacob looked up and met the dark brown eyes of one of the baristas. She wore a red apron and her blonde hair was tied in a short ponytail. She was mid-twenties, slim build, and reminded him immediately of Paulina.

He shrugged and smiled. "Nothing funny here," he said and nodded to the paper. "I was just thinking about something."

"I wish I were able to entertain myself like that," she jibed. "I'm Cally."

"I'm Jacob."

"Haven't seen you here before."

"Haven't been here before," he replied. "Is it always this busy?"

She nodded and collected three empty coffee mugs from an adjacent table with one hand. "Mostly college students who don't pick up after themselves. You don't look to be of college age."

"Thank you," Jacob replied. He probably looked 50 after the past two weeks.

"No, I didn't mean – "

He raised his hand to stop her and laughed. "It's okay, I'm well out of college. How about you?"

"Never went."

Even though she could have been a student, her mannerisms and language hinted at a maturity that comes from life outside academia. "You don't need a college degree to be successful," Jacob said.

"I would say this place is pretty successful," she said.

"This is your place?"

She nodded and shrugged. "Four years now."

"Impressive," he said. "Coffee is a great thing – and I like this Costa Rican dark roast."

"So I can count on your returning business?" she said and winked.

"I intend to make it a part of my daily routine."

"Good," she said. "Let me know if you need anything."

He nodded as she cleared another table, and watched her as she disappeared behind the espresso machines.

He looked around and noticed that there was another room

behind him with windows that faced the cross street. There were about 20 tables in the main room, and another 15 in the second. The place was two-thirds occupied, mostly with college students, as Cally had said, but there was a mix of others, including a few pensioners. It was a place where he could get some work done, perhaps even better than his old coffeehouse, Pine Perk. And it might come in helpful – constant background noise was sometimes better than the dead silence of 17 Swann. But he'd have to be careful if he were to make it a part of his routine. He was already feeling exposed being outside the facility, but cabin fever was stifling his progress. Thinking was a fickle thing for him: the environment had to be just right to get into deep thought.

He turned his attention back to his thoughts from before the interruption. The first signal coming in from space had arrived about a week after the outgoing transmission was sent. That meant that the origin of that signal was half of a light-week away, at most. The signal from the probe would take half of a week to get to whatever was producing the return signal, and the return signal, which was causing the interference in the AM band, would take another half-week to get to Earth. It was a small fraction of a light-year compared to the 100,000 light-year span of the Milky Way galaxy, but half of a light-week was still over 50 billion miles. The most distant, human-built spacecraft, Voyager I, was only about 12 billion miles from Earth, and it had been launched way back in 1977.

Jacob recalled a picture from an astronomy course he'd taken in college. It was an image of the Milky Way galaxy with its spiraling arms. The location of our sun is in a spur of the Orion arm. On the scale of the galaxy, our solar system is nearly indiscernible – a speck of sand on a vast beach. The earliest radio signal from Earth has traveled at most a hundred light-years, not even 1/1,000[th] of the way across the galaxy. The next closest spiral galaxy similar to the Milky Way is Andromeda, and it's 2.5 million light-years from us. The dimensions are unimaginable. That there were over 200 billion galaxies in the universe put Jacob's mind into overload. It was beyond comprehension. What it did put into perspective, however, was what a tiny fleck of nothingness was Earth and the human race. Why would anyone care about this tiny grain of life – other than those who lived here?

He glanced at his phone and noticed he had a text message: *We recommend you don't leave your Swann Street address at any time.*

Jacob huffed. What was he going to do, spend the rest of his life in solitary confinement? He walked to the coffee bar and got a refill from Cally. He glanced at a large clock on the wall near a poster of the cover of the novel, *The Count of Monte Cristo*: it was 10:30 p.m. He went back to his seat.

He took a sip of coffee and breathed its strong aroma out through his nose. He was starting to lose his appreciation for the importance of what he was doing. There were two things of which he had to continue to remind himself. One, there was a strange object in the Antarctic seas that had blasted signals into space, the likes of which were beyond human technology. And that didn't even include the device itself, which had disappeared into the seabed. And two, there were now signals coming in from deep space – although their origins still had to be confirmed. He wondered whether the Search for Extraterrestrial Intelligence, or SETI, had anything to say about what was happening. They had ongoing searches that included radio telescopes. He'd search online when he got back to 17 Swann to see if they were on to the signals.

As he took another drink of coffee and looked out the window, an alarming thought hit him so hard that his vision went to white static for an instant. Whatever was broadcasting the signal to Earth was a *maximum* of a half light-week away. But what if the entity that had detected the outgoing transmission from Earth just waited a while before sending the return signal? The sources could be sitting on Mars, or the moon, or somewhere even closer. And what was their next move?

Jacob finished his coffee, took his mug and the newspaper up to the counter, and left the Count Cristo Coffee House. His heart pounded as he walked back to 17 Swann.

As Daniel gazed out over the dark spruce trees below, he thought he saw an owl dive from the upper canopy and disappear into a thick mesh of branches. He craved the fresh air of the cool night but the windows of the Space Systems building did not open.

At 11:15 p.m. it was still early, and he and Sylvia were just catching their second winds. Neither would knock off until after 2:00 a.m. The only thing that would stop him early was a loss of focus to such a degree that sleep would be more productive. He was nearing that undesired state, but decided to switch to some other task for a while to give his brain a rest.

He grabbed the inventory list the others had compiled that cataloged the items brought back from the base. It had taken them the entire day to get through ten percent of the cache, most of which was written materials – books and files. The other things were objects that seemed to have some special meaning, such as items found in the vault room or some other out of the ordinary place. The Nazis were organized to the degree of clinical psychological disorder, and anything that had special status in terms of location or packaging deserved a close look. And there was a lot more through which to rummage still at the base.

Daniel didn't think they'd find anything groundbreaking in their original take, but it was good to get everyone doing something together that wasn't stressful. The interactions seemed to work. Sylvia had mentioned that she enjoyed working with Jonathan McDougal and, during lunch in 713, Will managed to crack a joke that made Thackett laugh. Of course, Thackett had also been the target of the joke, but it was made in a good-natured fashion. It seemed to Daniel that Will's intimidating exterior was a hard, but thin shell.

Daniel went through each of three lists, item by item. The books were all on codes, cryptography, and ancient languages. The files were mostly the medical records of torture victims, but a few were technical drawings of things like control panels, room designs, and various mechanical and electrical devices. None of it seemed to be out of the ordinary. The artifacts, however, included some odd things, including Hitler's urn. Daniel was still skeptical that it was authentic. Will believed it. Then again, Will believed he'd actually spoken with Hitler's soul. Daniel had given him the benefit of the doubt, especially with everything else he'd witnessed. But as time went on, he reverted to skepticism.

The other things they'd collected from the base included ordinary electronic components and other mechanical devices. There were a few, however, that could not be identified, and had no obvious function. Will was an experimental physicist, and should have been able to identify most common devices. However, as Will had admitted, some things might have been obsolete for such a long time that he'd never seen them before. But they piqued Daniel's interest, and he'd make a note to have CIA engineers take a look at the unidentifiable items after everything was cataloged.

He went back to his desk and read email. Two were from other independent researchers in their group, and another from Thackett, informing him that Hale had left 17 Swann and gone to a local coffeehouse.

Daniel shook his head. Hale was a risk taker.

Hale had also asked more detailed questions about the signals. In particular, he wanted to know why the government was lying about their sources and origins.

Daniel thought it was good that Hale was asking tough questions. But it was essential that he never release anything he'd learned to the public. Especially now that he had all kinds of other damaging information – like the CIA report on the Red Wraith project. That would be devastating.

Daniel retrieved the metal can that contained his good tea and scooped out a clump with a silver tea ball that he'd gotten from his mother when he'd graduated from college. Things regularly cropped up that made him realize he missed her and his father. The feeling was worse whenever he remembered that he was alone. Divorce was a bitter experience that lingered on for most people. For Daniel, it was sadness that prevailed. And he knew it was a mutual sadness.

As he walked over to the electric teapot, he nearly jumped when an image appeared in the window. He turned around in such a hurry that his neck popped like a knuckle.

"Sorry," Sylvia said. Her expression was of apology overlaid on a grin.

Daniel shook his head and sighed in relief.

"Why are you so jumpy?" she asked.

"You caught me off guard," he replied and looked at her feet. She had no shoes, just green socks. "I can see why I didn't hear you."

"I smelled tea."

"I haven't even poured the water," Daniel said and nodded to the can. "Help yourself."

Sylvia smiled and retrieved the tea container. She scooped out some tea with her own tea ball, which Daniel suspected she only used in his office.

He poured water into his cup and then filled Sylvia's. They walked out to the main room where Daniel sat in one of the two chairs and Sylvia took the left side of the couch, closest to him.

"Do you ever feel like you don't want to go home some nights?" she asked. "You know, just sleep on the couch."

"Sometimes," Daniel replied. He thought sleeping almost anywhere was better than going home to an empty house. It was even worse when he wasn't making progress at work.

"Every time I go home," she continued, "I have a feeling that what I am doing here – what I am witnessing – isn't happening."

"What do you mean?"

"I go shopping, I do my laundry, I wash the dishes, I think of my childhood days," she explained. "Then I call my parents, and we talk about everyday things in their lives, and I give them some of the benign parts of mine. But in the back of my mind, I think the parts that I am omitting aren't real. They only seem real when I'm here, in this building."

Daniel nodded. "I get that when I'm mowing my lawn, or raking leaves, or shoveling snow," he said. "I see my neighbor mowing his lawn every weekend in the summer and I know that his world is much different than mine."

Sylvia nodded. "Same for my parents."

"The rest of the world lives in the dark."

She shrugged. "Maybe they're lucky."

"We're lucky," Daniel said. "We're privy to things no one else can even fathom. Things so farfetched that anyone who would speak about them in public would be considered a crackpot. But these things will affect our entire world, and no one else will know until it happens."

"That knowledge isolates us," Sylvia said. "It makes me feel alone."

Daniel nodded but remained silent.

"I've been trying to connect my research on UFO sightings in South America to Antarctica," she said, changing the subject.

"I suppose there are many connections." The post World War II UFO reports in South America had been one of Sylvia's first projects. Daniel knew she'd thought it had been wrapped up long ago, but then came the events in Antarctica. They opened up new possibilities, and it became difficult to rule anything out, no matter how farfetched.

She shrugged. "Everything is circumstantial, of course," she said, "but there are some odd things that have come up."

"Regarding the UFO sightings?"

She shook her head. "More like objects being transported through Argentina."

"Such as?"

Sylvia shook her head. "Nothing specific. Just verbal descriptions of a few gadgets and a poor quality black-and-white photo – actually, a Xerox copy of it."

"You have it?"

Sylvia nodded, jumped off the couch, trotted to her office, and returned with a piece of paper and handed it to him.

The picture was grainy, like it had gone through multiple iterations of copying, but he could still make out the basic features of the object. It was metallic, cylindrical, and about the size of a large coffee can with a diameter of about eight inches. The scale was clear since someone's hand was grabbing it at the base. Circular patterns of bolts held flanges on the top and bottom, and the top face looked to have a small, circular port or window.

"This could be anything," Daniel said.

"I agree," she said. "But it's consistent with the stories of alien technology coming up through Argentina – some say from crashed UFOs."

"I wouldn't rule out anything at this point," Daniel said. "You have anything more than the photo?"

She nodded and grinned. "There were supposedly at least two devices, one of which was rumored to have been acquired by the United States in Argentina."

"Who has it?" Daniel asked. His nerves tingled with an excitement that he hadn't experienced in weeks.

She shrugged. "All I know is that its acquisition was ordered by Heinrich Bergman."

Daniel wrung his hands. Bergman had been the director of the Red Wraith project, and was now deceased. "Did he get it?"

She nodded. "It took a while to track the different codes and identification numbers, but it's listed in the inventory of the Red Wraith project."

Daniel took a sip of tea and set it down on the table. He rubbed his eyes with the heels of his hands. "We need to get it."

JACOB CONTINUED down Swann Street toward the facility. The sky was clear and the moon large with a reddish-yellow hue. Cool air filtered through trees and bushes that lined both sides of the empty street. A rare, overwhelming peace saturated his mind and body as he breathed and walked. It was something that occurred only when he was alone. He realized that he'd worked out a lot in his mind. It was clear that he'd needed to get away from the books and files – the details were cluttering his view and masking the severity of what he'd been learning.

The implications were *existential* – the word Theo had used.

He understood why his uncle had forced him into the effort. It had nothing to do with the will, or money. He'd done it because he believed that Jacob could help. It was clear that if rumors spread – such as the true origin of the signals – things could degrade quickly. The world might fall into chaos, and everything would break down – security, economies, and the rule of law.

The world was more fragile than most people understood. A thousand years ago, civilizations were dispersed – they were separate pockets of humanity that were mostly isolated from one another. The problems of one civilization didn't affect the others. But it was different now. Problems at one location on the planet were felt globally, and instantaneously communicated throughout the world. Advances in communication and transportation technologies had made the situation what it was. Progress had its advantages and disadvantages.

Jacob passed by 17 Swann and looked for potential stalkers before he turned back, walked up the sidewalk to the stoop, and inserted the key. He checked the mailbox – empty – and rode the elevator up to the flat.

He opened the email program on the computer. There was one unread email waiting for him from an address he didn't recognize. He opened it and read. The first sentence made the skin on his forearms pucker.

Dear Jake,

By now you have immersed yourself in the puzzle to which I have subjected you. It is now time that you learn more.

Until now, your view of the world has been based on empirical evidence, limited to the logic, physics, and mathematics developed and experienced by others. It was the same for me during my first 98 years. That changed six months before my voyage to the Nazi base as I started to make connections between seemingly unrelated occurrences from the far past to the present. My hope is that it won't take you 99 years to see the same. There is more to the world than what meets the eye.

There are things at play that you may find unbelievable. You should know about the Red Wraith project by now, and you might think it is a farce. It is not. I have met the only man who has emerged from the program with the ability to separate his soul from his body. He's the one who set all of this in motion – why the probe emitted a signal, and why we have received signals from deep space. His name is William Thompson. You and he will cross paths.

What you are working on now will be the most important thing you do in your life. Don't give up. – With love, Theo

JACOB FELT cold and hot at the same time. It was the shock of getting a message from the grave. After a few seconds, he realized that it saddened rather than frightened him. It seemed his uncle had confidence in him all along. Obviously, Theo had set up a delayed email message to be sent at what he thought would be the right time. There was no risk in sending messages to the secure address – no one else could get to the computer. The message would have arrived even if Jacob hadn't accepted his uncle's challenge.

Theo must have known that he wouldn't give up. Even when stymied by puzzles as a kid, Jacob would toil over them relentlessly until he'd solved them. They'd become obsessions. Sometimes his engineering projects in school and, later, as a professional, would challenge him. Solving such problems brought him some satisfaction since they often resulted in something useful. The project that he worked on now was already an obsession and, according to Theo, would be the most important thing he'd ever do. The knot in Jacob's gut told him that his uncle was right.

Theo's email was the only one he'd received in the past 24 hours. He was waiting on others, but now he knew the answer to at least one of the questions he'd asked: *Who is W.T.?* Now he'd ask, *Who is William Thompson?*

IT HAD BEEN two days since Lenny had arrived in Virginia Beach and checked into a hotel as close to the sand as he could get. He stood on the balcony of his sixth-floor room and lit a cigarette. The view of the lights on the boardwalk dissolving into the midnight ocean eased his mind, but his charged nerves made his hands shake.

In the old days, he'd be untraceable in the free world – in the United States, South America, and most of Europe. But not now. The world was networked to track his location anywhere on the globe, and DNA could identify him without ambiguity. Therefore, whether criminals or the authorities were pursuing him, he couldn't hide for long. If he stayed in one place, he'd eventually be found. If he kept moving, he'd eventually be tripped up at an airport, a border, or on some traffic violation. Nowadays, large metropolitan areas even had face recognition software that constantly monitored the population through cameras on the streets, public transportation, and at ATMs.

His mistake was that he'd carried on his work for too long – through the transition from the days of anonymity to the information age. He was a relic – an exposed, known, sought-after artifact of the Cold War. And now, even though he'd made plans, and had even attempted the first steps to escape his former life, he was trapped. He'd been sucked back in just as he was about to hit the beaches of Costa Rica.

But it was even worse than that. Unbeknownst to him, his services had somehow been transferred to China. But his allegiance, although somewhat fickle, had not. Lenny had worked for Bergman since the decommissioning of the Berlin Wall. Since that time, he'd been on the side of the West, and with the United States in particular. There were things he disliked about the Americans, but their governance was as close to non-oppression as he could imagine. He enjoyed the UK as well, but he'd quickly overstayed his welcome there. Other parts of the West were tolerable, but many countries still had the odor of the war in their societal fabric.

China was a threat to all of them. They had the largest undercompensated workforce in the world, and used it to build a dangerous economy. Together with industrial and military espionage, they used their economic muscle to impose a dark force upon the world. Lenny had lived through communism and believed it had no place in modern civilization. The Chinese were communists, and were now ruled by a dictator – which is what an unelected president without term limits was.

It had been a gradual change – almost undetectable at first – but he was certain now. He currently worked for communist China. But now, although it was a long shot, he might have an opportunity to make a change.

Even though he hadn't held a strong allegiance to any one country, working for the Chinese left a bad taste in his mouth. He'd rather be working with MI-6, like he'd done in the 1980s, or with the CIA, as he had with the late Heinrich Bergman. He should've retired when Bergman was killed and the Red Wraith project dissolved. But the business had a way of sucking a person back into the game.

Months ago, while he was a wounded prisoner in a hospital in St. Louis, the few remaining CIA operatives associated with the Red Wraith Project had arranged for his escape. They'd saved him from a life sentence – or execution – and he owed them for it. But he owed the Chinese nothing. They'd only taken over the project when the Americans ran away from it. It was another example of how the Chinese found shortcuts to technology that they themselves could not develop. It had been the former director of the CIA who had ordered Lenny's rescue and reactivation.

With being removed from the surveillance operation at the Space Systems building, Lenny had the feeling that his run with Chinese intelligence was coming to an end. He'd screwed up a few times, and that was all it took with them. He'd decided to lay low for a while until things cooled and they called him back. In that case, however, he wasn't sure what he would do. They might call him in to eliminate him – clean up a loose end. It was impossible to tell.

And he'd had another nightmare about his daughter: Misha's face on Jody Dixon's body. Lenny had never experienced a midlife crisis, as many people supposedly do, but it was possible that he was entering a late-life phase of remorse. His mind seemed to be changing – or at least becoming susceptible to his deeply buried conscience. He wouldn't call himself a sociopath – he had feelings in certain circumstances. He was more of an aspiring sociopath, and worked hard to suppress empathy for others. It was required for his chosen line of work.

Lenny's vacation was coming to an abrupt end. He'd already spotted two Chinese operatives tailing him around the city. He'd lost them, and would be careful not to allow them to pick up his trail again, but he was already being pursued and he didn't know their intentions. Silence from the Chinese network was exacerbating his paranoia.

He'd think about what to do next while he rested on the beach for another day, but he'd already made a major decision: he'd go back to DC and try to reconnect with his old network.

AFTER BREAKFAST, Will met with Denise, Jonathan, and Sylvia in the basement of the Space Systems building and continued cataloging the items collected from the base. It was going to take a few days to finish the task, but the work cleared Will's mind. More importantly, the company improved his mood. Last night had been the first in a long time that he hadn't had a nightmare.

Jonathan and Sylvia continued tabulating the written materials while Will and Denise worked on the artifacts and other objects. Just before 10:00 a.m., Jonathan made a coffee run and returned with a carafe and four paper cups with lids. He set everything on the table, and then pulled sugar and creamer packets out of his jacket pocket and tossed them next to the cups. He popped open the lid of the carafe and poured coffee into a cup.

"Self-serve," Jonathan said as he tore open a creamer packet and emptied it into his cup. He then reached into another jacket pocket and pulled out napkins and plastic spoons.

"You thought of everything," Sylvia remarked and walked over and poured coffee.

"How are you two doing?" Jonathan asked Will and Denise.

"Going slowly," Will replied. "It takes time to open the crates, and unpacking and repacking is tedious work. Some of the contents are fragile."

Will waived Jonathan over to a crate he'd just opened.

Will reached in and pulled out a molded cover that had originally been sprayed as foam into a plastic bag and then pressed into the top of the crate, where it had hardened in the shape of the contents. Three items were inset in a similar mold beneath it.

"Most of the crates have two or three layers," Denise added as she reached in and removed one of the items, and then extracted it from the zip-locked plastic bag that contained it. It was a clear glass vial, about the size of a saltshaker, with a white screw cap lid. Inside was a reddish-brown powder. She turned it in her hands and read the typed print on a yellowing label adhered to its side. "Marsstaub, 1947," she said.

Will, who had just started to pour coffee, turned his head back in her direction and spilled on the table. "Damn," he said and wiped the table and his hand with a napkin. "What did you say?"

Denise repeated the word. "What does it mean?"

"Mars dust," Sylvia replied as she emptied a packet of sugar into her coffee. "It's in German."

Will threw the damp napkin into a trashcan near the entrance and walked over to Denise. "Can I see?" he asked.

She handed him the vial and he read the yellowing label, which looked to be the original. The characters were typed, and the glass was thick.

"What is it?" Denise asked.

All three looked to Will for the answer.

"No idea," he said as he lifted it to the light. The powder was as fine as talc and slid over itself as he tilted the bottle. "But it can't be dust from Mars. It's probably the name they gave to some chemical."

"We've been to Mars," Sylvia said. "But we hadn't yet even been to space in 1947."

"Sputnik – our first excursion into Earth orbit – happened a decade later," Jonathan added.

"We've landed things on Mars many times," Will said, "but nothing has ever made the return trip." He handed the container back to Denise. "Don't open it – we have no idea what it is. It could be a dangerous chemical."

Denise put the bottle back in its bag and then into its molded inset in the crate, pulled out another, and took it out of its bag. "Phobosstaub," she said.

"Phobos dust?" Sylvia said.

"What is Phobos?" Denise asked and handed the bottle to Will.

"It's Mars' largest moon," Will said and held it up to the light. It was fine gray dust, slightly courser than the Mars dust. "I'm sure we haven't recovered anything from Phobos either. And I don't know if we've ever landed a probe on either of Mars' moons."

Denise put the bottle back in the bag and set it in the crate. "Any guesses as to what the others are?"

"There's more?" Will asked and went to the crate.

Denise pulled out a third bottle, and Will the fourth.

"Venusstaub," Denise said.

"Merkurstaub," Will followed. "Venus dust and Mercury dust." He looked to Sylvia who confirmed his translations.

Denise reached into the crate and pulled out the foam packing to reveal another layer of items. She pulled out two more bottles and handed one to Will.

Will read it through the plastic bag. "Mond der Erde," he said.

"Moon of the Earth," Sylvia said.

Denise read aloud, "Der halish comet," and turned the label to Will.

It read *Der Halleysche Komet*.

"It means Halley's Comet," Sylvia said.

Will took it and held it up to the light. The contents looked like black pepper, but more pointed and elongated than pepper grains.

"What does this mean?" Jonathan asked.

"It can't be real," Will huffed and smiled. "We've only brought stuff back from the moon, and the Nazis did not beat us there. And they most definitely didn't go to Mars and back."

"So what is this stuff?" Sylvia asked.

Will shrugged. "It all needs to be chemically analyzed," he said and handed the bottles back to Denise. He went back to his coffee cup and topped it off before adding cream and sugar.

"The only one we can check directly is the moon dust – Earth's moon," Will added. "We do have chemical data for Mars as well. The instruments that landed there did chemical analysis and transmitted the data back to Earth."

Although Will was convinced there was an explanation for the labeling of the substances – codes for some other materials perhaps – his mind seemed to churn in the background with apprehension. It seemed he'd gotten the distraction he needed.

As Lenny exited Interstate 64 onto I-95 North toward DC, he imagined himself on Costa Rica's Punta Leona sands, soaking up the sun. He'd been there multiple times in the past decade, and it was the kind of place where he'd hoped to spend the final chapter of his life. He'd tried to imagine the same scenario that morning while relaxing on Sandbridge Beach on Virginia's coast. But even as the hot sun had beaten on his face and penetrated his eyelids with a pink warmth that seemed to wash away reality, a holistic anxiety thrummed in the back of his mind. He couldn't tell whether it was the guilt of his past, or the ever-present uncertainty of his future.

There was the constant threat of being eliminated by his current employers, and the danger of being captured by those seeking justice for his crimes. In the two days he'd lived out a mock retirement on the beach he realized that he'd never be at peace. It forced him to make a decision. He did, and now he was on his way to carry it out.

In Fredericksburg, Virginia, he got fuel, a large soda, and a candy bar, and then got back on the road. It felt good to stretch his legs and get his blood moving. He had to get his mind straight before he made his move.

His first objective was to get on the right side of the battle. Neither China nor his former homeland, Russia, was the right side. He longed for the days of working with Heinrich Bergman. Even though that project had been the darkest of them all, every operation he'd carried out – even the hits – seemed to advance toward some principled objective. In the case of Red Wraith, Lenny wasn't clear what that objective was exactly, but he'd been convinced it was transformative. If its success meant the creation of some powerful weapon or tool, he preferred that it not get into the hands of China.

Even in his younger years, while working for the KGB, China was a foe. At that time it had been undeveloped. Now the massive country was awakening, and a global storm was rising with it.

Even though he accepted that the specific acts that he had carried out – including the most recent ones – had been evil, they'd been necessary evils. He wasn't to blame. Some deserved what they got. Others were just in the wrong place at the wrong time. He was just an instrument put into action by a higher authority. The organization handed down the orders. Who was he to question those who had a view of the bigger picture? That his current employer was China was something he hadn't figured out until it was too late. It was something that had been revealed gradually, as the former management was slowly removed from the organizational structure.

He had to get back to working for the right side – not necessarily the United States, but the West. At least then he could argue that his actions contributed to something that might better the world. It was that same argument that had convinced him to defect to the West in the 1970s, when the Cold War was in full bloom. He'd quickly gotten sick of rounding up normal citizens, whose lives were already horrible, for a trip to Siberia, or to take out a rising political adversary of the Soviet government.

When his work had expanded to Europe, and he'd been tasked with eliminating foreign intelligence agents, he'd started reading

Western newspapers and getting an idea of what was really happening in the world. It was then that he'd determined he was on the wrong side of the war and, therefore, on the wrong side of morality. Not long after that epiphany, a CIA case officer named Heinrich Bergman, who had led an effort to collect technical intelligence in East Germany, flipped him. Lenny had earned Bergman's trust over the next few years as they had together decimated the Soviet intelligence network in the area. Lenny had killed dozens of his former countrymen and women, many of whom were even more ruthless than he. By doing this, he had done the world a service. Bergman then invited him to work on a project in the United States.

After working a short stint with MI-6, he'd accepted Bergman's offer and was granted US citizenship through CIA channels. He then worked within a secret project called Red Wraith under the direction of Bergman. But now Red Wraith was terminated and Bergman was dead.

For the same reason he'd turned from the Soviet Union, he was now turning from communist China. His plan was to connect with whomever he could find who had been involved in Red Wraith when it was solely an American enterprise. There were a number of ways to do that. One way was to show himself.

It was around 4:15 p.m. when Lenny pulled his rental car into the parking lot of a large grocery store and assembled a disguise. He was aware that even the silhouette of his large head might give him away to the Chinese operatives staking out the CIA facility, and the only way he could change that was with a baseball cap and a fleece with a tall collar. He'd let his facial hair grow for three days, which amounted to a thick black and gray layer that he'd dyed red the night before. He put on some large sunglasses and the disguise was complete.

He navigated surface streets for 15 minutes before pulling his car up to the gate of the Space Systems building. He removed his hat and sunglasses as he approached, now out of sight of any Chinese watchers. An armed guard peered at him through a bulletproof window, seemingly searching Lenny's chest for something.

"Where's your tag?" the man asked through an intercom. "I'm not reading your car's chip."

An electronic proximity card must have been needed to get through the gate.

"Is this International Logistics?" Lenny asked, knowing that was the company next door, where he'd parked days earlier to stake out the place.

"No," the guard said and pointed in a direction indicating that Lenny should back out. "A block west."

Lenny backed out, and then slipped on his sunglasses and hat as he drove away. Space Systems security now had his face on video.

A brazen exposure of this sort was done for one of two reasons, and everyone involved knew it. Either he was letting them know that he knew about their covert facility, or he was attempting to contact them. Either way, when he returned the next day, they'd bring him in.

His concern, however, was that they might also arrest him. They'd likely have evidence of the murders he'd committed over the past year. The one that stood out in Lenny's mind was the shooting and dismembering of a man in a parking garage at Syncorp Headquarters, in Baton Rouge, Louisiana. William Thomson had been an eyewitness to that event. Denise Walker had also witnessed him killing a nurse in a hospital in Southern Illinois, half a year ago. They could put him away forever. It was risky.

He just hoped that what he had to offer would be enough to bring him back into the fold.

Will and Denise sat on the couch in his flat and gazed out the windows onto the forest below. The pine needles looked pale in the midnight moonlight, and a gusty wind swirled through the upper canopies of the trees.

Denise sipped a glass of merlot while Will sloshed a single ice cube around the bottom of a tumbler of scotch. It had been a tiring day of cataloging the items collected from the base, but neither of them felt like sleeping. He knew he'd be awake for another hour or two, and might catch a second wind.

Denise pulled her feet up on the couch and moved close to Will, resting her shoulder against his. "Each time I wake up here I can't believe where I am," she said. "Half a year ago I was working on DNA cases in a tiny office on campus and thinking about career options."

Will recalled where he was half a year ago and wondered how he'd survived. "I think everyone involved in this feels like you do," he said. "But my guess is that the strangest things are yet to come."

"Any ideas as to where all of this leads?"

Will shook his head. "Final destination, no. But I think it will go through Antarctica."

"Thackett is trying to make that work," she said. "But other things are also possible, right? Like Mars?"

Will shook his head. "I think the Mars idea was a knee-jerk response since the first incoming signal came from there. But the probe on the Mars surface was just resending the same signal that was being broadcast from Earth – the initial blast from the probe in Antarctica. The incoming signals detected a week later, which are still coming, are from multiple sources – one of which is Mars, but not from its probe. The probe on Mars' surface has disappeared. I'm sure they're rethinking their plans."

Denise seemed to mull it over. "Suppose we go to the base and we don't find anything particularly important. Where do we go next?"

"Maybe we won't need to go anywhere."

"What do you mean?"

"Maybe something will come to us," he said, and then flinched at the vibration of his phone on the coffee table in front of the couch. An instant later, Denise's did the same just a few inches from his.

They both leaned forward, collected their phones, and read the incoming text messages. Will's read: *Meeting in 713 in 10 minutes.* It was from Thackett.

Denise confirmed the same. "Kind of late for this," she said as she gulped down the final third of her wine. "What could it be?"

Will set his whiskey glass on the table and stood. "No idea," he said, "but we must be in for some news."

They took the elevator down to the seventh floor and arrived at the 713 entrance just as Jonathan shuffled down the hall behind them. As he caught up, Will flashed his proximity key near the keypad and opened the door.

He filed in behind Denise and Jonathan and closed the door. Thackett, Daniel, and Sylvia were already seated in the cluster of furniture on the far side of the room.

As they approached, Thackett gestured for them to sit. Denise sat on the couch, between Daniel and Sylvia, and Jonathan took an upholstered chair to Thackett's left, opposite the coffee table from Denise. Will took a wooden chair on the far end of the table, across from Thackett, which must have come from one of the offices.

"Sorry for dragging you all down here at this hour," Thackett said, "but I wanted you to have this update as soon as possible."

By their expressions, it seemed that Daniel and Sylvia were not yet informed of what was to come.

Thackett continued. "The incoming AM signals have ceased," he said and seemed to check each of their reactions.

"When?" Will asked.

"A few hours ago," Thackett replied.

"All at the same time?" Will asked.

Thackett shrugged. "I don't know the specifics – I will get that info to you – all I know for certain is that they have all subsided."

Will's mind churned with speculative projections, but then went into a state of intense, white noise anxiety. He stood and walked away from the others, toward the meeting table near the exit. Two-thirds of the way there, he turned around and walked back. He remained standing with his hands on the back of the wooden chair. "We have to get moving," he said. "We have to get to Antarctica."

Everyone turned their eyes to Thackett, who raised his hand and grinned.

"My feeling as well. We need to start moving again," Thackett said. "The crew has been given their orders, and the *North Dakota* will be out of dock in two weeks. At that time you all will be transferred to the *Stennis*, and will rendezvous with the *North Dakota* as soon as they get to the Weddell Sea."

Will was satisfied, but it didn't quell his anxiety. As long as the signal was active, he'd felt safe thinking that nothing else would happen until that stage was complete.

That stage was now over, and he didn't want to find out what came next.

CHAPTER 8

Jacob ate breakfast, brewed coffee, and powered up his laptop. He started the Wave Tempest program and set it up to analyze the outgoing electromagnetic signal from the probe. It was a long shot, but he had to let the program have a crack at decoding it. It was going to take hours.

As his computer worked on the data, he took *The Israel Thread* up to the dome. He leaned back on the couch and stared into the clear blue Friday morning sky. The meditations from the night before came back to him. What was he doing on this insignificant speck of a planet? And what did that make him?

His total insignificance to the rest of existence was, in one sense, liberating. In another, it made him feel lonelier than he'd ever been. But he realized that wasn't a new feeling; it had been there all along. Perhaps most people never recognized their irrelevance because of the distractions that come with life on this planet – hunger, pain, love, and a multitude of responsibilities. Once these were removed, the simple truth shone through. And that truth was that none of it mattered.

Earth could be destroyed – rendered down to its constituent atoms – and the rest of the universe wouldn't care. And we wouldn't remember. No one would remember. For him, maybe it was this, now overt, feeling that drove him. Maybe his craving for puzzles to solve was based in something other than entertainment. It could be that, at some deeper level, he was hoping that he'd discover something that alleviated that helpless feeling of isolation and insignificance.

He shook off his philosophical pondering and turned his attention to the book – his current distraction from an insignificant existence. He was getting close to the end, but felt he was behind schedule.

The book cited more interviews of Nazi war criminals by the Mossad, most of which backed up what he already knew about the Nazis' Red Falcon project and the Antarctic base. But there was one peculiar statement made by a U-boat captain who had run supplies to the base before surrendering at Mar del Plata, Argentina, after the Germans surrendered. The captain's name was Otto Wermuth and, under great pressure from his Mossad interrogators, he claimed that Hitler was on his way to the base and that they had the key to unlock some cataclysmic event – the *cleansing*, he'd called it.

According to Theo, the Israelis discredited the man based on his claim that Hitler was still alive – something they knew for a fact was untrue. They'd asked for the location of the base, but Wermuth only answered in generalities and, when pressed, couldn't give details. Now, Jacob realized, the U-boat captain had been telling the truth about the base – minus the details – and was possibly accurate about there being a "key" to initiate some event, whatever it was. In the margin, Theo had written something about that key being a physical object, not just an idea or a bit of crucial knowledge. Jacob's first thought was of the White Stone, but Theo would have mentioned it by name. It must have been something else.

He read all morning and into the early afternoon. It was slow going, as he had to follow some leads to background information, including monographs on the Ahnenerbe and the SS, located in the stacks.

At about five o'clock the sky clouded, and the patter of light rain on the dome lulled him into a nap. He awakened an hour later to a clear, purple sky. The late afternoon had turned into early evening, and he was hungry but refreshed.

He checked his computer's progress and found that it had crashed at around 4:00 p.m. It would be no use on the outgoing signal.

He reheated some pizza in the oven and took a quick shower before the oven timer chimed. He turned on the television as he ate at the counter.

The lead story at the top of the hour made him set down his pizza and stand up from his stool. He stared at the TV. According to BBC News, the Russians had fixed their rogue satellite, and the others it controlled, and stopped the transmission. The Russians still denied responsibility for any of it.

Jacob's chest tightened and he took a deep breath. He was confused: he knew it wasn't a malfunctioning spacecraft that had caused the radio interference. Did it mean that something else was about to happen? His trembling nerves gave him the feeling that time was running short.

It was near dusk as Lenny made the final turn toward the Space Systems building. He took a deep breath and hoped that he was making the right decision. If wrong, he might spend the rest of his life in jail, or lose it altogether.

He stopped next to the guard post at the gate and rolled down the window. Two rough-looking Special Police Officers, or SPOs, managed the entrance.

"They're expecting me," Lenny said.

One man exited the booth as the other spoke. "Mr. Butrolsky?"

He flinched even though it shouldn't have surprised him that they knew his real name. Lenny nodded.

The man came to Lenny's side of the car with his hand on his firearm. "Please exit the vehicle."

Lenny did as instructed, and the man guided him into a frisking position – hands on the hood of the car and legs spread. Lenny wasn't armed.

"Come with me," the man said. "We'll park your car."

Lenny knew they'd have to first make sure the car wasn't rigged with a bomb, and then lift fingerprints and whatever other biometric data they could find inside in order to catalog who might have been in the car previously. They'd find nothing suspicious.

From behind, the guard directed Lenny through doors and corridors as he spoke on the phone. A minute later they arrived at an elevator and waited. Thirty seconds later it opened: three additional guards were waiting inside. The man from the gate passed him off to the other three and Lenny stepped into the elevator. It descended.

From the indicator above the door, they dropped to Level D, four floors below ground. The door opened to a gray corridor that smelled like musty concrete. They passed heavy metal doors on both sides that had switchable signs indicating "Vacant" or "Occupied," like those seen on airplane lavatories.

As they walked, Lenny noticed that about half of the rooms were occupied, and it made him wonder how many people the CIA brought through the place.

They came to a vacant room on the right, and the man who'd led the way pulled out a proximity card and held it up to the lock. There was a beep and a click, and the man pushed the door open.

The room was larger than Lenny had expected, and had what looked like an old-fashioned jail cell in the back, left corner. In the center of the room were a table and four chairs, and on the right wall was a stainless steel worktable with a sink and overhead cabinets. A few feet away from the sink was a chair constructed entirely of welded one-inch pipe, bolted to the floor. Directly beneath it was a drain. Lenny was familiar with the setup, but from a different perspective.

"Don't worry," one of his escorts said, apparently sensing his thoughts. "We don't do that anymore." The man pointed to a chair at the head of the table. "Have a seat. Someone will meet with you shortly."

Lenny sat down as the men walked out. The latching of the door was followed by a click. He imagined the sign on the door now read "Occupied."

After 15 minutes he stood and paced. He fidgeted with his hands and wondered how long they'd make him wait.

Five minutes later, the door beeped and two men entered. One he recognized as the CIA Director, James Thackett. He figured the other one was there for the Director's safety.

"Shall we, Mr. Butrolsky?" Thackett said and nodded to the table.

Lenny went to the seat at one end of the table and Thackett took the chair opposite him. The third man stood against the wall behind Thackett.

"Perhaps you should begin," Thackett said as he interleaved his fingers into a ball of knuckles and rested them on the table in front of him.

Lenny hadn't organized his thoughts nor devised a way to start the conversation. He'd assumed he'd be answering questions.

"I worked many years for Heinrich Bergman," Lenny began and watched for a reaction. He got a deadpan expression and silence.

"I have intimate knowledge of the Red Wraith project," Lenny continued, "and I know how current events are related."

This seemed to stir the Director's mind.

"What do you know, and how are you involved?" Thackett asked.

Lenny rubbed the back of his head and then laced his fingers together and placed them on the table in front of him, mirroring Thackett. "It would be unwise of me to talk about anything incriminating without a lawyer or immunity," he said, and paused.

Thackett shrugged but remained quiet.

"Maybe I should start by explaining what I can offer you," Lenny said.

Thackett nodded for him to continue.

"I'm sure you know that there's an elaborate Chinese intelligence network operating in DC, and elsewhere in the country."

Thackett nodded.

"But perhaps you don't know exactly what they're after, and what they're willing to do to get it."

"They want a lot of things."

"True," Lenny agreed. "However, much of what was important just a year ago, is no longer important."

"Explain."

"The Chinese want something very specific and, from my understanding, they almost acquired it," Lenny explained. "In fact, they did acquire it, but couldn't hold on to it."

"Are you talking about a thing, or a person?"

"A person."

"And how do you know about this?" Thackett asked.

"I will explain all of that if we come to an agreement," Lenny said, "but you should know they now seem to be after other things as well."

"Go on."

"One is the book that belonged to Theodore Leatherby."

"Horace," Thackett whispered. "What else?"

"The location of a secret CIA facility in the DC area," Lenny replied. "And I'm not referring to this one."

"Why are they looking for it?"

Lenny shrugged. "I assume there's sensitive information stored there."

"Is that all? Don't they still want ... the person?"

"They want him dead," Lenny said.

Thackett's face seemed to flush and then lighten to a deathly pale. "How do you know this?"

"Because they hired me to do it," Lenny replied. "But there are others with the same task – other assassins to hedge their bets."

Thackett's eyes widened, and he was about to say something, but Lenny preempted his question.

"One million dollars," Lenny said. "That's what they offered me, and my safe dismissal from their employ."

"Do you believe them?"

"That they'd let me go?" Lenny shook his head. "No."

"How did you get the job to begin with?"

"It took me some time to figure out that CIA's Syncorp had changed hands. I've carried out a few odd jobs for them in the past year," Lenny explained. "I'd be happy to give you the details once we have a deal."

"What do you have to offer?"

"I've given you two things already," Lenny said. "One, I've warned you of their plans to terminate your ... asset."

"What's the second thing?"

"They already know about this place," Lenny replied, "and that Denise Walker – and therefore William Thompson – are here as well."

Thackett's expression flashed to that of horror for an instant, and then to a blank stare.

"They've known for a few days, and are staking out the place as we speak," Lenny added. "I disguised myself before I came in."

"Okay," Thackett said after a few seconds of what seemed like internal reflection. "What are you offering us now?"

"I'm deeply connected with the Chinese operation. I can damage their network," Lenny explained. "At the very least, I can pipe information to you."

Thackett studied him for a few seconds, seemingly mulling over his options. "Why are you doing this?" he finally asked.

Lenny closed his eyes and nodded his head, indicating he knew the question was coming. "Two things," he said. "First, I want out of this business. When I restarted my work after Bergman was killed, I assumed I was working for the CIA head – your predecessor."

"Terrance Gould," Thackett said.

Lenny nodded. "I did a few jobs figuring I was working CIA black-ops jobs. And I think I was for a while. But then it all changed."

"How so?"

"I got a different handler," Lenny said. "And then Syncorp was sold to a Chinese firm."

"It was a mistake arranged by Gould."

Lenny nodded. "After what happened to the facility in Detroit, and the bad press that followed, allowing the Chinese takeover was a stupid, panicked move."

"When did you find out you were working for Chinese intelligence?" Thackett asked.

"That's a loaded question," Lenny responded. "I *suspected* it when we captured your man at Syncorp headquarters, in Baton Rouge."

"And you met the Chinese operatives?"

"Yes, including the new Syncorp CEO at the time, Zhichao Cho," Lenny said. "I understand he's dead."

Thackett nodded.

"I've heard rumors about Cho's death," Lenny added, "and the others on the Chinese ship."

Thackett nodded but didn't elaborate.

"So you had an epiphany," Thackett said. "Why the change of heart?"

"Like I said, I want out," Lenny reiterated. "With the Chinese, there is no way out."

"Only one."

"Exactly." He wasn't counting dying as a way out. "After my services to you, I want out."

"That's it?"

"It goes deeper," Lenny replied. "I don't want to be on the wrong side of this."

"What do you mean?"

"As you may also have experienced in your work for the CIA, I have done things that I may regret in the future. At the time, they were for the right reasons – for the better good. The Red Wraith project had goals which, although I do not understand them all, were for the better good."

"You are a Russian, Mr. Butrolsky."

"No. I am an American."

Thackett shrugged.

"I am of Russian origin," Lenny continued. "I grew up in the former USSR during the Cold War, served in the Red Army, and worked for the KGB. I worked first in Germany and Eastern Europe, and then in England. That was where I was converted. It was where I experienced Western life for the first time. I never wanted to leave."

"How did you get here?" Thackett asked. "Why not stay in the UK?"

"I'd planned to stay on with MI-6," Lenny explained, "but it was Heinrich Bergman who convinced me to come to the US. We had worked together to dissolve a KGB network in East Germany before they took down the wall. Afterwards, he offered me a job."

Thackett remained silent.

"Like I said," Lenny continued. "I'll infiltrate the Chinese network, and supply you with whatever information I can obtain. And I'll destroy the network if the opportunity arises."

Lenny figured that was the only way he might live in peace. It would be a massive cleanup operation – something that was his specialty. Only this cleanup would be for him and, as a secondary consequence, of great service to the CIA.

"You'll have to if you want to live in peace," Thackett said. "At the very least, you'll have to decapitate the network – take out all of the top-ranking operatives."

It was as if Thackett had read his mind, and Lenny liked the tone of his voice. "So, do we have a deal?"

"I'm going to think about it," Thackett said and stood. "I'm sorry, but you're going to have to stay here this evening." Thackett nodded toward the small cell in the corner of the room and then gestured to the armed man behind him.

Lenny stood and walked into the cell. The guard closed the door behind him as Thackett left the room.

It was strange to Lenny that, at some level, he welcomed the confinement. He'd be safe for the night.

IT WAS 9:00 p.m. when Jacob closed the book. He had fewer than 10 pages left, but couldn't read another minute – he'd been at it all day and could no longer concentrate.

As he approached the end, he was glad he'd decided to work through it sequentially and pull in outside sources when needed. To get the full context, it had been important to study the references – especially the CIA files. He now had a good understanding of the story, and had at least a hazy view of the big picture.

According to Theo, extrapolating the so-called "Israel thread" from the past led to the series of recent events that accounted for everything that was currently happening. The Red Wraith project produced one subject who could transform. That man, William Thompson, had entered the probe at the bottom of the Weddell Sea and set everything into motion.

Jacob was skeptical of all of it, and didn't think he'd ever be able to accept it. Again, he acknowledged the difference between belief and assumption. For now, he'd assume everything he'd read was true, but he couldn't necessarily believe it.

Although it had been unclear what secrets the probe held, apparently no one had expected it to blast an electromagnetic signal into space to alert whoever might be listening that the probe had been accessed. Whoever was the intended recipient of that outgoing signal, it was clear to Jacob that the message had been received – because there had been a response. The problem was that both the incoming and outgoing messages had been encrypted.

And now the incoming signal had ceased. So the question was, *what was coming next?*

His laptop had been working on the outgoing signal all day with no success. The program had crashed, but he'd restarted it and would give it another few hours to process the data. After that, if it had made no progress, he'd move on to analyzing the incoming signal.

Jacob put the book in his backpack and headed out. He needed a walk and some air, and a change of environment. Fifteen minutes later he was in the Count Cristo Coffee House, sitting next to a large window with a view of Hyacinth Street, the cross street to Swann.

It was a Friday night. The traffic outside was more active than during his previous excursion, and the coffeehouse was more crowded. He overheard college students talking about upcoming exams for summer school classes, one in physics and another in organic chemistry. He was lucky to get a table.

He pulled out *The Israel Thread* and read the last 10 pages. It ended with a concise summary of facts that accurately reflected his understanding. But there was a page and a half of green-inked handwriting that followed on the final two pages. It was an update written by Uncle Theo.

On the first of the final two pages was a hand-drawn map of Antarctica. It showed the location of the probe, and that of a tunnel that started on the west coast, in the Weddell Sea, and led to a base labeled with a swastika. The base was about 50 miles inland and in rough terrain, near a ring of mountains and a lake. As he examined the details, the sight of his handwritten name startled him. Directly below the map was a note that read: "Jacob, people will kill to get this map. Guard it with your life. –H."

It suddenly occurred to him that this was what the man who'd shot at him – or those who'd hired him – really wanted: the location of the base. Anxiety started to drive him into a state of panic, but he took a deep breath and a sip of coffee, and managed to maintain his composure. He shouldn't have brought the book outside the facility. He made a mental note to never do it again.

He read on. Next, Theo summarized what they had known about the signals at the time. First, there had been an immediate response from Mars. A European satellite in Mars orbit took a picture of the source on the surface and beamed it back to Earth. The object was located near one of the planet's poles, and was a perfect replica of the probe beneath the Weddell Sea. More importantly, the Mars signal was identical to that emitted from the Earth-based probe.

Jacob realized that the signal from the Mars probe accounted for the echo, or "ghost signal" he'd seen in the data of the outgoing broadcast. It had in fact not been an echo at all – it was an identical signal being broadcast from a duplicate beacon on Mars.

Theo had written that the United States and its allies were now planning to send William Thompson to Mars.

Jacob was confused. Why would they do that? What was he going to do once he got there? Look for other structures on Mars? It made no sense. And there were other signals that had come from other places – probably deep space. And they certainly couldn't send anyone there. They probably couldn't even get Thompson to Mars anyway – they didn't have the technology.

Theo had been alive when they'd detected the signal from Mars. However, Jacob realized, he'd passed away before the incoming AM radio signals had arrived, over a week later. Jacob figured they'd likely put to rest any plans for Mars.

Jacob's suspicions were verified when Theo explained that, since the probe in the sea had required William Thompson to get inside and activate something, they'd assumed that something similar had to be done with the probe on Mars. It was grasping at straws, but they'd started planning a manned trip to the red planet. Theo noted that it was better than doing nothing, but that they'd probably develop a new plan when more information was available.

He finished reading Theo's monograph at 10:00 p.m. It had taken just over a week. The new knowledge he'd acquired had changed him. And now it was time for him to press onward, beyond what Uncle Theo had done.

His nerves tingled and his mouth was dry. He took a drink of coffee but it didn't help. While he was reading he was accomplishing something – getting up to speed. But now he'd passed on to the next stage, the one where all eyes were on him. Theo had brought him into the situation to solve a puzzle, and it was clear that it was matched to his expertise: signal analysis and encryption.

Jacob was up for the challenge but, in this case, there was the possibility that the encryption was beyond current technology. There were encryptions that would take all the computers in the world millennia to break. The point being, if an advanced intelligence didn't want us to decipher something, we wouldn't be able to. However, if they wanted us to get the message, they'd make it within our reach. Otherwise, what would be the point?

He twitched as a tap on the shoulder interrupted his thoughts. He turned to a smiling face. It was Cally, the owner of the Count Cristo Coffee House.

"Good to see you again," she said.

"I told you I was going to be a regular," he replied as he closed the book and slipped it into his bag. "Pretty busy tonight."

"There are some exams for summer classes next week," she said. "They're all cramming."

Jacob laughed. "Some things never change."

She nodded. "As long as there are exams to cram for, I can count on good business. But I've been getting some odd visitors lately. Secret service types, by the looks of them."

Jacob's vision blurred for an instant. "What? Dark suits, sunglasses?" He tried to smile as if he were joking.

"I actually saw a gun," she said as her eyes widened. "Two men ordered coffee together but sat separately, one where you are now, and the other in the other room. They seemed to watch the street and who was coming and going. Very strange."

Strange indeed, Jacob thought. "Were they Americans?"

She seemed surprised by the question. "Sounded like it," she replied. "But who knows around here. There are a lot of internationals – visitors and diplomats."

"Yes, but they aren't supposed to be carrying guns."

"I suppose not," she said and shrugged. "What? You think they're after you?"

It was clear that her question was a joke, but hit closer to a nerve than she could have imagined. "Sure, they're watching my every move. They gave up out of fear of dying of boredom."

She laughed. "I'm sure it's not that bad," she said.

His life was uncomfortably far from boring.

Cally went back to the counter to help with a line of customers that had suddenly formed.

Jacob calmed himself. It wasn't out of the ordinary to have CIA, FBI, or Homeland Security personnel milling about in Washington, DC. After all, they drank coffee, too. He put it out of his mind, pulled out his notebook, and read over his notes.

The discovery of the probe was a scavenger hunt through time in which each piece of the puzzle was solvable with current knowledge. He therefore had to assume that his piece, the encoded signals, was also solvable with current knowledge.

The part of the story that was beyond him, however, was how William Thompson had accessed the interior of the probe in the first place. It was deep in the ocean and composed of some kind of impenetrable material – which was a mystery of its own. And he wasn't buying all of the supernatural mumbo jumbo that a man separated his soul from his body and got inside it. It was preposterous. But it was also distracting: if true, it would change his perspective on his very existence. If false, it brought into question everything else they were doing.

Jacob pushed it to the back of his mind. He didn't have a choice, so he might as well embrace the situation. It was time to start deciphering the incoming signal – extract the digital components and look for patterns.

He read an abandoned newspaper as he finished his coffee. Ten minutes later he was in the cool night air and on his way back to 17 Swann.

JACOB RETURNED to 17 Swann and popped open a cola as he checked whether his computer software had made any progress deciphering the outgoing signal. It had crashed for the second time with no results.

He turned his attention to the incoming signals.

It was straightforward for the Wave Tempest software to identify and separate the seven signals. They were all of different intensities – probably because they were all located at different distances relative to Earth. For the same reason, they all started at slightly different times. Finally, and this was a little more challenging to explain, all of their frequencies were slightly different – corresponding to slight separations on the AM dial. Despite these differences, the signals were identical – meaning that the information they carried was exactly the same.

He chose the strongest of the signals for analysis, and then got to work on extracting the digital data from the signal. This part was straightforward – just routine signal analysis – but the resulting ones and zeroes meant nothing in their raw form.

It was 3:00 a.m., in the middle of his third Pepsi, when he noticed a gap in the raw data where there was no signal. There was nearly a full second of complete silence, whereas the signal on either side of the gap was continuous. The only other silent gaps were where the signal had gone through a full cycle and then restarted from the beginning.

He expanded the view to get one full cycle of data on the screen. The gap – which looked like a notch in the data – separated the first tiny fraction of the total signal cycle from the rest. He checked the other six incoming signals and, in every one, the notch appeared near the beginning of every cycle.

He figured the two parts were separated for a reason and it gave him an idea. What if the two pieces of the total signal were encrypted differently? In that case, he could try to decode them separately – starting with the shorter one. Even the simplest of encryption methods, however, could be nearly impossible to break, depending on the key size of the cipher algorithm. If it were a 256-bit key, as required by the Advanced Encryption Standard for US Top Secret information, then there was an outside chance that he could get CIA or NSA supercomputers to break it using brute force methods. But if it were of a less secure encryption, he might be able to do it on his laptop using Wave Tempest. The program had many functions, including special packages to decipher symmetric or asymmetric encoding. If the signal was from an advanced intelligence, however, the message could have been encoded using something beyond Earth-developed technology – such as quantum information algorithms.

Jacob stood, took off his sneakers, and thought as he walked the carpet runner barefooted from the table to the stairs and back. There were other problems.

Even if he were able to extract the correct binary data – decipher it from the message – it would still just be a stream of ones and zeroes. It would have no meaning unless he knew what kind of information the data represented. It could be text, numbers, audio, or images. Binary files often came with headers that identified what the data represented, and how to interpret them – a signature of some kind, or a so-called magic number.

And it could be even more complicated. In graduate school, he'd studied steganography, where a single signal could carry different messages depending on the interpretation algorithm. For instance, an audio or text message could be hidden in an image. The possibilities were endless.

He paced for a few more minutes and then grabbed his laptop and went up to the dome. Time to try to break the encryption of the short part of the incoming message.

It was 5:00 a.m. when Jacob grabbed his fourth soda, which helped him to work through to 7:00 a.m. It was his first all-nighter in a long time, but well worth it. He'd made some headway into cracking the first part of the transmission.

He had a large set of parameters to deal with and had to make assumptions as he went along. The first was the length of a byte. The standard was eight bits – each a "1" or a "0" – that made one byte. There were 256 different binary number combinations one could make with eight ones and zeros, which meant that one byte could represent any of 256 different characters. In that case, the translation to text would be straightforward.

But it didn't have to be eight bits to a byte. Nonetheless, Jacob assumed eight bits to start, and tried to extract text using the usual ASCII protocol – a table that translates bytes to specific characters. It was a long shot, and it failed. It was preposterous to think that a message coming from deep space would use English characters, or those of any other Earth-based language for that matter. It was good to try, however. If it had worked, it would have been strong evidence that the signal had a human origin.

He then approached it from another angle. He contemplated what kind of message he would send if he didn't know the language of the recipient. It depended on what information he needed to convey, but it wouldn't be a written language, and it wouldn't be audio either. It would have to be images, and he'd send them in the simplest format possible. That, he knew, would be in bitmap format, where each element of the file tells the recipient how to color in each tiny square pixel on a grid, not unlike the number-color painting he'd done as a kid. In this case, he'd start by assuming the simplest form that didn't involve colors – only gray-tones. That way, one value could be specified for each pixel that gave it a specific gray-tone somewhere between white and black. If that value were given by an eight-bit byte, there were 256 graduations between white and black, giving a reasonable quality black-and-white – or gray-tone – image.

He started an algorithm that searched for patterns that were consistent with bitmap image files. One strategy the program employed was to search for regularly repeated bytes – often the byte "00000000." In some types of bitmap image files, such buffer bytes separated the information for each pixel. For instance, each partitioned piece of data might first give the location on a grid, and then tell the recipient how dark to shade it. The concept was easy, the deciphering, however, was not. He got his computer working on it – it was going to be grinding away for hours.

He brought his laptop from the dome down to the table on the first floor and plugged in the charger. He then went to the kitchen and pulled a piece of cold pizza out of the refrigerator, took a bite, and turned on the TV. A BBC News panel reported that the Russians and Swedes were arguing again about the AM radio disturbance. This time the Russians were denying they'd fixed anything at all, and that the interference had stopped on its own.

The panel included the BBC anchor, scientists from Russia and Sweden, and an American so-called conspiracy theorist affiliated with the SETI Institute who argued that the AM disturbance had multiple sources, and that one of them was from Mars.

"You people are biased," the Russian said to the SETI panelist. "All of your hopes and fantasies depend on the existence of little green men."

"And women," the Swede added, provoking a chuckle from the anchor.

"How do you explain the glitches at the LIGO facilities?" the American rebutted. "They started at the same time as the AM interference."

It was an interesting connection, Jacob thought, but clearly a coincidence. Gravitational waves and electromagnetic waves were completely different. The former were not mechanical vibrations, like those produced by earthquakes. Gravitational waves were distortions of space-time itself, and humanity couldn't produce a measurable gravity wave if their very existence depended on it.

"That is a vastly distorted connection, which makes it clear that you do not know what you are talking about," the Russian said. "This is what you people do – draw wild conclusions from coincidences."

"Coincidence?" the American said. "Is it also a coincidence that the glitches stopped when the AM disturbances ceased?"

"What is your source on that?" the anchor asked. "Just yesterday we interviewed a scientist who was arguing for funds to fix that very problem."

"I'd like to know the source as well," the Swede said. "Information from the LIGO facilities is rarely leaked."

"I won't reveal my source," the American said, "but would such an occurrence convince you that there was more to it?"

The other two panelists immediately shook their heads in a negative response, and the anchor chuckled, shook her head, and said, "We'll have to end there. Top of the hour news just ahead ..."

Jacob turned off the TV and sat in silence at the counter as he mulled over his plan for the day. He finished his pizza at 7:20 a.m. and brushed his teeth.

He got in bed, set the alarm for 10:00 a.m., and closed his eyes.

It was the best sleep Lenny could remember.

A clock outside the cell on the opposite side of the room read 7:15 a.m., and the aromas of bacon and eggs made his mouth water. A young security guard slipped the meal through a slot in the door, followed by a mug of coffee.

"You need anything else for now?" she asked.

"No thank you," Lenny replied.

"The director will be with you shortly," she said and left.

A half-hour later, Thackett entered with two men. One of the operatives unlocked the cell and motioned for him to take a seat at the table. Lenny recognized the other as a member of the team that tried to capture him at the restaurant, where Lenny had failed to collect Jacob Hale for the last time. He was still embarrassed about that debacle.

"Mr. Butrolsky, you have quite a record," Thackett started. "A violent one."

Lenny just stared back at him. It wasn't something he'd deny – to himself or to the man who held his fate in his hands.

"You killed that lawyer in Boston, and Hale's brother," Thackett continued.

It was Hale's cousin, but Lenny wasn't going to reveal knowledge of any of it.

"And the former Red Wraith people who have been cleaned up," Thackett said. "That you, too?"

A full minute of silence passed before Thackett continued. "I take it by your silence that you're responsible for all of those hits."

Lenny didn't respond. He'd carried out those hits, but was not *responsible* for them. He'd been taking orders.

"I realize you weren't the one making the decisions," Thackett said, as if reading Lenny's thoughts. "In normal times I'd have you ... removed from service."

Lenny understood. He was a loose end that needed trimming, and the CIA would never have him arrested. He knew too much – and not just about Red Wraith.

"But these aren't normal times," Thackett continued. "The Chinese have been on our backs from the beginning, and likely know more than we do about Red Wraith. And, as you've confirmed, they're still pursuing William Thompson."

Lenny nodded.

"I want to know what they know," Thackett replied. "I want to know why they're after Thompson. And I want to know why they're after Hale."

"They don't want Hale," Lenny said. "They want the book he has, and access to the secret facility."

"What's so important in the book?" Thackett asked. "Does it contain something about Red Wraith?"

Lenny shrugged and shook his head.

"Here's the deal," Thackett said. "Your mission is to use your current position in the Chinese network to infiltrate it to the deepest level. When you have extracted all of the useful information, you'll take it down."

Lenny's gut tightened. Infiltrating the Chinese network was orders of magnitude more difficult than taking it down. Lenny had spook skills, but they were not fine-tuned. And he didn't know a lick of Chinese.

"Just to be clear," Lenny said, "by 'take it down' you mean in the way for which I was trained."

Thackett nodded, "But on my order, not at your discretion."

"Understood," Lenny said. "And what do I get in return?"

"Immunity, and a peaceful retirement," Thackett replied. "And you'll be given a modest pension for your service over the past decades."

Lenny hadn't even thought of a pension. Even if it were only a thousand dollars a month, it would seal his retirement funding.

"Sounds fair," Lenny said. "How will we communicate?"

Thackett nodded to the two operatives. "This is Nordstrom, and Bailey," Thackett said, nodding to each as he said their names.

"They are your handlers. You'll be given a secure phone and a laptop."

A half-hour later, Lenny was heading northeast on I-395 into Washington, DC. His Chinese contacts had called a meeting.

THE ALARM CLOCK woke Jacob at 10:00 a.m. His head pounded like he had a hangover, but he knew the remedy.

He trudged out to the kitchen and started the coffee maker, and then jumped into the shower. All-nighters could have long-term disruptive effects but he figured that, if he forced himself to stay awake all day, he'd get back to a normal sleep schedule.

Although his body was still exhausted, his mind was already running at top speed and his muscles twitched. The blanketing anxiety put his nerves in a high-voltage state that made them react to the smallest stimuli, including the sporadic splashing of water in the shower. The aroma of freshly brewed coffee eased the tension as he got dressed.

He went to the kitchen, turned on BBC News, and made scrambled eggs and bacon. It seemed that every story in the news was connected to his work. But he knew that wasn't true. BBC was also covering all kinds of humanitarian stories, as well as multiple conflicts around the world. However, his mind glossed over those, constantly trying to pick out connections to the probe, Mars, the signal, and conspiracy theories that weren't entirely false. It occurred to him that conspiracy theorists have a role to play in the world.

He finished breakfast, cleaned the kitchen, and went down to the first-floor table to see what his computer had accomplished since he'd initiated the processing on the incoming signal. He wasn't optimistic. The Wave Tempest program would only have been crunching the data for three hours. While in graduate school, he'd run deciphering jobs that had taken multiple computers many days of continuous processing to complete. Although he now had a much faster computer than he'd had then, he was sure the decoding would take some time. Nonetheless, he was curious to see the feedback Wave Tempest 8.0 was spitting out about the data.

As the software chugged along on a large data set, it would report what it had attempted to do, even if it had failed. Therefore, even though he might not know what the data was, he'd know what it wasn't. For instance, the program might report that the data were not expressed in 8-bit bytes, and then associate that conclusion with some level of confidence in the form of a percentage. Whether it returned negative or positive responses, they were only to be taken seriously if the confidence level was over 90%.

The screen was black when he arrived, although the software was working in the background. When he logged in and the screen came back to life, the first thing he noticed was that the program had stopped. This meant one of two things: the program had given up or it had identified a solution.

Jacob's vision blurred. Wave Tempest 8.0 had reported a solution.

The program had constructed a table of parameters with corresponding confidence levels, all of which exceeded 98%. The bytes were 10 bits long, and there were over 10 million bytes, or about 10 megabytes, of data. It identified various characters that were used to identify parts of the files, and separated the files. In the end, it identified the data to be three images in the simplest file format: bitmap. He frantically searched for the path to the files and, when he closed the window to the analysis program, he found what he sought. His heart seemed to misfire like a poorly tuned engine.

The program placed a folder labeled Output Files on the desktop. Jacob opened it, revealing three image files: A_001.bmp A_002.bmp A_003.bmp

CHAPTER 9

Lenny pulled the rental car into the parking garage, parked on the roof, and waited.

Strange meeting times and places like this had always given him headaches. Being late for this kind of encounter could be devastating, and it wasn't good to be too early, either. It was two minutes to noon.

At 12:01 p.m., a large SUV drove up and parked two slots down. The passenger-side window rolled down and a man waved at Lenny to come to the vehicle.

As Lenny approached, the SUV's back door on the passenger side swung open.

He got in and closed the door, and found himself with three Syncorp operatives who he knew were really with Chinese intelligence. Even though he was one of their employees, it was a precarious situation after his stay at "Hotel CIA" the previous night, not to mention his little beach vacation where he'd lost his Chinese tails. He might have to answer for that one. It also would have been better if he hadn't had a recent string of failures.

They ordered him to hand over his gun, which was standard for a meeting with the boss.

They were likely planning to do one of two things: terminate his service, which could mean terminating *him*, or give him another assignment. As for the first option, Lenny had backup in case things turned ugly: his two CIA handlers. It had been a long time since he'd had such a luxury and, although not foolproof, it gave him a sense of security.

Lenny had always appreciated the sophistication of first-world intelligence services. From the CIA to the KGB to MI-6, they were resourceful and efficient. Perhaps it was because intelligence services were somehow separate from their respective governments. They had some autonomy by virtue of their business – meaning they had complete control of personnel and operations and, most importantly, had an abundance of resources. In this case, he had confidence in his CIA backup.

If Chinese intelligence gave him a new assignment and kept him connected, it would take some time to collect anything useful for the CIA. However, he'd already accomplished something: the three operatives in the car were now marked and would be carefully tracked. Every place they'd go, and every contact they'd make, would be documented and mapped for as long as the CIA could keep them in their sights. An entire network could be uprooted in such a way. And now, if they were taking him to a safe house, a virtual hornets' nest of activity and personnel would be revealed.

"Where are we going?" Lenny asked.

After a few seconds, the driver answered, "A place where you can explain what you have been doing."

A spike of paranoia surged through Lenny's brain. Had they tracked him to the CIA facility? He wouldn't be surprised if they'd already known about the facility before Denise Walker was seen entering the place. The United States couldn't keep secrets. Perhaps it was a consequence of an open society. Rather, Lenny thought, it was due to poor vetting of those who were close to sensitive information. That wasn't the case for CIA employees, but it was for the contractors they'd hired – Edward Snowden and his public dumping of NSA information was an obvious example. Why take every precaution to make sure your personnel and information are safe while you collect intelligence, but then put it all in a virtual box and give it to a third party to store and organize? It didn't make sense. Lenny was happy that he was on the collection side of the equation.

Twenty minutes later they drove into an industrial complex. They pulled into a large metal building filled with crates and 55-gallon drums of all colors. Lenny got out of the vehicle and followed the men to an office with windows that faced the interior of the building. The blinds were closed.

One of the men knocked, and someone behind the door responded with a grunt. One man opened the door while the other two patted Lenny down for additional weapons. They sent him in and remained outside as they closed the door behind him.

The room was dirty and smelled of stale coffee grounds. It seemed to be a break room. It had white metal cabinets and stained counters, a stainless steel sink, and a flimsy rectangular table with plastic chairs. Some of the fluorescent ceiling lights were out, and one flickered at a frequency that would eventually give him a headache. A rusty refrigerator that he thought might be left over from the Cold War hummed in the far corner like a malfunctioning power transformer.

"I am Tao," the man said and directed Lenny to sit down.

Lenny knew that Tao was the new CEO of Syncorp. His predecessor, Cho, had resided in a fancy headquarters building in Baton Rouge. It looked like Tao preferred more of a blue-collar facility. Tao was at least 15 years older than the late Cho, and his gray-black hair was long enough to slick back on his head with some kind of hair product that maintained a shine.

The Chinese hadn't delayed in replacing the former boss of the operation. But it seemed that Tao hadn't come through the ranks: in the past months, Lenny had met over 10 of the senior operatives in the network, and Tao hadn't been one of them. He figured the senior man had been brought in from the outside, and therefore would not be completely caught up with what had been happening – at least he'd not be as well-versed as Cho had been. And Tao had already made a mistake by bringing him to the safe house – if that's what it was.

Lenny felt a little colder when he calculated the possibility that they'd taken him there to terminate the relationship. If the situation took a bad turn, he'd activate the distress call – an elegant safety device with which he'd been fitted before leaving the CIA facility.

"You have had some recent failures," Cho blurted.

Lenny didn't know what to say.

"Explain yourself," Tao added.

"Well," Lenny stammered. "I've had some unfortunate timing, and the man was a – "

"—Three times this man got away," Tao cut him off. "You do not understand the importance of the information he possesses."

"There were armed operatives with him the last time," Lenny said. "I walked into a virtual ambush – I was shot at."

"Are you afraid to die, Mr. Butrolsky?" Tao asked in a slow hiss as he reached for something below the table. "Let me show you something about death."

Lenny's arm tensed with an automatic reflex to grab his gun. He stifled it just in time. He didn't have it.

Tao slapped a thick file folder on the table and slid it to Lenny. Some photos slipped out along the way. "This man we need to find, William Thompson, is a mass murderer."

Lenny opened the folder and gathered the pictures. The one on the top caught his attention, not because it showed something particularly gruesome, but because he couldn't identify what he was seeing.

"That's Cho," Tao said.

Lenny looked back down at the image. He could make out some bones, and the general outline of a skull. Other than that, it seemed to be a black and reddish-brown amalgam with parts that looked metallic. "What the hell is this?"

Tao stared at him for a few seconds, nodding, and seemingly studying Lenny's response. "You have not seen this before," Tao said.

Lenny shook his head. "I don't know what this is – what am I looking at?"

"Flip through the others."

Lenny did as he was told, and it became clear. The other photos revealed bodies from different locations on the deck of a ship, taken from a variety of angles.

"Those 53 men were incinerated on the deck of our aircraft carrier near Antarctica," Tao said. "The metal melted beneath them, and their bodies continued to sizzle like fried eggs well afterwards, despite the horrid cold. Others were severely burned as their boots melted beneath them while trying to tend to the victims."

Lenny was flabbergasted. He'd never seen anything like it. It looked like the men had been thrown into a shallow pool of molten iron and left there while it solidified. "What happened? Was it a flamethrower, or some kind of laser weapon?"

Tao shook his head and reached out his hand for Lenny to return the folder. "I think you well know. It was the man you delivered to Cho. With your connections to Red Wraith, we thought you'd be the best choice to carry out his elimination."

"I still can – "

Tao raised his hand and cut him off. "You are too exposed right now. The CIA must be well aware of your presence."

That was an understatement, Lenny thought.

"Our people will work on this for a while," Tao continued. "You will be brought back when the time is right."

"Do you want me to go back to tracking down Jacob Hale?"

Tao shook his head. "You'll be given new tasks."

Lenny nodded but remained silent. It was exactly what he wanted to hear.

"There are stores of information at different sites around the country – Syncorp files and other things – that the Americans haven't yet collected," Tao explained.

"Important stuff?" Lenny asked. "Or just redundant?"

"As far as you're concerned, it's all important," Tao said. "You just need to retrieve it. Successfully this time."

Lenny cringed. "Where?"

"Your first trip will be to Long Island, New York," Tao said.

"What's there?"

Tao stared at him as if he should have known the answer.

It took him a few seconds. "Oh, yes, the compressed punishment facility that's there – in Riverhead," Lenny said.

Tao nodded. "That's only one of the locations you will be visiting. It's shut down, but otherwise undisturbed," Tao said. "You'll get detailed instructions soon."

It looked to Lenny like he'd soon have something to deliver to the CIA.

JACOB OPENED the first image file and his heart sank.

It was a uniformly gray square with no discernible features – no image, no structure whatsoever.

He opened the other two, and they looked the same.

He zoomed in on one of the bitmap images so that he could see the graininess of the pixels. They looked to be a random distribution of gray-tones, ranging from light to dark. When zoomed out, it all looked the same shade of gray, much the way the dots in Seurat's paintings blend to show the illusion of continuous colors.

Technically, the images were "pix-map" rather than bitmap, since each pixel could choose any one of numerous allowable shades. In contrast, in a bitmap image, each pixel could only take on one of two possible shades, usually black or white. Pix-map images provided much more detail. Most people referred to them both as bitmap images, unless there was a reason to make a distinction between them.

The upside was that Wave Tempest was able to identify and extract large bitmap images from the raw data. The downside was that the images looked to be a random distribution of pixels, and therefore provided no information. He'd have the software do a detailed analysis of the images, looking for patterns and calculating statistics of various types. But he doubted anything useful would come of it.

He knew it was likely that the images were encrypted. The problem was that there were numerous methods that could have been used to encrypt them, and none of them would be easy to break.

For instance, one encryption method involved changing the shade of each individual pixel based on some mathematical formula. The receiver of the image would need to input a parameter in order for the formula to operate correctly. This parameter was a key, or a password, which was usually a long number or a string of characters.

Jacob had neither the key, nor the decryption formula. He was dead in the water.

He set up Wave Tempest to crunch on the data from the longer part of the incoming AM signal, and went up to the dome with a Pepsi to think about what to do next.

Lenny flew into MacArthur Airport in Islip, Long Island, rented a car under an alias, and took Highway 27 east, toward Montauk Point. It was late afternoon, and the sun was at his back.

Twenty minutes into the drive, the city thinned into sparse suburbs and rural developments. He took the exit for the William Floyd Parkway and headed north. He passed the entrance to Brookhaven National Lab, and could tell by the new structure at the front gate that they'd bolstered security since 9/11. It was a good thing he wasn't trying to get into that place again. Some of his early work for Heinrich Bergman had been connected to the lab or, rather, to people who had been working there. As far as he knew, they'd never found the bodies.

It had been 10 years since he'd last been on Long Island, but it all came back to him. It amazed him how muscle memory for driving could be recalled and put into service even after a decade. In his case, he'd navigated out of Islip Airport without even thinking about it. Now he was approaching Highway 25 and knew he could go west, toward the trendy town of Port Jefferson, or east, in the direction of the old Naval Testing Grounds.

There were three targets from which he was to make acquisitions. The first was a set of climate-controlled storage buildings at the naval testing facility. He figured it would be the easiest of the operations due to location and lackluster security.

The second target was the deserted Compressed Punishment Facility in Riverhead, 15 miles east of Brookhaven National Lab, on I-495. He still needed instructions on what to find in the so-called "Stone Box." The name was rarely used in the news; it wasn't a flashy building like Detroit's Red Box, but it stood out like an ominous gray ruin on the eastern outskirts of Riverhead, on the bank of the Peconic River. The building itself was only a few years old, and was probably in perfect shape. It hadn't been damaged and gutted like the Red Box had been. But the grounds hadn't been maintained since the shutdown, making the place resemble an old, deserted asylum. He was familiar with the security measures taken at the Red Box and, if the Riverhead facility had the same, it could be a dangerous mission. His hope was that most of the sophisticated systems had been deactivated.

The third destination on the list was Plum Island. Located in Gardiners Bay, a mile east of Orient Point, off the North Fork of Long Island, the place was a convolution of oddities that included the Animal Disease Center and the Plum Island Light, a lighthouse. His fingers tingled at the thought of the place. It would be, by far, the most dangerous undertaking of the three.

Established by the US Department of Agriculture in 1954, control of Plum Island was assumed by the Department of Homeland Security at about the same time Riverhead, at the center of Long Island, was chosen for the location of the Stone Box Compressed Punishment facility. Both developments occurred in 2003 in response to the 9/11 attacks.

There were still top-secret activities on Plum Island, and labeling the security as tight was an understatement. It employed electronic, human, and canine surveillance, and there were measures taken in the surrounding waterways, including boat patrols and passive sonar detectors. It would be the most difficult place he'd ever attempted to access. He'd save Plum Island for last.

His first order of business was to check into his hotel, and then rent a truck. He'd hit the first place on the list – the Naval Testing Grounds – around 2:00 a.m. the next morning. It would be a bulk move of files and electronic storage media. The other two places would take planning, but he'd be after smaller, specific items that had yet to be detailed. He hoped the forthcoming descriptions would be better than what they'd provided for the book and keys.

He carried two phones now: one for the CIA, and the other for Chinese intelligence. It was like having one for the wife, and another for the mistress. Although he had neither, Lenny knew he'd better not mix them up. Making a mistake with the CIA wouldn't matter – they knew about the wife. If he said something out of place with the Chinese, however, things could get dicey.

By 5:00 p.m., he'd checked into the hotel and rented a box truck. He'd paid an extra fee for the company to deliver the truck to the hotel. At 6:00 p.m. he was on his way to Port Jefferson to get dinner. He thought about shellfish but decided he couldn't take a chance on getting sick. A burger and fries would have to do. Too much was at stake.

JACOB SPENT most of the day working on the long part of the AM signal. It was more complex than the short part, but he set up Wave Tempest to take a crack at it, and let it run. After dinner, he took a closer look at the three bitmap images the program had extracted from the short part of the signal.

The first thing he noticed was that there was a solid white square, 16 pixels on a side, in the extreme upper left corner of each image. It wasn't noticeable when the whole pictures were in view because they were 1,600 pixels on a side. The feature was a little odd, but he assumed that it had something to do with orienting the images.

Other than that, the statistical analyses of the images didn't reveal anything helpful. The average pixel shade was about the same for all three images, as was the distribution of shades.

What he needed was the decoding formula and the key. The operation would change each individual pixel by increasing or decreasing its tone level, which took on values from zero, which represented white, to 255, which represented black. The formula might add 10 levels to a pixel at level 115, taking it to 125, thereby making it darker, or subtract from another one, making it lighter. It would have to do that to over a million pixels. With the correct formula and key, the end result would be an image.

At 9:15 p.m., after running for four hours, the Wave Tempest program crashed.

Jacob was tired – he was running on three hours of sleep – and hungry.

He went up to the kitchen, put a TV dinner in the oven, and set the timer for 16 minutes. It was going to be Salisbury steak again, with mashed potatoes, gravy, peas, and cherry cobbler.

He turned on the TV and flipped through the channels. He watched the American networks for about ten minutes. They were covering upcoming elections and were focused mostly on domestic issues.

He then flipped to BBC News and caught the end of another squabble between Russian and French diplomats regarding the AM disturbances. The finger-pointing persisted even after the disturbance had ceased, making Jacob think that it must have been a slow news day.

BBC then turned to a related story, anchored by the same woman who had directed the discussion on gravitational waves the previous night, with the same panel that included the American from the SETI Institute, and the Russian and Swedish scientists.

The timer chimed and he headed for the oven.

The anchor first addressed the panel contributors and went right into discussion. "Seems you were right, Dr. Stills," she began. "The glitches plaguing the gravitational wave facilities have subsided."

Jacob whipped around and stared at the screen.

The man nodded. "I wasn't lying last night when I told you I had a reliable source inside one of the facilities."

The woman turned to the other two men. "So, do you still think it's a coincidence that the glitches began with the AM disturbance, and then ended with it?"

"A horribly unfortunate coincidence," the Russian replied. "It adds fuel to the conspiracy hopefuls such as this man."

Jacob's mind buzzed. There was something he was overlooking. An instant later, it hit him.

He started to run out of the kitchen, toward the stairs, but slid to a halt and turned around.

He went to the oven and turned it off, and stopped the timer. He then extracted the TV dinner from the oven and set it on one of the burners to cool.

He ran for the stairs.

LENNY GOT up at 6:30 a.m., arrived at a local used bookstore by eight o'clock, and ordered a coffee and a bagel. It was the only place nearby that was open this early on a Sunday.

He grabbed a newspaper and sat next to a window, pretending to read.

The mission from the night before had been uneventful. The storage facility was alarmingly unsecure, and he was surprised kids hadn't looted the place long ago. He figured it was so far out in the boonies that it didn't attract attention.

He'd had to defeat a few doors and padlocks. The latter he'd cut with a bolt cutter. He'd picked the locks of all the inner doors except one that was more complicated. For that one, he used a small explosive device that was triggered with a shotgun shell. Since he'd been deep inside the building, and had seen no one on the premises outside, he hadn't worried about the noise.

It had taken him over an hour to carry out the cardboard file boxes. He was grateful that the truck had come with a dolly, otherwise it would have taken him twice as long and his back would be aching. He'd flipped through some of the files to make sure they were the right ones; he'd seen the top-secret markings as well as mention of Syncorp and Red Wraith, so he knew it was the right stuff. There were also boxes of hard drives and other older storage media, like CDs and DVDs.

He'd hand off the truck to his Chinese contacts at a large grocery store at noon, after the CIA made copies and removed anything of particular importance. He'd then take a cab back to the hotel. The CIA had already fitted both the truck and its cargo with tracking devices. They'd use them to root out the Chinese network in the New York area and wherever they would lead.

What Lenny found disturbing was that the sensitive information stored on US government sites was unknown to the US government, but known to the Chinese. His job was therefore to use Chinese intelligence to help the Americans find their own information. It was an unsettling reality that there was no one in the US who knew everything that the government was doing. On one hand, it was dangerous: things like Red Wraith and other black projects could live in relative autonomy. On the other hand, it was a weakness: connections and synergistic interactions were missing from the big picture. Why hadn't the US known about this information? Was there anyone left who understood its significance? Not that Lenny understood the technical details, but he had an appreciation for the importance of Red Wraith information.

Now it was time to plan the Stone Box operation. In this case, he was after a stash of computer hard drives and storage devices. They would be easier to carry, but more difficult to obtain. And it would be more challenging to get into the building. Unlike the storage facility at the Naval Testing Grounds, the Stone Box still had security guards patrolling the premises, and some electronic surveillance and alarms in the building.

He pulled out his laptop and opened the map file provided to him by his Chinese contacts. It was time to develop a game plan.

He'd make the move tonight.

It was a Sunday morning and Daniel had arrived a little later than usual. He'd had some trouble getting to sleep and woke up after 7:00 a.m. He usually woke up without an alarm at 5:30 a.m., but he must have been more exhausted than usual. The stress didn't help.

When he got to 713, Sylvia and Thackett were already seated in the discussion area. There was a stainless steel coffee warmer on the coffee table, along with porcelain cups and dispensers for cream and sugar.

"Running a little late today?" Sylvia asked.

Daniel thought her tone revealed concern, but brushed it aside. Arriving after 7:00 a.m. was considered late for him, and it was already 8:30 a.m.

"I had a late night. Something going on?" he asked as he grabbed a coffee mug and sat next to Sylvia on the couch.

Thackett nodded. "The others are on the way."

Five minutes later, they had all arrived and were seated.

"Jacob Hale has requested data from the Laser Interferometer Gravitational-Wave Observatories, or LIGO facilities, in Livingston, Louisiana and Hanford, Washington," Thackett explained. "He warned that we should extract the data without drawing attention."

"Gravitational wave?" Denise asked.

Heads turned to Will.

Will nodded. "I'm no expert, but I do know that they are waves in space-time that are produced when massive objects move in certain ways, or collide," he explained. "The first observed gravitational waves were produced by two colliding black holes located somewhere in distant space. It resulted in a Nobel Prize in physics years ago."

"I've heard that gravitational waves will open a new world for observational astronomy," Sylvia said. "They can be used to study dynamic events – effects of supernovae and things like that."

Will went on to explain that when massive objects wobbled, collided, or exploded, they produced waves in space-time that could be visualized as circular ripples expanding around an agitated fishing bobber on the surface of a smooth pond. The gravitational waves would emanate outward in all directions, traveling long distances, and could be detected with specialized sensing equipment. The detection apparatus was enormous, and gathered data using an optical device called an interferometer that had two perpendicular arm-like components, each about four kilometers long. On top of that, two of these colossal devices, separated by thousands of miles, were needed in order to make measurements. A gravitational-wave observation could only be authenticated if it were detected at both facilities – a method that's called a coincidence measurement. There were two such gravitational-wave detectors in the United States, one in Livingston, Louisiana, and the other in Hanford, Washington.

"These are not mechanical waves, like seismic waves from earthquakes," Will added. "They actually distort space-time itself, and travel at the speed of light."

"So why would Hale want this data?" Daniel asked.

Thackett cleared his throat. "He said LIGO detected glitches that were diagnosed as electrical disturbances – giving them false readings that were hampering their measurements," he explained. "They started and stopped with the AM disturbances."

"Get him the data as soon as you can," Will blurted. "He's brilliant."

"Why?" Sylvia asked. "Is it important?"

"Any wave can carry information," Will replied. "Gravitational waves are no different."

"Can we get the data without anyone knowing?" Jonathan asked.

Thackett stood from his chair, winked, and pulled out his phone. "I'm on it."

AFTER SENDING the email the night before, Jacob couldn't concentrate on anything.

He'd watched BBC News and eaten his Salisbury steak TV dinner, and then munched on chocolate chip cookies until he could no longer keep his eyes open. He'd gone to bed at 10:30 p.m.

At 8:30 a.m. he rolled out of the bunk, took a quick shower, and was in the kitchen a half hour later. His mind was clear, and he thought his sleep routine would now be back to normal.

He ate banana nut oatmeal for breakfast as he watched the news. All of the stories were repeats except those that covered the American elections. He was afraid now that the BBC was going to get distracted from the real story, like all of the other networks. He hoped that the important events weren't going to fade away from the spotlight, but maybe that would be for the best. The general public didn't need to know what was going on for now. They couldn't do anything about it.

Overnight, he'd dreamt about the bitmap images from the AM data. The images were square with 1,600 pixels to a side, and had small white squares in their upper left corners. It could be that the images were supposed to be added together, pixel for pixel, kind of like overlaying two semitransparent slides. In the case of adding bitmaps, a pixel at one position in one image would be added to the pixel at the corresponding position in the second image to get the sum. That sum pixel, which would now represent a different shade than the constituents, would be located at the same location in the final image. This would be done for all of the pixels to form the final, summed image.

It could also be that the "decrypted" image was supposed to be the sum of all three images. And this could get even more complicated: since the images were square, one could first rotate an image by 90, 180, or 270 degrees and add it to another image. Finally, it might be that there was a complicated set of additions, subtractions, rotations, and numerous other operations that were needed to get the final image.

The nice thing was that Wave Tempest could do all of it automatically and quickly.

He went to the downstairs table and opened his laptop. He set up the program to carry out a long series of operations on the bitmap images that included all combinations of summing and rotations. In the end, he'd have over ten thousand bitmap images to peruse with the hope that one of them might be the decrypted version.

He went to the computer on the desk beneath the overhang and opened an email from the staff. It read, "Dr. Hale, we are currently in the process of acquiring the LIGO data you requested. It was a keen observation on your part, and we agree that it is worth checking out. More to follow."

He was encouraged by the response.

As Wave Tempest carried out its task, he decided to go for a run to clear his mind.

LENNY SWITCHED OFF THE LIGHTS, killed the car engine, and waited for his vision to adjust to the dark. He turned on his night-vision binoculars and scanned the parking lot behind the imposing building. It was 2:00 a.m., and there was no traffic, even in the commercial areas just a half-mile away.

The Stone Box was the largest structure in Riverhead, NY, and he'd imagined that it had attracted attention from the locals, even though it was on the outskirts of the city. It reached 25 stories, and had a few sublevels. It wasn't as tall as the Red Box but spanned a larger area. Of course, it had the same total space since it had 365 treatment rooms and preparation facilities identical to those in the Detroit facility.

The report that armed security guards patrolled the place was false. Lenny had staked it out all day and not a single car had entered the parking lot. He'd driven by numerous times since midnight, and it had been all clear.

His CIA backups were in the area if he ran into trouble, but he was otherwise on his own. Although, he knew his Chinese handlers might also be watching. The Chinese were strictly "hands-off" with their contractual work. It wasn't clear whether that was policy, or a peculiarity of the culture.

According to the building schematics, the security at the emergency exits on the north side of the building could be disabled without setting off alarms. Lenny had suspected the building would have this flaw, since the Red Box facility once had the same one. Long ago, he'd been tasked with overseeing the upgrade. He hoped that the lack of communication between government entities worked in his favor this time and that the Stone Box hadn't patched the problem.

He got out of the car and extracted a duffle bag from the back seat that contained his tool kit. There was also room in the bag to carry out the hard drives.

He made his way across the blacktop parking lot to the nearest emergency exit. There were three on the north side of the building, and he chose one bracketed by two large bushes to give him some cover.

The alarm-triggering mechanism on the door was like that found in most residences: a magnet or electronic chip, and a sensor. Since the sensor and chip were close together when the door was closed, the sensor would detect the presence of the chip. If the sensor didn't detect the chip, the door was assumed to be open, and the alarm would be activated.

Lenny understood the system well. The challenge came in separating the chip from the door while keeping it in contact with the sensor in the doorframe, and then mounting the chip to the sensor. Superglue worked perfectly for the latter. The former, however, was not easy. The chip was mounted flush with the inner edge of the door, and could only be reached by cutting through the door's outer panel. It was a steel security door, so it would take work, and make noise.

He located the sensor-chip pair high on the door. He grumbled to himself: this would be hard on his damaged shoulder. He found a small wooden crate next to a dumpster on the far side of the lot, giving him something on which to stand to reduce how far he'd have to reach.

After 40 minutes of careful cutting with a small battery-powered tool, the chip was nearly free. He then squeezed superglue between the chip and the sensor. He'd have to wait a few minutes before cutting away the last bit of metal holding the chip in place.

He packed up all of the tools except the electric cutter, and then leaned his back against the wall next to the door and lit a cigarette.

It still baffled him how they could design a building for high security, and then skimp on certain parts, making it vulnerable to simple methods of break-in. He glanced up at a camera and retracted his criticism: had the cameras been operational, his approach would not have been possible. That also went for what he was going to do inside.

He finished his cigarette, ground it out with his shoe, and picked up the butt and put it in his front pant pocket. He tested the hardness of the glue with a jackknife and was satisfied that it was cured. He then cut away the last sliver of metal that attached the chip to the door. Next, he pulled a set of lock-picking tools out of his tool kit and went to work on the lock. Again, it was standard work. Five minutes later, he was ready to open the door.

He put the tools in the bag and got ready to make a break for the car if it turned out he'd overlooked something. He pulled the door slowly in case something caught on the chip as it opened. When it was clear, he listened intently for a few seconds, moved inside, and closed the door.

The entire building was under emergency power. It was dim, but he didn't turn on his flashlight. He knew the layout, and his eyes adjusted quickly.

He made his way to the main security panel and opened it, exposing flashing green, red, and yellow lights, and switches and wires. The system was identical to that of the Red Box. Under normal conditions, it was controlled and monitored remotely, but that required staffing, and there wasn't any. The system had been reduced to its bare-bones settings.

Lenny jumped a few wires, flipped some switches, and went over it all again in his mind. He was most concerned about the motion detectors. There were a few laser traps, but he could see those in the low light. When he was sure he'd disabled everything between him and his destination, he moved on.

He had to go to Level D, four floors below ground. The elevators were not operational, so he took the stairs. It seemed to get darker as he descended, even though the lighting was uniform the entire way.

On the second flight down, he got a feeling that someone was following him. His senses heightened as if he were in danger. He stopped, held his breath, and listened for movement above and below him. He heard nothing for a full 10 seconds and resumed his descent.

He arrived at Level D and looked through a small window in the stairwell door. The other side was dark. He pulled the door and cringed as it opened with a screech that echoed in the stairwell.

He flipped on his flashlight and navigated through hallways until he found the main office. The door was unlocked, and he walked into the office of the former warden of the facility. He went to the far side of the office and opened two wooden cabinet doors mounted on the wall behind a large desk. The cabinet was a façade that concealed a safe.

He pulled out his phone and found the email that contained the combination for the safe. Chinese intelligence had extracted it from the former warden, which is how they knew of the safe's existence in the first place. He recalled that the warden had then been removed from the equation using their usual methods which, in this case, meant dissolving his body in acid to remove all biological evidence of his existence – or as close as they could get. In the business they'd say the man "got juiced." Lenny had been tasked with dumping the warden's liquefied remains in a garbage dump in rural South Carolina.

He dialed the combination and opened the safe. He unloaded seven hard drives and four small data storage devices and packed them in his duffle bag. There was also a thick file folder that wasn't on the list of items to acquire. That was ominous. Chinese intelligence could be testing him to see whether he'd deliver it: he'd not been there to hear what the warden had told them. He put the folder in the bag, closed the safe door, and spun the dial.

A sound like that of a pencil rolling off a desk came from the main office.

Lenny's fingers tingled. Now he had to get out of the place.

AT 10:00 P.M., Jacob took a stroll to the Count Cristo Coffee House. He brought his backpack, which contained a notebook that he used to jot down ideas and plans, and also an unclassified source – a book – on the mythical Nazi "Base 211" that was rumored to have been located in Antarctica. The book was riddled with conspiracy theory and conjecture, but he had a hard time discounting anything now that he'd seen things from his new perspective. Sometimes the conspiracy theorists were right, although they rarely knew it.

He left the coffeehouse at closing time, and got back to 17 Swann Street a little after midnight, just as Wave Tempest completed its full set of transformations of the images. There were over 10 thousand of them to examine. He worked through the first 5 thousand, but they were all gray, just like the original images, with no structure at all.

At 2:15 a.m. he took a break and went up to the kitchen and grabbed a soda from the fridge. He turned on the TV and found that all of the news channels were replaying their Sunday programs, most of which covered the US elections coming in November. However, BBC had again interviewed the representative from SETI around dinnertime, and was now replaying it.

The interviewer was aggressive and seemed to go out of his way to be disrespectful toward the man. Jacob felt bad for the SETI rep, especially since he might really be on to something regarding the gravitational-wave data carrying information. But Jacob felt it was beneficial for the media to squelch the man's ideas for now – he didn't want to get scooped on this one.

He went back down to the first-floor table and continued screening images. He finished at 4:00 a.m. They were all gray.

His only hope now was that the data from the gravitational-wave facilities would show up, and would provide something useful.

Before he headed upstairs for bed, he checked the desktop computer one last time to see if there was a message from the staff about the LIGO data. No luck.

That was probably good for now – he didn't want to go through another all-nighter.

Tao paced in his apartment with his hands behind his back. He breathed forcefully through his nose as he coaxed his mind to remain calm.

He hadn't eaten all day, and hadn't slept since 4:00 a.m. the previous morning. He was now approaching 24 hours without sleep, and his eyes burned.

He stopped at a liquor cabinet and opened it. He'd been drinking too much lately. This time it would be vodka.

He grabbed a fine wheat vodka called Double Cross, and poured two fingers worth into a whiskey glass. Ideally, the bottle would have been in the freezer for a few hours, but an ice cube would have to do. He took a swig, poured in a little more, and put the bottle away.

The American asset would be reporting back any time now, assuming there had been no complications. He wasn't sure there would be anything of importance in this new cache of information, but everything helped. Although he was up to speed on what his predecessor, Cho, had done, he was not confident in his own understanding of the big picture. It wasn't clear that anyone knew what was really happening.

If the American were to be successful in his collection tasks, Tao would reassign him to eliminate William Thompson. There was less risk with contracting an American to do it rather than a Chinese operative. The latter could initiate a war. But Tao thought he'd delay the decision until he'd assessed what Lenny had collected. And, if Lenny were to fail this time, he'd have to be *juiced*.

Tao didn't understand the importance of killing Thompson. He huffed to himself as he considered the possibility that the Chinese government might be trying to kill Thompson out of revenge. If he had really killed all of those men on the aircraft carrier – fried them like eggs – then he deserved a slow, painful death. But Tao couldn't get himself to believe the official story – the idea of a man turning himself into some kind of supernatural entity and killing everyone. It was more likely that there had been some kind of oil fire, or maybe an incendiary ordinance had somehow discharged on the ship.

Tao also doubted the accuracy of the intelligence used to locate the information that Lenny was currently collecting. That skepticism had arisen from a video he'd watched: Cho had tortured the former warden of the compressed punishment facility in New York – the one that was currently being burgled. Cho had performed a dental horror show in that video. He'd drilled the man's teeth, and pulled a few, while he'd asked questions. This was the source of the information on which Lenny was operating.

When Cho was certain he'd get nothing more from the warden, he played torture artist until the man finally convulsed, and died. The worst thing Tao had ever seen was Cho removing half of the man's lower jaw and then showing it to him, some of the teeth still in place.

Cho had been a horrible little man. Tao was glad he was dead.

He took a sip of vodka and stepped onto the balcony and into the muggy outside air. Whatever Cho had done, Thompson had probably killed more – at least that's what he'd been told. But he wasn't seeking revenge on anyone's behalf. His first responsibility was to the intelligence network, and collecting the information they needed.

Tao's superiors had given him a thorough briefing on Cho's Red Dragon project, but he felt there were omissions in what he was told – big ones.

He knew about the probes, the White Stone, William Thompson, and that they were searching for a secret Nazi base that the Americans had already discovered. He knew about the outgoing signals from the probe, and the incoming ones from deep space that everyone was playing off as a malfunctioning Russian satellite. The Russians were even playing their part by being targeted with the blame, and then denying everything, as usual. But they knew, and could prove, that the signal wasn't coming from them, and they still played along. *Why?*

Tao figured that, even though the Russians were constantly scuffling with other geopolitical powers, they wanted to avoid frightening the general public. That could lead to civil unrest. Even the United States kept it under wraps: maybe they too feared losing control of their population. Perhaps if this information became public knowledge China would have an additional advantage; they already had control of their people.

It was possible that everyone was holding on to their information because they knew something bigger was coming, even though no one knew what that was.

Tao was thrilled to be involved. He was at the ground level, collecting information, but also at a position high enough to see many of the larger pieces in motion. If there were a breakthrough, he'd be the first to see it. It was a privilege experienced by only a few people in the world.

He downed the rest of the vodka and winced as it seared his throat. Where was that report from the American?

LENNY SNAKED through the halls and then up four flights of stairs. He flinched at the slightest stimuli, and trembled uncontrollably. What was the origin of this fear?

He'd never felt afraid of anything – not like this – even when his life had been threatened. He wanted to run, but knew he had to proceed carefully which, in this case, meant slowly. The odor of his sweat only fed the fear.

A few minutes later he was at the security control panel. He reset all of the systems he'd deactivated. He then cracked open the exit door and peered outside. All clear. He set the door so that it would lock when he closed it, and then stepped out and eased it shut. The only blemish was the notch cut in its top left corner. Otherwise, it was like he'd never been there.

He went to his car, deposited the duffle in the trunk, and drove off the location using a back alley, between a warehouse and a fenced stockyard filled with excavation equipment. He wondered if it was there to demolish the Stone Box.

His trembling diminished as soon as he exited the property. What the hell was going on? It hadn't been simple fear that he'd felt; it was a nearly paralyzing fright. His skin still crept as if he were being stalked by something horrible.

He pushed it all to the back of his mind and concentrated on the next step. He took Highway 25 west, out of Riverhead, to Highway 25A, to his new hotel in Port Jefferson.

He parked the car away from the lights in the hotel lot and opened the trunk. He unzipped the duffle stuffed with the items he'd taken from the facility. He then unzipped an identical bag filled with hard drives, storage devices, and files given to him by the CIA. The manufactured items had information that the CIA was certain the Chinese already had, mixed in with well-designed misinformation to lead them astray. He made sure that the dummy bag had the same number of items in it as the authentic one. He zipped them both, and took the bag carrying the authentic items, and his tools, with him into the hotel room.

He sent an email to his Chinese handler indicating that he had the items and they could make the switch.

The handler responded with a time and location.

Lenny would have only a few hours to sleep.

JACOB OPENED his eyes and searched for the source of the noise that woke him.

It was his phone, beeping and buzzing.

He reached into the inset shelf above his head and grabbed his mobile, which was next to the clock that read 6:00 a.m.

It was a text message from "The Staff," but there was no phone number. It read, "Requested data on your laptop."

Jacob read it again as he sat up in the bunk and put his feet on the carpet. It was the gravitational-wave data, he concluded, and his heart rate elevated.

He took a shower, got dressed, started the coffee maker, and headed for his computer on the first-floor table. His mind felt clear even though he was going on two hours of sleep. He figured it was all adrenaline.

He opened up his laptop where he found a new folder on the computer's desktop labeled LIGO. Inside the folder were two files: one labeled "Read Me" and the other, "Raw LIGO Data." He opened the former and read it. It explained that the other file contained all raw data starting from one week before the outgoing EM blast from the probe, and ending yesterday, one day after the incoming AM signal ceased. It was exactly what he needed.

He started the Wave Tempest program, imported the LIGO data, and plotted it. The result was a graph that showed signal intensity versus time. The first peak in the data, which coincided with the outgoing blast from the probe, was much larger in magnitude than all of the others and was composed of a mess of complicated peaks. The rest were clustered together in groups of seven, the first of which started about a week after the outgoing EM blast had ceased. It was precisely when the incoming AM disturbance had started.

Jacob opened up graphs of all of the incoming and outgoing electromagnetic disturbances, and compared them to the gravitational wave data.

His heart pounded with excitement and anxiety. Everything matched.

The first, messy part of the LIGO data overlapped perfectly with the outgoing EM blast. And the groups of seven LIGO peaks that came later, matched with the beginning of each incoming AM cycle. There were seven gravitational-wave signals in each cluster, just as there were seven sources of the AM signals.

On the LIGO graph, he zoomed in on the most prominent signal in one of the clusters of seven and found it to be amplitude-modulated – there was information encoded in it.

Just as he had done with the AM disturbance data, he got Wave Tempest crunching the data. He had a hunch about what it was going to spit out.

All he could do was wait.

AT 6:15 a.m. Lenny carried everything out to the parking lot.

The previous afternoon he'd rented a second car, a blue Toyota 4-Runner SUV, and had the rental company deliver it to the hotel. He loaded the authentic items into the blue Toyota along with all of his belongings.

He went to the first car, a gray Kia sedan, and confirmed that the counterfeit materials were in the trunk. He then pulled the Kia out of the hotel parking lot and started driving to the rendezvous point, where he'd meet operatives of the Chinese network. For some reason, they'd always used diners, and he headed for one located in Patchogue, on the southern shore of Long Island. Thirty minutes later he was sitting in a booth in a strange chrome-finished diner that was already populated with pensioners at this early hour.

Lenny watched out the window as he sipped coffee from a porcelain mug. Just as the clock on his phone flipped to 7:00 a.m., a dark SUV pulled next to his Kia in the parking lot.

Lenny put a few bucks on the table, walked out to his car, and opened the trunk with the remote. Two Asian men got out of the SUV, and Lenny handed the bag to one of them.

Without a word, Lenny got into his car and drove away.

He grinned as he watched the SUV pull out behind him and head in the opposite direction. The hard drives and memory devices were rigged with two viruses. One was an easy-to-identify location program that would alert the owner to its location if stolen. It was something that the Chinese would expect to find on a high-security device. The second virus, however, had the same function, but was highly sophisticated and hidden in "erased" memory.

Computer-savvy people understood that most of the so-called

deleted data on a storage device was not really deleted, but just marked for overwriting when space was needed. This particular virus was hidden in that reallocated space. Lenny likened it to someone hiding by lying amongst dead bodies and pretending they were dead. The important point was that the decoy drives, if ever connected to the Internet, would discretely give away their locations. And then the Chinese network would start to unravel.

He went back to the hotel where he abandoned the Kia and drove away in the Toyota, never to return. He headed for a coffeehouse in Port Jefferson to plan the Plum Island mission. His first two tasks had been successful, but those were child's play compared to the one ahead of him. He still didn't know what he was supposed to collect. All he knew was that, although it was heavy, it wasn't large and could be carried in a knapsack or duffle bag.

The security on Plum Island was formidable. He'd need help from his CIA cohorts on this one. In fact, the operation was so difficult that he wondered if it would look suspicious to Tao if it went off without a hitch. He'd have to think about how to explain how he got around boat patrols, security fences, motion detectors, and dogs. And after that, how he got into the buildings – with a slew of their own security features. And then, how he'd found the items, which were probably locked away in a secure area within one of the buildings. Finally, he'd have to explain how he'd done everything in reverse on the way out. Lenny thought it was like *Mission Impossible*.

He parked the car, went into the coffee shop, got a dark roast brew, and sat in a comfortable chair across from two young mothers chatting about summer camps for their kids. He was running on less than two hours of sleep and hoped the coffee would give him enough of a boost to devise a strategy. It was a bad idea to work out a plan without a clear head – especially for a job of this complexity.

He took the laptop out of his backpack and opened a detailed map of Plum Island that Chinese intelligence had provided. He compared it to the one given to him by the CIA: they were identical, except that the CIA map had schedules of power outages, indicating when security measures would be deactivated in certain areas.

The CIA map was helpful, but it wasn't enough. At noon he'd meet with his CIA handlers to hand over the contents of the late Stone Box warden's safe. He'd ask them for assistance, even though he didn't know what they'd be able to do. Too many people would have to be involved for inside help, including Homeland Security, which would be risky. No matter how much they claimed to cooperate, the CIA did not play well with others, and that meant with Homeland Security and the FBI.

A small boat he'd reserved was ready for him at Orient Point, at the tip of Long Island's North Fork. He'd had some experience with boats, but didn't know how rough the waters would be. Even though he'd have to cover less than two miles on the water, it made him nervous. He'd have to monitor the weather and water conditions, and make plans accordingly.

The difficulty of the mission made him wonder what his Chinese clients thought of him. It was absurd that they'd send him into such a difficult situation without any instructions, or assistance.

His face seemed to heat up with his increasing displeasure. If it weren't imperative to learn exactly what it was they were sending him to find on Plum Island, he would have dropped the job altogether.

He got a coffee refill and a muffin, and sat back down and checked his watch. It was about time for the handoff of Stone Box materials to the CIA. He checked the email account he shared with Chinese intelligence and found a new message. It was a long one, and he read it carefully.

It looked like they had a plan for Plum Island after all, and a good one. He could cancel his boat reservation.

AFTER GETTING Wave Tempest going on the gravitational wave data from LIGO, Jacob went up to the kitchen, poured himself a cup of coffee, and turned on the TV.

He put a bowl of blueberry instant oatmeal in the microwave and paced in front of it while it cooked.

The microwave beeped, he pulled out the bowl, and sat at the counter in front of the TV. As he ate, he surfed through all of the news channels. None of them covered the AM signal, or anything about the gravitational-wave detection facilities. Those stories seemed to be dead, and even the BBC spent most of its airtime on the US elections.

He finished his breakfast, put the bowl in the sink, refilled his coffee, and headed back downstairs.

When he got to the computer, the screen was black so he brushed his finger across the touchpad, bringing it back to life.

Wave Tempest had stopped. On the screen was a table of parameters, and a single file. The program had a 99% confidence rating with the results: it was a 1,600 by 1,600 bitmap image.

Jacob opened it. It was gray, like all of the others.

He zoomed in on the upper left corner and looked for a 16 by 16 pixel white square. It was there, just like in the other images.

His fingers trembled as he set up Wave Tempest to use the new image to conduct image operations – adding and subtracting from the others in various combinations and rotations. He made sure the program started working with the images all oriented the same way – with the small white squares in the upper left corners.

The idea was straightforward. The three gray images extracted from the incoming AM signal did not come with an algorithm and corresponding key to decrypt them. One method of encrypting them was to add an image to them that was just noise – a random distribution of gray tones. The resulting image would be unidentifiable – scrambled. The random noise image that had been added to the others was now the decryption key: all you had to do was subtract it from the scrambled one to recover the original.

However, the encrypting process could be more complicated than just one addition or subtraction of the noise image. For instance, the noise image could first be added to the original, rotated by 90 degrees, and then added again, and so on. It would then require the exact reverse operation to decrypt it. But decryption would be impossible without the original random noise image that was used to do the encryption. He hoped that the image he'd just extracted from the gravitational-wave data from LIGO was the decryption key.

He watched as the program conducted the various operations and spit out the resulting images into a folder. The miniature pics formed an array in the output folder as Wave Tempest proceeded. After working for less than a minute, something caught Jacob's eye. Of the more than 100 images that had already been produced, all were gray except for three.

"Holy shit!" he yelled. There were decrypted images in the folder – pictures.

He opened the first. It resembled a drawing of an atom, but he quickly determined it was a schematic of the solar system. It showed all of the planets – including Pluto – and the moons of Earth and Mars, and what he thought was a comet.

The scale of the drawing was given at the bottom as a circle with a horizontal line through it. It was like a lower-case theta, the Greek letter, but circular. Next to the symbol was a series of solid and open dots that he figured represented a binary number, which probably functioned as a multiplier to set the scale. He had no idea how the units converted to meters, but he could figure that out later since all of the planetary orbital dimensions were known.

Next to Mars and Earth were small, water-tower-shaped icons that Jacob thought looked like the sketches Theo had made of the underwater probe. Wavy lines emanated from them that exited the solar system, and he concluded they represented the outgoing signal.

Wavy lines also came in from multiple directions outside the solar system and were directed toward Earth. He assumed that they represented the incoming AM signal. There was a similar set of waves that went from Mars to Earth.

His breathing had become progressively quicker and more shallow. He took a deep breath and tried to force himself to relax and not hyperventilate.

What was on the monitor before him might be the first evidence of life outside of Earth – intelligent life – and he might be the first human to ever see it. The image conveyed a simple message: Earth was receiving a signal from outside the solar system. And, most importantly, it was intended for Earth.

He opened the next image. It was a map of Earth that showed all of the continents and an expanded view of Antarctica. The locations of two probes were indicated off the Antarctic coast. A triangle was drawn such that one corner was located at one of the probes, another at the South Pole, and the third located inland, near the west coast of Antarctica. He suspected that the third point was the location of the Nazi base.

The only other highlighted point on the map was in Egypt. A line pointed to a location that he knew was near Giza. He zoomed in on the other end of the line and found a circle, inside of which were five concentric rings of illegible symbols.

His vision dimmed as his brain went into overdrive trying to assess the significance of the image. It represented the White Stone. To the right of it was the symbol for the length scale on the previous drawing – a circle crossed by a horizontal line. Two lines extended from the top and bottom of the symbol to the same positions on the circle, indicating that the unit of length shown in the first drawing was the diameter of the White Stone.

But the image did more than set the length scale for the drawings. It was a connection to the White Stone. It was a message: the White Stone and, more importantly, the probe, were not of this world.

He moved the image aside and opened the third one. It looked like an engineering blueprint of a flat, rectangular object. It seemed to have electrical leads – two on the right edge and two on the left – making it seem as if it were an electronic device about the size of his hand.

The wires coming in from the left – if that's what they were – looked as if they were connected to an antenna. Squiggly lines emanated from the antenna toward the input leads, seemingly indicating incoming electromagnetic signals. Near the leads on the right was a string of ones and zeros, and square waves, indicating data going out of the device.

The diagram was laid out like a typical engineering drawing, with top and side views so that all dimensions were clear. The overhead view showed what seemed to be electromagnetic waves impinging on the object's top surface, at the center of which was an equilateral triangle.

Jacob had no idea what the object was, but it was another piece of the puzzle. If he had the object in hand, he might be able to put his skills to work and determine its function.

He stared at the three images lined up from left to right on his computer screen. His friends would now get something in return for their hospitality.

LENNY READ THE EMAIL AGAIN. It beckoned the question, *how embedded were the Chinese?*

More alarmingly, how long would the United States continue to make the same mistakes? Chinese intelligence had one of their operatives working as a scientist at the Plum Island animal disease research facility. The plan to get him inside now seemed trivial.

Lenny would pick up false paperwork from his Chinese handlers that identified him as a technician brought in to repair a machine that was conveniently located in the same building in which the item of interest was stored. He still didn't know what that item was, but he hoped he wouldn't be exposed to anything that would make him sick. A wide variety of deadly diseases were studied at Plum Island, including those that could cross over to humans.

Lenny took Highway 25A west to a donut shop in Oyster Bay where he picked up mock ID materials, paperwork, and a specialized tool kit. He would be Leonard Strovsky, an X-ray fluorescence spectroscopy technician working as a subcontractor for a large scientific company.

His Chinese contact inside the Plum Island facility was Dr. Jennifer Chung. She had disabled the instrument he was being brought into repair, and knew exactly how to fix it. He therefore had a legitimate reason to be there, and the exit would be smooth – the malfunctioning system would be functional when he left. It was a good plan.

The paperwork included some technical information in case someone asked him questions. His response to anything he didn't know was to be, "I understand the electronics, not the physics." To be consistent with this cover, Dr. Chung had removed a plug-in chip from a large circuit board in the device. He would simply plug it in when he was finished. Otherwise, he'd only need to know the basics of X-ray fluorescence, or XRF.

He'd learned that the device was used to illuminate a material sample with X-rays. The sample would respond by emitting a unique spectrum of different X-rays that could be analyzed with a spectrometer. The peaks that appeared in the spectrum could then be used to determine the sample's atomic composition. That's all he'd need to know as a tech. No one should be suspicious.

The tension that had been building in Lenny's body and mind had faded. He was safely playing both sides of the coin. Now, even if he were caught in the act, the CIA would take custody of him. His connection with the Chinese would be over. On the other hand, if the plan worked, he'd continue unraveling the Chinese network. Either way, he wouldn't be shot trying to defeat the security of Plum Island.

After delivering the authentic data storage devices he'd collected from the Stone Box to his CIA handlers in Huntington, he drove back to Port Jefferson, had lunch at an outdoor deli, and drove toward Montauk Point to see the lighthouse on the easternmost part of Long Island. He had time to kill. The operation would begin at 6:00 a.m. the day after next – a Wednesday – when he'd board a ferry for Plum Island at Orient Point.

Just after 3:00 p.m. he entered the Hamptons on Long Island's South Fork and discovered a small public beach. He parked in a nearby lot, got out of the car, and stretched his back and shoulders. He then followed a path of thick boards embedded in the sand and sparse grass to wooden steps that descended to the beach. He walked up to the water, took off his shirt, and slung it over his shoulder. It was only about 70 degrees, but the sun felt good on his back as he walked east, next to the waves.

He thought about his last two jobs. Each was a success, and both sides were happy for the moment. But there would soon be an ugly divorce from one of the parties, and the Chinese network would not be happy when it was over. He wondered if he'd ever be free from them. The CIA could give him a new identity, but he knew there'd be limits to his security.

For starters, leaks within the CIA were inevitable, and he was sure that the Chinese, and other countries, had their sources within it. Next, someone could simply recognize him – anywhere in the world. An asset would then be sent to terminate him. And it would be an easy job.

One thing that kept him safe for now was his constant movement. However, when he was finally stationary, it all could sneak up on him.

He knew he had to put all of that out of his mind. Worrying about the future made no sense. He had to concentrate on the next job.

His Chinese phone chimed with a text informing him that a message was awaiting him in their shared email account. He sat on the edge of a wooden chair and turned away from the sun so that he could see the screen of his phone in his shadow. He navigated to the account and opened a message in the drafts folder. It was a final confirmation from his Chinese handlers with more details, including a description of the object he was to collect.

It was a stainless steel cylinder, about eight inches in diameter and a foot in length. The ends were sealed with knife-edge flanges and copper gaskets. Sharp edges on the rims of the cylinder, and on each cap, were designed to clamp on and cut into both sides of a flat, copper ring to make a seal that kept the cylinder under extreme vacuum – like that of deep space. The cylinder must have contained something sensitive to air.

What the hell was it? A bomb? More likely it was a deadly virus, he thought, considering the place it currently resided. Still, the containment was odd – he didn't think a deep-space-like vacuum was needed to preserve a virus.

He pulled out his CIA phone and typed a message containing all of the relevant information from the Chinese email. He knew the CIA would consider making a mock device for him to deliver to the Chinese so that he might stay plugged into their network.

Lenny sent the message and grinned as he looked out over the water. He'd already provided enough to the CIA to uproot a large part of the Chinese network. He'd always known how susceptible such a covert organization could be to a mole, but had never seen it from the perspective of the mole.

In less than a week, he'd exposed numerous operatives, located the headquarters and the network's leader, Tao, and delivered authentic information to the CIA and bogus info to the Chinese. Now, he'd just exposed a Chinese operative, one Dr. Jennifer Chung, at the Plum Island facility, and would soon deliver a mysterious device to the CIA. Although he wasn't finished, he thought he'd progressed toward his final release to green pastures.

He flipped his sunglasses down and leaned back against the chair. Green pastures. He shuddered as pain spread through his still-healing shoulder and down his arm. He'd be alone. It would be a time when everything buried in his mind would claw for the surface. And then he'd start worrying about where he'd be going next – that final green pasture. Although, he feared it might not be so green. Would he ultimately have to account for his life?

He wondered if those he'd eliminated over the years would come back to haunt him. The nightmares of Jody Dixon hadn't stopped. He'd popped her head like a cantaloupe on the floor. The problem was, in the dream, it wasn't Jody Dixon. It was his daughter. She'd be 31 years old and probably had kids of her own, he thought. But Jody resembled his daughter. Jody was someone's daughter.

He shook away his thoughts. This escalation of guilt and worry seemed to be inherent to the human psyche. He'd noticed that people would always solve one problem, only to replace it with another. The person who'd work three jobs and struggle to pay bills wasn't worried whether that mole on their back was cancer. On the other hand, wealthy people often became obsessed with their health because it was the only thing they couldn't control, and the only thing left to worry about. In Lenny's case, upon retirement, his focus would turn from survival to accountability. Perhaps it was the reason he'd turned back to the CIA: was he attempting to redeem himself? If so, he might die trying. And that might be okay.

His Chinese phone beeped. The message told him to check his email after 4:00 p.m. for additional details. Lenny stood and began retracing his path westward along the beach, into the sun and toward his car. He'd find a quiet place to mentally prepare for a few hours, get dinner, and then a good night's sleep.

He'd leave from Orient Point at 6:00 a.m. the day after next.

JACOB WOKE up and jumped into the shower. The night before, he'd taken his laptop to the coffeehouse and had gone back and forth between examining the three images and trying to decode the long part of the AM signal. The latter was unfruitful, but he developed some ideas about the former.

It seemed to him that the square object in the third image was a decoder of some sort – with the signal coming in one side, and decoded data going out the other. If that were the case, what would be its purpose – to decode the rest of the data in the transmission? Why not just send the data so that it could all be decoded the same way?

The problem with the physical decoder device was that he didn't have it. And he figured that his uncle would have at least mentioned it had he known about it. Jacob had searched 17 Swann for hours, but hadn't found anything that resembled the object in the drawing. It worried him: he might be at a dead end.

The implications of the images had kept his mind reeling all night: signals coming from outside the solar system, the decoder device, and the reference to the White Stone. He wondered if, like the White Stone, the CIA had the decoder stowed somewhere. Perhaps they didn't even know they had it.

He wrote up a report that displayed the images and presented his take on what they meant. He also described the process he used to decrypt them.

Decoding the three original images required multiple subtractions of the encryption noise image he'd extracted from the gravitational wave data from LIGO. The first subtraction was made with the white square in the upper left corner of the original image aligned with that of the encryption noise image. For the second operation, the noise image first had to be rotated by 90 degrees clockwise – a quarter turn – and then subtracted. It was then rotated another 90 degrees and subtracted, and another 90 degrees and subtracted, for a total of four subtractions. Each pixel had to correspond to a number between zero and 255 in order to match a defined gray tone, so any negative numbers resulting from each subtraction reentered the allowable range from the top. Wave Tempest did it all automatically, along with numerous other sequences, but this was the set of operations that worked. The software even created a new decryption image that could be used to decode each of the original images with just one subtraction.

As he wrote the report, he used his uncle's writing style, and emphasized that his interpretations of the images were purely conjecture, even though that should have been obvious.

He composed an email and attached the report file. He then attached all of the decrypted image files separately, even though they appeared as figures in the document. He also included the three original encrypted images, and the decoder noise image. There was always value in the raw data.

At the very end he wrote: *Have you found something that resembles the square decoder device shown in the third image? If so, could you send it to me?*

He took a deep breath and hit the send button at 10:15 a.m. It was as if his chest had been bound by a thousand rubber bands and they'd all broken at once. He'd finally delivered something useful. The stress was gone for the moment.

His report would be a bombshell. It documented the first contact from an extraterrestrial intelligence. But the thought had crossed his mind that maybe this wasn't the first encounter. He had no idea what secrets the governments of the world were keeping.

His neck tightened and he twitched. It occurred to him that he was currently witnessing, or even partaking in, a government cover-up. The struggle between those keeping the secrets and the so-called conspiracy theorists who were trying to pull them out of the shadows made his hands clench in frustration. Perhaps that was because he didn't know on which side of the equation he was positioned. He'd always been for transparency. In this case, perhaps it was better to keep the public in the dark – at least until the government knew what the hell was happening.

He wondered whether anyone else had decoded the images. It had only taken him a few days, so why hadn't the NSA or CIA figured it out already? Although, he was sure they wouldn't tell him if they had. But if they hadn't already decoded the images, their minds were about to be blown.

The key to figuring out how to decrypt the messages was being aware of current events, like Theo had instructed. The key – literally in this case – was the LIGO data.

The next question was what would *he* do next? He could continue working on the second part of the incoming message, but that might be fruitless. The device depicted in the image might be required to decode it. Perhaps he could turn his attention back to the outgoing signal – that which was emitted from the probe when it first broadcast its message to the rest of the universe. That might also be impossible since he figured it was intended for someone else – beyond Earth – but he'd take another crack at it.

JAMES THACKETT STARED at his computer. His hands trembled as he yanked a tissue out of the box on his desk and wiped the sunlit dust from the screen. He put on his reading glasses and looked more closely. Horace had been right: Jacob Hale was worth the risk.

The three images told a simple story. The signals originated from outside the solar system. The image of the Earth map connected the probe, the White Stone, and the Nazi base. And the square device seemed to be a decoder of some kind that would be needed to decrypt the rest of the incoming signal.

He retrieved his phone and sent out a broadcast text message to the group, calling a meeting in 713 in 15 minutes.

Ten minutes later, Thackett was sitting in one of the upholstered chairs in 713, trying to formulate how to deliver the news. He didn't know how they'd handle it. Evidence of alien intelligence could change a person's worldview, and that could be devastating to some.

Daniel came from his office and sat on the couch, across from him.

"More news?" Daniel asked.

Thackett nodded and glanced at the folder in his hand.

Daniel reached out, but Thackett waved him off.

"Let's wait for the others on this one," Thackett said. "I think it would be best if you all got this information at the same time."

Daniel's eyes widened. "Is something happening?"

"Nothing to be worried about."

Sylvia joined Daniel on the couch just as Denise and Jonathan arrived.

"No Will?" Denise asked as she sat next to Sylvia.

Jonathan took the wooden office chair near the end of the coffee table. "Two meetings in 24 hours," he said. "What's up?"

Thackett smiled and held up a hand. "We'll wait for Will," he said. "In the meantime, maybe you can catch me up on what you've been doing." Thackett wanted to diffuse the awkward silence, but he could barely concentrate as they gave him their updates. They were about to get the most important briefing of their lives.

A few minutes later, Will entered and took a seat in the upholstered chair to Thackett's left.

"About time," Denise said.

Will grinned and looked at his watch. "Actually, I'm a half-minute early – he said 15 minutes."

"Now that we're all here," Thackett broke in, "I have some new information that you might find … well, I'll let you decide how to judge it."

Everyone's eyes were on him, and their expressions were like those of captivated children, except Will's. Will's eyes seemed to look right through him.

Thackett turned his eyes to the folder in his hand and then held it up. "What I have here," he explained, "are the results of the data decryption efforts of Jacob Hale."

"Decryption of the incoming signal," Will said, seemingly wanting confirmation.

Thackett nodded. "He explains that there's a tiny part at the beginning of the signal that's separated from the rest by a short silence," he said. "Every time the signal repeats, it starts with this short piece, then a gap, and then a long portion – the rest of the message. Hale was able to decrypt the short part."

"And?" Denise said, moving to the edge of the couch. "What is it – what did he find?"

"He got three bitmap images," Thackett replied. "But they showed nothing – just gray."

"Encrypted?" Will asked.

Thackett nodded. "But then Hale noticed something."

"The gravitational wave glitches that coincided with the AM disturbance," Will blurted.

Thackett nodded.

"They contained information?" Will asked. "The gravitational-wave data?"

"Yes," Thackett replied. "He extracted another bitmap image from that data, but it too was gray, and seemed to be noise."

"It was the key needed to unscramble the other images," Will said. "Wasn't it?"

Thackett stared back at him, shocked. "How do you know this?"

"I've been thinking about it ever since you told us that he wanted the LIGO data," Will replied. "I take it that he was successful."

"What did he get?" Sylvia asked.

"Three unscrambled images," Thackett replied as he reached into the folder and pulled out the first figure and handed it to Daniel. "According to Hale, they are bitmap, gray-scale images. This first one shows the solar system, with some details that should be familiar."

"It looks like outgoing signals from Earth and Mars," Daniel commented.

Thackett nodded. "And incoming signals from multiple locations outside the solar system."

"Looks like there's one coming in from Mars as well," Sylvia added, as she leaned toward Daniel to get a peek.

Daniel passed the image to Sylvia and asked, "We are absolutely certain that this came from the incoming signal – not some reflection or something that originated from Earth?"

Thackett detected a tone of realization in Daniel's voice. "Yes, Daniel."

"So we're looking at the first direct, deciphered intelligent information from a source other than humans?" Daniel asked.

"I think that's exactly what this is," Thackett replied and handed him the second image. "This one is a map of Earth – it has some interesting details as well."

Daniel studied it for a few seconds. "My God, it gives the location of the base," he gasped. "And the zoomed-in part – is that the White Stone?"

"Looks like it," Thackett replied.

"Well, this confirms that the White Stone is not of human making," Sylvia said as she passed the first image to Jonathan. "Strange that the Nazis acquired it well before the war."

"And neither is the base," Daniel added. "Perhaps the Nazis deciphered enough of the White Stone inscription to locate it."

"Or they stumbled upon both," Sylvia said as she passed the first image to Denise on her right, and got the second from Daniel.

"Finally, the third image," Thackett said, holding it up for everyone to see before passing it to Daniel. "This is a drawing of a device that Hale thinks is a decoder of some kind. He thinks it's needed to decode the remainder of the signal – the long part of the AM signal."

Will gasped. His eyes widened and he seemed as if he wanted to jump up and run out of the room.

"What?" Thackett asked.

"That device is in the storage room," Will replied. "It's with the items taken from the base."

"I remember it too," Denise blurted.

"Really?" Now Thackett felt his own heart picking up pace. "Can you get it?"

Will looked to Denise and said, "Come with me."

Denise stood. "Won't take us long – everything is cataloged."

Will and Denise left, leaving the others to mull over the implications.

"Jonathan," Sylvia said, "you don't look well."

Thackett agreed. He looked both worried and disheartened. "You okay?" Thackett asked.

Jonathan took a handkerchief out of his pocket and wiped his head and mouth. "It's fascinating, but a lot to take in," he said. "Up to this point, there has been a lot of circumstantial evidence. Even the signal, while not deciphered, left room for other explanations."

"There's still room for other possibilities," Daniel argued. "This is undeniably strong evidence, but we should all know that there's still a finite chance that our conclusions are incorrect."

"Spoken like a true Omniscient," Thackett said, and grinned.

Jonathan seemed to settle.

Sylvia walked in from Daniel's office with an electric teapot and a tin.

Thackett hadn't noticed she'd left.

"I needed some tea," Sylvia said. "I thought you all might need some as well." She went into the kitchenette at the end of the room, to Thackett's right, and brought back two porcelain cups and set them in front of Thackett and Jonathan. She and Daniel already had cups on the table.

"Why do you think the message is split into two parts?" Jonathan asked as he scooped out some green tea with a tea ball and poured hot water into his cup.

"My guess is that the first part of the message is easily deciphered," Daniel explained. "And the second part may be impossible to decrypt unless one has the physical device depicted in the image."

"You think others have decoded the front end of the message?" Jonathan asked. "I mean, do you think anyone else has these images?"

"Like the Chinese and the Russians?" Daniel asked in a rhetorical tone. "Hard to say. They'd need the data from the gravitational-wave facilities."

"Yes, and they'd also need to know why they're important," Thackett said. "Do you think they've made the same connection Jacob Hale has?"

"Did our people make the connection?" Sylvia asked.

Thackett shook his head. "I don't think so," he replied. "And no one outside of this group is ever to know. We might be ahead of the game now."

"Will you confiscate the LIGO data?" Jonathan asked.

Thackett shook his head again. "It's too late," he replied. "The scientists already have the data, and it's everywhere in the community, although it isn't published. It's best not to bring any attention to it. Now that their so-called glitch problem is gone, maybe the data will be forgotten."

"If we have the decoder device from the picture, that also gives us the advantage," Sylvia said, "assuming there's only one of them."

The muscles in Thackett's legs tingled as if they were about to twitch. He was now convinced that he'd made the right decision with Lenny Butrolsky. Lenny had told him that the Chinese had first sent him after Jacob Hale to obtain a book and keys. Now they were sending him out to collect other things, including a *device* of some kind. Thackett suspected that the device the Chinese sought was the decoder, but that implied they'd already acquired the images he'd just received from Hale. He doubted it, but it was possible.

He just hoped that Will was right, and the decoder device was in the basement.

WILL PUSHED the button and the elevator began its descent. He flinched when Denise grabbed his hand.

"Do you think this is it?" she asked. "Will this tell us what's going on?"

He sensed fear in her voice. "You okay?"

She smiled, but it seemed forced. "I don't know. I'm feeling some strange anxiety."

"Me too," he said and squeezed her hand. "I'm glad you're here."

The elevator stopped and opened.

He let go of her hand and they hurried to the storage room. Denise found the notebook in which she'd cataloged the items from the base and searched through it.

"This is all on my computer," she said. "Would've been quicker if I had it with me."

Will went to the stack of over a hundred crates of various sizes and started moving them around. He recalled that they'd come across the item in question on the first day, and therefore its crate would be buried.

"Got it," Denise said. "We're looking for crate number six."

After about 10 minutes of moving crates and reorganizing, they located it. Will removed the lid with an electric screwdriver.

"It's item C6-2," Denise said as she lifted the foam molded cover from the first layer and set it on the table.

Packed in tight insets in the first layer were other items Will remembered cataloging, including a complex vacuum tube and some other electronic devices. The device they sought was wedged in a tight inset in the center of the layer.

"That's it," he said as he extracted it. He took it to the table, removed the flat box from its zip-lock bag, scratched off some clear tape, and unlatched the clasp that held it closed. He opened it.

"Looks just like the drawing," Denise confirmed.

Will closed the box. "Let's go."

Ten minutes later, they were back in 713.

Will set the box on the coffee table and opened it. The others sighed and gasped, but Will thought it was unimpressive. It looked like a square piece of gray metal.

"The dimensions seem right," Daniel said. "I found a scaled photo of the White Stone. That makes the object in the drawing a little over six centimeters on a side."

Will looked closely at the drawing and noticed something important. He then examined the device and flipped it over. "This has to be it," he said.

"How do you know?" Daniel asked.

Will pointed to one of the corners of the object. "You see how this corner is chamfered?"

"You mean the flattened corner?" Daniel asked.

"Yes," Will said. "All of the others are sharp."

"What does it mean?" Sylvia asked.

"First, it matches the drawing," Will explained. "That chamfer needs to be there, or this wouldn't be the right object. But that feature is there for a reason."

"To orient the object," Jonathan interjected.

Will nodded and pointed to the drawing. "You see the incoming and outgoing signals, and their respective connections." He rotated the object and pointed to the chamfered corner. "This is the proper orientation: the signal comes in on the left, and goes out on the right. The chamfered corner must be on the top left."

"Where do you hook up the inputs and outputs?" Denise asked as she looked back and forth between the drawing and the object.

Will shrugged. There were no connections for anything – the object was completely smooth, except for some areas on the outer edges that had a rougher texture than the rest. "It will have to be carefully studied to figure out how it works."

"I think we have someone who can help with that," Thackett said.

"Jacob Hale," Daniel said.

Thackett nodded. "Maybe it's time to bring him in."

THERE HAD BEEN A LIGHT RAIN.

Jacob breathed in the earthy air as he walked down Swann Street toward his building. Aromas of roasted coffee beans emanated from his clothes and mixed with those of wet grass. Even though it was past 11:00 p.m., it had been such a scorching day that the sidewalks steamed from the rain that had been too little to cool the hot concrete.

It had been 12 hours since he'd sent the images. His anxiety increased every minute that he didn't hear a response. He had to leave his flat for a few hours so that he would be forced to stop checking his email every 10 minutes. He'd check it one last time before he went to bed, maybe while he ate something and caught up with the latest network news.

The highlight of the unproductive evening had been chatting with Cally, the owner of the Count Cristo Coffee House. His interactions with her, and his increasing anxiety about his work, made him long for Paulina. He'd only heard from her twice in the ten days since she'd left. It was something he'd expected, but it still affected him. She'd been so busy that she'd never come back from London. She had intended to return to the States to pack up her belongings and close out her apartment. Rather, she sublet it to a colleague who had packed some of Pauli's belongings and shipped them to England. He was trying to be optimistic about the chances of working it out with her after his work was done, but that seemed to be a long way away.

Even though he knew that people were watching out for him – probably the CIA – he'd been diligent about taking different paths to and from the coffeehouse, and keeping close watch for anyone following him. Besides, he always carried his uncle's Glock 40.

He turned left, walked a block, and then turned right and continued walking parallel to Swann Street. He passed his building, cut right, through two yards, and then took another right onto his street. He walked 50 yards, turned right onto his walk, and inserted the key in the door.

He entered the foyer, checked the mailbox, and inserted the key into the receptacle next to the elevator. A half-minute later, he entered the elevator, inserted the brass key into the proper slot, and pushed button number four. He felt his eyelids become heavy as the elevator made its vertical and horizontal maneuvers to his place. He was more tired than he'd thought.

The elevator made fine adjustments indicating its final approach and stopped.

As the door opened and he stepped into the dark, his key ring fell to the floor. The lights came on as he bent over to pick them up. When he straightened up, his brain flooded with panicked alarm. He dropped his backpack and keys.

There was a man sitting at the far end of the large wooden table.

"It takes about 10 minutes of perfect stillness for the lights to turn off," the man said. "And the sensors are extremely sensitive."

Jacob fumbled for the Glock and eventually extracted it from his pocket and pointed it at the man.

"That's not necessary," the man said, holding up his hands. "I'm not armed."

Jacob frantically twisted his head back and forth, scanning the rest of the place for an accomplice, but found no one. "Who are you?" he said, hearing the trembling in his voice.

The man was in his early 40s, short brown hair, a millimeter of scruff on his face, and thick, like the CIA man he'd encountered in the parking lot of Paglio's Bistro.

"A friend," the man said. "Please lower your gun."

Jacob did it slowly, but kept it at the ready.

"You're Jacob Hale, Horace's nephew," the man said. "Your uncle was an extraordinary man."

"You knew him?"

"Briefly."

"Recently?"

"Yes. I was with him during his final mission."

"Antarctica?"

The man nodded.

Jacob's nerves calmed, but he kept aware of the gun in his hand. "And who are you?"

"It was ingenious to check whether the gravitational-wave data carried encrypted information," the man said, ignoring his question. "Can you imagine if this had happened at an earlier time, say 15 years ago? We wouldn't have been capable of detecting the gravitational waves."

Jacob had already considered it.

"But what's even more astonishing," the man continued, "is that someone somewhere was able to create gravitational waves. We certainly do not have that technology. We have to build facilities that are miles long just to detect them."

This was also in the back of Jacob's mind. It meant that whoever had sent the messages was far beyond human technology.

"Who are you?" Jacob repeated.

"Well," the man said and grinned, "you've already posed that question to our mutual friends – who were also friends of Horace's."

Jacob noticed two dimple-like scars on the far right and left of the man's forehead – high, near the hairline. He knew what had caused them. "You're William Thompson," Jacob said.

"Call me Will."

"How do I know you're telling the truth?"

"What reason would I have to lie?"

Jacob just shook his head as he tried to come up with an answer. He had no idea.

"And how else would I be able to get in here?" the man added.

"Duplicate keys." He immediately recalled that Uncle Theo had warned him that there were no copies.

"A logical possibility," the man agreed. "But don't you think that if they had keys, those who run this place would have gotten in by now and secured all of this sensitive information?" the man asked as he spread his arms and gestured to the stacks of books and boxes on the wall of shelves.

It was a good point, Jacob admitted. "Then how did you get in?"

"How much do you know about me?"

"You were supposedly the only success of the Red Wraith project," Jacob answered.

"What does that mean, exactly?"

"You are able to separate."

"And what does that mean?"

"Your soul can separate from your body," Jacob replied, hardly believing he was saying the words.

"Okay," Will said and nodded. "Then you should be able to explain how I got in."

Jacob was confused and remained silent. He knew what the man wanted him to say, but he couldn't do it. He didn't believe any of that crap. A few seconds passed and all he was able to do was shake his head in quick, erratic spasms.

Will looked down at his hands, which were now clasped together and resting on the table in front of him. "I don't blame you," he said. "I'd be skeptical, too. Even I sometimes wonder if it's real. However, I assure you, it is. Now, given that preposterous premise – that I have the separation ability described in the Red Wraith documents you've read – how could have I defeated the formidable security of this facility?"

Jacob could formulate the simple logic once he accepted the assumption that the man could separate. "To get in the main door, you separated, passed through it, and pressed the exit button on the inside," he guessed. "But I don't know what you did for the elevator: even if you got inside it, you'd need a key to activate a button to move to a specific floor. And the elevator might not have been on the first floor when you got into the foyer."

Will nodded and said, "My range extends beyond the dimensions of this building."

It took Jacob a few seconds to devise a solution. "You could have pushed the button inside the elevator to bring it to the foyer – that doesn't require a key – and the elevator door would open. You got in, separated again, and then pressed the button up in this room – as if someone were here and wanted a ride down – and the elevator took you here. You never needed the key."

Will nodded in approval. "They could improve the security in this place by requiring a key to ride the elevator from the room to the foyer, and adding something to sense whether someone is in the elevator."

"I still don't believe it," Jacob said, more defiantly than he intended.

The man laughed out loud. "I like you, Jacob," he said. "We're alike in some ways: you're an engineer, I'm a physicist. We're skeptical by nature. What can I do to eliminate your skepticism?"

By his tone, Jacob knew the question was sincere. "You must've had to do it before. What do you usually do?"

"I'm usually worried about frightening people," Will said. "But subtle demonstrations always result in people suspecting it's a trick of some kind. I end up having to do drastic things in the end anyway. So why don't I just skip to something convincing?"

"Okay," Jacob responded. His voice shook in anticipation.

"Perhaps you should take the gun out of your hand – put it back in your pocket."

Jacob put it in his backpack instead, and set it on the floor. "What are you going to do?"

"Just relax and trust me," Will said.

Jacob watched as the man's eyes rolled back in his head and his eyelids lowered so that only slivers of white were showing.

Jacob tensed as something enclosed around his entire body. It was as if he were instantly wrapped head to toe in duct tape. He couldn't move anything below his neck.

His feet were two meters above the floor before he even realized that he was elevating.

His natural reaction was to struggle, and he almost panicked. In what he could only describe as a paralyzing state of shock, he remained hovering, over 10 feet above the floor. The kitchen was to the right, and one of the dome skylights was directly in front and above him. William Thompson was below him, facing forward, and dead still.

A few seconds later, Jacob touched down gently on the floor, and the grasp released. The man's blue eyes opened.

Jacob remained still and quiet.

"You okay?" Will said.

"Holy shit!" Jacob finally yelled and fell to his knees. His mind seemed to collapse on itself as it processed the implications and conclusions that were spawning from the event. Between his successful decoding of what was likely a message from an alien intelligence, and the direct observation – experience – of a human separating his soul from his body, his worldview was in turmoil.

Jacob recoiled against something clamping on his upper left arm. Before he could pull away, he was up on his feet and the man was standing next to him, holding him steady.

"I'm sorry, Jacob," Will said as he let him go and took a step back. "I didn't mean to frighten you."

Jacob rubbed his arms and legs, trying to determine if he'd been hurt or if there were any marks on his skin. "It's really true."

"It is," Will said. "I guess your skepticism has been cured."

Jacob made a noise that was half laugh and half cough. He felt something on his face and rubbed it with the back of his hand and then looked at it. He expected it to be blood, but it was a tear.

"We found the decoder device," Will said. "It was recovered from the base – the one your uncle explored during his final mission. The Nazis had it."

Jacob nodded and looked back at him, trying hard to focus on what he was saying but his mind still reeled from what had just happened.

"Jacob?"

Jacob's mind seemed to scramble. "Did you use it?" he finally blurted after his mind could process Will's words.

Will shook his head. "No. That's why I'm here. They want you to come back with me."

"Who's 'they?'"

"Friends," Will replied. "Horace's colleagues."

"Where are we going?"

"It's not far from here," Will replied.

"When?"

"Tonight, if you're ready."

"It's late."

"They have a place for you to stay the night," Will said. "If it's anything like mine, you'll be very comfortable," he said as he looked around. "I have to say though, this place is beautiful."

"It's magnificent," Jacob agreed. "Let me pack my things."

"I saw a kitchen up there. How about something to eat before we go?" Will said. "I've been waiting for a while. I'm starving."

Jacob laughed. He felt like vomiting, but that would subside. "I have a frozen pizza."

"Sounds perfect," Will said. "I can fill you in on some details while we eat."

Jacob wasn't sure he'd be able to eat or think, but one thing he knew for certain was that everything was going to be different from this point forward.

CHAPTER 10

Lenny sat on a bench on the pier at Orient Point and stared to the east.

The rising sun glinted from the waves, and he shielded his eyes with his hand. The cool ocean breeze mixed with the aroma of coffee as he took a sip from a paper cup. He was unusually calm considering he was about to embark on a major mission.

The docked ferry gates opened and Lenny boarded with over 40 others who looked to be Plum Island employees, including a few dressed as security guards. They cast off and the boat accelerated eastward. The wind reached an impressive clip that made Lenny's eyes water, but invigorated him, and sharpened his mind.

Thirty-five minutes later they were docked at Plum Island, and he watched as the other passengers went ashore. A cluster of armed security guards checked their IDs as they stepped onto the dock. When it was Lenny's turn, he handed a guard his paperwork, and a worn driver's license indicating that he was from California. The guard looked it over and let him pass.

Lenny spotted Dr. Jennifer Chung in a golf cart near a concrete pad next to the pier. She was scanning the passengers as they came down the ramp. She'd somehow missed him and he approached her.

"Dr. Chung?" he asked.

The young Asian woman jerked around and looked at him for a few seconds before speaking. "You startled me," she said with a New York accent.

"Sorry," he said and forced a smile. "I'm Leonard Strovsky."

"Call me Jennifer," she said.

She was young, maybe 30, and petite. Pencils held her black hair in a bun, and her thin eyebrows hid behind the thick black rims of her rectangular glasses.

"Call me Lenny," he responded as he shook her hand. He put his bags on a carrier in the rear of the cart and sat in the passenger seat.

"The fluorescence spectrometer is in Lab 157," she explained as she turned the cart around and pushed the accelerator to its maximum, crawling speed. "It's in a high-security area, but close to the place you need to access. I hope you brought the right tools to get into it."

"I should have what I need," he said. "Is the place wired?"

"What do you mean?"

"Is there electronic monitoring – motion sensors, cameras, or access codes?"

"Yes, of course."

"Which ones?"

"All of them."

It was going to be a busy day, and evening, he thought.

Jennifer drove the golf cart off the asphalt road onto a dirt path that weaved through a sparse grove of pines. The mixed scents of the trees and the thick layer of dead needles on the ground reminded him of summer army training in Siberia as a young lad. It had been a stressful time for most, but he had enjoyed his time in the forest.

The vegetation got thicker and Lenny held up his arms to block branches that invaded the open cab of the vehicle. A minute later they emerged in a parking lot behind a cement-gray building scattered with a half dozen golf carts and a diverse collection of lawn equipment. She parked in a space next to a flatbed trailer loaded with a sprayer and a large tank of weed killer.

They sat quietly in their seats for a few seconds before Jennifer broke the silence. "The spectrometer you will be repairing is in this building, but the thing you're after is on the far end," she explained and pointed to the east side of the main building.

The main structure, located just behind the building where they'd parked, was a red brick, three-story building that sprawled over a hundred yards, east to west. He knew from the satellite images that there were numerous buildings around the aging main structure, some of which looked to be add-ons, and others that were connected via tunnels or catwalks. He'd better be careful not to get lost and find himself being questioned by security guards or other personnel – especially ones with technical backgrounds.

"After you get checked in, I'll take you to the lab so you can start on the repairs," she explained. "Do you have a multimeter in that bag?"

Lenny nodded. That was the one instrument he would have in his hands the entire time. It was used to measure electrical current, voltage, and resistance, as well as perform other diagnostic functions. It would all be for show, of course.

"I figured you'd stay in the X-ray fluorescence lab and pretend to read schematics for most of the day. If anyone comes in, you can just stick your head into the housing of the instrument and probe around. Just don't touch anything."

Lenny nodded.

"At lunchtime," she continued, "I'll take you past the room you need to access. After that, I'll show you to your dorm."

"Dorm?"

"You'll be spending the night."

"I can do that?"

"This isn't as high security as you might think," Jennifer said and chuckled.

Lenny's stomach tightened. He thought it should have been more difficult, considering that the type of research done at the facility could have other uses. Animal diseases could devastate entire countries. And some could even cross over to humans.

"You'll be working late," she continued. "The building will be mostly empty after 5:00 p.m., and you can stay the entire night if you need to. When you have what you need, go to the dorm. I'll pick you up in time to get you on the ferry back to Orient Point in the morning."

Seemed easy, Lenny thought. Disturbingly easy.

They walked to the main building and climbed concrete stairs to a steel door. Jennifer held an access card up to a white pad next to the handle, prompting a click and a beep. She opened it and led him through a labyrinth of hallways to the main office. Lenny filled out paperwork, got a visitor's ID and access card, and was given his housing information.

Twenty minutes later they left the main office and Lenny followed Jennifer through a large foyer. They passed a semicircular array of tall windows giving a wide view of the front of the main building. The front drive was a roundabout with a flagpole at its center. The American flag flapped wildly in the ocean breeze and snapped so loudly that he could hear it through the windows.

They passed into a brightly-lit corridor that smelled like the confluence of a hospital and a horse barn. After about 50 meters, they entered the eastern wing and then went two-thirds of the way to the end of the building before turning right, into a small lab.

He recognized the gray cabinet of the Model 400Z Fluorescence Spectrometer on the wall opposite the entrance. It was larger than he'd imagined: about the size of a refrigerator, except wider, and the upper half had two leaded glass doors that opened outward on hinges to reveal the innards of the device. The massive structure was turned away from the wall, and an access panel in the back had been removed to reveal a half-dozen circuit boards and other complex internal electronics.

"This is the instrument," Jennifer said as she swung open the glass doors on its upper half. "The problem is the X-ray source – it won't turn on. If someone asks, you can say that you already checked the X-ray tube and the power supply, and now you're troubleshooting the electronics. Maybe you can put the electronics schematic on the table and spend the day pretending to mull it over. If someone comes in, you can get behind the cabinet with your multimeter and probe around. Before you leave, you can plug the missing chip into the board."

Lenny agreed as he unfolded the electronics schematic like a large map and spread it out on a table next to the instrument. It was a mess of circuit diagrams with parts labeled with codes. He hoped no one quizzed him on it.

"Where's the chip?" he asked.

Jennifer opened a drawer, pulled out a small plastic box, and removed the lid. Inside was a black chip the size of a domino pressed into a piece of Styrofoam. She then showed him exactly where to insert the chip in a large circuit board in the rear panel of the instrument.

"I really don't expect any trouble," she said. "I'm one of only a few that actually uses this instrument. I'll come to get you at lunchtime and we'll take a walk."

Jennifer left and Lenny sat at the table. It was going to be a long day.

A RATTLING noise startled Jacob out of his slumber.

He sat up straight and took in a deep breath through his nose. It took him a few seconds to realize where he was. He grabbed the vibrating phone from the coffee table in front of the couch and read the incoming text message: *Room 713 at 8:30*. He had 30 minutes to get ready.

He was still groggy – it had been a late night. After arriving at the Space Systems building he'd gone through two hours of security protocols. He'd ended up falling asleep on the couch in the room he'd been given.

He showered and dressed. He only had shorts and jeans. He chose the latter with a polo shirt, ate a bowl of cold cereal, and went to the elevator. On a number pad located next to the floor selection buttons, he punched in the code he used to get into his room and selected the seventh floor. He emerged from the elevator and approached a receptionist behind a desk. The man stared at his chest.

"Oh, sorry," Jacob said and took his ID badge out of his bag and clipped it onto his shirt.

The man pointed to Jacob's right and said, "Room 713, on the right."

Jacob walked down a carpeted corridor, arrived at the door, and punched in the code for his room again. It beeped and clicked, and he walked in. To his right was a group of people clustered around a circular coffee table. The only one he recognized was Will.

"Come on over," said a man in his fifties. He was the only person wearing a suit.

There were four men and two women. They stood as Jacob approached, and they were all smiling.

"I'm James Thackett, CIA Director," said the man in the suit as he stuck out his hand.

To Jacob, he looked like a politician.

Jacob shook his hand. "Jacob Hale."

"You've already met Will," Thackett said and then proceeded to introduce Jonathan McDougal, Denise Walker, Sylvia Barnes, and Daniel Parsons.

"We all knew your Uncle Horace," Sylvia said. "He must have had great trust and respect for you."

"Before we tell you who we are, exactly, we'd like to tell you about who your uncle was," Daniel explained. "I'm sure it has been a perplexing mystery to you – perhaps for most of your life – but it might go even further than you've imagined."

It already had, Jacob thought.

"Looks like we need more furniture," Will said as he stepped into an office and returned with a wooden chair. He set it down in the cluster of furniture that surrounded the coffee table.

"Shall we sit?" Thackett suggested.

They all took their seats around the coffee table, and Jacob took one of two wooden chairs.

"In World War II," Daniel began, "Horace was a member of the British Special Air Service, or SAS. After the war he moved into intelligence, MI-6 and the American OSS and CIA. He held dual citizenship with the US and UK, which we found to be strange at first, but we became more comfortable with the idea when we realized how the relationships had developed over of period of more than 50 years. He would eventually come to the US and be appointed the head of a special group called the Omniscients, or Omnis."

"Sounds pretentious," Jacob remarked.

Sylvia laughed out loud.

"The 'omniscient' part of the Omniscients derives from the type of clearance they – *we* – have," Daniel explained.

Now Jacob knew with whom he was working: the *Omniscients*. "What level of clearance is that – Q-clearance with SCI or SAP access?" Jacob asked.

"The Q-level clearance gets you top-secret access," Daniel explained. "The 'Sensitive Compartmented Information' and 'Special Access Program' designations are mainly terms used by outsiders."

"Let's get to the point," Thackett broke in. "Omniscient clearance means you have unlimited access across all platforms, all agencies, and all security levels. If Daniel wanted to walk into Area 51 right now, it would happen."

Jacob stared back at Thackett with no words forming in his brain. This broke all the rules of information security. "How is anything secure?"

"At any given time, there are only about a dozen Omnis in existence," Daniel explained. "It's a lifetime appointment, and we're not allowed to leave the country."

"Although, that rule has been relaxed recently," Sylvia commented.

Daniel added, "And we're not supposed to know one other's identities. We broke protocol when we met Horace, when Sylvia and I met each other, and when Sylvia and I met Jonathan and Denise, and – "

"Okay," Thackett cut in, "we've been ignoring the rules ever since the probe was discovered in Antarctica and we realized its significance."

"You see, Jacob," Daniel continued, "in the words of your uncle, all of the events leading to where we are now have existential implications. There's too much at stake now to let our usually effective, but sluggish, protocols impede our progress."

"Toward what, exactly, are we progressing?" Jacob asked.

"That's a part of the puzzle," Will said. "We need to figure out how to use the decoding device, if that's what it really is, and hope we learn something new. Otherwise, we've just been stumbling around in the dark." Will pulled a polished wooden box out of a backpack on the floor next to his chair and handed it to Jacob. "This was recovered from Antarctica – your uncle was on that mission."

Jacob knew what it was. He set it on the coffee table, unhooked the latches, and opened the box. A square piece of gray metal was pressed into a felt-lined inset. He got his fingertips around one of the edges and gently pulled it out.

It was about two inches on a side, over a half-centimeter thick, and heavy. He turned it to view it from different angles. "Did you scan it for radioactivity?"

"Yes," Daniel said. "Nothing."

Jacob held it up to the light and looked along an edge. "The only feature that I can see is one of the corners is chamfered – and only on one side."

"To orient it," Will suggested, "like an electronic chip."

"So you know where the input and output signals get wired," Sylvia said.

"In principle," Jacob said, nodding. "The problem is that I don't see a place to connect the wires – there are no features at all, other than the one chamfered corner."

"We know this is your area of expertise," Thackett commented. "We have signal and electronics analysis labs here, as well as a full contingent of technicians. We'd like you to figure out how this thing works."

Jacob's hands and feet tingled. He wanted first crack at the device.

If it worked like he suspected it did, he'd be the first to see the decoded message in the long part of the AM transmission.

Jacob looked to the others. "When do I start?"

It was 12:30 p.m. when Jennifer picked up Lenny for lunch, and he felt as if his stomach was starting to digest itself.

"What kind of food do you have in the cafeteria?" he asked.

"Not much to choose from," she replied. "Mostly premade sandwiches and some microwave meals. That's why I bring my own." She tapped a red insulated container suspended from a strap that hung over her shoulder.

They climbed a flight of stairs and passed a dozen doors before they got to 207, near the end of the corridor.

"This is it," she said as they passed it. "Inside is a locked closet. The outer door from the hall is wired, but the closet is not. The thing you're looking for is in a safe in that closet."

A safe? It was going to be a challenging night, he thought. "Do you have the combination?" he asked.

She shook her head.

Of course not, he thought. "Are there cameras?"

"Yes, on each end of the hall," she said. "I'll show you the security control room. It's all automated – nothing monitored by human eyes. If you make a mistake, you'll have to take the hard drive that stores the video. I'll give you the code to get into that room."

"Is there a camera inside the security room?" Lenny knew that highly secure facilities often monitored their main security rooms from another location.

She smiled. "It's currently not functioning."

Lenny was impressed.

"I don't have the code to get into lab 207," she explained. "I assume it won't be a problem for you."

"Nope." The safe might be another story, he didn't add.

They got to the end of the hall, went down a flight of stairs, and exited the building into the cool ocean wind.

"Are there janitors?" Lenny asked.

"They take the five o'clock ferry off the island."

They followed a path that went past what looked to be a three-story college dorm and a smaller, brick building that had no windows.

"That's where you'll stay tonight," she said, pointing to the dorm.

"What's that?" he asked, nodding to the smaller structure.

"You don't want to know."

"Okay."

She sighed. "We do some research on human subjects here," she said and shrugged. "I'm already committing treason, I suppose I can tell you that as well."

"What kind of research?"

"The effects of drugs and various biological agents," she replied. "But we only use volunteers."

Lenny nodded and shrugged. Sure, volunteers. Thoughts of the infamous MK Ultra project came to mind – the CIA's drug experiments. He could tell that Jennifer expected a more pronounced reaction. She didn't know what he'd seen in his lifetime. The Red Wraith project had produced about the worst humanity had to offer.

Another five minutes and they were in the cafeteria. He purchased a foot-long sub sandwich, a bag of chips, and a fountain drink. Jennifer suggested he buy something for dinner as well, since he'd be staying the night and would only have access to a vending machine after 5:00 p.m.

They sat at a large round table and ate.

"Are you sure the object in question is in the safe?" Lenny asked.

She nodded.

"How do you know?"

She blushed and looked down at her bowl of noodles. "I knew the man who used to work in that lab."

"How?"

"He was my Ph.D. research advisor."

"Where is he now?"

Jennifer chewed slowly and swallowed. "He's dead."

"Oh, sorry. How?"

"Ricin."

Lenny knew a lot about ricin. It was an old, well-known poison produced from castor beans. A few salt-sized grains could kill an adult human. "Accident?"

She stared at him and chewed without answering.

"Is it made here?"

"Not anymore," she replied, "but we have a stockpile."

"Back to my question," Lenny finally said. "How do you know the object is in the safe?"

"I was screwing my advisor," she said. "The old pervert told me all kinds of things. And he actually showed it to me."

Lenny was starting to see the real Jennifer Chung. She was a spy, probably nurtured from a young age to infiltrate American society and position herself in a place where she'd be useful. It was not unlike the Russian strategy, or that of many other countries. There were probably thousands of Chinese loyalists in the US doing the same, but only a handful would climb to places where they could make a difference. Jennifer Chung was one of them, and this might be her only real mission in life. Unfortunately for her, she was going to fail, and it was going to end badly for her.

They finished lunch and returned to the main building where Lenny resumed his mock repairs.

By 5:00 p.m. the place was deserted. At 9:00 p.m. he walked the halls, pretending to look for a bathroom. Having the security control room in the same building it was monitoring was a mistake. Not keeping all of the cameras operational was another. Not properly vetting your employees, however, was the biggest mistake of them all.

He found a bathroom and relieved himself, took a long swig from a water fountain in the hall, and made his way down a dark corridor to the security control room. The access code worked, and he entered the room and closed the door. With the overhead lights off, only flashing buttons and indicators on control boards and circuit breaker panels illuminated the small room.

Three large computer monitors were dark until Lenny moved a mouse to bring them out of screensaver mode. The center screen prompted him for a password, and he entered the one Jennifer had given him. One monitor showed a detailed map of the building, identifying various zones and their respective security statuses. The zone for the control room was shaded yellow, indicating that the cameras were not functioning and no motion sensors were active.

Most of the hallways, including the one where room 207 was located, were shaded green, indicating they were covered by active cameras and there were no breaches. There were other symbols that identified various gadgets such as motion detectors, contact detectors for doors, and glass-break sensors. There were additional sensors that weren't meant for security, such as water and humidity detectors and, in one lab, a fluorine gas detector. It seemed that the third floor had the highest level of security. He wondered what they were protecting up there.

He deactivated all of the cameras on the first and second floors, as well as the door sensor on 207 and the motion detectors inside. As Jennifer had indicated, the internal room with the safe wasn't wired and the safe wasn't even represented in the diagram. He hoped that meant it had no security gadgets. It might not need anything, he thought. He might not be able to break into it.

He double-checked that all security features were deactivated and exited the security room. He stopped by the lab with the fluorescence spectrometer, picked up his tool kit, and walked down the hall and up a flight of stairs.

The hallway on the second level was vacant and dimly lit. He tried to make as little noise as possible as he made his way down the hall. If he unexpectedly encountered someone it could be a big problem. Killing someone was out of the question this time.

He easily defeated the lock on room 207, went inside, and closed the door behind him.

The overhead lights were off, but enough light spilled out of the five chemical fume hoods situated on the room's perimeter to allow him to navigate around the lab tables in the center of the room. He pulled a flashlight from his bag and scanned the beam around the laboratory. In metal pans on the tables were what seemed to be chunks of rocks, some of which looked like melted metal. They reminded him of the meteorites he'd seen in a science museum in Chicago a few years prior while waiting to make contact with another operative.

In the fume hoods were arrays of test tubes in racks, and petri dishes on shelves. Each contained fine powders that had the brown-tan colors of ground-up rocks. He thought it odd that a geologist worked in such a place, but then he recalled that there were scientists who studied both rocks and life science. Biogeologists? That the samples on the tables seemed to be meteorites captured his imagination for a second but then he got back on task.

There were four side rooms in the lab. The two on the left side, relative to the entrance, were storage rooms. One on the right, furthest from the entrance, was an office. And the one on the near right was the one he was seeking.

The room that contained the safe was closed, and the square window in the door was dark. He walked over and tried the knob – it was locked, as Jennifer had warned. He pulled out his tools and picked the lock in a few minutes. He opened the door, clicked on the flashlight and found the light switch. He closed the door and flipped on the overhead lights.

The safe was inside a cabinet, which was also locked, but Lenny just forced it open, tearing through the particleboard door and splintering the wood veneer near the latch. The safe was 18 inches square at the base and two feet tall. His heart sank as he examined the safe's door. It had an electronic lock – with a white keypad.

"Shit," he muttered under his breath. How was he going to get through this one? He'd acquired some safecracking skills on dial-type safes – although the sophisticated ones could still be a problem – but nothing on digital locks.

He pulled out his phone and did a quick search on the Internet for information on digital safes. For the specific safe in the cabinet in front of him, it was either a four- or five-digit code followed by the hash symbol, meaning 10 thousand or 100 thousand possible codes, respectively. On top of that, entering three consecutive incorrect codes would lock out the system for up to five minutes.

Next, he looked for information on drill points. These were vulnerabilities in the safe design that made it susceptible to drilling in specific locations – secrets carefully guarded by the manufacturers. But there were all kinds of strategies to bolster such mechanical vulnerabilities, such as glass re-lockers, where a tempered glass plate was embedded in the safe door that actuated a secondary locking mechanism when broken. Lenny had no idea about the features of the safe in front of him. But it didn't matter since he didn't have a drill capable of the job.

He sat on the floor and stared at the safe. It was bolted to the floor and to the wall behind the cabinet. Even if he could dislodge it, he still couldn't open it without the code, and he couldn't take it with him on the ferry. He thought about contacting Jennifer for help, but he knew she would have already given him any assistance she could.

He was in a thinking daze when something struck him. He sat up and looked closely at the white buttons on the safe's number pad from different angles. He did a quick calculation in his head and smiled: he might be able to open it.

IT WAS 9:00 p.m. when Jacob was finally at the stage where he could start examining the device. He downed a canned espresso drink and hoped it would keep him going for a while. It looked like it was going to be another late night.

The laboratory reminded him of his lab at Interstellar Dynamics, except this one was much larger and better equipped. The smell of solder and burnt electronics permeated the place.

The CIA lab in Space Systems' sub-level A had every device imaginable, from high-tech wire bonders for making tiny electrical connections to state-of-the-art network analyzers for signal analysis. The lab bay was about the size of a tennis court with numerous testing stations spread throughout the area. Other labs of similar size but with different specializations were located on the floor, as well as on lower levels. It seemed that the CIA had its own forensics labs – for electronics and humans – as well as development and reverse engineering labs. Some of the work was contracted out to companies such as Interstellar Dynamics, but the most sensitive work was done in-house.

He was paired with an electronics expert named Hank, a self-proclaimed night owl, and they sat next to each other on stools at a lab bench that butted up against a wall. The surface of the bench was covered with all sorts of instruments, including an oscilloscope and a spectrum analyzer.

Jacob opened the wooden box and placed the square device on a static-free stage. He and Hank wore bracelets connected to electrical ground in order to avoid damaging any sensitive electronics inside the object. He hoped he and the others hadn't already damaged it by handling it without taking such precautions.

They moved the stage and device to the platform of a microscope, and then systematically examined every square millimeter of the object's gray surface. Other than the chamfered corner, the device had no features indicating places to connect wires. The surface was smooth, except that two of the four edges were rough, or textured in some way.

Next, they touched two needlelike probes of a voltmeter to the surface – about a centimeter apart – and measured its electrical resistance. This would reveal whether or not the object was made of metal, which conducted electricity, or an insulator, which did not. Even though the object looked like it was made of tungsten, which was a metal, the top and bottom surfaces were electrically insulating, like the plastic coating of a power cord.

Next, they checked the edges of the device, near the positions where the input and output wires were shown in the drawing. Jacob methodically poked the two probes along the edge, keeping them about a centimeter apart. With the chamfered corner oriented on the upper left, he traced the bottom edge and found it to be electrically insulating. He slowly proceeded up the right edge and, when the probes were about halfway to the top, something happened that made him freeze in place and stare at it.

One of the voltmeter's metal probes sunk into the surface, and the gray material hardened around it.

"What the hell?" Jacob said aloud.

"Never seen anything like that," Hank gasped, wide-eyed.

Jacob disconnected both probes from the voltmeter so that there was no chance of damaging the device, and traced the sharp end of the second probe along the same edge. At a position about two centimeters above where the first probe was stuck, the second one sunk in and froze in place.

"Strangest thing I've ever seen," Jacob remarked.

"Makes for easy connections," Hank commented. "But how do you get them out?"

Jacob carefully pulled on the upper one with increasing force. Just as he was about to stop, it moved outward slowly, like pulling a stick out of mud. When the probe separated from the device, the void it left behind immediately disappeared as if it had filled in with liquid metal, and then hardened.

He pulled out the other probe and proceeded to trace the upper edge – no connections – and then down the left side. When he reached the connection positions shown in the schematic, the probes again sunk in, just as they'd done on the opposite side.

"According to the drawing, the left side is the input, and the right is output," Jacob said.

"Easy enough," Hank agreed. "We flow in the encrypted data on the left, and collect the decrypted data flowing out on the right. What do we do with it?"

"I hope it will be in the same data format as the signal we decoded to get the images," Jacob replied.

"Bitmap images?"

Jacob nodded. "I think the first part of the signal – which we've already decoded – was designed to tell us how to decode the rest of it."

"Decryption is not possible without this device?"

"Right," Jacob replied, recalling his many failed attempts at decoding the long part of the AM signal using his software. "My guess is that the remaining part of the signal either has a very long key, or it has undergone some kind of quantum encryption."

"Beyond our technology," Hank remarked.

All Jacob could do was nod and shrug.

"Never dealt with anything like this before."

"You really expect me to believe that? You're CIA," Jacob jibed.

Hank remained quiet.

"I'm sure you know all about Area 51 as well," Jacob said.

Hank chuckled nervously.

No sense of humor, Jacob thought. "Maybe you can set up an external drive with a copy of the input signal while I configure the network analyzer and recorder for the output," Jacob suggested.

Hank left to get the required equipment, leaving Jacob to his thoughts. With any luck, they'd start decoding the data in the next few hours.

LENNY THOUGHT he'd found a way to cheat the safe – or at least reduce the number of guesses he'd need.

On the white buttons of the keypad were smudges from years of greasy fingertips pressing them. It was a grimy residue similar to that which accumulates on computer keyboards. The buttons for the numbers 2, 4, 5, and 9, and the "#" symbol, were darker than the others. If it were a four-digit code, then there were only 24 possible combinations with those smudged buttons. If it were programmed with a five-digit code, it got a lot messier. He'd worry about that if the four-digit plan failed. If they'd recently changed the code, he was screwed.

He wrote down the 24 possible combinations on a piece of paper he'd unpinned from a corkboard on the wall opposite the door. The first combination was 2-4-5-9-#, and he punched it in. A red light flashed for three seconds and then went off. Incorrect code.

Next, he punched in 2-4-9-5-#. Same result.

After the third combination, the light flashed red and then turned yellow and remained lit. He entered the next code anyway, but this time got no reaction after he pressed the # sign. It was frozen.

He sat down and started a timer on his phone so that he'd know how long the safe would time out. After four and a half minutes, the yellow light flashed for 30 seconds and then went out. It seemed that the safe was reset, but it meant that he'd have to wait five minutes every time he entered three incorrect combinations. That wouldn't be horrible for 24 combinations, but if it were a five-digit code he'd be in trouble. In that case he'd also have to consider the possibility of repeat digits, and then the number of possibilities skyrocketed.

He tried three more combinations and sat back to wait for the yellow light to go off.

The first code he entered after the fifth timeout – a half hour after he'd started – resulted in a beep and a green light. The electronic lock hummed and the door cracked open. Lenny's heart rate picked up as he opened the door and scanned the flashlight around the safe's interior. Inside were stacks of files and a cylindrical aluminum case that was over a foot long, and eight inches in diameter. It had a flat along its length so that it wouldn't roll.

He extracted the case and put it on the floor. It was about 25 pounds, and he figured it would be easy to carry in his duffle bag. He positioned the case so that it rested on its flat, and then unsnapped the latches that held the two halves together. He lifted the upper half, and it pivoted on hinges, like a casket.

The object inside looked exactly like the description he'd been given. Inset in the cushioned interior was a stainless steel cylinder about the size of a tall coffee can, capped with heavy-duty flanges on both ends. One flange had a circular window at its center that was about two inches in diameter. At the center of the opposite flange was a threaded hole, about an inch in diameter, at the bottom of which was the head of a bolt. He thought the bolt probably actuated a valve used to pump out air, or to leak air back into the evacuated vessel when it was to be opened. A ring of 16 twelve-point bolts fastened each flange to the cylinder. He recognized them as aircraft bolts.

Lenny tipped up the device so he could look through the window. It was too dark inside to see, so he directed the flashlight through the window, into the interior. Suspended by brackets inside the vessel was a silver cylindrical tube, about two inches in diameter and eight inches long, with black rounded end caps. Seven or eight equally spaced black grooves encircled the body of the tube.

With his CIA phone, he snapped pictures of the device from all angles and tried to get some shots of the tube suspended inside. He then took a picture of the case, and sent everything to his CIA handlers. He closed the case, slipped it into his duffle bag, and then searched the inside of the safe for anything else of importance. There were only documents of various sorts, most of which seemed to contain financial information, except for one file marked "top secret," which he took.

There was also a small handgun hidden above a panel in the safe's ceiling. He left it.

He closed the safe, turned off the lights, exited the room, and closed the door. He then left the lab and went to the security room and reactivated all of the cameras and sensors.

Lenny then returned to the lab that housed the fluorescence spectrometer and inserted the missing chip into the electronics board, as Jennifer had instructed. He packed up his tool kit, closed the instrument's cabinet, and pushed it back against the wall. The so-called repairs were complete.

He closed the lab and exited the building into the cool night.

The air was filled with the fragrances of dry pine needles and ocean, and the midnight sky was a dichotomy of the blackest black speckled with shimmering stars. A gentle breeze caressed the trees and cooled his face. He stopped, pulled a pack of cigarettes out of his pocket, and lit one. He hadn't been able to smoke all day and just realized the craving that had crept up on him. He took a deep drag.

The horizon to the east formed where the black sea met the abyss of space. There was nothing but ocean between him and Europe. He exhaled smoke as he sighed. That was one place to which he could never return: too many dead bodies.

He finished his cigarette, ground it out on the pavement with his foot, and picked up the butt and put it in his pocket. He then followed the path west, through a grove of pine trees.

Lenny checked into the dorm, which he quickly assessed was better than his usual dive motels, bought a candy bar and a soda from a vending machine, and went to his room and ate the extra sandwich he'd purchased at the cafeteria. Jennifer would be picking him up in five hours for the ferry ride back to Orient Point.

JACOB AND HANK looked over the setup one last time. It had taken longer than expected to rig the system to stream the encrypted signal into one side of the device, and collect the output, and hopefully decrypted, data from the other.

The mechanical setup was straightforward, but there were questions about stream rates and signal strengths to consider. They eventually agreed on all of the parameters, taking into consideration the rates and strengths of the signals as they'd originally arrived from space. They could always amplify the signal intensity gradually, if needed, but they had to be careful not to damage the device.

"Shall we connect the wires?" Jacob asked as he grabbed a copper wire with small pliers.

"Let's do it," Hank replied.

One by one, Jacob took the wires from the programmable amplifier that had been loaded with encrypted data files and pressed each wire against the left edge of the square decoder. In each case, the material swallowed the tips of the wires and solidified into a strong connection. He repeated the process on the right edge for the output wires, which were connected to the input of a sophisticated signal analyzer and recorder.

"Turn on the signal input," Jacob instructed.

Hank powered up the amplifier and pressed a button to initiate the input signal.

Jacob watched the display monitor on the output analyzer that was supposed to flash snapshots of the data expelled from the output of the decoder. It showed nothing.

"Increase the input amplitude," Jacob said.

Hank increased it by ten percent, then twenty. Still nothing.

"What the hell?" Jacob huffed. "Keep increasing – slowly."

After five minutes of gradually increasing the input amplitude, Jacob told Hank to stop and reduce the signal strength. There were no data streaming at the output and he didn't want to damage the device – it was something he'd never be able to repair, much less reverse engineer. It made him wonder whether the object had tamper-proofing mechanisms – through self-destruction or lethal booby-traps. It didn't matter: they had no choice but to tamper.

"Do you find it odd that there's no external power source?" Jacob asked. "There's no way an internal battery would last this long – 50 years or whatever it has been – and we've already checked for radioactive sources."

"Yes, it's odd," Hank replied. "I wouldn't have expected it to be a passive device."

By "passive," Jacob knew that Hank meant the device didn't require power for its internal circuits to function. "Active" devices, however, required external power or an internal battery. "I think it should be active as well," Jacob remarked. "But I didn't see anything indicating that in the diagram."

Jacob pulled out his laptop and brought up the image of the schematic and studied it closely. There were only two sets of connections, one for the input data and the other for output data. Any other connections should have been revealed when they'd mapped all of its surfaces and edges with the multimeter probes.

"We should take a closer look at the surface," Jacob suggested as he set the device on a viewing platform, making sure not to dislodge the wires. The platform had clamps to secure the object, as well as an overhead light and large magnifying glass, each mounted to separate articulating arms. He positioned the light over the device, turned it on, and reached for the magnifying glass.

"Look!" Hank gasped.

Jacob twitched and then looked to where Hank was pointing.

The outer edges of the decoder glowed bright green.

"Holy shit!" Daniel said and turned off the light. The edges glowed for a full 15 seconds and then slowly dimmed, leaving no trace on the gray surface. He rushed over to his computer and reexamined the schematic. "Look here," he said, pointing at wavy lines on the diagram. "Those must represent light."

"That's the power source," Hank said, smiling. "It just needed to be brighter than the overhead room lights."

"Let's give this another shot," Jacob said and reset the data input and recording devices.

They positioned the fluorescent lamp about a foot above the device and turned it on. The outer edges of the square object glowed green. A few seconds later, a green equilateral triangle illuminated in the center of the face of the decoder and rotated clockwise at about one rotation per second.

"We have data at the output," Hank said.

Jacob's heart seemed to sputter as he watched the data stream across the buffer screen. "It looks to be multilevel, digital data," he said. If that were true, the new data were different than the data he'd extracted from the short part of the AM signal used to generate the three bitmap images.

After ten minutes, Jacob asked, "How much input data has gone through?"

Hank looked at the display on the input device and said, "About one gigabyte of over 100. How much is in the output buffer?"

"Just over 70 gigs."

"That's a seventy-to-one compression ratio," Hank said.

"That's huge," Jacob noted. "I hope there's no data loss in the conversion."

"That's a possibility," Hank agreed. "It's going to be a lot of data – seven terabytes."

"At this rate, it's going to take 17 hours."

"We're limited by the rates of our input and output devices," Hank said. "Should we leave it and come back?"

"The output buffer can only handle one terabyte," Jacob said. "We'll have to come back every two hours or so to transfer data to another storage device to make room."

"I'm here until midnight," Hank said. "I can show the tech on the next shift how to execute the transfer."

Jacob's hands trembled and his stomach soured. He'd been running on minimal sleep for days and felt like he had zero blood sugar. If he could sleep through until morning he could get back on a normal sleep schedule, and his mind would be fresh for analyzing the new data. But he couldn't get himself to leave.

At 11:50 p.m., Hank informed the next technician of the data transfer routine as Jacob listened. Hank left at 1:45 a.m.

Still in awe of the implications of what was happening, Jacob hung on until 3:00 a.m. before making his way back to his flat. He made it to his bedroom, fell face-first onto his bed, and fell asleep without taking off his clothes.

LENNY BREATHED in the cool morning breeze as he walked toward the dock. It seemed that Jennifer Chung was running late.

Other than getting off Plum Island and delivering the goods, his assignment was complete. But he'd had trouble sleeping.

As he'd been getting ready for bed, it had occurred to him that he'd previously seen a device like the one in his bag. But he couldn't place it, and it bothered him.

He was also uneasy about the possibility that Chinese operatives might be waiting for him at Orient Point, or even on the ferry, intending to take possession of the object right away. He didn't have a plan for that contingency and would have to improvise.

Jennifer rolled up behind him in a golf cart and he got in.

"Everything work out?" she asked as she pushed the accelerator.

"Some minor complications, but I managed."

"It was there?"

Lenny nodded and patted his duffle bag. He'd packed clothes around it so that the edges didn't protrude. As they approached the dock, his curiosity got to him. "Do you know what it is?"

She shook her head. "Only that it was acquired by US intelligence operatives in Argentina after World War II. The rumors were that it had originally been brought back from Antarctica by a Nazi U-boat."

Lenny flinched.

"There might be part of a meteorite inside it," she added.

The brakes squeaked and Lenny had to put his hand on the dash to keep upright. "Why did your advisor have it?"

"He was an expert on astrobiology."

"What's that?"

"They're pulling the ropes," Jennifer said, nodding toward the ferry.

Lenny hustled up the ramp.

JACOB WOKE up at 6:00 a.m. and headed down to the lab. The data transformation wouldn't be finished until the evening, but he couldn't stay in bed any longer. When he arrived, Hank was already there, and the assistant was gone.

"I thought you weren't coming in until this afternoon," Jacob said.

"I got in at 5:00 a.m.," Hank replied. "Couldn't sleep."

Jacob understood. "Still a long ways to go."

"Better to be here in case there's a glitch," Hank said.

Jacob felt the same, and was glad the technician was there. He decided to go back up to his apartment and work on the outgoing signal from the probe. Those data differed greatly from the incoming signal, and he wanted to study them.

By mid-afternoon he'd had no luck, and decided to call Pauli at

4:00 p.m., which was 9:00 p.m. in London. The call was short since she was already piled with work, but she filled him in on her progress. Her apartment hadn't yet been furnished and she'd been sleeping on an inflatable mattress. She was in good spirits, and it seemed that she'd missed him.

After they hung up, he called Hank to check on the data, and then located the Space Systems gym. During a 45-minute run on the treadmill, he worked out some of the lingering grogginess, and his mind seemed to clear.

He showered, ate a healthy dinner for a change, salad with chicken breast, and headed down to the lab at 7:15 p.m.

He found Hank seated at the lab bench and took a stool beside him.

"About an hour to go," Hank informed him.

They decided to get some coffee in a nearby break room to pass the time.

They returned 50 minutes later and, after five minutes, the green-illuminated triangle on the square device turned white, but continued to rotate.

"Something's happening," Hank said.

"The input stream has stopped," Daniel noted. "The device must still be crunching the last batch of outgoing data."

Five minutes later, the triangle stopped rotating and disappeared. The screen on the output analyzer turned to a flat line – no more data was streaming.

"I guess that's it," Jacob said.

"What now?" Hank asked.

"I'll have to take the hard drive," Jacob said. "The one on my computer doesn't have enough space."

Hank seemed to make a calculation and then huffed. "It will be 17.3 terabytes total. We're lucky we had a 25 terabyte portable drive."

Jacob was going to have to figure out how to use the Wave Tempest software with streaming input data before he could even attempt to decipher it.

"How long will it take to decode?"

Jacob shrugged. "The first set took a few hours. But that was just a fraction of what we have now. These data also seem to be of a different type – multilevel digital rather than standard, two-level. It could take days, and that's if the encryption isn't too complicated."

Hank transferred the remaining data from the analyzer buffer to the portable drive, and then did the same with an identical storage device. "We currently have two copies of the data, and we'll make more," he said as he handed Jacob the original.

They parted ways and Jacob rode the elevator up to his flat. He powered up his laptop and set it on the granite countertop in the kitchen. He put on a pot of coffee and started the Wave Tempest software as it brewed.

It was 10:00 p.m., but it felt earlier to him. He took a seat on the couch that faced the northern wall of windows. Far below were patches of trees and parking lots and, in the distance, a brightly-lit commercial area filled with restaurants and traffic. It reminded him of Paulina. If she only knew what he'd been doing in the past weeks and, more so, where he was now.

The coffee pot beeped, and he poured some of the brew into a porcelain cup and took a sip. He sat on the couch and leaned back. He tipped his head back and sighed. It was nice to have accomplished something and have some time to breathe, even if only for a few minutes.

It would take days to process all of the data. It was going to be an excruciating wait. The three images he'd already decoded were the first messages of alien origin ever seen by humans. But they weren't the real message.

He moved to the counter, hooked up the external hard drive that contained the extracted data, and began configuring the Wave Tempest program to handle the colossal amount of information. Once he figured out how to do that, he'd start the decryption process.

The real message was still to come.

Tao examined the device on the rickety table in the break room. He touched the cold metal with his fingertips.

It was a stainless steel cylinder about 15 centimeters in diameter and 30 centimeters tall. The top and bottom were each sealed with a flange fastened to the outer rim with a ring of 16 bolts. There was a two-inch diameter window in the center of the top flange, but the interior was dark.

Tao found a small flashlight and directed it through the window.

Inside, brackets suspended a cylindrical object about five centimeters in diameter and 15 to 20 centimeters tall. It had rounded black end caps, and eight equally spaced black rings that encircled its midsection. It didn't look particularly complicated, but what did he know? He was no engineer. How would he even know whether it was the right thing? He wondered if anyone would know, considering that no one in China had seen it either. Even the Chinese mole on Plum Island had only gotten a glance at it, and she hadn't even managed to get a picture of it.

He packed his new acquisition back into its protective case, pushed it aside, and pulled a pack of cigarettes out of his inner jacket pocket. He lit the unfiltered Pall Mall, took a long drag, and exhaled through his nose as he stared at the case. What was he supposed to do with this thing? He cringed at the idea of just putting it in the safe house's underground vault and forgetting about it.

It made him think about the other prizes his Russian-American asset had retrieved. It seemed to be a waste to expend such an effort to collect them, and then hide them away and forget about them. He shrugged as he blew dual streams of smoke out his nostrils. These things, and many others, would soon be transported to China where they'd supposedly be put to use.

Still, it confused him. His predecessor was dead. Cho's Red Dragon project, however, was still alive. But Tao knew neither who ran it, nor its objective. And things had changed drastically in the past weeks with the events involving China and the Americans in the Southern Seas. It was a victory for the Americans. But how did that affect China's plans? They must have recalculated their course.

A knock on the door startled him from his thoughts.

He looked up to see one of his men peering through the small window in the door of the break room.

Tao nodded for the man to enter.

Two of his operatives escorted Lenny inside. The available space in the break room was instantly reduced to an uncomfortable volume.

"Good morning, Mr. Butrolsky. Please have a seat," Tao said. "Would you like some tea?"

Lenny politely declined.

The plastic chair creaked as Lenny sat, and the two escorts took posts inside the door with their hands folded in front of them.

"First, I commend you on your flawless work in New York," Tao said. "Your final payment will be transferred by the end of the day."

Lenny nodded and grinned.

"I am quite aware of your desire to end our relationship," Tao said, and studied the Russian's face.

Lenny's face remained blank, but he nodded slowly.

"Unfortunately, you are currently too valuable to us," Tao explained. "There are many things to do. For one, William Thompson is still alive. We need you to finish that job."

Lenny shrugged. "It will be difficult."

Tao nodded. "Also, there's Jacob Hale."

Lenny seemed to grimace.

"Is that a sensitive topic?" Tao asked, knowing the answer.

Lenny didn't respond.

"He has become a high-priority target as well," Tao added.

"I don't understand," Lenny said. "I thought we just needed the book and keys from him."

"It has come to our attention that there is much more to Mr. Hale," Tao explained. "And there's new information that we need to collect."

"What kind of information?"

Tao shrugged. "It's not clear right now, but we have reliable sources providing us with intelligence. The Americans are trying to break a cipher of some kind. Something connected to their Red Wraith project."

"I thought Red Wraith had expired."

"I think not," Tao said, raising his voice. "Clearly, recent events in Antarctica refute that notion."

"How so?"

"We have learned that the *Stennis* carrier group is heading back to the Weddell Sea," Tao explained. "They're going there for a reason, and we suspect it is connected to their Red Wraith project."

"How is killing William Thompson, or Jacob Hale, going to forward your initiative?" Lenny asked.

Tao lit up a cigarette and took a drag. "Thompson is the key to everything," he said as he exhaled smoke. "We must eliminate him so that the Americans do not have him. It would be better to acquire him, but that has proven to be impossible."

"And Hale?"

"We've been informed that he is of great utility," Tao said. "At this point, more for his talents than his possessions."

"What are his talents?"

"Signal analysis, encryption, complex reverse engineering," Tao replied. "It would be most desirable to collect him. Again, we will be satisfied with eliminating him."

"How do you want me to proceed?" Lenny asked as he shifted in his seat, making the chair groan and slide on the floor.

"We need to get you inside the facility," Tao said.

"What facility?"

"The one to which you followed Ms. Walker – Space Systems."

"That will prove to be difficult."

"You will have some help," Tao said.

Lenny's face seemed to go blank for a split second before he spoke. "You have someone inside?"

"We have people everywhere, Mr. Butrolsky," Tao said as he exhaled his final drag. He ground his cigarette into a dirty paper plate and dropped the smoldering butt onto a pile of others. "We will be in contact soon. Do not leave the DC area."

Tao nodded to his men who escorted Lenny out and closed the door behind them.

It was a gamble. All of his assets would be at risk. Orders from above indicated that it was an all-or-nothing situation. China was prepared to go to war, if needed, putting their very existence on the line. But that was a last resort.

They were already in a war of a different kind. The current war was more of a race, although it was not clear toward what they were racing, or what would happen when a winner was declared.

IT HAD TAKEN Jacob past midnight the night before to figure out how to stream input data from an external hard drive using the Wave Tempest software. He'd realized he needed another drive on which to stream the output data – his laptop didn't have enough storage space. He requested one at 1:00 a.m. and received it 15 minutes later.

He did the final setup in the morning, and his kitchen counter now had three objects on it: the raw data storage device, his laptop, and an output drive with a 100-terabyte capacity. His laptop was now acting like an intermediate processor, working to decrypt the data as it had with the short AM signal and the gravitational-wave data. He hoped the procedure would be the same, but he'd rely on Wave Tempest to figure it out.

He had intended to take a short nap on the couch, but it had extended to almost three hours and through lunch. The severe sleep deprivation over the past few days had caught up with him, but he felt better after the nap.

He went for a run on the treadmill in the gym and showered, and then spent the rest of the afternoon and early evening going over his notes on *The Israel Thread* and periodically checking his computer's progress. The feedback parameters seemed to be converging, meaning it was on track to identifying the file formats. If that was done successfully, the rest was just mathematical operations – data conversions and packaging of data into usable formats, like bitmap images.

In his experience, new information often ended up raveling into new puzzles rather than solving the original one.

The first puzzle solution was the realization that the incoming AM signal was split into a short part and a long part – and that the two parts were different. Next, that short part had to be decrypted – it was fortunate that it wasn't complicated – resulting in three bitmap images. But those images were gray – they were scrambled or encrypted – so the next step was to unscramble them. The next part required the revelation that the glitches observed by the gravitational-wave detectors also carried a signal. It was important that he'd known what to look for at that stage – another bitmap image – and then known what to do with it. Performing multiple subtractions and rotations of that image from the other three resulted in three decoded images, one of which identified the decoder device needed to decrypt the long part of the AM signal.

And now he was waiting for the next puzzle – whatever Wave Tempest was currently concocting – and there would be more after that.

He wasn't complaining. In fact, he was more worried about what would happen when the final puzzle was put together.

His stomach burned and he suddenly felt famished. It was going on 10:00 p.m., and he hadn't eaten since lunchtime.

He turned on the oven and slid in a frozen pizza. He grabbed a Pepsi from the refrigerator, popped it open, and took a long swig. He went over to the windows and gazed out at the traffic in the distance. Just as he was about to sit on the couch, the doorbell rang.

He padded over, peered through the peephole, and opened the door. It was Will.

"You awake?" Will asked as he stepped inside.

"Barely," Jacob responded as he closed the door behind him. "Something going on?"

Will shook his head. "I heard the decoding device worked and wanted to see how things were progressing."

Jacob explained how they'd used the device to extract data from the signal. "I was able to convert the short part of the AM signal – which is what gave us the image of the decoder device – using my software. In that case, the encoding was simple. The rest of the signal, however, is extremely complex. It's multi-frequency, and my software found nothing in the raw data."

"The device extracted digital data from the long part of the incoming AM signal?" Will asked.

Jacob nodded. "Yes, it's a multilevel digital signal."

"So, not just two levels – ones and zeros," Will said. "How many levels does it have?"

"One section has 16," Jacob answered. "That's the highest I've seen so far."

"Any idea how the decoder device works?"

"Beyond our technology, and I've seen a lot on the cutting edge," Jacob replied. He described how the electrical connections were made.

"It just oozed around the tips of the wires and hardened?" Will seemed astonished.

Jacob nodded and explained how light was used as a power source.

"In my own research I've come across some interesting materials, but never anything like that," Will said.

"Me either."

"How much longer to decrypt the data?"

"Could be hours or days, but it seems to be converging."

"Do I smell something burning?" Will asked, tilting his head back and sniffing the air.

"Crap," Jacob said and hurried into the kitchen area. He hadn't set the timer on the oven. He turned the oven off, opened the door, donned an oven mitt, and pulled the pizza pan out and set it on the stovetop.

"Salvageable?" Will asked, laughing.

"Just in time," Jacob replied. "Got distracted. Want some?"

He did, and Jacob cut up the pizza and put the pan on a hot pad on the counter. He pulled a Pepsi out of the refrigerator and set it in front of Will.

"Thanks," Will said and popped the top on the can and took a swig. "Think the data will again be in the form of images?"

Jacob shrugged. "It could also be text in some alien language, but that would be trouble."

Will nodded. "We'd need an illustrated dictionary to decipher it."

"Even then, we'd probably need a whole team of language experts to crack it," Jacob added. "It makes me wonder about the time scale of things. It could take months, or years, to decipher a new language."

"It could just be diagrams, like that for the decoder," Will suggested.

A loud beeping sound came from Jacob's right, making him sit upright and lose his train of thought. It was the computer, on the counter. He stared at Will.

"What?" Will asked, wide-eyed.

"I think it finished something," Jacob replied. "Or maybe it crashed."

They stood simultaneously, and Jacob nearly tipped his plate onto the floor. He hit a button on the laptop, bringing the screen back to life. A new folder labeled "Extracted Files" was on the screen. "Program's still running, but it successfully extracted some files," Jacob nearly shouted and opened the folder. It contained three image files.

He opened the first, labeled "Image.001."

An unscrambled picture appeared on the screen. At the top were two lines of ten characters. The first character on the left was a single open dot – a circle – beneath which was another open circle. Next was a solid dot with a vertical line beneath it. Next were two closely spaced solid dots with a symbol beneath them. Next were a triangle, a square, and a pentagon, and onward up to a nine-sided polygon, all with corresponding symbols beneath them.

"Looks like a number system," Will remarked.

"Base ten, numbers zero to nine."

Below the numbers was a four-by-eight array of characters.

"Looks like an alphabet," Jacob said.

"Numbers are easy," Will said. "A new alphabet is another story."

"Defining a language for what is to follow?"

"That could be a mess," Will said. "There are languages we've been working on for centuries that still haven't been deciphered."

"Hopefully we'll be given enough information to figure it out," Jacob said as he closed Image.001 and opened Image.002. It seemed to be a page of pictorial definitions with script. The order of the "words" seemed to follow that of the alphabet characters given in the previous image. "This looks like the picture dictionary you anticipated."

"Strings of characters meant to describe pictures. That only works if you know what the pictures represent," Will noted. "The first one looks like a spring."

"Look, a saw blade," Jacob said and pointed. "It seems to be in motion."

"Maybe it's defining a verb, meaning 'to cut.'"

Jacob closed the figure and opened the next. The dictionary continued. "These files are small," Jacob said. "At this rate, there will be thousands by the time it's finished."

"If my worldview hadn't been shaken so drastically in the past year, this would have done it," Will said. "This is an alien communication. How are you doing with this?"

Jacob glanced at Will and then retracted into his mind and tried to assess what was happening. He quickly came to the conclusion that he exhibited no outward symptoms of shock or astonishment because, deep down, he still didn't believe it. "It just seems too convenient," he said. "It mimics too closely all the predictions of how intelligent extraterrestrial life might contact us. They'd first send us definitions of numbers and an alphabet, and then a picture dictionary. Do you think it's real?"

"No idea," Will said as he picked up his phone. "But I think we need to meet with the others."

CHAPTER 11

By 4:00 a.m., just before Jacob went to bed, Wave Tempest had decoded nearly 750 images. Most of those images seemed to be pages of picture definitions. The last few files, however, looked like engineering drawings.

When he awakened at 6:00 a.m., the image count had risen to 1,000. The newest ones again looked like engineering drawings, but were becoming increasingly complex. He had no idea what the diagrams represented, but he didn't have time to look at them closely.

By 7:00 a.m. he was in room 713 to report on what was happening.

He stammered through some preliminary information. His mouth felt like it was full of soda crackers and peanut butter. He took a swig of water and collected his thoughts. He was otherwise a confident public speaker, but he'd never addressed a group of people like this one.

James Thackett, the CIA director, sat at the head of the long conference table, opposite Jacob, who stood at the other end, near a projector screen. Seated along the length of the table on Jacob's left were Daniel and Sylvia, and then Jonathan and Denise. Closest to him, on the right, was a tall, middle-aged man with black hair and dark-rimmed glasses. He was a CIA ciphers specialist. Further down was a linguistics specialist – a thin woman in her sixties wearing a green sweater. Her gray hair was tied in a tight bun and had two criss-crossing pencils sticking through it.

The last person on the right was William Thompson. Will made him the most nervous.

To calm himself, Jacob imagined Uncle Theo was in the room with him. It helped.

He spent the next hour explaining how they had decoded the message and converted a small fraction of it into readable data in the form of images. He was instructed by Thackett to omit any mention of gravitational-wave data, as that was the key to deciphering the main message. The ciphers and linguistic specialists were not cleared for that information. It was also data that was easily obtainable by foreign intelligence if its importance were revealed.

Jacob displayed sample images on the screen as he spoke. "Most of what we've obtained so far seems to be a list of definitions – a picture dictionary of sorts," he explained. "Next came a long string of characters – about 100 dense pages of which seems to be text."

He paged through a few slides until an image that looked like a blueprint for some complex device was displayed. "Finally, as you see here, there are technical drawings," he said, and then went on to explain that they had not yet identified anything in the drawings.

"How many more images are there?" Sylvia asked.

Jacob shrugged. "There's still a long way to go – most of the data has not yet been processed. My computer is working on it as we speak. My guess is that there will be thousands."

"How long will it take to finish?" Jonathan asked.

"At this rate, maybe 48 hours," Jacob replied. "I've requested a second computer to cut down on the time."

"It will take years to understand this information and learn the language," the linguist said. "I don't think it's possible to translate the message in the amount of time you've given us. Even with the dictionary."

Everyone turned their heads in unison to the ciphers specialist.

It took the man a few seconds to realize that eyes were on him.

"Sorry," he said, "I'm still trying to reconcile that this information came from ... not Earth."

"That has not been verified," Daniel said.

"I agree with my colleague," the man continued as he nodded to the linguist. "Although we should be able to proceed immediately, it's the sheer volume of material that's concerning."

"Tell us more about the engineering diagrams," Daniel said.

"There are hundreds of them so far. They range from simple to complex, and some look like electrical circuits," Jacob explained as he rummaged through a folder on the computer desktop to show them. "I only downloaded a handful for this presentation."

The first one he opened resembled a complex printed circuit. The next one looked like a parabolic antenna housed inside a sphere. It had hundreds of labeled parts – language unknown – and the image was large. He zoomed in on one small area, revealing intricate details that were also labeled in foreign script.

"The physical dimensions given here are referenced to the diameter of the White Stone, which is about 67 centimeters," Will said. "So this object, whatever it is, is about a meter tall."

Jacob opened another file. "I looked at this one before. It's part of a series of related diagrams. Note the scale of this one."

It took a few seconds, but the gasps came in unison.

"That's over 50 meters in diameter," Director Thackett said.

Jacob nodded.

"What is it?" Denise asked.

Jacob shrugged and shook his head. "We'll need hundreds of engineers to work on these if we're going to understand these drawings in a reasonable amount of time." It made him think of his former employer, Interstellar Dynamics. This type of thing was right in their wheelhouse, but it was beyond their scale. Unfortunately, he also no longer trusted them. If his former supervisor, Terrence, would accept a payoff to fire someone, perhaps he could also be bribed for information.

"Can you go back to the text part of the message?" Will requested. "Not the dictionary, just the text."

Jacob showed the first page of text. He zoomed in on the horizontal lines of script so that the characters were clearly resolved. Everyone stared at the screen, but it was Will who drew his attention.

Will's eyes glassed over and rolled back partway, so that the whites showed below, but his pupils were only half covered by his eyelids. His lips moved almost imperceptibly, as if he were reading. After a few seconds, he seemed to shake out of his trance.

"Okay, thanks," Will said and took a swig of coffee.

Denise looked at Will as if she were trying to ask him something. Will responded by shaking his head, "No."

Thackett stood and walked to the front. Jacob took a seat in a chair next to the wall with the screen to his left.

"For now, everything will stay in CIA. No other agencies," Thackett started. "This is all top secret, of course. Unfortunately, we don't have time to enact all of the usual security protocols. Each of you, and your respective work, would normally be separated and compartmentalized, but we need to work together on this. We have about 20 CIA engineers cleared, as well as a dozen linguists and cipher experts. We'll get them started immediately. Daniel and Jacob will organize the engineering effort."

Jacob nodded. He found it unusual that he'd be thrown right into such a role, but he was probably a good choice. First, he'd deciphered the original signal. Second, this was certainly a reverse engineering task, something of which he'd had much experience. The CIA's technical efforts focused mostly on new development, rather than figuring out how old stuff worked. They usually contracted out the latter to places like Interstellar Dynamics.

"We'll gradually expand," Thackett continued. "When we do, we'll start with NASA and Department of Defense scientists and engineers. And then to NSA language and cipher specialists."

"What about us?" Daniel asked, and gestured to Sylvia and Will.

"We'll talk about that next," Thackett replied, and dismissed Jacob, the ciphers specialist, and the linguist.

Jacob took the elevator back up to his flat. On the way, he thought again of the implications of what he'd seen, and what he was doing.

For him, the world had changed.

AFTER THE GROUP SPLIT UP, Will moved with the others from the conference table to the cluster of furniture on the opposite end of room 713. Everyone was there except for Jacob, who had been dismissed and gone back to his flat to check on the data.

Will poured a cup of coffee from a pot in the kitchenette and sat in one of the two leather chairs in the cluster. Thackett sat in the duplicate leather chair to Will's right, and Daniel took the wooden chair to his left. The others filled the couch.

Everyone seemed nervous.

"The president has given me complete authority over this operation," Thackett explained. "He's scared to death."

"The president is frightened?" Denise asked. Will read fear in her eyes and voice.

Thackett nodded and continued. "The idea that we have received a message from an extraterrestrial source has riled more than just him. And leaks are starting to occur. Right now they're in the form of rumors and conspiracy theories, and haven't gotten much traction. But it's just a matter of time."

Jonathan shook his head. "It won't be kept a secret."

Thackett shifted in his seat, apparently agitated by the comment. "The rumors might not be coming from us," he explained. "Too many people know about this already, including foreign governments. It's a miracle the exposure is as limited as it is. However, none of that is our problem. We're here to find out what the hell is happening, what is going to happen, and what to do about it."

After a few seconds of silence, Denise asked Will, "Could you read any of it?"

The others looked to him with anticipation, including Thackett.

The message consisted of strings of foreign characters, some of which resembled those in the Greek and Russian alphabets. Others reminded him of hieroglyphs. But the message didn't contain any of those common "Earthian" characters, and he could read none of the text. He shook his head. "A few of the symbols resemble some of those on the White Stone, but I can't read them."

If he were to just magically acquire the ability to read the language, they could bypass the linguists altogether. It would compress the process from years to weeks. "I do feel a sense of familiarity with the script, but no comprehension," Will added. "I'll keep looking at it."

"You should study the technical drawings as well," Thackett said. "Another set of technically-trained eyes couldn't hurt."

Will agreed. The drawings would also give him some context for the language, and they intrigued him. Were they supposed to build those things? Something occurred to him and he turned to Thackett.

"If the drawings represent large, complex devices, there will be separate diagrams for each constituent piece, with highly detailed drawings for individual parts, and larger scale plans for the entire device," Will explained. "Ever see the breakout drawings for the transmission of a car? There are hundreds of pieces – gears, gaskets, bearings, shafts, and other things. Think how difficult it would be to assemble a transmission if you also had to fabricate every part from scratch – every tiny gear and bolt. I think that's what we have going on here."

"Worse," Sylvia said. "The plans are in an unknown language."

"We'll have to reverse engineer every part," Thackett said. "We'll need a lot of engineers."

"The engineers' objective should be to determine the functions of these devices," Will said. "Not to actually build anything – not yet anyway."

Thackett nodded.

"With security in mind," Daniel said, "it would be prudent to keep the main drawings in the hands of a select few. Those for the individual parts can be assigned to lower-level personnel."

Will agreed. "No way to know that you're working on a transmission if you're only reverse engineering a single gear."

"Unless the engineers talk to each other," Daniel said. "We'll have to enforce compartmentalization."

"Do we really have the time to worry about security?" Jonathan asked.

"If it hampers progress, we'll make adjustments," Thackett said as he pulled out his phone. "For now, we'll go with Daniel's plan."

The meeting ended and Will headed for Jacob's flat. His nerves tingled with anxiety – he had to get a look at the drawings.

His gut told him that they were crucial to their survival.

WILL'S stomach soured as he stared at the pile of information on the table.

After their meeting the previous morning, it had taken the rest of the day to print the files that had been decoded and extracted, and the computer was still running. The night before, he and Jacob had separated the technical drawings from the rest and had them bound.

On the table were nine, three-inch-thick volumes printed on oversized pages. They were filled with technical drawings interleaved with text that seemed to have the format of technical manuals. Jacob had five additional volumes, and there was much more to come. More than half the data had yet to be decoded.

The printed copies were bulky, but Will preferred paper to computer screens. He liked to write notes on things, and paper copies seemed much more convenient than electronic documents. They were also easier on the eyes.

The coffee maker beeped simultaneously with the doorbell. It was 8:00 a.m., and he was expecting Jacob.

Will let him in, and they both grabbed coffee and went to the table near the southeast wall of windows.

"Nicer view than I have," Jacob quipped.

"I know people," Will responded. He grabbed one of the volumes and handed it to Jacob. "We should sort through these and identify which drawings we can hand off to the engineering team. We'll need to keep the 'big picture' diagrams under wraps."

Jacob nodded. "How should we proceed?"

"I thought we'd just start paging through them and try to identify what we can," Will suggested. "We'll make plans when we know more."

Jacob agreed.

Will grabbed a volume and the two men started working.

Will had the first of the nine volumes. The drawings were arranged according to the order in which they were decoded. He'd added page numbers when they were printed so that they could easily locate them later. He opened the cover and peeled away the first onionskin-thin title page to reveal the first drawing.

The first thing he noticed was the intricate detail of the print. The lines were razor-thin and sharp, and the symbols and text were perfectly clear. It was something he hadn't appreciated when viewing the digital versions. Since the files were bitmap images, the file sizes of the more intricate diagrams were enormous.

The first drawing resembled the breakout plan one gets with the instructions for a home-assembled piece of furniture. However, this one was orders of magnitude more intricate and complex.

Although the more than 100 parts were separated, the lines connecting them to their respective final positions allowed Will to visualize the object when fully assembled. This one formed a sphere with a hemispherical bowl on the topside, reminiscent of the Death Star from *Star Wars*, but miniaturized. A pedestal protruded from the bottom of the sphere with mounting brackets branching off it in all directions.

The scale on the bottom of the page was defined by a line, about an inch long, next to a symbol that was a circle with a horizontal line through its center. It was the diameter of the White Stone, which was about two-thirds of a meter, or two feet. With this scale, the object in the drawing was about 20 feet in diameter, and the recessed bowl on its topside had a diameter of about six feet.

Each constituent part was labeled with a set of symbols – probably the name of the part in the alien language. The text seemed familiar somehow but, no matter how much he concentrated, he was unable to read it.

The next page showed a more detailed drawing of one of the components on the previous page. It was a complex shape that was roughly cylindrical, like a barrel, with a square recess in the top. The drawing showed a view from the top and two projections from the sides, like a conventional technical blueprint. All of the dimensions were given, and the scale on the bottom of the page indicated that the whole piece was about two feet tall and one foot in diameter.

The object's interior components were broken out like those on the previous drawing, revealing the details of the parts. There were about 20 new parts and, as Will expected, the next drawings detailed them. It was clear that the device on page one was going to be composed of thousands of pieces, each of which would have to be reverse-engineered and constructed from scratch. It was daunting.

"Damn," Jacob said.

Will looked up from his work. About 40 minutes had passed since they'd begun. Jacob looked pale. "You all right?" Will asked.

"This is impossible," Jacob replied.

Will's chest seemed to tighten as if bungee cords were wrapped around his upper rib cage. He didn't want to reveal his own feelings of futility. "It won't be easy," he said.

"It will be impossible," Jacob reiterated, this time with a tone of conviction. "I do this for a living. It would be easier to have the object and no plans, rather than plans in an unknown language, but no object. I can see already that this will take decades, and I've only been through five pages. Not even one complete piece."

"Just keep going," Will said. "We can make a better assessment once we've seen it all."

"We don't even know the materials used to build these things," Jacob said. "Even if we had the chemical formulas, some parts might be composed of unique alloys that require special fabrication techniques. That alone could take years to figure out."

Jacob's rant made Will think of the White Stone, and the material of which it was composed. He agreed that it could take years to figure out what it was. Although, it would be much easier to reverse engineer a material in hand than to discover a new one. The latter might take a century. "You're getting ahead of yourself."

"You have Pepsi?"

Will shook his head. "Sorry."

"I'll be right back," Jacob said as he stood and walked out of the apartment.

When the door closed, a sense of gloom seeped into Will's mind. Jacob's hopelessness had its foundation in experience. He was an expert. But it made Will think that there must be another way. Whoever had sent the message could not have expected them to learn the language and build the devices in any reasonable amount of time. As Jacob said, it would take decades.

Will's estimate was longer, considering they'd both come to the same conclusion after examining fewer than 25 of the thousands of drawings.

He paged ahead for ten minutes, scanning another 50 pages. He was still on the individual components of the first major piece. He flipped ahead another 200 pages until he came to the last component of the piece. Fifteen pages of tiny script followed. He couldn't read it, but he assumed – hoped – that the text provided detailed explanations of the fabrication and assembly of the device, and perhaps its intended function, which was most important.

He flipped to the next major piece. This one was an electronics schematic, larger than anything he'd seen before. The ensuing pages were filled with detailed sub-circuits, and he was able to deduce the types of some of the individually labeled components, such as resistors and capacitors. But they were all parts of miniaturized, integrated circuits.

He flipped through another 100 pages of intricate and complex circuits and concluded that it would take a team of electrical engineers years to sort it all out. He feared the circuitry might even be beyond human technology. And, again, it would come down to the materials. What was worse, however, was that the device might be designed to apply physics that humans did not yet understand.

He paged ahead to the next major piece. It was a cylinder with a dish-like object on the top and thin rods protruding around its perimeter, like a cactus flower. He gasped. According to the scale, it was over 150 feet tall and 50 feet in diameter. He paged ahead and found an interior drawing. The first things that struck him were features that resembled ladders.

The subsequent pages contained a multitude of complex components. At the end was a 30-page section of script.

Jacob was right. Will was familiar with large-scale construction of scientific equipment, and knew that the plans before him marked decades of work – even if they could read the language and understood the functionality of the devices.

The doorbell broke Will from his train of thought. He walked to the door and let Jacob in with a case of soda.

"Sorry, locked myself out. You want one?" Jacob asked as he nodded toward the case.

Will declined and went back to the table while Jacob put the Pepsi in the refrigerator.

"The rest of the data is finished processing," Jacob said as he returned to his seat at the table. He then pried up the tab of the soda can, producing a slow hiss, and then a pop. "I sent it to be printed. It's a little more than what we have here."

Will nodded. After taking a few seconds to digest Jacob's words, he said, "You were right. It will take thousands of people years to build what I've seen so far – even if they understood the language, and had the ability and materials to build it all."

"I was thinking about it on the way to my apartment," Jacob said. "We might employ an incremental strategy."

"What do you mean?"

"Identify one part that seems central to the whole thing and solve it."

"Solve it?"

"That's reverse engineering lingo," Jacob said. "It means cracking the function, control, materials, and construction of an unknown device. The solution is a functional replica."

Will nodded. "Go on."

"Once you've solved one central part," Jacob continued, "it may define the context for the entire device. If not, you target another part to solve, and so on."

Will agreed but was still pessimistic. There were thousands of parts, and some of the devices were large. However, he was glad that Jacob's attitude seemed less defeated.

"It's a good strategy," Will said, "but we should go through all of these drawings before making any decisions."

"That's going to take a few days."

"At least," Will agreed. "Better take good notes as you go."

Jacob opened his volume of drawings as Will flipped back to the first page of his. This was going to fill their waking hours for a while.

AT 10:00 P.M. Lenny parked his rental car in the rear parking lot of the hotel and got out. He weaved his way around parked cars until he arrived at the black SUV that was concealed behind a large laundry truck. He made sure it would be impossible for Chinese operatives to follow him due to the darkness, the speed at which he moved, and the proximity of the vehicle to the hotel entrance. He doubted that they were following him at this point – he should be in good standing after his recent successes – but he always followed his safety protocols.

The rear door on the passenger side of the SUV opened, and Lenny got in and closed it. A half-hour later they checked through the gate of the Space Systems building and parked in a sublevel of the garage. Two men led him to an elevator and accompanied him to a level five floors below the surface. They exited the elevator into a hallway that looked similar to the one he'd encountered during his first visit. A scent reminiscent of wet cement solidified the familiarity.

They brought him into a small room with a table and chairs and left him alone. Although they locked the door, this room didn't have a holding cell. Seemed his status had been upgraded.

A few minutes later, the CIA director and two security personnel entered. James Thackett took a seat across from Lenny as one of the other men retrieved two bottles of water and set one in front of Lenny and the other in front of Thackett.

"Congratulations on your string of successful missions," Thackett said.

Lenny nodded and grinned. "I wish I could take credit for them." It was easy to accomplish something when both sides wanted you to succeed.

"You had our help, but it was still a complex operation – Plum Island, I mean. I take it that your Chinese contacts were satisfied."

Lenny nodded. "I don't think they even know what it is – the device," he said. "Do you?"

"It's being passed into the right hands."

Lenny grunted. He interpreted that as a no.

"You requested this meeting," Thackett said. "What do you have?"

Lenny shifted in his seat. "They still want me to kill William Thompson."

Thackett shrugged. "I'm sure they do."

"And also Jacob Hale."

"Oh?" Thackett said and raised an eyebrow.

"They have someone inside."

"Inside," Thackett repeated. "Inside where?"

Lenny looked around, spread his arms, and said, "Here."

"Space Systems?" Thackett turned pale.

"That's what they told me."

"Who, exactly, told you that?"

"Our friendly local head of Chinese intelligence," Lenny replied. "Tao."

Thackett twisted open his bottle of water and took a drink. "Bullshit."

"I hope so," Lenny shrugged, "but they also had someone on Plum Island that no one knew about."

"Plum Island is not Space Systems," Thackett retorted, his face flushed. "People that have access to this place are vetted extremely well."

"People can be turned," Lenny argued. "People lie."

"Perhaps Tao is lying."

"Maybe. Can you take that chance?"

"We don't take any chances," Thackett said. "Thompson is isolated from all but a select few in this building."

"Then you should be okay."

"Quit playing me," Thackett said.

"Please, Director," Lenny said as he shook his head and held up his hand. "I came here to see how we can use this to our advantage." He wasn't playing the man. Lenny had chosen sides. It was the same as when he'd worked with his former boss, Heinrich Bergman. Bergman had given him a way out of a horrible situation in Europe, and Lenny had shown his gratitude with loyalty.

"I managed security for the Red Wraith project under Heinrich Bergman, as I have explained," Lenny continued. "When Bergman was killed, and Red Wraith went under, I was in no-man's land for a while. In fact, for some time I thought I was still working under the auspices of Red Wraith. By the time I noticed any peculiarities, I had carried out jobs under new leadership. Chinese leadership. For that, I blame the CIA. They should have terminated the project, including loose ends, rather than allowing it to get into the hands of an enemy."

Thackett looked at him with an expression of alarm.

"Yes, enemy," Lenny reiterated. "I'm not playing you, Director. I'm concerned. And I have chosen sides."

"Okay, Mr. Butrolsky," Thackett said. "Do you think it's true that they have someone on the inside?"

"I don't know," Lenny admitted. "It could be a trap. If you start a large-scale probe to find a mole they'll know this info got to you, and who gave it to you."

Thackett nodded and sighed. "And what would you recommend?"

"I can tell you what Bergman would do."

"Go on."

"He'd take out the entire Chinese network."

Thackett stared at him, silent.

"You don't have the stomach for it," Lenny said, reading Thackett's horrified expression.

Thackett remained quiet, seemingly searching for a response.

Lenny preempted him. "This asymmetry in tactics has always been a problem," Lenny said.

"What do you mean?"

"Our enemies – and I used to be one of them – pursue their objectives using any means necessary," Lenny explained. "The United States – and the West in general – impose arbitrary moral standards that impede their advancement, and erode their safety. I cannot speak for the Chinese, although I know they'd do the same, but I know that Russian intelligence would not hesitate to take down an entire network. I was personally involved in a counterintelligence operation that eliminated over 100 operatives."

"That was the Cold War," Thackett said.

"Is our current situation not as vital?" Lenny asked.

Thackett settled back into silence, and this time Lenny followed suit, waiting for the director to derive his own conclusions. Lenny figured there were many options, most of which ended with him cleaning up the Chinese network. But he was sure a more complicated option would be chosen.

"How are you supposed to use their source inside Space Systems?" Thackett asked.

"Their asset is supposed to get me access to this building."

"And your only objective is to assassinate Will Thompson?"

"And Jacob Hale," Lenny reminded him. Though once that hit might have been satisfying, he'd turned the page on Hale. They were now on the same side. "And anyone else of importance if the opportunity should arise."

Thackett seemed to think it over for a minute. "I think you should follow through, and infiltrate Space Systems," he said. "If need be, we'll catch you along with the mole."

Lenny nodded. He knew the plan. And he knew how it would end.

"Maybe we're just not smart enough," Will said, looking up from the volume of drawings. It was closing in on midnight, and they'd been at it the entire day.

"What do you mean?" Jacob asked and took a long swig of soda.

Will stood from his chair, yawned, stretched, and walked to the window. The moon was bright, and the night was clear. The details of the moon's surface were vivid and he located the Sea of Tranquility. "We might not have what it takes."

Will saw Jacob's reflection in the window. Jacob shrugged and stared at Will, seemingly expecting an explanation.

Will continued. "You know that chimps can learn sign language, match written words to pictures or physical objects, and even do simple arithmetic. They can use basic tools, and even pass knowledge to their young."

"I don't understand. Are you calling me a chimp?" Jacob laughed. "I'm trying as hard as I can."

Will huffed and turned to face him. "Seriously. What is humanity's most significant intellectual accomplishment – from a scientific or technological perspective?"

Jacob seemed to search his mind for a few seconds, and then replied, "Flight – the airplane."

Will nodded. "Certainly near the top. But I would have taken it to its extreme. I'd say it was the first moon landing."

"There are other things that were just as important," Jacob argued. "The transistor – it's responsible for every computer and communications device that we have. The Internet wouldn't exist without it."

Will nodded. It was a valid argument. "The Internet has changed our world considerably. It has effectively made the world smaller."

"I feel claustrophobic sometimes when I think about it," Jacob confided. "But what about medicine? We've made huge advances there."

Will nodded. "Far from a solved problem, however. But we're digressing. Back to the apes," he said. "Suppose all humans were removed from the Earth for some reason. Perhaps a virus wiped us out and there were no survivors."

"Not sure where you're going with this."

"What are the chances that the apes would ever make it to the moon?"

"You mean evolve as we did over millions of years? Like in *Planet of the Apes*?"

"Not exactly," Will said. "We leave them all of our knowledge. They have all of the books – dictionaries, language books, and technical books. Will they ever be able to learn the language and develop intellectually to the degree that they could get to the moon?"

Jacob just stared back at him.

"Suppose we simplify it for them," Will continued. "We give them all of the information to learn just one language. We then provide them with detailed instructions in that language to build a rocket that can get them to the moon. Will it happen before they overpopulate and starve themselves out of existence? Will it happen before some catastrophic event occurs? Will it happen before the sun burns out?"

"What's your point?"

Will detected concern in Jacob's voice.

"We are the chimps in this story," Will finally said.

Jacob stared at him. His face seemed drained of blood and his eyes became glassy.

They were quiet for a full minute before Jacob broke the silence.

"During my years reverse engineering complex military devices for the government, I never questioned my ability to accomplish any task," Jacob explained. "Without even thinking about it I knew that, whatever the level of sophistication of the device, it could be understood by humans. After all, every one of those devices had been created by humans."

Will walked back to his seat and tapped the top cover of his book of drawings. "What if there are things in here that we are not capable of understanding?"

Jacob took a deep breath and exhaled. "I agree that the sheer volume of material and magnitude of complexity make this a formidable undertaking. However, I haven't yet seen anything that we're incapable of understanding."

"So far, I agree," Will said. "But only regarding the building of the physical devices. Where we might have more difficulty, however, is in the functionality of the devices. What do they do, and how do they work? How will we test them?"

"Maybe we just need to trudge forward and focus on the task at hand."

Will agreed. What else were they to do? He opened his volume and resumed studying. Jacob did the same.

Will's toes tingled and his leg muscles twitched. He was starting to feel anxiety about something he could not isolate. It was a time pressure of some kind. They needed to decipher the language to have any chance at understanding the drawings.

He hoped it would just come to him and he'd be able to read the text – like what had happened with the White Stone script. He had a sense of familiarity with the script in the images: it was a feeling like recognizing someone's face but forgetting their name.

They continued until 1:15 a.m., when Jacob got a phone call and packed up his things as he talked. The call ended a minute later.

"That was my girlfriend – I need to call her back. I think I'll pack it in for the night," Jacob said and headed for the door.

"Don't forget your soda in the fridge."

"Got another case at my place," he replied. "Anyway, I'll need it here tomorrow."

As Jacob approached the door, the doorbell rang. He stopped and looked to Will.

Will walked to the door and opened it. It was Denise. He opened the door wider and let Jacob out.

"Oh," Denise said. "Hello, Jacob."

"Hello, Denise," he said and started down the hall. "And good night."

Will let Denise in and closed the door.

"We have to talk," she said.

It was a look he'd seen before. Something was happening.

DANIEL POURED hot water into his cup and submerged a tea ball filled with his favorite Earl Grey. He set the cup on the window and let the tea steep while he gazed out over the treetops below.

The evergreens swayed gently and the silvery undersides of their needles glistened in the moonlight. He imagined their fragrance, and it reminded him of summer vacations on Washington Island, Wisconsin, as a child. He'd always brought a stack of books with him, but he'd also enjoyed many of the things that normal kids liked.

He smiled as a happy memory surfaced in his mind. A girl named Emily had kissed him one night while they sat on the pier. The stars had been crystal clear that evening, with no moon to be seen. He could almost smell the scent of pine mixed with her perfume. It had been a better time – a time of obliviousness. Sometimes he wished it would return.

"Can I get some of that?" a female voice chimed from behind him.

Daniel turned around. Sylvia stood in the doorway.

"Of course," he said and nodded to the metal can on a shelf near the door. He pulled the tea ball from his cup, emptied it in the trash, and started to hand it to her before he realized that she had her own.

"Anything from Will and Jacob?" she asked as she scooped tea.

Daniel shook his head. "Not yet," he replied. "It's an enormous amount of information."

"You seem concerned."

"I am."

"About what?"

Daniel poured hot water into Sylvia's cup. "I can't see where this is going," he said. "I'm lost now more than ever. And I have a feeling that Will and Jacob are as well."

"You think they should have reported something by now?"

Daniel nodded. "I'm afraid this might be too much for us."

"You mean we need more people working on it?"

Daniel shrugged. "Maybe."

"What do you mean by 'maybe?'" she asked. "It would go faster with more engineers."

"I'm not so sure about that," Daniel replied. "What if we can't figure it out? What if we aren't capable of producing the things in those drawings?"

Sylvia stared back at him, expressionless.

"Consider the beacon," Daniel argued. "We can't even identify the material of which it's made, much less reproduce the probe itself. We can hardly even reach the ocean depths where it disappeared into the seabed. And we have nothing that can broadcast electromagnetic waves at the intensity it did. The closest thing we have is a nuclear explosion – and that only lasts for an instant."

Sylvia nodded. "And the gravitational waves."

"Yes," Daniel said. "We can barely detect them, much less produce them. It's far beyond our technology."

He took a sip of tea and set his cup on the sill. He spotted on his desk a printout of the original three images Jacob had decoded. One showed the diagram of the square decoder device.

"And then there's this," he said as he picked up the paper and pointed to the diagram. "We have no idea how it functions," he explained as he put it down again.

"But we got it to work."

"I think we were lucky," Daniel rebutted. "Jacob, whose profession is to reverse engineer the most advanced technological devices, has no idea how it works. Will said it might be a quantum encryption device – something beyond human capability at this point. That's speculation, but it has important implications."

"Whoever constructed it is far more advanced than we are," Sylvia said.

Daniel nodded. "But it's not just the technology," he explained. "It could be that we're incapable of understanding what they understand."

"They?"

He shook his head and sighed. "Aliens perhaps – depending on how you define them." He was embarrassed to use the word "aliens," but there were other possibilities that were even more difficult to openly consider.

"What else could they be?" Sylvia asked.

Daniel made eye contact with her and raised an eyebrow.

She shook her head.

"Why not?" he asked. "We've already seen a lot of strange things."

"But ghosts?"

"Not ghosts," he scoffed. "More like what Will has seen – the so-called wraiths in the Red Box facility where he was tortured, and the being in the probe."

"Not to mention the beings he witnessed in the graveyard," she added. "Seems like ghosts to me."

"If you define it that way, then yes, ghosts," Daniel admitted. "But it seems that there's an entire world that we cannot sense. Dimensions we cannot access. I'd prefer to call them aliens."

"But what's the purpose of these things we're supposed to construct?" Sylvia asked. "As you've said, we can't even understand the ones we've already acquired – like the decoder – much less build new ones."

"That reminds me," he said as he reached around the side of his desk and pulled out a black, hard-shelled suitcase about the size of an airplane carry-on. He set it on the desk and opened it, revealing a cylindrical metal case about eight inches in diameter and over a foot in length. It had a flat along its length so that it wouldn't roll when placed on a level surface.

He pulled the case out of its padded container, placed it on the desk, and released three clips that held the two halves of the cylinder together. He lifted the upper half of the container and it pivoted on hinges like a small suitcase, revealing its interior. A stainless steel cylinder, about six inches in diameter and 10 inches long, fit snuggly inside a form-fitted inset. He removed the object and set it upright on the desk.

Caps on each end were studded with a ring of bolts. The top flange had a small window.

"My God, that's exactly like the picture," she said and bolted out of the room.

She returned 30 seconds later and handed him a grainy copy of a photo. He recognized it as the one she'd shown him over a week ago when discussing so-called alien artifacts in South America.

"It's one of the devices stolen from Argentina after the war," she said as she stepped closer and tried to look through the window in the top of the cylinder.

"Here," Daniel said and turned on the flashlight on his mobile phone and handed it to her. "It's pitch black in there."

Sylvia looked through the window as she shone the light in at different angles. "What is it?"

"No idea. Looks like a tube with black rings and rounded end caps."

"Why is it encased in this metal canister?"

"It's a vacuum chamber," Daniel explained. "They say some parts might be sensitive to air, and the vacuum chamber protects them from oxidation."

"Where did they find it?"

"The CIA acquired this from Plum Island, off the coast of Long Island," Daniel replied. "Otherwise, we know nothing about it."

"Yet another object we can't explain," she noted.

"I'm about to hand it off to Jacob and Will," he said. "Maybe they can determine its function."

"That still tells us nothing about its origin."

"I know," Daniel said and grinned.

"What?"

"That's going to be your job."

"Oh?" Sylvia smiled. "Where do I begin?"

"Plum Island," Daniel said. "This thing was hidden in a safe located in a lab run by a well-known astrobiology professor."

"Why don't we just talk to the professor?"

He shook his head. "Only Will can talk to him now."

"He's dead?"

Daniel nodded.

"Then how did we learn it was there?" she asked, seemingly confused. "How did we get it?"

"We've infiltrated Chinese intelligence," Daniel explained. "They have an operative in place on Plum Island – the professor's former graduate student."

Sylvia was silent while she seemed to process the situation. After a few seconds, she nodded. "I'm supposed to go there?"

He smiled. "You up for an adventure?"

"I'm not an operative."

"You'll have some help."

"I suppose it's not a very dangerous operation," she said.

Daniel sensed his expression change even though he fought against it.

"What?" Sylvia asked as her eyes widened.

"We're fairly certain that the student assassinated her professor," Daniel replied.

Sylvia seemed to slouch and her face turned pale. "How?"

"Poison."

"That's just great," she said and shook her head. "What will I be looking for?"

"Papers, notebooks, computer files, other devices," Daniel replied. "Search everything."

"How do I get access?"

"That's already been worked out."

An electronic beeping sound followed by that of a closing door came from the main room. A few seconds later James Thackett stood in the doorway of Daniel's office.

"You explain it to her, Parsons?" Thackett asked.

Daniel nodded.

Thackett looked to Sylvia. "You ready to go?"

Sylvia looked to Daniel with a panicked expression, and then back to Thackett. "Now?"

"Your flight leaves at 6:00 a.m.," Thackett replied. "You won't be alone."

Thackett left.

Sylvia turned to Daniel. Her expression revealed feelings of betrayal. "You could have warned me."

"Sorry, I just found out myself," he said. "But you'll be traveling with friends."

"Who?"

"Denise and Jonathan."

He sensed her relief as she smiled and said, "I better get packing."

IT WAS LATE, and Will was exhausted, but he was always happy to see Denise. She seemed both agitated and excited.

"What's going on?" he asked as he led her to the kitchen counter and handed her a beer.

She held up her hand. "I'm leaving early in the morning."

"Where you going?"

"Plum Island."

"The research facility?" Will asked.

Denise nodded.

He'd heard of the place when he'd visited Brookhaven National Lab, on Long Island. The Plum Island facility was isolated, as well it should have been. Potentially dangerous biological research was conducted at the facility. "Why are you going there?"

"The CIA recovered a device of some sort from the place," Denise continued, "they want us to dig up more information."

"Us?"

"Jonathan and Sylvia are going as well."

His neck muscles relaxed. He knew Denise wasn't afraid of anything, and that's what worried him. It was best she didn't go alone.

"What kind of device?"

Denise shrugged. "Sylvia will fill us in on the way. They think it's related to our work here. You and Jacob are going to get a look at it tomorrow."

"How long will you be gone?"

"A few days," she said as she grasped his hand and led him to the couch in front of the window.

They sat.

"They said you and Jacob will stay here and continue working on the schematics."

Will winced as a queasiness pinched his stomach.

"What is it?" she asked.

He shook his head.

"Tell me."

He was reluctant to talk about it, but obliged. "I don't know," he said. "It seems like too much for us. Too complicated."

"I heard the CIA linguists have made progress translating the language," Denise said. "That will help, right?"

Will shook his head. "It's not the language I'm worried about."

"What, then?"

"We have no idea what these devices are supposed to do," he replied. "Even if we did, we might not be capable of constructing them."

"Are they too large?"

"No."

"Too complicated?"

"Probably, but that's not all," Will replied. "The technology itself could be beyond us. We may not even have the scientific knowledge to understand the physical principles under which they operate."

"Do we need to understand how they work in order to operate them?"

"Perhaps not," he admitted. Most people didn't understand how combustion engines worked, but they could still drive cars. "But we still probably cannot construct them."

"Why?"

"You remember how we couldn't even scratch the surface of the probe, or the White Stone?"

She nodded.

"The material is harder than diamond," he explained. "Although we should be able to determine its chemical composition, we still don't know how to make it. It might take years to figure it out. And that's just one thing. I'm sure there are countless others that we haven't yet identified." He leaned back on the couch and sighed.

She nodded and leaned back with him. She lay her head on his shoulder and said, "It doesn't matter though, does it?"

"No," he replied. "We have to keep pressing forward."

She kissed him on the cheek, and then on the lips.

He put his arm around her shoulder and pulled her closer. "What time do you leave?"

"Heading for the airport in three hours," she said. "We'll have to continue this when I get back." She kissed him loudly on the cheek and stood.

He led her to the door. "Be safe," he said.

"I'll be in good hands," she said as the door closed, leaving Will in numbing silence.

It was times like these when he thought back to his earlier life, when he could enjoy the present and have hope for the future. If only he and Denise had met under different circumstances, where they both continued to live in complete obliviousness to the rest of existence. But now he could hardly imagine living a traditional life in this world, and with the threats that existed within it.

The world was getting smaller every day, and that was just a result of human development. Within a matter of seconds, a person could communicate with any other human being on Earth and, in about a day, get to any inhabited place on the planet. A little more than a century ago, none of this was possible. No airplanes, no telephones. The world had been vast – effectively infinite – to those who'd lived at that time.

It made Will think again about the drawings, and the possible disparity in knowledge. Humans had gone from being surface dwellers to space travelers in about 100 years. In the last 50 years, we'd made enormous advances in medicine, electronics, communications, computers, transportation, and in general scientific knowledge. It was difficult to imagine where we'd be in another 100 years. Maybe we'd solve all of our biological problems – disease, aging and the like. We might also make enormous advances in space travel, artificial intelligence, and energy. What about 200 years from now? A thousand years? Ten thousand years? It was difficult to fathom that alien technology could be a hundred thousand or a million years ahead of ours.

He yawned and rubbed the back of his neck. His head ached thinking about the task before him. But he had to try to figure it out, even if the technology was a million years ahead of him.

It had all started with the probe. And it was always in the back of his mind that he had been the one who had triggered it.

DENISE FINISHED her granola bar as the ferry approached the Plum Island dock. The salty wind was cool and made her hair course and flat, and the smell of brine filled her sinuses. She squinted into the morning sun as she followed Sylvia and Jonathan to the ramp.

Devising a plan to get into the facility hadn't been difficult, but they had to be careful not to raise the suspicions of the Chinese mole, Jennifer Chung. And they assumed there were others.

She, Sylvia, and Jonathan were posing as experts sent by the Center for Disease Control to inspect the labs of scientists who had funding from the Department of Defense or NASA. This covered only two researchers at the Plum Island facility, one being Jennifer Chung's advisor, the late Professor Stanley Miller. Professor Miller's research had been funded by NASA for nearly three decades up to his untimely death.

A tall, thin man in his early sixties met them as they came ashore. Wisps of his white hair floated in the wind and his lips were red and cracked. He wore a white lab coat with a plastic badge that read: Dr.

Carl Beck, Sr. Safety Officer. His wire-rimmed glasses were fogged with the humidity.

"I'm Dr. Beck, welcome," he said and directed them to a golf cart. "I'll get you checked in and show you to the facility."

They all put their luggage in a basket on the back of the cart. Sylvia sat in the front passenger seat, and Denise and Jonathan took the rear bench seat. Dr. Beck pointed out various buildings on their ride through the sparsely wooded roadway. Five minutes later, he parked near a green dumpster at the back of a large building.

"You'll get your badges here," Beck explained, "and then we'll get you to the labs."

An hour later, they'd dropped off their luggage at a dormitory, donned badges, and were on their way to the main research building.

As they approached Professor Miller's lab, Dr. Beck asked, "What is your objective here? What are you looking for, exactly?"

Sylvia answered, "We're here to assess the lab conditions, record the equipment and supplies inventory, and document any safety procedures that are in place."

Beck cleared his throat. "I'm sure you understand that we're concerned about having safety inspectors coming in from the outside. The general public is already frightened by this facility. There are a lot of nasty rumors."

"You can relax, Dr. Beck," Sylvia said. "When it comes to astrobiology, there's little formal protocol regarding biosafety. Most of the current safety procedures are designed to protect samples from earthly contamination – meteorites, moon rocks, space dust, et cetera. We're now in the process of developing more formal protocols regarding threats coming in from the other direction."

"You mean viruses coming in with the extraterrestrial material?" Beck asked. His expression showed both surprise and skepticism.

Sylvia nodded. "We'll eventually want to bring back materials from other planets, or deep space. So the Center for Disease Control is coordinating with NASA to prepare, and we want to carefully document what our federally funded astrobiologists and astrogeologists are currently doing. This is a good place to start."

A look of relief came to Beck's face as he stopped at a door on his right. "Let's get you started on Professor Miller's lab," he said and punched a number on a keypad next to the door. "You know he passed away not too long ago."

"We heard," Sylvia said. "Very sad."

"It's quite a mystery," Beck said. "Some say he was poisoned. You don't think it was something he had in here?"

"Doubtful," Sylvia said. "He studied mostly meteorites and moon rocks, neither of which should have been a threat."

Denise was impressed with Sylvia's calm demeanor, and fluid responses. Denise recalled when she'd had to talk her way into a few places while conducting investigations for the DNA Foundation. It could be nerve-racking.

Dr. Beck led them into the lab and turned on the lights. "All of the doors to the connected rooms are unlocked, and the equipment is all unplugged. How long do you think you'll be in here?"

"At least a day," Sylvia said. "We may split up later to get started on the other lab."

Denise knew they'd have to spend some time in the other lab to alleviate any suspicion. That lab, however, was still active, so they'd have to convincingly play their parts in the mock mission.

Dr. Beck gave Sylvia his phone number and said he'd check back at lunchtime. He left and closed the door.

"Where do we start?" Denise asked.

"The safe," Sylvia replied.

They walked into a small side room, located immediately to the right when entering the laboratory, and opened a tall cabinet. The latch was bent and the wood veneer was splintered as if it had been forced open. Inside, partially built into the wall and bolted to the floor, was a massive gray safe.

"Looks like they built the cabinet around it," Jonathan commented. "Have the combination?"

Sylvia nodded. "One of our operatives provided it," she replied. "This is where the device was stored." She punched in four numbers followed by the pound symbol on the safe's keypad. It beeped, a green light illuminated, and the door hummed and clicked. She pulled it open and they all peered inside.

It was mostly empty.

Sylvia reached in and pulled out two file folders and handed them to Denise. She then reached inside and opened the door to a small compartment on the safe's ceiling and pulled out a black gun.

"That's a Beretta Nano," Jonathan said and reached out his hand.

Sylvia handed it to him.

He pulled the magazine, slid open the chamber, and a round fell into his hand. "One in the chamber," he said. "Someone was ready for business." He placed the handgun and ammo on an upper shelf inside the cabinet.

Sylvia turned on her mobile phone flashlight and examined the inside of the safe. A few seconds later, she stood up and said, "That's it, just the files." She took one of the folders from Denise and opened it.

Denise opened the other folder and examined its contents as Jonathan watched over her shoulder.

"Looks like accounting ledgers," Denise said.

"Looks like payoffs," Jonathan corrected. "And large amounts – they total over a million dollars."

"You think this could have something to do with Professor Miller's murder?" Denise asked.

Jonathan nodded and shrugged. "Maybe."

"This one looks like passwords to something," Sylvia said and handed her file to Denise.

"Maybe passwords to encrypted files. Look here," Denise said and pointed to the column of file names next to the passwords. "These have file extensions for word processing and spreadsheet programs."

"What do these asterisks mean?" Jonathan asked, pointing to a filename with an asterisk next to it.

Denise looked at the bottom of the page where "* = Printed" was displayed in bold type. "I think it means there are hardcopies of those files," she concluded.

Denise handed the files to Sylvia who slid them into her bag.

Sylvia then returned the gun and its loose round to the hidden compartment, and closed the safe.

They exited the safe room and went into the main lab.

"There are three other side rooms," Sylvia said. "One is Professor Miller's office, and the other two are for storage – mostly samples and equipment. Denise, you start in the office and I'll check one of the other side rooms. Jonathan, you can start in the main lab with the wall-mounted cabinets."

"What am I looking for, exactly?" Jonathan asked.

Sylvia shrugged. "Written materials, strange objects, anything that seems odd."

Denise went into Professor Miller's office and closed the door. In the center of the room was a large wooden desk covered with a mess of papers. A tall, gray filing cabinet was in one corner, and a trashcan overflowing with papers stood near the door. An old computer was on a small table, against the wall behind the desk. The dingy tiled floor looked like it hadn't been cleaned in decades, and a large cobweb occupied one corner of the ceiling. It bothered her that its creator was nowhere in sight.

A large window overlooked a shabby courtyard speckled with sparse tufts of grass on packed dirt. Fallen branches from the surrounding trees were scattered about. Yellow dirt was caked on the outer sill, a buildup of years of windblown soil and rain. Discarded equipment, including an air conditioner and a vacuum cleaner that looked like it was from the 1960s, was piled next to a green dumpster on the opposite side of the yard, and the pulsing buzz of a weed trimmer came from somewhere in the concealed distance.

She turned back to the room and examined the items on the desk. She started by taking a picture with her phone's camera. There was sometimes information revealed by the final state in which something was left. On top of the pile was a receipt for a plane ticket from New York's LaGuardia Airport to Los Angeles. She wondered if the late professor had lived long enough to take that trip. It reminded her of how the old man had died, and she went to the main lab and found an unopened box of latex gloves and donned a pair. She convinced the others to do the same before returning to the office.

She filtered through the stacks of papers on the desktop. Most were scientific articles from astrogeology and astrobiology journals. Others were brochures advertising scientific instruments and supplies. There were handwritten notes that looked like lists of daily tasks, and calculations of chemical formulas and reactions. As she sorted the papers, she piled the ones she'd already examined on a wooden chair next to the desk.

She lifted a thick chemical catalog located at the far left corner of the desk revealing a file that her brain first identified as not abnormal. But that was because she'd read hundreds of files marked in a similar fashion.

On the outside of the folder was a swastika, and the German phrase for "top secret." She flinched when she flipped it open, even though she knew what she was going to see. In the header of the first page was the emblem for the Nazis' Red Falcon project. It was dated 2 December 1951.

WILL FOLLOWED Daniel and Jacob out of the elevator and into a dark corridor that smelled like musty concrete and floor wax.

Will and Jacob had been working all morning on the drawings in Will's flat until Daniel called at 10:00 a.m. and told them he had something to show them in one of the labs. Will had an idea of what it was – Denise had mentioned it the night before.

They passed a dozen doors before reaching one labeled F-19.

Will squinted in the bright fluorescent lights as they entered an expansive, immaculate lab that reminded him of a medical operation room.

Daniel led them to a lab bench on which was a cylindrical metallic object, about the size of an elongated coffee can, with flanges bolted to the ends.

"What's this?" Will asked as he peered through a small port

window on the top of the stainless steel cylinder. He partially shielded his eyes from the overhead lights so he could see inside the chamber. Suspended by brackets from the inner wall of the vessel was a ringed tube with black, rounded end caps. He stepped aside to give Jacob a look.

"One of our operatives recovered it from Plum Island," Daniel said.

"That place off of Long Island, where they study mad cow disease?" Jacob asked as he peered inside.

Daniel nodded. "They evidently do more than that."

"The vessel and viewport are standard vacuum parts," Will said. "They're an older vintage of what I used for my research when I was at the university." It seemed to him that his university career had occurred in another lifetime, but it had only been two years. "The vendor's part numbers are stamped into the edges of the flanges."

"Why does the device need a vacuum-sealed environment?" Daniel asked.

"It's probably a preservation measure," Jacob said. "Some things might be sensitive to air or water, and this keeps sensitive parts from degrading. If you put a piece of iron in there, it would never rust."

"It could also be to keep something from leaking out," Will said. "After all, this came from Plum Island."

"Any idea what it is?" Daniel asked.

Will looked to Jacob and they both shook their heads.

"No clue," Jacob said. "We'd have to take it apart and have a closer look."

"That's your field," Will said to Jacob. "You'll have to do it in a glove box purged with a dry, inert gas, like argon."

Jacob nodded. "I'm sure they have the appropriate facilities here."

"Is this why you sent the others to Plum Island?" Will asked.

Daniel nodded. "One reason. Perhaps they'll find more info on this thing. But maybe they'll find more than that. It's obvious that the scientist who possessed this device was connected to Red Wraith. He may have had more information relevant to our work."

"We have a lot of work to do on the message and technical drawings," Will said. "What's the priority?"

"I thought you could both work alone for a while," Daniel replied. "Jacob can start reverse engineering this device while you work on the technical plans. You should get together regularly to discuss what you've learned."

Will would have welcomed some mechanical hands-on work after days of staring at mechanical drawings, but he had to keep studying them. It could turn out that the device on the lab bench in front of him was not important, and time spent on it would be wasted. The drawings, on the other hand, were undoubtedly of importance considering their origin alone.

Will snapped a few pictures of the object with his phone and found his way back to his quarters. He took one of Jacob's Pepsis from the fridge, popped it open, and took a swig. He was beginning to understand Jacob's taste for the elixir.

Specks of dust floated in a beam of morning sun that glinted from the wooden table where his half of the drawings was stacked. As a child, he'd lain on the carpeted floor of his bedroom and watched bits of fuzz and dust defy gravity in the sunlight. It would put him into a daydreaming state in which his thoughts would meander into the dark crevasses of his mind. Things would emerge from the depths that could not surface while playing baseball or watching cartoons. Some thoughts would only reveal themselves when he was in such an introspective state. When he was alone.

He recalled internal dialogs he'd had during his childhood about the concepts of time – the infinite past and future – and the vast expanse of space. They'd played out over and over, continually evolving. He'd mulled over concepts that played profound roles in physics, such as the speed of light, and mixed them with philosophical thoughts. But these internal investigations, when taken to their logical ends, had always led to existential questions that he could not answer. Where did he come from? Why was he here? And where would he go? Past, present, future. None were really known. But Will now knew there were answers to those questions, which was a profound revelation on its own. He didn't have the answers, but they would come. They'd come to everyone.

He opened a pack of drawings and continued his work. After two hours of studying, he went to the refrigerator and grabbed another of Jacob's Pepsis. He popped it open and swallowed a large gulp. A surge of refreshment overcame him as the cold carbonated beverage attacked the back of his throat. He sighed and walked back to the table.

The drawings were becoming increasingly complex. The current one was for a round, domed object, the size of a large basketball arena. It was riddled with ramps, corridors, and what seemed to be electrical conduits. It looked like a building designed for humans. And there were other drawings that showed similar features.

He flipped to the next page and read: *This structure is located adjacent to the matter-antimatter concentration unit* ... and then gibberish.

It took him a few seconds to realize what had happened.

He'd been reading the alien script. And then he'd lost it, and the text returned to unreadable symbols. He stared at them and concentrated as hard as he could. Nothing.

"Damn," he said aloud.

He grinned and took a sip of soda as a surge of adrenaline coursed through his bloodstream. The language was in his mind somewhere.

It took Denise two hours to get through the stack of papers in Professor Miller's office. She managed to get a paper cut, despite the latex gloves.

Next, she moved to the desk drawers and found them locked. She scanned the desktop and other surfaces but there was no key in sight. She'd had a finicky desk in her office at the university and knew the remedy. She found a paperclip and made a few bends. She stuck the makeshift key into the lock in the top drawer, the long narrow one where pencils and paper clips are usually stored, and rattled it around.

After a few minutes of futility, she rolled the chair away from the desk and yanked the drawer with both hands. On the second try, it broke free, making the metal rods and other mechanisms inside the old desk clatter.

The top drawer was filled with a medley of paperclips, pens and pencils, and old, yellowed sticky-notes. The two side drawers now opened freely and she found a stack of notebooks in one, and densely packed file folders in the other.

She extracted one of the notebooks and examined the cover. It was labeled *Apollo 17 Sample 298,* and dated February 1st, 1973. She flipped through it and read random pages.

She learned that Professor Miller had conducted numerous experiments on a moon rock brought back from that mission including chemical and structural analysis, and tested numerous physical properties such as electrical conductivity and magnetism. The majority of the research, however, was of the biological sort, looking for proteins and other evidence of life. On the last page, dated December 4th, 1975, was a note indicating that a manuscript had been submitted to a scientific journal.

The next notebook contained Miller's notes on a similar analysis of a meteorite discovered in Siberia. This project was dated recently, just two years ago, and again ended in a publication, this time with Jennifer Chung as a co-author. Denise thought she'd like to speak with Chung, but it might blow their cover.

The most recently dated notebook described a project on space dust, and Jennifer Chung seemed to be involved more prominently. The project was unfinished.

There were over a dozen other lab books, and Denise sorted them according to date, with the most recent on the top of the stack. She went to the third one from the top and opened it. The pages were filled with sketches that resembled the device from the safe, which now resided in the Space Systems building. She paged through it quickly and found that Jennifer Chung was not involved in this research. It was curious, however, that Chung had entered the scene immediately after Professor Miller had started the project. He'd been working on it until his death.

She flipped back to the first page and read. The words written halfway down the page made her head spin.

In Miller's words: *How can we be certain that this device has not been contaminated? Although the Argentine authorities claim they never opened the original vessel that contained the object, how can anyone know whether the German sub crew hadn't opened it? (Even though the captain of the captured U-boat claimed that he'd kept it locked away in his quarters the entire time). The device changed containment vessels multiple times after being taken from the Nazis in 1945. It can only be hoped that this was done in a proper sterile environment. Another concern is the environment in which it was discovered in Antarctica.*

AFTER LUNCH, Will went to the gym for an hour, and then returned to his flat. He paged through the mechanical drawings for hours before he found it. It was a drawing of the Plum Island device. It hit him that the discovery confirmed that they were all connected: the base, the probe, the device, and the incoming radio signals.

The first of the five pages of drawings displayed the cylindrical device from four perspectives, with smaller breakout drawings showing circuit diagrams and other components in more detail. The rounded ends seemed to be electrical connections, as did the eight grooved rings. There were also some features that they hadn't noticed at first look, including a ring of tiny holes on the outer rim of each end cap. It seemed like their function was to run air or fluid through the device. They also showed that the entire inner core was composed of the same material, which seemed odd, as it would be an inefficient use of space, and made the object heavy.

His cell phone chimed with a text message from Jacob indicating that everything was ready in the lab, and that there was something that he should see.

With his phone camera, Will snapped photos of the drawings and headed for the elevator. When he arrived, Jacob had his head down and was writing in a notebook.

Jacob flinched when he noticed him, and his expression conveyed excitement and anxiety.

"What's going on?" Will asked.

Jacob nodded to a metal box about the size of a small refrigerator, with windows on all sides and flexible tubes and steel pipes attached to the top. Arm-length rubber gloves were connected to sealed ports on each side so that four people could work on the same object and not contaminate the internal environment.

"The glove box is purged with a constant flow of dry argon gas so that no humidity or ambient air can get inside," Jacob explained. "And all of the tools inside have been sterilized."

Will looked inside. The cylindrical device rested securely in a V-shaped groove cut into a Teflon slab. The object was eight or nine inches long, including the black hemispherical end caps, and about two and a half inches in diameter. The eight black grooves that encircled the body of the cylinder were equally spaced along its length.

"It's radioactive," Daniel said.

"Oh?" Will said. It was both surprising and unnerving.

"The carrying case is lined with lead, but I got negligible readings from the Geiger counter from outside the containment vessel, so I don't think anyone was exposed," Jacob explained. "However, there is some radioactivity inside the glove box now that the object has been removed from its vessel."

Will looked inside and spotted a Geiger counter. An identical one was on the bench next to the glove box.

"It's weak inside the box," Jacob continued, "and there's no measurable activity out here."

Will wondered why it was radioactive – if only slightly – but then figured it could be for any number of reasons. Even smoke detectors and emergency exit signs contained radioactive substances.

"There's something else," Jacob said. "Go to the other side and stick your hands in the gloves."

Will did as Jacob instructed.

Jacob inserted his hands on the opposite side, where Will could see him through the windows of the glove box.

Jacob picked up a red needle. "The shaft of the needle is made of aluminum – it's not magnetic," he explained as he twisted it in various directions so that Will could get a look at it. "Attached to the tip, however, is a tiny magnet. This crude tool is used to check whether things are magnetic. We use it all the time in reverse engineering."

Will nodded that he understood. If the tip were brought to the surface of a piece of iron, which is magnetic, it would be attracted to it and deflect toward it, or even stick to it. If it came close to a piece of aluminum or plastic, or any other nonmagnetic material, there'd be no deflection. Simple, but effective. "So what did you find?"

Jacob touched the tip to the silver-gray body of the device and pulled it away. "Not magnetic," he said. He repeated the process in a few other places – between the black, grooved rings. "None of the gray-colored material is magnetic."

"Are they made of metal?" Will asked.

"No, the gray parts don't conduct electricity. But this is interesting," Jacob said as he brought the magnetic tip close to one of the black, rounded caps but did not touch it.

The needle deflected away from it.

Jacob then moved the needle near one of the black rings. The needle again deflected away from it.

"Magnetic?" Will asked.

Jacob set the needle on a small shelf inside the glove box. "Check for yourself."

Will had often worked on sensitive instrumentation, but this was different. If he damaged something, it would be irreparable.

He retrieved the needle and brought it up to the device with great care. As the tip approached the black end cap, the needle was repelled and deflected away from it, making it slide slightly between his finger and thumb. He approached the cap from another direction, same effect. It had the feel of trying to force two bar magnets together when they were aligned to repel.

"You feel it?" Jacob asked.

Will nodded.

He moved the magnet near the other end cap. Same result.

He then moved the tip near one of the rings. It also deflected away – the needle was repelled.

"Now, see the blue needle on the shelf?" Jacob asked and pointed to it. It also had a tiny magnet glued to the tip. "That one has the south pole of the magnet at the tip. The red one has the north pole at the tip."

Will set down the red needle, picked up the blue one, and repeated all the checks. The gray parts were nonmagnetic, and all of the black parts repelled.

He set the needle down and pulled his hands out of the gloves. His thoughts seemed to fracture and move in many directions at once.

"Is it possible?" Jacob asked and came around to Will's side of the glove box.

Will shrugged. "We'd need more measurements."

"Can you imagine?" Jacob said, grinning.

"A room-temperature superconductor," Will said. He knew that most people had seen the demonstration of a tiny magnet levitating above a puck of material being cooled by liquid nitrogen. In that case, the superconducting puck repels the magnet from below, so that the magnet levitates above it. The phenomenon is a characteristic of superconductivity: a superconducting material repels all magnets, regardless of how they are oriented.

A room-temperature superconductor would show exactly the same behavior, but it wouldn't have to be cooled. Such a discovery would revolutionize many technologies, from energy to electronics to levitating trains.

"Is it possible?" Jacob asked again.

Will shook his head and sighed. Thousands of scientists had been working for decades to find a material that superconducted at room temperature. "It would change the world."

Jacob stared at him with a concerned expression. "What's wrong?" he asked.

Will realized he was frowning. It took him no time to understand why. If the material was in fact a superconductor, it wasn't the work of humans.

It didn't surprise him. It was a confirmation. It meant that there was something lurking in the distance, or in the dark. It meant that he was right; they couldn't build what was in the drawings, even if they translated the language. They lacked the knowledge.

Will looked to Jacob, whose expression seemed to turn toward resignation.

"We can't build any of those things, can we?" Jacob asked. His voice seemed to crack like that of a man first realizing he is old. He was referring to the drawings.

Will shook his head. "No."

IT WAS GOING on 6:00 p.m. by the time Denise finished packing up the materials.

The notebooks and files from Professor Miller's office filled three cardboard shipping boxes. She'd gone through everything, and even went to the extreme of removing drawers, picking through the garbage, lifting ceiling tiles, and looking behind the pictures on the walls for possible hidden items. She was about to place the lid on the last box when Jonathan called from the main lab.

She went out to see what was happening.

Jonathan was standing at a counter next to a fume hood at the far end of the lab.

Sylvia came out of one of the other side rooms. "What's going on?" she asked and walked over to Jonathan.

"Does this look familiar?" he asked and nodded to a molded plastic box on the counter, about the size of a small briefcase.

Inside the box was a set of six glass ampules secured in felt-lined insets.

Denise looked closer. Each was about the size of her pinky finger and melted on both ends so that they were permanently sealed. The ampules contained fine powders: four were various shades of gray, one almost black, and the last was reddish brown. Each had a sticker with a number, one through six, and a legend of contents was adhered to the inner cover of the box, which read: *1. Merkurstaub 2. Venusstaub 3. Mond der Erde 4. Marsstaub 5. Phobosstaub 6. Der Halleysche Komet.*

Denise's nerves tingled. "Yes, of course – the powders in the basement of Space Systems that were brought back from Antarctica," she said. "The professor must have been studying them. But how did he get them?"

Jonathan shrugged and closed the lid of the box. "Look at the label."

"*Die Bestätigung,*" Sylvia read aloud.

"What does it mean?" Denise asked.

"The confirmation," Sylvia replied.

Denise's mind buzzed for a second as it searched for the reference. "That term was mentioned in one of the notebooks, and I saw a file labeled the same in English. But everything is packed – it would take a while to dig it up."

Sylvia shook her head. "We'll take everything back to DC and sort it out there," she explained. "I'll notify Thackett to get a team out here by helicopter to pick it up." She pulled out her phone and went into one of the side rooms.

"Didn't I tell you when you started interning with me that you'd have an interesting time?" Jonathan teased.

Denise smiled and rolled her eyes. "I don't think you meant anything like this."

Jonathan laughed. "More exciting than DNA Foundation research?"

"A little more dangerous."

"If I recall, you had some dangerous encounters before this,"

Jonathan argued. "But the foundation research eventually brought you here."

Denise shrugged. It brought her to Will – or him to her. He was constantly in her thoughts. And now she just wanted to get back to DC to dig into Professor Miller's files, and to be with him.

Sylvia came back into the main lab. "They'll be here around noon tomorrow to pick up everything."

"Will we leave in the morning, or wait for the evening ferry?" Denise asked.

Sylvia grinned. "Neither," she said. "We'll be traveling by helicopter."

"DESPITE OUR FEELINGS OF HOPELESSNESS, we need to press forward," Will said and nodded toward the glove box. "I found the drawings for this device. They were in the third volume of my stack."

Jacob's eyes widened and his look of despair subsided. "That's incredible," he said. Then, in one breath, he ran through the same implications that Will had – everything was connected: the signals, the device, the probe, and the base.

"There are some details in the drawings we need to check out," Will said as he pulled up the images on his phone and zoomed in on the tiny holes around the perimeter of one of the end caps. "It looks like something is supposed to flow through these, gas or liquid. But look here," he said as he zoomed in on a feature near the center of the object.

"Looks like a valve of some kind," Jacob said.

Will nodded. "A one-way valve designed to let something out of the inner volume and into one of the tubes that leads outside. It would be nice to know what is coming out of the device and, more importantly, what's inside it."

"Any ideas on how to do that?" Jacob asked

"You can do a gas analysis on what's leaking out of the tube," Will suggested.

Jacob nodded. "I can set something up to collect it."

Will shook his head. "You're going to have to put the whole thing back into the vacuum vessel it came in and connect it to a sensitive gas analyzer."

"Why?"

"Because you're going to be looking for helium gas."

"How do you know that?"

"Afterwards, you can feed a thin fiber into one of the vent tubes to collect residual material near the inner valve," Will continued. "A chemical analysis will tell us what's inside the inner core."

"You know what this is," Jacob said.

Will grinned. "Maybe."

CHAPTER 12

After a day and a half on Plum Island, and a two-hour flight in a Sikorsky VH-60N helicopter, Denise was happy to be back in DC. The ride was noisy, but well worth skipping the airports and Washington traffic. She had no idea that the Space Systems building had a helipad on its roof.

Even though she enjoyed her quarters in the Space Systems building, she missed her cozy apartment in Chicago. But that wasn't home for her anymore. It seemed that home was no longer a static location. It had more to do with people. Now it was Will and Jonathan that defined home.

While at 8,000 feet above the Atlantic Ocean, approaching the East Coast, she decided she was going to tell Will how she felt about him. She'd become increasingly restless about something ever since they'd returned from Antarctica many weeks ago. It was a feeling like time was running out for her to tell him.

Now was the time, and she'd been anxious to arrange time alone with him ever since the chopper had touched the rooftop.

After unloading and sorting the cargo they brought from Plum Island, Denise went back to her flat, unpacked her suitcase, and took a shower. Now she sat with the others around the coffee table in room

713 and chatted while they waited for Will to arrive. Her stomach churned with hunger. It was going on 7:00 p.m.

"Did you see Jennifer Chung while you were there?" Thackett asked.

"Twice," Sylvia replied. "Both times she was eating with a coworker in the lab's cafeteria."

"Was the coworker this man?" Thackett asked as he pulled a photo out of a file folder and showed it to her, and then to Denise and Jonathan.

Denise recognized the Asian man in the photo: extremely thin, glasses, tall, and in his early 30s. He had a military-style haircut.

"That's him," Sylvia confirmed. "Is he significant?"

Thackett nodded. "Now that Dr. Chung has been identified, we're tracing all of her connections. This man is both her lover and her liaison with Chinese intelligence. And there are other suspicious connections on Plum Island, as well as at nearby Brookhaven National Lab on Long Island, and at some of the local universities."

"What are you going to do?" Daniel asked.

Thackett shrugged. "For now, nothing other than map the network. The FBI will be brought in when the time is right – when we know they won't disrupt other operations in progress."

The door beeped and Will entered. His eyes were puffy and his hair was as disheveled as short hair could get. He made eye contact with Denise and seemed to force a smile. He then made eye contact with Jacob who, Denise just noticed, seemed to be as stressed as Will.

Will got coffee and sat in the chair to Thackett's right. Denise was on the couch, directly across the coffee table from Will.

Thackett cleared his throat and started the meeting. "I think we should start with what Jacob has learned about the device from Plum Island, and then get an update from Will on the drawings. The new information gathered from the Plum Island visit may take some time. Jacob?"

Jacob glanced to Will, and then set his coffee mug on the table and slid to the edge of his chair. "To start, we have not identified the function of the device. However, we've concluded that we cannot replicate it – it's beyond our technology."

"How did you determine that?" Daniel asked.

"We need to do more tests," Jacob explained, "but we think there is a superconductor in this device – a room-temperature superconductor."

"What does that mean?" Thackett asked.

"We – humans – have not yet discovered a room-temperature superconductor," Jacob replied. "And scientists have been searching for them for a long time."

"It would change the world," Will added. "Just identifying that material would be the most significant scientific advance in modern times – in terms of impact on society. It would be an instant Nobel Prize."

"We conclude, therefore, that the device is not of human making," Jacob said.

"And it's doubtful that we can replicate any of the major devices in the technical drawings," Will added. "Like the Plum Island device, I think they are all of extraterrestrial design."

"Explain," Thackett said.

"I've been going over them for days, and have only scratched the surface," Will explained. "The drawings of some of the individual components look manageable – such as bolts and supports, and other nontechnical pieces. But, even for those, we can't identify the materials used to make them."

"That might be described in the text," Sylvia said.

"Which we cannot read," Daniel added.

Will went on, "Some of the drawings seem to be of large structures – one is the size of a basketball arena. Others are electronics – circuits and controls, and probably advanced computers."

"Even so, we've had two major breakthroughs," Will continued. "First, we found the diagrams for the Plum Island device in the drawings."

Everyone seemed to gasp in unison.

Will explained the implications and how they confirmed connections that were otherwise speculative. He also argued that the discovery of these drawings upgraded the mutual authenticities of the decrypted signals and the decoder device.

"Any guesses as to the function of the Plum Island device?" Daniel asked.

Will shook his head. "I don't want to speculate at this point," he said and glanced at Jacob. "First, we need to conduct a few tests."

Everyone seemed to ponder what they'd just heard when Sylvia broke the silence. "You said there were two breakthroughs. One was finding the drawings of the Plum Island device, what's the other?"

Will took a deep breath, and said, "For a split second, I was able to read the text."

There was a collective gasp from the group, except for Jacob, who looked confused.

"What do you mean?" Jacob asked.

After a couple of seconds, Will responded directly to Jacob. "I'll explain it to you later," he said. "We should move on to what was discovered on Plum Island."

LENNY CLIPPED the counterfeit badge onto his lapel as he pulled the Honda Civic up to the entrance gate of the Space Systems building.

With the help of an asset on the inside, it had taken Chinese intelligence only two days to get him access. It was clear, however, that neither Tao, nor their inside man, understood the importance of Space Systems.

When briefed by his Chinese handler, Space Systems was described to Lenny as a company subcontracted by the CIA for domestic surveillance and counterespionage. The mole, who went by "Fred," was a low-level surveillance engineer. His main duty was to configure surveillance packages for operatives who would go into the field and install them in residences and cars. It was a skill that Lenny had also acquired as a young KGB agent in Eastern Europe as a part of his professional development. He'd come a long way since then.

One of the three security guards at the gate examined his badge and scanned the chip. If they decided to take it to the next level of security, the fingerprint and iris biometric data on the chip would match his own. And if they searched the car, they'd never find the gun. It was stowed inside a special compartment mounted near the engine that looked like a fluid reservoir. The only risk was that one of the guards would recognize him. He assumed that Thackett would have thought of that and informed the guards of the operation.

The guards let him pass, and his next worry was moving around inside the building. Not only did he not know the layout, he didn't know where his security card was valid. Denied attempts to enter unauthorized access points were monitored, and would activate warnings.

Lenny parked the car in the most remote spot he could find on the second sub-level. He popped the hood, got out, and gently closed the door. The front end of the car was close to a wall, so it was easy to use his body to block the view of any cameras that might be around. He extracted the gun and put it in a special holster inside his jacket, and then lowered the hood with care and pressed it closed. He stood still for a few seconds and watched to see if anyone had seen the maneuver. The area was clear.

As he approached the elevator, his phone rang – the one for the Chinese network.

Fred had an American accent – Midwestern he figured – and explained how to operate the secure elevator. Lenny did as instructed, and the elevator took him to floor C, the third sublevel, where the door opened. A man, blond hair, six feet tall, with dark-rimmed glasses stood in front of him.

"I'm Fred," the man said. "Follow me."

He then led Lenny through a network of cubicles and into a large workroom, and then closed the door behind them.

In the center of the room was a counter-height table filled with oscilloscopes, circuit boards, and other electronics tools. On the far wall, opposite the entrance, was a workbench with partially assembled electronics gadgets that Lenny recognized as custom-built surveillance devices.

"How did I get past main security?" Lenny asked.

"It's just a matter of programming your security card with the needed settings, and updating the computer system with your status," Fred explained. "You have a duplicate of Kevin Boudreaux's badge. He's a security guard who has already gone through central security for the night – at least according to the computer."

"A security guard?" Lenny asked. "Isn't that kind of risky considering that the other security guards, like those at the gate, might know the man?" Lenny was quickly losing confidence in the operation.

"Different security sections," Fred explained. "The man you replaced is internal security, and the ones at the gate are in the perimeter security group. They don't talk much."

Lenny wasn't convinced. He looked again at the badge. "Where is Kevin Boudreaux?"

"Let's just say Kevin is no longer with the company," Fred replied.

Lenny knew what that meant, and found it to be unprofessional, and risky.

"I need to know where William Thompson is located, and how to get to him," Lenny said. Rather than take down Fred right away, he wanted to go through with the operation as far as he could in order to root out any other assets Tao might have in the facility.

Fred sat on a stool at the central table and opened a laptop. His fingers moved in a blur on the keyboard as he explained what he was doing. "Logging into central security ... searching for access ID 00190523 and ... he's currently in room 713."

"Okay, let's get going – "

"Wait," Fred interrupted. "Searching for access ID 00190622 ... and ... he's in the same place. Room 713."

"Who?"

"Jacob Hale."

Lenny's mind whirred. They were both in the same room? He

figured they were connected in some way, but he'd never imagined that they knew each other.

It was a scenario that made Lenny salivate. The rarest of opportunities.

"How are you getting this information?" Lenny asked. "I thought you dealt with external surveillance instrumentation."

"I do," Fred replied and smirked.

The man seemed proud of what he was about to say.

"I've turned one of the internal security people," Fred boasted. "She gave me access to the system and taught me how to do a few things with it. She does the more complicated things – like your access badge. And she'll be helping us tonight."

"She's our only asset in the building?"

Fred nodded. "With her, we have everything covered."

Lenny's thoughts went to the task at hand. "Who else is in 713?"

Fred typed for a few seconds. "It looks like Director Thackett is there. Also, Denise Walker, Jonathan McDougal – "

Lenny gasped and then quickly disguised it as a cough. He rubbed his aching shoulder. How nice it would be to put a bullet in the old man's brain. "Sorry," Lenny said. "Who else?"

"That's weird," Fred said as he squinted at the screen. "It says two others are there but they have dynamic ID numbers."

"What does that mean?"

"Dynamic IDs change continuously," Fred explained. "It means that security is not allowed to know their identities."

It was intriguing. "Why aren't they doing that with Thompson? You'd think they'd keep him anonymous as well."

"They did keep him anonymous," Fred said and smiled. "He has a static ID, but his name isn't connected with it."

"Then how do you know he's there?"

"My friend in security was able to identify him visually – we got a picture that we checked with Chinese intelligence – and she connected him to the ID number with face recognition software."

Lenny thought it was a testament to the damage that could be done by just one well-placed mole.

"It doesn't matter who else is there," Fred said. "In fact, the more the merrier."

"Why?"

"They'll all be dead when this is over."

"Those weren't my orders."

"They were mine," Fred said.

"I'm going to be a bit outnumbered up there," Lenny said. "I'm supposed to take out Thompson, and maybe Hale, and then get out – you're supposed to get me out of here."

"The plans have been altered slightly," Fred explained. "We're supposed to take out anyone of significance – but Thompson is first priority, then Hale, then Thackett and the rest."

"What do you mean 'we?'"

Fred opened a drawer in the worktable and extracted a handgun with a silencer attached. "I'm going to assist you, and my security contact is going to help us." He pulled out two sets of earbuds and microphones, and handed one to Lenny. "She'll guide us out when it's over, and erase all digital evidence so that I can remain in place as an asset – no access card tracing and no video will survive."

"Doesn't seem like your kind of work."

Fred's expression changed. He seemed insulted.

"I've only killed one so far," he said. "But two gives me 'double-O' status, right?"

The man was clearly mocking the profession. "Are you referring to the security guard, Kevin Boudreaux, as your first?"

Fred shrugged and grinned.

Lenny was going to enjoy putting an end to this hack. "When does it start?"

WILL REFILLED his coffee mug as Sylvia started her report. She was wringing her hands, which made his own hands become restless – a tingling that came with anxiety. They'd found something.

"Our search focused on Professor Miller's lab," she explained. "He was an astrogeologist – or astrobiologist – with a Ph. D. in geology and a master's in biology. The bulk of his research concentrated on meteorites, space dust collected by satellites, and moon and Mars rocks."

"We brought back samples from Mars?" Daniel asked.

"No," Will said. "We've never had a craft return from Mars. The Mars material must be debris that came to Earth after a large impact on the Martian surface – meteors composed of Mars material which landed on Earth."

"That's right," Denise confirmed. "I read it in one of his scientific papers."

Sylvia continued, "The rumor is that his graduate student, who is now a known Chinese spy, poisoned him with ricin."

"Nice woman," Thackett quipped. "But Jennifer Chung will remain in place for now."

"The device Jacob and Will are examining was found in the professor's safe, along with some files," Sylvia continued. "The files are not of great importance, but we discovered other information in the office in the professor's lab." Sylvia nodded to Denise.

"Professor Miller's office was a mess, but seemed to be as he'd left it," Denise explained. "There were Nazi Red Falcon files in his desk dated after the war had ended."

Daniel gasped. "The professor knew of Red Falcon?"

"It's astonishing," Jonathan added.

"As it turns out," Thackett said, "Professor Miller was on the CIA payroll – through the Red Wraith project."

"The more important point here," Denise continued, "is the content of the Red Falcon files, and the related notes in the professor's lab books."

Will suddenly felt like he could no longer remain in his seat. His neck broke out in a prickly sweat.

"The Nazis did not build the device he had in the safe – the one Jacob is studying," Denise said.

"Then how did they get it?" Daniel asked, moving to the edge of the couch.

Denise shook her head. "They discovered it."

"What?" Daniel asked. "Where?"

Denise smiled. "Antarctica."

Everyone looked up in unison at the sound of a chime coming from the direction of Thackett.

Thackett reached into his jacket pocket, pulled out a vibrating phone, and seemed to read a text message. He tapped a short response and sent it. "Excuse me, I'll be back shortly," he said and went to the door.

EVEN THOUGH LENNY thought he'd made a permanent decision regarding the path his life was to take and, more accurately, how he'd like to end it, he was at a crucial junction.

A person really couldn't know how they'd act in an extreme circumstance where a rare opportunity outweighed principle. Such a dilemma could only be tested when one was forced to face it directly.

Lenny stood next to Fred, who chattered constantly as the elevator rose from the bowels of the Space Systems building toward the seventh floor. As Fred prattled on, Lenny contemplated the situation.

Although he knew that his mind was trained to consider all options, and weigh the corresponding outcomes, he sometimes wondered how it worked. He'd concluded it was locked in a mode of logic and survival.

He could kill them all: Will Thompson, Jacob Hale, Jonathan McDougal, Denise Walker, the CIA Director, and whoever else was with them.

Although he would have liked to repay Jonathan McDougal for the damaged shoulder, he had no animosity toward William Thompson, or Jacob Hale, although punching the latter in the nose might have been satisfying. Emotion had to stay out of certain aspects of life, and that included his professional life.

Another rule he'd formulated was to not deviate from plans made of sound mind unless new information was added to the equation. He'd chosen to take a side, and end his career on good terms. He hoped that would help him to cope with his past once the distractions were removed.

The elevator door opened and the men exited and walked up to the reception desk. The young man behind the desk looked up and glanced at both of their badges.

"You aren't expected," the man said.

Fred started to reach into his jacket, but Lenny reached out his hand and stopped him.

"Please send a message to the Director and tell him that we are here," Lenny said.

The man stared at him for a second, and then looked again at their badges and sent a text.

Fred gave him a confused look and again eased his hand toward his gun.

The response came a few seconds later, and the receptionist waved them past and notified them that 713 was on the right.

They walked down the long, carpeted hall and, as they approached 713, Lenny pressed the barrel of his gun against Fred's left temple.

"What are you doing?" Fred asked, wide-eyed.

Lenny pulled Fred's gun out of his jacket and threw it on the floor behind him. He pulled the earbud and microphone off of the man's head and crushed them with his foot. "Looks like we're both moles," Lenny whispered. "Now shut up."

A half-minute later the door to room 713 opened, and Thackett stepped into the hallway and closed the door behind him. He looked at Lenny, and then to the gun and crushed communications devices on the floor behind him.

"This is your mole," Lenny said.

Thackett pulled up his phone and called security.

"There's another one – a woman in internal security," Lenny added. "I'm sure you can get it all from this guy."

Lenny pulled off his badge and handed it to Thackett.

"By the way, he also killed this guy," Lenny said, pointing to the name on the badge. "A security guard."

Thackett looked at the card, then to Lenny, and then to Fred.

Before Lenny knew what was happening, Thackett cracked Fred in the mouth with a straight right, making a hollow popping sound. Fred crumpled to the floor. Blood leaked out of the man's nose and through his fingers as he cupped his hand over his face and groaned.

At that instant, Lenny liked Thackett a little more than before.

Seconds later, four operatives sprinted down the hall, guns drawn. They seemed to assess the situation quickly and didn't view Lenny as a threat. He wasn't.

They secured Fred's hands behind his back with zip ties. One man collected the gun and pieces of broken communications equipment from the floor.

As he was being led away, Fred shouted, "They're going to get you for this!"

Lenny put his gun in his jacket as three of the four operatives dragged Fred around the corner. One man remained, seemingly awaiting orders.

"We can now play this a couple of ways," Thackett said. "We could redefine your mission, or you could escape from Space Systems right now, and inform your Chinese contacts that your plan was disrupted and the mole captured. We'll make sure to locate the woman." He turned to the remaining operative and said, "Lock the place down until we locate her, and shut down outside communications immediately." He then nodded to Lenny. "And make sure this man gets out discreetly."

Lenny figured the woman couldn't have known what had happened anyway, especially with how quickly it all went down. The question now was what he was going to do. He reasoned it out quickly.

"I'll escape and maintain my relationship with the Chinese network," Lenny said. It was the only way that he could be sure to clean up the entire spy ring and leave no loose ends. "I take it that we'll be starting the dismantling procedures soon."

Thackett nodded.

Lenny and the CIA operative headed toward the elevator.

"It's the only explanation," Will said. "The Nazis must have discovered it at the base. They could not have built it themselves."

"And neither could we, here, in the 21st century," Jacob added.

Will flinched in response to a beep from the entrance. Director Thackett returned and took his seat. "Where were we?" he asked, as he massaged his right hand with his left.

"Everything okay?" Will asked. Something had changed with Thackett. He had a sense of ease compared to when he'd left a few minutes earlier.

"All's well, now," Thackett replied. "Do the documents from the professor's office explain the function of the device?"

Denise shook her head, "No."

"How did it get into the professor's possession?" Thackett asked.

"It was first collected by the Argentine Navy," Denise replied. "It was on a German U-boat that surrendered at Mar del Plata after the war."

"U-530," Daniel blurted. "The captain was Otto Wermuth. This object was not on the list of contents taken from the vessel."

"And what about the decoder?" Jacob asked. "The Nazis couldn't have made that, either."

"We found it at the base – stored in the vault room," Daniel replied. "Whether the Nazis discovered it at the base is unknown. They could have found it somewhere else and taken it there."

"Regarding the device from Plum Island, the Red Falcon file states that the object was discovered in Antarctica," Sylvia clarified. "Not necessarily at the base."

"Although the Nazis explored the area extensively by air, they landed only a few times," Daniel explained. "And only for a short duration each time – less than an hour. I don't think they had time to discover the device elsewhere on the continent."

"It's not surprising that the objects were there," Will said. "After all, the base is in the same general area as the probe, and we're convinced that the probe is also of alien origin."

"But what about the White Stone," Sylvia added. "That was discovered far away, at Giza."

Will wondered why only the White Stone had been found outside Antarctica, and in such a globally visible place. "Perhaps the White Stone was placed there so that it would be discovered first. It led to everything else."

"Plausible," Daniel said. "But speculative."

"Speculation is all we have right now," Will retorted. Pressure built in his temples and he was on the verge of screaming in frustration. He didn't know where the agitation originated, but he had to get back to the drawings on the table in his flat. "I have to get back," Will said as he stood.

"Please, Will," Thackett said and gestured for Will to sit. "Stay a few more minutes so that we can get updates and hash out a plan."

Will sat but his skin crawled with impatience. Denise made eye contact with him and it seemed to calm him.

"We have more from Plum Island," Sylvia said as she reached into a duffle bag at her feet and pulled out a black plastic box with a handle. It was shaped like a small briefcase. She set it on the coffee table, released two latches, opened the lid, and turned it so that Will and Thackett could view its contents. "This was discovered in a cabinet in Professor Miller's lab."

It took Will a few seconds to process what he was seeing. When it finally hit him, he gasped an explicative and reached over the table to bring it closer.

"What's this?" Thackett asked with a confused expression.

"We found a set of vials in the crates brought back from the base that contained powders just like these," Denise explained. "The labels suggest that they are material samples from various celestial bodies in the solar systems – from planets and moons."

"And Haley's Comet," Will added.

Thackett seemed confused. "Is that possible?"

"For Earth's moon, yes, and possibly Mars," Will replied. "We've brought materials back from the moon, and it's possible that Mars fragments reached Earth when objects impacted its surface."

"But what about the others?" Thackett asked.

"Not possible," Will replied.

"Then what are these?" Thackett asked.

Will shrugged. "We'll have to get them tested. We do have some data on the chemical makeup of the planets, but the comparisons won't be definitive."

"What does that say on the inside of the lid?" Daniel asked as he leaned in closer.

"*Die Bestätigung*," Sylvia said. "It means, *The Confirmation*."

"What is it supposed to confirm?" Daniel asked.

"Perhaps Professor Miller was supposed to confirm that the materials were from the places indicated by the labels," Sylvia suggested. "Is that possible?"

"He might have been the best choice of experts to do it, but it was probably not possible," Will said. "At best, he might have been able to determine whether the samples were consistent with what we know about these objects."

After a few seconds of silence, Thackett said, "Let's move on with the updates." He looked to Daniel.

Daniel nodded and began. "The language experts are working on the translations," he began. "They're optimistic, but it will take time. Next, a subset of the technical drawings, selected by Will and Daniel, have been distributed amongst a small set of CIA engineers."

"Internal people?" Jacob asked. "Or subcontractors?"

"Internal," Daniel responded. "We don't need any of this getting out."

"And we know what Denise, Jonathan, and Sylvia have done on Plum Island," Thackett said, seemingly wanting to wrap things up. "Now, how are things going to continue from here?"

"Sylvia and I will study the files brought back from Plum Island," Daniel said, "and Jonathan and Denise will go through the professor's lab notebooks."

"There are over 50 of them," Denise added.

"Finally, Jacob and Will should continue with the technical plans and studying the device recovered from Plum Island," Daniel said.

The meeting adjourned, and Will headed for the exit.

As he approached the elevator Will sensed something behind him.

He spun around to face someone rushing toward him. In an uncontrollable reaction, he started to separate but stopped when his pursuer halted.

"You have to relax," Denise said. "What's wrong with you?"

It took him a few seconds to gather his thoughts and temper his state of extreme anxiety. His fingers trembled as he pressed the elevator button.

Denise stepped in as the door closed and pushed the button for her floor.

"I don't know," Will replied, although he'd felt this way on numerous occasions as of late. In each case, his mind had been grinding on a problem in the background. He'd also been on edge ever since Thackett left 713 in response to a text, and then returned a few minutes later. "I'm agitated."

"I can see that," she said. "I haven't seen you in almost two days. You got out of there so quickly, I had to run to keep – "

"It's not possible," Will blurted.

"What's not possible?"

"We can't build a single item in those drawings."

"There are going to be a lot of people working – "

"– I don't care if the entire world is working on it," Will cut her off. "It's beyond our knowledge. It might be thousands of years beyond us. And the sheer volume of it – I doubt we could build it all in a decade even if we were capable of constructing everything."

Will stopped his rant and remained silent as the elevator ascended.

"Can I come up to your place to work?" she asked as the elevator stopped at her floor. "I could use the company."

"Me too," he said. "I'm going to throw in a frozen pizza."

She stared at him for a second and then asked, "Since when do you eat frozen pizza?"

"Jacob got me hooked," he said. "See you in an hour?"

"Half-hour. I'm anxious to get going on this," she said as she got off the elevator.

The door closed and the elevator continued its ascent to his floor, where he got out and entered his flat. The oven clock read 8:38 p.m. when he turned it on to preheat. He walked over to the windows and stared out over the forest.

The tops of the spruce trees swayed in a light wind. It calmed him. The moon was bright enough for him to see a bat navigating the trees, swooping unpredictably and making slight adjustments in the breeze. It finally disappeared into the darkness below the silver-needled branches.

The event brought a wave of despair to his mind. That bat was oblivious to what was happening in the world – or *to* the world. On some level, he envied the creature. On another level, it added to the pressure: Will had started this, and he might be the only one who could affect the outcome. And even that bat – and every other living thing in the world – would suffer the consequences of his decisions.

He broke from his meditation when the oven buzzer and the doorbell sounded simultaneously, and was caught for a split second between the kitchen and the door. He went to the door, and Denise stepped in and handed him a covered bowl.

"What's this?" he asked.

"Salad," she replied. "We should eat at least one thing that's healthy. What's that sound?"

"The oven – just finished preheating," he said as he hurried around the counter and turned off the buzzer. He then led her to the table where they would work after dinner. It was stacked with a dozen thick volumes of drawings. He cleared space for her to work as she set her over-packed backpack on a chair.

"That's a lot of drawings," she commented. "How far along are you?"

"About halfway through the first one," he replied.

She raised an eyebrow. "You mean halfway through only one of those volumes?"

"I've paged ahead through some of the others, but only studied half of volume one," Will explained. "They're complicated. Jacob has a dozen others."

They went to the kitchen where Denise sat on a stool at the counter and Will operated on the other side. He put the pizza in the oven and offered Denise a soda. She chose water instead, as did he.

As the pizza baked, Denise filled him in about the trip to Plum Island. It seemed that she enjoyed working in the field, which is what she had done for Jonathan when she'd interned with him, carrying out investigations for DNA Foundation cases. It also seemed that she needed a little danger in her life to keep her interested. She was in the right place.

Eighteen minutes later, the oven timer chimed and Will pulled the pizza out of the oven and sliced it. Twenty minutes later they'd finished the whole thing along with the salad.

"I was hungrier than I thought," she said.

"I think you're going to develop a taste for frozen pizza."

She huffed and rolled her eyes.

He put on a pot of coffee and nodded toward the table in the study. "Shall we?"

"Sure," she said as she stood from the counter and hugged him. She kissed him on the cheek and looked him in the eyes. "I'm glad to be back."

The coffee maker beeped, indicating that the brew was complete, and Will pulled two mugs out of a cabinet. He filled one with coffee and handed it to her, and did the same for himself. He led the way to the table, turned on an array of inset lights directly above it, and adjusted the intensity to near the maximum.

"It's lit up like a football stadium," Denise jibed. "You need it that bright?"

"There are fine details in the drawings that are hard to see otherwise," he replied and grabbed the first tome from the top of one of the stacks.

Denise unpacked the contents of her backpack and organized them on her side of the table. They both settled into their work.

Will resumed from where he'd left off, somewhere in the middle of the first volume. The current drawing was of a circular structure about the size of a small house. It was filled with complex electronics and didn't seem to have any moving parts. There were uncountable objects within the structure that he couldn't identify. Perhaps the drawing was for a communications device.

For the next hour, he examined more than 30 pages of breakout diagrams of components within the circular object. He went to the counter and retrieved the coffee pot, refilled their cups, and returned it. He took his seat at the table and flipped to the drawing of the next device. He gasped.

"What?" Denise asked, looking at him over her glasses.

"This is the decoder device," he replied. "You know, the one we used to decipher the incoming radio signal."

His face warmed as his heart pumped harder.

Denise walked around the table and looked over his shoulder.

The square device was depicted in every detail including the strange external electrical connections that would swallow up wires, as well as intricate internal circuits. Some circuit elements were represented by small rectangles, like integrated chips in human-developed electronics, and were labeled with characters that Will knew were numbers. He flipped the page and found the circuit diagram for the first circuit element. It was complicated.

He found the electrical connections to the two "hidden" connectors on each side of the device. More interestingly, however, there seemed to be hundreds of tiny internal electrical connections leading to the other two edges – the ones that seemed slightly rougher, or textured, relative to all of the other surfaces.

"This is incredible," he said. "We now have two devices represented in the drawings – this and the Plum Island device."

"You don't think the Nazis were capable of building this, either?"

"No way – they must have found it somewhere," he replied. "The circuitry is way too complicated, and the materials are too advanced. We couldn't construct this either."

"Can't it be figured out now that we have the plans?"

Will shrugged. "Maybe years from now, if we were lucky. But I've noticed something else. The drawings get more complicated as I go along. At this point, halfway through volume one, it's clear that they are all beyond our capabilities."

Denise's eyes widened as she looked over to the stack of drawings. "There are over 10 volumes here," she said. "What do the diagrams look like at the end?"

"There are 24 volumes total," Will said, "Jacob has the other half. But I have looked forward, into the last one I have. They're incomprehensible. They get larger in scale, and refer to the earlier drawings for some of the component parts. Some are enormous – the size of sports arenas."

"What could it be – I mean, in its entirety?"

He shook his head. "We're not even sure if the whole thing is supposed to be a single object when fully assembled, or multiple separate ones."

After a few seconds of silence, he nodded toward her stack of lab notebooks and asked, "What have you learned?"

"Listen to this," she said and flipped a few pages back in the notebook she'd been reading. "This is in Professor Miller's notebook on the Plum Island device." She read verbatim:

"THE OBJECT WAS DELIVERED *in a stainless steel vacuum vessel as they were concerned that it might contain contaminants, the type for which I will be testing. It is also mildly radioactive. That it was discovered in a remote cavern and immediately vacuum sealed lends confidence that whatever biological materials that were on the object when it was placed there might be preserved, safe from heat and the elements."*

. . .

"So they knew it was discovered, not constructed," Will concluded. "But by whom, the Nazis?"

She nodded and read on:

"*Discovered near the excavation, the German team made the precautionary assumption that the device was of extraterrestrial origin. The device, along with the so-called verification materials, were to be sent to Germany in 1945, but were instead intercepted in Argentina.*"

"It says here that the device and the space-dust samples – the verification materials – were taken from the German sub, U-530, when it surrendered at Mar del Plata," Denise continued.

"How did the US get them?"

"The Argentine government didn't want to part with the objects," she explained, "but everything was stolen soon after being confiscated by the Argentinians."

"Who stole them?"

"Miller claims it was a concerted effort by MI6 and the OSS," she said. "And that the United States took possession. The devices and powder samples were handed off to NASA sometime in the 1960s, and then to Los Alamos National Lab to make a replacement part for the device."

Will's mind seemed to light up with activity as if it were falling over itself to connect pieces of a puzzle that didn't quite fit. The connection between MI6 and the OSS made him think of Horace. As a dual citizen of the US and UK, he'd been a member of both MI6 and the CIA. Since the latter was created in 1947, he must have been with the OSS at the time the devices were stolen. He'd also been in Argentina and Antarctica during that time.

"Professor Miller had the device and the powder samples," Will said. "Where is the replacement part?" He was intrigued by the possibility that someone might have been able to replicate something, and therefore might have understood the function of the device.

Denise paged forward in the notebook and turned it around to show Will. It was a black-and-white picture of three objects laid out on a table. One was the Plum Island device, still inside its protective vacuum chamber. Next was a set of large clear vials, filled with dusts of different colors.

"Looks like they split up the dust samples," Will said. "Professor Miller got some, and we have some in the basement."

The third was a cylindrical object that seemed to be a little larger than a one-gallon paint can. It looked to be made of lead and had a large eyebolt on the top so that it could be lifted by a hook or chain. It had 'NASA' spray-painted on the top and side, along with the international warning symbol for radiation. "That must be it," he said.

Denise shrugged. "Maybe."

Will took out his phone and snapped a picture of the photo in the notebook. "I have to talk to Jacob."

JACOB STOOD with a cold cola in hand and stared at the sketches in his lab book on the kitchen counter. He was making no headway.

He'd mapped all visible parts of the Plum Island device and made notes, but still had no idea of its function. The most intriguing features were the black rings and end caps that he and Will thought might be room-temperature superconductors, but they couldn't know for certain without further tests.

The device was now in the hands of a CIA scientist who specialized in residual gas analysis, and a sample of the material from inside the device, near the valve, had been given to a materials composition analyst. All he could do now was work on other things as he waited.

He took a long swig of soda and glanced at his phone on the counter next to the lab book. He wondered what Pauli was doing. It was at times like these that he missed her badly. They'd often worked together for hours without speaking a word. It was a calm in which they could both think in clarity, and yet enjoy each other's company.

A loud chiming sound broke him from his thoughts. It took him a few seconds to realize that it was the doorbell.

He walked to the door and peered through the peephole: it was Will. He let him in.

"Sorry to bother you so late," Will said.

"It's barely past eleven," Jacob replied and closed the door behind him. "I'm just getting started. What's going on?"

"When I met you at 17 Swann," Will explained, "I noticed some things on the bookshelves that weren't books. There was something that looked like a machine, and some boxes and crates."

Jacob nodded. "There's a lot of stuff there – and I never got around to exploring most of it," he said. "You think there's something important there?"

"Denise found some evidence that there is another object. It's a replacement part – probably for the Plum Island device – made by NASA and Los Alamos National Lab. Have a look at this," Will said and showed Jacob the picture on his phone.

"I see the powder samples and the Plum Island device," Jacob noted. "The third thing – the one with the radioactive warning symbol – is that the replacement part?"

"I think so," Will replied. "The powder samples and the Plum Island device were stolen from the Argentine government in a joint mission carried out by MI6 and the OSS immediately after the war. Can you think of someone who might have been involved with that?"

"My uncle," Jacob said without hesitation.

"All of these items were in NASA's possession, but then given to the CIA in the late 1970s," Will explained. "We have two of the three. Do you think the third could be at 17 Swann?"

"Possibly," Jacob replied. "I think we should check it out at soon as we get a chance."

"How about now?"

"Can we get out of here?"

Will shrugged. "Let's see," he said as he placed a call on his phone.

Jacob listened as Will explained the situation to Director Thackett.

The discussion carried on for a few minutes while Will negotiated the terms, and then ended the call and said, "We're good to go. A car will be waiting for us in the parking garage, ground level."

"I'm surprised Thackett is okay with this."

"I wouldn't say he's okay with it, exactly," Will responded. "You have the keys to 17 Swann?"

"Do we need them?" he asked.

Will seemed to get the joke. "They're for your benefit."

Jacob retrieved the keys from his backpack. Fifteen minutes later they were on the highway with Will at the wheel of a government-issued SUV.

Will pulled out his phone and called Denise. The conversation lasted less than a minute.

"Kind of left her in my flat," Will explained.

"Not happy?" Jacob imagined Pauli would not have reacted well.

"She's okay," Will said. "She'll probably still be working there when I get back. Another night owl."

While they drove, Will filled in Jacob on what he'd discovered in the drawings.

"The decoder was there?" Jacob reiterated in an excited tone.

"The internal electronics are complicated," Will said, and explained that the two rough edges of the square device – the ones without the hidden connections that swallow up wires – had hundreds of electrical connections leading to them. Like him, Jacob had no idea as to their function.

The traffic was lighter than normal and they made it to Swann Street in 25 minutes. Will parked the car on a side street and they meandered their way to the building, casually avoiding streetlights as they went along. The night air was cool but comfortable, and the leaves of the oaks rustled in the light wind, creating shimmering shadows in the moonlight.

They arrived at the stoop of 17 Swann and Jacob inserted the cylindrical key. The door swung open a few inches and he grabbed the edge with his fingertips and pulled. They entered the foyer, and the door pivoted closed behind them.

Jacob inserted the elevator key, the door opened, and they got inside.

As the elevator made its maneuvers, Jacob asked, "Any idea what this thing might be?"

Will shook his head. "We'll have to figure it out once we have it."

The elevator opened and they stepped out, triggering the automated lighting. They both stood and stared at the scene. It had been a week since Jacob had been inside.

"This place is unbelievable," Will said, as he tilted his head back and gazed at the skylights in the high ceiling. "I can see why Horace liked to work here."

"I think he might have actually lived here for periods of time," Jacob said. "I think I could live here full time – and work from home."

"Yeah, me too. It's even better than Space Systems," Will said. "Where should we start?"

"Some of the upper shelves are filled with objects and boxes," Jacob said and pointed to the second-level stacks. "There are only books on the floor level. You can take the stairs to the second level on the far side and we can work toward the center."

Jacob watched as Will walked around the table on the first floor and down the narrow rug to the opposite side, and then climbed the stairs to the second level.

"It's like a narrow scaffolding," Jacob warned as he watched. "No guardrail. Be careful."

Jacob went up the ladder on the near side and stepped onto the second-level walkway. He pulled the first box he encountered from its shelf, and placed it at his feet. It was cardboard, and weighed about 20 pounds. He knelt in front of it and removed the lid, which squeaked as he worked it off.

Inside was an object wrapped in cloth and packed in form-fitted white Styrofoam. He removed it from its packing and placed the cloth-wrapped item on the lid he'd just removed. He took care as he unwrapped, exposing a mechanism the size of a toaster and riddled with metal tubes and valves. He thought it resembled the carburetor of a car, but figured it was for something less ordinary, probably an airplane part. He packed it up, returned it to the shelf, and moved to the next thing to its right.

The next item was a large envelope, the kind used to pack large quantities of documents. It was clear from its weight that it wasn't filled with paper. He opened it and slid out six rectangular wooden boxes, each about four by eight inches, and an inch thick. He opened one, revealing a chrome-plated engraving. He tilted it in the light so that he could see its intricate features, and figured out what it was: a printing plate for currency. It looked to be in British one-pound notes, but differed from what he recalled from his trip to the UK last year with Pauli. The date on the plate was 1943.

He put it away and opened another. It was the plate for the backside of the previous note. He put it back and was about to close up the envelope when he noticed a folded piece of paper that had yellowed with age. He opened it and immediately recognized his uncle's handwriting. It read: *Acquired during Operation Rat Trap. Nazi castle on Italian border. Counterfeit operation by Nazis on the ratline after the war. See monograph titled ODESSA (1952).*

Jacob put the note back into the envelope and returned it to the shelf. His uncle had led a secret life that made his own look like a waste of time. He had the impression that every item on the shelf that wasn't a book was some kind of memento of one of Theo's adventures.

As the night progressed, Jacob found a variety of odd things, from gun parts to samples of top-secret magnetic alloys to a special nozzle for magneto-hydrodynamic submarine propulsion.

After three hours of rummaging through everything on the shelves, they hadn't found anything resembling the gray cylindrical object from the picture. They spent the next hour scouring the rest of the place, but found nothing.

They ended the search in the kitchen.

"Time to get back," Will said as he pulled two sodas from the refrigerator.

He handed one to Jacob, and they popped them open and drank.

"Amazing things here," Will said. "I found gadgets from Germany's V-2 rocket program – one was a gyroscope of some kind, for navigation. I'd like to know the story behind that one."

Jacob felt the same. He told Will about the British currency plates while they rode the elevator down.

It was a few minutes past 4:00 a.m. when they got to the SUV, and Jacob was looking forward to getting back and getting a few hours of sleep.

Searching 17 Swann had been a good idea – it had to be done. But Jacob had an empty feeling in his gut having come up with nothing. In the end, it had been a waste of time, and it seemed that every minute mattered.

Tao didn't know what to think.

Both of his assets inside the Space Systems building had been discovered and apprehended, and he'd heard nothing from them. His only source of information was Lenny, who made a terse report by email. It seemed his mole had botched the mission and Lenny had barely escaped. Tao was skeptical.

Four operatives, two teams of two, were to pick up the American and bring him to the safe house by 9:00 a.m. That gave Tao an hour to drink his tea and think about the questions he was going to ask.

If the answers weren't satisfactory, it would be time to remove Lenny from the game board.

Daniel had no idea that Will and Jacob had ventured out to 17 Swann the night before. He would have been against it, but it was Thackett's place to make such decisions. Jacob was a great asset, and it would be a huge loss if something were to happen to him. Will, however, was irreplaceable. If something happened to him, all hope would be lost. To top it off, they hadn't found what they were looking for.

By 8:00 a.m. everyone except Director Thackett was seated in their usual spots around the coffee table in room 713. It seemed that neither Will nor Jacob were in good shape for the meeting.

"How long were you guys out last night?" Sylvia asked.

"Until 5:00 a.m.," Denise answered and looked at Will.

"And you were still working when I got back," Will rebutted.

"I was worried," Denise replied. "You should've called."

"You sound like my mom," Will replied, and smiled at her.

"More like his wife," Jonathan said and laughed.

"You both need to shut up," Denise said, eliciting chuckles from everyone.

The door beeped and opened.

Thackett walked in, filled a coffee mug for himself, and took his seat. "You guys find what you were looking for?" he asked.

"Unfortunately, no," Will said and handed him a picture. "We have two of the three objects in that picture. We were searching for the third. Perhaps it's stored at another facility."

Thackett studied the picture for a few seconds and said, "I'll get someone on it."

"It looks like it's radioactive," Jacob added.

Thackett nodded. "Now, the Plum Island information," he said. "What have you found, Denise?"

"I read Professor Miller's notes on the so-called verification materials," she said.

"You mean the moon dust and the other powder samples?" Thackett asked.

Denise nodded. "He carried out all of the compositional analyses using modern techniques, and came to the conclusion that the moon dust in the vial – from Earth's moon – was authentic. He was also convinced that the Martian material was authentic, but this was based on meteorites found on Earth, and materials analysis data beamed back to Earth by various Mars landers."

"What about the others?" Daniel asked.

"For the other planets, one of the Martian moons, and Haley's Comet, all he could do was say that their compositions were consistent with what we know about them," Denise replied. "And he found no evidence of life in any of them."

"Why would the Nazis have this?" Jacob asked. "What's the significance?"

"That's what I am getting to," she replied. "The samples in Miller's lab, as well as the ones we found in the items in the crates, were siphoned off the original 'verification' set, which was discovered at the Antarctic base."

"Same ones recovered by MI6 and the OSS in 1945?" Sylvia asked.

"Seems so," Denise replied.

Will shook his head and muttered, "How can that be? That was before we even landed on the moon."

Denise continued, "They were originally discovered in sealed tubes made of quartz, and backfilled with an inert gas to preserve the contents. The original tubes were cracked open, and multiple sets of the powders were made and sent to various places. Looks like we now have two sets in our possession."

"What were the powders doing at the base – what was their purpose?" Daniel asked.

"I found something about that in one of the Red Falcon files we took from Miller's office," Sylvia replied. "The so-called 'verification' worked as follows: if we were to authenticate the origins of the materials in the tubes, it would be proof that everything else there – at the base – was of extraterrestrial origin. The materials were placed there by someone who intended to convince us of this."

The room was silent while everyone seemed to contemplate the ramifications of Sylvia's response.

"I think we were leaning that way already," Sylvia continued, breaking the silence. "Ever since the probe rose up into the sky and blasted a signal into space. And maybe even before that happened."

"The question arises as to whether there are more such objects to be found at the base," Daniel said. "Everything we have in our possession, save the White Stone, which was found at Giza, came from the base."

"We need to go to the base," Will said.

No one responded, but they all looked to Thackett, who set down his coffee mug and edged forward in his seat.

"That's in the works, as you know," Thackett responded. "In the meantime, let's carry on with the work here."

Thackett went on to explain that there had been a security breach and that everyone should take extra precautions, especially when leaving the facility. The internal problem had been solved, but those on the outside were still there. It was Chinese intelligence.

Thackett then heard the plans for going forward and adjourned the meeting, leaving Daniel and Sylvia to themselves.

"Things are happening," Daniel said, "but are we really accomplishing anything?"

"They're making progress with the text," Sylvia replied.

Daniel nodded. "And we now have over 100 engineers cleared and working on the drawings," he said. "I get daily reports from the group leaders. They're making almost no progress."

"They're not learning anything?" Sylvia asked. Her expression was a conflation of surprise and worry.

"Small things," Daniel said. "Nothing in electronics or materials. And, most importantly, they can only speculate as to the functions of a few of the devices. In the end, we don't know how to build any of it, and we don't know what any of it is supposed to do."

"Perhaps now that we have a few of the actual pieces, along with their corresponding drawings, we can make some advances."

Daniel shrugged. "Maybe. But I've been told that it would take 20 years to build everything even if we knew exactly what it all was."

"Will said something along those same lines," Sylvia said.

"As did Jacob," Daniel added.

"It seems like an insurmountable task."

"And it might be," Daniel said. "It leads me to question whether we're going in the right direction."

"I don't understand."

"Are we being directed to recreate everything in those plans?" he asked. "Was that the intention?"

"Why else would they have been sent to us?"

Daniel shook his head. He didn't know the answer to that question, but his brain was grinding away at something he couldn't yet identify.

There was something big that they were missing.

LENNY CRAVED A CIGARETTE. He was nervous, and the smoke residue in the car amplified the urge.

They'd assigned extra operatives to bring him in this time. The second team of two was a few cars behind the SUV in which Lenny was currently riding.

They pulled directly into the warehouse, and the garage door rolled down behind them. The operatives patted him down – even though they'd already taken his weapon – and then led him into the break room where Tao was waiting.

"Please take a seat, Mr. Butrolsky," Tao said. "Tea?"

Lenny turned down the offer and sat in the plastic chair.

"We lost two assets yesterday," Tao said as he poured water from a dented aluminum teapot into a mug that was intended for coffee. "The operation was a complete loss. Please explain what happened at the Space Systems building."

"Your inside man screwed up," Lenny started. "I was not informed that I was to have a partner in this operation. He was not a professional."

"Details," Tao ordered.

"We took an elevator to the floor where Thompson and Hale were supposed to be attending a meeting," Lenny explained. "It opened to a front desk that was manned by a security guard. Your asset, Fred, panicked and pulled his gun. The guard pressed an emergency alarm button and scrambled. The operation was over at that point and I managed to get back to the parking garage. I got out before the place was shut down."

Tao seemed to mull over what Lenny had told him.

"And how did the second asset get caught?" Tao asked.

Lenny shrugged. "I never saw the second person," he explained. "Fred was communicating with someone the whole time – he was wearing earbuds and a microphone."

"Did you see him get captured?"

"No," Lenny lied. It made him wonder where Fred and his cohort were now. Probably in the basement, he figured, behind a door labeled "Occupied." "If I'm not informed of the entire plan for an operation, I do not want to be a part of it. This man was a hack with a James Bond complex."

"He did not follow instructions!" Tao yelled and swiped his cup off the table. It collided with the bottom of the refrigerator and shattered, causing tea and ceramic shards to scatter everywhere. Tao breathed heavily for a few seconds and then seemed to calm down. "We know nothing about that facility," he said. "Our people were highly compartmentalized and isolated. What was your assessment of the place?"

Lenny had to come up with something quickly, and Jacob Hale's former employer came to his mind. "It reminded me of a classified military engineering subcontractor. I've been in a few of those places."

Tao stared at him for a few seconds and then nodded slowly.

Lenny thought Tao was trying to convince himself of what Lenny had told him. The story was plausible. All of those places looked alike, and he was sure that few people had knowledge of the deep innards of Space Systems – like the holding cells in the sublevels. Although he was sure Fred was learning about them now.

"You have put me in a difficult situation," Tao said. "You have failed me three out of four times."

Lenny stared back at him. "New York worked out well," he finally responded, although it was far from luck.

"Were there any other successes?" Tao asked.

Lenny would have loved to have broken it to him that he was

successfully carrying out a mission as they spoke, but only smiled to himself in his mind. The question was how much was Tao worth to him? What did Chinese intelligence have that the CIA needed?

What Tao didn't know was that he was at the end of his rope. If he didn't have another mission for Lenny, the CIA was prepared to simultaneously move in on multiple Chinese safe houses – places traced through Lenny's work – and would round up more than a hundred people. It would be a move so devastating that it could cause a war. And, in light of current events in Antarctica, war was not a big leap.

"I think you need to get out of the DC area for a while," Tao said, finally. "Maybe one final task for you before we authorize your retirement."

Lenny's heart sank. He was literally minutes from getting to the final stage – terminating the Chinese network and fulfilling his obligation to the CIA. Now he would have to follow up on a new lead – an assignment that would probably not reveal anything new. And this new mission would only be his last if Tao had him terminated. The Chinese let no one retire.

"What do you have in mind?" Lenny asked.

"Something more suitable to your skills," Tao replied. "A recovery mission."

Tao's words grated on Lenny's nerves. The condescending little bastard would eventually witness his most developed skills firsthand.

"You'll get instructions in the next 24 hours," Tao said and then spoke to his men standing at the door. "Take him back."

The men led Lenny back to the car. He didn't understand how there could be any other information, devices, or equipment that could change anything at this point. It seemed to him that everything related to Red Wraith was either already collected, or not worth collecting.

He'd await his new instructions and then inform Thackett of the plans.

Will got a call from Jacob in the late afternoon, and then met him in the lab.

"You were right about the helium," Jacob said. "From radioactive decay processes, right?"

Will nodded. Over long periods of time, radioactive substances produce helium gas as a byproduct of radioactive decay. It comes from a type of radioactive process called alpha decay. "What did you get from the chemical analysis of the internal materials?"

"I had to get some help with that," Jacob explained. "At first we tried to use an optical fiber to scrape material from the inside of the device to get a sample. That didn't work, so we used a thin tungsten wire instead."

Will nodded. Tungsten metal was extremely hard. "The fiber might have been too soft to scrape away any material."

"There were heavy elements inside the device, and the analysis required special methods," Jacob explained. "Also, the sample size was very small."

"What did you do?"

"The CIA has everything," Jacob said, grinning. "Of course, radioisotope analysis is important for national security. Their experts got a clean analysis."

"What did they find?"

Jacob led him to a table with an open laptop. He opened the image of a graph that had multiple sharp peaks, and a table identifying the radioactive isotopes.

The one on the list that caught Will's attention was Am-241, along with U-233 and Th-229. He knew the first one was a radioactive isotope called americium, and the others were uranium and thorium, which were products in the decay chain of americium. His conjecture had been correct.

"Interesting," Will said as his heart picked up pace.

"You know what this is?"

Will nodded. "It's a radioisotope thermoelectric generator."

"Of course," Jacob said. "Like those used in the voyager spacecraft."

Will nodded. "Those devices have been producing power for over 40 years. They're ideal for long-term power, although they carry some risk."

"Yeah, radioactivity," Jacob said.

"We'll need a little help," Will said, "but we can use this to get some important information."

"Like what?"

"Like how old this thing is," Will replied.

CHAPTER 13

Lenny's new assignment was taking him back to the scene of a crime – one of his own.

In less than a half hour after the meeting with Tao, he got instructions from the Chinese network for the next mission. He barely had time to get to the airport.

The trip from Reagan International to Baton Rouge had a four-hour layover in Atlanta, where he met a CIA operative. Lenny was impressed with how quickly the CIA reacted to set up the contact and devise an alternate plan.

The Chinese had ordered him to burn a former Syncorp storage facility to the ground, whereas the CIA wanted him to preserve its contents – computers, digital storage devices, and crates that contained a range of things, from paper files to exoskeleton parts. But it wasn't about the things they knew were there. It was about the unexpected.

In addition to his CIA orders to collect the materials *en masse*, he was to search for a specific object. The picture given to him by his CIA contact in Atlanta was a photo of a photo, the original in black-and-white. Most of the image was blacked out – clearly there were other items in the image that were classified – leaving just one object visible.

He was told it was about the size of a one-gallon paint can, probably made of lead, and had a large threaded hole in the top, which may or may not have a heavy-duty eyebolt screwed into it. The eyebolt was present in the photo. The top and main body had NASA painted on them, as well as the universal radiation warning symbol. The latter made him twitch.

As he sat in the terminal waiting to board the flight to Baton Rouge, he tried to discern details in the poor-quality picture. The more he studied it, the more familiar it looked to him. After a few minutes, he was convinced that he'd seen it before, but couldn't place it.

That the Chinese network had assigned him to carry out a scorched-earth mission worried him. When an intelligence network started torching things they'd collected, or destroying things that had value to the enemy, it usually meant one of two things. One was that they were about to disband and disappear. If that happened before the CIA made a move to collect them, all of the work that had been done to identify and track the foreign network would be lost. The second possibility was that Chinese intelligence had a major final mission planned: they'd strike once more before they'd dissolve. Their next step would be to clean up any loose ends, and Lenny was one of them. In either case, the CIA would have to move quickly. As the operative in Atlanta had conveyed to him, they were aware of the situation, and were on edge but on the ready.

Lenny knew this was his final mission for Tao – or him posing as Tao's asset. Even if he followed through with the plans, and the contents of the warehouse were destroyed, Lenny was at the end of his rope. Tao was going to retire him.

The CIA version of his mission – the one he was actually going to carry out – was to determine if there was anything of value in the warehouse. He couldn't imagine that the Chinese had left anything important unguarded, but things had changed after Tao's predecessor had died.

It reminded him of the great lengths to which the US government had gone to develop the Red Wraith technology through Syncorp, and to preserve it and keep it secret. He thought his late boss, Heinrich Bergman, would be rolling in his grave at the half-century of research lost – given away, or destroyed.

He wondered what had really been happening in the Red Box, and why it was worth the colossal effort and money. He'd known about the torture – that was no secret – and that it was supposed to induce some kind of psychological or physiological transformation in the subjects. But he'd always been confused about the details. Did it give someone the ability to burn people? Images of the charred bodies on the Chinese carrier came to mind. Seemed like a lot of money, time, and risk to produce another physical weapon that could otherwise be carried out by a conventional flamethrower, or a laser.

But Lenny knew it was deeper than that. It was somehow related to the object he'd acquired from Plum Island, and to other such things that everyone seemed to want from the former Red Wraith sites, of which there were dozens.

A thought materialized from Lenny's subconscious that caused him to jerk his leg and nearly tip over his carry-on bag. As the head of security for the Red Wraith project, he'd been to all of the Red Wraith facilities. He wondered, *had anyone remembered the missile silo?* He didn't know why that came to mind, but his memories usually surfaced for a reason.

TAO SWIRLED a single ice cube in a tumbler of 10-year scotch as he looked down at the night traffic. It had rained, but people were still milling about at the midnight hour. It was a Wednesday, and he was still baffled by how so many people were out late during the workweek.

But he had more important things to think about.

Tao had decided during their last encounter that Lenny would embark on his final mission, and that his retirement was going to be of the sort from which one does not return.

The deserted Baton Rouge facility – the former Syncorp headquarters – was still being surveilled by Chinese intelligence, but was not active. It was used only as a storage facility until the time was right to collect what was useful to send to China, and then destroy what wasn't.

Once the Baton Rouge facility was cleaned up, he'd organize a final operation to infiltrate the Space Systems building and eliminate William Thompson once and for all. Those were his orders. He'd then follow the proverbial ratline back to China, as would more than a hundred of his operatives. Whoever was left would relocate to other sub-networks in the United States.

But Tao knew that such a mass exodus wouldn't be possible. The magnitude of what was being planned, if it didn't cause an all-out war with the United States, would at least lead to an underground war against all of the Chinese networks, including those in other countries. But he knew that, whatever this fight was really about, it was worth it.

DANIEL WAS in a comfortable morning trance as he gazed out the window and steeped his tea. He was alone in 713. Sylvia would be there in ten minutes, as would everyone else, for the meeting Will and Jacob had requested late the previous night. They'd found something.

The tea was just a warm-up for the strong coffee that would follow. He'd had a terrible night's sleep. His mind had been grinding away at something, but the thought wouldn't crystalize. The feedback he'd been getting from the engineers was uniformly disheartening, but that, too, was revealing something. He just didn't know what it was.

At five minutes to eight Sylvia arrived and went directly to her office. Thirty seconds later she appeared at Daniel's door with a notebook in one hand and an empty cup in the other.

"You're looking for tea," Daniel said and nodded to the metal canister on the cluttered shelf near the door.

"Thanks," she said as she prepared her English Breakfast tea. "I woke up about six times last night. I'm exhausted."

"Stuck on something?" he asked. It was a stupid question. They were stuck on something their entire careers. But she knew what he meant: *stuck on something that is bothering you?*

She shrugged. "Not more than usual," she said. "But it's bothering me that everyone else seems to be stuck as well. Usually some of us are at least making incremental advances."

"I couldn't sleep either," he admitted. "And for the same reason. Although it was worse because of the impromptu meeting."

"Same here," she said. "It creates an element of hopeful anticipation."

Daniel thought it was a good phrase. How many times in his life had he felt "hopeful anticipation?" Many. And how many times had the result lived up to the hope? He'd say never, but that wasn't completely true. Things sometimes came close to matching expectations. And, occasionally, there were times when things worked out unexpectedly well. But he'd learned that it was never good to get up hopes.

By eight sharp everyone had arrived. Will and Jacob looked like they'd had nights as bad as his. Denise's hair was wet, and she looked like she'd been to the gym. Jonathan looked well rested, as if he'd already been up for hours.

Director Thackett was in a suit, as usual. He poured coffee as he started the meeting. "Will and Jacob, you asked for this meeting, so why don't you start?"

Will nodded to Jacob.

Jacob cleared his throat and began. "We think we may have determined the function of the Plum Island device," he explained.

Will pulled out some stapled packets of papers and passed them around.

Daniel paged through his copy. The first page was a color photo of the cylindrical object collected from Plum Island by the CIA operative. The second was an intricate technical drawing of the device that was riddled with foreign script. The last page had two graphs with some curves and peaks, along with some calculations.

"The first page," Jacob began, "is a pic of the Plum Island device. The second is a technical drawing we got from the decoded signal."

"The drawing clearly matches the object," Jonathan commented. "That's incredible."

It was a positive development, Daniel thought, but there were thousands of other drawings for which there were no existing devices.

"What's on the last page?" Sylvia asked.

"Some of the materials inside the object are radioactive," Jacob replied, "and this is the analysis identifying those materials."

"So what does it do?" Daniel asked.

Jacob nodded to Will to answer.

"It's a radioisotope thermoelectric generator," Will said. "Or, for short, an RTG."

Daniel roughly understood the function of RTGs from one of his past projects. However, the others remained silent with wide eyes, seemingly awaiting further explanation.

"It's a power source," Will said. "It's like a battery. Only this battery can last a very long time. Centuries, in principle."

"How does it work?" Jonathan asked.

"The short version is that the radioactive material heats up as it undergoes its radioactive decay process," Will explained. "Another part of the device – a thermoelectric component – can produce electricity if one side is warm and the other side is cold. The radioactive material provides the warm side, and the environment provides the cold side. In a spacecraft, the cold side can be provided by deep space."

"Deep space is cold?" Sylvia asked.

"Yes," Will replied. "And so is Antarctica, which is where this was supposedly found."

"So we've already built these devices?" Sylvia asked.

Will nodded. "A long time ago. Voyager I and II used them," he explained. "They were launched in 1977 and their thermoelectric devices are still working."

"So this isn't beyond our technology," Sylvia said.

Daniel thought he saw a spark of hope in her eyes.

"Yes and no," Jacob replied. "We cannot replicate this device."

"Why not?" Sylvia asked, the hope draining away from her face.

"You see those black rings and end caps in the photo?" Jacob asked.

Pages rustled as everyone flipped back to the image.

"As we reported a few days ago, we think those are composed of superconducting materials," Jacob said. "And we have not yet discovered a room-temperature superconductor."

"So what have we learned from this?" Daniel asked. "That the device matches one of the technical drawings, and that we cannot replicate it since the materials are too advanced?"

"And that it's a power source – it functions as an RTG," Sylvia added.

Will shook his head, sat forward, and said, "We haven't told you the most important part."

"There's more?" Daniel asked. The tips of his fingers tingled with anticipation.

"Flip to the second graph on the last page," Will instructed.

Pages rustled once again as everyone flipped pages.

"This is a graph of data taken with a sophisticated radioisotope detector that tells us what kinds of radioactive materials are inside the device," Will explained.

"What are the peaks?" Daniel asked.

"They correspond to the various isotopes in the sample," Will continued. "There are peaks that correspond to uranium-233, thorium-229, bismuth-209, and trace amounts of americium-241. The two most common isotopes used in human-made generator devices are americium-241 and plutonium-238."

"So this device uses americium-241," Daniel concluded aloud.

"Correct," Will replied. "But knowing this information allowed us to figure out something else that may shed an entirely new light on our situation."

"What is it?" Daniel blurted, hearing the tone of desperation in his own voice. He'd been awaiting new information for weeks.

"I assume you are all familiar with the idea of carbon dating," Will said.

"You mean like they do with ancient artifacts to determine how old they are?" Thackett asked.

"Yes," Will replied. "When something dies, it starts with known amounts of the radioactive isotope carbon-14, and its non-radioactive isotope carbon-12. As time goes on, the carbon-14 decays into carbon-12, and the ratio of the amounts of the two isotopes changes. Since we know the rate at which carbon-14 decays into carbon-12, we can determine how long it has been since it died. You just measure the ratio of the amounts of the two carbon isotopes."

"So you carbon-dated the device?" Sylvia asked.

"Same procedure," Jacob said, "But different elements."

"You see, carbon-14 has a half-life of 5,730 years," Will explained. "A half-life is the time it takes half of a given amount of the substance to decay."

"Carbon dating is accurate for aging things on the order of 50 thousand years, or about 10 of its half-lives," Jacob added.

"The half-life of americium-241 is 432 years," Will said.

"So it's accurate to about 4,000 years?" Sylvia asked.

"That's right. But carbon dating is also somewhat different, perhaps less accurate in many instances, because the starting amount of carbon-14 is so little to start with," Will explained. "Our case is a little different. We're assuming that the material inside the RTG was near 100% americium-241 when it was inserted. And, even though americium has a half-life of 432 years, its decay products have longer half-lives. For instance, uranium-233 has a half-life of almost 160,000 years. Looking at the relative ratios of the americium, and the decay products, we got an estimate of its age."

"How old is it?" Daniel asked, barely able to maintain his composure.

"Remember," Will said, "we assumed it started at 100 percent americium –"

"—please," Daniel interrupted.

Will took a deep breath before he spoke. "It's just over 40 thousand years old. Give or take a few thousand."

Daniel just stared back at him in silence, despite the gasps of the others.

"How can that be?" Jonathan asked with an expression of disbelief.

"I think we all know how that can be," Will replied.

"That's around the end of the Stone Age," Sylvia said. "Roughly the time the Neanderthals disappeared."

"Are you sure you haven't made a mistake?" Daniel asked. His voice was so quiet he wasn't sure whether Will had heard him over the chattering of the others.

Will shrugged. "Of course we could have made a mistake," he replied. "We made assumptions. However, there are checks that are used to verify the results. Namely, the specific ratio of the decay products matches the decay chain of americium-241. The main decay product of americium-241 is uranium-233, which has a half-life of 159,200 years."

"Which means there won't be much error in this estimate," Jacob added. "Besides, we got an expert from Michigan State University to recalculate the results. It's her numbers that we reported since her method was more refined. Ours and hers agree to within 300 years."

"Besides, what if we'd found that it was only 100 years old?" Will argued. "It would still be a shocking result. Americium wasn't discovered until 1944."

"So this thing was here before we even knew americium existed," Daniel said.

Will shrugged. "Is that so surprising?" he asked. "The probe was first discovered by Captain Cook. So it was here in the 1700s. It was beyond our technology then, as it is now. Our newest discovery just confirms that none of these devices were created by us. We already knew that – for God's sake, these devices might contain room temperature superconductors."

"So it's confirmed," Daniel said. "We cannot reproduce anything in the drawings."

"I've come to the conclusion that it doesn't even matter," Will said.

"What do you mean?" Daniel asked.

Will stared forward with blank eyes, seeming not to look at anyone or anything for a length of time that soon became awkward.

"What do you mean, Will?" Denise asked, repeating Daniel's question.

"We're not capable of building anything shown in those drawings," Will said. "And based on that fact, and on our discoveries of some of the devices depicted in those drawings, I draw two possible conclusions."

"And those are?" Daniel asked.

"First, the knowledge conveyed in the incoming message was intended for a much more advanced civilization," Will explained. "The outgoing signal from the probe alerted someone outside of Earth that it had been entered and activated. That meant that someone – in this case, me – had the ability to separate. We were supposed to be technologically advanced enough to build these things by the time we achieved the ability to separate. And we're not."

"We cheated the test," Daniel said, "and now we're not prepared for what comes next."

Will nodded. "Yes, we cheated. "

"What's your second conclusion?" Denise asked.

"Well," Will said and took a deep breath. "I don't think we'll have to build any of the things depicted in the drawings."

"Why – what do you mean?" Daniel asked.

Will set his packet of papers on the coffee table and took a quick glance at everyone before he said, "I think everything has already been constructed."

LENNY DROVE around all five levels of Syncorp's parking garage to check for anything suspicious. The facility was mostly empty except for a few utility vehicles that belonged to Syncorp. He parked his rental car on the second level of the parking garage so that it couldn't be seen from the ground-level entrance, got out, and made his way down the ramp to the ground level.

He took in a pollen-infused breath of hot air as a bead of sweat tumbled down the side of his face. He wiped it off with his sleeve. It was 9:00 a.m., but already 83 degrees in Baton Rouge. The high for the day was going to be 96 with 90 percent humidity. He hoped the buildings still had power, and the air conditioning was on.

He walked past a small moving truck that he recognized. A nearby drain in the floor marked the location of a too-recent hit. One of his own. Something came over him as he walked by the scene. It started with guilt and shame, and transformed into fear. The man he'd shot and dismembered in that very spot had been an unwitting participant in a deadly game – one with rules he didn't know. He was an idiot but probably hadn't deserved to die.

The last image Lenny had in his mind as he walked away was that of the man's head dissolving in a barrel of acid, his lifeless eyes melting away to some other world. He was sure it was a memory that would resurface for the rest of his life, along with countless others just as ghastly.

He made his way down to the ground level, stood in the shade at the garage entrance, and surveyed the scene. The lawn had recently been cut, so he should still expect people to show up unannounced – but not the lawn service. A private security company patrolled the campus of six buildings in the evenings. Therefore, the daylight hours were safe, but he had an ID card in case he crossed paths with anyone.

Directly opposite the garage entrance, fifty yards away, was the Syncorp headquarters building. It was twenty stories tall, all glass, and only the emergency lighting was on.

He took a few steps out of the garage, but remained in the shade. Fifty yards to his left was the front of a recently built storage building.

To the right was a shipping building with a loading dock. He knew there was another warehouse near the back of the campus which was for incoming shipments – mostly supplies for the things they were building in the colossal underground lab complex.

Lenny walked out of the shade and into the morning sun. It was like a blast from a heat lamp that directed the rest of his senses to convey immediate discomfort. The smell of the freshly mowed grass filled his sinuses, and the buzz of cicadas and the groan of a distant lawnmower threw him momentarily into a scene of a domestic life. A part of him longed for an existence where mowing the lawn in the sweltering heat was the worst thing you had to do that day. Lenny recalled mowing a lawn only once in his life. But that had only been a part of his cover as a maintenance man. He'd killed a woman that afternoon and thrown her body into a dumpster.

He turned left and made his way to the storage facility.

The white, two-story building had a footprint of 60 by 100 feet. He reached into his pocket and extracted a white proximity card given to him by one of Tao's men. He flashed it near a pad next to the door, a small green light illuminated, and a beep and a click indicated that the door had unlocked. He took a deep breath and blew it out hard. That he wasn't going to have to break in and defeat the security system was going to save him some sweaty work.

As he opened the door, a cool current of air blew over his arms. The air conditioning was functioning.

He pulled out his gun and a flashlight, stepped inside, and closed the door. He was well aware of the possibility that some of Tao's goons might be planning to take him out, but he estimated that to be unlikely. They were well equipped at their DC safe house to make him dissolve from existence. But he still had to be alert.

He scanned the flashlight around until he found a circuit-breaker box next to the stairway to the second floor. He put his gun back in his jacket pocket, opened the metal box, and energized the circuits for the interior lights. The entire space lit up like a football stadium.

He was astonished.

The entire first floor was completely empty except for a few wooden crates that were damaged beyond use. What was going on?

He took a few steps up the metal staircase and looked up to the second floor. The lights were on. His senses heightened when he noticed the second breaker box on the wall at the top of the stairs. Someone else had turned on those lights.

It seemed that his hand was reaching for his gun before his brain processed the sound that hit his ears: something was making noise upstairs. A shuffling. Then nothing.

As he proceeded upward in sloth-like movements, the air temperature rose. He approached the top and ducked his head under a railing to get a peek at the second level.

Two men were standing over a body, but looking directly at him. Their guns were drawn.

"Of course!" Daniel blurted.

Will stared back at blank faces. Only Daniel seemed to understand what he'd just said.

"What do you mean, 'of course?'" Sylvia asked with a tone of irritation.

"All of the objects we have in hand were discovered by the Nazis," Daniel explained. "They didn't build any of them, they found them."

"And they found them in Antarctica," Will added. "Most likely at the base."

"I'm still not following," Thackett said. "We've already settled on that, haven't we?"

"I think Will is implying something a little deeper," Denise said, and looked at Will with wide eyes.

"I think everything depicted in the drawings has already been constructed," Will explained. "And it's all at the base."

"Some of the objects are as big as buildings," Daniel argued. "Wouldn't we have seen them?"

"What's on the other side of the mountain?" Will asked. "The one directly above the base, next to the lake."

"A valley and more mountains," Daniel said.

"And a lot of ice," Thackett added. "Horrible landscape. It's why the Chinese and Russians couldn't explore the area on foot."

"How thick is the ice?" Will asked.

"As you go inland, it gets progressively thicker," Daniel said. "Up to two kilometers in places."

"Enough to conceal objects the size of buildings?" Will asked.

"What are you suggesting?" Thackett asked. "That all of this stuff is buried in the ice somewhere?"

"I hope it is," Will said. "Because we're incapable of constructing any of it."

Thackett looked to Daniel, seemingly prodding him to comment.

Daniel shook his head and shrugged. "No luck from the engineers," he explained. "Over a hundred of them have been working on the drawings for many days. Can't do much more than identify nuts and bolts."

"The linguists have made headway converting to English words," Sylvia added, "but syntax and sentence structure is going more slowly."

"What about you, Will?" Denise asked.

Will knew she was referring to his potential to read the language directly. He shook his head. "I thought I was getting something for a while. But no, I can't read it. Not yet."

"Why should he be able to read it?" Jacob asked, apparently confused.

Will was supposed to have explained it to him, but he'd never gotten around to it. He was just about to fill him in when Sylvia broke in.

"His mind was implanted with information, including the ability to read various languages, when his soul possessed a body that had previously been occupied by a being that had possessed that knowledge," Sylvia said.

Jacob just stared back at her.

"I'll give you more details later," Will said.

"There's still a lot to explore at the base," Daniel said. "We weren't there long enough to do a thorough search."

"It's enormous," Sylvia said. "It would take weeks."

"Or years," Thackett added, "especially if the search led you to the outside."

"Maybe we should get satellite images of the area and study them before making any decisions," Will suggested.

Thackett shook his head. "I can tell you that our best CIA analysts have been working on that for months and have found nothing in that area other than mountains and the lake. I doubt you'll find anything."

"If we can't see any of these things with high-resolution satellite images, then they must be buried under the ice," Will argued. "And since the Nazis have already recovered some of the devices, they must have been in the right place."

"How would these enormous objects have gotten into the ice?" Jonathan asked as he refilled his coffee mug.

"Maybe the ice came afterward," Daniel said. "Could be the case if it all was constructed 40 thousand years ago."

"And the ice formed around it," Denise said.

"It must be accessible from the base," Will argued. "How else would the Nazis have acquired the devices? I doubt they were digging in the ice. We need to get to the base."

Thackett cleared his throat. "Repairs to the *North Dakota* are complete," he said. "They'll be heading out to sea soon. I'll push for an itinerary. The first step is to get you all to the *Stennis*. You can wait there until the *North Dakota* arrives.

Will's gut churned and stomach acid seemed to work its way into his throat. He'd been struggling to sustain a moderate level of patience, but his anxiety had nearly breached its containment during the past few days. But now the stress diminished. They were finally going.

"In the meantime," Daniel said, "we should review everything we know about the base, and study the satellite photos, even though experts have already analyzed them."

"Who's going this time?" Sylvia asked.

Daniel panned his head around the group, and made eye contact with Jacob, as he spoke. "We're all going."

LENNY STEPPED TOWARD THE MEN, keeping his gun elevated but not aimed directly at them. "What's going on here?" he asked.

"Come over, Lenny," one of the men said as they both lowered their guns.

Lenny recognized one of the men by his short blonde hair. It was like thick carpet glued to his oversized head. The man went by "Benjamin," and was one of the CIA operatives he'd worked with on the Plum Island operation.

Lenny lowered his weapon but kept it in hand as he approached with caution. He didn't recognize the second operative, a tall African-American man, but he did recognize the man on the floor. He was from Chinese intelligence and, Lenny knew from experience, an assassin.

"Looks like they had some plans for you," Benjamin said.

"Why are you guys here?" Lenny asked.

"You're welcome," Benjamin said and then nodded towards his partner. "This is Hal."

"Oh, right," Lenny said, instantly ashamed. He wasn't used to having anyone look out for him. "Of course, thanks. I'm just confused, I thought I was alone on this – "

"— We got a tip," Benjamin explained. "We hacked into Tao's email, as well as those of all of his connections, thanks to some of your previous work."

Lenny recalled the digital storage devices he'd collected from the old Naval Testing Grounds on Long Island. The CIA had replaced them with decoys infected with Trojan Horse software before Lenny had turned them over to Chinese intelligence.

"You may have saved your own ass on this one," Hal added.

Lenny looked down at the man on the floor. His hands and feet were zip-tied, and duct tape was wrapped around his head and mouth. "What are you going to do with this guy?"

"We have people coming to collect him," Benjamin said, "but you and I should take a look around while Hal waits for them. We've been ordered to clean the place out and to take anything of value."

"The first floor is empty," Lenny said as he looked around the second floor. There was a stack of about 20 large cardboard boxes lined along one of the far walls, and three five-gallon cans labeled as kerosene a few feet from them. "There were supposed to be computers down there – Tao wanted me to retrieve the hard drives, and whatever else looked important."

Benjamin nodded. "Everything got cleared out before we arrived last night. At that point, we watched the place closely because we knew something was up. And then this guy," he said and nudged the man in the small of the back with his heel, "crawled in and set up shop. Seems he was going to snipe you outside the building."

Benjamin pointed to a small window that had a direct line of sight to the entrance of the parking garage. A rifle was on the floor beneath it.

"We managed to get in through a service door in the back, and hit him with a dart from the stairwell," Benjamin continued. "He just came out of it a few minutes ago."

"You bring the kerosene?" Lenny asked, nodding in the direction of the cans.

Benjamin shook his head. "Nope," he said. "I think our friend here was going to set the building on fire – along with your corpse."

Lenny doubted that. The Chinese didn't like evidence of any type – even the charbroiled kind. "Have you looked in the boxes?" Lenny asked. He needed to search for the object in the picture Thackett had sent him.

"Not yet," Benjamin answered. "Let's have a look."

Together they pulled a box off the top of the stack. It was heavy, as if it were stacked with books. They opened it to reveal files so densely packed that Lenny had to use two hands to extract one of the folders. Stamped across the front and back were the words 'TOP SECRET' but he didn't hesitate to flip it open. His blood stirred with anger when he recognized the documents as Red Wraith files. This was information that, not too long ago, he'd been charged with protecting. He recalled the feeling of satisfaction he'd get when assassinating someone for leaking documents of this sort. His former boss would have been furious. The next image in his mind was that of his boss roasting in hell, and how he might be there with him before long. It seemed he'd nearly been delivered there today.

For the next hour, they rummaged through every box until they'd gone through all 22 of them. It was a mixture of Red Wraith, Red Falcon, and technical files. Lenny figured they'd all be considered important, but not crucial.

"You're going to take everything?" Lenny asked.

Benjamin nodded. "We're supposed to be on the lookout for equipment as well."

"Like this?" Lenny asked as he pulled out his phone and showed him the picture of the object."

"That's the one," Benjamin acknowledged. "And anything else that looks strange."

Lenny glanced back at the picture and it jarred another image in his mind. He suddenly remembered why the object looked familiar to him.

He had to get to Devils Lake, North Dakota.

THE NEWS ANNOUNCER on the crackling AM radio said it was 3:00 p.m. The reception wasn't very good in the break room, but the constant sound of voices soothed Tao's nerves.

He'd heard nothing from his asset since early morning, when the American was supposed to have arrived at the dormant Syncorp facility. It was supposed to be a short-range shot, and then the usual disposal of the body. Everything was there at Syncorp – the chemicals, and large-scale containment and waste removal equipment. If everything had gone as planned, the American asset would be in liquid form by now, and seeping down the pipes and into the Baton Rouge sewer system.

Tao's hand trembled as he took a sip of tea.

His decision to remove Lenny wasn't because the man had failed. In fact, he'd done better than the average Chinese operative, considering the difficulty of the missions. Tao knew this had something to do with Lenny's familiarity with the American system, and that he blended in. He would not have fared as well in Beijing.

Tao had to eliminate Lenny because it was time to clean up. The American had been a valuable tool, but now it was time to make a move and get out. It reminded him of what the Americans had done with their many wars abroad – leaving their equipment behind. The mistake they'd made was to leave that equipment functional. In many cases, it got into the wrong hands. Tao would not leave an asset such as Lenny to be reclaimed.

The unknown outcome of the morning's operation concerned him. If Lenny had somehow survived the ordeal and identified his would-be assassin, he could be a problem. He knew the location of the safe house and, more alarmingly, he could identify Tao. But Tao had to put those thoughts aside. He had a major operation to coordinate.

The Ministry of National Defense, the MND, was stepping up its efforts regarding the Americans' Red Wraith project and the conflict in the Southern Seas. Although Tao did not fully understand how those things were connected, one thing that linked the two was William Thompson. And he knew that Thompson was in the Space Systems building. It was the one useful piece of information he'd gotten from his mole, Fred, before he'd disappeared. The MND had given top priority to killing Thompson at all costs – even if doing so would lead to war.

With his inside connections lost, Tao would have to formulate a more brute-force strategy. He had more than 40 operatives in the Northeast, and he was calling them in. And the Ministry of State

Security was sending a special-forces unit. They were all expected to arrive in the DC area in the next week. Orders would then be communicated to the individual teams, and they'd hit Space Systems in an early morning operation. It would be an all-or-nothing effort. Escape plans for the high-ranking officials had already been formulated.

Tao was going to take a route through Mexico. Some would be routed through Canada, and others would go dormant for a few months, hopping through numerous safe houses scattered about the country. Cities with large universities were the best places, as well as the so-called sanctuary cities. Tao would have enjoyed staying in San Francisco for a while, but his orders were to get out as soon as possible. He knew too much.

Tao flinched and spilled a few drops of tea when his phone vibrated on the table. It was his asset in Baton Rouge. The conversation lasted less than ten seconds.

The American was dead.

DANIEL HAD SPENT the whole night poring over satellite images of the Antarctic surface within a one-mile radius of the base.

Antarctica was like another planet. It had a lonely beauty he associated with the vastness of deserts and oceans. He realized that the pictures before him could be thought of as both: desert and ocean. However, there was little life in Antarctica.

His eyes burned and it was approaching time to close them for a while. It was 2:00 a.m., and he thought he might spend another night on his office couch. He'd been considering talking to Thackett about getting living quarters in the building. The trip back and forth to his house was just a waste of time, and often dangerous considering his usual sleep-deprived state.

He'd found nothing strange in the satellite photos. The lake was considered somewhat unusual because there were times of the year when it was open water. This was supposedly the result of a rare geothermal source that both warmed the water to a temperature just above freezing, and kept it moving. The lake would still freeze over in the winter, but the ice would be thin. They were fortunate, however, that the lake wasn't easy to locate. It covered an area of just a few acres, and Antarctica was enormous: it was larger than the continental United States. At this time, the lake was covered by a thin layer of ice on which snow would accumulate, making it blend in with the rest of the white landscape. It also was difficult to find in satellite images if the viewing angle wasn't directly overhead: steep mountains sloped in on the north and east. The lake would show up with more contrast in thermal imaging, but not much more than other warm areas on the map. All of this was good: he was convinced that the Chinese and Russians would not be able to find it on satellite images.

There was a plateau on the west side of the mountain that overlooked the east side of the lake. The eastern side of that mountain, opposite the lake, sloped sharply into a valley of snow and ice. A mile further east, the rocky peaks of a dense mountain range rose out of the rippling ice that curved back to the west, forming a rough semicircle. The edges of the arc gradually sank into the white rippling blanket of snow and ice. Daniel estimated that, if the arc were completed to form a full circle, the mountain directly above the base would be on its perimeter.

Although it was an interesting geometry, it was not unique. He'd been looking for patterns of features the entire time, and had found many. He'd located some ordered formations, like mountaintops that formed rough squares or triangles. Some features even looked like pyramids protruding from the ice, but examining images of the same area taken at different angles quickly disqualified such illusions. After many hours, he'd found nothing of importance.

The sound of light footsteps came from outside his office door. He looked up to see Sylvia standing in the doorway. Her black and red hair was in such extreme disarray that he was sure it contained irreversible tangles. Her eyes looked swollen, and her lips dry and on the verge of cracking.

"You have any coffee made?" she asked.

"Sylvia, you need rest."

"Coffee."

He pointed to his French press on a low shelf near the door. A bag of coffee was on an upper shelf next to a can of tea.

"You find anything?" she asked as she scooped ground coffee into the press.

"No."

"Me either."

"I doubt we'd see anything anyway," he said. "Might be completely buried, if it even exists."

"I think Will's conjecture is a real possibility," she said. "All of the BHC devices came from the base."

"B-H-C?"

She grinned as she poured hot water from the tea kettle into the press. "My own terminology. It means Beyond Human Capability. I think it sounds better than alien, or extraterrestrial."

Daniel nodded as the strong aroma of coffee saturated his olfactory system. He liked the term 'alien' better. It was a word that seemed to excite people – it excited him – but that's probably why Sylvia's term might be more appropriate.

"They all came from the base," she continued. "And we know the Germans didn't build any of them."

He nodded. "It's not inconceivable that aliens built them."

"Sounds crazy."

"Everything sounds crazy," Daniel argued. "We got a message from deep space with drawings that match objects collected from the base."

"Does it make sense to go to the base at this point?" she asked. "Seems we're starting to make some progress – Will and Jacob identified the Plum Island device and the decoder."

Daniel shrugged. "The engineers and linguists will still be working while we're gone."

"It takes such an enormous effort to get there," she said. "The crew of the *North Dakota* can't be too pleased with the plans."

"They're well informed now," Daniel said, "they know that whatever is happening is important."

"Is it important?"

It was a question to which no one really knew the answer. He didn't know anything more than the others. But his subconscious mind conveyed an anxiety that tightened his chest. It was a tension that was always there, and intensifying.

"I can't answer that," Daniel replied. "Only way to know is to go there and find out."

Lenny lifted his sunglasses and squinted into the sunlight that beamed through the windshield of his government-issued SUV. There was something of a bright yellow color spread out on the horizon. It was too far away to identify, and the landscape was so flat that it was difficult to judge the distance.

He'd flown directly from Baton Rouge to Minneapolis, and then taken a prop plane to Grand Forks, North Dakota. The SUV was waiting for him at the airport, and he started the two-hour drive west at about 2:00 p.m. The drive was flat the entire way, and it was hotter than Baton Rouge, although not nearly as humid.

The plains seemed endless. The only features were the occasional silo and farm machinery that protruded from the fields. Sometimes a tall grain bin would appear on the horizon, and it would take an agonizing amount of time to get to it.

It was at the one-hour mark that the horizon acquired a yellow tinge so that the skyline went from the green of the fields to yellow to sky blue.

Ten minutes later he was engulfed in a sea of golden sunflowers – dense fields as far as he could see in all directions. It was a surreal moment, as if he'd been transported into a fantasy world. It was better scenery than the beach, or at least more rare. Awestruck, for a moment he thought he could live in such a place. Then he remembered that North Dakota was not much different than Siberia in the winter.

He was one hour from his destination, a small resort on Lake Alice.

Welcome to Wonderland, Alice, he thought, still in awe of the endless fields of sunflowers. Lake Alice was close to Devils Lake, a popular fishing location. This worked in his favor since there were many small motels and rental cabins available for outdoors enthusiasts. He'd reserved a cabin for a week, although he was hoping to complete the operation in a couple of days.

Lenny breathed in deeply and took a sip of a "Gallon Gulp" soda. A gas station attendant had told him it was what the serious truckers used. He thought those truckers probably also had a bottle to pee in so they could stay on the road. Lenny did not, and he pulled the SUV into a small gas station called *Jiffy Stop-n-Go*, and parked next to a gas pump.

As he topped off the SUV's tank, his cell phone vibrated in his breast pocket. It was a text message with two long strings of characters. He grinned. They were the access codes for missile silo A-51. He knew there were only about a dozen silos in the "A" group, so the last one in the group would be A-11 or A-12. Silo A-51 didn't exist on lists that normal military personnel were allowed to see. But that was okay – it didn't contain missiles.

He went into the store, relieved his straining bladder, and bought a few snacks to get him through the rest of the drive.

The silo itself was located 25 miles northwest of his cabin on Lake Alice. When he'd gone there the first time, over ten years ago, the silo entrance had been located in a small clearing in a wooded area on a large farm. His previous visit had been in the late fall, and the crops had already been harvested. He wondered if there would be sunflowers there this time.

His task on that first trip had been to deliver a wooden crate that contained a cylindrical device that Heinrich Bergman had informed him was not dangerous if kept in its case. Only he and Bergman knew that it was stored there. And now only Lenny knew about it – Bergman was dead.

All Lenny knew for certain was that the device was connected to the Red Wraith project, and it was important enough to hide away in a safe place. Even though he'd transported a multitude of sensitive cargoes during his service to Bergman, the importance of this one was something he should have appreciated at the time he'd originally transported it. After all, he'd brought it to a nuclear missile silo in the middle of nowhere.

It wasn't difficult convincing Thackett to authorize the venture after he'd presented him with the details. Lenny had only seen the top of the object in its crate when he'd delivered it the first time. But he recalled the hole for the eyebolt and the radioactivity symbol, and the size seemed to match.

Lenny hoped his hunch was correct. He owed Thackett. The CIA had just saved him from an almost certain fate. He had real hope now that the CIA and Thackett might allow him to fade away gracefully from the business. And by gracefully, he meant alive. But he wasn't finished yet. They still had the dangerous task of bringing down the Chinese network.

At about 4:00 p.m. he pulled into the front office parking lot of the summer resort and picked up the keys to his cabin. He navigated a network of unpaved, sandy driveways through the woods to cabin Number 9. He parked the SUV and got out.

The smell of pine trees and lake water brought a warm feeling to his mind. He wished he were there to relax and fish. But those activities were for those who led normal lives.

He grabbed a large black duffle bag from the back seat of the SUV, stepped onto the cabin's wooden deck, and opened the back door. He stepped inside and closed the door behind him. He was in a small utility room with a clothes washer and dryer, and the air was filled with the scents of laundry detergent and dryer sheets. It wasn't an unpleasant smell.

When he walked into the main room he was astonished by the view. Floor-to-ceiling windows faced north over an enormous lake. A boat pulled a water skier in the distance, and the muffled sounds of jet skis penetrated the cabin walls. Everything was wood – cedar he thought – walls, floors, and ceiling. There were two bedrooms, each with two sets of bunk beds, and the kitchen and living room were furnished with the basics. There was a large flat-screen TV mounted on the wall opposite the windows, and a stone fireplace built into the east side of the cabin. It was comfortable.

He opened a patio door in the kitchen and stepped onto a deck that overlooked the lake. The shoreline was about 100 feet away, and a line of tall pines to either side separated his cabin from the others. The only hints of other cabin dwellers were the sounds of squealing kids beyond the pines, and the smell of grilling meat.

He stepped back inside and headed for the back door. He needed to do some reconnaissance on the silo site. He wasn't concerned about security – there shouldn't be any – but he knew the landscape might have changed. For all he knew, the entrance had been buried since his delivery a decade prior, and overcoming something like that would take some planning. On his way back, he'd pick up some food.

WILL FIGURED it took some heavy leaning on Thackett's part to get things moving so quickly on the Antarctica trip. However, the CIA director did have the president's ear: according to Thackett, the man hadn't gotten a good night's sleep since the incident on the Chinese carrier. That was something Will tried not to think about.

A little after 8:00 p.m., Denise came up to his flat with a bottle of wine and green tea ice cream, the latter having sentimental value from one of their last nights together in Chicago.

They ordered Chinese – which was a strange ordeal since security personnel had to pick it up from the restaurant and deliver it to them.

During dessert, Denise's demeanor changed from excitement to something Will couldn't read. She didn't seem upset. It was something else.

"Ever think of how it would've been had we met under different circumstances?" she asked.

"You mean if you hadn't had to rescue me from the Red Box, and I hadn't developed strange abilities, and I hadn't brought the world into some dire situation that required everyone to scramble as if our very existence depended on it?" he replied. "Oh, and that you hadn't gotten shot in the process?"

She grinned. "Yeah."

"Well," he said. "Without all that, I think you might have found me a bit boring."

She laughed loudly, and pressed gently on one of the scars on his forehead. "They're almost gone," she said.

"My God, I was a physics professor," he continued. "How would you have handled that?"

She took a sip of iced tea and then grabbed his hand. "I hope I would have been intuitive enough to discover the man that was hidden inside. But my feeling is that you knew he was there all along."

She might have been right. He'd always had a sense of purpose and a drive for adventure, but he'd had few venues in which to exercise it. "I think I've made up for the years of calm," he said.

"And then some," she said. "I just want you to know – if it isn't obvious – that I want us to be together when this is over."

Will was not surprised by her words, but they hit him harder than he'd anticipated. He felt the same, and it made him feel regret and shame for creating a situation that would put his – and her – hopes in jeopardy.

"I have already fallen for you, Denise," he said. "I want more than anything for us to be together. But you must know there's a chance that all of this will end badly."

"I know," she said as she stood, and then pulled his hand so that he did the same. She hugged him and put her head on his chest. "I just want you to know how I feel about you."

He squeezed her tightly.

"Besides," she said, "maybe we can figure out a way for it not to all end badly."

"Are you hinting that we should get to work?"

She pulled her head off of his chest so that he could see her face. She smiled and nodded as a tear ran down her nose. She caught it with her sleeve.

She kissed him and went to the worktable and unloaded her backpack.

Struggling to maintain his composure, Will went to the kitchen and brewed a pot of coffee. Ten minutes later, they got to work.

Denise resumed poring over Professor Miller's notebooks and the files from Plum Island. She'd also ordered additional files from the CIA archives that were related to the murdered professor's work.

Will continued studying the drawings. However, it was not the blueprints that interested him. Instead, he concentrated on the text that accompanied them. He'd had flashes where a few words had materialized in his mind. He recognized the strings of symbols that referred to the words circuit, connection, wire, fastener, and conductor, and the full sentence, "Connect the cable before energizing the circuit."

He'd examined a series of ten drawings, doing his best to visualize the object in three-dimensions given the drawings' different perspectives. Each one had multiple pages of text that he assumed were instructions on how to fabricate and assemble the parts. He stared at the text and tried to concentrate, but it felt forced. It occurred to him that he might be trying too hard, and this reminded him of the posters of three dimensional objects that could only be seen if you relaxed your eyes a certain way. He'd never been good at those.

Denise's voice interrupted his thoughts. He looked up, then at his phone. An hour had gone by. "Sorry, what did you say?"

"Your eyes were rolling back," she said. "Were you separating?"

"No," he replied. "Just trying to think." He smiled and shook his head.

"Why are you smiling?"

"It's just strange that you would ask that question as if it were a normal thing."

"It's normal now."

He supposed their small group was getting used to the idea. It still wasn't normal for him. "You making any headway?" he asked.

She nodded. "I think the life of an Omniscient would suit me."

"That so?"

She nodded. "I love the mysteries," she explained. "I guess that's what I thought I'd be doing as a lawyer."

"You were doing that as a lawyer."

"Yeah, but that was a fluke," she said. "Under normal conditions, I'd just be reviewing old cases and looking for problems."

"I suppose you're looking forward to our trip," he said, knowing the answer.

"Can't wait," she replied as her eyes widened.

"Good," he said. "We leave in six days."

"What?" she exclaimed. "How do you know that?"

"Thackett told me today."

"And you made me wait all the way through dinner to tell me?"

She kicked his shin under the table.

"Ouch," he said and laughed. "We'd be leaving sooner, but Thackett said we had to wait on something."

"What? Delays with the *North Dakota*?"

"No, the sub and crew are ready," he explained. "It's something else. He said he hoped it would be important, but didn't give me any more info."

"Intriguing," she said and flapped closed the notebook on the table in front of her. "Do you want to take a break and open that bottle of wine?"

"You get the glasses."

A LITTLE AFTER 8:00 p.m. Lenny was in the general vicinity of the GPS coordinates that Thackett had given him for silo A-51. He'd have daylight well past nine o'clock this time of the year, especially this far north.

He pulled off the country road and parked the SUV in the grass beneath low tree branches that leaned over a barbed-wire fence. The narrow road cut through a densely wooded area through which he'd be trekking west for about two hundred yards. After that, it should be farm fields, at least according to the satellite images. It wasn't odd that he'd seen no evidence of the silo in those images. The area wasn't just blurred or blacked out. Rather, the photos seemed to be altered so that everything looked natural. He hoped that was the case anyway – otherwise the silo might be buried.

He got out of the SUV, doused himself with mosquito repellant, and put on a floppy hat to keep the ticks out of his hair. As he climbed over the rusted barbed-wire fence, he broke one of the strands and would have fallen had he not grabbed a tree branch. He then pushed his way through brush and over fallen trees up a gradual slope that continued for over 75 yards.

He winced at the noise he made as his feet crushed sticks and dead leaves. He struggled through nets of vines and entangled branches, and burrs attached themselves to his pants and shoes. He recalled that it had been easier going the first time. Not only had it been late fall for that first trip, so much of the foliage was gone, but he'd been a decade younger.

After ten minutes of climbing, the hill leveled off and the tree population turned to evergreens. Lenny took a deep breath. The smell of pine made him think of Christmas. It also reminded him of his summer military training in the former USSR.

The pines and spruce branches were thick, but easier to push through than vines, and the ground was covered with needles and long soft grass. He pulled out his military-grade GPS device and checked his progress. He was close.

He walked another 30 yards west and then due north. A few minutes later he pushed through the low-lying branches of a cluster of large, closely spaced pine trees and into a clearing. Long, soft grass carpeted the floor of the glade, and tall evergreens formed a semicircular wall to the north, east, and south. To his pleasant surprise, the west side bordered a farm field filled with tall sunflowers.

In the center of the clearing was a concrete disk, about six feet in diameter and a foot thick. Long grass grew over its edges, but would not be a problem. He went to the north edge of the disk, took ten steps north, and settled to his knees in the soft grass.

He reached into his backpack and pulled out a hand-sized garden shovel, the kind used to plant flowers, and eased it into the ground until the handle prevented it from going further. He pulled it out, and then pressed it back in, this time about six inches to the north. He repeated the process about 20 times, moved six inches to his right, and made another row of stabs all the way back. In the middle of the fourth pass, the shovel hit something solid about two inches below the surface. He didn't know why his heart sputtered in excitement – he knew he'd find what he was seeking.

He yanked out the grass with his hands and removed the soil around a circular receptacle that looked like the end of an eight-inch pipe with a hinged metal cap. He knew the cap was hermetically sealed so that the internal electronics would not get wet. A sophisticated closing mechanism was secured with an integrated combination lock that had rollers, like a cable bike lock, rather than a dial, like a padlock.

He took out his phone, found the combination that Thackett had sent him, and rolled the ten indicators to the proper digits. A spring-loaded mechanism inside the port forced the lid upward on its hinge, revealing a number pad and a small screen that illuminated and brightened as it warmed up. An underscore symbol flashed on and off, prompting him for the access code.

Lenny pushed the lid down until it latched, and the lock dials spun and randomized automatically. He spread some dirt on the lid, along with some of the grass he'd pulled, and stood.

He took a careful look around to make sure no one was watching, something that was more of a habit than a necessary precaution. He'd hear someone coming no matter from which direction they came. There were too many branches and sticks on the ground, and the sunflower field would be difficult to navigate.

As he walked back through the clearing and into the woods, all he could think about was getting back to the cabin and resting before the night's operation. Food was on his mind as well, and he decided on fish.

Daniel left Space Systems at midnight.

He then drove 40 minutes in DC traffic before parking his Toyota Corolla in the driveway of his empty house. He turned off the engine and stared at his garage door in a fatigue-induced daze. The only sounds were the ticks of his car's cooling engine and exhaust pipes.

He looked up to the second floor. Seeing the dark bedroom windows night after night was a stark reminder of what he'd lost over the past year. His wife wasn't coming back. He'd been served with divorce papers two weeks earlier. They were sitting on his kitchen table. He'd sign them and mail them in the morning.

He still had almost a week before the journey south, but he liked to pack early. Before going to bed, he'd collect some things to take to the office in the morning, and then spend the rest of the night on the living room couch, trying to fall asleep. He could no longer sleep in the bedroom. His mind needed a rest, but it wouldn't let him.

He got out of the car and opened the back door of his Corolla. As he reached in for his briefcase a voice whispered behind him. He hit his head on the doorframe as he wheeled around.

"Relax," the voice said.

"You," Daniel said. The man was six feet tall with dark hair and a millimeter of scruff on his face. It was the same man he'd met under identical circumstances months before. His heart went from nearly exploding to a pace that was no longer life-threatening. "What do you want?"

The man stared at him in silence.

"Sorry," Daniel said. "You startled me – I didn't mean to sound rude. I should thank you for what you did for us." The man had given him crucial information the last time they'd met. "And you helped Jonathan McDougal in the airport in Chicago. You're Avi."

The man nodded. "Shall we go to the diner?"

"Yes," Daniel said as he closed his car door and followed Avi to the sidewalk. The diner on the corner of the adjacent cross street was where they'd conferred last time. Avi had given him a thumb drive with useful information on the Red Falcon and Red Wraith projects and, of particular importance, transcripts of interrogations of Nazi war criminals.

They arrived at the diner and sat across from each other in a booth next to a window. The server brought two mugs and a carafe of coffee, and left them alone.

"I have some disturbing news that you should forward to your director," Avi said. "Chinese intelligence is aware of your facility, and is planning a major operation in the next week."

Daniel stared at him, unable to speak. After a few seconds, he was able to verbalize one of the many questions that ran through his mind. "What's the objective?"

"To kill William Thompson," Avi replied, "and whoever else is valuable to your operation."

"It would mean war."

Avi nodded. "They believe it is worth the risk."

"How do they know that?" Daniel asked. "Nobody knows what any of this means."

"There's more," Avi continued. "Along with the internal attack, they're considering an all-out attack on your naval forces in the Southern Seas. And that would also initiate a war – possibly go nuclear."

"Do you have any proof of this?"

Avi reached into his breast pocket and slipped him a thumb drive. "I'll send you the decryption code in an email."

Daniel put the drive in his pocket. "You have my email?"

Avi grinned. "One more thing," he said. "Tell your director that a hit has been put out on his mole. They are searching for him."

Daniel knew nothing about a mole, but he'd forward the message to Thackett immediately.

Avi finished his coffee and stood. "I'll let you pick up the tab on this one."

Daniel nodded and smiled. "Thank you."

Avi nodded and smiled back, but his eyes were deadly serious. "We're in this together."

ON HIS WAY back from the silo, Lenny picked up a takeout fish dinner from a local restaurant and ate it while he watched the news on the TV in the cabin. The BBC was reporting on maneuvers and countermaneuvers between the American and Chinese navies in the Southern Seas, and also in the Pacific, near some artificial islands constructed by China. It seemed that things were heating up.

At midnight he drove out of the resort and fueled up the SUV at a gas station, where he refilled his travel mug with soda and purchased a few nutrition bars. He'd need sustenance for the hours of work that lay ahead of him.

He turned on AM radio for the half-hour trip and tuned into a program about aliens and UFOs. The host discussed various conspiracy theories with callers about what was happening in Antarctica. Lenny chuckled. If they only knew that they were really on to something this time.

After 15 minutes he lost the signal and turned off the radio. It was at undistracted times like this that his mind often went to uncomfortable places. This time, however, the feeling was more mild than usual: he was on the right side again, and his task didn't involve killing anyone. However, there was going to be plenty of that in the near future.

He wondered if he could ever make up for his past. It was impossible to measure how much a life was worth, but he'd come up with a crude way of quantifying it. He'd killed 264 people. So far. He estimated their average age to be about 35, and knew the average person lived to be roughly 75. That meant, on average, he'd robbed each of those people of 40 years of life. Multiplying that number by the number of people he'd terminated meant he'd extinguished over 10,500 life-years from the planet – from the human race. It was a staggering number. He figured he only had 20 years left of his own life, so there could be no equal justice brought to him, based on that simple math. They could put him to death, but he'd still owe a debt of 10,480 life-years.

But what if he saved lives? What if he saved 1,000 people from certain death? Would he earn 40,000 life-years? Of course, he had no answer to that question but it wouldn't hurt to try to pay back some of those lost life-years. To him, it would be okay if he were only able to break even somehow. He didn't want to think about how he'd be punished in the afterlife for extinguishing over 10,000 life-years.

At 12:40 a.m. he parked the SUV in the same location as he had that afternoon, except he stayed on the shoulder of the road this time. It would look less suspicious to someone passing by, as if the SUV had broken down. It was a country road that had very little traffic, but it was best not to make it seem as if someone were trying to hide the vehicle in the ditch, under low-hanging tree branches.

He got out of the SUV and doused his head and entire body with mosquito repellant. He slipped on his backpack, donned his hat, and pulled a hand truck out of the back of the SUV. It was the same method he'd used to haul the crate up the hill when he'd delivered it to the silo a decade ago.

He had a powerful flashlight in his backpack, but the moon was so bright that he didn't need it. He locked the SUV, put the keys in a front pant pocket, and walked through the ditch to the edge of the woods. He raised the hand truck above his head and lowered it to the ground on the opposite side of the barbed-wire fence. He stepped onto a strand of wire about two feet above the ground, grabbed a tree branch, and stepped over to the other side. He had wire cutters in his backpack for the return trip with the heavy crate.

Leaves and sticks crunched beneath his feet and the wheels of the hand truck as he made his way west, up the hill. Branches occasionally got caught in the handle of the dolly, and vines tangled in its wheels, but he just gave it a hard tug to keep it moving. Twenty minutes later, he was up the hill, out of the dense deciduous forest, and into the pines. Another 75 yards north and he emerged in the glade.

The sunflowers to his left swayed in a gentle breeze that also ruffled the tops of the pines. The moonlight attached itself to the sunflowers making them resemble a black-and-white photo.

He breathed in deeply through his nose, taking in the scents of the pine needles that covered the ground. He locked the scene in his mind so that he might recover the memory someday.

He lowered the hand truck into the grass, walked around the concrete disk to the buried circular port, and peeled off his backpack and set it down. He cleared off the dirt and grass from the lid, and then took a deep breath and blew away the residual debris. He pulled the flashlight out of his bag, as the trees to the southeast cast shadows in the moonlight over the clearing, making it impossible to see the numbers on the lock. Lying on his belly in the grass, he held the flashlight with his left hand and rolled in the combination with his right.

The metal cap sprung open, revealing the green, illuminated screen and input pad. He turned off the flashlight, pulled out his phone, found the code, and punched it in. Nothing happened.

He looked closely at the code and confirmed it matched the one on his phone. He directed the flashlight beam back into the hole and noticed an un-illuminated, green "Enter" button and pushed it. A second later, a grinding sound came from behind him. His heart pounded.

Lenny went over to the concrete disk. It was sinking into the ground. He knew it would take 20 minutes to move down a meter, and then another 10 minutes to slide laterally to expose the access ladder. He was amused that most people thought this entrance was the missile launch silo. It wasn't. The actual launch site was more than 100 yards to the north and not discernible to the naked eye. The reason that the launch port was buried was that this particular silo was never completed, and had never housed any missiles.

Lenny sat down in the grass and admired the stars over the sea of sunflowers. He pulled a nutrition bar out of his backpack and started crunching on it. It would be his last opportunity to rest for the next few hours.

The sky was perfectly clear and, with the moon at his back and behind the trees, even the faintest stars were visible to the north and west. The idea of the abyss implied by every black part of the sky was one of the few things that had ever impressed him with a feeling of hope. He'd always thought it odd, but the concept that our little planet was an insignificant speck of dust meant that there might be better things out there. Better things to come. Perhaps even for him.

The disk completed its vertical motion and started moving to the side, in the direction of the sunflower field. Ten minutes later, it completed the process and ground to a halt.

Lenny shone the flashlight down the hole and looked inside. The steel ladder was as he remembered it. Dim red lights lined the walls as far down as he could see.

He donned his backpack and grabbed the dolly. He'd have to climb with one hand and hold the dolly with the other. He swore under his breath: he'd used a hand truck to deliver the crate in the first place and left it inside. But he remembered that the axle had cracked. He couldn't chance it going belly-up as he carted the heavy cargo through the woods, so he had to bring a new one. The new one was sturdier.

During the slow, painstaking downward climb he had to switch hands multiple times. His damaged shoulder hurt no matter which hand held the dolly, and the ache was radiating through his neck and chest by the time he reached the bottom, over 70 feet below the surface. He massaged it with his hand as he searched for a light switch. As he recalled, it was located on the north wall, a few feet away from the access ladder. He felt around for it with both hands for a minute without success. He took off the backpack, extracted the flashlight, and beamed it around until he located the switch. There were two, and he flicked them both.

Fluorescent overhead lights flickered and then brightened quickly, illuminating control consoles and a wall of dead computer screens. The room was about 20 by 40 feet, and the ceiling was more than 20 feet tall.

He rolled the hand truck across the floor to an elevator and pressed the down button, which was the only way it could go. He'd worried that there might be problems with the electrical power since there was no regular maintenance, but he was relieved to hear the motors humming. The elevator door opened, and he went inside and pushed the button labeled "Engine Access." It was the deepest level.

It was a slow elevator, as it was designed for heavy loads, and took almost 10 minutes to get to the bottom, over 200 feet below the surface. The elevator door opened and he turned on his flashlight and scanned the area. It was a hallway. The caged lights on the wall were dim, but good enough. He turned off the flashlight and rolled the dolly behind him as he walked.

After about 75 meters he came to a large steel door with a one-foot-diameter wheel instead of a handle. He rotated the wheel counterclockwise. After about five full turns, air whistled around the door's edges and his ears itched, as if there was a change in pressure. Another five turns and the door was loose. He pushed it inward, and went through the doorway and into pitch darkness.

Using the flashlight, he found a panel of ten switches, flipped them all, and watched as over a hundred fluorescent lights illuminated the space. The floor was circular, and about 100 feet in diameter.

As he stepped onto the floor, he tilted his head back and looked up the launch shaft. The surface was more than 200 feet above, and he couldn't see the top, despite the well-lit base. It was an impressive engineering feat, even without considering the rocket science it was designed to support.

At the center of the floor was the wooden crate, seemingly undisturbed since it had been delivered a decade earlier. It was cubic, 2 feet on a side, and its weight was stamped on the lid: 183 pounds. The only markings were the stenciled black words "Property of The United States Government" and "Property No. US-78905803."

The crate's lid was secured with Phillips-head screws. He pulled an electric screwdriver out of his backpack, selected a matching bit, and went to work. A few minutes later, he pulled off the lid and removed form-fitted packing material to reveal the upper half of a gray metal cylinder. Stenciled in yellow paint on its top and sides were the acronyms NASA, LANL, and ORNL. He knew the latter two stood for Los Alamos National Lab and Oak Ridge National Lab, respectively. Directly beneath "ORNL" was the symbol "Am-241." The universal symbol for radiation was painted in numerous places on the top and side of the cylinder.

Everything matched the picture sent to him by Thackett, except that the eyebolt on the top was missing. The tapped hole for the eyebolt, however, was there.

He snapped pictures of the object, replaced the packing material, and closed up the crate. As he went to replace the lid, he noticed a piece of paper stapled to its underside. It read: *Replacement Core. ORNL ID# 77540932800-1*. He took a picture of the note, and then replaced the lid and screwed it down.

After packing up his tools, he wedged the platform of the dolly under the crate. He then pulled three sets of ratchet straps out of his backpack, wrapped them around the crate and dolly, and tightened the ratchets to secure the crate firmly to the dolly's frame. Three ratchet straps was overkill, but better safe than sorry, especially considering that his cargo was radioactive.

It was going to be a struggle pulling over 200 pounds – including the weight of the hand truck – through the forest. The first major feat, however, would be getting it to the surface.

He rolled the crate to the elevator and punched the button for the control room. Ten minutes later, he rolled the hand truck into the control room and positioned it against the wall, near the ladder to the surface.

A cardboard box on one of the desks contained a heavy-duty

hand winch with 100 feet of cable, and a chain. The cable on the spool was rated for 300 pounds and seemed to be in good condition – no rust or fraying. It was the same rig he'd used to lower the crate down the shaft when he'd delivered it a decade ago.

With the winch and chain – together over a hundred pounds – crammed into his backpack, he climbed the ladder to the surface.

After taking a minute to catch his breath, he secured one end of the chain around the base of a nearby pine tree, and hooked the other end through an eyebolt on the winch. The hook on the chain had a spring-loaded clip to ensure that it wouldn't inadvertently detach. He then spooled the cable out of the winch and lowered it down to the control room floor, and then climbed down again and secured the cable to the dolly so that it would be stable during the upward tow.

The climb back to the surface winded him again, and he took a break. Cranking the winch was going to be hard on his damaged shoulder, regardless of which arm he used. But there was no avoiding the pain. A few minutes later, he started reeling.

After 20 minutes of grinding pain, the top handle of the dolly protruded from the opening and leaned toward the tree to which the winch's chain was attached. Lenny locked the winch and sat in the grass to catch his breath. He pulled a bottle of water out of his bag and started drinking.

The moon had moved to a position above the treetops and lit the area with a ghostly pale light. The air was cooler now, and the breeze had diminished. Isolated sounds of rustling of leaves and branches emanated from various directions; it seemed that the nocturnal wildlife was active.

After he finished his water, he put the empty bottle in his backpack, and then stretched his legs and lower back for what was coming next.

He went to the opening, reached down, and grabbed the handle of the dolly with one hand, being careful not to get his feet too close to the edge of the hole. Dew had formed on the grass and made the footing slick.

Lenny secured his second hand on the frame of the dolly, adjusted his feet, and pulled with all his strength. As the hand truck moved upward, its wheels got stuck on the lip of the opening. He quickly readjusted his footing, gave it another strong tug, and almost fell backwards as the wheels rolled over the edge, but recovered just in time.

He reeled the rest of the cable into the winch and put it into his backpack along with the chain. He then climbed back down the ladder, put the winch and chain in the box from which he'd gotten them, turned out the lights, and climbed back to the surface.

He crouched in the grass next to the small control port and pushed the "Close" button on the pad. The circular door started its half-hour closing operation. While he waited, he consumed the last of the nutrition bars and relieved himself behind a tree – even though he knew no one was around.

By the time the port had closed, he'd become uncomfortably cold. It was the combination of sweaty clothes and decreasing temperature – he figured it had dropped to about 60 degrees. He'd welcome the imminent physical activity to get him warm again.

He closed the lid of the control panel and covered it with dirt and grass.

He then grabbed the handle of the dolly and dragged it behind him through the pines. The wheels occasionally wedged in a hole, or on a pinecone, and would bring everything to a jolting halt. This caused sharp pain in his bad shoulder, and foul language to come out of his mouth. He kept the latter to a whisper.

The moonlight penetrated the dense canopy of the deciduous woods, but he still had to use the flashlight on occasion to navigate more complicated terrain. Since it was a shallow grade downhill, he pushed the hand truck ahead of him and let gravity assist, but it was slow going. In the numerous instances where he encountered holes and fallen limbs, he turned the dolly around and tugged it. It had almost tipped over a few times, but in each case he'd saved it. His back ached – in addition to his shoulder – and he knew it was going to be trouble for him in the morning.

After struggling for almost an hour, and out of breath, he finally made it to the barbed-wire fence. He took wire cutters from his backpack and snipped the two lower strands. The top strand had been broken during his earlier recon visit when he'd almost taken a spill.

He pushed the dolly through the fence line, down one side of the ditch, and then turned it around and dragged it up the other side and to the shoulder of the road, behind the SUV.

He opened the rear door of the vehicle and, keeping the crate strapped to the dolly, slid them into the back. He covered everything with a blanket and closed the door.

At 3:45 a.m., Lenny was on his way back to the cabin.

"WHERE'S THE DEVICE NOW?" Will asked as he passed the photos across the coffee table to Daniel. It was 6:30 a.m., and everyone was present for the impromptu meeting.

"Somewhere in Wisconsin by now," Thackett said. "The operative should have it here early tomorrow."

The others looked exhausted, and Will was going on three hours of sleep. Even though his brain wasn't yet functioning well – despite the strong coffee – he could see that the cylindrical object in the photos matched the so-called replacement part.

"It has to be a replacement americium core for the RTG," Will said as he examined the second picture that showed a piece of paper that read: *Replacement core. ORNL ID# 77540932800-1.*

"Where was it found?" Denise asked.

"North Dakota," Thackett responded. "In a missile silo."

"That's strange," Jacob said. "Why there?"

"The former director of the Red Wraith project – "

"– Bergman," Will blurted without thinking. "Heinrich Bergman." He was the first person Will had killed – the first of many.

"Yes, Bergman," Thackett continued. "He moved it there so it wouldn't be found if anything went wrong with the Red Wraith project. The missile silo was unfinished, but parts of the facility were operational. No missiles, of course. It was a good, long-term hiding place."

"Why are we just now learning of its existence?" Daniel asked.

"Because I just learned of it myself," Thackett said. "A new asset came forward with the info."

"Are we going to have time to examine it before we go?" Jacob asked.

Thackett shook his head. "A day if you're lucky. You're scheduled to embark for Argentina in three days. But you'll be taking it with you."

"Can't we delay a day or two to give us some time to study it?" Jacob asked. "If it's a replacement core for the RTG, we might learn how it works. All of the testing equipment is here."

Thackett shook his head. "You have to get out of here on time," he said, "and with everything of importance – all of the devices and whatever testing equipment you need."

"Why?" Denise asked, seemingly picking up on something Thackett was omitting.

Thackett repositioned himself in his chair and took a deep breath. "We got a tip that Chinese intelligence is planning something."

"Here?" Will asked, astonished. "They know about Space Systems?"

"Not exactly," Daniel replied. "They know you're here, and they know the CIA is involved. They do not know the extent of Space System's functionality."

"What are they going to do?" Will asked. "Conduct an all-out assault?"

Thackett shrugged. "Maybe."

"How did you learn this?" Denise asked.

"Two independent sources," Thackett replied. "One was a Chinese operative we captured at the Syncorp headquarters in Baton Rouge."

"And the other?" Will asked.

"Israeli intelligence," Daniel said.

"We're going to disrupt their plans," Thackett continued, "but it's best to have you out of here before then, just in case."

"Just in case what?" Denise asked.

"There's a chance that China may sell out on this," Thackett said. "They could bomb Space Systems. They could be gambling that we lack the resolve to go to war."

"Do we?" Will asked.

Thackett shrugged. "That's up to Congress," he replied. "China would bet on a retaliation of the same magnitude. If that were the case, then they'd be the winners because everything we have here would be destroyed, and it's irreplaceable."

"Then it's best we get out now," Denise said. She was becoming animated, and louder. "Why wait any longer?"

Thackett put up his hands and gestured for her to calm down. He smiled. "We deal with threats like this constantly – not at Space Systems, but elsewhere. We're monitoring them closely now, and we know they're not ready to go. They need four or five days, but you'll be out in three."

That seemed to relieve her.

The others continued to discuss plans in the background as Will's attention receded to the inside of his mind. The tension was building just as it had before he'd entered the probe and put everything into motion. It was something he wished he hadn't done. Now it was as if his subconscious mind was telling him that he was going to do something else he was going to regret. But regret wasn't quite right. It was more like he was about to do something irreversible.

He wondered if the feeling derived from his own thoughts, or from those that had been imprinted upon him. And it wasn't clear whether the premonition was positive or negative. He did know that, whatever it was, it had to happen, and that he had to do it.

It was 10:00 a.m. when Lenny pulled the SUV up to the gate of Space Systems. He was exhausted but had made good time. It was a Sunday, so traffic had been light.

He handed the car keys to a group of men in white lab coats and was then escorted to the elevator. Ten minutes later he was with Director Thackett in the same basement-level room in which they'd had their last meeting.

"From the pictures you sent, we believe that the device you collected will be crucial to our efforts," Thackett began. "Thank you for recovering it."

"Thanks for taking out that sniper before he blew my head off," Lenny replied.

Thackett nodded. "I have some news."

Lenny's neck muscles tightened.

"We interrogated the sniper," Thackett explained. "Chinese intelligence is preparing for a major operation."

Lenny shrugged. "They're constantly on the move."

"This is different," Thackett responded as he moved his chair forward and leaned his elbows on the table. "They're planning to take this place out in an all-out effort to eliminate William Thompson."

Lenny was not surprised. "In addition to me," he explained, "they allocated another six to eight special ops types for the task."

"Bigger," Thackett said as he shook his head. "They're planning a military-style attack, and then they'll disband."

"It would be an act of war."

Thackett nodded.

"You can't trust the information you got from the sniper," Lenny argued. "They're pre-loaded with false information."

"We verified it through an independent source who had warned us of the same before we got it out of the Chinese operative."

"What independent source?"

"Israel – Mossad."

Lenny nodded. An extremely reputable source. "Okay," he said. "What's your plan?"

"Your position in the network has clearly been compromised," Thackett said. "And we had a plan for what happens in that case."

"A massive cleanup. It's a large ring."

"Over 100 people," Thackett said and nodded. "You'll have a specific task in our preemptive move."

"Get Tao," Lenny said without hesitating. "And you'll want him alive."

Thackett nodded. "We want his safe house intact – the rest of their network should think everything is operating normally."

Lenny knew the tactic. They could then capture everyone going into the place. He figured the maneuver might work for a while. If things weren't coordinated well, however, it could all blow up in their faces, and the ring could scatter. Chinese intelligence always had a plan in place for that. "When?" Lenny asked.

"Friday."

Lenny raised an eyebrow. Only five days to prepare.

It was still early to be packing for the trip, but Jacob started organizing the things he'd be taking on the bed. It eased his mind.

He didn't know whether it was nervousness or excitement that kept his heart beating at such a quick pace, but he imagined that his uncle had experienced the same on many occasions. It was difficult now to imagine Theo as the man who had raised him. That whole time, Horace – as those in his professional world knew him – had been going from adventure to adventure. And now Jacob had been brought into Uncle Theo's world.

He was told not to take many clothes – except underwear. Everything else would be provided. He'd made a list of electronics to bring along – mostly test equipment. He decided to bring along the square decoder device as well. Everything had to fit inside a cubic crate, four feet on a side.

The Plum Island device, and the so-called replacement part, had to be stored in special containers since they were radioactive. The previous afternoon they'd had a look at the replacement part brought back from the missile silo. Painted on the side of the lead container was "Am-241". It was americium, as Will had suspected, and they were now confident that it contained a replacement core for the Plum Island device.

Jacob had been emailing and texting Paulina daily since he'd moved to Space Systems. She knew nothing about his move, but that was about to come to an end. His phone rang.

"I tried to call you today," Pauli started without saying hello.

Jacob saw where the conversation was leading. He knew she hadn't tried to reach him on his mobile. "So you tried to call me at work," he said. It was where he should have been on a Monday morning.

"They said you were fired three weeks ago," she said. "What the hell is going on?"

Jacob took a deep breath. "I can't tell you the details," he began, "but I can tell you that I have a new job. And I no longer live in the apartment on Pine Street – so don't ever go there again."

"And when were you planning on telling me this?" she asked in an angry voice. "We've been communicating this whole time."

"I was going to tell you when everything was settled."

"Settled? What does that mean?"

"Pauli, I work for the government now," he explained. "I can't tell you where I am or what I'm doing, but they brought me in because of my technical skills."

"Does this have anything to do with that man at the restaurant coming after us with a gun?" she asked.

Jacob didn't want to answer the question, but did anyway. "Yes. He was after some things I got from my uncle."

"The book?"

"Yes, and other things," he replied. "I'm going to be out of touch for a while."

"Is everything okay?" she asked. Her voice took a softer tone.

"Everything's fine," he said. "I'm just going to be out of the country for a week or two."

"What's going on? Are you working for the CIA or something?"

After some hesitation, he replied, "Not exactly. I'm sort of a freelance subcontractor at this point – kind of doing the same things I did when I was with Interstellar Dynamics."

"Why all the secrecy then?"

"I'm working on some highly classified stuff, and they want me to be isolated until the job is done," he explained. "All of us here have to follow the same rules."

Her nearly imperceptible sigh and subsequent silence told him that she was satisfied with his explanation. But he was sure it would come up again later.

"I miss you, Pauli," he said. "I want to go back to what it was like in grad school." It was where they'd met, her being in law school at the time.

"I want to come back to DC," she blurted. "I hate it here."

He laughed. "It's only been two weeks," he said. "Give it a chance."

"I know," she said. "We'll talk about it when you get back from your trip."

They chatted for a few more minutes and ended the call.

A deep pain swelled in Jacob's chest. Sadness and despair overwhelmed him and he broke down. He wept in screams into one of the pillows on the bed.

After he calmed down and came out of it, he analyzed what had caused the drastic reaction. A part of it was that there was a real possibility that he wouldn't make it back from Antarctica. But that wasn't completely new: every time he drove his car there was a finite chance that he could get into an accident. This, however, was different. They were meddling in things they didn't understand. There was a sense of darkness in all of it – intellectually and existentially.

Uncle Theo's words came back to him: *existential implications.*

CHAPTER 14

Will took in a deep breath through his nose and rubbed his eyes. He zipped up his coat and stepped out of the helicopter and into the cool ocean air.

They'd landed at Argentina's Ministro Pistarini International Airport at 3:00 a.m. local time and boarded a CIA helicopter for Mar del Plata. They'd now await another chopper to pick them up and take them to the *USS Stennis*.

The sky to the east was giving up its darkness to the impending dawn, and the light drowned out the stars on the horizon. The packed gravel helipad crunched beneath his feet as he walked to the cargo hold of the helicopter, pulled out pieces of luggage, and handed them to their respective owners.

They traveled lightly. Their Navy hosts would provide all of the essentials, including clothes. The most important items were their laptop computers. The crates containing the devices and testing equipment had shipped out two days earlier and were already onboard the *Stennis*.

They walked to the open end of a large metal Quonset hut that faced the sea. The opposite end was closed, and Jonathan seemed nervous as he peered into the dark interior of the structure.

Denise nodded in Jonathan's direction. "This is where we were attacked last time."

"You were attacked?" Jacob asked with a surprised expression.

Denise nodded. "And I was hit," she said and pointed to her thigh.

Will's temples pounded at the thought of Denise being struck by a bullet fragment. She'd been lucky she hadn't bled to death. Jonathan's quick actions had probably saved her life.

"You okay with being here?" Will asked.

"I hardly remember it," Denise replied. "But I'm nervous around dark places now – even small ones, as if a snake is going to strike out at me."

Will thought moderate paranoia was a good thing – an overt manifestation of experience. The paranoid had a better chance of survival than the naïve. He had started his life naïve, but had transformed to paranoid. He'd transformed in many ways.

He glanced in the direction of the helicopter and the four, armed operatives that traveled with them. He was glad they were there, but he knew that anyone showing up with ill intentions would have more to worry about than those four men.

Two cast iron benches faced the sea. Denise and Sylvia took one, and Daniel, Jacob, and Jonathan took the other. Will paced back and forth between them as the others talked.

Denise seemed excited as she fidgeted with her fingers and bounced her feet on her toes. She stared out to sea as she chatted with Sylvia.

A few minutes later, a pinpoint of white light blinked on the horizon in front of a backdrop of brightening sky. The sun was rising, and static beams of light seemed to burst around a white cloud that Will imagined as a colossal mountain on another planet. A half-minute later, the echoing chops of the incoming helicopter were perceptible over the waves lapping on the rocky shore.

"This is about the time we were attacked last time," Denise said.

Will turned and noticed everyone was now standing. Daniel, Sylvia, and Jacob were looking out to sea. Jonathan and Denise faced the Quonset hut and seemed to peer into the shadows deep inside.

Will tensed and his nerves seemed to tingle.

"I think we're safe," Jonathan said, as if he'd sensed Will's anxiety.

Daniel turned to Jonathan. "Sylvia and I are armed this time."

Jonathan patted his chest and smiled. "Me too."

"What the hell – am I the only one without a gun?" Denise asked.

"I'm not armed," Jacob said.

"Me either," Will added.

Denise looked at Will in silence for a few seconds before she replied, "You don't count – you have other ways to defend yourself."

Jonathan laughed, "If it's that important to you, maybe we can get you a weapon when we get to the *Stennis*."

"It is that important," she said.

Will felt the need to badger her. "I don't think they'll allow you to have a weapon on the ship."

Denise looked at him with an expression of betrayal.

"They can't have just any yahoo wielding a gun," he continued.

"Shut up," she said, smiling.

"Actually, he's right," Daniel said. "Only official CIA personnel will be allowed to keep their weapons. Jonathan will have to turn his over."

Jonathan shrugged and nodded.

"And no one will be allowed to carry on the sub," Sylvia said.

Will couldn't imagine a sidearm discharging in a submarine.

He glanced up and noticed that there were now two helicopters. The first one, with the lights, was about a half mile out, and another one was about a quarter mile behind it – no lights.

"The first one is our ride, the second is protection," Sylvia said as if she were reading his thoughts. "Taking no chances this time."

The wind surged as the first chopper landed on a large concrete pad, while its menacing brother hovered in eerie silence a few hundred yards offshore. Minutes later they were in the air and heading out to sea, southeast.

Daniel's first voyage aboard the *USS Stennis* had ended nearly two months ago. He never thought he'd be back.

He'd dreaded his first time aboard the massive aircraft carrier but that had subsided quickly, and he'd become quite comfortable. It was much better than life on a submarine, but he'd also acclimated to that more quickly than expected. Now, he was gearing up for another uncomfortable transfer to the *North Dakota*.

His nerves were better this time. Not only was he more comfortable in the confined quarters of the sub, but also there were fewer threats in the area than during that first voyage. Two days earlier, however, a couple of destroyers in the group had been forced to fire warning shots at Chinese surface ships that had been edging back into the area. The intruders vacated, and the seas were now clear.

It was the dead of winter in Antarctica, so there was little chance that anyone would venture very far into the contested area – land or sea. The weather was horrible everywhere, and land exploration was virtually impossible. The ice flows in the Weddell Sea were worse than in previous decades, and any vessel that would purposely enter the treacherous icescape would have to be on a suicide mission. The *Stennis* group, or *Carrier Strike Group 3*, stayed on the outskirts of the flows and monitored the waters closely for stray icebergs.

After 24 hours on the *Stennis*, Daniel and the rest of the CIA group boarded a helicopter that ventured out a half mile from the carrier and hovered above the surfaced *North Dakota*. The shadowy sub rocked from side to side in the rolling waves. It was just as dark, but the seas were calmer than the first time he'd undergone the exercise.

Daniel watched as the helicopter crew strapped Sylvia to a sailor and then lowered the pair to the *North Dakota's* deck, where a man used a long stick with a hook to pull them closer. A second sailor on the deck grabbed the pair and secured Sylvia before she was released from her escort. It was a safe system, as long as the helicopter maintained a stable position in the gusty winds, and the waves weren't too large. Denise went next, followed by Jonathan, and then Jacob.

Daniel knew that a fall into the icy water meant certain death, but he trusted those around him. As he descended to the deck, the wind seemed to cut through his clothes and his vision blurred. Gusts from the helicopter blades blasted a mist of seawater into the air, some of which he tasted on his lips. Once on deck, he was guided to the hatch and brought directly to his quarters where he changed into a jumpsuit – called a poopy suit – and white sneakers. Jonathan was already there and nearly dressed.

"Not too many people can say they've done that," Jonathan said, grinning.

Daniel knew he was referring to the open-sea transfer, and nodded. "Not something I'd like to do on a regular basis."

Ten minutes later, the dive order was announced, and the *North Dakota* submerged. A few minutes later, a young sailor escorted them to a small meeting room where Captain Charles "Chuck" McHenry and his first officer, Lieutenant Diggs, were waiting for them. Neither man looked happy.

"This must be crucially important," McHenry started, implying that it had better be. "We were deployed for six months and were supposed to get six months off. We got five weeks. We're all a bit exhausted."

"It didn't make sense to swap crews," Lieutenant Diggs added. "Gold crew already knows about the base, and they've navigated the tunnel."

"And they have combat experience," McHenry said.

Daniel recalled that the *North Dakota* had been attacked during its previous deployment. It was something that would have terrified him, and he respected the people who had gone through it and were willing to come back.

"The crew is tired but excited," McHenry said. "Many have the feeling that history is being made somehow. Frankly, I'm excited as well. My orders came from the president himself."

"Last time, we had to leave before we could properly explore the base," Diggs added.

"You have any idea what we're looking for?" McHenry asked.

"Not exactly," Daniel replied. "We have cargo that we retrieved from the base that dates to well after the war. We'll be looking for similar things."

"I saw your cargo," McHenry said. "Some of it's hot."

By "hot" Daniel knew McHenry meant "radioactive." "Those items are well contained," he assured him.

"What are they for?" McHenry asked.

"We think one is a radioisotope thermoelectric generator," Will replied.

"An RTG?" McHenry said with an expression of surprise. "What does it power?"

Will shrugged. "We're not sure. But we think the second radioactive piece is replacement material for the RTG. It was assembled by NASA over a decade ago, with the help of Los Alamos and Oak Ridge National Labs."

"Did they have any additional information?" Diggs asked. "Like who ordered the replacement material?"

"The short answer is no," Daniel interjected. "I searched all NASA records – including restricted information – and found nothing."

"How do you know it belongs to NASA?" Diggs asked.

"Only by the tagging," Daniel admitted.

McHenry got a call on his communicator. They were at depth and ready for orders.

The captain stood. "Let's get this show on the road."

A GROUP of sailors vacated the *North Dakota*'s galley for their shift as Will sipped chicken soup from a plastic mug. After nearly 35 hours, he was getting used to life aboard the sub, but wondered how he'd feel after six months beneath the waves.

Despite what the captain had told them about the crew's excitement, Will imagined they would not have been pleased about the incursion on their surface-dwelling lives and being sent back to the dark Southern Seas. But it looked like McHenry's assessment was accurate: most seemed openly excited and optimistic. Part of that enthusiasm might have been because of the perks they were going to get afterwards. According to McHenry, they were going to get some kind of salary bonus. Also, because of deferred repairs, and the fact that another crew would take over when the *North Dakota* was redeployed, they'd get a full year off. Will just hoped that they'd all make it back to enjoy their rewards.

He watched as Denise poured hot water for tea and took a seat across from him. "We're going to enter the cavern in the next hour," she said. "They said the lake will be frozen."

"Should be," Will said. "It's winter."

"But there will only be a thin layer of ice because the water is warm."

"Yeah, there's probably a geothermal heat source," he said. "But nobody knows where that is exactly."

"Do you think the *North Dakota* could break through the ice?"

Will recalled an image of the sail of an American sub breaking through ice in the Arctic. "They can break through ice that's pretty thick – up to a meter, I think. But we don't want to do that."

"Might be spotted," Denise said.

Will nodded.

She looked over his shoulder and smiled and nodded.

Will turned his head as Daniel and Sylvia passed by. They both got tea and, as they sat, Jacob and Jonathan arrived. Will was hoping to spend more time alone with Denise, but he knew that would be nearly impossible. Their time together was always rushed and almost never private. There were things he wanted to tell her.

"I hear we're about 45 minutes from the cavern," Jonathan said to Will and Jacob. "I think you'll both be fascinated."

"I already am," Jacob interjected. "I can hardly believe I'm here. A few weeks ago," he paused and glanced down at his watch, "I'd be stuck in traffic on I-95 on my way to work."

Will had seen pictures of the cavern. He was aware of the size of the base, as well as the engineering involved in its construction. Those things, combined with its dark history, might make it more than fascinating for him. It might overwhelm him, in the most negative way.

"How are we going to proceed once we dock?" Sylvia asked, and looked to Daniel.

"I think we should show Will the basic layout while the crew unloads the cargo," he said and looked to Will.

Will nodded. Although he'd seen maps and pictures of what had already been discovered, he needed to see it first-hand. There was more to the place than what images could convey.

"After that," Daniel continued, "I thought we'd split up and explore – search for anything that might be connected to the devices we've brought along, or anything else that's peculiar."

It was as good a plan as any, Will thought. But his task also included searching his mind.

He sensed excitement in the others while they anticipated getting the call to go to navigation to view the cavern. As they chatted, Jacob left and returned with a book.

"You wanted to see this," Jacob said and handed it to Daniel.

Daniel examined the cover. "It's one of Horace's monographs," he said and grinned as he opened it. "And it's annotated in his handwriting – he has a unique script."

"You said the man that was hunting me down worked for Chinese intelligence," Jacob said.

Daniel nodded. "They wanted this, and access to 17 Swann."

"I think I know why they wanted the book," Jacob said and reached out his hand. "Let me show you."

Daniel handed him *The Israel Thread* and Jacob paged through it.

"This," Jacob said as he handed it back.

It was open so that opposite pages showed two maps. They were both of Antarctica.

Daniel stared at them for a few seconds. His first expression went from confusion to horror. Finally, he just looked ill.

"Thank God they didn't get this," Daniel said and pointed to one of the pages. "This map shows the general location of the tunnel entrance in the Weddell Sea and, worse, the location of the base. This is what the Chinese – and Russians – have been seeking this entire time." He looked to Will. "And they've been looking for you."

"So no one has seen this besides you?" Sylvia asked.

"Only me and my uncle," Jacob replied.

"May I keep this for a while?" Daniel asked.

Jacob shrugged. "Sure," he said as a sailor came into the mess.

"Captain said you can come to the navigation deck," the man said. "We're entering the cavern."

Will's neck tensed. A feeling of dread filled his mind. It seemed he was about to get answers to some longstanding questions, some of which might be shattering. But he also sensed that he was again about to do something that was irreversible.

LENNY WATCHED through a dirty exterior window as the small SUV pulled into the gravel drive that led to the safe house. Tao always arrived a half-hour before the guards' shift change at 8:00 a.m. As usual, he pulled up to the building's two roll-up doors and waited.

His night security team consisted of four men. They'd been hit with tranquilizer darts and carried off by a special-ops team, and then replaced by a four-man team of Asian CIA operatives. There were only two guards on the daytime team, and they'd get a big surprise when they showed up for work in the next 30 minutes.

Lenny wondered how well Tao knew his low-level security personnel. If he discovered the imposters early, he might be able to get out a message. In that case, Plan B would be executed, and that would be a bloody mess.

The roll-up door opened, and the SUV pulled into the building and parked. One of the guards opened the driver's side door and Tao stepped out.

In one swift move, the guard spun Tao around and locked his arms above his head, far away from his pockets.

Tao yelled something in Chinese, and the faux guard yelled something back. Lenny had no idea what they were saying.

Lenny walked out from behind a stack of crates. "Hello, Tao," he said. "Or should I call you Chang Wei?"

Tao seemed to flinch at the sound of his real name.

"You probably didn't expect to see me this morning – or at any other time, for that matter," he continued as another CIA operative searched Tao's pockets, found a cell phone, and handed it to him.

Tao's eyes seemed to refocus multiple times on Lenny's face. After a few seconds, a look of recognition came to his face before it drained to a sickly pale. "It was only business," Tao stammered.

Lenny nodded. "And so is this," he said. "We're going to need the password for your phone."

Tao shook his head, and the CIA operative who was holding him pulled Tao's hands behind his back and fastened them together with zip ties.

"We noticed you have a soundproofed room in the back," Lenny said. "Some nice equipment there as well. I wouldn't call myself an expert or anything, but I know my way around some of the tools."

Tao looked at him blankly.

"As you well know, I'm not the squeamish type," Lenny said. "But we can avoid that for the time being if you give us the password. There's a lot more we want from you, but that's for later."

Tao remained silent.

Lenny nodded to the operative, who then spun Tao around and pushed him toward the rear of the facility.

Lenny looked at his phone. The morning guard rotation was in 15 minutes, and they weren't known for being late.

JACOB NOTICED his jaw was hanging open and closed it. He had to keep reminding himself that what he was seeing was real – that it was all really there – and not just an image on the screen.

The exterior lights of the *North Dakota* lit up the cavern like a football stadium. There were eight video monitors, each showing a different view. The water was perfectly clear, giving the illusion that the sub was hovering in air.

The monitor for the camera that faced downward was dark, as if there were no bottom to the cavern. No lights were aimed upward, toward the frozen lake, for fear that satellites might pick up light that filtered through the ice and snow on the surface. But the most fascinating view was that of the manmade structure built into the cavern wall and ceiling, about 200 yards from the edge of the lake. He'd known it was coming – he'd seen the photographs – but it was different seeing it live, and knowing he'd soon be inside.

"What do you think?" Sylvia asked from behind him. "I find it eerie."

Jacob nodded. "Especially knowing who's responsible for it."

"I'm not so sure anymore that the Nazis were the only ones responsible for this," she said. "Although, I'm sure they're responsible for the disturbing parts."

"Like the torture rooms," Jacob said.

Sylvia nodded and stared at the screen. "And who knows what else is in there."

Indeed, he thought. He wondered how the alien devices they'd brought along would fit in. Those had nothing to do with the Nazis.

THE TENSION DRAINED from Lenny's temples when Tao finally gave up the password to his phone.

Lenny would have ripped out the man's fingernails to get it. Although it was a procedure he'd carried out numerous times, especially as a KGB agent in Europe, it wasn't something he'd relished. It was just business, not unlike the gunner at a slaughterhouse.

Lenny gave the phone to a CIA operative of Chinese origin, who took it away to be analyzed. The agent would crosscheck codenames on the phone with information the CIA had gathered through electronic surveillance, and then devise a scheme to call Chinese intelligence ops into the safe house, one by one.

It was going to be like a roach motel, Lenny thought, recalling the humorous commercials for cockroach traps in the 1980s with the slogan, *Roaches check in, but they don't check out!*

"Now we need to get to other orders of business," Lenny said as he grabbed a wooden chair from the corner and slid it up to Tao. He turned it around and sat on it backwards, leaning his heavy arms across the chair's back. "Now it's time for you to tell us why you are so interested in our Red Wraith project," he said.

As the words left Lenny's mouth, flashbacks to his work with Bergman resurfaced. How many people had he interrogated starting with that statement? He stood, walked over to a workbench, and then returned to his seat.

"What do you know that we don't?" Lenny asked as he snapped the needle-nosed pliers in his right hand.

WILL COULDN'T TAKE his eyes off the structures built into the cavern walls. He wondered how the Nazis had managed to construct them under such harsh conditions, not to mention doing it secretly during wartime. He had doubts that such a feat could be carried out in the present day. It made him wonder how much of it had been there before the Nazis had even started.

"We're approaching the access door," Daniel said and pointed to one of the monitors.

Will walked over to Jacob who stood close to the monitor. His eyes were wide and his mouth was hanging open.

"You all right?" Will asked.

Jacob glanced at him and closed his mouth before his eyes shifted back to the view of the structures built into the ceiling. They were slips for submarines.

"This is incredible," Jacob said.

The dark windows in the structures built into the wall near the slips made Will shudder. It was as if someone was behind the glass, watching them.

"Those are Nazi U-boats in those slips," Jonathan said.

Jacob shook his head. "This is unbelievable."

"Wait until you get inside," Jonathan added.

"Look, the doors are opening," Jacob said as he pointed to another monitor that had an upward view.

Above the *North Dakota*, two doors swung downward, giving it a vertical path to the slip inside the base.

Will's vision faded and he got light-headed. Something was wrong.

DENISE GRASPED WILL'S ARM. The bare skin on his forearm was unnaturally warm. "You okay?" she asked.

With a slight turn and tilt of his head, he glanced at her. His eyes were black – fully dilated pupils – and wide. Without responding, he turned back to the monitor displaying the view from the deck camera. There was no image – just black with flickering white static. They were ascending to the dock, but still submerged, and it was too dark for the deck cameras.

"Will?" she asked again.

He put up his hand, shook his head, and kept staring at the monitor.

A minute later the pilot announced that the *North Dakota* had surfaced inside the facility.

The screen was still black.

"It will be another half hour before anyone can go ashore," Captain McHenry said from behind them.

Will flinched and turned to face the captain.

"We need to run the power cables from the ship to the base's electrical grid," McHenry continued. "Once we have the area secured and the lights on, I'll give you the green light to come ashore."

McHenry barked some orders to his crew as he walked away.

Will looked again to the black screen. It was as if he were in a trance.

Denise squeezed his hand hard. "What is it?" she asked, this time not letting go.

He broke his gaze from the monitor and looked at her. "I've been here before."

"You know that's impossible," she said, "maybe it's familiar because you've seen the pictures."

Will shook his head.

Jonathan interrupted, asking her to help him locate something on the cargo list. When she returned, less than a minute later, Will was gone.

She looked up to the monitor just as the camera caught the ceiling lights flickering to life inside the base. It was a dim image, but she could see men milling around outside. Her attention focused on someone walking the roped platform from the submarine deck to the dock. It was Will.

It was clear to Lenny that Tao had no interest in having his fingernails removed with needle-nosed pliers.

Lenny worked from a script that had a mixture of questions, some of which had verified answers, and some which did not. If Tao gave conflicting answers to the verified questions, Lenny would know he was trying to misdirect them. But there were also questions to which the CIA knew that Tao had answers. In this case, if Tao claimed he didn't know the answer, Lenny would know he was lying. So the interrogation script had built-in checks. And he knew that Tao was well aware of the tactic.

After a half-hour of crosschecking Tao for truthful information, Lenny got a text message notifying him that the replacement security guard detail had been successfully neutralized before they could send a distress message.

Lenny moved on to new questions – questions to which the CIA needed answers, and it wasn't clear whether Tao knew them.

"Is there a plan to attack our naval forces?" Lenny asked.

Tao mumbled.

"Speak up," Lenny said as he nodded to the audio recorder on a nearby cart.

"Yes," Tao replied, more loudly this time.

"Are they coordinated with your operation, here in DC?"

"Yes," Tao replied. "If it is clear the United States is going to retaliate on the China mainland, then more extreme actions will be taken."

"Are Chinese forces on the Antarctic continent?"

"I think you know that already," Tao replied.

According to Lenny's interrogation sheet, that was an unknown. "Answer the question."

"Yes," Tao said. "About a hundred special forces were deployed two days ago."

"What are they looking for?"

"A secret base – whatever the US is hiding there."

Antarctica was worse than Siberia this time of the year. "Where are they deployed, exactly?" Lenny asked.

Tao shook his head. "I do not know," he said. "That information is too specific, and I did not need to know it for my mission here."

A CIA officer, a tall Asian man with a shaved head, took a chair and sat with Lenny and Tao. His name was Lin. "I have a few questions now," he said.

Lenny nodded for Lin to proceed.

"Have you broken the code?" Lin asked

Tao's eyes widened. "What code?" he asked.

Lin shook his head in feigned disappointment. "The incoming message from deep space."

Tao stared at him for a few seconds. "Yes," he said, finally. "But only a small portion of it."

"How?"

"We have good cryptologists, just as you do," Tao replied. "It was not very challenging, but it provided no information. The decoded signal was in the form of gray images, nothing more."

"What about the second part – the longer portion of the message?" Lin asked.

Tao shook his head. "I do not believe they have – the encryption is too difficult."

"What do you know about Antarctica?" Lin asked. "What do your superiors think is there?"

Lenny shifted in his chair and Tao seemed to flinch.

"We have Nazi files that claim that there is an alien base there," Tao explained. "It is rumored to be filled with wondrous technology that would lift any country to invincibility if they were to acquire it."

"Then why didn't the Nazis take over the world?" Lin asked.

"They couldn't access it," Tao said. "It's rumored that one had to be a ghost to get to it."

Lenny stood. This was getting over his head. The CIA would have to continue the interrogation at Space Systems, or some other facility. He pulled out his phone and placed a call to Director Thackett.

THE FIRST THING that Will noticed when he emerged from the *North Dakota's* hatch was the banner that covered nearly a third of the far wall of the enormous bay, opposite the dock.

Inscribed in a white circle on a field of blood red was the black swastika-like symbol of the Nazis' Red Falcon project. Although he hadn't reacted to the pictures he'd seen, being here sparked a dark *déjà vu* that he could only describe as primal fear. He controlled it. He needed to learn.

During his last hours of life, Horace had delivered a message from Landau, the being Will had first encountered during his tortuous stay in the Red Box, telling Will that this place was significant to him. And Will could feel it. There was something here.

The overhead lights buzzed as they warmed, spilling a yellow hue on the enormous carved-stone rectangular void. The floor spanned an area equivalent to three or four average-sized basketball courts laid side by side, and the ceiling was over 50 feet high. The wall to the left, when facing away from the sub and toward the wall with the banner, was sheer, solid stone with no features, and the wall to the right had two massive sliding doors that were as tall as the ceiling.

He turned around and faced the *North Dakota*. Carved in the wall behind and high above the sub were dark windows that overlooked the dock. The slip looked like it could fit two German U-boats, but was barely large enough to accommodate the massive *North Dakota*.

He turned again and faced the far wall. Beneath the banner, on the floor level, was a set of six steel doors. A set of metal stairs led to a second level of doors, and a bank of ominous-looking dark windows that overlooked the entire bay. The bottom of the banner almost touched the top of the second-level doors.

He looked up and spotted a steel I-beam track that was anchored to the ceiling and carried two movable cranes. He followed the track as it curved from above the dock, directly above the *North Dakota*, through the open bay, and through a notch between the top edges of the giant sliding doors on the right wall. It looked as if one of the cranes was used to lift things from the dock and then transport them into the space behind the doors.

"I thought I told you to wait until I gave the all-clear," a raspy voice came from behind him.

Will turned. It was Captain McHenry.

"Sorry, Captain," Will said. "I'm drawn to this place."

McHenry seemed to mull it over for a moment before he spoke. "You sense something here?"

The captain was aware of his abilities – it was the *North Dakota* that had taken him to the two probes when he'd activated them.

Will nodded slowly as he replied, "It's like I've been here before. I feel the urge to flee – the place makes my skin crawl."

McHenry nodded. "It should. Horrific things have happened here. And I feel like we're being watched."

Will sensed the same.

"Everything seems in order," McHenry continued. "You're clear to move about as you need. I think Daniel and Sylvia can get you to the important places – the vault and the library. And the torture chamber."

The muscles in Will's back twitched a few times and then relaxed. His head turned toward the doors beneath the banner. "The second door from the right, on the floor level, leads to stairs that lead to the torture rooms," he said and pointed to the door.

McHenry's face turned blank for an instant, and then he nodded slowly. "Yeah, that's right."

Will's gut twisted and his heart seemed to sputter like an engine running out of fuel. "Thanks, Captain," he said. "I'll wait for the others."

McHenry nodded and headed in the direction of the sub.

Will walked around the bay. After being cooped up in the sub for almost two days, he felt like running. But there were also things brewing in his mind that urged him to run.

All but one of the more than 50 ceiling lights were fully illuminated now. McHenry had mentioned that they'd found a large cache of electrical supplies during their previous visits and had done some maintenance. Additional supplies, including light bulbs, were brought along on the *North Dakota*.

The gray-brown stone of the cavern walls and ceiling looked as if it had been chiseled, with large facets and gouges that were evidence of large cutting machines. The floor was rough, but perfectly level. Will figured it was a natural void in the rock that the Nazis had modified. But where were the tools and machinery?

He went over to the large sliding doors and tried to pull them apart. When they wouldn't budge, he peered through the two-inch crack that separated them, but couldn't make out anything in the dark. It was almost unnoticeable, but air seemed to be drawn into the crack.

He then proceeded to the far end of the bay, opposite the dock, and climbed the metal stairs to a metal mesh platform directly above the set of six ground-level doors. On the wall, to his right, was a bank of dark windows. Directly in front of him, to the left of the windows, were two metal doors. He reached up, just above the steel frame of one of the doors, for the bottom of the banner. As he made contact, a bolt of static electricity snapped between the banner and his fingers, making him flinch.

He turned around and looked out over the bay. The scene was surreal. In the distance was the massive submarine. Men were scurrying about under the bright lights, carrying supplies and running cables and other equipment. A sailor maneuvered one of the overhead cranes to a position above the *North Dakota* and lowered a cable. A man on the deck latched a hook from the end of the cable to a strap on a crate and gave the operator a nod. The cable tightened and lifted the crate from the deck. The crane then moved along the track and lowered the load onto the floor next to a stack of others that had already been unloaded.

He imagined a similar scene from three-quarters of a century earlier – this time with Nazi soldiers scurrying about, and the *North Dakota* swapped for a German U-boat. He could almost hear their orders being barked out in German.

Out of the dozens of people milling around on the floor below, Will's mind detected something in his peripheral vision. Someone was pointing at him.

It was Denise. She led the others toward the stairs. Will met them at the bottom.

"You were supposed to wait," Denise said.

Will looked at her but didn't respond.

"We should get you familiar with the layout," Daniel said. "We can start with the torture facility."

Will shook his head. "Not ready for that yet. How about the library?"

"Okay," Daniel responded.

Daniel led the way through one of the steel doors beneath the banner. They walked 50 feet down a dimly-lit corridor, and then climbed two flights of metal stairs.

"How many levels does this place have?" Denise asked.

"At least five," Sylvia replied. "Maybe more."

After five minutes of weaving through hallways, they entered a room with a large wooden table at its center. It stood on a thick rug embroidered with the Red Falcon emblem – the same design as the banner in the bay. To the right were rows of shelves stacked with thousands of books. On the wall to the left was a detailed map illustrating the tunnel, base, and the location of the first beacon. On the wall to the left of the map, adjacent to the entrance, was a print of a disk on which were five concentric circles of strange writing. It was an image of the White Stone artifact. Its procurement in Egypt by the Nazis had started everything – the Red Falcon project, the base, and everything since then, including what had happened to him.

"Last time, we took everything that was on the table," Daniel explained. "We were in a hurry, and figured that whatever they'd been working on last was probably the most important."

After ten minutes of exploring the stacks, they decided to move on to the vault room.

Sylvia led the way as they filed out of the library. They took stairs up a level and, after a few minutes of navigating hallways, entered an office. The lights in the room were fully warmed, but their glass covers had yellowed with time, giving the place a dingy look.

Sylvia steered them into a narrow room with cabinets and shelves on both sides. "This is where we found the White Stone and some of the other artifacts, including the decoder device," she explained, pointing to one of the cabinets.

"Good thing you brought everything back," Will said as he opened the cabinet and looked inside. "Otherwise we'd still be stuck on the message."

"We didn't have time to look closely at anything," Sylvia said. "We were in a hurry. We packed as much as we could and got the hell out of here."

Will closed the cabinet and looked to the entrance to the next room. It was framed by torn steel. "Where's the door?"

"They took it away after blowing the vault," Sylvia said.

Will walked inside and went to a bank of file drawers. There were 49 of them – an array of seven by seven. He pulled one out. It was nearly six feet long, and empty.

"That's the one that contained the box with the urn," Daniel said.

"Urn?" Jacob asked.

They all looked at each other waiting for someone to respond. Denise finally said, "It supposedly held the ashes of Adolf Hitler."

Jacob's face went blank for an instant and then asked, "How is that possible?"

Sylvia explained it to him as Will closed the drawer and rolled out another.

This one was packed with hundreds of file folders. He pulled one out from somewhere in the middle and opened it. The cover page was on Red Falcon letterhead, and signed by someone he didn't know – someone named Nestler. It was dated 5 January 1952.

He flipped through the approximately 30 pages and quickly surmised that it was a file on one of the test subjects. Her name was Jessica Rosen and she was 32 years old when she'd passed "... due to complications resulting from excessive electrical currents being passed through her body." And there were pictures. The bastards had hooked up electrodes to her right hand and right foot and burned them to a black-and-red crackled crisp.

Will handed the file to Denise and pulled another file. This was that of a man in his 20s who had suffered a slow death by the "nascher," which translated to "nibbler" in English. It was an automated device that slowly amputated limbs – taking an inch at a time. What a horrible death, he thought, but probably no worse than being cooked by electricity.

"This is awful," Denise said, clearly exasperated. "What happened to her?"

"They ran an electrical current through half of her body – the right side to avoid the heart," Will replied. "It carried on for hours – they were trying to get her soul to separate."

"Where does it say that?" Denise asked.

Will put the file he was reading back into the drawer. He took the file from Denise and flipped through the pages. "It says right here," he said, pointing to a paragraph beneath one of the pictures. He read on, "It says here that the room smelled of burnt pork – a smell that lingered for weeks afterwards."

"I didn't know you read German," Denise said.

"I don't."

"So how do you know what that says?"

Will looked closer, concentrating on each word. It *was* in German. He'd never studied the language, and had never been exposed to it other than hearing some of his German scientist collaborators converse from time to time. He'd certainly never learned to read the language. But he knew how he knew.

Sylvia stepped in and took a look at the file. "That's what it says," she confirmed and then stared at Will along with Denise.

Will said, "I told you that I learned things when I – "

" – It was implanted," Sylvia said.

Will nodded.

"It's amazing," Sylvia added. She seemed dazed.

"I still don't understand," Jacob said.

"I suggest we move on," Daniel interrupted. "We need to give Will the full overview of the place so that we can decide where to concentrate our efforts."

"Are we in a hurry?" Jonathan asked.

Will felt the urgency to move as quickly as possible.

Daniel shrugged. "Never know what's happening on the outside. Pays not to dawdle."

"Where to?" Jonathan asked.

"The torture facility," Daniel replied.

Will's heart picked up pace. It was time.

LENNY SHIVERED in the late afternoon sunlight and breathed in the fresh outdoor air. They'd set the air conditioning to the maximum inside Tao's building to make it as uncomfortable as possible for those being questioned.

He watched as three CIA operatives put Tao into an SUV and

carted him away. Another CIA team loaded a half-dozen others they'd duped into coming to the safe house into another vehicle and drove off. The operation had been going on for over ten hours.

Lenny lit a cigarette, took a deep drag, and held it in for a few seconds before blowing smoke through his nostrils.

"Those will kill you," a man said from behind him.

Lenny turned around.

It was Schroeder, a CIA special operative with whom Lenny had worked on two operations – Plum Island, and the break-in at the defunct Stone Box facility, on Long Island.

"Unless Tao gets to you first," Schroeder added, and grinned.

Evidently, Schroeder had heard Tao threaten Lenny an hour before, just as they were wrapping things up and about to deliver their catch to Space Systems. Lenny had told the Chinese chief that now he'd get his chance to see what was going on in the mysterious CIA facility.

"There are plenty of others who'd like to get their hands on me," Lenny said. "What's one more?"

Schroeder laughed. He reached into his pocket, pulled out a business card, and handed it to him.

Lenny took it. On one side it read: DMS, Inc. Inquiries@DMS-Inc.com

On the opposite side, it read: When absolute safety is not possible.

"What's this?" Lenny asked.

"It's something for people like us," Schroeder replied. "I'm not allowed to tell you anything else – just have a look. I'll sponsor you."

"Sponsor?" Lenny said. "Sounds like a counseling program."

Schroeder laughed. "Far from it," he said as he pulled out a pen and put his hand out for the card. "Not that I don't need it."

Lenny handed it to him.

Schroeder wrote something on the card and returned it.

It was a string of numbers and characters.

"That's my sponsor code," Schroeder explained. "When you're ready, send them an email. The subject line should read 'Safety

Deposit Box,' and only my sponsor code should be in the body of the message. You'll eventually get a reply with instructions."

Lenny's phone buzzed. He put the card in his pocket and answered the phone. It was Director Thackett.

"The team in place at the safe house will finish up there," Thackett said. "You need to come in ASAP."

Lenny agreed and the call ended.

He figured there were two likely reasons for the urgency. The first was that the CIA operative who had assisted in interrogating Tao had provided Thackett with information that needed immediate attention. They had been going back and forth in Chinese and Lenny only got the parts that Lin translated. Lin had been sending Thackett information the entire time. The second possibility was more serious: word had gotten out that the safe house was compromised, and the Chinese network was scrambling. But they rarely scrambled without torching what they could – and doing some personnel cleanup of their own. Either way, Lenny knew he had some work to do.

On the way to Space Systems, he pulled the card Schroeder had given him and glanced at the backside. *When absolute safety is not possible.* What the hell did that mean? No one could protect him better than the CIA at this point.

He flipped the card over and noted the email address. Maybe he'd send them a message when there was a break in the action.

WILL FOLLOWED Daniel and Sylvia through a maze of corridors and stairwells. Denise, Jonathan, and Jacob followed.

They came upon a set of two steel doors. Carved into the stone above the doors was a string of German words.

Will recognized the entrance, and the words: *Der Tod ist der Hirte der Menschheit.* "Death is the shepherd of mankind," he said. Seeing the words conjured an ominous feeling of *déjà vu* that triggered a fright reaction. It made him want to run, or separate. He held the impulse at bay, and stared at the words.

The night he'd died, Horace had asked him if that phrase meant anything to him. It had not. The image of the words before him, however, struck him with fear and anger. Evil resided behind those doors.

Daniel and Will pushed the double doors in unison. The hinges complained with a rusty squawk as they pivoted.

They stepped into a long foyer with a line of a dozen doors on each side, and another set of double doors at the far end, opposite the entrance. It resembled a prison block, or a high-security mental facility, and smelled like rotting tallow from a rendering plant. It was the stench of ancient death.

They went to the center of the foyer and Daniel turned to face the others. "All of the rooms are similar, although there are some differences in the specific equipment they contain," he explained. "They all have cages – exoskeletons – and some rooms have two or three of them."

A door on the right attracted Will's attention, and he went to it. The number *19* was engraved in the casing above it. The lock mechanism crunched as he turned the handle, and the door squealed as he pulled it open. He stepped inside.

In front of him was an archaic exoskeleton tilted at an awkward angle as if it had been damaged. There was nothing inside the device, but a few piles of inch-long bone slices were distributed below where the arms and legs of its inhabitant would have been. The largest chunks were more than an inch in diameter, undoubtedly femur slices. A nibbler was still locked on the left arm of the exoskeleton.

Jacob gasped as he entered, and Will turned to see his horrified expression. The others seemed unfazed – they'd seen it before.

Will stepped closer to the exoskeleton and examined it.

A thick cable suspended the cage from a winch on the high ceiling so that the feet dangled two feet above the floor. Electrical cables spewed out from the upper spinal area of the Exo and recombined in ceiling-suspended conduits that guided them to different parts of the room. He followed the conduits to their respective destinations, and it was clear that they were separated into power, control, and sensing channels, the latter of which went to a lab table with an oscilloscope and other instrumentation.

Another table, on the left as they'd walked in, was equipped with a vise, sink, and soldering equipment. A partially disassembled nibbler with its wires exposed was locked in the vise. It seemed to have a burned-out motor.

On the wall above a third table and a sink, on the right side and closer to the exoskeleton, was a pegboard on which various hand tools, cutters, and saws were mounted. The tabletop had more of the same, many of which were piled into a large ceramic pan. The purpose of the tools was clear from the brown stains and the leather-like dried material in the teeth of the saws: they were for manual use – up close, and personal.

Will got light-headed for a moment as the image of a face came to the forefront of his mind. It was a man with dark hair and eyes, and he was smiling, exposing a gap between his two front teeth.

"What did you say?" Sylvia asked

"What?" Will looked at her, confused. "I didn't say anything."

"Yes, you did," Daniel said. "You said 'Todesengel.'"

"What does that mean?" Denise asked.

Sylvia turned to her and said, "It means *Angel of Death*."

THACKETT TOOK the elevator to the sublevels of the Space Systems building. His nerves were firing at random and he was developing twitches in parts of his body, the most annoying of which was in his right eyelid. He'd heard that a stiff drink could help, but he didn't want to start down that rabbit hole.

The elevator stopped at Level D, and a security guard met him in the corridor on the way to meet Leonard Butrolsky. When they entered the room, Lenny was seated in a chair and sipping a bottle of water.

"Good job collecting Tao," Thackett said. "We've already nabbed

17 other operatives, and word still hasn't gotten out about the safe house being compromised."

"Something else must be up," Lenny said.

Thackett knew that Lenny was intelligent. Otherwise the man could not have survived in the business for as long as he had. He'd had to adapt. The Cold War era, and its old ways, was long gone.

Lenny was an irreplaceable asset: he had the intelligence to succeed, and the will to do what was needed to carry out a job. If such a man were ever to go rogue and go on a killing spree, he'd be difficult to stop. He didn't mean a killing spree carried out by a serial killer. He meant a binge of assassinating politicians, celebrities, judges, and business tycoons. The man was an animal, but one that had constrained himself to the business of intelligence and security. He was the perfect tool for the war that was to come or, better yet, to stop that war before it got going.

"We've managed to follow up on something you and Lin got out of Tao today," Thackett said. "Actually, it led us to capture another Chinese op who had information about the operation they were planning against Space Systems."

Lenny nodded. "What do you want me to do?"

Thackett sighed. "All we know at this point is that the task force they're putting together is going to assemble in the next few days. We're working on the when and where. For now, get out of sight. We'll contact you when we have a plan."

Lenny nodded. "Is that all?"

"I think these next jobs are going to be tough, but they'll be decisive," Thackett explained and looked Lenny in the eyes. "But when this is over, and we've cleaned up this mess, I will personally see to it that you can safely leave the business."

Thackett nodded to the security guard, who then escorted Lenny out of the room.

Most of his CIA ops were capable of killing during military-like operations where the shooting would be going both ways. But a true assassin that was capable of mass murder, up close and personal, was rare. A true assassin could kill people as they slept, and not think twice about it. Lenny was a true assassin. And Thackett was going to need him.

He'd wait five minutes to make sure Lenny and his escort were on the elevator. After that, he'd go two doors down and check on the Chinese op who was spilling information. Thackett wouldn't ordinarily allow the methods that were being employed. In this case, however, lives were on the line, and much more.

"TODESENGEL," Denise heard Will whisper again.

She tugged his arm but it was like trying to move a 1,000-pound statue. She went around his right side and faced him. She gasped. His eyes were wide open and white – rolled back in his head.

Daniel went around to the other side and his expression turned to confusion, then fear. "Is he ..."

Before Daniel could finish, Will's eyes rolled into their natural positions and he turned to Denise. "What?" he asked.

"You were ... your eyes ..." Denise stammered.

"Were you separated?" Daniel asked.

"I've been here before," Will said. "An image entered my mind. I was in one of these cages – in an exoskeleton. I saw the doctor."

"Mengele?" Daniel asked.

Will nodded. "The 'Angel of Death' himself."

"You've been through some horrible things," Daniel said, "maybe you were having some kind of psychological event, or maybe you remembered the pictures – "

"No," Will cut him off.

He edged closer to the exoskeleton and turned so that he'd have the same view as its last occupant. He pointed to a closed cabinet door to his left, below a sink. "That's where they keep the acid."

Denise looked to Daniel, who nodded.

She walked over to the cabinet and pulled on the wooden door, but it didn't budge. Jonathan started her way, but she put up her hand and he stopped. She grabbed the handle with both hands and yanked. The door flew open with a wooden yelp. She knelt on one knee and peered inside as the others gathered behind her. Inside were three liter-sized glass bottles: one empty and cracked, one completely full, and the last just a third full. She started to reach in.

"Don't pick them up," Will said. "They might leak."

Denise reached in and carefully turned the closest bottle – the partially filled one – so that they could see the label. The label was yellowed and cracked, and the ink had faded, but she read what she saw, "H-C-L."

"That's hydrochloric acid," Will said.

Denise stood, closed the cabinet door, and looked for a label or sign which would have revealed its contents. There was nothing. A chill ran up her back and into her scalp. "How did you know that was there?"

Will had already turned to the other side of the room and was staring at a coiled cable on top of a small table. He pointed to a drawer on the table. "There's a large soldering iron in that drawer," he said as he rubbed his fingertips together.

Sylvia went to the drawer and pulled out the object. It was a foot long, an inch in diameter, and had a cork handle with a cord sticking out of the back end. The metal tip was cut to a wedge, like a giant screwdriver, and was rusted. On closer inspection, the tip of the iron had other debris on it, and Denise knew what it was.

"That wasn't used for soldering," Will said, still rubbing his fingers and palms.

"How do you know these things?" Daniel asked. "Is this a part of your implanted memory – from your encounter in the probe?"

Will shook his head.

"Then how?" Sylvia asked.

"I've been here before," Will replied. "This isn't like the implanted knowledge. It's more like starting your car when it's dark – you somehow know exactly where to put the key."

"Like muscle memory," Daniel suggested.

Will went across the room to the wall near the cabinet that contained the acid.

Until now, Denise hadn't noticed the red button that now seemed to mesmerize him. It was about the size of a circular drink coaster and inset into the wall.

Will got his face close and rubbed his finger over it, leaving a trail where it cleared away a thin coat of dust. He wiped off the rest of it with his sleeve and then pushed it. It actuated with a loud click. He held it down and looked around, seemingly to see if anything had energized.

He let the button pop back to its original position, and scanned the room again. Nothing. He popped the button a few more times with no effect. He then stepped back a few paces from the wall, closer to the exoskeleton. Denise stayed near him, but the others gathered closer to the exit.

Will's shoulders slouched forward slightly, but then Denise's attention was drawn to a sound. It was the button. It clicked inward, all by itself.

Sylvia gasped behind her and Denise glanced back to see everyone staring at the button with wide eyes.

After a few seconds, the button popped out. Will remained motionless.

"Will," Denise said and started to take a step in his direction, but the sound of the button depressing again made her freeze in place.

A second later it popped out again. Then in, and out, and repeated. The frequency increased rapidly until it reached tens of repetitions per second and then, in a final explosive act, the button fractured into fragments along with a part of the wall.

After the action ceased and the debris settled, Denise approached him. His eyes were open and white. She started to reach out and touch his arm, but then retracted her hand.

After almost a minute of still silence, Will fell to his knees and inhaled as if he'd been holding his breath the entire time. Tears spilled down his cheeks and he coughed as if he were drowning. After a few seconds, he got to his feet, went to the sink near the wall-mounted hand tools, and vomited.

Denise followed him and put her hand on his shoulder. He reached back and gently pushed her away.

"What's wrong?" she asked.

Will answered with another bout of heaving that lasted thirty seconds. When it ended, he remained with his head bowed over the sink and spat over and over.

Sylvia walked over with a half-full bottle of water and a small package of tissues.

Will accepted them without turning from the sink.

Another minute passed before he turned, still wiping his mouth with tissues. His face was sickly pale.

"What just happened?" Daniel asked.

"I was supposed to push that button while being tortured in there," he said, nodding to the exoskeleton. "But that's not all," he continued as he looked around at the walls and ceiling. "There are others here."

"Others?" Daniel asked. "Who?"

"Those who were tortured to death," Will replied.

"You mean like those you saw in the cemetery?" Denise asked, referring to when they'd returned to Baton Rouge after the probe in the Weddell Sea had blasted out its signal. Will had seen hundreds of souls in the cemetery near his apartment.

Will nodded. He turned to Sylvia. "You said you felt as if you were being watched the last time you were here. You were."

Will reached down, picked up a circular slice of bone from the floor, and examined it. "Is there any way we can find out who was the last victim in this room?"

Daniel nodded. "There are thousands of files still in the vault. However, the file for the last person in this room might have been on the table in the library when we came here the first time. If so, we'll have that one on the *North Dakota*."

Will swayed and took a step to the side to steady himself. Denise grabbed his arm. He turned to the others and said, "Let's get the hell out of here."

As they made the final turn in the corridor that led to the bay, Will nearly jumped out of his skin as Captain McHenry and another sailor rushed around the corner. Will's composure was balancing on the edge of a knife and his nerves were hot, like bad wiring.

McHenry came to a sliding halt. "Come with me," he said. "I need to show you this."

A minute later they were all in the main bay. Sailors milled about near an opening in the wall on the right side of the bay when looking from the direction of the sub.

"We finally got these doors open. They were jammed," McHenry explained as he walked toward the dark void in the rock. "Last time we were here, we didn't have time to examine this area very closely."

With his eyes, Will followed the crane rail on the ceiling that led from the submarine slip, directly above the *North Dakota*, through the main bay, and through the center of the large opening. The two sliding doors, nearly 50 feet tall and 20 feet wide, had been moved to each side. One was off its tracks and leaning against the wall.

"At first we thought it might be a repair or assembly bay – maybe for subs," McHenry continued and then waved them to follow him inside. "Now, we have no idea."

They walked in and everyone seemed to gasp at once. There was an enormous circular hole in the high ceiling. It was about 60 feet in diameter, and a rope ladder hung from its edge and dangled a few feet above the floor.

Beams of light whipped back and forth in the darkness far above them – five or six men were climbing four built-in ladders placed symmetrically inside the rising cylindrical cavern. It seemed to go on forever, like an inverted abyss. The feeling then flipped, and Will felt as if he were at the bottom of a colossal well.

"The hole was covered with perforated steel," McHenry explained. "We thought it was just a part of the ceiling until one of my crew noticed a draft. Air is being sucked up into the shaft."

Will noticed a pile of perforated steel panels at the far end of the chamber. "What's its function?" Will asked. "Is it a missile silo?"

McHenry shrugged. "Don't think so – we'd expect to see burns on the walls and floor from rocket engines, or V-2 rocket parts somewhere in the facility."

Will followed the crane rails coming in from the outside. The room was square. The opening was circular, over sixty feet in diameter, and nearly took up the room's entire ceiling. The crane track curved halfway around one side of the opening and terminated.

"That's solid stone," Jonathan said, eyes wide. "How could they have done this?"

McHenry shook his head. "My men are about 250 feet above the floor and still don't see the top. It's probably not open to the surface – otherwise it would be colder down here."

"What's directly above us – terrain-wise?" Sylvia asked.

"A mountain," Daniel replied.

Will grabbed a flashlight from a duffle bag on the floor and directed the beam up the wall of the shaft. It was smooth, but there were signs of where the stone had been cut. Some of the gouges were vertical, as if a large drill had been used to make a circular pattern of holes that traced the opening in the ceiling. Other grooves encircled the inside perimeter of the shaft, as if a giant auger had been used to bore it.

"Where did they put the removed material?" Jacob asked.

"Maybe they used the crane to remove large pieces of rock and dropped them through the submarine dock," Will suggested.

"Could be," McHenry said, nodding. "Regardless of how it was constructed, it was a major feat. The more important question, however, is what's it for?"

McHenry's communicator beeped. "Sir, we're at 300 feet," a man's static-ridden voice crackled from the device. "There's a horizontal tunnel cut into the wall. Should we explore it?"

"That's a negative," McHenry replied. "Maybe on the way down. Can you see the top?"

"Negative."

"Keep climbing," McHenry said and then turned to the others. "Looks like we have a lot to learn about this place."

Indeed, Will thought. He hadn't told McHenry about the souls.

"I want to go up there," Will said.

McHenry looked confused for a second but then recognition surfaced in his eyes. "Climb? Why?"

Will had to move, do something physical. But that was just an excuse. Something was pulling him. "I just need to take a look for myself."

McHenry shook his head. "I don't think that's advisable. You realize I'm responsible for you?"

Will sighed and nodded.

"Let's talk about it when the exploration team gets back," McHenry said. "If you still think it's important after their report, I'll let you go."

"Okay," Will said. "How long do you figure they'll be?"

"They've been climbing for 45 minutes and don't even see the top. I'd say a couple of hours," McHenry explained.

Daniel stepped to Will's side. "Let's have a look at the files while you wait," he suggested. "We can figure out who was the last subject in Room 19."

Will's mind shifted gears. "I need to go back to the vault room. If you locate the file, find me there."

Daniel agreed.

Will and Denise made their way to the vault room as the others went back to the *North Dakota*.

When they arrived, Will went directly to the cabinets in the room that preceded the vault. There were some artifacts there, and a few books. He then recalled that, while trying to decipher the message on the White Stone, the wraith had told him to find a book by Schwinger. There were six books in the cabinet and Will picked them up and examined them.

"You've already seen this," Denise said. "What are you looking for?"

"The book by Schwinger," he replied. "It's not here."

"We can search the library," Denise suggested.

"Maybe later," Will said. "Has anyone checked this place for radioactivity?" He knew the Nazis had been working on the atomic bomb and might have produced some partially enriched uranium. And he knew Dr. Mengele wouldn't hesitate to study the effects of extreme radiation exposure on his subjects. The Plum Island device was also radioactive, and he thought there could be more such objects.

"I know someone checked things with a Geiger counter the last time they were here," Denise replied. "But I'm not sure how thorough they were."

He walked into the vault and pulled out one of the 49 drawers from somewhere in the middle. He pulled a file from the center of the stack and opened it. It was the treatment file of one of the female subjects. She'd been injected with a concoction of chemicals. She was 28 when she'd died. He returned the file and pulled another.

After reading random files for over an hour, Will felt a warm breath drift across the back of his neck. He turned, expecting Denise to be leaning over his shoulder, but she was five feet behind him, fully engaged in reading.

"We're being watched," Will whispered.

"What?" Denise whispered back, her eyes wide.

Will needed to see who was there with them. He sat on the floor next to the file cabinet, concentrated, and separated.

Two wraiths were in the room.

He tingled with edginess, but they seemed to be more curious than threatening. One was examining Denise, and the other watched him. The latter looked to be female, and seemed to sense his awareness of them.

"Where have you been?" she asked.

Will didn't know how to respond. Rather than answering her question, he asked, "How long have you been here?"

The wraith shook her head.

"Where is your body?" Will asked.

She pointed to the floor.

Will couldn't tell what she meant. "Buried?"

She shook her head and pointed downward more emphatically.

It took Will a few seconds to understand, but then it hit him hard. The Nazis must have weighted the bodies down and dropped them through the submarine access door.

The wraith then turned to the one with Denise and seemed to call him. As she moved, her long, translucent-white hair was more evident, and flowed like she was submerged in water. She looked young and beautiful, as she might have been before her soul had been ripped from her body.

The other one came close to Will and seemed to study him.

"I have seen you before," he said.

Will was starting to feel uneasy about being recognized by them. What the hell did that mean? "How?" Will asked. "When did you see me?"

In an instant, the souls scattered and he found himself back in his body and staring up at the face of Daniel. He was in mid-sentence and Will asked him to start over as he stood.

"We found the file on the last victim in Room 19," Daniel repeated, and looked over to Sylvia, who had walked in behind him with a manila file-folder in hand. She handed it to Will.

He opened it. The face in the small photo clipped to the first page looked familiar somehow, but he couldn't place it. The signature at the bottom of the page indicated that the man had been one of Josef Mengele's subjects. His name was Saul W. Kelly, an RAF bomber pilot hit by antiaircraft flack on a bombing run over Germany. He'd made it 50 miles off the German coast into the North Sea before he had to bail out. A German ship spotted the burning craft and found him in the icy waters before hypothermia set in.

Will thought dying in the North Sea would have been better than the slow, miserable death he'd experienced in this place. The rest of his crew never made it out of the plane – they had all been dead when the pilot had bailed.

Handwritten notes indicated that Kelly spoke perfect German and that he'd sometimes plead in the language of his tormentors, trying to summon their sympathy. He'd been subjected to the nibbler and lost his left arm at the shoulder, and his right leg up to the middle of the thigh.

Will cringed. The man's limbs had been taken an inch at a time. He thought it was worse than anything he'd gone through in the Red Box. He paged ahead and saw that Kelly had also been burned, and electrical currents had been run through various parts of his body.

He went to the end of the 100-page file and looked for the time and cause of death, but those parts of the report were blank. "No word on how he died," Will said.

"The file looks unfinished," Daniel suggested. "According to the notes, the Nazis were trying to duplicate whatever they'd done to this man."

"And it seems like there was a gap in their activity," Sylvia explained. "The last entry in this file is June 27th, 1952. The next closest entry we've come across – found in another file left on the library table – is December 1953. Also seems the Nazis cycled their personnel after that – all new names in 1954, except for Mengele."

Will closed the folder and tucked it under his arm – he'd look at it more closely later. He then explained to the others what he'd seen and learned while separated.

"How horrible," Denise said, seemingly looking around for evidence of their observers. "They were killed and their bodies were just dumped into the water?"

Will nodded. "Probably tied to rocks," he added.

"And they said they'd seen you before?" Daniel asked.

"Yes," Will said. "And asked where I've been."

A young sailor burst into the room, startling everyone, including Will.

"The captain sent me," he said. "The climbing team is back."

Lenny sat back in one of the upholstered chairs in his ratty motel room and flipped open his laptop. Sunlight came through the thin curtain and illuminated the dust on the screen. He brushed it off with his sleeve and repositioned himself so that the shadow from his body shielded it from the sun.

He wondered if there was anything more bleak than being alone in a cheap motel as the sun set.

He figured he might as well do something while he awaited orders from the CIA, so he set up an email account that he'd use as he transitioned into civilian life, if that ever became a reality.

He took out the business card that the CIA operative had given him the day before and read it again. "Something for people like us," he said aloud.

What had Schroeder meant by that? And what did he have in common with that man? Lenny had no family, although his adult daughter was out there somewhere. His parents were gone. He was sure he had distant relatives in Russia, but no one who would recognize him. Perhaps he'd find a way to bequeath his life savings to his daughter after he'd passed on to Hell.

He composed an email to Inquiries@DMS-Inc.com. The subject line read "Safety Deposit Box," and the main body was a string of 12 characters: Xt5H9*m#f739 – the sponsor code Schroeder had written on the card.

Lenny looked it over to make sure he hadn't made any mistakes, and then sent it.

He set his laptop on the bed and turned on the television. He tuned in at the kickoff of a pre-recorded football match between Manchester United and Chelsea, and watched as he ate a bag of chips and drank a bottle of soda. United scored an early goal and kept their lead for most of the first half until Chelsea got the equalizer in the 43rd minute. That's when the message telling him to check his email came in on his CIA phone.

The instructions came directly from Director Thackett. There was a safe house in Washington, DC where more than 15 high-level Chinese intelligence operatives were assembling to make final plans to attack the Space Systems building. The information had been extracted from Tao and another Chinese operative.

Thackett's orders were to eliminate the network using whatever means necessary. He'd have any assistance he needed.

Lenny knew exactly what that meant.

It would mean complete decapitation of the Chinese network in the United States. They already had Tao – he was the head. The ones holed up in DC were the spinal cord. If his task were executed in full, it would do three things. First, it would thwart their immediate mission. The remaining operatives would scramble to get out of the country, but many would be rounded up before escaping. Second, it would take the Chinese network a decade to recover, even though they had assets in every university, government lab, and technology company. Third, and most directly applicable to him, there'd be no one left in Chinese intelligence to find him – or even identify him. He was a local asset that they'd supposedly assassinated – hence the reason Tao had been so surprised to see him.

Their assault on the Space Systems building was scheduled for Monday night. That gave Lenny 48 hours to devise a plan.

WILL FOLLOWED the sailor through a labyrinth of halls and stairwells and finally into the bay. About half the crew had assembled near the entrance to the side room where the vertical shaft was located.

"It leads all the way up to the surface," McHenry explained. "There's a large circular door – as wide as the shaft itself – at the top. We did not open it, nor figure out how to do so."

"How do you know it opens to the surface?" Daniel asked.

"Because they opened a small hatch that's next to it," a man said from behind them. It was the first officer, Lieutenant Diggs. "It's hellishly cold out there: negative 65 Celsius."

They went into the shaft room and approached the rope ladder that hung from the edge of the circular hole.

"Once you get up there, there are steel ladders anchored in grooves cut into the stone," McHenry explained. "It seems like a lot of extra work – to cut those grooves – but nothing sticks out into the circular cross-section of the shaft."

"Nothing to get caught on," Sylvia said. "Like it's supposed to launch something."

"Maybe," McHenry said and shrugged. "But we still haven't found any evidence of rockets."

"Did they find anything dangerous?" Will asked.

McHenry's expression indicated that he didn't want to answer the question, probably because he knew where it was leading.

"I don't see the point in your climbing," the captain argued. "We have video and hundreds of pictures."

Although he knew he'd need to climb it eventually, Will agreed that they should first look at the video and photos.

They went back to the *North Dakota* and assembled in the mess hall, except for McHenry, who had to check on something on the bridge.

Although it was early evening in DC, Will's perception of time was skewed and he craved breakfast food. The leader of the climbing team sat with them as they ate, and set up a laptop at the head of the table so everyone could see the screen.

"All you're going to see at first are the ladders and flashlight beams," the young ensign, Smith, explained as he started the video.

Indeed, the upward view of the shaft was filled with a half-dozen beams of white light dancing on a black background. Some men had lights strapped to their heads, others onto their forearms.

"You can see why the climb went so slowly," Smith said.

The men had worn harnesses and methodically latched onto each rung with clips, one in each hand, as they ascended. The incessant clicking was complicated with echoes of the same.

Smith fast-forwarded the video and stopped on an image of the wall next to the ladder. Two horizontal grooves, about a foot wide and six inches deep, were cut into the wall of the shaft, and followed the perimeter to the adjacent ladder. The grooves were separated in height by about six feet and, inside the grooves, were thick rebar rails anchored to the stone.

"Those perimeter rails appear every 200 feet," Smith explained, "and allow you to shimmy around the perimeter of the shaft, from one ladder to another. The ladders and perimeter rails are all inset into the stone so that nothing will obstruct an object passing through."

"Again, like a missile silo," Sylvia said.

Smith shrugged.

"What good would it do to launch from Antarctica?" a voice boomed from behind them. It was McHenry. "The range of the V-2 rocket was only about 200 miles."

McHenry sat at the end of the table and instructed Smith to continue.

Smith fast-forwarded to the next point of interest. Next to the ladder was an oval inset cut into the wall. It was about six feet tall, and four feet wide. The man carrying the camera – which must have been strapped to his head along with a light – stepped into the recess. It looked like it continued on as a tunnel.

"This first one is about 300 feet above the floor," Smith explained. "In total, there were 18 of them, evenly spaced all the way up. On the way down, we ventured about 50 feet into one of them. It was a smooth tunnel – no features – and level. There looked to be a junction deeper in, but we didn't venture any further."

"Maybe they're service tunnels," Will suggested. "Maybe the shaft is accessible from other parts of the facility."

"Not much else to see until we get to the top," Smith said and fast-forwarded the video.

"How high is the shaft?" Denise asked.

"It's 2,760 feet from floor to ceiling," Smith replied. "It was strange that our laser rangefinders didn't work from the floor – we had to range it from top to bottom. You'll see why when you see the door at the top. The shaft is as straight as an arrow. Impressive feat of engineering." He forwarded to a point where everyone stopped climbing and seemed to gather. "Here's the top."

The circular door on the ceiling was 60 feet in diameter, same as the tunnel, and shiny, like a chrome bumper. It was concave when looking from the bottom, faceted, and came to a shallow point at the center, as if it were pressed into shape by a giant diamond-shaped object.

"I can see why the rangefinder didn't work from the floor," Will said. "Smooth and faceted."

Smith nodded.

"What does that mean?" Denise asked.

"He's talking about the door," Smith said.

Will explained that the rangefinder first sent out a light pulse, and then measured the time it took the light to travel to and from the object being ranged. Knowing the speed of light and the time of travel, the device calculated the distance to the object. There was no problem getting a return signal from objects with rough, irregular surfaces, since a part of the incident beam would scatter back to the detector. However, with faceted, reflective surfaces, like the door, no light would reflect back to the detector.

"What material was used to construct the door?" Will asked. "And why is it polished?"

Smith shrugged. "No idea. But there's more," he said and forwarded to another part of the video. "Here's an inset chamber off to the side of the door. It has a ladder that leads to a hatch."

To Will, it looked like a tunnel from a city sewer up to a manhole cover.

"It opens inward," Smith continued, "which I'm sure was by design since there was about three feet of snow and ice on top of it."

The video showed a man opening the hatch and shining a flashlight on glittering ice.

"It took us an hour to chip our way through it," Smith said. "Made a hole just big enough to squeeze through and get some video. It was strange seeing the stars. It was horribly cold."

The video was of low quality – poor lighting – and there was nothing but snow. The hatch was located on a mild slope, the mountain rising to the left on the screen.

"Where's the door to the shaft?" Will asked.

"It's covered with snow," Smith replied and froze the video. "The edge of it is about 20 feet directly forward in this shot."

Will nodded. There was nothing to see. "Is that everything?"

"Yes," Smith replied.

"There are obvious things missing from this," Will said.

"Such as?" McHenry asked from the far end of the table.

"Power," Will replied. "How does the door open? Were there no conduits for cables?"

"No," Smith said. "And we looked for them."

"And what about a control room, or at least a control panel?" Will asked.

Smith nodded as if he had already worked through those questions. "Maybe we'll find something in one of the side tunnels," he suggested.

"What if the project is just unfinished?" Daniel asked. "Maybe they ran out of time."

"Or ran out of resources," McHenry added. "Their supplies must have diminished when the war ended."

"Is there anything else in this place that's unfinished?" Will asked, skeptical. "Even in the shaft, was there any evidence of unfinished business – brackets for pipes or conduits, loose wires, anything?"

Smith shook his head.

Will was more suspicious now than ever. He'd have to climb the tunnel himself. "I want to take a look," he said.

McHenry seemed to mull it over until he sighed and shook his head. "Fine," he said. "Get some rest and you and my best climber can hit it in the morning."

Will nodded.

"As for the rest of you," McHenry continued, "you should split up and start searching for anything connected to your cargo." He turned to Jacob. "You should assist my crew in unloading your crates, and then start assessing what we have to do with the equipment. You mentioned that something had to be assembled – the radioactive device."

"Yes, sir," Jacob said. "It's the RTG – we think its americium core needs to be replaced with the one from NASA."

"We have nuke engineers to assist with that," McHenry said. "For now, let's just devise a plan of operation."

Jacob nodded. "We'll need radiation shielding."

The captain nodded. "We'll start at 0500 hours, when my climber is on duty," he said as his communicator beeped. He nodded and walked out.

Will looked at the clock on the wall next to the entrance. The climb was going to start at 5:00 a.m. It would give him time for some much-needed rest – his internal clock was out of kilter. They were all readjusting to be on the same schedule as McHenry, who had hours that straddled the shifts of the crew.

"Are you sure you want to do this?" Denise asked.

"It's a ladder," Will replied. "I think I'll be okay."

She kicked his foot under the table and gave him an annoyed look. "It's a tall ladder."

"I think you should be careful while you explore," he said, and wasn't joking. "Who knows what the Nazis have here – and there could be booby-traps. And you should have a Geiger counter with you."

"I'm sure the captain will set us up with what we need," she said.

Will was happy to have a task that required some physical activity. From the alien devices to the shaft to the souls who roamed the ancient base, his mind was a web of confusion.

CHAPTER 15

Will was eating breakfast in the mess hall with Denise when a young sailor entered and approached him.

"Sir, I'm Ensign Sims," the man said. He was a wiry guy with gnarled hands. "Captain said we can start the climb whenever you're ready."

Will stood and shook his hand.

"I'm going to grab some nutrition bars and water for us while you finish breakfast," Sims said and then disappeared into the kitchen on the far end of the mess.

Will took another bite of scrambled eggs and followed it with the last of his orange juice.

"Be careful," Denise said, and kicked him lightly in the shin under the table.

"It's just a tall ladder," Will replied and stood as Sims reappeared.

He followed Sims off the *North Dakota* toward the room with the shaft. On the way, he learned that Sims had an abundance of climbing experience including ice climbing – an extremely technical sport. He was also a Machinist's Mate whose main responsibility was to conduct damage assessment and repairs of all mechanical systems.

"You should lead the way and make navigation decisions," Sims proposed. "We'll be linked in case either of us falls. It shouldn't be a problem – it's just a ladder – but the place is old. Something could break."

They went inside the shaft room and donned harnesses and gloves, and hats fitted with flashlights and cameras. They also strapped on light backpacks with the food and water Sims had collected, as well as other supplies.

They linked together with a 15-foot line, and climbed the rope ladder that led to the shaft.

The last time he'd been on a rope ladder, Will recalled, he'd been dodging gunfire and had fallen into the icy Weddell Sea. This time he shouldn't have any problems.

A minute later, they transferred from the rope to the metal ladders and climbed by clipping onto each successive rung with wrist latches. The devices were nylon straps that wrapped around the wrist with a climbing carabiner clip positioned against the muscle between the thumb and forefinger. The clip had a well-positioned trigger release. The idea was to clip onto each rung, rather than grabbing them with their hands, and to make sure one carabiner was engaged at all times. In addition to being safer, this would keep them from cutting their hands on sharp protrusions on the rungs, such as jagged welding spatter. After the first 50 feet, Will had already sliced one of his gloves.

At 300 feet they came to the first side tunnel, and Will stepped off the ladder into an oval inset carved into the rock. It was tall enough for him to stand, and had a flat floor.

"Let's take a look," Will said and moved into the passage, which was the same height as the entrance but was round, as if it had been cut with a circular boring machine.

The shaft angled slightly upward. Fifty feet in, it made a slight bend to the right. At 100 feet they came to a junction and could go either left or right. The new passage angled upward from left to right at a steep grade. The floor was flat and rough, and the footing was solid.

"What do you think?" Will asked. "Should we continue upward?"

Sims shrugged. "Maybe all of the service tunnels are connected."

That was Will's suspicion as well. "It would beat climbing the ladder all the way up."

As they proceeded, the tunnel inclined and followed a continuous curve to the right. After 10 minutes, they came to an entrance on the right and followed it. After about 100 feet, it terminated at an inset that was open to the main shaft. It was the next service channel up the shaft, a quarter of the way around the perimeter relative to the first one, and 150 feet above it.

"Guess they're all connected," Sims said.

They checked every access tunnel on the way up, but found them all to be similar – just featureless holes that led to the main shaft.

The final access tunnel led to a square, room-sized cavity that was open to the top of the main shaft.

Will peered over the edge. "It's a long way down," he commented.

The enormous door that capped the main shaft was faceted, but it looked like it opened and closed like an iris, or a camera shutter.

On the left wall of the inset when facing the shaft was a metal ladder that ascended to the hatch shown in the video. The question now was whether they were going to go outside and explore the surface.

"What do you think, Sims?" Will asked, nodding toward the hatch.

"Let's go for it," Sims said as he peeled off his backpack and started pulling things out.

"What are you looking for?"

"Don't tell the captain," Sims said as he threw a black, ski-mask style hat and a black thermal shirt to Will. "I figured you'd want to go outside. These are thermal clothes our Navy SEALs use. Don't know if they're good enough for winter in Antarctica, but they can't hurt."

"Good thinking," Will said as he and Sims donned the garments.

Will climbed the ladder and pulled the latch on the door. "Good thing the hatch opens inward," he said.

"Because of the snow?"

"That," Will replied, "and so we can't lock ourselves outside. How big of a mistake would that be?"

"Let's not do that," Sims replied, laughing nervously.

Will knew that there was no chance of that happening with him there – he'd just separate and open it from the inside.

Will lowered the hatch and was greeted with a blast of cold air and ice crystals that forced him to cover his eyes. "We forgot goggles," he joked as he climbed upward and squeezed through a narrow tunnel of ice to the surface.

Bits of ice and snow crunched beneath his feet as he moved out of the way for Sims.

In his six hours of early-morning surveillance, Lenny counted 11 Chinese operatives entering the apartment. He recognized three of them. They composed the head of the dragon – minus Tao – and they were all in one place. That was a mistake.

It was just 9:00 a.m., so he figured it was unlikely everyone was present, considering that their operation was planned for the following evening. However, it was a good time for him to start setting up.

If he were to eliminate everyone in the apartment, there'd be no one left who knew him – at least not in the upper echelon. He'd be free of Chinese intelligence. He was assuming that the CIA would keep its promise and make sure that Tao, and the assassin they'd captured at Syncorp in Baton Rouge, would never see the light of day. To him, that meant they'd be juiced. He wasn't sure what it meant to the CIA.

The Chinese ops were gathering in a two-bedroom apartment on the top floor of a five-story brick building. If they'd been in a house, he would've considered burning it to the ground with them trapped inside. But he couldn't burn down the entire apartment building. Although some collateral damage was usually inevitable, that much was not professional.

The previous evening, Lenny had disguised himself as a maintenance man and taken the building's elevator to the roof. After some brainstorming, he'd devised a way to accomplish his task.

He'd recalled seeing an assortment of equipment and supplies in the back of Tao's safe house. It seemed that the place used to be a large repair shop for heavy machinery, such as earthmovers and trucks. Tao had most of the place cleaned out, but some of the old contents had been kept and stored in a shed behind the building. This included tools, tanks of used oil, and a large assortment of compressed gas cylinders. It was the gas cylinders that interested him.

Lenny leaned back in the seat of the van and lit a cigarette. It was a cool morning, and a light breeze passed through the open windows. He was parked on a cross street with a good line of sight to the entrance of the building. He'd mounted a camera on the van's side mirror and wired the feed into his laptop. It was easier on the eyes, and was better for the forthcoming nighttime surveillance.

The night before, he'd also threaded a camera through an air vent on the roof of the building to a vent in the living room of the apartment. It was a CIA device that had a wireless transmitter capable of transmitting the 100 yards to his computer. It also had a microphone. Although Lenny did not understand Chinese, the feed was streamed to a CIA team in Space Systems.

The group of Chinese operatives had been congregating for days. Lenny figured the CIA should now have a good idea of what they were planning.

He'd notified Thackett of his cleanup method, and was awaiting his approval. Lenny would make his move around midnight.

THE COLD WAS like nothing Will had experienced before.

That wasn't completely true. It was like nothing he'd experienced in nature. He'd been exposed to a lot during his time in the Red Box, including hypothermia.

The wind howled somewhere in the distance, but the air was calm.

He looked to the sky. Constellations of stars that were foreign to him sparkled with an intensity he'd never before witnessed, and they reached all the way down to the horizon.

"I've never seen anything like it," Sims remarked, his face tilted upward and panning back and forth. He was already shivering.

"We're looking almost directly along the South Pole," Will said, tilting his head directly upward. "Strange."

They were standing on a level plateau about the size of a football field.

To Will's right were Sims and the hatch. To his left was the main door, buried in snow. About 40 meters behind him, the mountain sloped upward and peaked at about 500 feet above the plateau. He panned the flashlight along the surface in front of him until it disappeared about 50 or 60 meters away. It seemed that the plateau dropped off at that point.

The two men were still tethered together, giving Will about a 15-foot leash to explore the surroundings if Sims stayed near the hatch. It would give him enough range to get to the edge of the large door.

Will scanned the light on the surface where the main door should have been. He couldn't tell if his eyes were playing tricks on him, but he thought he saw its circular rim. He got on his knees and dug through the snow with his hands. The climbing gloves protected his fingernails, but they did nothing to keep his hands warm.

After a few minutes, he reached frozen gravel, and peeled back a stone-impregnated shard of ice to reveal a gray, metallic surface. It seemed that the door was painted and covered in gravel so that it couldn't be spotted from the air. "We should snap a few pictures," he said.

"On it," Sims said and pulled out a small camera and began snapping.

When he was finished, Will figured Sims got over 30 shots of the main door and the surrounding area.

"What do you think?" Will asked and nodded toward the western horizon. "Have a look over the edge?"

Sims was silent for a few seconds. "You think it's okay?" he finally asked.

"The plateau looks pretty flat all the way," Will said. "And I think I see bare rock in places, so I doubt we'll have any trouble."

Will noticed that Sims was shivering as badly as he was, but he thought this was a rare opportunity to get a look over the lake beneath the plateau, and they should take advantage of it.

Maintaining their separation, Will led the way.

The footing remained solid and the breeze picked up as they approached the drop-off. When he got close, he crawled on his belly and peeked his head over the edge.

Will waved Sims over. They were on a flat ledge of solid rock, with no chance of sliding off with a loose sheet of ice.

Sims slid in next to him and peered over the edge.

It started with a sheer drop of about 1,000 feet, and then sloped gradually to the lake they'd previously seen only from below its surface.

The lake was black except for the reflection of the sliver of moon on the horizon, which was out of view when they were away from the edge. The lake was frozen and clean. Perhaps the wind kept the thin skin of ice free of snow.

"I can hardly believe I'm seeing this," Sims said. "It's beautiful."

"It's like another planet," Will remarked and then turned his head back, in the direction of the hatch. "We've got a long climb down."

"Yup," Sims said as he took a few snapshots of the lake and backed away from the edge.

As they made their way back to the hatch Will took a few deep breaths of the clean cold air. The black silhouette of the mountain peak rose into the blanket of stars above. The Earth was an inconsequential speck of dust on the windshield of the universe. Did any of it mean anything? – the planet, or the life that resided upon it? And what about life elsewhere, in other parts of creation? Did it matter to him? Did it matter to anyone? All he could do was live locally, in time and space. He had to deal with what was happening around him in the present and the immediate future.

The mystery was becoming increasingly convoluted. Why the probe? Why the signal? And, now, what was the purpose of the shaft? What did this all have to do with Landau's instructions for him to find answers at the Nazi base? What did this have to do with the "existential implications" professed by the late Horace, and by Landau?

Will had no answers. Only intuitions. He was in the right place for now.

THE CLIMB DOWN was swift as Will and Sims followed the tunnel that spiraled around the main shaft. They stopped when they got to the lowest access tunnel, which was marked with an empty water bottle. The tunnel continued past it, leading further downward.

"We should see what's at the bottom," Will said.

Sims agreed. "It's another 300 feet to the floor," he commented.

The tunnel continued to corkscrew downward, around the shaft. Ten minutes later, they came to a doorway cut into the stone, but it was blocked off.

"Dead end," Will said.

Sims examined the edges of the doorway. "That's strange," he said. "There's a seam."

Will stepped closer and aimed his flashlight at the inner edge of the doorway. "It looks like a slab of stone is blocking it," Will said.

Sims pushed on it in different places, but it didn't budge.

"Let me have a look," Will said as he sat on the floor and leaned against the wall.

"What are you doing?" Sims asked, confused.

Will concentrated and separated. He passed through two feet of stone and found himself in the shaft room, near the rope ladder, where they'd started their climb. Directly above was the opening to the main shaft. Sailors were milling about, moving out the perforated steel sheets that had previously concealed the shaft.

Will turned around to get a view of the slab through which he'd just passed. It was enormous, and spanned one entire wall of the shaft room – to the left of the room's entrance when entering from the bay. From inside the shaft room, it looked just like all of the other walls.

The blocked doorway through which he'd just passed was on the far left of the slab. He instead passed back through the center of the slab, and entered a dark circular tunnel of the same diameter as the vertical shaft.

He continued down the tunnel until he'd exhausted his range – about 100 meters – and then returned to his body.

He opened his eyes, and Sims was staring at him with a concerned expression. He had a water bottle in his hand and looked as if he was going to douse him.

Will held up his hand. "Please, don't."

"You okay?"

Will stood up. "Beyond this slab is the main shaft room," he explained and then patted the wall to the left of the doorway. "To our left is a hidden tunnel."

Sims stared back at him with a bewildered look. "How do you know that?"

Will shook his head. "You were on the *North Dakota* when the probe was triggered, right?"

Sims nodded.

"How do you think that happened?"

Sims shook his head. "Only rumors."

"The rumors are true," Will said. "We need to get into that tunnel."

LENNY LIT a cigarette and took a deep drag. From his rooftop perch, he looked out at the stars as he exhaled. A stiff breeze dissipated the smoke.

It was 11:30 p.m. He'd hauled a large cylinder of carbon monoxide gas to the roof via the building's service elevator earlier that evening. It was a newer cylinder than the others in the shed behind the former heavy equipment repair shop – now Chinese safe house – and Lenny had the suspicion that Tao had purchased it for his own use. He'd noticed gas connections to one of the shop's hidden rooms. It must have been a kill room.

Lenny wore a pair of overalls and had placed a sticker that read "Nitrogen" over the carbon monoxide label. If anyone asked, he was an air conditioner repairman. It fit the cover perfectly since AC repairmen often used compressed gas to clear out blocked drainage systems.

There were now 17 people in the apartment – thirteen men and four women. Most were Chinese operatives, but there were a couple of Americans, and at least one Russian. It made him wonder if the Russians and the Chinese were cooperating.

Lenny found the air handling system for their fifth-floor apartment. It was the top floor, so he was able to verify the path of the ductwork. The AC supply and return ducts were labeled with apartment numbers, but he'd made sure that they were labeled correctly. The last thing he wanted to do was kill off an innocent family.

The CIA had been monitoring the group's conversations through the tiny camera-microphone device Lenny had installed in the apartment the previous evening. The Chinese network was finalizing plans for the assault on Space Systems, and was coordinating special ops that were gathering in two other locations. The CIA and FBI were on both scenes and ready to pounce.

He fed about 10 feet of hose through a tight-fitting hole in the supply duct that took cooled air into the apartment. When the time was right, he'd start the gas flow, and monitor the return air for carbon monoxide content. He was fortunate that the building was recently renovated, and the smoke and carbon monoxide detectors were on a dedicated circuit that was accessible from an external breaker panel. It saved him from having to devise a way to get into the apartment beforehand to disable them.

He was waiting on two text messages. The first came at 11:36 p.m., indicating that both apartment exits, the inner door and fire escape exit, were sealed. The next came at 11:38 p.m. informing him that all communications would be jammed in 60 seconds.

He waited a full minute after he lost cell phone reception before opening the cylinder's valve. He dialed the regulator to fully open. The flowing gas hissed deep in the duct.

After 10 minutes, he inserted a carbon monoxide monitor into the apartment's AC return duct. It was already at a dangerous level.

He picked up a hand-held monitor that received the camera feed on an unjammed frequency. Ten of the 17 occupants were in view, four of whom were standing and pacing. The others were seated on a hodgepodge of furniture. One was attempting to make a call on his cell phone and looked frustrated with the loss of service.

After 20 minutes, they had all found places to sit or lie down. A few minutes later, a woman sitting on a stool and resting her head on the kitchen counter rolled to the side and hit headfirst on the tile floor. One of the men got up from an upholstered chair and stumbled over to help her, but instead fell on the woman and rolled onto his back. One man staggered to the exit and tugged at the door in futility. He collapsed a few seconds later and sprawled face down on the floor. Lenny figured the same was happening to those in the other rooms since no one came out in response to the noise.

He looked at the gauge on the regulator. It would take another 10 minutes to empty, and he'd let it all go. After that, he'd pull the hose, turn off the AC blower, and wait for 15 minutes. He'd then restart the blower in order to clear the deadly gas out of the apartment, and take the empty cylinder down to the building's rear parking lot where a CIA operative was waiting with a van.

Lenny lit a cigarette and took a deep drag. He'd have another 17 souls to add to his long list. He wasn't proud of it – it had to be done – but he did get some satisfaction that the world would be a better place without those people in it. China was going to lose this battle.

AFTER RETURNING from the climb late that afternoon, Will and Sims reported what they'd found. The captain had been aggravated that they'd ventured out to the surface, but his displeasure seemed to be offset by their discoveries.

Going on midnight, the whole CIA group along with McHenry, Diggs, and a few of the crew faced the wall beneath the vertical shaft.

"The Nazis went to great trouble to conceal this," McHenry said. "It's not clear how they even got such a massive piece of rock in here."

"They also hid the opening to the shaft," Daniel added as he glanced to the hole in the ceiling.

Will thought mounting perforated steel on the ceiling was nothing compared to moving a slab of stone the size of the foundation of an average-size house.

"We'll probably have to blast it apart," McHenry said.

"How long will that take?" Will asked.

Thackett nodded to Diggs, who returned the nod and left.

"Probably a few hours. Diggs is on it," McHenry replied. "Otherwise, I have some other important information."

Will didn't like the tone of the captain's voice, nor his guarded expression. He seemed anxious.

"China has people on the ground," McHenry explained. "They're searching for us, and the base. About 100 special ops types."

"In this weather?" Daniel asked. "It's a suicide mission."

"They seem willing to risk anything at this point," McHenry said.

"What do you mean?" Sylvia asked.

"As you know," McHenry continued, "they were planning to attack a CIA facility on US soil. That, I've been informed, is under control. However, the target of that operation is now here."

"What do you mean?" Sylvia asked.

"He means me," Will said. His anxiety ratcheted up a click, even though he had the feeling that the Chinese ops didn't pose the greatest threat.

McHenry nodded.

"If they were willing to attack on US soil," Daniel said, "what's stopping them from doing the same here?"

"Precisely," McHenry said and nodded. "And without restraint."

"What does that mean?" Jonathan asked.

"We need to keep moving forward," McHenry said, seeming to ignore the question. He turned to Daniel. "What's your plan?"

"We need to find out what's at the end of that tunnel," Will said before Daniel had a chance to answer.

Daniel nodded. "Yes, and the rest of this place needs to be explored and mapped."

"My crew will continue exploring," McHenry said.

Daniel nodded. "It's clear that this project – the construction and operation of this base – was much larger than we'd imagined," he said. "And it seems that the Nazis weren't the ones to construct it."

Will was certain they hadn't.

THE CYLINDER WAS EMPTY. Everyone inside the apartment was motionless.

Lenny pulled out the gas tube and coiled it up.

Cell phone jamming had ceased, and he sent a text informing his collaborators that he'd start airing out the apartment in 15 minutes. The additional time would ensure that everyone in the apartment got a heavy dose of the deadly gas.

When it was time, he powered up the AC unit and blower, and informed the rest of the crew that the apartment would be clear in 20 minutes.

He carted the five-foot-tall cylinder to the service elevator, and rode it down to the mechanical maintenance room on the first floor. He exited into a parking lot in the rear of the building, and loaded the empty cylinder into the back of a van.

As the van drove off, he approached a small gray car. As he got close, the trunk popped open and he extracted a black canvas duffel bag, slung it over his shoulder, and gently closed the trunk. The man in the driver's seat glanced at him through the rearview mirror.

Lenny checked his watch, walked over to a dumpster, and lit a cigarette. He took a deep drag and looked at the moon, which had just come into view through the trees. He hoped that what he was about to do would be his last task in this line of work.

He finished the cigarette, ground out the butt with his boot, picked it up, and slipped it into his front pocket.

He went back into the building and rode the passenger elevator to the fifth floor.

He found apartment 504 and knocked softly. The door opened, he entered, and the door closed behind him.

"Ready to clean this up?" said the man at the door.

It was Agent Schroeder, the CIA operative who had given him advice on the retirement service, if that's what it was.

Lenny nodded as he pulled out a hand-held carbon monoxide detector and pressed a button to analyze the air. All was clear, although he knew there could be residual pockets of the gas trapped in closets and cabinets. That would dissipate with time.

"Three of these people are native-born Americans," Schroeder said. "Two Caucasians – a male and a female – and an African-American female."

Lenny nodded. He wasn't surprised. Anyone could be turned if offered enough, or threatened with the right thing.

"There's also a Russian – definitely an intelligence op," Schroeder added.

Lenny knew the Russians had their noses in everything, but was surprised and concerned that they'd cooperate with China. It was unusual.

Lenny turned his head in the direction of a rummaging noise coming from a back room.

"They're collecting all of their laptops, storage devices, and papers, and exchanging their mobiles with burner phones containing evidence that fits the story," Schroeder explained as he walked over to two duffel bags on the dining room table. He unzipped one of them, revealing rolls of cash. They looked dirty and used. "This is about 25 thousand."

"I'll put that in one of the closets," Lenny said.

"I was thinking in the pullout bed in the couch," Schroeder suggested.

All the same, Lenny thought.

Schroeder opened the other duffel, revealing bricks of brown powder packed in clear plastic bags and wrapped in transparent packing tape. It was heroin.

"The toilet tank?" Lenny suggested.

Schroeder shrugged and nodded. "That works. We put the fentanyl in the freezer," he said, and then pointed to the duffel bag that hung from Lenny's shoulder. "You ready to go with that?"

Lenny set the bag at his feet and unzipped it, revealing a large nail gun.

"You know the method?" Schroeder asked.

"Two in the head, one in the eye."

"It's a brutal world."

Lenny nodded. This particular display of brutality would be a reenactment of a scene carried out by a Mexican drug cartel in Juarez. It wasn't difficult to get guns down there, especially for the cartels, but guns were noisy – even with silencers – and traceable. Nail guns, on the other hand, not so much.

Lenny waited as the operatives in the back rooms completed their collection of materials and left.

"Try to get out in 15 minutes," Schroeder said as he exited. "We'll be nearby."

Lenny knew that they'd be keeping watch for anything unusual from the outside as he finished the job. It was a luxury he appreciated.

He took Schroeder's advice and put the drug cash in the foldout bed. Next, he put half the heroin in the toilet tank, and the rest behind the refrigerator.

He then went back to the living room and took the nail gun out of the duffel and connected the battery. He then loaded a stack of 3.5-inch framing nails.

He walked over to the couch and put the first shot into its wooden arm. It popped a little louder than he liked, but the head of the nail was buried a quarter inch below the surface.

He examined the array of bodies scattered about the floor and devised an efficient order in his head. He walked over to a man near one of the windows in the front room. He was on his side, so Lenny pushed him over with his foot. He recognized the man: he had been one of his handlers in the past. He put the first nail in the center of the man's forehead. It ended up going through the skull and popping out behind the left ear. Blood ran out of the holes, making Lenny suspect that he wasn't dead. He was going to be.

Lenny reduced the power slightly and then popped the man on the top of the head. It still went through. He reduced the power again and fired the final one into the man's eye. He pushed on the man's head with his boot to check something. It was as he'd suspected: the nail had gone through the back of the skull and nailed it to the floor.

He dialed the power back another click and gave the others the same treatment. He only had to reload once.

There were two other rooms.

When he entered the first one he nearly screamed. A man stood next to the wall, dazed. He'd somehow survived the carbon monoxide and must have been recovering.

Lenny put the nail gun up to the man's forehead and pulled the trigger. The nail drove in all the way, making a dimple in the skin. The man just stood there while blood trickled around the nail head and down his nose.

Lenny put the second nail in his right eye, and the man dropped heavily to the floor and convulsed.

He put a third nail in the top of his head, but the convulsions got more violent.

Lenny had seen enough. He held the man's head to the floor with his foot and put the nail gun to his temple. He popped him three more times before the convulsions stopped. The body continued to twitch.

When he took his foot off the man's head, he could tell it was nailed to the floor. He was probably going to have nightmares about this one.

There were two women on the floor in the second room, and Lenny finished the job.

He went back to the front room, disassembled the nail gun, and put it in the bag. He checked the peephole to make sure the hallway was clear, and then exited and went to the elevator. He went out the back door, into the parking lot, and walked casually to the back of the gray car from which he'd acquired the nail gun. The trunk popped open as he approached. He set the bag inside and closed the trunk gently. The car started and drove off as he walked through the gate of a chain-link fence at the back of the property.

He emerged on a dirt path in an empty lot that meandered through tall grass and bushes. He stopped, removed his overalls, and balled them up under his arms. He followed the path to the back of a restaurant and threw the overalls into a reeking dumpster. He then hiked to the next street, got into his CIA-issued SUV, and headed to Space Systems.

It was done.

LENNY WAS TAKEN to a room he hadn't been to before, deep in the bowels of the Space Systems building.

There were at least a dozen people sitting at computers and wearing headsets. Monitors showing live camera feeds were arrayed on the front wall. He recognized one of the feeds. It showed the scene of his latest cleanup operation.

"Everything has gone as planned," Thackett said as he walked up to him. He pointed to one of the live feed monitors on the wall.

The image was dark, but Lenny could make out the silhouette of a large building.

"That was where a contingent of Chinese special ops assembled," Thackett continued. "They made it easy for us by gathering in an abandoned barn about 40 miles outside Alexandria. There were 24 of them, and we took 20 alive."

"No police?" Lenny asked.

Thackett shook his head. "The whole thing took about 90 seconds. There was a lot of shooting, but most of the weapons were fitted with silencers. Everyone was out of there 10 minutes after the shooting stopped."

Lenny thought it seemed to be a well-planned operation. But it would only take one person with a phone to get a video of the whole thing. Every operation carried that risk.

"There's something else," Thackett said. "I want you to be around for a couple more weeks."

Lenny was hoping to be on his way to the airport in the next few days, but knew that it never worked out like that. Big messes turned into medium and then small messes before they were fully cleaned up. "Something else happening?"

Thackett nodded. "Of the 24 operatives in the barn, four of them were Russian – one was killed in action."

Lenny nodded. "There was a Russian in the apartment as well."

"He was Russian intelligence," Thackett said. "It's unusual for China and Russia to cooperate in this way."

Lenny thought it was more than "unusual." It was unnerving.

"With the Russian involvement, you can see why I want you to stick around for a while," Thackett said.

Lenny nodded. He had intimate knowledge of how Russian intelligence operated, and had the advantage of knowing the language.

"Once the local threats are eliminated," Thackett continued, "you'll be out of the business. It will be a couple of weeks, at most."

Lenny knew the deal he'd made with Thackett, but the idea that he'd be out in "a couple of weeks" still took him by surprise. This time the light at the end of the tunnel was real. The Chinese network was decimated. His criminal record would be cleared. He had enough money to live on until he died of old age. The next question would be where to go.

"When will you know things are complete?" Lenny asked.

"Our problems with the Chinese – and possibly the Russians – are about to enter a new phase," Thackett said. "Once that occurs, the conflict will be elevated to a new level, and concentrated elsewhere. This will mean that we can employ new methods domestically. That's when you will be free to disappear."

"Is this heading for war?" Lenny asked. "With the apartment operation and the four killed on the farm, that's 21 gone."

Thackett shrugged. "Even our domestic law enforcement will know something's up," he said. "But autopsies will show those in the apartment all died of carbon monoxide poisoning, and were then plugged with a nail gun to make a statement. The method will be traced back to a drug cartel – or to one of their copycats – not to us."

Lenny figured that as well. But he didn't think it would matter. Conspiracy theories were ubiquitous.

"And the barn scene is completely cleaned up – no bodies to find," Thackett added. "Besides, we're already at war with China on a number of levels."

"What happened at the third location?" Lenny asked. He knew that three operations were supposed to occur simultaneously.

"A warehouse in Alexandria," Thackett said. "Captured eight operatives. They had chemical weapons – enough to kill thousands."

Lenny flinched. "They were going to kill everyone in Space Systems?"

Thackett nodded. "We're interrogating them now," he explained. "And Tao, too."

"What are you looking to get out of them?" He'd hoped Tao was already dead.

"If we can confirm an order from the level above Tao, there might be further action."

"In what sense?"

"In the military sense," Thackett said. "We'll hit their navy, or the China mainland."

Lenny's mind seemed to pickle in the information. He'd seen a lot, and done a lot, but he'd never been involved in such a high-stakes, geopolitical skirmish. It was events like these that could escalate to world war.

"We can't let something like this pass," Thackett continued. "Otherwise our enemies will think there are no consequences for their actions. It weakens us – makes us more vulnerable."

Lenny understood. "What do you want me to do?"

"Make yourself scarce for a while," Thackett said. "Be reachable – by phone and secure email. I don't foresee any big operations, but I might have some smaller things for you to do – off the books."

Lenny nodded. Every mission he'd carried out was off the books.

WILL SAT up and almost hit his head on the bunk above him. Jacob was at the door.

"They blasted through the wall," Jacob said, clearly excited. "There's an enormous tunnel."

Will already knew that. He looked at the clock fastened to the bunk above him. It was 8:00 a.m. – he'd slept for six hours. The climb must have taken its toll. "On my way," he said as he pivoted and put his feet on the floor.

He donned his Navy-issued clothes, and stopped by the mess hall to grab a bagel on the way out. The others were waiting in the bay.

"It's huge," Denise said as they walked into the chamber where the vertical shaft was located.

The first things Will noticed were the smell of sulfur and the fine white dust on the floor. A jagged hole had been blown in the stone slab that had concealed the tunnel. The hole was large enough for a car to pass through.

"We drilled holes in the hope of forming a symmetric opening," a sailor explained. "But the slab is over two feet thick, so it didn't form the way we intended. And we still need to blast a hole to the doorway leading to the service tunnel."

Will stepped over some rocky debris and through the opening. The ceiling was arched, as if the passage had been first bored as a circular tunnel, and the floor had been leveled afterward. Caged lights were inset into the walls, less than half of which were illuminated.

"This is unbelievable," Will said. He hadn't noticed the lights when he'd separated. "Were the lights on when you blasted through?"

"No, sir," one of the sailors said. "We found a switch."

Will walked up to one of the lights. It was a filament bulb inside a wire cage. A conduit above the fixture extended to his left, deeper into the tunnel and toward the next light, and to his right, where it terminated at a hole in the rock. Wires emerged from the end of the conduit and disappeared into the hole.

"The tunnel looks like it was cut the same way as the shaft," Will said.

Daniel looked over Will's shoulder, and Will turned to see what had distracted him.

Six crewmembers walked in from the bay. They were armed and wearing backpacks. McHenry followed.

"I thought you'd want to get started right away," McHenry said. "These guys are going along. They have tools, and food and water. And, just in case, weapons."

There was no way of knowing how far the tunnel went into the mountain, or what they'd find at the end. But Will agreed that it was possible they'd encounter Chinese ops.

Minutes later, they were trekking down the tunnel. The sailors led the way with flashlights, which they turned on only when a long string of the wall-mounted lights was out.

They headed away from the lake, inland, toward the geographic South Pole. It was easier to specify directions relative to permanent landmarks, since using a compass near one of the Earth's magnetic poles was unreliable, and GPS signals did not penetrate the mountain. The other option was the hand-held inertial navigation device that one of the crew carried. The device employed a high-precision gyroscope, which measured relative changes in direction. Before they'd started down the tunnel, the initial direction had been defined by a line connecting two rock features in the bay. It kept an electronic log that would later be used to generate a map of the tunnel system.

Two hundred meters in, the tunnel started to slope downward at a noticeable grade.

As they descended, nearly a kilometer in, the air cooled to the point where Will could see his breath. Their Navy-issued jumpsuits were insufficient for the temperature, but they kept moving forward.

After a half hour of walking, nearly two kilometers from the entrance, something seemed to change in the distance. About 100 meters ahead, the lighting seemed different, and the tunnel leveled and widened. Everyone seemed to pick up pace.

When they were 50 meters away, it was clear that the tunnel terminated in a bright chamber.

When they were 20 meters from the end, one of the armed sailors stopped them. He then moved forward, scanning his head in all directions as he proceeded.

When Will thought it was clear, he joined the sailor.

The passage widened sharply at the end. The lights were the same as those in the tunnel, but were haphazardly mounted about irregularly shaped walls. In the center of the wall that marked the end of the tunnel was an enormous steel slab. It was actually four plates, each eight feet tall and four feet wide. They were welded together, side by side.

"That looks like submarine steel," Jacob remarked. "Extremely hard."

"And welded to a steel frame that's anchored into the stone," Will added. "No handles or hinges."

"How did we not know anything about this tunnel?" Daniel asked.

"It wasn't mentioned in any of the files or notebooks," Sylvia said. "Although, we haven't read everything yet."

"Perhaps this was done at the very end," Daniel added.

Will touched the metal with his hands. It was warmer than the air. He turned his eyes to the ceiling, where stone blended into the metal structure behind the plate. The stone there had been chipped away in a fashion that didn't match the rest of the tunnel. It was as if the Nazis had retrofitted a frame and metal barrier into an existing opening.

Will noticed something in the corner to the left of the steel barrier, and went to examine it. It was chunks of metal and spent welding rods. He picked up a small piece of the metal and handed it to Jacob. "Looks like it was cut with a torch."

"Crude construction," Jacob said. "Seems like they were in a hurry to seal it off."

"Where are we exactly?" Will asked.

"Close to the other side of the mountain, opposite the lake," Daniel replied.

"How thick is the ice here?" Will asked.

"Between two and three kilometers," Daniel said.

"So there could be things buried so deep in the ice that they've never been seen by humans?" Will asked.

Daniel nodded.

"What are you getting at?" Jonathan asked.

"Not sure," Will said. "But it's time someone had a look behind that steel plate."

Will sat on the floor near the steel barrier, and separated.

Lenny had been ordered to lay low while things cooled down, and decided to head out of town. He'd narrowed down his destinations to Myrtle Beach or Key West. At the last minute, he chose Florida.

The heat could be miserable to some people, but it kept his pain at bay. The dull aches of old injuries, especially gunshot wounds and broken bones, resurfaced when it was cold and damp. The heat softened it all. He also planned to consume some alcohol.

As he waited at the gate in Dulles Airport, he caught the news on one of the many televisions mounted about the terminal. One story was of a horrible massacre in the DC area carried out by a drug cartel. More than 15 members of a Chinese drug ring had been executed in a horrific way – no details given.

Lenny thought that the targets had actually suffered very little. It looked ugly in the end, but it was one of the more humane mass assassinations he'd carried out.

Another story popped up that he knew was significant. The conflict between the US and China was heating up. China was making maneuvers in international waters in the Pacific, and readying military aircraft for action – including nuke-capable bombers. There was no doubt in his mind that their movements were in response to the extermination of the Chinese intelligence network. They were all dead or missing. As Thackett had said, the next round of events would be on another level – one where Lenny's skills would not be as useful.

The last time Lenny had been in an airport, attempting to leave his professional life, he'd been reeled back in at the last minute. Chinese intelligence had marked him the entire way, and, just before his flight boarded, an old man had slipped him a business card with a thinly veiled warning. He couldn't help but imagine that they were on his tail again, only this time they'd be there to eliminate him. His edginess was natural: a little paranoia was healthy.

He had an hour before his flight was to board, so he took a stroll through the shops as he searched for coffee. What he really wanted was a smoke, but the airport had eliminated the smoking room. Caffeine would have to do.

After a few minutes, he located a coffee kiosk and got into a line behind a dozen other customers. Five minutes later, he'd placed his order and moved to another counter where he waited for his beverage. The man in line immediately behind him stepped to his side and sighed.

"Always a line at this place," the man said.

Lenny grunted and nodded. He glanced at the man and turned back to the counter. He processed the image in his mind. The man was about six feet tall, dark hair and eyes, mid-50s, olive skin, and with a dark gray scruff on his face. Lenny had detected a weak accent and was trying to identify it.

The barista called Lenny's alias – Leon – to get his coffee, and followed with "Avi," who followed closely behind.

Lenny started to walk away when Avi said, "Leon, may we chat for a minute?"

The muscles in Lenny's forearms tensed, and his hand clenched and popped the plastic lid off of his cup. He adjusted his grip just in time to save it from falling to the floor. He noted that the man had emphasized his name in a way that brought its authenticity into question.

"Name's Avi," the man said and nodded toward an empty terminal across the walkway.

Lenny followed him to a window overlooking the tarmac. He had the feeling he was going to miss another flight.

"How can I help you?" Lenny asked.

"It's urgent that you get this to your employer immediately," Avi said as he handed Lenny a small data storage device. "The Chinese are about to initiate coordinated operations in the US and Antarctica."

The accent was Israeli. "I think we've eradicated the domestic threat."

"No," Avi said. "You've foiled plan A. Plan B is about to start."

"All of their operatives have been eliminated – or are on the run," Lenny argued. "Not sure how they could reorganize – "

"It only takes one person to distribute a biological agent through the air handling system of the Space Systems building," Avi cut in.

"We've already disrupted those plans."

"Again, there's a backup," Avi said. "This one originates on Plum Island."

Thoughts of Jennifer Chung came to Lenny's mind, along with those of her deceased professor, who had allegedly been poisoned with ricin.

"And bigger things are occurring in the south," Avi added. "And it's not just China."

"Russia," Lenny said.

Avi nodded.

"Why not deliver this information directly to the US Government?"

"My government is in the process of doing just that," Avi replied. "However, the US president is not well informed of the details of what has transpired here in the past days, and my usual go-between with the CIA director is currently in Antarctica. Besides, you'd be the asset they'd call upon for this kind of operation."

"I was on my way out."

"Yeah, so am I," Avi said and grinned. "And I have been for the past decade."

Lenny sighed and put the data device in his pocket.

"Good luck," Avi said, and then disappeared into foot traffic.

Lenny sat down and gazed out the window as he took a sip of hot coffee. He tried to relax as he thought about how to proceed. He was being sucked back into the fray. Again. But it was clear that his services might be required.

He took out his CIA phone and sent a text to Director Thackett.

WILL PASSED through the steel plate and into a room the size of an average movie theater.

Light emanated uniformly from the walls and 40-foot ceiling.

Everything was smooth and white, and the floor was polished, but riddled with footprints near the steel barrier.

The wall opposite the steel-plate barrier was curved like a movie screen. A few feet above the floor, a horizontal surface jutted outward – like a countertop or desktop – that spanned the entire 50-foot width of the room. He thought it might be an instrument console, but there were no buttons or controls, except for one round hole, about three inches in diameter, located near the center.

He moved in closer and examined the surface around the hole. They were faint, but symbols were etched into the surface. They were of the same script as that in the alien drawings. He could almost read them – like words on the tip of his tongue that he just couldn't verbalize.

He turned his attention to the rest of the console and followed it to each of its ends, where it curled around the corner on each side and continued another few feet down the side walls.

He passed through the wall behind the console. The space was jammed floor to ceiling with circuitry and mechanisms that he could not identify. He continued deeper, through another wall, a few feet of rock, and then into ice, and then continued until he exhausted his range, which was another 75 yards.

He explored in all directions and confirmed that the tunnel went through the mountain, as they'd suspected. The rock above the ceiling of the room was about 20 feet thick, beyond which was ice.

He reentered his body and stood. Everyone was staring at him.

"It's a control room of some kind," Will said and described in detail what he'd seen. "Looks like there's a missing component."

"Nazis took it?" Daniel asked.

Will nodded. He thought he knew what that missing part was.

"We need to get inside," Sylvia said. "We need to cut through this plate."

The walkie-talkies were of no use in the tunnels, so they headed back toward the *North Dakota* to inform Captain McHenry of their find.

They'd return with a cutting torch, and warmer clothes.

WILL TWITCHED with every step as they trekked back to the *North Dakota*.

It was as if his nerves were held at high voltage and every stimulus caused them to fire in unison. His brain processed multiple thoughts in parallel and he couldn't keep track of everything. But they were converging toward something. Images of the symbols next to the empty port on the console kept coming back to him.

"Power encoder key," Will whispered under his breath.

"What?" Denise asked. She was walking next to him.

"The open port," Will replied. "The script reads 'power encoder key.'" The meaning came to him from the place in his mind where foreign thoughts were stored – memories that had belonged to someone else.

Denise must have assumed that he was guessing, and he left it at that.

A half hour later they arrived at the *North Dakota* and informed McHenry of what they'd found. The captain said a team would be ready in a few hours with the equipment needed to cut through the steel barrier.

Will went back to his quarters and opened his laptop. The decrypted drawings and text were stored on the drive. It was the long text that interested him this time.

Until now, everyone had concentrated on the drawings, and the text associated specifically with them. He was now convinced that the drawings didn't matter – everything was already constructed. In his mind, it made the numerous volumes of technical drawings nothing more than a colossal maintenance manual, like that which comes with a new car. But he thought the extensive amount of text, which seemed to be separate from the drawings, might provide information about the purpose of whatever was behind the steel barrier.

He found the text document. It was 128 pages of dense script. He zoomed in on the first page, stared at the title, and concentrated.

A few minutes passed as his eyes switched back and forth

between the title and the first line of the main text. It was right at the edge of his mind. Another minute passed and he grunted in frustration and set the laptop on his bunk. He stood and ran his fingers through his hair as he took in a deep breath and blew it out with force.

He paced in the small room for a few minutes and tried to calm his mind, and then went back to the text.

The title had four sets of characters – four words, if that's what they were – and he stared at each for a few seconds and tried to read them aloud. He was about to give up before he widened his view and concentrated on the entire title at once. It was like a switch had been thrown.

The four foreign words translated to "To the Next Generation." He scrambled to his backpack, pulled out a notebook and a pen, and wrote it down. He went back to the screen and kept his vision wider, taking in a few words simultaneously. The first line beneath the title read: "If you have received this message, you have triggered a series of events that will annihilate all life on your world."

His stomach churned as he considered the meaning of what he'd read. It was a confirmation of what, deep in his mind, he'd already known.

His hand trembled as he wrote down the words.

He looked to the next sentence and was convinced he could continue reading, but the process of writing it down was too slow.

He grabbed the laptop and notebook and navigated the narrow walkways to Denise's quarters. He knocked, and a female voice told him to come in. It was Sylvia.

"Where's Denise?" he asked.

"Mess hall," Sylvia replied.

"Come with me," he said and exited for the galley.

He found Denise rummaging through a pile of meal replacement bars.

She turned and looked at him with wide eyes.

"I need your help," he said. "I need you to type as I read."

"What's going on?" she asked. "What are you reading?"

"The text from the decrypted AM signal," he replied. "I translated the first line." He handed her his notebook.

She looked at it and then back to him. "I can't read this," she said and handed the notebook to Sylvia."

"What?" he asked. "Why?"

"It's in German," Sylvia said and handed the notebook to him.

Will stared at his scribbling. It read: *Zur nächsten Generation. Wenn du diese Nachricht erhalten hast, hast du eine Reihe von Ereignissen ausgelöst, die alles Leben auf deiner Welt vernichten warden ...*

He was confused. He'd translated a language no one had ever seen into one he'd never learned. However, the meaning was clear in any language: it was a threat – it meant imminent danger.

Sylvia came to his side and started to translate the German writing.

Will stopped her. "The title reads: 'To the Next Generation,'" he explained. "The first line says, 'If you have received this message, you have triggered a series of events that will annihilate all life on your world.'"

"Can you read more?" Denise asked.

Will opened his laptop and went to the next line. He nodded. "It says, 'We are the generation that preceded yours on this planet. What follows is an account of what happened to us, and what is about to happen to you.'"

Denise put her hand on his forearm. "Will," she interrupted. "I don't understand what you are saying."

Will stared back at her.

"You're speaking in German," Sylvia said.

He was hearing his voice, and thinking, in English, although he wasn't absolutely certain. Perhaps he comprehended the ideas in his mind and ignored the medium through which they were conveyed. "Get a translator," he said. "And an audio recorder."

Sylvia understood and left.

"What does this mean?" Denise asked.

"It means I can read it now," Will said. "Just like the script on the White Stone."

"What is it saying – what does it mean?"

"There are over a hundred pages there," Will said, "but the opening words imply that there were inhabitants of Earth before us – preceding the human race – and they're warning us of something."

"How can that be? Wouldn't there be evidence?"

Will shrugged. "I need to read."

Denise touched his hand, and Will flinched and withdrew it. He realized what he'd done and said, "Sorry, I'm a little jumpy."

"You're scaring me," she said.

"I'm a little scared, too," he said.

She kissed him firmly on the lips, and then squeezed his hands and let them go.

"I'm glad you're here," he said.

His heart seemed to cramp in a wave of guilt. He'd been the one to trigger whatever was going to happen, and therefore may have sealed the fate of the world.

He shook away the thoughts and looked into Denise's eyes. "I'm going to do everything I can." He put his hands on her shoulders and returned the kiss.

Sylvia rushed into the mess hall. "Follow me."

Will and Denise followed her through the narrow corridors to the planning room. Sylvia set a hand-held audio recorder on the table.

Will set down his laptop. "Please go," he said, looking to both Denise and Sylvia. "I need to concentrate. You can listen to the recording when I'm finished."

Denise hesitated, but then both women left and closed the door.

Will sat at the table, opened his laptop, and tested the recorder.

He started from the beginning and read aloud.

DENISE SAT WITH SYLVIA, Daniel, and Jacob at a table in the empty galley. She sipped tea as the others ate a dinner of pasta and marinara sauce. What she'd learned had disturbed her, and she felt the need to do something. But she could only wait.

"I know you explained it to me before," Jacob said. "But I still don't understand how he can all of a sudden read the language."

"And he's translating it to German," Daniel added.

Jacob stared back at him.

Denise laughed out loud.

"He never learned German, either," Sylvia explained.

"I don't get it," Jacob said.

"There was some sort of transfer of information to his brain," Sylvia said.

Jacob shook his head and sighed, seemingly resigned to the notion that he was not going to get a satisfying explanation. "How long is the translation going to take?" he asked.

"A few hours," Denise said.

"They should have finished cutting through the steel barrier by then as well," Jonathan said as he took a seat with the others.

"Will wants us to bring the Plum Island device with us when we go back down the tunnel," Jacob said. "I'll make sure that's ready to go."

"Maybe we'll have some answers in a few hours," Jonathan said. "How long has Will been at it?"

Denise knew Jonathan well, and could tell from his voice that he was concealing anxiety. "About an hour," she replied.

"All we can do is wait," Daniel added. "We should try to get some rest. I think we're going to need it."

Denise felt the same, but she knew her mind would not relax.

WILL'S HEAD POUNDED, and his stomach knotted up like a snake coiling around a rodent. He'd lost track of time. His brain had been working on overdrive for over four hours.

He pressed the play button on the audio recorder and listened.

It was odd to hear his voice speaking German. As he listened, his brain flickered between incomprehensible German and clear English. It must have been the implanted resources automatically translating the German he was hearing to the English the rest of his mind understood.

He stood from the table and stretched his back. He packed his computer in its case, grabbed the audio recorder, and headed for the door. As he exited the planning room he barely avoided colliding with a sailor standing in the corridor, making the man flinch.

"I'm the translator, sir," the young man said as he combed his trembling fingers through short blonde hair that barely concealed his shiny scalp. "Ensign Cheney."

Will handed him the audio recorder, and then turned in the direction of his quarters.

"Sir, you're supposed to report to the captain," Cheney said. "He's on the bridge."

Will reversed course, passed by the sailor, and headed for the bridge.

"Sir?"

Will stopped and turned.

"I heard some of what you were saying," Cheney said.

Will saw fear in his eyes. "Please keep it to yourself," Will said. "The captain will share info with the crew when he's ready."

"Of course," Cheney said. "But there's something else."

"What's that?"

"You speak German with a Berliner's accent."

"Oh?"

"It's a dialect that has faded in modern German," Cheney added. "How can you speak like that and still need a translator?"

"That's a complicated question," Will said, and one he didn't want to answer. "Let me know when you've finished the translation. If there are any ambiguities, make sure they're noted clearly. We'll need to study this carefully."

The sailor nodded and then headed in the opposite direction.

As Will walked toward the bridge, some of the info he'd translated went through his mind. His lack of reaction confused him until he realized that his emotional fatigue was tempering his ability to respond. The information was devastating.

He found Captain McHenry and Lieutenant Diggs on the bridge, studying a map on a computer monitor.

"You've completed the translation?" McHenry asked when he spotted Will approaching.

Will nodded. "I gave the recording to the translator," he said. "We need to get everyone together."

"Something wrong?" McHenry asked.

"Not sure," Will replied. Something was very wrong.

McHenry pulled out his communicator and gave the order for an immediate meeting. "Let's go," McHenry said and nodded to Will to lead the way. "The planning room."

Ten minutes later everyone was seated around the table, including Lieutenant Diggs and McHenry, putting the small room at an uncomfortable capacity. Will stood at the head of the table in front of a small whiteboard. They all observed him with anxious eyes.

"I've translated the text," Will explained. "It's now being converted from German to English."

"Did it reveal who sent it?" Daniel asked from Will's right, at the far end of the table.

Sylvia, who sat to Daniel's left, nodded that she had the same question.

"I'll get to that," Will replied. He paused for a moment to gather his thoughts and then began. "As we already know, the outgoing signal was sent by a single Earth-based source – the probe. That signal was not intended for us."

"There was also an identical probe on Mars which relayed a duplicate signal," Jacob explained. "They were both intended for a recipient far away – not Earth. And we haven't been able to decode them."

Will nodded. "The incoming AM radio signals, however, originated from multiple sources located far outside of the solar system," he explained.

"There were seven of them," Jacob added. "They all came from different directions, but the signals they transmitted were redundant – maybe to make sure we got them."

"Those are the ones you decoded – the drawings and text came from these transmissions?" McHenry asked.

"Yes, and they were intended for us," Will replied. "The outgoing signal from the probe, however, was intended to alert someone far away that we had actuated the probe."

"Alert someone?" Sylvia asked. "Who?"

"I don't know," Will replied. "However, the incoming signals, the ones that contained the drawings, and the text I just translated, were intended for us."

"Who sent the incoming message?" Daniel asked again.

"There are spacecraft located outside the solar system that were designed to detect the outgoing signal from the probe, and then respond by sending the incoming AM signals to us," Will explained.

"Was the outgoing signal intended for those spacecraft?" Daniel asked.

"No," Will replied. "Those spacecraft were placed there to watch – they were hidden observers. They have been there, concealed and dormant, for a long time. They became active, and sent us the AM signals, only when they detected the outgoing signals from the probes on Earth and Mars."

"How long have they been there?" Jonathan asked.

"About forty thousand years is my guess," Will replied, eliciting gasps from around the table.

"How did you come up with that?" McHenry asked.

"It's the age of the radioisotope thermoelectric generator – the RTG," Jacob said before Will could reply.

Will nodded. "The RTG was constructed at about the same time the spacecraft were placed at their locations."

"What is the intent of their message?" Sylvia asked.

"It's a warning," Will replied.

"Warning?" McHenry asked. "What's supposed to happen?"

"It's a warning that the outgoing signal from the probe initiated some kind of regeneration procedure," Will replied.

"Regeneration?" Sylvia said. "What's going to be regenerated?"

Will took a deep breath and said, "Earth."

Will let his words sink in.

The first to speak was Jonathan. "Regenerate Earth?" he asked. "What does that mean?"

"It means that the planet will be wiped clean of all life," Will replied, "and then restarted from scratch."

Will thought he could see recognition hit each of them separately. Their faces took on varying expressions of confusion and fear.

"How is this supposed to happen?" McHenry asked. "And who will carry it out?"

"I don't know who or what will carry it out," Will replied. "But I do know that it starts with the removal of the atmosphere."

"It becomes a vacuum?" Daniel asked.

"Like that of deep space," Will affirmed.

"But we could prepare for that," Daniel argued. "Build pressurized facilities, like they do with spacecraft."

"Not for very long," Jacob argued. "It would be like trying to live on Mars with our current technology."

"It's a moot point," Will said. "That's only the first stage."

"What comes next?" Sylvia asked.

"Radiation," Will replied.

"You mean like a dirty bomb?" Denise asked.

"More like the process we use to sterilize food," Will replied. He imagined giant radiation sources hovering above the Earth, out of reach of human technology, cooking the planet alive.

"But can't we use shielding to protect ourselves?" Lieutenant Diggs asked. "Like lead walls?"

Will shrugged. "Depends on the intensity and the type of radiation," he explained. "A wall of lead a couple of feet thick would reduce gamma ray intensities by a factor of a billion. But that wouldn't matter if the source is a billion times more intense than anticipated."

"Besides," Jacob said, "very few people will have access to that kind of shielding."

"And they'd need both – the shielding and a pressurized vessel – to survive," Sylvia added.

"Again, doesn't matter," Will continued. "The next step is extreme thermal cycles – hot and cold. Hot enough to melt rock, cold enough to liquefy nitrogen."

"It would take an unbelievable amount of energy to do all of these things," Jacob argued.

"I agree," Will said. "It would be impossible for us, but that doesn't mean it can't be done."

"Is that it then?" Jonathan asked.

Will shook his head. "The final step in the destruction process is to remove the top layer of the Earth's entire surface – two kilometers thick in places. The material is then reprocessed and redistributed."

"The magnitude of such an operation is unthinkable," Jonathan said.

Everyone remained silent. Denise's eyes were glazed, as if she were daydreaming. Daniel's forehead wrinkled in thought, Sylvia squinted, and Jacob's eyes were closed. Jonathan massaged the scruff on his chin. McHenry looked angry.

"After that, Earth will be gray, and dead," Will continued. It was just like in the nightmares he'd been having. "It will be devoid of life, water, atmosphere, and its protective magnetic field. In the end, it will not only be lifeless, but incapable of supporting life altogether."

"Like Mars," Sylvia said.

"In fact, it will be precisely like Mars," Will said.

"What do you mean?" Denise asked.

"Mars had developed intelligent life," Will replied. "About 50 thousand years ago, it suffered the steps I just described."

"That was in the message?" Jacob asked with eyes opened wide.

Will nodded. "Its civilization was failing – like we are – and the planet was wiped clean. But it hasn't yet been regenerated – as we know. Earth and Mars will be regenerated simultaneously."

"That might be as colossal an event as the destruction process," Jacob said.

"And more complex," Will added. "The planets will be given new atmospheres, and protective magnetic fields to shield from harmful radiation. In the end, they'll be seeded with life and, for the most part, left to develop without interruption."

"Who sent the warning?" McHenry asked. "Could this all be a hoax?"

Will had already considered this idea and dismissed it. "It's too elaborate – it's not a hoax," he argued. "As for who sent us the warning, it was the generation that preceded us."

At first there were gasps, but then they all stared at him with expectant expressions.

"The process I just described is cyclic," Will explained. "Another intelligent civilization was here before us. The planet was regenerated and we took their place. The previous generation replaced the one that preceded it, and so on."

"The previous generation was subjected to the same test?" Denise asked.

"Yes," Will replied. He knew she was referring to the test administered by the Judge in the probe.

"And they failed?" Sylvia asked.

Will shook his head. "No, they passed."

"Wait," Jacob said, "you just said they were regenerated."

Will held up his hand. "You'll understand in a moment," he said. "Our generation failed because we used the wrong means to initiate the metamorphosis – to develop the ability to separate."

"By 'wrong means' you mean torture," Denise clarified.

Will nodded. "The previous generation instead achieved separation through intellectual development."

"They were more advanced than us?" Daniel asked.

"By far," Will responded. "The text lists reference points in their development that we can compare to our own, starting with the first radio transmission of information. For us, that occurred around 1900, more than a century ago. The next reference point was the first powered flight."

"Wright brothers, 1903," Jonathan said. "About the same time."

"For them, powered flight occurred 20 years after the first radio transmission," Will said. "Next was the first moon landing. For them, this occurred 65 years after the first powered flight, or 85 years after the first radio transmission."

"So they were about 20 years behind us," Sylvia said. "Referenced to the first radio broadcast, it would be like our moon landing had occurred in 1989 rather than 1969."

Will shrugged. "I'm sure there's a lot of uncertainty in the technological development of a civilization," he said. "Suppose the Wright brothers hadn't existed, and there had been no one else with the intellectual curiosity, drive, and resources to develop powered flight. How long would it have been delayed? Decades?"

"A natural disaster, or war, could do the same," Daniel said. "Or an overbearing government – a ruthless dictatorship."

"Or a debilitating religion," Sylvia added. "One that consumed a society and put development into stagnation."

"Their next milestone was the first manned Mars landing," Will continued. "It happened 40 years after their moon landing."

McHenry huffed.

Will looked to him in anticipation.

"Didn't take them long to pass us by," McHenry said and shook his head. "We hardly even have a manned space program. If we'd kept pace with our predecessors, we would've landed on Mars over a decade ago."

"It's fascinating that we're getting a glimpse of what our own future may hold," Daniel said.

Will considered Daniel's comment as his blood seemed to thicken in his veins. He made eye contact with Denise and immediately regretted it as her expression turned from fascination to alarm.

"What's happening, Will?" Denise asked.

Will shook his head and turned to Daniel. "Although a part of their past is similar to ours, our future is going to be very different."

"What does that mean?" Sylvia asked.

Will ignored the question and continued with the timeline. "Their next major development was the manned exit of the solar system, 25 years after the Mars landing."

"Which, if we were on pace, would be about 15 years in our future," McHenry added.

Will nodded. "Perhaps," he said. "But then things take a leap. About 50 years after the exit of the solar system – about 65 years into our supposed future – they'd eradicated natural death."

"What the hell does that mean?" Jonathan asked.

"It means they'd cured all disease," Will responded, "or had a way of correcting any biological issues, including aging."

"Fascinating," Daniel said. "Their society must have undergone drastic changes after that."

"It did," Will said. "They maintained a stable population and focused their efforts on development – internally and externally. Their internal focus was on intellectual development, including science and engineering, but also on trying to answer deep philosophical questions of origin and purpose."

"And externally?" Denise asked.

"They became aware of their isolation," Will explained. "Even though they were able to explore beyond the solar system, they found nothing but debris and empty space."

"They searched for extraterrestrial life?" Daniel asked.

Will nodded. "They sent out radio signals in all directions," he explained. "And listened intently for centuries, but never heard anything back."

"And neither have we," Daniel added. "Well, until now."

"We've been listening for incoming signals for a long time before this," Sylvia added. "At least SETI has."

"SETI?" Lieutenant Diggs asked.

"Search for Extraterrestrial Intelligence," Sylvia explained. "It's an institute that was set up in the 80s."

"In the 200 years following their Mars landing," Will continued, "they made breakthroughs in advanced propulsion systems and energy sources. Their exploration capabilities advanced exponentially. They expanded their ventures outside the solar system for over 200 years before they eventually visited the Alpha Centauri system – our name for it – over four light-years from Earth. At that time, they could reach a significant fraction of the speed of light, so the round trip took them 12 years. They knew it was a lifeless system, but went anyway. Their missions continued to other nearby stars, and their methods of space travel continued to improve for another 200 years."

"Please," McHenry interrupted. "I don't see how this is relevant – even if this story is true."

"I'm getting to it," Will said, as he felt the frown forming on his face despite his efforts to conceal it. "I've just outlined a 600-year timeline of their technological milestones beyond their moon landing."

"So, at this point on their timeline, they're over 600 years ahead of us technologically and intellectually," Jacob said.

Will nodded. "That's if we're as intelligent as they were – otherwise our relative rates of development could be very different. But let's assume that our intellectual abilities are about equal so that the rates are the same."

"Again, how is this relevant?" McHenry asked.

"It's to set a point of reference – to give you perspective," Will replied.

Will couldn't tell if it was impatience or fear he saw in the captain's expression.

"At the same time they were exploring the space around them, they were contemplating other things – philosophical ones – such as their origin, existence, future, and intellectual development," Will explained. "It was at this point, around 600 years after their moon landing, that the first of them separated. They called it the 'evanescent transformation.'"

Everyone was silent, contemplating what he'd just said.

A few seconds later Jacob said, "You separated."

Will nodded.

"So we're ahead of them," McHenry said.

"Yes," Will said but shook his head. "But it works out badly for us."

"We did it the wrong way," Daniel blurted.

Will nodded.

"What does that mean?" McHenry asked.

"Our predecessors achieved the ability to separate through enlightenment," Will replied.

"And we did it through cruelty," Denise said. "Torture."

"That was the test we failed," Will said.

The others stared at Will with agitated expressions.

"Not long after the previous generation's first separation," Will continued, "a probe appeared in the ocean."

"The same one we discovered?" McHenry asked.

Will nodded. "They sent the first 'person' of their race to develop separation abilities to the probe. That person entered it and flipped the switch, just as I did. The probe sank into the seabed and, a few days later, a second probe appeared."

"The one with the Judge?" Sylvia asked.

"Yes," Will responded. "And, unlike us, they got a positive judgment."

"So they passed," Denise said.

"I don't understand," Jonathan asked. "Then why are they not still here?"

This was the part that frightened Will more than anything. "Despite their advanced, and more peaceful, development, Earth was regenerated 75 days after their judgment. They were given a warning, but it wasn't enough time to save everyone."

"They were destroyed anyway?" Denise asked, confused.

"Most of them," Will replied. "Clearly some survived since they returned 40 thousand years ago to set up a system to warn us."

"So what the hell was the point of the judgment?" Jonathan asked. "Pass or fail, everyone dies?"

"Not exactly," Will explained. "The probe alerts whoever is carrying out the judgments and regenerations – the 'regenerators' – that the occupying race on the planet has undergone the 'evanescent transformation.' At that stage, that race should be technically advanced enough to evacuate the planet, given enough warning. In this case, they had 75 days."

"That's not a lot of time," Denise said.

"They packed as many as they could onto every ship they had, and left," Will said. "Thousands escaped. Billions died."

"Billions," Sylvia repeated. "That's an incomprehensible number of lives."

"Where did they go?" Jonathan asked.

Will shook his head and shrugged. "I don't know."

"The previous generation got the warning from the Judge?" Sylvia asked.

Will nodded.

"But we never got such a warning," Daniel said. "Did we?"

Will shook his head. "No. I think that's the point of us failing the test," he speculated. "We're not given the opportunity to evacuate."

"We're supposed to be exterminated," Daniel said.

As everyone contemplated Daniel's words, each of their faces took on different distorted expressions of panic and horror.

"The text warns us of what is coming," Sylvia said. "Does it tell us what this facility is supposed to do?"

Will shook his head. "It only said that the base was constructed to 'assist us.'"

"Assist us?" Jonathan said. "That could mean anything. Help us hide? Defend ourselves? What?"

"I think the drawings were supposed to be more obvious to us," Will replied. "I think we were supposed to understand them, and figure it out for ourselves."

"We're too stupid," Jonathan huffed.

"Even if we were 1,000 years ahead of where we are technologically," Jacob said, "they still couldn't expect us to construct all of that stuff in 75 days."

Will thought the same, and that's why he hoped it was all there already, under the ice.

"Back to the point," McHenry said, breaking the silence. "How much time is left before someone shows up to destroy us?"

"If the destruction phase starts 75 days after the judgment, as it did for the previous generation," Will explained, "then we have less than a week."

Daniel looked at his watch and seemed to count in his head. He swallowed hard and said, "Four days."

At that instant, McHenry's communicator chirped.

"McHenry here," the captain said.

"We're set to cut steel," a man responded, referring to the barrier at the end of the tunnel.

"What about the radioactive material?" McHenry asked.

"We're set to make the transfer," the man replied.

"On our way," McHenry replied and looked to the others. "Let's go."

CHAPTER 16

Will looked over the drawings of the Plum Island device as a few sailors made final adjustments to the makeshift workroom they'd constructed in the main bay to handle the radioactive americium-241 replacement core. They had to deal with both the old material, still contained in the device, as well as the replacement core synthesized by NASA and Los Alamos National Lab. Will learned that the engineers aboard nuclear subs like the *North Dakota* were well versed in such operations.

Although the original americium in the RTG device had mostly decayed, the device was still dangerously radioactive. Will and Jacob had only been mildly exposed since the device, and the case in which it was stored, provided shielding. Replacing the core, however, required additional shielding and better handling tools.

Will, now able to read the script in the drawings, had discovered a note indicating that one of the device's end caps could be removed to "replace the charge." The charge was the radioisotope – americium.

The end cap just turned off like the lid of a jar. In this case, however, two holes were strategically placed – one in the body and one in the end cap – so that rods could be inserted, providing handles so that a sufficient amount of torque could be applied to twist the cap.

McHenry walked off the gangplank and joined them in the center of the bay. "Ready to make the transfer?" he asked.

Will nodded and explained that, to loosen the lid, they needed to turn the cap clockwise when looking from the top, which is opposite to that of most screw fasteners and jar caps. Evidently, the previous generation hadn't followed the "righty-tighty, lefty-loosey" rule.

Daniel and Denise joined them.

"The question is," McHenry continued, "how do we proceed once the transfer is complete? You said this is a power key of some sort. We really have no idea what will happen when, whatever it is, gets powered up."

It was a good question, and Will had already thought about it. "I think we should not hesitate to move forward, and insert the device," Will said. "But first, the *North Dakota* should leave the area – maybe head for the tunnel."

McHenry stared at him for a few seconds, his expression shifting from blank to alarm.

Daniel cleared his throat and said, "I don't know if we should rush into anything – "

"We might only have days left," Will cut him off. "If activating it – whatever it is – can save us, we need to do this now. If it's going to destroy us, we were about to be destroyed anyway."

"He's right," McHenry said. "We have to figure this thing out now. In addition to the clock on the regeneration, the Chinese are on the ice. The Russians are lurking in the southern waters, and might be on the continent as well."

"You got a transmission from Naval Command?" Daniel asked.

McHenry nodded. "Satellites have not yet spotted anyone on land, but the information comes from reliable intelligence sources," he explained.

"Are you going to get out of the area?" Will asked.

McHenry shook his head. "We're not leaving."

Will shook his head. "There's no way to tell what will happen – "

" – We'll get the *North Dakota* ready to run before you power that thing up. We're staying for the time being."

Will nodded. It was clear there'd be no arguing the point. If things got dangerous, he'd have to do whatever he could to help everyone get out.

"You and Jacob should oversee the radioactive material transfer while I get the crew prepping for a quick exit," McHenry said. "We'll set up a chain of communication through the tunnel with walkie-talkies so that we can know what's happening from the dock." He glanced at his watch and looked back to Will. "They should have started cutting steel on the other end."

It was a good plan. Inside the tunnel, the walkie-talkies would work for line-of-sight communications only. However, by stationing a few sailors along the tunnel, they could get messages to McHenry much more quickly than someone running through it. Will just hoped that, if something drastic occurred, there would be enough time to get the *North Dakota* and crew out of harm's way.

The others left, and Will and Jacob examined the work area. The main safety component was a lead blanket draped over a wall of stacked rock fragments from the slab that had concealed the tunnel. The engineers had leaded gloves, and one wore a chest shield, making him look like a baseball umpire. The final important component was a piece of curved leaded glass that was about the size of an automobile windshield.

The crates that contained the Plumb Island device and its replacement core were both open and located near a wooden worktable scavenged from somewhere in the base. On the table were hand tools, leaded gloves, and masks.

A man with a Geiger counter notified Will that everything was safe, and they were ready to proceed.

Another engineer walked up. "I'm Lieutenant Taggert," he said. "You and Mr. Hale should disassemble the RTG before we open NASA's americium container. No sense in getting the new material ready until we know you can open the device."

Will nodded to Jacob. They went to the table and donned gloves and masks. Will extracted the cylindrical Plum Island device from its container and set it on the table, where Jacob took a hold of it so that it wouldn't roll. Will grabbed two steel rods, each a quarter of an inch in diameter and a foot long, and inserted one into a hole on the side of the end cap. Another hole was located an inch away from the first, in the main body.

He stuck the second rod into the hole and assessed the situation. The two holes were staggered so that the rods were separated enough to get a solid grip on each. The rods would provide a lot of torque; it was like having a long handle on the lid of a pickle jar, and another long handle on the jar itself.

He grabbed the rods and recalled that he'd have to twist in the opposite direction of a typical jar lid. He repositioned his hands and looked to Jacob, who was holding the device on the surface of the table with both hands.

"Ready?" Will asked.

Jacob nodded.

Will pulled the rods in opposite directions, slowly increasing the force. Just as he was about to give up, the lid moved about a quarter of a turn and stopped. He pulled out the rods and set them on the table. He grabbed the cap with the thick glove and it slid out. It was shaped like the stopper on a thermos, except the top was rounded.

"That wasn't too bad," Will said.

Jacob tipped the device until a heavy chunk of material slid out and landed in a makeshift box made out of lead sheet.

The spent core was about the size of two D-cell batteries stacked end-to-end, but slightly larger in diameter. It was metallic, but riddled with gray and yellow where it seemed to have oxidized.

"Not bad for 40 thousand years," Jacob said.

Will grabbed the empty device and tipped it so he could examine its innards. The inside was shiny and black. He tipped it over and some gray-yellow dust fell out and into the lead box. He hoped NASA had gotten the dimensions right for the replacement. He then placed a lead lid on the box.

"Ready for the replacement?" Taggert asked.

"Yes," Will answered as he went over to the improvised handling area to observe the engineers as they disassembled NASA's containment vessel.

They'd strapped it to a short section of steel I-beam. There was a large threaded hole on one face of the cylindrical vessel, and a deep slot at the center of the opposite face. The former Will recognized as the threaded hole from the pictures. It was used to handle the object by attaching a threaded hook, or an eyebolt. The slot on the bottom face was for a threaded plug, behind which was the cavity that contained the radioactive material. The vessel was oriented so that the slotted plug was on the top.

An engineer twisted the plug with a tool that resembled a giant flat-head screwdriver that fit snugly into the slot. It was tight but, after some struggling, it broke free and rotated with little resistance.

When the cap was removed, another man inserted steel tongs into the exposed hole, pulled out a silvery-white metallic cylinder, and set it in a metal pan.

"Looks good," Jacob said.

"Let's hope so," Will replied as he retrieved the empty RTG device and handed it to Taggert.

"Let's do this," Taggert said as he took the device to the shielding wall and secured it to a meter-long piece of heavy I-beam with a clamp. The device was oriented vertically, with the open end up, so that the americium could be inserted from the top.

The same engineer who had extracted the americium from its containment vessel grabbed the new core with the tongs, lifted it above the device, and lowered it. When it got to the opening, it hit the edge and stopped. He lifted it again and lowered. Same result.

"Might be a tight fit," Will said to Jacob.

After a dozen failed attempts, the engineer set the americium back in the pan and set down the tongs. "It's heavy," he said and shook his arms. "Give me a minute."

Will was beginning to worry that it wasn't going to fit when the engineer picked it up again and inserted it on the second try.

Another man took a pole with a Geiger counter mounted on the end and monitored the radioactivity from multiple directions.

"Well shielded," the man said, "except at the top. We'll need to check it out again with the cap in place."

Will retrieved the cap from the table and handed it to the engineer, who then walked around the shielding and placed it on the device. He was only able to twist it part of the way with his gloved hand, but waved Will over to finish the job with the steel rods.

Will inserted the rods and twisted them until he felt the lid click into place. At that instant, small white lights appeared on the body of the cylinder. At each midpoint between the eight evenly spaced black rings that encircled the body of the device was a dot of bright white light that orbited its circumference. The dots circulated about twice per second but did not move in unison. After a few seconds, they disappeared.

"Looks like that did something," Taggert said in an excited tone.

Will nodded. "I guess we'll find out soon," he said.

Taggert glanced at something behind Will.

Will turned. Captain McHenry walked off the deck of the *North Dakota* and approached.

"*North Dakota*'s about ready to go," McHenry said. "What's the status here?"

"We're ready," Will said.

"Let's get this show on the road," McHenry said, and then instructed his engineers to clean up their tools and prepare the sub for departure.

"There's still some time," Will said. "They still have to get us through the steel barrier at the end of the tunnel."

McHenry nodded. He then looked to the device, and then to Will. "I hope you know what you're doing."

Will shuddered. He had no idea what he was doing.

WILL PULLED a cart that carried the crate containing the Plum Island device. As they headed down the tunnel, the others bombarded Will with questions.

"Do you think the previous generation still exists?" Sylvia asked.

"Maybe," Will replied. "If they do, I can't even imagine how advanced they've become."

"What do you mean?"

"They were 600 years ahead of us when they had to vacate Earth," Will replied. "How far do you think they're ahead of us now?"

"At least 40 thousand years," Jacob immediately replied.

"At least that," Will said. "It was 40 thousand years ago when they set up the warning system. Their original exodus from Earth might have occurred thousands of years before that. They could be 100 thousand years ahead of us now, or maybe a million."

"Imagine how much they would have developed after a million years," Jonathan said. "When they were just 600 years beyond us they'd already eliminated natural death and developed interstellar travel."

"And they could separate their souls from their bodies," Will added.

"Yes, the 'evanescent transformation,' as they called it," Daniel said. "I wonder how a society would change if everyone had that ability."

It made Will wonder how the previous generation had continued to evolve in the thousands of years after developing separation abilities. Did they even need physical bodies anymore? It made him contemplate the ultimate endpoint of the evolution of life. Without the need for a physical body, how long would life last? Would it exist forever, or would it dissipate into nothingness as the universe eventually dimmed into a dark afterglow?

Nothing is forever, he whispered spontaneously under his breath. He didn't know from where the thought had emerged.

His attention was redirected to the intermittent flashes of white-blue light that illuminated the tunnel ahead of them. The crew was still cutting steel.

A few minutes later they approached the end of the tunnel. Will shielded his eyes as a sailor cut through the steel plate that sealed the doorway with a cutting torch.

"It's submarine steel," a sailor informed him. "Plates are two inches thick. It took us a while."

Ten minutes later, one of four heavy plates crashed to the stone floor with a horrible clanging noise that echoed in the chamber and up the tunnel.

The crew cleared away, and Will walked inside. The others followed.

Although he'd seen the interior hours earlier while separated, the experience from inside his body was different. First, the cold air made his nostrils dilate as he breathed. Traces of smoke from the cutting torch remained in the air, but there was another scent in the background that reminded him of hot electronics, or melted plastic.

The floor was perfectly smooth, but had footprints from the last people who were there – probably the Nazis who had blocked off the entrance. The high ceiling was composed of the same white material as the walls and floor. Light seemed to emanate directly from the walls and ceiling, and it was bright enough to make him squint.

He crossed the theater-sized room to the wall opposite the entrance. About three and a half feet above the floor, a horizontal shelf protruded about two feet from the wall. It was about the height of a standing desk. He figured it was a control console of some kind.

On the surface of the console, near the midpoint of the wall, was a circular port that was about three inches in diameter and a foot deep. He couldn't tell if the script that was next to it was painted or etched into the surface, but it translated to "Power Encoder Input."

Will rehashed what he'd told them about the room, and explained what he thought they had to do with the Plum Island device.

"Looks like it will fit," Jacob commented as he examined the port.

Everyone assembled in the widened part of the tunnel just in front of the entrance. Jonathan and Jacob removed the lid to the crate as sailors wielding walkie-talkies positioned themselves along the tunnel, establishing a communications link to McHenry, back on the *North Dakota*. They'd only needed to place one man at the tunnel's midpoint, since it was so straight. A few others had to be positioned closer to the base, totaling four relays for communication. They'd established a code word for immediate departure: *giraffe*. In that scenario, all was lost, and the *North Dakota* would try to save itself.

Will was uneasy with everyone being present for the device insertion. He had no idea what was going to happen, and didn't know if he'd be able to protect them, or himself, if something drastic were to occur. But there was no talking anyone into leaving. Denise was by far the most stubborn, but the others were just as determined to stay.

Everything was ready.

Will took a firm hold of the RTG device and brought it into the control room.

"Look!" Jacob gasped and pointed. Something had illuminated on the console.

They went to it and found a ring of white light flashing around the empty port.

"It must be detecting it," Jacob said.

It was a good thing that the americium had been depleted when the Nazis had discovered it, Will thought. Otherwise, they would have gotten to this point.

"Shall we?" Will asked.

Jacob nodded.

The RTG device was symmetric – no distinct top or bottom except for the holes used to remove the cap – so he moved to insert it in the orientation in which he was holding it. As the leading end of the cylinder approached the opening, the white ring of light stopped flashing and the port closed – as if it filled with a white liquid which quickly solidified.

"What the hell?" Jacob said.

Will pulled the device back and the port opened again. The white flashing light resumed.

"Let's try it the other way," Will said and flipped the device.

As the leading edge approached the port, the flash frequency of the light increased. It was a tight fit, but he took care not to hit the sides as he inserted it. When the RTG was about a third of the way into the port, something seemed to take hold of it and pull it down.

Will let go as it sank below the surface. The port closed, and the light ring remained illuminated and no longer flashed.

An instant later, the console and the entire wall to which it was attached lit up with brightly colored buttons, indicators, viewing screens, and controls.

"Holy shit!" Jacob exclaimed simultaneously with prolonged gasps from the others who were standing a few feet behind them.

Will concentrated on what was happening in front of him. Images formed on the previously opaque, white surfaces of the console and wall. The buttons and indicators were labeled with high-resolution characters in the same script as that of the text he'd translated. He could read them: one read "Reactor Power," and another read "Flow Rate." Both indicators read zero. There were hundreds of similar readouts.

He stepped back a few feet and looked up at the wall. A map had formed in its center that represented the base and the surrounding area. Arrayed around it were multicolored schematics, some of which he recognized from the thousands of technical drawings he'd studied. He still had no idea of their functions.

"Where is that?" Denise asked. She was pointing at something in the upper right corner of the wall.

It was a camera view of the Antarctic surface. It seemed to be night-vision enhanced due to the low light.

"It's the mountain valley opposite the base and lake," Daniel explained. "I've carefully studied the satellite images of this area."

"I'm surprised the camera still works," Jonathan noted.

"I'm surprised any of this works," Will said. "It's 40 thousand years old."

"I'm still having a hard time believing that," Sylvia said.

Will didn't know what to believe.

Daniel took out a camera and snapped pictures of the console and displays.

There were numerous camera feeds. Some showed other views of the mountains. Others showed tunnels that must have been inside the mountain, or embedded in the surrounding terrain.

Will directed his attention back to the control console. He started on the left, reading the labels above indicators and controls as he moved to the right. As he approached the center he encountered a large yellow button encircled by a pulsing white ring. The label was in bright white script, and pulsed in unison with the ring. It read: *Initiate Startup Sequence.*

"This is it," Will said.

"This is what?" Jacob asked.

The others gathered around him.

"It says 'Initiate Startup Sequence,'" Will said as he pointed to the button. "We need to notify the captain. Maybe we should think this through."

Will discussed it with the others and they agreed to send a message to McHenry through the line of walkie-talkies. It was a few short sentences, but the main line read: *Have the option to, quote, initiate start-up sequence, end quote. Advise whether to proceed or stand down.*

It took a few minutes to get a response.

Will let the sailor repeat the return message even though he'd heard it as it was delivered.

The sailor said, "Captain's response: Chinese forces in the area. Proceed immediately."

Will nodded. It was time.

"This is your last chance to get out of here," Will warned.

A frown formed on Denise's face, the kind that he knew meant she wasn't budging. Similar expressions appeared on the faces of the others.

"We're all in," Daniel said. "Push the button."

Will walked over to the console. The bright yellow button was about the size of the top of a soda can.

He reached out and pushed the button with his forefinger. It was like pressing on a smooth countertop – there was no tactile response like that which occurs with a mechanical button. He looked up at the screen. Nothing.

"Anything happen?" Will asked.

He and the others searched the schematics and video feeds that filled the screen and console. It seemed nothing had changed.

"Look," Jacob said and pointed to the console.

The white ring around the yellow button was still flashing. It seemed that pressing it had no effect.

Will pressed it again, harder this time.

No effect.

"What the hell?" he said, frustrated.

Jacob walked over and pressed it multiple times. "Why would a button show up like this if we weren't supposed to press it?" he asked.

Jacob's words resonated in Will's mind ... *if we weren't supposed to press it ...*

It seemed to Will that the console and all of the room's other surfaces were composed of the same material as that of the probes – extremely hard, impenetrable.

He knew what to do.

WILL RECALLED something that the Judge had said during their fateful meeting inside the probe. He'd said that Will was in an *evanescent state* when he'd entered the first probe and triggered everything else that was to follow.

In physics, the idea of an evanescent field referred to the extension of a field beyond its confines. For instance, in some cases when a light wave reflects from a surface, a part of the electric and magnetic fields of which the light is composed can penetrate into the surface.

Will was going to apply this concept to himself. Instead of fully separating, he was going to try to extend beyond his physical reach.

He walked up to the console and leaned his hip against the edge to maintain his balance. He put his right hand on the surface with his middle and index fingers at the center of the yellow button. He went through the mental process of separating, but concentrated on the fingertips of his right hand. He imagined them growing and extending through anything they encountered.

His eyes started to roll backwards, but he fought it. His vision defocused but he concentrated on maintaining the position of his fingertips on the button. After what felt like a few seconds, a cold sensation seemed to flow through his fingers, as if he were dipping them into water. At that moment, they seemed to encounter a hard object with a flat surface. He exerted more effort. The object moved inward and abruptly stopped.

He pulled his hand back. It took him a few seconds to notice that the button had turned from yellow to white, and the ring that encircled it stopped flashing and remained illuminated. He'd actuated the button.

"What just happened?" Denise asked. She was staring up at the screen along with the others.

"You pressed the button," Jacob said. "How?"

"Things are changing!" Sylvia exclaimed. "What's happening?"

Will looked back to the screen. The numerous schematics now had parts that were flashing or moving. The indicators all fluctuated, including the gauges on the console: they were reporting information.

A new yellow button appeared, about a foot to the right of the first one. There was no ring around it. Next to it was a display that seemed to be a countdown. The number changed regularly, but it seemed to take longer than a second. He glanced at his watch and found that the number changed about 20 times in 30 seconds. So it was about 1.5 seconds per change.

He glanced back to the counter and translated the current number to be 20,200. That meant, at the rate it was counting down, it would reach zero in about eight and a half hours. He translated the flashing label above the counter: *Time to Online*. The label above the button read *Activate Pumping Sequence*.

"The next button will activate in about eight and a half hours," Will said, and told them what the labels meant.

"Pumping sequence?" Jacob repeated. "Have any pumps been found in the facility?"

No one answered. They all seemed mesmerized by the multitude of activity on the console and screen.

"A new schematic appeared," Denise said and pointed to the lower center part of the screen, not far from the button Will had just pushed.

Overlaid on a map outline of the mountains was a colorful assortment of lines that resembled an electrical circuit. Next to it was a cross-section that showed the mountains and the valley. Ice filled the bowl-like void in the semicircle formed by the mountains. At the very bottom, where ice met rock, was a complex of structures from which the lines emerged.

"That must be the pumping mechanism," Will said and pointed to the structures.

"What does it pump?" Jonathan asked.

"Water," Will said without hesitation.

"But there is no liquid water," Sylvia said.

"There's going to be," Will replied.

He wondered how the ice was going to melt, and where the water would go. But there was a bigger question. What was going to be revealed when the ice was gone?

AFTER AN HOUR of studying and snapping pictures of the complex mess of displays, gauges, and controls, everyone except Will and Denise went back to the *North Dakota* to update the captain.

Will was the only one who could read the displays and actuate the controls, so he had to stay. Denise snapped pictures of the screen and console at regular intervals so that they'd have a reference for how things changed with time.

With four hours left in the countdown, Will sat on an empty crate about 20 feet away from the screen. Denise dragged another one over and sat next to him.

"It's like a movie date," Will joked.

"Yeah, all we need is popcorn," she added. "See any water yet?"

Will shook his head. "Might take a while to melt the ice."

Denise's eyes widened. She moved her crate closer to him and hooked her arm around his.

"You okay?" he asked.

"Do you think we'll ever have a chance to be together?" she asked and put her head on his shoulder.

His chest tightened. He wasn't prepared for the question. And he wasn't prepared for his own answer.

He pulled his arm out of her grasp and put it around her shoulder and pulled her against him. "I can only hope," he said.

The noncommittal answer revealed to him what he really thought. He didn't deserve to be with her. Because of what he had done there were billions of others who also wanted to be together who might not get that chance. Perhaps he should have died in the Red Box like all of the others. The world would have carried on as it had – the good and the bad.

But he knew that would not have gone on forever, either. Even if there were no Judge to decide whether the world had met some arbitrary standard that determined its right to exist, a natural threshold was already in place.

In order to transcend its extreme isolation, the human race had to make enormous leaps in knowledge and technical ability. At some critical point, the balance between population, resources, and global destructive capabilities could go one of two ways: liberation, or destruction. The previous generation had gone 600 years beyond the current one before it had been judged. They had been advanced enough for some of them to escape what was to come next – the regeneration. Whether they still existed, he didn't know. But at least they hadn't been exterminated like intrusive pests. In their current state, humans were harmless to the rest of existence. They could hardly affect anything beyond the Earth's atmosphere. Perhaps the impending extermination was to ensure that they never would.

"Are you scared?" Denise asked.

Will shrugged. "I'm worried, not frightened," he said. "How about you?"

"I'm not worried for my life," she said. "I'm worried that ..." She paused and took in a deep, trembling breath.

"What?" he asked and pulled her tighter and looked at her. A tear streamed down her cheek. "Denise, what is it?"

She started to speak but stopped.

"What?" he repeated.

"I love you, Will," she finally said, and wiped her cheek with her sleeve.

Will's heart knotted in his chest. He'd sensed it in her from almost the first time they'd met. She'd almost single-handedly brought him back to a normal existence – at least to one as normal as someone like him could have. The hate in his soul had been so immense by the time he'd been released from the Red Box that he'd considered destroying the world on his own. And, although success was unlikely, he would have done much damage. She had changed him. She was one of the reasons why he was now trying to save it.

Denise tugged on his shirt and pointed to the screen. "Something's changed."

They both stood and got closer to the display. It was the cross-sectional view of the valley behind the mountain – an orange icon had emerged, and some flashing script appeared below it.

"What does it say?" she asked.

"Antimatter reactor online," Will replied. He was not surprised. The most efficient release of energy occurred when antimatter and matter came into contact and annihilated each other. It harnessed the full essence of Einstein's famous equation, $E = mc^2$.

"What's an 'antimatter reactor?'" Denise asked.

They took a few steps closer to the screen.

"It's a power source," Will answered. "Like a nuclear reactor, but better."

A box appeared on the screen with three lines of text. From the top, they read: power decoder activated, antimatter reactor online, melt commencing. The last line alarmed him.

"It's starting to melt the ice," he said. "We need to notify McHenry."

Will hurried out of the room and told one of the sailors keeping watch to send the message that a melting operation had started, and that the command to start the pumps in three hours was to remove the liquid water.

He went back into what they were now calling the "control room."

Denise pointed at one of the live camera feeds that viewed the iced-in valley from one of the mountains, and said, "Something's changing."

Will stepped closer. The surface seemed to glimmer.

"It's melting," he said. He didn't understand how it was being heated. Although he had no idea how to go about melting such a colossal volume of ice, he figured it would have to be done in small patches. How the whole surface could melt at once made no sense unless it was heated evenly from above.

It looked like the ice level was higher inside the ring of mountains than it was on the outside. Therefore, he figured the water forming on the top should run off on its own – through the lower mountain passes. It was the water that was low in the valley that would have to be pumped away.

Another message appeared on the screen: *Reactor 2 starting up.*

Things were moving on their own, and Will started to feel like everything was already out of his control.

"I think it's going to go fast now," he said and explained the message on the screen. "McHenry should get the *North Dakota* out of here. I think we'll be okay here. I doubt they'd design the control room to be flooded."

They both turned at the sound of footsteps.

Jacob rushed into the room. "McHenry is staying until the last minute," he said.

Daniel, Jonathan, and Sylvia entered. They were all out of breath as they set fully packed backpacks on the floor.

"Nutrition bars and water," Sylvia said.

"If the *North Dakota* is threatened, he'll get out," Daniel added. "They're ready to go right now. The captain ordered you to proceed – start the pumps, or whatever else is necessary. No more delays."

Will looked at his watch. The next stage would begin at 9:00 p.m.

WILL COULDN'T MONITOR all of the information on the enormous screen and console by himself. The others couldn't read anything, but they could at least alert him when things changed.

The live feed of the ice valley now showed a lake that was draining through the mountain passes. In the wider areas between the mountains, where the ice had been thick, were sheer vertical borders between water and ice, and more of the ice wall was revealed as the water drained. It was as if whatever was melting the ice was sharply localized, like the focused spot of a magnifying glass burning a hole through a piece of paper.

He looked at the console just as the countdown went to zero and a white ring started flashing around the button that actuated the pumping phase. It was time.

"This is your last chance to get out," Will said.

"Push it," Denise said.

Will touched his forefinger to the button and contemplated for a moment what he might be doing. He concluded that he had no choice but to trust those who had constructed the facility. He concentrated on extending his finger through the surface and actuated the button. The white ring remained illuminated, but stopped flashing.

"A new display appeared," Jacob said, pointing to the center of the screen.

It was a window that had a graph of volume versus time, and a series of gauges that indicated pumping rates, pressures, and some diagnostics. A schematic appeared that showed a network of pipes and pumping stations that riddled the mountains and terrain that surrounded the valley. Pumps illuminated as they started up, and the pipes changed from black to light blue as the water flowed through them.

"The pumps are starting," Jacob commented. "Where's the water going?"

That was the first thing Will had looked for, but it wasn't yet clear. The progressing flow through the web of lines resembled the course of blood through capillaries. The capillaries merged into larger ones, and eventually joined main pipes. He had no reference for their size, but he imagined the largest ones were close to the size of large sewer pipes.

After a few minutes, all of the pumps in the schematic were energized and operating. Will followed two main channels that led to final exits. One led to the cavern beneath the base. The other fed through the mountain, below the plateau that he and Ensign Sims had explored, crawling on their bellies to get a look over the edge. The duct truncated at an exit port about 50 meters below the surface of the lake. That water would also go to the cavern below the base.

A display showed a map of the cavern that revealed structures at depths far beyond those that could be reached by submarine. They were massive, and seemed to be a part of the pumping system. There were also channels at that depth that appeared to be a part of the drainage apparatus. He wondered if the main tunnel that led from the base out to sea was a part of the system.

The question was whether the base itself would get flooded, and whether the *North Dakota* would be in jeopardy. He knew that the current in the cavern beneath the base led out to sea, but couldn't see exactly how that happened. He figured the engineering of the fluid flow was complicated, and that the previous generation's design would work as intended.

If the objective were to remove all of the ice from inside the ring of mountains, there'd be an enormous volume of water to disperse. According to his estimates, with the average thickness of the ice at two kilometers, there'd be almost four trillion gallons of water to pump, maybe less considering that some of the water was spilling through the mountain passes. Once he knew the pumping speed, he could calculate how long that would take, but that information was not yet available.

"Looks like the water level in the valley is descending," Jacob said.

Will looked up at the live camera feed. Indeed, the water level had dropped by a noticeable amount.

After another 10 minutes, the schematic on the screen showed that the entire network of pipes was filled with water. All of the gauges now read nonzero values for pressure and flow, and did not fluctuate.

A new message appeared on the screen.

"What does it say?" Denise asked.

"All phase-two systems operating at full capacity," Will replied.

"Another button appeared," Daniel said.

Will went over to Daniel and looked at the console. There was a new button with a label and another counter. The label on the button translated to "Initiate Phase 3: Elevation." Above the counter, it read, "Time until access." He translated the number from the counter and did a quick calculation in his head. "The time remaining is about 52 hours," Will said.

"More than two days?" Jonathan repeated.

"What do you think the 'Elevation' stage is?" Daniel asked.

Will shrugged.

"You were right," Jacob said. "I bet all the stuff in the drawings is already constructed. It's encased in the ice."

That was Will's guess. But even if it were all there, he had no idea what to do with any of it. It was as if some apocalyptic event wiped out humans except for a group of eighth graders, and they were supposed to go to Cape Canaveral and revive the Space Shuttle program.

Then again, he thought, everything had been user-friendly up to this point. That wasn't completely true: it was easy as long as the operator had the ability to separate, and could read the language. Neither had been easily acquired. If something happened to him, they'd be dead in the water. It was comforting to know, unequivocally, that the Nazis had not gotten to this point: they had no one who could read the language, or press buttons in the console.

"Everything's safe in the bay, for now," a sailor reported. "The water level in the dock rose about a foot. The *North Dakota* will stay put for the time being."

The tension in Will's neck softened. The water extraction system must have been designed to bypass the base. The sheer volume of the cavern beneath the base and lake, and the steady current leading out to the ocean, must have been sufficient for the pumping speed of the melting water. By his reckoning, the pumps had to remove water at a rate of about 75 billion gallons per hour. There were no human-built pumping systems on the planet that could get even close to that. He recalled that the flow rate of the Amazon River was about 200 billion gallons per hour, so this system was a shockingly impressive feat of engineering.

It was fortunate that the *North Dakota* hadn't been on its way back through the tunnel when the pumping began. There must have been dangerous currents swirling through its nooks and crannies, making it impossible to navigate and producing dangerous debris.

He glanced at a camera view of the lake near the base. It seemed to have remained unchanged. It was frozen, but the ice was thin. It wouldn't take much pressure from below to break it up. To maintain the water level with such a large rate of flow, there must have been additional pumps in the tunnel that led from the base out to sea.

Will was exhausted, and he could tell everyone else was as well.

"Maybe you should all head back to the sub and get some rest," Will suggested. "We have two days before the next phase."

"What are you going to do?" Sylvia asked.

"I'm the only one who can operate the buttons," Will said. "I'll have to stay."

The others left, including Denise, leaving Will alone with his thoughts. He tried to put the last few days into perspective, but there was no tangible point of reference. He was witnessing – and actively participating in – the revival of an ancient technology that was not developed by humans.

His thoughts returned to what had happened to the previous generation. Did they still exist, or were their warning transmissions just messages from the grave, like the emails Horace had sent to Jacob?

The room had warmed to a comfortable level after the console had powered up. He'd be able to stay for a while, but the next stage wasn't set to occur for another 50 hours. He was running on six hours of sleep in the past 48. He'd eventually have to go back to the sub to sleep, eat, and shower.

He paced back and forth in front of the screen and picked out various features with each pass. The display looked like NASA's mission control, densely packed with fluctuating gauges, graphs, and schematics. He was looking for something that might indicate a malfunction, but found nothing.

After an hour by himself, he was startled by Denise's abrupt entry, and flinched at the sound of her voice.

"I thought you'd want something hot to eat," she said as she approached. She was carrying an oversized insulated mug. "Vegetable soup."

She handed it to him along with a spoon.

"Thanks," he said as he grabbed it, popped open the lid, and took a whiff. "This is perfect."

"Any changes?" she asked and nodded toward the screen.

He shook his head. "Seems to be running smoothly. Not that I'd know if something was wrong."

She followed him to the crates and sat next to him.

Together, they watched.

THE FIRST EVIDENCE of a structure appeared on the screen when the counter read 20 hours remaining. At first, Will was convinced that his eyes were playing tricks on him. But Denise saw it as well.

A dark, conical object protruded from the water. He recognized it from the drawings and, if he recalled correctly, it was over 200 meters tall. He had no idea of its function, but it was clearly the tallest of the objects. It also implied that there were about 200 meters of water left to remove.

According to the gauges, some of the pumps had powered down, and the rates of others had decreased.

Voices echoed from the direction of the entrance, and scuffing shoes alerted them that someone approached. Thirty seconds later, Daniel and Sylvia entered. They both glanced back and forth between Will and the screen.

"What's happening?" Daniel asked.

Will nodded to one of the camera views of the valley. "You see anything there?"

Daniel concentrated on the screen and a few seconds later he said, "My God. Is something emerging from the water?"

Sylvia gasped.

Jacob walked in, set a backpack on the floor, and looked up at the screen. "Something sticking out of the water?"

Will nodded. "Looks like something from the drawings."

"You were right," Sylvia said. "It's all been constructed."

Will had hoped that this would be the case, and that everything was completed and functional – whatever it was. He knew it would be nearly impossible to complete anything that was unfinished. They were fortunate that NASA and Los Alamos National Lab had already prepared the replacement americium core for the radioisotope device. Otherwise they'd be at a dead end. Of course, NASA and Los Alamos had no idea of the end purpose of the device. They just knew it was a radioisotope thermoelectric generator, and probably wanted to see how it worked. He was grateful for their curiosity.

"How's the *North Dakota* faring?" Will asked.

"They tried to open the doors to the slip, but they wouldn't budge," Jacob explained. "They managed to snake a camera with a water speed sensor through a crack near a hinge. The water is cloudy, and the currents are horrendous."

"McHenry is going to stay put until it slows down," Sylvia added. "He's worried that there might be debris in the tunnel leading out to sea due to the turbulence."

It conjured more serious thoughts: what if a part of the tunnel had collapsed and the *North Dakota* was now stuck? He wiped it from his mind – he had enough to think about.

"Look," Sylvia said, pointing to the screen.

Another structure was emerging on the right side of the screen, near one of the mountains. It was spherical with dimples, like a gigantic golf ball.

"It's in the drawings," Jacob said with a tone of excitement and agitation.

"We have no idea what any of this is supposed to do?" Denise asked.

"No," Will replied. "Whatever it is, I hope it's as easy to operate as this setup was."

"It was easy for you, not us," Denise argued.

Her words made him nervous. He knew that, if something happened to him, they wouldn't be able to do anything. But what if something came up that he couldn't understand, or couldn't do even with separation abilities?

"Some other news – McHenry got a transmission from the *Stennis*," Sylvia said. "First, one of our subs was attacked by a Russian sub outside the tunnel. The Russian sub was sunk, and now they're sending a carrier task force of their own. They'll be in the Weddell Sea in a week."

Geopolitical conflict was out of Will's control, but it still raised his anxiety.

"Next," Sylvia continued, "the bodies of dozens of Chinese soldiers washed through the tunnel and out to sea, mixed in with debris."

Will mulled it over. "They were close," he finally said. "They must've been in the valley when the ice melted."

"The bodies were pretty mangled," Sylvia said.

"Probably went through the pumps," Jacob said.

"That, and they would have been battered against the tunnel walls on the way out to sea," Will said.

"Tensions are high," Sylvia added. "More Chinese vessels are also on their way to the Southern Seas."

"Last time they tangled with the *Stennis* group it didn't go well for them," Denise said.

It was something Will was trying to forget.

Sylvia shook her head. "It's more likely that they're planning to attack this place, or whatever is appearing out there," she said and nodded to the screen.

Will looked at the counter and did the conversion in his head – there were still 19 hours left. When it came time to initiate the next phase, he would not hesitate. He just hoped he got the chance.

Will's anxiety swelled as the water level decreased.

His eyes did not deviate from the screen as more and more structure emerged.

What was being revealed could have been anything – a small city, or even a colossal spacecraft. The base of a conical tower, the first feature that had emerged, was now surrounded by sleek pieces of construction that he barely recognized from the drawings because they blended so seamlessly with each other. There was more symmetry than he'd first imagined, and there were multiple copies of some of the components. One of the larger, dome-shaped objects that he recognized was repeated six times, and arrayed symmetrically around the base of the tower.

"The whole world must be seeing this," McHenry said.

Will turned just as the captain snapped a picture of the screen. He'd hardly noticed that the others had arrived, and was surprised that McHenry was away from the *North Dakota*.

"What is this technology?" McHenry asked, pointing to the screen and the cluttered gauges and controls on the console.

Will shook his head. "Not ours."

McHenry had been in on many of their conversations, but still didn't seem to accept what he'd been hearing. Will didn't blame him: it was one thing to hear about it, and another to actually see it. McHenry had probably forced himself to believe that it was something our Earth-bound adversaries had developed. Even Will barely believed what he was witnessing, and he'd seen more than anyone else on the planet.

"It looks like a sunken city," Daniel remarked.

Will thought the ring of mountains looked strange with the ice removed from its interior. The mountain peaks resembled the cusps of a large molar tooth, and the structure was at the bottom of a large cavity at its center. Even the top of the tallest feature was more than a kilometer below the original surface of the ice.

"Look!" Denise said and pointed to the console.

The button to initiate phase 3 "Elevation" was encircled by a pulsing white ring. There still seemed to be a lot of water around the structures, but that evidently didn't matter. The pumps were still running.

"The next phase is ready to be initiated," Will said to McHenry. "Should you get back to the *North Dakota*?"

McHenry nodded but seemed reluctant.

"How long do you need?" Will asked.

"Everything's ready to go," the captain replied. "I'll just need time to get back. Give me twenty minutes to be safe."

Will nodded.

"By the way, they found the mangled bodies of Chinese ops in the debris expelled from the tunnel," McHenry said.

"I heard," Will said. "Must've got caught up in the melt."

"It means they were dangerously close," Daniel said.

"Chinese and Russian naval forces are moving into the area," McHenry continued. "They're heading for the Weddell Sea – some are already there – and the Chinese have been preparing for air attacks – nuclear-capable."

"To accomplish what, exactly?" Daniel asked.

Before McHenry could respond, a sailor rushed in and blurted, "Captain, Lieutenant Diggs requests that you come back to the *North Dakota* immediately."

"What's going on?" McHenry asked.

"I don't know, sir," the man replied. "But he said you should hurry, and that you should bring the crew along."

McHenry's face turned pale. He looked to Will and said, "This doesn't sound good."

Will's fingers tingled. He had a bad feeling. "I'm going with you," he said.

McHenry started to respond and then seemed to reconsider what he was going to say. "You should all come along," he said and looked to the others. "If anything should go wrong – flooding or something – you'd be trapped back here."

Will had a feeling that it wasn't flooding that worried the captain.

WILL FOLLOWED behind McHenry and four armed sailors. The others trailed by 50 yards, except Denise who lagged by fewer than 20.

Still in the tunnel and 100 yards from the shaft room, off the main bay, an eruption of gunfire caused everyone to take cover by sprawling on the floor. Men yelled back and forth between blasts from automatic weapons. A lull in the noise was interrupted by yelling that terminated with a flash of light and an explosion from the shaft room.

"That was a fucking grenade!" McHenry exclaimed. "Give me the radio."

One of the sailors handed him a walkie-talkie. Will figured they were close enough to communicate with anyone in the main bay.

McHenry got Diggs on the radio. "What's going on?"

"There was an explosion somewhere up the shaft," Diggs said. "I sent a team up the service tunnels to check it out. Now we're being attacked. Russian ops got in through the hatch at the top."

"How many?" McHenry asked.

Diggs' reply coincided with another burst of gunfire, followed by multiple single shots.

"Repeat."

"Between 30 and 50," Diggs said. "There are six of ours up there. The intruders leapfrogged them by rappelling to service tunnels below them. They're trapped in a service tunnel at 900 feet. One man down."

One man down. Will's mind ramped into a rage.

He ran back to Denise and said, "Stay low, and stay here." He grabbed her arm and squeezed it hard. "I mean it, and don't let the others move forward. Understand?" He stared her in the eyes until she nodded.

"What are you going to do?" she asked.

"You don't want to know," he replied and then ran forward and crouched next to McHenry.

"What the hell are you doing?" McHenry said. "Get back."

"Remember what happened on the Chinese carrier?" Will asked.

McHenry stared at him for a second, and then his expression turned to recognition.

"Trust me," Will said as he stood, making no attempt to take cover as another explosion rocked the walls.

Will ran the final 100 yards to the end of the tunnel, near the shaft room entrance. All of the action was overhead, except for some stray bullets and one grenade that had fallen to the bottom.

When there was a break in the action, he leapt into the shaft room and into the doorway that led to the spiraling service tunnel. He sat against the wall and separated.

In an instant, his consciousness flashed through the spiral tunnel to an elevation of 300 feet from the floor, to the first access tunnel that led from the upward spiraling corridor to the main shaft. All was clear. He returned to his body and sprinted upward until he reached the first tunnel access entrance. He ran in a few steps and sat against the wall, out of breath. He concentrated, separated, and followed the spiral corridor upward another 150 feet. All was clear.

He repeated the process twice more before he encountered the first group of intruders. They were Russian special ops, and 13 of them were attacking the next service tunnel up.

Will passed through the rock and into the service tunnel. All six of the *North Dakota*'s crew were there: two defended the entrance to the spiral tunnel, two defended the opening to the vertical shaft, and one other tended to the downed man who was on his back and bleeding from the chest and mouth.

Will's rage caused his vision to turn into a sparkling fire.

He passed through the rock and into the spiral tunnel above the trapped men, where he found another 18 Russian intruders. He passed into the shaft and found another 12 rappelling down the shaft.

At that instant, Will heard someone yell "Fire in the hole!" followed by an explosion.

Will flashed back to the service tunnel and saw what had happened. The Russian ops had rolled a hand grenade down the spiral shaft with the hope of timing it so that it would explode at the opening of the service tunnel where the *North Dakota*'s men were holed up. It had detonated too late.

Gunfire erupted again, from above and below the service tunnel, and another grenade rolled down the spiral corridor.

Will concentrated on shielding the entire entrance as the men again yelled and dove away from the opening.

The grenade exploded directly in front of the entrance, but the blast and shrapnel were deflected. It would have been a direct hit.

Less than a second after the blast, Russian soldiers charged toward the service tunnel from both directions.

Will's mind went into a white-hot rage, and he screamed through his very soul. The first of the storming soldiers, who was coming from above, blew apart as if he'd run into an airplane propeller. The first one coming from below crumpled into a mangled mess and started on fire.

Those who followed seemed to be confused and attempted to reverse course, but it was too late. Will simultaneously grasped them all – those from above and below – pressed them into a physically impossible conglomeration, and rung them with all of his might, as if he were trying to get the last drop of water out of a dish rag.

Before he knew what was happening, he'd dragged them to the next service tunnel up, and thrown their mangled bodies down the shaft. His consciousness followed them down until they struck the stone floor.

He flew back up the shaft and found the attackers that were rappelling. He cut all their ropes at once. Their bodies spontaneously ignited into flames on the way down, and their screams were silenced, one by one, as they struck the floor.

In an instant, he soared all the way up the spiral corridor – all was clear – and went to the hatch that led to the outside. The lid wasn't there – it had been blasted apart – and he went through the opening and into the cold. There were four soldiers standing around the large iris door that covered the shaft. They'd removed most of the snow and gravel.

Will forced them all through the small hatch simultaneously, and threw their broken bodies down the shaft. He screamed with them as he burned them all the way down to the floor.

All was silent.

JACOB MADE his way up to McHenry and listened as the captain and his first officer talked over the radio in between flurries of gunfire.

They'd moved to within 15 meters of the shaft room when an explosion boomed from high in the shaft.

"Sounds like another grenade," McHenry said into the radio. "How many do we have going up?"

"We have twelve men ready," Diggs replied. "Small arms only."

"Damn," McHenry hissed.

A second explosion rumbled from above, after which a high-pitched wail sounded in the tunnel. To Jacob, it sounded like a cross between a jet engine and a braking train. A torrent of fear surged through him as if he were in imminent danger.

An instant later something bright hit the floor with a "splutt" sound, like that of a pumpkin being smashed on the sidewalk. A dozen more hit the surface in quick succession. It took him a few seconds to realize what they were.

"My holy God," McHenry said.

They were mangled bodies and body parts, and they were all on fire. Even the smaller pieces that blew apart on impact were ablaze as if they were rags doused in oil.

Others started to hit, only these were preceded by their screams as they fell. In less than thirty seconds it stopped. At the center of the floor beneath the shaft opening was a blazing pile of mangled humanity – 40 or 50 bodies in total. All was silent except for the crackling of the flames.

Denise rushed up, followed by the others. Her expression turned to horror as her eyes seemed to recognize what they viewed. It was when she covered her nose and mouth that Jacob noticed the stench. It smelled like burnt hair and feces.

"Look!" Daniel said and pointed to the burning mound.

Through the wavering heat was the silhouette of a man. It was Will. He stood perfectly upright on the opposite side of the shaft room, closest to the main bay. His head tilted slightly upward and his arms were at his sides.

The quiet was then broken by a deafening wailing sound – the same as before but louder. Jacob covered his ears and turned to see the others doing the same.

The mound of smoldering bodies flared up, and then the intensity instantaneously increased to such a degree that everyone ran deeper into the tunnel to escape the heat. It roared like a rocket engine blasting up the shaft in a blue-white flame.

In 20 seconds it was over, and all was quiet and dark.

They all moved toward the shaft room with great caution. The smoke was gone, but heat still radiated from the floor and walls. The odor was still present, but not as strong. The bodies were gone.

Ash fluttered in the rising air currents and swirled like a light snow in a breeze.

Will stood on the opposite side of the shaft room, near the entrance to the main bay. It was as if he were in a trance, and only the whites of his eyes showed under half-closed lids.

Jacob bent at the waist as his stomach quivered, wanting to expel its contents. His mind flashed back to the memory of him pointing a gun at the man when he'd first met him.

WILL SAW them through the falling ashes.

It was Denise's eyes he met first, and he saw confusion and fear. Shame entered his mind for a second, but it dissipated in an instant.

"It's safe now, Captain," Will said to McHenry. "Your man needs help right away."

McHenry walked toward him and nodded to someone over Will's shoulder.

Will turned to see Lieutenant Diggs with a dozen young sailors. Their eyes were wide and on Will. They all carried weapons, and two carried packs with medical supplies.

"The hatch at the top was blown away," Will said to McHenry. "It should probably be closed off."

"You heard him," McHenry said. "Go!"

The men hurried into the shaft.

McHenry looked to Will, up the shaft, then back to Will.

"I can't explain it," Will said, preempting the captain's question.

"Is this what happened on the ship?"

Will nodded. "Similar," he said and then had to take a step backward to keep his balance. Dizziness nearly overtook him and he suddenly felt famished, dehydrated, and exhausted.

"You okay?" McHenry asked and took a firm hold of Will's upper arm with a strong hand.

Will stabilized himself and McHenry let loose.

"I need a few minutes to rest," Will said. "And eat something."

Will then noticed that the others had gathered around.

"What the hell was that?" Jacob asked.

"That was him saving our asses," McHenry said and looked to Denise. "Take him back to the *NoDak* and get him some food."

Denise nodded.

McHenry patted Will on the shoulder and then hurried into the service tunnel to go to his men.

AFTER EATING a bowl of beef stew with Denise in the mess hall, Will grabbed a nutrition bar and finished it before he got to his bunk.

He needed to rest his mind for a few minutes. He didn't remember falling asleep, but recalled the nightmares when he awakened two hours later.

He stood and, before he could exit his quarters, a sailor stepped inside. It seemed he'd been standing at the door.

"Name's Anders – I'm a Hospital Corpsman," the man said. "Captain McHenry wants me to look you over before you head back out."

"You a medical doctor?"

The man shook his head. "Not yet, sir."

Will sat. "How's the wounded man?"

"Petty Officer Dunlap is doing okay," Anders replied. "Bullet hit him on the right side of the chest, but missed the lung. The bleeding is under control. If we can keep infection out, he'll be fine."

It was a relief.

Anders took Will's blood pressure and shined a light in his eyes. As he listened to his heart, he said, "What's causing Dunlap the most pain is a broken tooth. Broke when his face hit the floor."

Will understood dental pain better than anyone. "No dentists on board?"

Anders shook his head. "Nope, but I can cap it – seal it with a composite. He'll get it properly fixed when we get home."

Anders put his gadgets in a black bag. "Everything looks good," he said. "They're waiting for you in the mess."

Will thanked him and headed for the mess hall. When he arrived, he grabbed some scrambled eggs and bacon and took a seat with the others, across from Denise. Everyone was there, including McHenry and Lieutenant Diggs.

"We got a radio update – still can't reply – indicating that the Chinese are asking about their personnel, and they're getting antsy," McHenry explained. "As we know, their people are gone, and it's just a matter of time before the Chinese make another attempt."

"The next one will be more drastic," Diggs added.

"What about the Russians?" Daniel asked.

"Nothing from them yet," McHenry replied.

"We need to move forward," Will said.

"I agree," McHenry said. "When you're ready, head back down the tunnel to the control room and initiate the next phase. The *North Dakota* is ready to go."

WILL PUSHED the button to initiate the "Elevation Phase."

Everyone watched as the gauges and controls on the console moved in unison to the far left and rearranged themselves. An array of new ones filled the center third of the screen, and additional controls and gauges appeared on the console. The video feeds and schematic diagrams also rearranged – some faded away, and new ones appeared.

The complex schematic of pipes, valves, and pumps disappeared and a new one took its place. It looked like the three-dimensional diagram of a colossal contiguous structure.

"Look at the water!" Denise exclaimed.

The view from the top of the mountain above the Nazi base gave the best view of the valley, which was now mostly empty. The water at the bottom churned like a boiling pot.

A few seconds later, all of the structures ascended in unison.

"It's moving," Will said.

No one spoke as the massive components rose. Shorter features emerged from the water, which now seemed to drain around the outer edges of a platform on which everything was mounted.

Ten minutes later, the structure stopped moving, and everyone stared and remained silent, seemingly studying the massive, complex object and anticipating more to happen.

The base of the structure was subtly curved, like a shallow, inverted circular bowl. Six hemispherical domes were arranged in a symmetric ring about its center, each with a channel that extended radially outward, following the downward curvature of the circular base. Will estimated that each of the six domes was as large as a professional basketball arena.

The tallest feature, the 200-meter-tall, tapered tower structure, emerged seamlessly from the center of the base – inside the ring of domes. Other satellite features – smaller towers and complex antenna-like spikes – were arrayed around the main tower and aligned parallel to it. Innumerable intricate devices were scattered about the base, but constructed in a manner that gave the overall structure a sleek look. Everything seemed to be the same color, but Will couldn't tell if that was gray, or white.

"What is it?" Denise asked.

No one spoke.

A few seconds later, the screen changed, rearranging many of the displays and inserting new ones. A message appeared: "Ramping Up Subspace Power: Ready to Initiate Final Phase." A new button appeared on the console. A white ring pulsed around it.

Will pushed the button.

WILL STARED AT THE SCREEN. The last of the water ran off the base of the colossal construction as it ascended another 100 feet above the mountain valley. Its wet surfaces glimmered in the low light.

"What now?" Denise asked.

Just as she finished speaking, three lines of text scrolled up from the bottom of the screen.

Will read them aloud. "It says, 'Shield and facility fully operational.' Second line, 'Encoded communication sent.' Third line, 'Proceed through corridor to transport chamber.'"

"Corridor?" Denise said. "Where?"

At that instant, an opening formed in the wall to the left of the screen. A white ring-shaped light flashed above it.

Will walked toward the entrance.

"Wait," Daniel said. "Shouldn't we think about this?"

"We have to go," Will responded. Both anxiety and excitement were building in him.

Daniel stared at him with an expression that changed from concern to agreement.

Will led the way, followed by Daniel, and then Denise and the others.

The passage was large enough to drive a bus through it, and its walls were smooth and white, like those in the control room. Light seemed to emanate uniformly from the walls, and there was a mild downward grade as they walked in the direction of the valley. It seemed they were heading toward a position near the exposed base of the structure.

After five minutes of walking, the downward grade leveled off and then turned into a slight upward grade. Five more minutes and the passage widened and terminated at a flat wall, similar to that which served as the screen in the control room, minus the console. As they got closer, the wall lit up with the image of a doorway, and a large ring-shaped white light pulsed at its center. A message appeared above it in alien script.

Will read it aloud, "Separate to Enter."

"What does that mean?" Jacob asked.

"It means only I can get in," Will said as he sat on the floor and crossed his legs.

He concentrated, separated, and passed through the wall – through the image of the door – and into a small compartment about the size of an airplane lavatory. On the wall to his left was one illuminated button encircled with a white flashing ring. The word for "open" flashed above it. He pushed it.

The wall behind him – the one through which he'd passed to enter the small chamber – split and shifted, and a physical doorway to the corridor appeared. He returned to his body and stood.

"The wall spontaneously parted in the middle and slid apart," Jacob said with a look of astonishment.

The others gathered around the newly exposed opening and stared with expressions of excitement and anxiety.

Will stepped through the opening and into the compact compartment. He pointed to the button, which had changed.

"When I entered while separated, the button read 'open,'" he explained. "I pushed it, and the doorway appeared. Now it says 'close.'"

As he stepped out, the button disappeared.

Denise stepped in to look, and nothing happened. "Where's the button?" she asked and stepped out.

Will went inside and the button reappeared. "It's back."

Denise stepped in, and it disappeared before she even got to the doorway.

"Take a few steps back," he said.

As Denise did so, the button reappeared.

"Looks like it's set up to make sure only one person goes in at a time," Will said. "Also seems to sense who pressed the button that opened it."

"But you had to separate to press that button," Daniel said.

Will shuddered. It was a screening mechanism, and it was apparent that only he could get inside and close the door behind him. He didn't know if that was good or bad, but it might complicate things.

"Stand back, I'm going to close the door."

"What are you doing?" Denise asked, as she reached in and grabbed his shoulder. She was clearly agitated.

"Time is running out, Denise," he said. Looking into her concerned eyes, a surge of affection nearly overcame him.

"I'll be okay," he said. Although he had no way of knowing that, it made no sense to him that he should be in any danger.

Denise squeezed into the compartment, kissed him on the lips, and took a step back. A tear rolled down the side of her nose to the corner of her mouth. Will wasn't sure from where her emotion was coming, but he was sure she sensed something. So did he.

Will turned to his left, extended his fingertips through the smooth surface, and pushed the button. The door closed.

JAMES THACKETT SAT in a leather chair that faced the window of his Space Systems office. The information his interrogation team had extracted from Tao had been verified by other CIA sources. He'd been skeptical in the beginning, and felt the information they'd spilled about future operations was too farfetched. He'd been wrong.

Lenny Butrolsky had delivered information from an Israeli source that helped the CIA to thwart yet another chemical attack on Space Systems. It also provided details of broader Chinese military plans. The Department of Defense knew what to look for, and now it was starting.

Chinese bombers had taken to the air and were headed to various locations in the southern hemisphere. Whether their actions were a mere threat could not be known until it was over. If a real attack, the targets were unknown: it could be the Nazi base – they now seemed to know its approximate location – or the carrier group in the Weddell Sea.

The United States' naval forces in the region had been warned and advised to take evasive and defensive action. This included an encoded message for the *North Dakota*, which was listening but could not transmit.

The *Stennis* would scramble fighter jets as soon as the Chinese bombers and escorts were in range. American nuclear submarines near the Chinese mainland were on notice for possible launch. It was not looking good.

The disappearance of the Chinese commandos on the ice in Antarctica, and the subsequent discovery of some of their mangled bodies off the coast, in the Weddell Sea, seemed to be the stimulus for the action. The fact that they'd sent bombers rather than launching missiles left a sliver of hope that they'd turn back. If they'd instead launched missiles, American missiles would already be in the air.

The world was on the brink, and the public was oblivious.

Every country was at full alert and ready to react. Thackett thought it was strange that the worldwide news media had barely covered any of the latest developments. Perhaps their respective governments were keeping them in the dark. It made sense: China and Russia wouldn't want to rile their populations, and the rest, including the United States, would have difficulty explaining what was happening to their citizens.

The Russians had lost contact with a submarine, and Thackett knew that it was at the bottom of the Weddell Sea. Its fate would have to be investigated further before the Russians would take action.

A thermal anomaly had been detected by satellites on the Antarctic surface, in close proximity to the base. Thackett, and the rest of the world, was in the dark about what was happening, since the *North Dakota* had strict orders not to communicate.

Thackett stood from his chair and hurried over to a small kitchenette and vomited into the sink. He hadn't eaten anything in over 24 hours, so only a small volume of noxious fluid emerged. He followed with some dry heaving and then turned on the faucet and rinsed out his mouth. He wiped his face with a towel, extracted a can of ginger ale from a small refrigerator, popped it open, and took a swig. It burned on the way down, but it perked him up so that he might be able to think again. Although, it was unlikely any amount of thinking on his part could affect anything.

Even though the Nazi base was deep inside a mountain, a direct hit with a thermonuclear device would likely kill its occupants.

Thackett winced as his stomach churned again. He took another sip of soda and averted another vomiting episode.

He never should have let them all go together. He'd loaded the bases, setting up China for a grand slam. He could lose Daniel and Sylvia, the foremost experts on the Red Wraith project and everything that had happened in Antarctica. Most devastating, however, was the possibility of losing William Thompson. He could not be replaced.

What did China know that everyone else didn't? Was the Chinese government acting out of fear? Did they think that the United States might gain something that would give them an advantage on the geopolitical board? He doubted that was the case: whatever the United States gained, China would eventually steal, just as they'd done with intellectual property for decades.

Thackett walked back to the window and gazed out at the lights below. It was 2:00 a.m. and the traffic on the surface streets was sparse. He pulled out his phone and dialed the leader of the interrogation team. He explained the situation and directed the operative to refocus his line of questioning.

An urgent update had been transmitted to the *North Dakota*, and the order given to extract everyone. Things had been escalating for a long time. Thackett just hoped the Chinese hadn't become desperate enough to drop a bomb.

DENISE SIPPED water out of a plastic bottle and paced back and forth near the door where Will had disappeared nearly 40 minutes earlier. She tried to participate in the conversations of the others, but it did little to comfort her. Acute anxiety saturated her mind and body because things were accelerating, and she knew there was nothing she could do about it.

The sound of people running in the passage behind them made everyone reach for the side arms given to them by Lieutenant Diggs. A few seconds later, two sailors rushed into the room.

"We have to evacuate," one of the men managed to say, despite gasping for air. "Captain's orders."

"What's going on?" Daniel asked.

"Chinese are going to attack," the other sailor answered as he looked at his watch. "Bombers. They'll be here in 30 minutes – it will take us 20 minutes to get back. We have to board and get the hell out, now."

Denise's mind froze for a few seconds without being able to form a single thought. Her mouth seemed to act without her brain. "I'm not leaving without Will," she said.

"What?" the taller of the two sailors asked as he looked around.

"Where is he?"

"He's inside," Denise answered, and pointed to the image of the door on the wall.

The man rushed over and pushed on it. "How long has he been in there?" the sailor asked.

"A little over 40 minutes," Daniel responded.

"Call him back," the sailor instructed.

Denise yelled for him, and the others joined in. They pounded on the wall.

After a full minute with no response from Will, the taller sailor said, "No time. Leave a note. Let's go."

Daniel tore a piece of paper out of a notebook and started writing.

"I'm not leaving without him," Denise said.

"Ma'am, I have a direct order from the captain to carry you if you do not come willingly," the shorter, but thicker, of the two sailors said.

As Denise sized him up, the man shook his head.

"The captain ordered me to come back with everyone I can find, no exceptions," he explained. "Please, Ms. Walker."

Jacob stepped next to her. "Denise," he said. "We'll leave him a note. He'll know what's happening. I think we'd only slow him down if we stayed. He can do things that we can't."

Denise stared at Jacob as her brain processed his words. He was right. Will would try to keep them safe at the risk of himself. "Okay," she said. "Let's go."

They ran a few hundred yards through the tunnel to the main control room, and then entered the long tunnel that led back to the *North Dakota*. Denise's side ached with a kilometer to go, but she thought she was feeling better than Jonathan. Jacob hardly seemed winded at all as they crossed through the shaft room and into the main bay.

As they approached the dock, Denise stepped aside and let the others cross the gangplank onto the deck of the *North Dakota*. At the last moment, she had a change of heart and turned back toward the shaft room.

The stocky sailor was waiting for her.

She tried to press past him, but he grabbed her arms. She made a move to knee him in the groin, but he blocked the strike with his thigh. He spun her around and squeezed her in a tight bear hug, her arms trapped at her sides. He lifted her off the ground and carried her to the gangplank.

"Will!" she screamed.

"Please, Ms. Walker," the sailor yelled into her ear. "We have to go!"

"Will!" she yelled again and burst into a frantic scream. She struggled as tears streamed down her face.

THACKETT WENT to the main communications center in the Space Systems building. The monitoring arrangement mirrored that of the CIA's Langley facility, and conveyed the same information.

Thackett maintained an outward appearance of calm, but his guts were on fire.

A large monitor tracked a group of a dozen Chinese bombers and their fighter escorts, 32 in total, as they approached the southwestern coastline of Antarctica. At that point, the group split into two, one heading for the Weddell Sea, toward the *Stennis* carrier group, and the other inland, in the direction of the Nazi base.

The *Stennis* had over 40 of its 70 aircraft in flight, 25 of which were heading on a course to intercept the Chinese planes that were on a direct line for the carrier group. The rest pursued the Chinese aircraft heading for the base.

The carrier group took a defensive posture, encircling the carrier with guided missile destroyers and other vessels. American subs patrolled the depths. Others shadowed a Chinese carrier heading toward the area.

Thackett felt confident that the carrier group would be okay. He thought it was likely that the contingent of aircraft directed toward the *Stennis* was a diversion. We'd have to send half of our birds to intercept them. The real target was the Nazi base. Since they probably were able to narrow down its location to the thermal anomaly in the valley, the Chinese might think that a thermonuclear weapon would be their best option.

It was odd that satellites could not get pictures of anything in the valley. Only thermal images were available, and they showed no structure whatsoever. It seemed that the area was just warming uniformly.

A young CIA analyst approached him. The name on his badge read "Thomas Brickman."

"Sir, are we going to war?" the young man asked.

"Not sure yet, Brickman," Thackett replied. "We'll know soon."

"What can we do?"

"Just do your job the best you can," Thackett said. "Everything will work out."

The man nodded and returned to his place at a console monitoring satellite feeds.

Thackett wasn't sure how things were going to work out. It was out of his hands, and in the hands of the military experts. All he could do was make sure the CIA provided them with any new information that appeared.

DENISE WENT to her quarters as the *North Dakota* descended through the doors and into the still-turbulent waters of the cavern. She buried her face in a pillow and screamed.

She was not angry with anyone. She wasn't angry with the sailor who had probably saved her life. She'd apologized to him as soon as they were both inside the sub. The young man smiled and told her not to sweat it.

A few minutes later, Sylvia entered the room they shared. "You okay?" she asked.

Denise sat up. She knew her burning eyes gave away the emotions she was trying to conceal. "I have to be okay," she replied.

"Will is pretty resourceful," Sylvia said.

"I doubt he'd survive a nuclear blast, Sylvia," Denise snapped. "He's still human."

Sylvia looked down.

Denise reached out and grabbed Sylvia's hand. "Sorry," Denise said. "This was the right thing to do. We couldn't wait. And Will wouldn't have wanted us to."

Sylvia sat on the bunk across from her. "It's too late to go through the tunnel," she explained. "McHenry said any major explosion could cause a collapse, and the currents still have not died down. There could still be dangerous debris flowing around."

"So where are we going?"

"Deep into the cavern, near the mouth of the tunnel," Sylvia explained. "They've determined it to be the most structurally stable location."

"How long will we wait?"

"They have a mini-sub that's going to poke a hole in the ice on the lake," Sylvia said. "It will stick an antenna and some sensors through the hole, including a camera. That way they can get radio transmissions and also monitor what's happening outside."

"Guess we'll just have to sit tight," Denise said. The wait was going to be excruciating.

JAMES THACKETT STARED at the screens as the team of over 50 CIA analysts yelled things out as they occurred.

The Chinese bomber squadron that was heading for the *Stennis* carrier group turned away without a shot. Some short chases occurred between the US and Chinese fighter planes, but nothing more. A few minutes after the engagement, both groups headed back to their respective origins. The Chinese plan to divide the American fighter assets had succeeded.

The Chinese bomber formation heading toward the Antarctic mainland would encounter a swarm of American F-18 fighter jets ten miles from their target. Thackett knew that was cutting it too close. If one of the bombers managed to squeeze through, it would be a matter of minutes before they'd be in bombing range of the base. And, if they were dropping thermonuclear devices, they'd only have to get close. If that happened, he wondered if the US would wage all-out war on China. The answer would be revealed in the next 20 minutes.

All attention turned to the video feeds from Naval Command. Both aircraft formations converged over a mountainous region ten miles northeast of the valley. The various aircraft could be distinguished on the screen by their colors, with a legend indicating their nationality and type. Red airplane symbols represented the Chinese H-6 bombers. There were eight of them. Thackett knew it was likely that only one or two of them actually carried thermonuclear devices, with the rest serving as decoys.

The legend also indicated the number of each type of plane. In addition to the eight bombers, the Chinese had 38 J-15 Flying Shark fighter jets. The US had 42 F-18 Super Hornets.

"They're separating," one analyst commented.

Thackett watched as a contingent of Chinese fighters increased speed, pulling ahead of the bombers in an aggressive move toward the approaching American planes. The bomber group then split into three parts, each with a few fighters in support. One headed along a vector straight for the base. The other two split left and right in an attempt to avoid the direct path of the incoming US jets.

The American squadron matched the move with a split of its own.

Just as the fighter jets were about to engage, the bombers veered sharply from their heading and reversed course. Thirty seconds later, the Chinese fighters followed suit. They were leaving the area.

"What the hell?" Thackett exclaimed. "What are they doing?"

At that moment, Brickman called to Thackett. "There's something strange in some of the satellite feeds," Brickman said as Thackett approached.

Thackett looked over and saw something odd on the monitor. He hoped they weren't Chinese intercontinental ballistic missiles.

CHAPTER 17

Will pressed the close button. The door behind him closed, and another one opened on the opposite side of the tight compartment.

He stepped through and was instantly taken aback by the size of the space he'd entered. It was circular but had enough floor space for a soccer field. The ceiling was dome-shaped and 50 feet high at its center. Everything was white, and the lighting was uniform and seemed to radiate from the walls, floors, and ceiling. An array of over 200 smooth, casket-sized pods bulged seamlessly from the floor.

It was dead silent, and the air was still and comfortable.

The wall on the left was a display of the same design as that in the main control room, riddled with schematics, messages, and indicators of various types. A large image at the top center of the screen indicated he was in one of six identical domes arranged in a circle around a conical tower. It was the same tower that was the first to break the surface as the water was pumped away.

Something caught his eye on the display and, as he started to move closer, a noise came from behind him.

The hair on his neck and arms bristled and he whirled around. It sounded like a voice – a whisper.

After a few seconds of silence, he turned again toward the display screen. At that instant, the whisper sounded again – louder.

He spun around. "Who's there?" he yelled. After a few seconds with no response, he yelled again, louder.

He listened intently and, a few seconds later, he heard it.

"William," it said.

He recognized the voice.

He sat on the floor and separated.

Denise felt more anxiety than ever in her life. Sleep had eluded her, she couldn't eat, and her mind couldn't focus on anything.

She sat in the mess hall and sipped tea while the others gathered for an update.

The last to arrive was McHenry. "The mini-sub poked through the ice on the lake and received a transmission," he explained.

The captain seemed sick as he updated everyone on the events since leaving the base. He mentioned that he'd gotten a strong reprimand for leaving Will behind. Even though Denise was adamantly against it at the time, she thought the captain had made the right decision, and told him so.

She also felt guilty for leaving Will, but she knew he would have forced her to go anyway. His argument would have been that he had more tools to cope with whatever happened, and that she'd just get in the way. He would have been right.

"The Chinese bombers turned around," McHenry continued. "We'll be heading back to the base when we're given the all-clear."

"Why did they call it off?" Daniel asked. "Was it just a threat?"

McHenry shrugged. "We're awaiting more information."

"How long before we get the all-clear?" Denise asked.

"Four to six hours," McHenry replied. "They'll do a comprehensive search for threats – air, land, and sea – before giving us the go-ahead."

Denise's nerves settled with relief, and she suddenly felt exhausted. Now she just wanted to get back to the base.

"Landau," Will said.

A white, wraith-like apparition hovered above the floor and seemed to consider him.

"You have come a long way, William," Landau said. "You are again where you are supposed to be."

"Again?" Will asked. "I don't understand."

"They are almost here."

"Who?"

"Those who will end your world – your generation," Landau replied.

"Can they be stopped?"

"It is why you are here," Landau said.

"We're running out of time," Will said. "I can feel it." His anxiety ratcheted as he felt the clock getting closer to expiration. "Tell me what to do. What is this place?"

"The previous generation passed the judgment, and was allowed to continue to exist," Landau said, not answering his question.

"Billions died." Will recalled from the incoming message that only thousands of the previous generation had escaped the execution.

"Even so, it was different for them than it will be for you."

"How so?"

"You failed the judgment," Landau replied. "The very essence of your race is to be extinguished."

"The essence? I don't understand."

"The core of each living being, and of those who have passed from physical existence, will be destroyed."

"You are talking about souls," Will said. He'd heard this before. "You mean our souls will be destroyed?"

"Yes," Landau replied. "They have been deemed tainted – a poisonous intrusion on the rest of existence – and must be destroyed."

"The souls of the previous generation were allowed to survive?"

"Yes," Landau said.

"Where did they go – what happened to them?" Will asked.

"I cannot answer that question."

"You told Horace that I should come here," Will said. "Why am I here?"

"The previous generation constructed this portal to facilitate a mass exodus when it was your generation's time, so that more than just thousands might be saved," Landau explained. "But they made the assumption that your generation would be at the same stage of development – technologically and evolutionarily – at which theirs had been at the time of judgment."

"By 'evolutionarily' you mean they assumed everyone would have developed separation abilities," Will said. "What is this place?"

"It breaks down your body and duplicates it in another location," Landau explained. "Your soul will travel separately, and recombine with the duplicate."

Will understood. He'd heard the conjectural theory before. The reason the body had to be broken down was to gather all of the information about it – how the DNA was constructed, how the various atoms and molecules were bonded together, and how the synapses in the brain were arranged. That information could then be conveyed to another location at the speed of light. The hypothetical question that had always come up regarding what would happen to the soul in this process. Would it be lost? Now he knew: the soul would have to travel separately.

"You're talking about teleportation," Will said.

"Yes."

"But you have to be able to separate to use it," Will said. "No one else can escape."

"This facility was designed to transport millions in just weeks," Landau confirmed. "But, yes, only you can use it."

"So I leave, and everyone else gets destroyed?" Will asked. "I will not do that."

"That you are the singular being of your generation to transform might be precisely what saves the rest," Landau said.

"I don't understand," Will said. His patience was waning.

"If there are no evanescent beings on the planet, or in its vicinity, when they come to execute the regeneration, everything may be reset," Landau said.

"Reset? What do you mean?"

"The regeneration may be suspended. In that case, the probe will revert to the state it was in before you activated it, and go dormant for centuries," Landau explained. "Your race will continue on, and might finally recover from its poisoning."

"The Nazis were the poison," Will argued. "They started this. But they're gone now."

"The consequences of vile acts never diminish," Landau said. "And, although you might think that the mass killing, torture, and attempted exterminations of your past are isolated events, they are also indicative of a holistic sickness within your race. Even so, there is a remote possibility your leaving gives those left behind another chance."

"How 'remote' of a possibility?"

"Does it matter?"

Will knew that it did not. He'd have to do whatever he could even if the chances were miniscule. "So I am supposed to be gone when the executioners arrive. What am I supposed to do?" Will asked. "Figure out how to use this device and transport out of here? What if it doesn't work – or I can't figure it out?"

"In that case, there's another possibility," Landau said.

"What's that?"

"You could die."

Will's mind seemed to darken as it converged on the meaning of Landau's words. "You mean kill myself."

"Yes."

Will was confused. "Why didn't you just let me die when I was in the Red Box?"

"It had to be this way," Landau explained. "In order to save your world, the probe had to be actuated, the judgment had to be made, and the destroyers would have to come here and find nothing."

"So why not just kill me now?"

"Because a great opportunity would be lost," Landau said.

Will couldn't conceive how anything positive could come out of what was happening. "What opportunity?" he asked.

"I cannot say more."

Will didn't like the uncertainty, but there was only one choice. He had to go through with it – the transport, or the ugly alternative.

"Does the previous generation still exist?" Will asked. "This place is 40 thousand years old."

"I cannot say," Landau replied.

"Where is this thing going to take me?"

"I cannot say."

Will would get no more information. He had to take a leap of faith into the abyss – into death, or into some other world – wherever the transport device would take him. Both were unknowns, but he had more confidence in the former. Death was certain. The device might not even function after millennia of dormancy.

"Who are you, Landau?" Will asked.

After contemplating Will's question, Landau answered, "I am the caretaker, the guardian, and the timekeeper."

The answer only confused Will, but he knew that Landau would reveal nothing more. Time was running out. "How will we know when they are coming?" Will asked. His mind twitched with the ramping anxiety. If they arrived unexpectedly and he was still on the planet, all would be lost.

"Gravitational disruptions will be detected hours before they appear," Landau replied. "This facility will destroy itself when it senses their imminent arrival."

"Why?"

"There can be no evidence that a being with separation abilities escaped," Landau explained. "In that case, the world would be immediately regenerated and the hunt for you would begin."

"What do I do now?"

"I will give you no more information. As you said, time is running short," Landau said. "I hope you succeed, William."

With those final words Landau vanished, and Will returned to his body.

He stood up from the floor and rubbed his eyes. He looked at his watch: two hours had passed in an instant. The combination of the near instantaneous passage of time and not knowing what was happening on the outside drove his mind to the brink of panic.

He now knew what he had to do. He had to be off the planet, or dead, when the executioners arrived.

DANIEL FILLED his mug with hot water, grabbed a bag of English Breakfast tea, and joined Captain McHenry, Sylvia, and Lieutenant Diggs at a table in the galley. It had been two hours since their last update.

"The good news is that there have been no further moves by Chinese or Russian forces," McHenry said. "It's all clear."

"How long before we go back?" Sylvia asked.

"Another two hours," Diggs responded.

"You said that was the good news," Daniel said. "What's the bad?"

"This doesn't mean anything to me, but it might to you," the captain explained. "The message said that multiple large-magnitude gravitational events – gravitational waves – have been detected at the Livingston and Hanford facilities in the past three hours."

Daniel looked to Sylvia, whose face seemed to turn pale before his eyes.

"What does it mean?" Diggs asked.

Daniel swallowed hard and had to force his words through a tightening throat. "I think it means our time is up."

WILL EXITED the transport facility through the small room and found a handwritten note on the floor.

They were gone. They did the right thing.

He grabbed a flashlight and his backpack and started the long walk toward the bay. His walk turned to a jog as the anxiety welled in his mind.

It went from light to dark as he passed through the control room and into the long tunnel that led back to the main bay. The tunnel lighting had been powered by the base's power grid, which, in turn, had been energized by the *North Dakota's* nuclear reactor. The darkness was a clear indicator that the *North Dakota* was gone.

After 20 minutes of walking at a brisk pace, he emerged into the bay and shone the flashlight in the direction of the dock. There were two large crates. He went to them and found a note tacked to one. It read: *A week's supplies. Will return ASAP.*

It looked like he'd have to carry out the plan before they got back. According to his estimate, he had a day left, two at the most.

He would have liked to have seen Denise one last time. The reality of what was to happen seemed to crush his soul, and his physical innards along with it.

The lid of each crate was held shut with four screws that stuck out about an inch, and were loose enough to turn with his fingers. He opened the first to reveal stacks of bottled water and boxes of food, including military MREs and nutrition bars.

He removed the lid from the second crate. The item on top was something that he needed, and they'd likely saved him a lot of time scrounging around the facility in the dark to find one. It was a Glock 9-millimeter handgun with a holster and an extra magazine. He doubted he'd need the extra ammo.

Beneath the gun were gloves, a parka, a blanket, and extra flashlights and batteries.

He packed his backpack with food, water, and batteries, and wrapped whatever he could in the blanket and tied it up.

The last thing he did before starting the long walk back was to strap the holster around his waist and load a round into the chamber of the Glock. It was an insurance policy: a quick exit.

DENISE FILLED her mug with coffee and sat across the table from Sylvia in the *North Dakota*'s galley. All of the others had gone.

It had been almost five hours since their evacuation. They were still at the mouth of the cavern but planned to ascend to the base in the next hour, after they received another update via the mini-sub.

"Do you love him?" Sylvia asked.

Denise's hand twitched and she stabilized her mug with the other just in time. She stared at Sylvia. Her mind was locked. She couldn't speak.

"Sorry," Sylvia said, her face reddening in what Denise interpreted as embarrassment. "I didn't mean to – "

"I do," Denise cut her off. "I'm a nervous wreck. It must be obvious."

Sylvia smiled. "Very much so."

Denise laughed as she caught a tear that streamed down the side of her nose with her hand. "It seems like I've known him for a long time. I investigated his case when he was still in the Red Box facility."

"He's a remarkable man," Sylvia said. "I can see why you feel this way about him."

Denise suddenly felt embarrassed. "It's selfish of me to be wrapped up in my own feelings when there is so much at stake."

Sylvia reached over the table and touched her hand. "Don't worry," she said. "We're only human."

At that moment, Daniel walked in and sat down next to Sylvia. He set his computer on the table along with a bagel and cream cheese. Denise must have missed him when he'd entered.

"We'll be back in an hour," Daniel said. "Everything's a little safer now that the Chinese and Russian ops are out of the picture."

Denise wondered if anyone would ever mention the Russian

soldiers who had been incinerated at the base. The vertical shaft had acted like the chimney of a crematorium. It was a scene that would come back to her in her nightmares but, even now, she wondered if it had really happened.

"I've been trying to find the report on the gravitational waves to give to Jacob," Daniel continued. "He should be here soon."

They had been updated on all fronts. The area around the base was clear, Space Systems was out of danger, and all aggressive military movements had not only ceased but reversed course. The latter was welcomed, but baffling. Something seemed wrong.

"What's going on with gravitational waves?" Denise asked.

Daniel looked to Sylvia who shook her head. "I haven't updated her yet," she said.

"The captain informed me that they've detected gravitational waves again. Intense ones."

"What does that mean?" Denise asked.

"When the probe rose into the sky and broadcast the electromagnetic signal, it also emitted gravitational waves – or at least they were emitted at the same time," Daniel explained.

"Recall that gravitational waves were also a part of the incoming radio signal," Sylvia added. "They carried information that was crucial to decoding the first part of the message."

"So what's the significance of the new ones?" Denise asked.

"We – humans – cannot produce gravitational waves," Daniel explained. "In fact, we've only just recently acquired the ability to detect them."

"So the latest detected gravitational waves might have been generated by whoever created the probe," Sylvia said.

Daniel nodded. "I think it means that something is starting – something is going to happen."

"We need to get back to the base," Denise said.

When they finally docked and the "all clear" was given to go ashore, Denise headed directly for the tunnel.

Leaving everyone else behind, she jogged down the long corridor toward the room where they'd left Will hours before. Her pace and anxiety increased as she approached the end of the two-kilometer tunnel. She had no idea what she'd find at the end but, in the back of her mind, she feared Will might not even be there.

Out of breath, she flew into the main control room and slid to a halt with a gasp.

Will stood in the middle of the room, facing her, expressionless. His eyes were open, but he seemed to be unaware of his surroundings. A full second passed before his eyes revealed recognition and he looked at her.

He rushed to her and lifted her in a tight hug.

She tried to respond, but his arms were crushing her ribs and all she could do was grunt.

He set her down. "Glad you're safe," he said. "Everyone else okay? What happened with the attack?"

"Everyone's fine," she replied. "China sent bombers to hit the base."

"What happened?"

"They turned around."

Will shook his head and seemed to go into deep thought.

"Maybe it was to intimidate us," she added. "I didn't want to leave you here."

"You had to," he said. "About time you made a smart choice."

"Are you starting already?"

She pointed to his hip. "Where did you get that?" She was staring at the gun. She recalled that, after the Russian attack in the shaft, everyone carried a weapon except Will. He didn't need one.

"The crew set me up with supplies," he explained. "Best to be prepared."

"No Chinese or Russian ops on the surface," she said. "Everything's okay at Space Systems, and the fleet seems safe for the moment."

Will nodded, but she noticed something in his eyes. Something wasn't right.

"What?" she asked.

"I need to talk to the others," he said.

"What did you find out?" she asked and grabbed his arm. "What happened when you went inside? What was there?"

Before he could answer, Daniel arrived, followed by the others, including Captain McHenry.

"You okay?" McHenry asked.

Will nodded. "Thanks for the supplies," he said. "I heard we were nearly attacked."

McHenry nodded. "Not sure what happened," he explained. "Naval Command informed us that a Chinese plane was carrying a nuke. For no reason, they called off the attack. What have you learned?"

"We need to get everyone together," Will said. "And we need to hurry."

THE BRIGHTLY-LIT BAY and the sight of the *North Dakota* gave Will a sense of comfort as they arrived.

He went aboard, showered, and headed for the galley. What he really needed was a good round of sleep, but he knew that would not be possible.

He ladled hot vegetable soup out of a steel pot into a bowl and grabbed a slice of pizza, and then sat on a bench directly across the table from Denise. The others were due to show up any minute.

Before she could speak, Will grabbed her hand. "You know that I love you," he said.

Denise flinched. She nodded. "What's wrong, Will?" she asked, seemingly fighting fear.

Will's chest tightened, and his hunger subsided. "Just remember that, okay?"

Daniel walked in with Sylvia. A half-minute later, Jacob arrived, followed by Jonathan and then McHenry.

McHenry asked the few sailors who were seated on the far end of the mess to leave. He then nodded to Will. "You have something to say?"

Will nodded and took a deep breath. He described what he'd seen in the transport room and explained its function.

"You have to be able to separate to use it?" Jacob asked.

Will nodded.

"They expected us to be more advanced," Daniel said.

Will then told them about his conversation with Landau, which induced looks of confusion in Jacob, McHenry, and Diggs, but he didn't have time to explain it to them.

"The final point is that I have to be gone when they come to regenerate the planet," Will said. "If they don't find anyone that can separate, they might cancel the regeneration, and reset the probe."

"You'll use the device to transport off the planet?" Daniel asked.

"That's one way," Will said.

"Where will it take you?" Denise asked.

"I don't know," Will replied.

"You said 'that's one way,'" McHenry said. "What's the other?"

Will avoided Denise's eyes and spoke directly to McHenry. "To not be alive when they arrive."

Denise gasped loudly.

"Kill yourself?" Daniel asked, seemingly appalled.

Will nodded.

"When will you have to transport?" McHenry asked, seemingly dismissing or wanting to divert attention from the second possibility.

"There will be a warning before they arrive," Will replied. "There won't be much time after that. The facility will self-destruct, and I'll have to be gone by then, and so will you."

"What's the warning?" Daniel asked.

"Gravitational waves," Will replied, "similar to those detected when the probe blasted out its signal. The process will start just hours after they're detected."

"How many hours?" McHenry said with an expression of alarm.

"My God," Daniel said.

"What?" Will asked.

"They just detected them," Daniel replied and looked to McHenry.

McHenry pulled out his laptop and opened it. A moment later he said, "They were detected at Livingston and Hanford at 14:38 – that's 2:38 p.m. That's just over 6 hours ago."

To Will it felt as if he were running off a cliff. He stood. "I have to get out of here, now. They'll be here at any moment. And I still need to learn how to use the device."

Denise stood and looked him in the eyes. He stared back at her. Everyone was silent.

"I'm sorry," Will said and dashed for the door.

WILL RUSHED BACK to his quarters to get the handgun he'd removed when he'd boarded. He sensed Denise following him, and she came in a few seconds later.

"Why are you taking that?" she asked, pointing to the pistol he'd just strapped to his side.

"Just in case," he replied and then caught the look of terror in her eyes. "It's not my first choice."

"Where will you go? Where will the transporter take you?" Denise asked, shifting her eyes from the gun to his eyes. "A spaceship? A planet?"

Will looked away. The sadness caused him physical pain. "Don't know," he replied. "Could be either."

"And after that?" she asked.

He looked back to her and knew immediately that it was a mistake. Tears were forming beads on her eyelashes.

"I don't know after that," he said.

"Couldn't you just come back after it's over?" she asked.

Will shook his head slowly. "The transport facility will be

destroyed. Besides, I don't know if it was designed to work in both directions."

Someone knocked at the door. It was McHenry.

Denise pushed past him and disappeared down the corridor.

McHenry nodded. "What are you going to do?"

"What do you mean?"

"Are you going to do it – are you going to transport?"

Will stared back at him, confused. After a few seconds, he caught on that McHenry was asking him if he was really going to go through with it. "I have to," Will said.

"What's the plan?" McHenry asked.

"I'm going now – I have to figure out how it operates."

McHenry nodded. "What if you can't figure it out, or if it's damaged in some way?"

With his hand, Will patted the gun that was strapped to his hip. "I move on to plan B."

McHenry grimaced, reached over, and squeezed Will's shoulder with a thick hand. "You're a brave man," McHenry said. "I hope it doesn't come to that."

CHAPTER 18

Will found Denise in her quarters. She was sitting on a bunk with Sylvia, who seemed to be consoling her. Sylvia left, and Will sat next to Denise and grabbed her hand.

"Things have always worked out this way for me," Will said.

"What do you mean?" she asked as she wiped her nose with her sleeve.

"I finally find you, and I have to go away," he said. "I've always had bad timing."

"Mine hasn't been so great either."

"You saved me, Denise," he said. "I'd already be dead if you hadn't found me. You gave me extra time."

It seemed that she wanted to speak but couldn't.

"If what I'm going to try actually works," he continued, "you will be responsible for saving many lives – maybe everyone's."

She shook her head. "Why are you trying to make me feel better?" she asked. "You're the one who's making the sacrifice."

"If it works," he said, "everyone will have played an important part. You included. If it doesn't work, we'll all be dead anyway."

"Can you promise me something?" she asked.

"Anything."

"Will you try to come back?" she asked.

Her dark brown eyes seemed to pierce through his and directly into his soul. He loved her. He loved her with a strength that made his a fate worse than dying.

"I promise," he said.

She kissed his lips and put her head on his shoulder. "I wish I could go with you."

"And I know you would." He hugged her tight. "I have to talk to Jacob."

He kissed her and hurried back to his quarters.

When he entered, Jacob was sitting on the bunk opposite Will's, looking at his laptop.

"I'm trying to find anything that might help you," Jacob said. "There are just too many drawings."

"I want you to be there when I try to figure this out – the transporter."

Jacob nodded. "Of course."

Will thought Jacob made an excellent addition to the group, and that the CIA better find a way to keep him in the fold if they survived the coming days.

"I heard Denise isn't taking it well," Jacob said.

"Neither am I," Will said. "It's been a strange life."

Jacob nodded. "And maybe an interesting one going forward," he said. "You might end up with the previous generation. It will be like living thousands of years in the future."

"That's one way to look at it," Will said. "Or I might be alone for the rest of my life, on some ship in the middle of nowhere. Remember, it was supposed to be a mass evacuation. Now it's just an evacuation of one."

A young sailor rushed into the room.

"Sir, the captain wants you on the bridge immediately," the sailor said. "It's urgent – something on the radio."

Will rushed through the narrow corridors of the sub, squeezing by crewmembers along the way. When he arrived on the bridge, the captain and Lieutenant Diggs were listening on headphones. When McHenry saw him, he waved him over.

"You need to hear this," he said as he handed him a headset.

Will slipped the headphones over his ears. He was already starting to perspire.

A woman's automated voice was in the middle of a statement when the headphones settled on his ears. It was similar to weather warnings that would interrupt TV and radio broadcasts. The voice said, "At 12:51 a.m. GMT, 37 spherical objects, 2 kilometers in diameter, were detected at a distance of 4,400 kilometers from the Earth's surface. At 1:17 GMT, the number of objects increased to 44. The nearest object closed to a distance of 3,200 kilometers. The objects appear to be maneuvering to symmetrically-located positions at that distance around the planet."

The voice then started to list location data for each of the objects with angles, distances, and speeds. They were coming in from all directions.

He ripped off the headphones and tossed them to McHenry. His heart thumped so hard he thought he might be having a heart attack. "This is it," he said. "I have to go. Now."

He turned from McHenry and raced to the hatch. Just as he started to climb, he caught a glimpse of Denise approaching from the other direction. Her eyes were wide, and she seemed confused.

"What's happening?" she asked, her voice revealing panic.

He stopped and looked at her. "It's time," he said. "I love you."

He heard her voice behind him as he climbed, but he didn't stop. He emerged from the *North Dakota*, ran across the gangplank, and sprinted across the bay and into the room with the vertical shaft, and then through the hole they'd blasted in the wall that had concealed the tunnel to the control room.

He was already winded by the time he was 100 yards into the passageway, and settled into a high-paced jog. The adrenaline that coursed through his body exacerbated the problem, but he knew he couldn't sprint two kilometers anyway. Every time he felt himself slowing down, panic forced him to increase his pace.

After what seemed like an eternity, he arrived at the control room. He raced through it to the side door at the front left, and then down the corridor that led to the small room through which only those who could separate could pass. He pressed the button to open the door. Just as he was about to step inside, a frantic voice and a rush of footsteps made him turn.

It was Denise.

She was breathing hard and crying and trying to speak.

He rushed over to her and grabbed her.

"I love you, too," she said, still winded.

He kissed her and let her go.

"Don't forget your promise," she said, tears streaming down her face.

As he turned to look at her one last time, he felt hot tears streaming down his own face.

He entered the small room and closed the door.

WILL RUBBED the tears from his eyes with his sleeve. He had to focus on his task.

He opened the door to the transport room, stepped out, and rushed to the control console below the large display screen on the wall to the left. He searched the console for a control that would initiate the transport process, and found a button encircled with a flashing white ring that was labeled "Board for Transport." Will pushed it.

A message appeared on the screen that read "Passengers Detected: 1," followed by "Proceed to Pod 107." A map of the pods appeared, and the one that represented Pod 107 flashed.

He turned around to search for the pod and noticed that a white line had illuminated on the floor in front of him that led into the pod array.

Following the line, he weaved his way through the array toward Pod 107. As he approached the oblong pod, stairs spontaneously formed on its nearest long side. The rounded top surface then tilted open like the canopy of a fighter jet. He peered into the open canopy as he climbed the steps, expecting to see an open space into which he would settle. What appeared instead, surprised and confused him.

The image, and the stench of ancient death, made him scream in horror as memories flooded his mind. Terror turned to rage, and he cursed. Tears filled his eyes as he knelt at the edge of the opening, and stared at what was inside.

It was a mummified corpse clothed in the rags of a prisoner. The skin was stretched and torn like an animal hide drawn tightly over its off-white skull. The lips peeled back and exposed teeth, some of which were broken off at the jawbone, and others seemed to have been drilled. The left arm was gone – cut off near the shoulder joint. The scoring from a saw blade was clear in its cross-section. The right leg was missing below the hip. A tourniquet lay loose around the stub.

There was a German Mauser pistol in its right hand. A rolled piece of paper was on its lap.

He picked up the yellowed and fragile paper and gently unrolled it. The handwriting was shaky, but in English.

When this facility was discovered, some of its systems were operating under battery power, but it was never fully functional. The Nazis tortured me, and forced me to follow their orders by threatening to murder my fellow inmates. With my unique abilities, I was eventually able to access this room, but I was the only one. For weeks, I did whatever I could do to satisfy them, but I eventually realized the extent of my new powers. I am responsible for the 347 dead Nazis at the bottom of the abyss. Josef Mengele was not among them. He should be brought to justice for what happened here. This place is not of this world, and neither am I. Infection has taken over, I am near death, and can do no more in this life. God, have mercy on us all.

Captain Saul W. Kelly, RAF
19 July 1952

WILL STARED AT THE DATE. A sense of horror flooded his mind that frightened him nearly to panic. He could see the distorted faces and hear the screams of the Nazi soldiers as they were torn to pieces.

Landau's question from the Red Box echoed in his mind: *Where were you on July 19th, 1952?*

He looked back at the corpse. There was a small hole in the top of the skull, near the back. The man must have shot himself in the mouth, or under the chin.

He studied the dried remains of the man's face. There was an element of familiarity in everything.

He remembered the name. It was in the file Daniel had shown him of the last man tortured in Room 19 – the file that was on the table in the library when they'd explored the base the first time. But Will seemed to know the face in the file from somewhere else.

He stood up and looked around. "Landau!" he yelled.

His words echoed throughout the facility, and he waited for a response. There was none.

He yelled again, "Captain Kelly!"

He separated to see if any souls were present. The place was empty.

He was confused. Captain Kelly needed separation abilities to get into the transport room. Will thought he'd been the only one to transform – Landau had said so himself. Now he worried that there'd be others on the planet when the executioners arrived.

He recombined with his body and screamed again, "Landau!"

After the echoes dissipated, he realized he had to move on.

He climbed onto an adjacent pod – no stairs formed – and tried to open the lid. There weren't even seams in which to get a grip.

He went to another pod, and then another, with the same results.

The only open pod had a corpse in it.

He hurried back to the control panel and found the map of the pods. A white blinking ring encircled Pod 107. All the rest were dim.

He pressed his fingers on the icons that represented the other pods, hoping to activate them, but it had no effect. He tried again, this time extending beyond his fingertips and into the surface, as he'd had to do with the buttons in the main control room. No effect.

"Fuck!" he yelled and ran to the open pod, and up the steps.

He reached into the pod and pulled up the corpse by the shoulders. It got jammed, so he tugged with force until it finally gave way. The cured skin held the rest of the body together better than he'd anticipated, and it came out as one piece. The Mauser was still clutched in its right hand.

"Sorry Captain Kelly," he muttered as he dragged the corpse down the steps and laid it on the floor.

He climbed back up the steps and slid into the pod. It reeked like rotting tallow, and a brown flaky film of dried blood obscured the interior consul that glowed beneath it. He scraped off the blood, revealing two buttons. One read "Close," the other read "Transport."

He hit the "Close" button. The top lowered, and his ears popped when it sealed.

A message appeared that translated to "Ramping for Transport," and a horizontal bar, like that which appeared when downloading a file on a computer, grew beneath the message.

When it was at 100 percent, the transport button disappeared, and a message appeared that translated to "Communication Error: Decoder Malfunction."

"Shit!" Will yelled.

He tried to repeat the sequence, but the transport button didn't respond.

He pushed the "Open" button. The top opened, he leapt out, and ran over to the control panel on the wall. Multiple error messages flashed on the screen: Decoder Malfunction, Improper Command Sequence, Unknown Command, and Translation Module Error.

They reminded him of the types of errors that would occur when interfacing scientific equipment for computer control. If you wanted to use a computer to control an instrument, you had to send commands through wires or fiber optics using some kind of communications protocol. All kinds of problems could crop up, and were often difficult to track down. Errors could arise from something as simple as a disconnected cable, or as complicated as damaged electronics or corrupted software. The one thing they had in common was that they all took time to fix. And time he didn't have.

A few feet from the edge of the screen were a desktop console with controls and a keypad riddled with foreign characters. He hoped he wouldn't have to enter any information, or respond to anything using the keyboard. He was able to read the language, but he knew there was no way he could write it. It seemed the translation abilities programmed into his brain only worked in one direction.

Something caught his eye on the console desktop, and his heart sank. It was an open slot with a white flashing ring around it. Something was missing.

He looked closer at the slot. Thousands of hair-like wires stuck out of it, some of which looked silver, and others which were clear, like fiber optics. It was a frayed mess, and it seemed to be damaged.

"Damn," he muttered.

He paced back and forth a few times, trying to decide what to do. Twice he removed the pistol from its holster and put it back.

Suddenly, an idea came to him. It was his last chance.

He pulled out his phone and snapped pictures.

JACOB STUDIED the screen in the main control room.

Things were changing. It looked like some pumps were reactivating, and some lines of script appeared that flashed like warning messages, but he couldn't be sure.

The temperature in the room had decreased since they'd arrived.

He snapped pictures of the screen at regular intervals as Daniel and Jonathan gathered remaining supplies to take back to the *North Dakota*. Denise and Sylvia were in the bay, helping the crew pack files and artifacts to be taken back to the States. Nothing of importance was to be left behind, and they were in a frantic hurry.

Will had warned them that the base was going to self-destruct, and they needed to be far away when that occurred. If the matter-antimatter reactors released all of their energy at once, it would have the same effect as detonating a thermonuclear weapon. The flashing messages only escalated the tension, and he had no idea how he was holding himself together.

"You think he's already done it?" Jonathan asked as they worked.

"You mean has he transported?" Jacob asked. "No way to know. Maybe the messages showing up on the screen would tell us something – too bad we can't read them."

At that instant, Jonathan and Daniel both flinched at something over Jacob's shoulder.

Jacob wheeled around, and it took him a second to comprehend what he saw. "Will!" Jacob nearly yelled. "Didn't the transporter work?"

Will rushed over to him, holding out his phone. "No," he replied. "It's malfunctioning." There was a look of panic on Will's face. He seemed to be sweating despite the decreasing temperature.

Jacob looked at the phone. It showed a picture of a screen with controls, and messages in a foreign script.

Before Jacob could ask, Will read the messages aloud as they all listened.

"They all sound like programming errors – corrupt code or unknown commands," Jacob said. "This can happen when a software translator is either missing, or is not the correct one. The translator could also be corrupted."

"There's something else," Will added as he scrolled down the screen on his phone and handed it to Jacob.

It was a photo of an empty slot that had what looked like coarse fur sticking out of it.

"What is that?" Jacob asked, pointing to the fur.

Will zoomed in closely on the edge of the slot.

"They look like fine wires and optical fibers," Jacob said.

"The light around the slot is flashing," Will said. "It means something is missing – looks like it was ripped out."

"If this is what's causing the errors," Jacob said, "the missing piece might be a dongle, or at least have a similar function."

"A dongle?" Daniel asked from behind them.

Will flinched at Daniel's voice, and then responded. "It's a device you plug into a computer that authenticates its software, or contains decryption information or passwords. It protects devices like a physical key."

Jacob's brain focused on the word 'decryption' in Will's explanation.

"How big is it – the port?" Jacob asked, his heart picking up pace as he grabbed the phone to take another look at the empty slot.

"About half as long as my phone – three inches or so," Will replied, "and between a quarter and a half inch wide."

"We only have one thing left," Jacob said and looked at Will.

Will's eyes darted back and forth a few times. When they stopped, they locked in on Jacob's, and his expression was that of recognition. "Where is it?"

"I have to go," Jacob said. "It will take the others too long to find it."

"What's he talking about?" Daniel asked.

"Radio ahead and tell them to stop packing!" Jacob yelled as he ran past a sailor and into the tunnel toward the *North Dakota*.

JACOB KNEW he couldn't sprint the entire two kilometers, but adrenaline kept him going at top speed for 400 meters before he settled into a fast, but sustainable, pace. He also had to be ready for an immediate return trip.

During the ten-minute run, he tried to visualize where he'd packed the object. Things got moved around when they'd unpacked the other devices and equipment, but he hoped he'd put everything back into their original crates.

He rushed into the bay and saw the crate he needed suspended by a cable from the overhead crane.

"Put it down!" he yelled as he slid to a stop near Sylvia and Denise.

"What's happening?" Denise asked.

"We need something from that crate," Jacob said. "Hurry!"

The sailor operating the crane reversed course and set the crate on the bay floor.

"What's going on?" Denise asked again.

Jacob explained as he worked.

Denise took off running.

Sylvia yelled to her.

"Let her go," Jacob said as he and a sailor removed the screws from the lid on the crate. "Let her see him one more time. We'll bring her back with us."

They removed the lid and unloaded the foam packing that protected the contents. Jacob threw things out with no discrimination as he frantically searched for the object he sought. A minute later, he found it: a small, flat box. He opened it and made sure the object was there – even though it was evident by the weight – and then closed it and sprinted through the bay and back into the tunnel.

WILL KEPT a hand on the butt of the pistol as he studied the activity on the screen. The indicators were bouncing around, and schematics would appear when something turned on or off. The pumps were reenergizing, and valves opened and closed.

The water level was rising.

Just as he was going to update Jonathan on what was happening, new warning messages appeared that verified the problem: "Warning: Water Level Rising" and "Energizing Auxiliary Pumps."

He read the messages to Jonathan.

Just as Will was about to explain, he turned toward the sound of someone running from the direction of the bay. He glanced down at his watch: 25 minutes had passed since Jacob had left. His anxiety was becoming unbearable.

A few seconds later, Denise rushed into the room, out of breath.

"Will," she said, in between deep gasps. "I wanted to see you once more."

Will's anxiety and sadness combined into a painful state of confusion.

She hugged him and nearly squeezed the breath out of him. Her sweaty face and hair brushed against his cheek.

At that instant, Jacob rushed in and went directly to Will. "Here it is," he said, out of breath. "Good thing I was a cross-country runner."

"The fibers in the console looked damaged," Will said, "but this is worth a final try." Especially since the only alternative was a bullet.

Jacob pointed to the screen. "What's happening?"

A new message had appeared.

Will read it, made a quick conversion in his head for the time, and said, "It says 'Reactor antimatter convergence in 48 minutes.'"

"What does that mean?" Jonathan asked.

Just as he was about to explain, another message appeared. He translated it in his mind as he read aloud, "Evacuation mandatory. Meltdown in 48 minutes. Transport facility nonfunctional in 32 minutes."

Will shuddered and panic started to take hold. It was happening. "You guys have to get the hell out of here, now," he said. "Get the *North Dakota* and everyone away from this place."

He grabbed Denise and kissed her on the lips. "I love you," he said and pushed her toward the tunnel. "Go!"

"Remember your promise," she said as Jonathan grabbed her arm and pulled her toward the tunnel.

Will rushed in the direction of the transport room.

WILL SCRAMBLED down the corridor and passed through the small chamber that preceded the enormous transport room. He rushed to the damaged console. On the screen was a new message conveying the same warning as on the display in the main control room: the facility would be nonfunctional in 31 minutes. Self-destruction would occur in 47.

He set the box on the console, opened it, and extracted the square object. It was the device they'd used to decode the incoming radio signal. It seemed unlikely that the same device would be needed to operate the transport system. His only hope was that everything had been encrypted in the same way, and that the decoder device was some kind of universal decryption key. It was his last hope.

He brought the device up to the open slot and was reassured to see that it was about the same size: it looked like it was supposed to slide in like a coin into a slot.

As he brought it closer, the fine frayed wires and fibers that spilled out of the opening spontaneously bent away from it, and a red ring illuminated around the slot. It seemed that the console was sensing the device. His hopes elevated.

The square decoder had one chamfered corner to indicate its orientation, much like that which appeared on the defunct computer floppy disks of the 90s. He turned it a quarter turn and tried to insert it again. The result was the same, except this time something pushed it away that felt like the repulsive force between two magnets.

He rotated it another quarter turn and the ring around the slot turned white and blinked rapidly. The frayed wires and fibers stretched out in the direction of the decoder as if reaching out to grab it, and something seemed to tug the square device toward the slot.

As he guided it in, some of the wires spontaneously attached themselves to the edges of the device. He let it slide through his fingers as it was tugged into the port. When the outer edge of the decoder was flush with the console's surface, the white ring around the slot remained, but stopped blinking, and a solid seal formed over the opening of the slot.

His eyes were drawn to the screen above the console, which now displayed a string of new messages. One read "Encoder Downloading," and another read "Destination Key" followed by a long string of numbers and characters that made no sense to him. Another message read "Preparing to Transport."

Will turned around to check if anything had changed with the pods, and spotted the illuminated line in the floor that led to the one that had contained the corpse. Nothing had changed, and it seemed he didn't have a choice but to use that particular pod.

He ran to it, passed by the remains of Captain Saul W. Kelly, climbed the stairs, and got inside. All of the error messages that had been on the console when he'd left the first time were now gone. He pressed the button to close the lid, and then the one labeled "Transport."

A message on the screen appeared that read "Ramping for Transport," with the bar graph showing its progress.

At that instant, a vibration rattled his whole body, which he was sure originated from outside the pod. He hadn't experienced any such effects the first time.

Seconds later, a message instructed him to separate and go into the adjacent pod to his right. The pod to his right was now illuminated.

He separated, passed through the wall of his pod, and entered the adjacent one. It was identical to the first, and had the same messages on the console.

After a few seconds, the message "Initiating Transport" appeared on the screen. If it worked as he suspected, the device would destroy his body to get all of its structural and quantum mechanical information, which would then be sent at the speed of light to some other location, along with his soul. His body would then be reconstructed, and his soul would recombine with it.

The anticipation was like nothing he'd ever experienced before. He wondered if it was how the first astronauts to land on the moon had felt just before blastoff.

Lights flashed in his peripheral vision, and he quickly located them. Identical messages had appeared on the screens in both pods, and his excitement turned to devastation. The new message read,

"Power Interruption Failure," and then, "Emergency Shutdown Imminent."

He went back to his body. The tremors had increased in intensity and frequency. There was no way to tell what was causing them. He looked at his watch: the facility would be nonfunctional in 12 minutes, and the meltdown would follow soon thereafter.

He hit buttons on the console to restart the transport process. It started to ramp, but the same errors appeared. This time there was a message that prompted him for an answer: it read "Repeat Command Until Success?" He pressed the "Yes" response button and watched it fail two more times.

The shaking became more violent. There were 6 minutes left. He had to get out immediately. It was time to move to Plan B.

"So much for your great technology," he muttered as he reached to his side and retrieved the Glock 9-millimeter. A round was already in the chamber.

He had to lean far to his left to make room for his shooting arm on the right. He put the gun to his right temple, and positioned it to ensure that the path of the bullet was through the center of his brain.

He took a deep breath and, as he pulled the trigger, he felt himself begin to separate. It was involuntary, and concentrated at his head.

From that point onward, everything moved in slow motion. His soul seemed to form a barrier between the bullet and his temple.

An instant later, he returned to his body, and caught the bullet as it fell from his head to his lap. Smoke filled the pod's interior, and the odor of ignited gunpowder made his sinuses burn. His ears rang at a high pitch.

"Holy shit," he muttered. It was clear that there was a lot more to learn about his separation abilities. But it didn't matter anymore.

Four minutes left. If he couldn't transport, and he couldn't kill himself, everything would have been for naught. Everything that everyone had done in this world – alive or dead – would be wiped from existence.

Existential implications.

An idea came to him.

He wedged his right elbow against the interior of the pod with the gun in hand and pointed at his right temple. His finger was on the trigger. He rested the side of his head against the barrel.

He separated and went to the adjacent pod. He then stretched what would be his left arm back into the pod that contained his body, and grasped the hand that held the gun.

He found the trigger finger and slowly increased the pressure, taking care not to misalign the barrel of the gun.

Nothing is forever, he thought.

He increased the pressure more and more and more ...

Hundreds of faces suddenly flashed through his mind: his parents, his sister, his childhood friends, the crew of the *North Dakota*, his CIA cohorts, and, lastly, Denise. Next came images of blue skies, green fields, and sunny beaches. He smelled lilacs and freshly cut grass and the ocean. And then there were magnificent fields of stars – billions of them – on an infinite black backdrop.

He sensed that he was smiling.

And then there was no sound, and there was no pain – just a flash of white light, then static, and then nothing.

DENISE WAS DOING BETTER than Jonathan, but she couldn't keep up with Jacob. He was striding effortlessly ahead of them, just enough to keep their pace at a sustainable maximum.

The sailors who operated the walkie-talkie communication line joined the run as it passed them, picking up the rear.

Denise felt vibrations in the floor as she ran, and they got more frequent and intense as they progressed.

When they emerged in the bay, there were two sailors on shore, and two others on the deck of the sub.

As she ran for the dock, Denise nearly fell as ice-cold water seeped into her shoes. The bay was flooding. As they approached the gangplank, Jacob slowed to let her cross first.

She looked back to see Jonathan trudge through the water,

panting hard and holding his side with his right hand. The four sailors would be the last to board.

A sailor grabbed her arm as she stepped onto the deck and rushed her to the hatch. Half a minute later, everyone was inside, the hatch was closed, and the dive order was given.

Although the adrenaline in her brain wouldn't let her contemplate the situation, she knew they'd never come back to the base. She also knew that Will wouldn't make it out, either. She just hoped he wasn't still in there.

He promised.

JAMES THACKETT ARRIVED at the Pentagon at 5:15 a.m. A security team had arrived at his house and nearly broken down the front door to get him. He'd barely had a chance to get dressed.

He'd been to the headquarters of the Department of Defense on numerous occasions, but this was the first time he'd ever been inside the bunker.

The main war room was larger than a basketball court, only circular, with display monitors around the perimeter, and a cluster of monitors suspended from the center of the ceiling. People toiled in front of computer screens and consoles that covered most of the floor space.

The first person Thackett recognized was the Secretary of Defense. The second was the President of the United States. He then spotted the Chief of Naval Operations, who ran over to meet him. Thackett knew him from the Naval Academy: it was Admiral George Sexton.

"James," Sexton said as he approached, "glad you're here."

"What's going on?" Thackett asked.

Admiral Sexton pointed to the largest screen, located on the opposite side of the room. Thackett squinted at first, but then pulled his glasses out of his pocket and put them on.

It was a satellite view from high Earth orbit. It showed dozens of white-metallic spheres in an array above the Earth.

"What the hell are those?" Thackett asked.

"We hoped you might have some idea," Sexton replied.

"You've been involved in the *North Dakota*'s activities during the past months," Thackett said. "This has to be connected. As you know, they're in Antarctica right now."

Sexton nodded. "The *North Dakota* has been unable to transmit for days, although we've been sending them updates," he said and pointed to another monitor. "At this point, there are 72 spheres, equally spaced around the planet. At first, they came much closer – around 4,000 kilometers from the Earth's surface – but now they're at about 50 thousand kilometers. There's a large oblong object behind the moon – almost 20 kilometers long."

Thackett felt his heart sputter. "Did we not see these coming?" he asked.

Sexton shook his head. "And, as you well know, we're always watching. We didn't detect them until they were inside the moon's orbit – they seemed to appear out of nowhere. And that the largest one seems to be hiding behind the moon is somewhat disconcerting. Intense gravitational waves were detected hours before the first of them was sighted."

"Is this why the Chinese called off their attack on Antarctica?"

Sexton shrugged. "Most likely. They turned back about the same time we spotted the first object."

"Do our sensors detect any communications from the objects – or anything else?"

Sexton nodded. "We've picked up some microwave emissions, as well as some other electromagnetic disturbances from the spheres. There has been elevated seismic activity around the planet, and anomalous tidal behavior. There's also been constant gravitational-wave activity, although not as intense as when they first arrived."

"Any craft sightings at the surface?"

"In the past hour, Navy fighter jets have been tracking small, oblong objects that move in ways that defy physics," Sexton explained. "They're about the size of the fuselage of a 747 passenger jet, but have no visible propulsion systems, no airfoil lift surfaces – wings – and no heat signatures. They make instantaneous turns, and undergo accelerations that would kill human pilots. Some have even gone into the water."

"Have they been spotted by civilian planes or radar?" Thackett asked.

"Undoubtedly," Thackett replied. "They initially rained out of the sky at hypersonic speeds – up to 30 times the speed of sound – and were detectable by radar. There are hundreds of them, maybe thousands, and sonic booms have been reported everywhere. They're all over the planet, but there have been no hostile encounters. Not yet."

Thackett shook his head. "The population is going to go crazy."

"It will be difficult to hide this," Sexton said. "But that's the president's problem. I need to focus on defense."

"Sorry, George," Thackett said and shook his head slowly, "but our technology might be outmatched on this one."

"I know," Sexton admitted. "I'm here to do my best."

Thackett nodded his head and patted Sexton's shoulder. "Yeah. Me too, my friend."

DANIEL SIPPED hot soup from a mug and tried to maintain his composure. It was difficult being in the dark when the fate of the world was in the balance.

He glanced across the table at Sylvia who'd been nibbling at a bagel for the past 20 minutes. He knew she must be feeling the same way.

They just had to hold it together for another two hours. The *North Dakota* would make the entire trip through the tunnel in less than 32 hours.

When they'd departed, the pumps at the base were on again. However, even though the water was directed into the base and, eventually, back into the valley, it wasn't coming in from the sea. Instead, it was fresh water being pumped from the abyss below the lake and into the base. Now there was a slow current through the tunnel, out to sea.

Jonathan joined them, followed by Denise, and then Jacob a few minutes later.

Even though they all felt the loss of Will, everyone was aware that Denise was especially distraught, even though she was acting strong. Her face was puffy, as if she'd been crying. Her hair was loosening from the knot on the top of her head, and some strands hung along the side of her face.

"We've not received a communication in the past 30 hours," Jonathan said. "I'm a bit anxious to see what's waiting for us out there."

Daniel was more than just "a bit" anxious.

"We're still alive," Jacob said, "so the regeneration hasn't started."

"What do you mean?" Jonathan asked.

"You remember what Will said," Jacob continued. "The first step is to irradiate the planet and kill all life."

"Wouldn't we be safe in the tunnel, and underwater?" Sylvia asked.

"Depends on the type of radiation, and the intensity," Jacob replied. "My take on it was that it was supposed to kill all life. And I assume that it would be done with technology that we've never seen before. It would be intense enough to get to us."

"Maybe they're waiting," Jonathan said. "Still preparing."

"Maybe Will succeeded," Denise said.

No one spoke for a few seconds. Daniel knew they were all thinking the same thing: Will was gone – either transported irreversibly to a distant place, or dead. And, despite all that he'd witnessed in the past year, Daniel thought it was most likely the latter.

"Let's hope so," Jonathan finally said.

As they ate, they speculated about everything from the evolution of the previous generation to what they were going to see when they emerged from the tunnel.

Daniel overheard random conversations as contingents of the crew passed through the galley to get food. They were all fully informed of what was happening. Some expressed fear about what they'd witnessed in the shaft room during the Russian attack, but their accounts seemed to have already devolved into rumors. Many worried about their families.

Daniel overheard a young sailor repeat something the captain had said to calm one of the young men. He'd said, "What you're doing right now is the best thing you can do to protect your family."

Hearing those words seemed to calm Daniel as well, even though he didn't have anyone to worry about on the outside. That wasn't entirely true – he still cared for his ex-wife – but he had no kids, and his immediate family had all passed.

But then he remembered what Will had said about the lingering souls. They too would be destroyed in the regeneration. Daniel didn't know what to think about that – there was no way to understand what that meant. But he hoped they'd done enough to prevent it from happening.

Two hours later the *North Dakota* emerged in the Weddell Sea and proceeded another ninety minutes toward the rendezvous point with the *Stennis*. Before they were in the vicinity of the carrier group, the *North Dakota*'s crew picked up the sounds of ship engines. It was a good sign in light of what Will had described; perhaps nothing had happened yet.

A sailor walked into the galley and informed Daniel that the captain wanted him on the bridge. When he arrived, the *North Dakota* was already at periscope depth. They were still 50 kilometers from the rendezvous point.

McHenry pointed to one of the many monitors mounted to the walls. "Look at number 17," he said. "It's an image from a spy satellite."

Daniel found the monitor and studied the image. It was a view of the night sky. There were stars. And there were other things. At first, they looked like large stars, but the color was off, and they were arrayed like a net over the entire viewable sky. There were at least 15 of them in sight.

"What are they?" Daniel asked.

"I was hoping you might be able to answer that question," McHenry replied.

Daniel shuddered. Up to this point, everything he'd learned from Will about coming events had been images conjured in his mind. They were renditions of ideas described to him, and his brain had fashioned them to be harmless. But what he saw before him was reality. Now his mind was working to conceal the horror that was rising.

"What are we going to do now?" Daniel asked.

"I'm going to radio Naval Command," McHenry said. "My guess is that we'll deliver you and your colleagues to the *Stennis*. Afterwards, we'll probably dive and await orders."

Daniel nodded. "How long before we meet with the *Stennis*?"

"I'll let you know after I talk to command," McHenry replied. "Maybe you should let the others know what's going on."

Daniel nodded and started back for the galley.

JAMES THACKETT sipped coffee and watched the large screen. The distribution of spheres resembled a net cast around the planet. Sensors picked up electromagnetic signals of various kinds, but they were sporadic. In the past 24 hours, sightings of small, oblong craft were reported all around the world, from land and sea.

The latest development was that the gravitational wave detectors were now going berserk. Spokespeople from both the Livingston and Hanford gravitational-wave detection facilities were providing regular updates. Whatever the objects were, they were doing something that scientists did not understand.

His phone vibrated in his chest pocket, and he extracted it and answered it.

It was the captain of the *Stennis*. The *North Dakota* had returned. Will Thompson had not. The base was expected to self-destruct. More information to follow.

Thackett put the phone back in his pocket and went to the restroom, where he vomited in a sink.

DENISE FLAILED ABOUT in panic and confusion. Someone was screaming at her and she couldn't orient herself.

Two strong hands grabbed her by the shoulders and shook her.

"Denise!" a voice yelled. "Get up!"

Denise squinted in the bright light and eventually focused on the face of the agitator. It was Jonathan. She remembered – they were on the *Stennis*. They'd been there for over a day, during which she'd spent most of the time sleeping.

"Something's happening," he said. "Let's go!"

She glanced at her watch: it was 3:15 a.m. She'd been sleeping in her blue, Navy-issued, overalls. She stood and put on her hat.

"Take a coat," Jonathan instructed.

She grabbed her coat and followed him. She'd never before seen him move so quickly as he maneuvered through corridors and around people. Five minutes later, they were on the deck of the *Stennis* in the freezing cold. The sea was wild, as it had been since they'd arrived.

Waves slammed against the ship's hull and an unwavering freezing mist blew over them. The cold seemed to penetrate her bones and she began to shake.

Jonathan grabbed her arm and led her to a partitioned area on the flight deck that safeguarded them from being washed off the ship by a rogue wave. There were at least 100 others with cameras and binoculars looking upward.

She looked to the twilit horizon. Less than a mile from the ship were hundreds of small, white oblong objects less than 500 feet above the water. In quick succession, they darted into the sky and then spiraled toward each other. Sounds like that of crackling thunder made her cover her ears. In less than a minute they coalesced into a single point and, in a final blinding flash, they were gone.

Other flashes came from all directions, like lightning on the horizon, followed by a continuous rumbling reminiscent of a diminishing storm.

At that instant, darkness returned, the seas calmed, and the air became still.

Everyone stared into the sky in silence.

"I'm not sure," Jonathan said, "but I think Will might have accomplished his mission."

Denise wiped tears from her face, hugged Jonathan, and buried her head in his parka. She laughed and cried at the same time.

JAMES THACKETT COULDN'T BELIEVE his eyes. The packed room was silent.

He'd been holed up in the bunker for nearly three days, anticipating the worst.

The alien objects were leaving. The small, oblong ones on the surface seemed to spiral upward and coalesce in various locations around the planet, and then evaporate in a flash. The larger ones that formed the array around the Earth just disappeared. The largest one behind the moon – the one they'd been calling "the mother ship" – was gone.

Orders started ringing out from different directions, instructing people to check satellites and sensors. Many were on the phone, getting reports from various places. All indications were that the alien objects had disappeared. The electromagnetic signals were gone. The gravitational wave detectors were quiet.

The reports and verifications continued for over three hours before the official "all clear" status was declared.

After another hour, George Sexton started to send people home. Most had been awake for over 72 hours, catching catnaps on the floor by their desks when they could no longer function.

Sexton walked over to Thackett with a cup of coffee and handed it to him. "You lost your operative," Sexton said. "But it seems that he accomplished his mission. My feeling is that we've barely averted something unimaginable."

Thackett nodded. He still felt sick.

"I have no idea of the details, but whatever you've managed there at CIA was complicated," Sexton said. "Well done, James."

Sexton stuck out his hand, and Thackett shook it.

"Go home," Sexton said. "I'll be in contact if anything happens."

Thackett nodded and headed for the exit. He was exhausted, but knew he would not be able to sleep. He just wanted to see his wife.

CHAPTER 19

It had been a week since Jacob had witnessed what he thought was the most significant event in modern history. He'd seen it with his own eyes from an aircraft carrier in the Southern Seas.

William Thompson had succeeded.

What Uncle Theo had done for him was beyond anything Jacob could have imagined. The "existential consequences" Theo had conveyed applied in the widest sense – to the entire world – and also directly to Jacob. The world would forever be changed, and so would he. No matter what happened from this point forward, his life would have meaning because of what he'd been able to contribute to the world.

When he arrived in DC, he went directly to 17 Swann and booked a flight to London. He arrived at Heathrow at 6:00 p.m. and took a taxi to a tall apartment building in London's Kensington W8 District. He walked in with a group of strangers and made it past the front desk and into an elevator. He exited on the 9th floor, found apartment 9A, and knocked.

A few seconds later, the light behind the peephole dimmed, and he heard a gasp from behind the door.

Pauli opened it and stared at him with an astonished and

confused expression for a full second before embracing him. "Jake!" she screamed.

She hugged his neck tightly and wouldn't let go. Her body shook as if she were shivering, and he could tell she was crying.

"I'm so glad you're here," she said, still hanging onto him. "I tried to call you a hundred times after those objects appeared. On the news, people were saying they were aliens."

Jacob knew for a fact that those people were correct.

"Others were saying it was some kind of trick," she continued.

"They're gone now," he said as she released her grip and they separated far enough to see each other's face. "And I don't think they're coming back."

"Where have you been?" she asked. "I've been worried sick – "

"Can we go inside?" he asked.

As she led him inside, he said, "I have a lot to tell you, Pauli."

"Like what?" she asked as she closed the door.

"To begin with, I got a new job ..."

LENNY DROVE up to the cabin and shut off the car.

He'd rented fishing poles and a small boat at the main office, and purchased a North Dakota fishing license. It was the same cabin in which he'd stayed the night he'd carried out the collection mission on the mock missile silo.

He'd visited popular vacation areas during the past few years, but this would be the first time in decades that he'd truly be able to relax. He was going to go fishing, maybe swim, grill hamburgers, and drink beer.

He had the place for a week, after which he'd continue to the West Coast, and then south to San Francisco, where DMS, Inc. had a safe house. It turned out that Schroeder had given him some sound advice. The service his CIA colleague had recommended specialized in "unconventional retirement management," as they'd described it. Once the accounts were set up and financial assets were transferred, he'd make his final decision as to where to go. He was leaning toward Costa Rica, but Belize was also in the running. From what he'd seen so far, North Dakota might not be a bad choice either, but he doubted he could handle the winters.

He considered contacting his daughter and, although his mind could change in the future, decided against it. Of all things, he didn't want to make a connection with her that could be exploited by his enemies. He hoped most of them were now permanently out of the picture, but he couldn't take the risk and put her in danger.

It reminded him of his final cleanup job for the CIA. He'd tracked down Jennifer Chung and her boyfriend in Manhattan. As far as Lenny knew, they were the last of the Chinese network who could identify him. They were now both in the Space Systems building. Thackett promised that they'd never see the light of day.

The long drive from the East Coast to the Central Plains had been good for his demeanor. The last time he'd made the drive he'd formulated a way to quantify his impact on the world. Was a life saved worth a life taken? He didn't know the answer to that question, but he figured the numbers might now be in his favor. He estimated his last effort might have spared the lives of hundreds in the Space Systems building alone. Perhaps it had also prevented a war.

His initial thought when he'd seen the objects in the night sky was of the Red Wraith project. He knew William Thompson had something to do with their presence, but he had the impression that the mysterious man had also been responsible for their disappearance. William Thompson was the fruit of the Red Wraith project, the government entity that Lenny had been charged to protect for nearly two decades. Perhaps Heinrich Bergman's life's work had unintended consequences that had led to all of it. Red Wraith had both created the problem, and solved it.

Lenny's life was a microcosm of this larger dichotomy. He didn't know if he'd made up for his past transgressions – deep down he secretly thought he probably had not – but at least he'd tried. He knew he might still pay a price for what he'd done, in this life or the next, but he was satisfied for now.

Perhaps he could rest. Perhaps he might enjoy a little peace for the first time in his life.

Daniel scooped out a ball of Earl Grey tea and submerged it in a cup of hot water. He looked out the window of his Space Systems office and admired the silvery moonlight on the wavering tops of the spruce trees below. A bat fluttered out, made a few acrobatic maneuvers, and dipped back into the canopy.

Daniel's reflection no longer alarmed him. He'd aged. But he'd lived through it all, and had something to show for his efforts.

His conclusions about what had happened over the past year were extrapolated from his own perspective of the events. It went against every synapse in his brain to put such a heavy weight on conjecture. It went against his instincts as an Omniscient. But it was what he wanted to believe.

The CIA – through the Red Wraith project – had provoked William Thompson to put the entire world in jeopardy. But then they'd helped him to save it. William Thompson had sacrificed his life for everyone.

It reminded him of a story he'd heard as a child in parochial school. They'd simplified Fyodor Dostoevsky's *The Parable of the Onion* into an easily understood story for first graders.

The idea was that a sinful woman was given a chance to be lifted out of Hell by hanging onto an onion. As she started to rise, others in Hell saw their chance and grabbed onto her legs. The onion held, and more and more people hung onto the others, until millions were being raised out of the fiery abyss. Even with the immense weight, the onion held. But when the woman looked down and saw the long chain of people dangling below her, she got worried: they might be too heavy for the onion and it could break, ruining her chance to be saved. She then became angry: those who hung below her might not be as worthy as she to be saved. In her fear and anger, she kicked until they started falling, and continued until there was only one person left. But even that single person worried her, so she kicked violently to get that last person to fall. With a final kick, the onion snapped, and she fell back into Hell.

The story reminded Daniel of William Thompson. He'd provided a proverbial onion to billions, despite the fact that he could not use it to save himself. He wondered if the world would use the onion he'd provided, or cause it to snap.

It would be difficult to convince some that what had happened wasn't a tragedy. After all, none of it would have happened had they not meddled in things that they shouldn't have. That had started with the Nazis, and it could have stopped with them. But then the Americans had discovered the project and kept it alive, and then a small group of Omniscients brought it to maturity. But it had been William Thompson who had finally ended it.

The tragedy was that many people had died for no apparent reason. Pockets of humanity had been doing that since the beginning of recorded history. There had been countless wars that had killed millions, but accomplished nothing. He didn't know exactly how many lives the Nazi Red Falcon project, and that which had followed in its wake, had claimed, but he was sure it was in the tens of thousands. He had a feeling that the world had somehow changed for the better now that it was over. What would they do with their second chance?

Daniel believed that helping to guide William Thompson to his destiny was the defining accomplishment of his own life, and it was the reason why he'd sacrificed everything for his work.

He turned in response to a light knock on the door. It was Sylvia.

"Tea?" she asked and pointed to the empty cup in her hand.

He smiled and pointed her to the can of Earl Grey on the table.

She grabbed a stainless steel tea ball from a cup of clean silverware and scooped some out. She walked over to him and squeezed his hand. "Are you doing better?"

He nodded. "You?"

She smiled. "I'm just happy to be here with you," she said as she poured hot water into her glass cup. "I'm looking forward to getting back to our late-night routine."

A chime sounded in the main room.

"James is here," she said, and nodded toward the door. "Shall we?"

He followed her out to the cluster of furniture in the main room.

"Would you like some tea?" Daniel asked as Thackett approached.

Thackett smiled and shook his head. "No, thanks, I only have a few minutes," he said. "I wanted to give you some updates."

Daniel sat on the couch, directly across the coffee table from Thackett. Sylvia sat to Daniel's right.

"First, about the time the *North Dakota* left the base, satellites reported a thermal anomaly – as if a nuclear device had been detonated – in the valley where the structure and base were located. Since then it has completely flooded, and is now frozen solid," Thackett explained. "Scientists are completely baffled as to how such a thing is possible."

"I don't get surprised by much anymore," Daniel said.

"I suppose not," Thackett said and laughed. "Me either."

"Next," Thackett said, "your recommendation to make Jacob Hale an Omniscient has been granted. He should follow in the footsteps of his uncle."

"Horace was a great man," Daniel said.

"Finally, Daniel," Thackett said, "I'll forward a list of potential projects that you can assign to our Omni group as you see fit. Best to get on with our business."

Thackett stood. "That's all I have," he said, "other than I want to express my gratitude for what you two have done."

Daniel stood and held out his hand. "James," he said as Thackett grasped his hand. "We think you did well in all of this. In the end, I think even Will trusted your judgment – and trusted *you*. And so do we."

Thackett smiled, and then chuckled. "He really didn't like us much at first, did he?"

Sylvia laughed and shook her head. "And he could be quite an intimidating fellow."

"We should be grateful to have crossed paths with him," Thackett said and started for the door. "I'll get that list to you tomorrow morning."

Thackett walked out and closed the door, and Daniel and Sylvia sat back on the couch.

"I'm glad we crossed paths as well," Sylvia said as she smiled and took a sip of tea.

"Me too."

DENISE POURED hot water into her cup and looked across the coffee table to Jonathan, who was packing his pipe with cherry tobacco. It was strange being back with him in his campus office in Chicago.

"You think you finally got the adventure out of your system?" Jonathan asked.

It seemed to Denise that the past year had been an entire lifetime. She'd gone from a green law intern to going on missions with the CIA. She'd been in a submarine. She'd explored a Nazi base in a tunnel beneath Antarctica. She'd been shot. She'd seen direct evidence of the existence of life beyond Earth, and witnessed alien technology which exceeded that of humans by thousands of years. She'd experience the supernatural. She'd seen the world on the edge of destruction, and then survive. She'd fallen in love.

"Not yet," she said.

Jonathan laughed loudly as he lit his pipe. "I suspected not."

"I could use a break, though."

"Back to some DNA work for a while?" Jonathan suggested. He'd been reinstated as the director of the DNA Foundation. "This time as a full-fledged employee?"

That was a change she'd welcome. Chicago wasn't a cheap place to live, and an intern's salary didn't get you much. She'd been staying with her former roommate for the week and, although it was a comfortable environment, it was time for her to upgrade her living conditions.

"I bet our friends in the CIA would be happy to bring you on," he added.

"Maybe in the future," she said. "For now, I think I'll get back to some slower-paced DNA Foundation work."

Jonathan nodded. His pipe had gone out and he set it in an ashtray on the table. "I'd better get going home," he said as he glanced at his watch. "Julie will be waiting for me. She wants you to come for dinner on Saturday."

"I'll be there," she said as she followed Jonathan to his desk and then out of the office.

"Can I give you a lift?" he asked.

"I think I'll stay and get my office organized," she said. It was going on midnight, but her internal clock had still not yet adjusted to a normal sleep routine. Besides, she needed to keep her mind occupied.

They parted ways and Denise found her keys, opened her office door, and turned on the lights. It was an utter mess. Piles of papers and file folders littered every horizontal surface.

She started by sorting the loose papers, and putting the trash into a pile for recycling. As she moved a stack of files from the desk to a side table, a picture slid partway out of a folder somewhere in the middle of the pile. She managed to squeeze the stack to prevent it from falling all the way out, saving herself the time to locate the folder from which it came, and then set the pile on a chair.

She then removed files from the top until she got to the one with the protruding photo. When she opened it, a flood of emotion overtook her. It was the file she'd compiled on Will during the investigation of his case for the DNA Foundation.

The picture was upside down, and she flipped it over. His boyish face and blue eyes seemed both stressed, and wise.

Tears streamed down her face, and she sat at her desk, buried her face in her hands, and bawled until her emotions were under control. She rested her forehead on the desk as she recovered.

After a few minutes, she lifted her head, sat up, and wiped her eyes with her sleeve.

She looked out the window into the clear night sky. The moon was nowhere to be seen and the stars glittered in elegance. But it was the space between the stars that captured her attention.

That was where he was: somewhere in the black.

The light was too bright to open his eyes. He was on his back and maneuvered to his hands and knees. The floor was cool and smooth, and the air was comfortable. A low-pitched rumble was barely detectable.

He wobbled to keep his balance as he stood.

After a few failed attempts he was able to keep his eyes open for a few seconds. He was in a room the size of a warehouse. All of the surfaces were white, and light seemed to emanate uniformly from all directions.

His body was stiff, as if he'd slept in an awkward position for a long time, and his feet ached. He clenched his fists a few times and stretched his arms as he walked in a circle, trying to decide where to go.

It occurred to him that he had no idea where he was.

It then occurred to him that he didn't know who he was.

He then spoke aloud in a voice he recognized, but he did not know from where the words came. "I promise."

Nothing is forever.

THE END

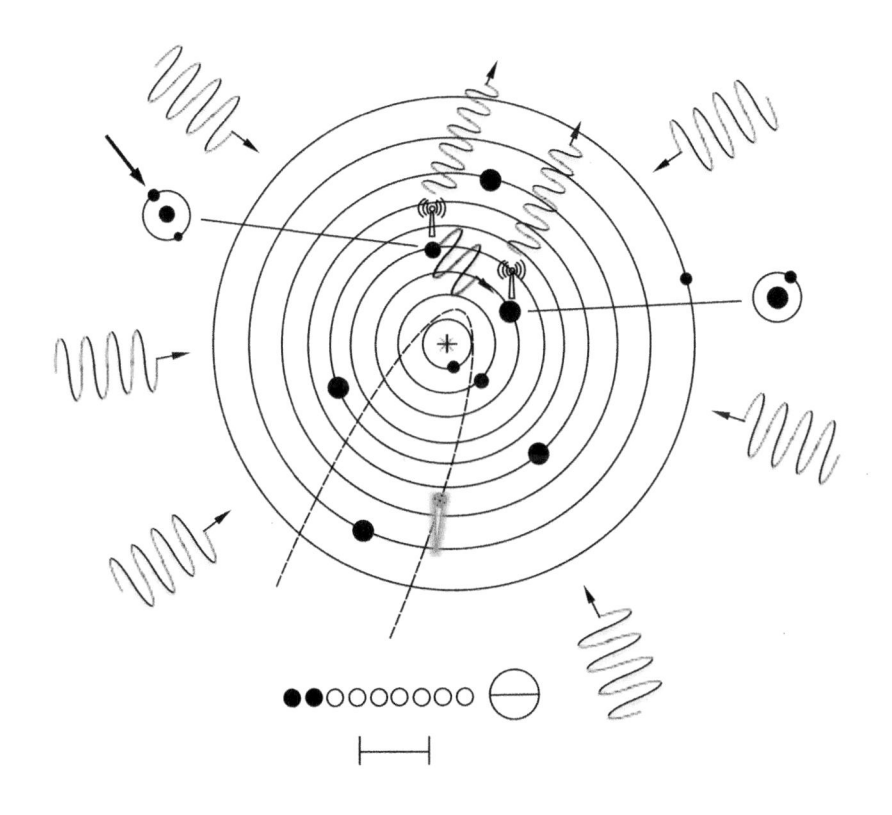

DECODED IMAGE 1

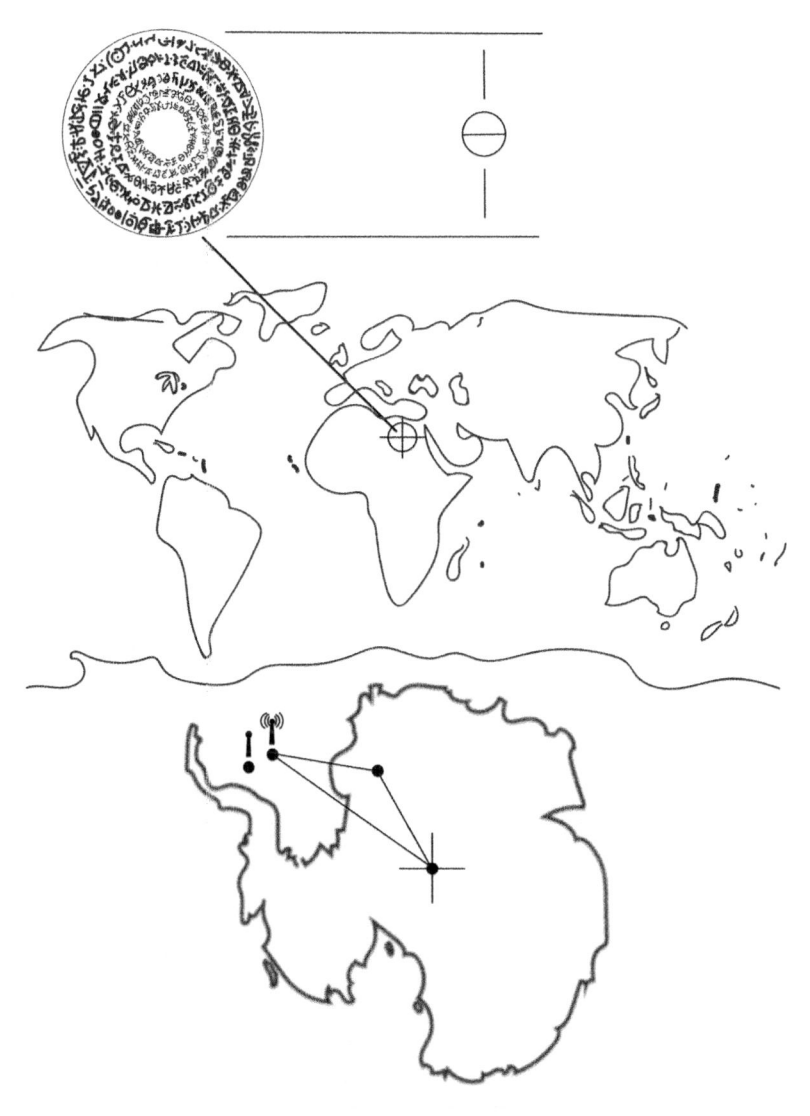

DECODED IMAGE 2

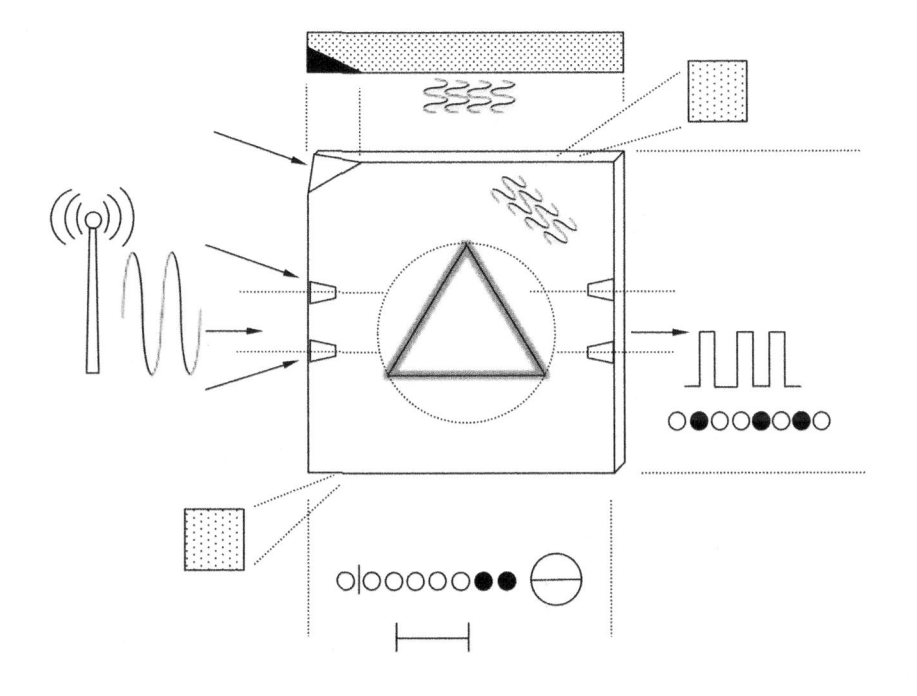

DECODED IMAGE 3

ACKNOWLEDGMENTS

The author would like to thank Jessica Fiorillo for her invaluable input, editing, and constructive and uplifting support. It is no surprise that one part of her professional life is as a "handler of authors." Thanks are also due to Nayeli Zúñiga-Hansen for a full reading of the final manuscript.

ABOUT THE AUTHOR

Shane Stadler is an experimental physicist and university professor. He spent his early career at the US Naval Research Laboratory where he conducted research on artificially-structured magnetic materials. His current research is on magnetic and quantum materials, which is funded by the US Department of Energy. He has written five novels, including *The Peregrine Conjecture* (2023) and the four-book, sci-fi *Exoskeleton* series. He is a coauthor of a well-known college physics textbook and has published over 250 scientific papers on topics that range from magnetic cooling to spintronics to superconductivity.

You can contact Shane at www.ShaneStadler.com

ALSO BY SHANE STADLER

Printed in Great Britain
by Amazon